Ashen Sky

Ashen Sky

Book Two of:

The Arcadian Complex

Paul James Keyes

ISBN 978-1-952872-07-5

Published in the United States by Verge Publishing.
VergePublishing.org

Cover artwork by Paul James Keyes and Raven Wade Keyes.
Internal artwork and design by Paul James Keyes.

This is a work of fiction. Names, characters, places, and
incidents either are the product of the author's imagination or
are used fictitiously. Any resemblance to actual persons,
living or dead, events, or locales is entirely coincidental.

You can follow Paul on Twitter **@PaulJKeyes**,
TikTok **@PaulJamesKeyes**,
or visit **ArcadianComplex.com** to become an honorary
Arcadian!

"To the elements it came from
Everything will return.
Our bodies to earth,
Our blood to water,
Heat to fire,
Breath to air"

-Matthew Arnold

Table of Contents

The Nation of Aragwey

Kingdom of Taris
Kingdom of Kovehn
N
W
E
S
Ebsdale
Ennen
The Altrese River
Saldrone
Jarum
Besterio
Hordle
Ketsmill
Odenbar
Darrenfield
Becfield
Ghromyl
Besbuin Peninsula
Felington
Vermholt
Tavallon
Gulf of Nerim
Torus Desert
Denherm
Hurspen
Gestrcho
Bronam
Melvona
Salenport
Benmoth
Telvarse
Zenbrogh
Rasile
Silden
Cerivon
North Galdren
Barslewn
Tephlona
Bouchen
Yelmis
Whepton
The Crimson Waters of the Minthune River
South Galdren
Cheslyn
Quono
Fort Bastion
Sarnoma
Ilvanelle
Lithillo
Parnith
The Bastion River
Oeslum
Epero
Nesbern
Mesilo
Aderna
Erotos
Uhlomn
Shian Point
Lake Baratoa
Anosil
Ersalyn
Faehiln
The Rivers Etto
Elswani Monastery
Shian City
Scar of Phandrol
Kingdom of Phandrol

Hotel Willows
Blue Fox Inn
The Etwel River
The Etwon River
Arcanum Cathedral
The Queen's Palace

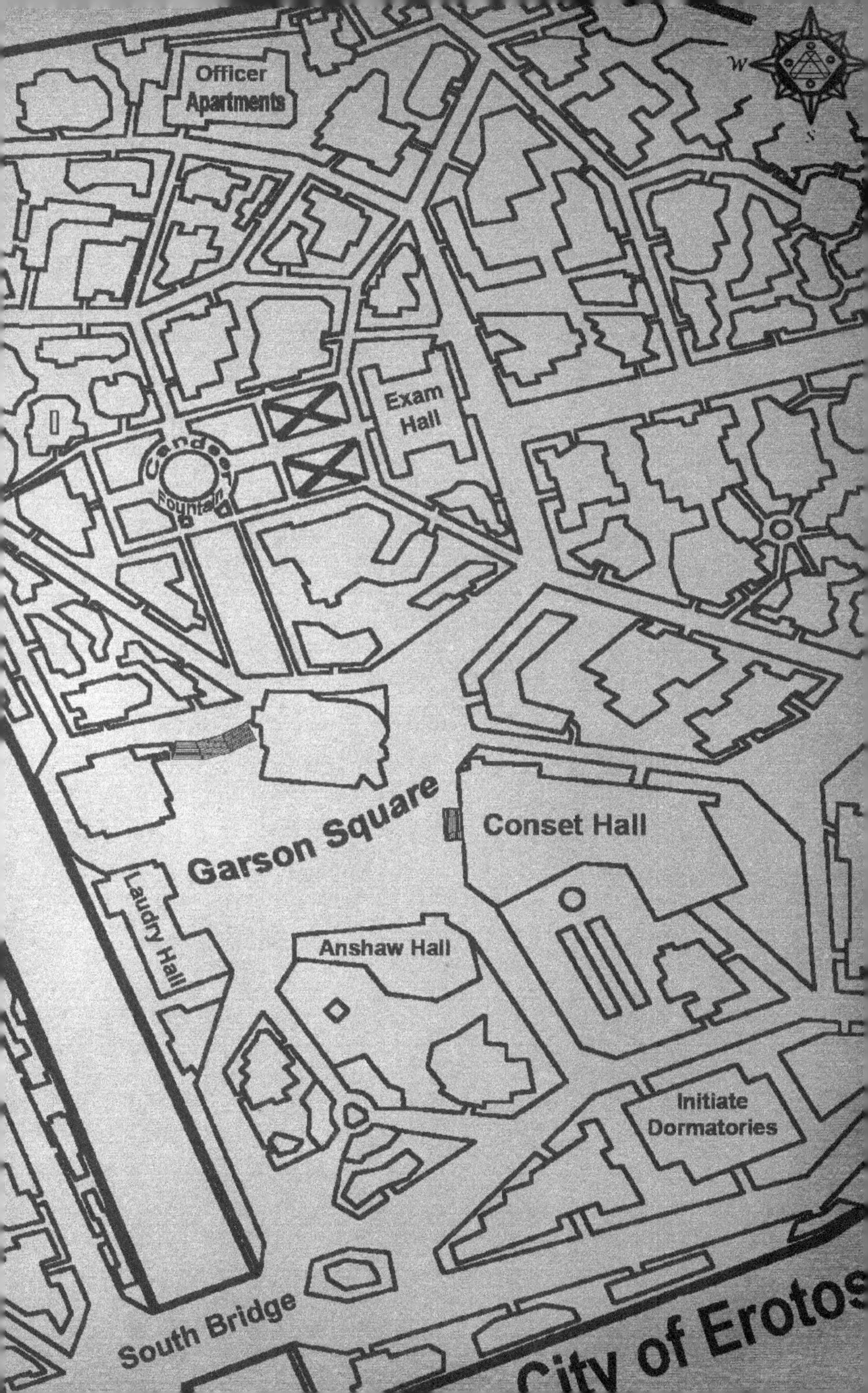

Officer Apartments
W
Exam Hall
Candeer Fountain
Garson Square
Conset Hall
Laudry Hall
Anshaw Hall
Initiate Dormatories
South Bridge
City of Erotos

CHAPTER
1

Reborn

The earth shuddered in Erotos as another tremor raked through the palace's foundation. It came as a dull vibration, not unlike the massive Machina of old, though most knowledge of those grand devices had been lost to the bowels of history—few references remained, even within the ancient Archives of the Arcanum deep beneath the grand cathedral just north of the palace.

The tremor was an Echo of the Power—the properties of matter could fluctuate in countless ways once a vortex began to form; random, invisible undulations turning stone into liquid or drawing energy into uncontainable lightning storms. Loose objects could find their mass reduced to nothing and float away in defiance of the laws of physics, breaking rules even the most powerful Ver'ati could never hope to challenge. At times, whole sectors of the city needed to be shut down until particularly offending Echoes had time to dissipate. It was not uncommon to hear of deaths during such occasions, but Lord Ethan and his Ver'konus operatives did their best to obscure the truth when it came to matters of the Power.

The walls of the royal chamber groaned in distaste as the Echo, too wide to pinpoint its exact origin, threatened to rattle every door from its hinges and sent each of the richly colored tapestries that lined Queen Havorie's bedchamber swaying back and forth in vaunting ripples of cloth. The draperies, now centuries old, were still as vivid as the days they were first woven. Their threads were tempered to outlast countless generations of inhabitants by careful workings of the Power.

Havorie woke as the tremors grew stronger. She sat up in bed, pushing the down-filled blanket off her upper body. A flash of light drew her attention to her left wrist. She pulled up the sleeve of her frilly nightgown, exposing the golden clasp of the device that was cinched around her arm like a wristwatch. Its function had nothing to do with the time of day. It was a Power Artifact—similar to the trio of Charisms that guarded the palace's entrance hall with their abilities to detect the presence of the Power. The device had a crystal face that was positioned on the inside of her forearm. She held it up to get a better look at its glowing dials.

The Detector was her personal version of the Charisms. One hand detected individuals in the process of channeling, another determined one's strength in the Power, and a third identified the presence of Artifacts in the vicinity, just like the three Charisms. The dials would glow and point in the direction of whichever property they were honed to detect, similar to a compass finding north. There was a fourth hand on the Detector, but it did nothing, or at least had done nothing for as long as Havorie could recall, but three out of four working dials wasn't bad considering the age of the relic.

All of the known Artifacts had histories older than Aragwey, their origin as much of a mystery to their keepers as the Power itself. They outdated even the oldest records kept by the Arcanum historians, which meant they existed well before John Graven, the first Ver'ati, walked the lands a thousand years ago. Havorie discovered the Detector, along with a number of other interesting trinkets, among her mother's possessions a few years after her passing.

It hadn't taken long for Havorie to figure out how the three working dials operated. The Power was as common in Erotos as honey mead. One of the three working dials was always glowing at least faintly. The hand that sensed one's strength in the Power had been pointing towards Aaron Levy, the odd man with the Mark of Kings on his arm, ever since his arrival in Erotos a little over one month ago.

Havorie met him briefly on the day he revealed his mark to the world. The dial rapidly spun in circles as soon as she was within twenty paces of him. The Detector glowed so intensely that she was forced to slide it up her arm and fold back her sleeve, doubling the layers covering it to conceal the illumination from the public during her introduction speech. Farther away, as she was now, the dial remained fixated in his direction, but the glow was diminished.

That young man is the most powerful Ver'ati in the city, she mused. Before his arrival, the Detector had always pointed towards Lord Ethan.

That was not the only hand glowing tonight, however. The dial that detected active channeling was shining with bright pulses of light. Someone nearby was using the Power. Only a massive display could bring such brilliant flashes to the dial. It was forbidden to channel within the palace—someone was clearly breaking the law. All that energy flowing through the halls was most certainly the cause of the tremors.

Through the window, Havorie could see that the Echo stretched far beyond the palace grounds. All across Erotos, buildings swayed with the motion of the earth. Within the harbor directly south of the palace, a segment of the dock had broken loose and several ships were capsized and in flames. Smoke from the fire covered the harbor like a thick fog. First responder Ver'ati were doing their best to squelch the flames, but the fire was spreading too quickly for them to handle without reinforcements.

What an utter mess....

"Step back from the window, my queen."

The stern voice of Damian Sarvo, her head of security, caught her by surprise. She would recognize it anywhere—always gruff and emotionless. Damian had watched over her for her entire life and over her mother for half of hers before that as well. She quickly hid the Detector under the sleeve of her gown before turning around. Damian was poised in the doorway of the chamber. His steps were always eerily silent.

"The glass could shatter from all the rumbling," he said. "Best if you return to bed and wait out the Echo."

Havorie frowned, but did as she was told, walking back to the bedside. Damian approached as well, drawing the canopy around the edge of the bed so that Havorie would be fully enclosed as she slept.

"A butterfly, trapped in a net," said Havorie.

Damian ignored the comment.

With the Detector fluctuating so brightly, Havorie had to place her hand over top of it so Damian wouldn't notice its shine. Power Artifacts were quite rare, even in Erotos, and tightly controlled by the Arcanum. If anyone learned she had several in her possession, they would most certainly be taken away. Havorie was queen, but she was young, only eighteen years old. She was still treated like the heiress—a fragile ornament that must be kept locked away to ensure her survival into queendom.... No one seemed to care that she had already arrived.

It had been fourteen years since her mother's passing, Mast guide her soul. Everyone still acted like Havorie was the poor, four-year-old girl she had been when she first took the throne. Her duties had increased since that time, of course, but in the last few years, little had changed. She occasionally met with officials who had traveled across Aragwey to visit her court, but through the urging of her aids, every decision had already been made for her. She had daily coaching lessons on the conditions of her kingdom as well as continued classes on etiquette and public speaking from Lord Resoldo Byron, her steward, but still she was little more than a figurehead.

Lord Ethan, despite his deteriorated state, headed the military, and all real decisions went through him and his men—the worst of which was that despicable general, Guther Aldune. Havorie was glad General Aldune was out of the city leading a war march along the Minthune River, as it meant she no longer had to tolerate him during her weekly briefings with the Ver'konus. Lieutenant General Cale Fisman had taken over in his absence. At least he treated her with some respect, even though he too was versed in hiding the truth.

"Try to get some rest," said Damian after Havorie was once again under the covers. He silently exited the room, shutting the door behind him.

If it wasn't for the threat of losing her Detector, Havorie would have told Damian about the illegal channeling. Lives could easily be lost if the shaking got worse. Whoever was abusing the Power this recklessly needed to be stopped before it was too late.

With a sharp clink, a diagonal crack formed across the bedchamber window.

Havorie frowned. She couldn't tell the guards what she knew without explaining how she knew it, but she couldn't just allow this to continue either.

She slipped out of bed once more. She positioned one of her pillows perpendicularly beneath her covers so that its silhouette resembled her sleeping body. Stepping gingerly over to her dresser cabinet, she retrieved another one of her late mother's Power Artifacts from its perch. It was hidden atop a ledge inside the central cabinet drawer.

She peeked out her chamber door—Damian had begun his rounds. He would circle back around shortly. Now was her chance. She checked the pulsing dial. It was pointing east, towards Lord Ethan's wing of the palace. With her heart racing, she stepped briskly down the corridor, using the shaking as cover to move from room to room without notice.

Damian's warning about the glass had not gone ignored. Havorie skirted the hallway along the wall opposite the bank of windows. The maids and servants had paused in their duties when the vibrations first struck a low rumble in the panes of glass that faced the inner sanctums. They took cover away from the windows and the luminescent bulbs that Lord Ethan invented several decades ago. Until the shaking stopped, they would huddle in dark rooms beside walls they knew would not crumble, no matter how violent the tremors became.

Like the rest of the city, the palace was indestructible, built with Calvenite, an unnatural stone developed by Ver'ati Builders many centuries ago. The obsidian-colored material gleamed in the light—a modified version of slate; only the Power could mar its dark façade. Under pressure from the tremors, the walls would flex, but they would never crumble, no matter the strain.

Though tremors had been a common occurrence in the capital for as long as Havorie could remember, their frequency had increased significantly in recent memory. With the Power being summoned hundreds of times a day within the city's vicinity, it was a wonder they didn't occur more often. The quakes were usually among the easiest Echoes to manage, but Havorie had never experienced any this violent before.

While pausing to catch her breath, she risked a glance out of one of the rattling windows. The garden atriums were well lit, even now as the night air cooled the eaves, drawing the heat up and out into the cloudless sky. Towering lamps illuminated the gardens in splotches of light that shifted with shadows as mostly bare branches wavered like spindly fingers in the crisp breeze. The air had a bite to it, leaving a light frost on the few leaves that still lingered within the brush. Winter was fast approaching—the days becoming shorter.

Havorie barely managed to keep her footing as the ground lurched violently to the side. She threw herself into the nearest room as the rumbling momentarily grew stronger. She had to wait until the shaking diminished enough for her to continue deeper into the east wing.

Chancing only a fleeting look back to check that no one was following, Havorie couldn't help but smile to herself. The corridor was still completely vacant. She had half-expected to see Damian barreling after her, hand on his hilt, always ready for a fight. Little escaped him—he was the head of palace security and captain of the royal guard for a reason. Though her ruse had not yet been discovered, she knew her absence would not go unnoticed for much longer. It was only a matter of time before Damian or one of the other palace guards found her snooping out of bounds.

She looked at the Detector once more. The light was growing brighter as she closed the distance to the source of its attraction. The pulses were like a living heartbeat—invisible currents of energy flowing everywhere around her. The Detector picked up the subtle charges in the air.

"My queen?" came a confused voice from behind her in the dark.

Havorie jumped at the words. Spinning around, she breathed a sigh of relief as the light from the corridor lit the face of a young maid, no older than Havorie herself. She did not recognize the girl, which was fortunate. Many of her own maids would have turned her over to Damian on the spot. If the unfamiliarity went both ways, perhaps the girl could be intimidated into leaving her be.

There was a chance that the east wing maids were not fully briefed on her "voluntary" captivity. She had been all but a prisoner in her own home ever since the Whunes infiltrated the Underground with their tumorous flesh and deadly claws. Havorie had to admit that King Garrett's hulking slave beasts getting so close was a truly frightening reminder of his vast reach, but the lapse in security had been addressed. The only lingering result was that she now had to be sequestered away to keep her "safe" from the dangers of life. In reality, she knew it was just an excuse to minimize her rule.

Havorie couldn't help but think things would have been different had she developed the Gift of the Arcanum like her mother. The queen of Phandrol being Ver'ati was considered a good omen, and Havorie's mother, Nestra, had been a very good omen indeed. She brought a light to the people of Phandrol that Havorie could only aspire to. Havorie's subjects rained praise upon her. They rallied around her, cheered her every spoken word, but it was mostly just wishful thinking—the last stranglehold of hope lingering after her mother's unexpected demise. Queen Nestra's death was still mourned heavily, which was all the more reason for them to hold Havorie up in her place, apparently. They wanted to love her, needed to perhaps, simply because of the hope for peace and justice her mother had represented.

Havorie felt the disappointment in the air—saw it on the faces of every official she met with. She could never quite live up to their expectations. Her blood tested negative for the gene that controls the Power. It skipped over her. She was just a regular person, where her mother had been barely one step short of Mast herself. Queen Nestra Elveres had been a kind leader—decisive, elegant, beautiful; she commanded the people and the military with grace. She gave Lord Ethan his title and allowed him to form the Ver'konus in her name, and the light shone brighter on the people of Phandrol for it. She was steadfast against King Garrett's threats and the military hordes of Kovehn—they had not been allowed to step one foot across the Crimson Waters during her reign.

The same could not be said for Havorie. The Whunes crawled through the Underground just last month! Even though every last Whune had been purged from the sewers, people were still scared to go out at night. The streets of her own capital were unsafe! Havorie could hardly fault her subjects for their fear.

She stared at the young maid. The girl's brown hair gathered beneath a cream-colored bonnet before running behind her ears in two short braids. She had a look of fear in her eyes, though Havorie couldn't tell if it was from the increased intensity of the earthquake or if the girl was simply shocked to see her queen sprinting through the hallways dressed only in a nightgown. No one could blame her if it was the latter. Havorie glanced around the room—it was one of the many linen closets that serviced the guest rooms along this corridor—she could think of no plausible excuse for her presence in such a place.

"What is your name, girl?" Havorie asked the maid, being sure to speak in the most stately, regal tone she could muster. Lord Byron would have been proud—old Resoldo had spent countless hours trying to mold her into a proper queen during their daily lessons together, starting back before she even knew how to walk. He probably thought it all landed on deaf ears.

"Ervia. Ervia Sindel… my queen," said the maid, her voice escaping as a squeak. "Pardon me, but what… is that?" Her eyes were locked on the amber glow of the Detector, its light pulsating under the thin lace of Havorie's sleeve.

A pile of folded linens toppled over in the corner of the room as the intensity of the quake grew stronger.

Havorie swept an annoying lock of flaxen hair out of her eyes as it dangled into view. The fluffed out nest of hair that was usually styled into dense curls by Madam Jusair, her personal maid, was beginning to fall flat at this hour. Ervia was staring back at Havorie questioningly. She had to say something….

"Ervia," Havorie said, trying to construct a better excuse than simply speaking the truth outright, but nothing came to mind. "I can't have you telling anyone that you've seen me," she said simply. Ervia waited for her to continue, but Havorie realized she wouldn't believe a word of her explanation until she witnessed the reading on the Detector firsthand.

Havorie pulled up the sleeve of her nightgown, fully exposing the glowing Artifact on her wrist. She held it up to Ervia so the young maid could get a look at what had drawn Havorie from her chambers at such a late hour. "It's like the Charisms," she explained. "Someone is channeling a vast amount of Power within the east wing."

"But that's forbidden within the palace," said Ervia, frowning.

Havorie nodded. "I'm on my way to investigate…. And you're coming with me." She didn't want to risk leaving the girl behind. Ervia had a nervous look on her face again, but Havorie couldn't resist smiling. It was clear from Ervia's expression that she didn't want to go against her queen.

Just as Havorie expected, Ervia smiled meekly back at her. Most people had no idea of the diminished state of the queen's authority and would never risk openly antagonizing her. Together, they went into the hallway as the intensity of the tremors finally waned. Havorie ran as fast as her legs would carry her. She was more than a little surprised to see Ervia keeping up as they rounded the corner, entering Lord Ethan's residence within the palace. Ethan's study and personal chambers were one floor down, leaving the floor Havorie and Ervia were on open for use mostly by the wait staff.

Havorie glanced at the Detector. The channeling was directly ahead now. There were a few rooms to pick from. The doors were all closed—any one of them could be concealing the source of the dial's attraction.

"Not that one," Ervia whispered. "Cherry and Silvia were still tidying up in there when the shaking started."

Havorie pointed questioningly at the next room over. Ervia shrugged. There was only one way to find out…. Havorie turned the knob delicately. The clicking sound it made was too soft to be heard over the rumble of the quake. The door opened inward. Havorie pushed on it slightly and peered through the crack. It was too dark to see anything. She gave up on caution and pushed the door fully open, letting the hallway light fill in the shadows. She hit a switch on the wall just to the left of the door and several luminescent bulbs flickered on overhead, lighting the empty meeting hall in its entirety. They were directly above Lord Ethan's quarters now.

Checking the Detector again, Havorie watched as the dial began spinning in circles. She was too close to the channeling to get any further information from the device.

We must be directly above the culprit.

Havorie reached into a pocket in her nightgown and pulled out what appeared to be a rolled up scroll with ornately engraved silver end caps—the Power Artifact she retrieved from her dresser. Havorie crouched to the floor and pulled the scroll open. Where one would expect to see canvas, a thin film of translucent material reflected the luminescent bulbs overhead. As she pressed the see-through sheet to the floor of the meeting hall, a curious thing began to happen along the film. The tile beneath shimmered and started to disappear. It was as if the floor had turned to glass. Looking into the translucent material allowed Havorie to peer directly into Lord Ethan's bedchamber as if through a window. Her view was blocked slightly by a cabinet below, so she slid the scroll across the tile to a location with a better vantage point. The tile was still intact—not actually altered at all.

Havorie glanced up at Ervia. The girl was dumbfounded, her jaw held partially askew. It must have been a strange sight for a commoner, even in the capital of magic. Havorie smiled faintly. "You can't tell anyone about this either," she said.

Peering through the floor, she could see Lord Ethan lying motionless in his bed, his thin, white hair matted to his brow by perspiration. Doctor Hilven Crane—head physician and Ameliorator of the Ver'konus—and Lieutenant General Cale

Fisman—acting commander—along with several other men Havorie did not recognize, all stood over Lord Ethan. He was strapped to his bed.

At first, it appeared that Ethan was entirely doused with a thick layer of sweat, reflecting the room's lights off his skin, but after a moment, Havorie realized that it was his skin itself that was glowing with shimmering, white light and not a reflection at all. The men standing over him were drawing on the Power, and together they were doing something to Lord Ethan's body.

Ethan suddenly convulsed, his chest ratcheting up despite his restraints. Havorie could clearly see he was screaming in pain, but no sounds carried through the floor or her little window. Calvenite could deaden even the harshest screams.

"What are they doing to him?" asked Ervia, her complexion becoming ashen as she sat beside Havorie, watching intently through the window.

Before Havorie could answer, Ethan stopped convulsing. The lull lasted only a moment before Ethan's skin, along with his clothes, started melting off his body. His wispy hair fell away as his scalp drooped off and something black began poking through. His entire body was turning into gray goo, his skin shearing off in piles on the bed.

Ervia screamed.

Ethan's fingernails detached and fell away from his hands.

Havorie felt like she was going to be sick. She gagged slightly, covering her mouth with her hand as she watched his pink insides bubble to the surface and spill out all over.

They were killing him and there was nothing she could do but watch....

Without warning, a face emerged from the mound of sticky flesh that was once Ethan's old face. A chill ran down Havorie's spine. The new mouth gasped for air and eyelids shot open, revealing new eyes that sparkled like blue gems. They appeared to stare straight at her, though she was pretty sure there was no way anyone below could have known she was watching.

She suddenly realized that she was actually witnessing a new layer of skin forming beneath the old. Ethan was shedding his old body like a cocoon. The black fibers poking through his old scalp were a full head of new hair. His new skin was smooth and unblemished; youthful and vibrant. He was rosy-pink like a newborn baby. Despite having been around Ver'ati her entire life, Ethan's transformation was by far the most remarkable thing Havorie had ever witnessed.

As the men standing around Lord Ethan lowered their hands, the glow vanished from Ethan's skin and, simultaneously, the earth stopped trembling. Their concentrated use of the Power had caused mayhem all across the city.

Havorie's heart fluttered mercilessly as she took in Ethan's naked form. Doctor Crane stepped up to Ethan's side and released the restraints holding his arms and legs in place, allowing him to rise up from his bed. The remainder of his old skin slopped onto the floor as he took his first steps around the room. He appeared to be about twenty-five years old now, fresh muscles bulging in his arms and shoulders. He was perfectly healthy, in the prime of his youth—handsome didn't even begin to describe him! Havorie could feel her cheeks warming as she spied down on him. She dared not glance over at Ervia, though she knew the girl was watching her now with a curious smile on her lips.

A click sounded from the door. Havorie immediately scooped the scroll off the floor, causing the little window to vanish as soon as it was lifted. She shoved the Artifact under her gown.

"There you are!" said a voice from the hallway, both girls turned around.

Havorie did her best to look innocent. She'd been so engrossed in watching Ethan as he twisted and flexed his new body that she'd nearly been caught with her Artifact out. She hoped the blush had faded from her face; she wished she could get one more glimpse of his sculpted body…. He looked like a statue, molded out of clay.

"I see you've made a new friend," said Damian, stepping forward, allowing his large frame to fill the doorway. "It's perfectly alright if you want to see more of her. In fact, I think it is good for a young lady such as yourself to have friends, but I can't have you running away like this again, especially not during a quake."

"I'm sorry, Damian," said Havorie, playing on his assumptions. "I just didn't think I would be allowed to be friends with a maid."

"Nonsense," said Damian. His stubble-covered chin wrinkled slightly as if Havorie had insulted him. "You are queen and may choose your own company. Let's just make next time an official visit."

"Alright," said Havorie as she stood up from the floor.

She slid the scroll back into her pocket, being sure to call no notice to it as she followed Damian out through the doorway. He stayed a pace in front of her, his watchful eyes always searching meticulously for hidden threats, even here within the safety of the palace.

"See you tomorrow, Ervia!" She shot the girl one last meaningful glance before stepping out of sight entirely. She hoped it would be enough to keep her silent about what she had seen, at least for the time being.

CHAPTER

2

A Sinking Feeling

Javic Elensol sat in the tiny dimly lit closet, devoid of distractions apart from the commotion of the class just on the other side of the door. He needed to focus if he was ever to connect to the Power without first delving into his emotions. It seemed an impossible task—he had only ever made the connection whilst driven by overwhelming emotion and necessity—but this was the assignment given to him by Professor Arius Vanton: To find his anchor—something that would allow him to enter a peaceful state of mind where he could reach the Power.

The other initiates and cadets in the class were doing an activity where a sphere of matter was passed around, each student taking turns transmuting it into different substances, after which they were judged on the purity of their work. They were all having quite an enjoyable time if the jovial ruckus coming through the closet door was any indication.

Professor Vanton considered Javic's purely emotional connection to the Power to be a weakness. The professor was attempting to remedy this by segregating him from the rest of the class until he learned to access the Power without drawing on his feelings. He spent every one of Vanton's classes thus far locked away in the supply closet with the extra books and training apparatuses.

He was not to come out until he could break down the door on his own, free of emotion, but every time he felt like he was getting close—

A hissing noise sounded from the other side of the door, followed by a burst of laughter, shaking Javic's concentration once more.

This was not how he imagined his training would proceed. Professor Vanton's transfiguration class was his worst subject by far. At least he got to participate in his other courses.

Javic yawned as boredom settled over him. If he were back home in Darrenfield he would be asleep right now. It was the middle of the night—an ungodly hour. The rising and setting of the sun always dictated the start and finish of Javic's day when he was a farmer. He had spent a long summer and fall planting and harvesting crops, and now during the cold months when everything green retreated back into the earth, life was supposed to finally slow down so that Javic and his grandfather, Elric, could rest up before preparations for the next season of planting needed to commence. Apart from maintenance and repair work around the farmhouse, there was little else to do during the winter months but sit back and read a book, or perhaps go out hunting if the mood struck. With the hours of sunlight so short, most of Javic's time during previous winters was spent indoors in front of a carefully maintained fire, just keeping warm and listening to his grandfather recite fanciful stories. They all seemed fanciful anyway, until the day they became a reality.

It had been a little over two months now since Belford, with the Mark of Kings on his arm, appeared in the old rock quarry near the Elensol farm, and Javic hadn't had a normal day—or night—since. Far from home, in the Glowing City of Erotos, the sun may as well have not existed. The hours of the day were marked by the amount of time the moon lingered above the horizon. Wizards could use their abilities only when the moon was up. With so many Ver'ati in the city, things tended to run on their schedule.

Dazzling glowing bulbs created by Lord Ethan—true works of wonder—were placed at the tops of Calvenite lampposts all along the city's walkways, flooding the streets with unnatural light no matter the position of the celestial bodies. It was a strange concept for Javic to get used to—not waking with the sun. In some ways, he supposed, the bulbs were like miniature suns themselves—they hurt Javic's eyes if he stared directly into their luminance, leaving green and purple blotches across his vision which drifted about for a few moments before subsiding. Their glow even hid some of the dimmer stars from view—but unlike the sun, they did not provide significant warmth, which was becoming increasingly noticeable with the recent turn in the weather. Javic could see his breath, even now while indoors.

Erotos and the kingdom of Phandrol had always seemed like such a distant land, a place of magic and mystery where Ver'ati trained and performed their miracles. As much as Javic always daydreamed of traveling across the five kingdoms, he never truly expected to go on such a journey. Adventures were for people far braver than he, people who could stare into the face of darkness and never flinch—people like Arlin Calary; no Power to speak of, but a sword on his belt and a flame in his heart. When he fought, he became one with the earth, the steal of his blade springing out from his flesh as if it were fused to his bone. It was a sort of bravery which most men could only interpret as crazy, but Javic had grown to admire him for it.

Arlin was the kind of man who could get a woman like Mallory Worvon to fall in love with him, and that was quite the feat. Arlin could have any woman he wanted, really, but Mallory was a truly special prize. Her soft-brown hair, when the sunlight hit it just right, reminded Javic of the dense fields of barley back home, blowing in the wind in late spring just before harvest time. Her rosy cheeks held a natural blush that gave her a shy, girlish appearance, but she was far from shy. She was older than Javic, and had a flirtatious attitude that he found hard to resist, and even harder to read. They were only friends, and she clearly had feelings for Arlin, but recently Javic couldn't get her out of his head. Mallory had a motherly quality about her that he found quite attractive. She was caring, kind, brave—not fearless like Arlin, but courageous nonetheless, never faltering even when faced with real danger.

Javic had watched Mallory coddle Kara through her regressed state for several weeks after Belford turned her back from being a Whune, right up until the girl's passing. Seeing the loss in Mallory's eyes had been the hardest part to bear, but the kindness she expressed towards the girl in her final days was exactly what drew Javic to Mallory.

The closet door began to rattle slightly at its hinges. Javic could feel the rush of pure exhilaration that came from touching the Power. The sensation was addictive, though it took a lot out of him, both physically and emotionally. The tingling feeling flowed through his chest and out through his limbs like a torrent of ice-cold water threatening to sweep him away.

He always felt as if he were about to lose himself when the Power flowed through his veins. He forced his mind to release the connection, which was twice as difficult as grasping it in the first place. A part of him never wanted to let go. It had been the thoughts of Mallory surging through his head that allowed him to find the Power—that subject was too emotionally charged.

Professor Vanton had made it very clear that if he broke out using his emotions, it would not count, and right back into the closet he would go. The crisp awareness that the Power brought along with it slowly began to fade. The edges of the room dulled with his waning perception. The faint light seemed to fall flat as his world dimmed. Javic could still sense that the Power was there, available for the taking, but without his emotions to draw it in, it stayed just out of reach, as surely as if the moon were beneath the horizon. Javic let out a sigh.

He hadn't seen Mallory in over a month—hadn't seen anyone he knew since his brief meeting with Shiara and Belford several weeks ago. He couldn't wait until he passed his proficiency exam so that he could finally have outside visitors again. It still made his stomach flutter to know he would one day become Ver'ati like Shiara Nighfield. She would have been pleased to know that he learned much from watching her attempts to teach Belford how to use the Power, even if Belford hadn't. The teachings had aided Javic greatly in his training thus far—at least in his other classes where his teachers didn't care how he reached the Power, just as long as he was able to.

He was already stronger in the Power than Thorin McGowlin—that much was clear from the extensive testing he underwent during his first week as an initiate. Thorin was strong in other ways, but when it came to the Power, he was lucky if he could affect anything beyond his own body. The same was true for most initiates these days. Connections to the Power were becoming weaker with every passing generation. Javic, on the other hand, had extremely high potential according to Doctor Hilven Crane, the lead doctor at the academy. It was not as high as Belford's of course—his blood responded too strongly for the doctor's machinery to accurately measure—but it was still higher than any of the other initiates this year. Doctor Crane told him his strength would continue to grow with age and practice.

He already caught the eye of a few of his professors, leaving his classmates simultaneously jealous and eager to befriend him—another new experience for Javic. He never had much luck making friends back in Darrenfield, other than Salvine Welin…. Javic immediately pushed the thought of his almost-girlfriend out of his mind before the fresh wound of her loss could pull him back down again.

Things wouldn't have been so difficult at the academy for Javic if only Belford had been allowed to stay by his side. The powers that be had roped Belford into their web. While Javic was forced into initiate training, Belford—equally unrefined—was fast-tracked straight into officer classes. There was no time to waste for the bearer of the Mark of Kings. Javic had expected to go through the academy with Belford—the only familiar face left in this place. Ever since their parting, Javic was becoming more and more homesick. It was a hollow feeling in his gut. He longed for days past— of being on the farm with his grandfather, Elric, and his horse, Olli. He couldn't even keep his most loyal companion with him! Olli probably didn't miss him all that much. She was stabled at an extended stay enclosure just outside of the city with Amit and the packhorses that had made the journey south with them. There, she could roam around more freely than if she was placed at the Hotel Willows with Elric. She probably did miss their long rides along the countryside, though—Javic knew he did.

The latch on the closet door scraped open and light from the classroom filled the chamber. Javic blinked several times before his eyes started to adjust. Professor Vanton stood in the doorway with a scowl on his face. He was easily Javic's oldest teacher, but when he got into his lesson plans he was also his most animated professor. Appearances could be deceiving when it came to the age of Ver'ati. They often looked considerably younger than they really were. Vanton seemed to be pushing eighty, so Javic could only imagine how old he actually was—ancient, most likely. His gray eyebrows floated above his sharp eyes like wisps of cotton. He silently fastened up the last few buttons on his jacket, preparing to go out into the cold. He stared over at Javic thoughtfully.

Javic glanced around the empty classroom. The lesson had ended… he had failed once again.

"Rylin has volunteered to help you find your anchor," said Professor Vanton, gesturing over to the boy sitting at a table in the corner of the room.

Javic had overlooked him. He knew Rylin Gansly well. He was Javic's bunkmate in the dormitories. The boy flashed him a sympathetic grin. He was only thirteen years old, the age at which children in Phandrol were required to be tested for the Gift of the Arcanum. He joined the academy shortly after Javic's induction, and Javic had listened to him cry himself to sleep every night for the two weeks that followed. It was partially Rylin's crippling homesickness that had set off Javic's own longing for simpler times. It wasn't until Javic started walking with Rylin to their classes together and sharing old stories from Darrenfield that the boy slowly began to overcome his fear of being away from home. Rylin's family lived in Shian City, all the way over on the Phandolian coast, and, like Javic, this was his first time in Erotos. The fact that he was an initiate and not allowed visitors didn't matter; his family lived too far away to make the journey very often.

"Practice," said Professor Vanton, "all the time you can. It could save your life one day. Emotion is unreliable… too slow."

Javic nodded reluctantly. It hardly seemed to matter. He would spend every day in that closet just wasting his time until the date of his proficiency exam came up. Then he just had to hope that what he had learned in his other classes was enough to get him promoted to cadet status. After that he would be allowed to choose his own courses and professors.

Rylin lead the way out of the classroom. He was a small thirteen-year-old. His head didn't quite reach Javic's shoulders. They walked silently down the hall. Rylin was a fast learner, already ahead of most of the other students in their class, but Javic couldn't help being a bit embarrassed to have such a small child as his tutor.

"It's really not that hard once you get the hang of it," said Rylin in his somewhat screechy voice. "You just have to let your mind go blank, ignoring everything but your task."

Javic grunted.

"Your anchor is what relaxes your mind—gets it ready to access the Power," he added.

Rylin used to be such a quiet boy, but he had opened up quite a bit to Javic since they started walking together. He was a sweet little kid, but he talked too much for Javic's taste. Javic didn't have any siblings and wasn't used to so much chatter. Rylin, on the other hand, had several brothers and sisters back home. He came from a family of seven, all fishermen, and Rylin claimed being vocal was part of the job. As much as Rylin annoyed Javic at times, Javic had to admit that he was starting to care for the boy. He imagined this was what it felt like to have a little brother.

Javic pushed open the heavy door at the building's entrance with a creak. A blast of cold air hit him in the face. He stepped through and held it open for Rylin to follow behind him. They exited Conset Hall, descending the eight marble steps that led to the promenade, bundling their jackets up around themselves even tighter as they went.

Most of the architecture in Erotos was formed from unbreakable Calvenite, though some of the peripherals were made from natural stone. The white of the marble staircase offset the glossy-black sheen of the Calvenite structures around it. The walkways throughout the academy were expansive, though no carts or carriages were allowed to enter onto many of them.

Around the side of Conset Hall, Rylin hopped onto the edge of a long planter box. He walked along, balancing on the narrow stretch of stone with his arms held out to his sides. He stopped as he wobbled slightly, but then continued forward, placing one foot in front of the other.

"My anchor is my mother," said Rylin, not looking back as he stepped gingerly along the ledge in front of Javic. "When I think of her it calms me enough to accept the Power."

Javic frowned. Lately, he had been trying not to think about his own mother, Kali, who died in service to the Ver'konus and left him to be raised by Elric, but everything kept reminding him of her. She was a student here once, before Javic was born. Javic used to love thinking and talking about his parents. They represented adventure and true romance in his mind, among other things. Simply knowing that he was going through some of the same experiences as them gave him a warm, fuzzy sensation that was as close to fulfillment as Javic could ever recall feeling.

Since learning the truth about their deaths—that Wilgoblikan was their murderer—and coming so close to enacting revenge upon the Goblikan Whune, the subject of Kali and Bartan had become tainted in his mind. Javic did his best to push the hatred he felt towards the dark wizard back down inside of him, but knowing that Wilgoblikan was still alive—and not only that, but that the Whune was currently being held somewhere in this very city, and yet infinitely beyond his reach—was very difficult to get out of his head. He could only hope that the Ver'konus had him locked away in some dank, dark cell where they tortured him regularly. They were dark thoughts, he realized, but after what that monster had done to Salvine and to his parents, and to so many other innocent people over the years in King Garrett's service, being tortured was the least he deserved.

Javic had not shared any of his thoughts about Wilgoblikan or the Whunes with Rylin, nor with anyone else for that matter, and he was not about to start now. He pushed the darkness to the back of his mind.

"Using memories of your mother?" asked Javic. "That sounds a lot like emotion to me."

Rylin shook his head and had to stop walking again for a moment as his ankle wavered. "Not the same. Emotion makes you act with pure instinct, but when you're calm and aware of your surroundings—yet not distracted by them—you have more control. It's like being in a fight," Rylin added, giving a nervous laugh. "If you're too scared or excited you might miss something or take a wild swing."

Though it was hard to imagine Rylin in a fight, Javic understood the sentiment. It was the same concept he enacted while hunting. If he didn't first steady his breath and clear his mind of distractions before releasing an arrow, he usually missed. He had never thought about approaching the Power in the same way.

The ground lurched beneath Javic's feet in an intense, sideways sheering motion that made the tops of the buildings sway eerily above him.

Rylin fell from the planter's ledge, landing on his hands and knees. "An Echo!" he exclaimed. He seemed unfazed by his awkward landing, but Javic helped him regain his feet anyway.

There was a terrible crash a couple of paces away as a marble statue smashed into unrecognizable chunks on the ground, thrown from the eaves of Conset Hall by the violent motion of the building.

Javic and Rylin stumbled along, moving away from the building's edge and farther out into Garson square as quickly as they could manage over the unsteady ground. Several more barrel-sized statues came loose and met their end on the Calvenite walkway below. This was the most intense earthquake Javic had experienced so far.

Protocol for an Echo was to move away from the location as swiftly as possible. This point was stressed several times during Javic's orientation. Echoes were unpredictable; they altered reality around them in seemingly random ways. What started as an earthquake could end with a city block frozen in stone. There really was no telling how bad it could get.

Echoes occurred quite often in Erotos, though with varying degrees of scope and severity. It was said that there was always at least one Echo going on at any given moment around the city, though many were so tiny that they were never detected. This was not Javic's first tremor, in fact there were several smaller ones earlier that very night, though Professor Vanton had ignored them and continued on with his lesson. This Echo, on the other hand, consumed the entire city. Looking across the square and over the buildings on the opposite side, Javic could see the tops of the towers of the Queen's Palace in the Central District, illuminated by glowing bulbs, wavering precariously back and forth.

The shaking continued on for what felt like ages, at one point even growing so strong that Javic almost lost his footing altogether. His heart was racing when the tremors finally retreated down to a low rumble. After a moment, even though slight vibrations continued, people began pouring out from the buildings around the square, cuts and bruises abound.

Everyone stood in groups, nervous laughter erupting sporadically from around the square as people began to recount their individual experiences of the shaking. They were all clearly relieved the worst of the Echo had passed. Most Echoes only lasted seconds, but some could go on for relentless hours. The calm only lasted a moment before a deep rumble sent shrieks through the crowd. The building across the way from Javic, Laudry Hall, creaked and groaned as it twisted over, its backside rearing up into the air. The whole structure was turning onto its side and sinking into the earth! Calvenite could not break, but the quake must have hollowed out a portion of the ground beneath the building. It was sinking into the abyss, all in one giant chunk.

Javic watched in horror as people threw themselves from the slanted windows of Laudry Hall before the earth could swallow them up. Some scampered away after landing in the square, others did not rise again. There was nothing any of the bystanders could do as the building quickly disappeared beneath the surface with a terrible scraping sound that filled the otherwise quiet night. A cloud of dust emerged from the hole as the building settled, and by the time the air cleared, only the northwest corner of the structure remained above ground.

When the rumbling finally ceased, in place of Laudry Hall, only a view of the Queen's Palace remained, its magnificent towers jutting high into the sky above the Old City on the opposite side of the Etwon River, as if nothing had happened at all.

A Familiar Face

The waking nightmares that plagued Belford's mind when he first appeared in Aragwey hadn't resurfaced in quite some time, but even so, last night, when the tremors became especially violent, he prepared himself for a reoccurrence of the visions. He expected to see pillars of fire springing up from the ground, showering him with sparks of molten lava, or the corpses of the dead staring up at him with their dark, accusatory eyes. He hadn't understood what was causing the tormenting hallucinations to manifest at first, but after his talk with the dishearteningly old Lord Ethan, he now knew exactly where his demons came from.

He could still see the missiles in his mind, sending streaks of blinding white light arcing across the sky—precision strikes devouring whole cities in monstrous mushroom clouds—but the eyes of the dead no longer followed him everywhere he went. They were memories, he now knew, not ghosts—though sometimes he wondered if the distinction really made any difference at all. There was no solace in understanding his trauma. He saw his world end, and only two other living souls could understand how that felt. Lord Ethan was one of them, and King Garrett, the man who ordered Belford's assassination, was the other. He could confide in neither. The three of them were part of the generation that developed the Power, now masked in mysticism and legend. Few knew the truth about the Power's scientific origin. To the Aragwians, it was all magic.

Belford leaned back in his cot in the little apartment he shared with Lieutenant Canbel and Captain Grine. He gripped a thin golden chain hanging around his neck and pulled the attached butterfly pendant out from under his shirt. It had been Kara's. He made it for her—a token of trust—calling upon the Power to form its intricate curving design back when they first met at the bath in Bronam. He knew now that the creation of gold was illegal under strict penalty from the Arcanum, but he could not bring himself to part with the trinket.

After Kara's death, Belford considered dropping it over the edge of the Rosa Marsa into the Crimson Waters below, but he didn't have the heart to do so. It was all that remained of the poor girl. He couldn't just throw it away, no matter how bad he wished to rid himself of it. He still had reoccurring nightmares about her death, though he could never quite remember the details upon waking.

One of his roommates, or overseers as Belford liked to call them, Lieutenant Sulinton Canbel, asked about Kara a few nights ago. Belford had awoken from a particularly awful dream crying out her name. No one knew anything about Kara except for the people who'd been aboard the Rosa Marsa, and Belford preferred to keep it that way. Canbel and Grine were Guther Aldune's watchdogs while the abominable general was away on his war march along the Minthune River.

There wasn't anything particularly wrong with Lieutenant Canbel, other than the fact that he asked far too many questions, but Belford found him to be utterly irritating, especially when he asked about things Belford couldn't remember from his past. The lieutenant couldn't get it through his thick skull that Belford simply didn't know the answers. Most of what Belford did know came from his singular meeting with Lord Ethan on the day he arrived at the city. The things Ethan told him—about the past, the Power, the computer on the moon—they were all closely guarded state secrets.

In the forty years since Ethan appeared in Aragwey, only a handful of his most trusted advisers had been told the truth about such things. Before leaving on his war march, Guther Aldune made it clear to Belford that he was not allowed to tell anyone about his conversation with Ethan, Lieutenant Canbel included, nor was he permitted to talk about his dreams.

Belford's dreams gave him glimpses into his past every now and then, but even after much reflection he only understood fragments of what he saw there. The majority of his memory had not yet resurfaced. There was, of course, Claire Birch—all of his most vivid memories revolved around her. Even before Belford could remember anything else—who he was; where he came from—he already knew he loved her, more than anything in the world.

Whenever Belford's mind started to wander, it was a sure bet as to where it would eventually wind up. Without Claire, he felt like a physical part of him was missing, torn violently from his flesh. It left him deadened to the world around him; detached. He kept thinking about the freckles on her nose; the sheen of her auburn hair in the sunlight; the perfect arch of her feet; the way she smiled whenever he spoke her name out loud. She made him a better person just by knowing her.

He didn't know whether she was alive or dead, or somewhere in between—locked away in the memory banks of the super-computer that directed the Power. There were no answers. He had nowhere to look. If there was any hope of ever seeing Claire again, it was to somehow access the memory banks of the computer up there, hundreds of thousands of miles away through the vacuum of space. Beyond reach. Harder than watching the world burn was the hopeless pangs of sorrow he experienced from missing Claire.

He had tried to track down where the Ver'konus was keeping Wilgoblikan. He desperately wanted to question the Whune. Somehow, Wilgoblikan had managed to predict Belford's return to Aragwey, showing up at the Elensol farm less than a day after the computer placed Belford in the nearby quarry. The idea that Wilgoblikan might know how to find Claire in a similar manner was the only thing that kept Belford going. So far, though, his efforts had been fruitless. Wilgoblikan had vanished into the system—swallowed up by the military machine. Nobody who knew anything about him would say a word to Belford on the subject. The secrets of the Ver'konus were vast and plentiful. Belford was left feeling frustrated and bitter.

With a sigh, he reached for the morning news bulletin, still covered in crumbs from Lieutenant Canbel's breakfast. He shook the paper over the floor before diving in.

The deadliest Echo in years, read the title on the first page. Belford skimmed the article. Apparently, last night a building along Garson Square had fallen into the earth, taking with it three faculty members and at least a dozen students. The casualty figures were still coming in. Deaths caused by the Power were hardly a new occurrence. Laudry Hall had been one of the larger lecture halls on the south side of campus. Belford was unfamiliar with the building. He knew very little of the academy south of Candeer Fountain. All of his officer training classes took place within a three block radius of his apartment at the far north end of campus. South campus was mostly for underclassmen. The lecture halls there were built so that a single teacher could babble on to a room full of students for an hour or two about some dead king or long-forgotten war and pretend everyone was gaining something useful out of the whole ordeal.

Luckily, no classes were in session within Laudry Hall at the time of the sinking, or else the death toll would have been far greater. Ver'ati cut in through the roof and recovered dozens of survivors throughout the night, but the violent fall broke more than a few backs. Not even Ver'ati healing could fix a person once life entirely drained out of them.

Death is death, and there is no coming back.

He'd been told that several times now. It didn't matter how powerful he was, some things were unfixable. Even so, he couldn't stop replaying Kara's final moments in his head. There had to have been something he missed, some way he could have saved her. She deserved so much better than to die, alone among strangers....

A rap at the bedroom door snapped Belford back to his senses. He stuffed the butterfly pendant necklace under his shirt before responding. When the door opened, he was relieved to see Captain Sharith Grine calling upon him, rather than Lieutenant Canbel. Grine, like Canbel, annoyed Belford when they first met, but he'd been much less persistent than Canbel when it came to pestering Belford with questions. Grine's main area of study was Amelioration—healing and body alteration—and as such, his interest in Belford was limited to related queries. Grine was a scrawny guy. Belford was pretty sure he could easily pick Grine up and carry him over his shoulder if he felt so inclined. Their relationship had become one of mutual distance; their only interactions revolved around the basic pleasantries required to maintain civility while living and working together.

"There's a summons for you," said Captain Grine as he flipped through the stack of mail delivered that morning. His bangs had become overgrown and were beginning to fall overtop his glasses. He swept his hand through his hair, brushing it to the side as he glanced through the rest of the messages before handing the summons over to Belford.

Like the morning news bulletin, the summons was written in English, though no one called the language by that name any longer. Belford had marveled briefly over the unlikelihood of being absent from the planet for countless millennia only to return and find people still speaking English, but the mystery had resolved itself: The legendary John Graven, also from Belford's time, instated it as the official language during his reign as High King of Aragwey after his return to Earth about a thousand years ago. Each subsequent returnee with the Mark of Kings—Emily Fox, Hannah Davis, King Garrett and Lord Ethan—reinforced the tradition, and spread their own familiar culture throughout the land. The language changed surprisingly little over the years, especially in Erotos.

The summons was straight forward enough, though it lacked any explanation. He was to proceed to the palace, where he was to meet with Lord Ethan about an urgent matter. There was no hint as to what the urgent matter might be. The fact that Lord Ethan wanted to meet with him was somewhat surprising in itself. The man was hardly coherent during their first meeting and Belford honestly hadn't expected him to live much longer, let alone recover enough in his delirium to request Belford's presence. Perhaps he was having a moment of lucidity and was ready to impart more details about their past. Whatever the reason for the summons, it was the most exciting development for Belford in weeks, and he did not intend to keep Ethan waiting a moment longer than necessary.

Belford gathered his jacket, made from fine embossed leather, and a curved ceremonial blade that he had taken to wearing on his hip, despite not having any training on how to properly wield the weapon. Both were gifts, among many delivered to him by the various lords and ladies of the thirteen houses of Erotos. Ever since revealing the Mark of Kings on his arm to the world, the presents had been pouring in. Each house bombarded him with contributions in an attempt to gain his favor, none wanting to be forgotten when the day came that Belford took over Lord Ethan's position as leader of the

Ver'konus. The only house not to bestow seemingly endless gifts upon him was the Nighfield house. It was also the only house of which Belford could remember the name, because of Shiara Nighfield's mentoring. She must have told her family not to bother trying to buy his affections. *Smart lady.*

The air was brisk outside as Belford made his way to the taxi station across the street from his apartment. Squinting in the bright blue morning light, he chose a foot-pedaled taxi—a cart hooked to the back of a bicycle. The foot taxis tended to be significantly faster than the horse-drawn carriages for travel within the city due to their tighter maneuverability. They also smelled significantly better than the horses. He paid his driver with a portion of his weekly stipend, given to him by the Ver'konus, and they were off towards the Queen's Palace.

Belford enjoyed the aesthetics of the Old City. Although the style of the architecture was consistent throughout all the districts, nothing in the newer sections could top the massive scale of the Queen's Palace or the Arcanum Cathedral. The extravagant buildings with their ample towers, decorated with Calvenite spires and colorful stained-glass windows, were pleasantly mixed with the contemporary electric light bulbs that Ethan introduced to the city several decades ago.

Ethan really outdid himself with those. Every person north of the Scar of Phandrol praised him like a god for reinventing electricity. None of the other kingdoms even had the technology to figure out how the bulbs worked yet. Most people just assumed they were an extension of the Power— just more magic to them—but Belford recognized the hum of turbines during his brief stint in the Underground last month when the Whunes attacked. Ethan built a secret power plant somewhere beneath Erotos. Belford was sure of it.

With all the opportunity for reinvention, Belford was starting to wish he'd learned more about the technology of his time back when he had the chance. The Power gave him a tool to reproduce anything, as long as he knew how it worked.

For instance, despite having been in many cars in the past, he knew nothing of how combustion actually worked, other than the basic concept of controlled explosions pushing out pistons or some such process. Even with his distaste for horse-travel, he didn't really feel like dedicating his life to the re-perfection of the automobile engine. He wondered how Ethan managed to recreate a power plant under everyone's noses. He was gifted—Belford had to give him that.

The taxi wheeled past the entrance of the palace without a hint of slowing.

"Here is fine," said Belford.

The driver ignored him, or perhaps didn't hear, continuing on down the street.

"I said you can drop me off here," Belford reiterated as the distance from the palace increased.

The driver began peddling faster in response.

Belford gripped the leather seat with both hands. "Where are you taking me?" he demanded. His heart began beating faster in his chest. The moon was down; he was Powerless. He watched the dark mud-and-clay-streaked street whiz past as he contemplated jumping from the moving cart. It would be a rough tumble at the speed they were traveling. His hand went to the hilt of his sword instead, fumbling nervously on the unfamiliar grip of the new blade.

The driver, spying upon him through a side-mirror attached to the handlebar, saw the intention in his eyes. "Not very observant today, are you?" she asked—her familiar voice escaping from under the brown cap that held back her long, raven-black hair.

Belford caught a glimpse of her steel-blue eyes in the mirror. "Shiara?!" He already felt stupid. She was dressed in a baggy tunic and trousers that masked her feminine curves. She turned the taxi around the corner, heading towards the docks. Belford had been so lost in thought when he first got in that he hadn't noticed the obvious disguise. He felt his face redden.

"I've been trying to figure out how to meet with you for days," said Shiara. "You've been designated a top asset. No one is allowed to speak to you without express consent from General Aldune's office." Shiara brought the taxi to a stop shy of the bustling harbor, pulling up on the sidewalk before turning around in her seat. "My requests to see you were denied." There was a slight crease in her forehead as she frowned. Her eyes shined as she looked upon him.

Belford felt uneasy under her gaze. He cared for Shiara as a friend, but her eyes held more than friendship in their stare. His heart belonged to Claire and Shiara knew it. She was outwardly respectful of his wish to remain platonic with her, but there was no hiding the truth of her feelings in her eyes.

"You disobeyed commands in order to see me?" he asked in awe as he realized the risk she was taking just to have this meeting. Belford had never seen her disobey orders before— she was a dog of the military, loyal to a fault.

"Of course not," said Shiara. "I was never ordered not to see you. My requests to set up an official meeting were simply denied. An incidental run-in on the streets isn't insubordinate."

"Incidental run-in?" asked Belford. "Is that what you call dressing up as a man and driving a taxi around outside my apartment building?"

Shiara pointedly ignored him. "Do you want to hear what I've found out about Wilgoblikan or not?" she asked, placing a hand on her hip in irritation.

Belford focused in with seriousness. "You know where they're keeping him?" In the two months since Wilgoblikan's capture, Belford had not heard a single peep regarding the dark wizard's whereabouts. He still believed questioning Wilgoblikan was his best chance at finding Claire. Belford felt a nervous pinch form in his gut as he waited for Shiara to tell him what she had discovered.

"Not exactly," said Shiara, softening her posture. "He's in a secret lab, somewhere, probably in the Underground, but I do know who's looking after him," she said. She didn't force him to inquire. "Doctor Hilven Crane." She gave a slight grimace. "He's overseeing all of the captured Whunes directly—experimenting on them."

Doctor Hilven Crane. He was the lead Ameliorator within the Ver'konus. Belford interacted with him on an almost daily basis. The doctor constantly picked and prodded his mind, trying to learn how Belford managed all of his incredible medical feats with the Power. He had directly asked Doctor Crane about Wilgoblikan on several occasions and the doctor claimed he would look into it for him, pretending to know nothing—now to find out he had been blatantly lying to his face the entire time!

"You can thank Thorin for the information," said Shiara. "Aldune still has him doing menial dock work, but it's amazing how much information can be deduced from reading shipping itineraries and talking to the right delivery boys. When someone is asked to haul something as unusual as nine indestructible Calvenite cages, it's not soon forgotten."

Belford truly was grateful. He owed Thorin many thanks, but his mind was already churning away, contemplating how he might go about getting what he needed from Doctor Crane—unabated access to Wilgoblikan.

Shiara seemed to read his thoughts. "Be cautious of Crane," she said. "Were I in your stead, I would not approach him openly. He is close with Aldune, and cares for little beyond his craft."

Belford nodded slowly to himself.

Turning back around in her seat, Shiara steered the taxi towards the palace entrance for a few quick pumps of her feet. She stopped again suddenly, gesturing for Belford to get out. "You can walk from here," she said. "I have other duties to attend to."

Belford stepped out of the cart, slightly miffed by the sudden dismissal. "Can I have my fare back?" he asked.

"Seeing as you're not a real taxi driver, and didn't even drop me off where I requested."

Shiara shook her head, a thin smile on her lips. "And risk blowing my cover?" She blew Belford a kiss before peddling off down the street without so much as a glance behind her.

Belford trudged back towards the palace entrance, shaking his head. Despite Shiara's abrasiveness and the awkward energy still lingering between them, it was good to see a friend. He always had people around him, but somehow he had been feeling more alone than ever at the academy.

He walked past the guard checkpoint out in front of the palace. The guards saluted Belford despite his lack of an official rank. Everyone recognized him now. The Mark of Kings had made him an overnight celebrity. He entered the palace's anteroom, its grand ceiling arching high above, and began making his way along the columned walkway. Before he reached the end, a steward wearing the royal crest—a blue fox with golden trim—emerged from a side room and hurried over to Belford.

"Ah, Aaron Levy, sir," the man said, calling him by his true name. "Right this way. The lord is expecting you."

Since remembering his birth name, Belford still hadn't quite gotten used to hearing people say it. It didn't fit him anymore, but Ethan knew him as Aaron, so that was what all of the officials called him. The steward led him off to the side, bypassing the Charisms chamber and instead directed him down an adjacent hallway filled with wooden crates. The steward walked quickly. At the end of the hall, Belford spotted the opening of a freight elevator.

"Do not be alarmed," said the steward, "this is not merely a tiny room. In actuality it's—"

"I know what it is," interrupted Belford, uninterested in hearing the man's explanation of what an elevator was.

If the steward was insulted by Belford's interjection, it did not show on his face. He pulled down on a lever and they rode in silence. The lift descended slowly into the earth. The door to the elevator was a metal grate, allowing Belford to watch the solid wall of the shaft shift by in front of him. After a while he lost track of exactly how far down they'd gone. Deeper than he'd been in the Underground before, surely.

Suddenly a tunnel appeared in front of them in the elevator shaft. The steward released the lever as the lift became level with the tunnel's floor, halting their descent. He slid the grate open and led the way out, continuing down the narrow corridor ahead.

Belford could hear the hum of machinery nearby—Ethan's hidden power plant, if he was to venture a guess. The tight walls and thick air made him feel like he was in a mine, but there were barred gates along the halls and chambers that spider-webbed off of the main shaft which gave Belford the distinct impression that he had descended into some kind of dungeon. The steward removed a key from a pouch on his belt and led Belford through several locked gates before stepping into a room with a deceptively high ceiling.

It looked to be a natural cavern, though it was decorated to suit a king—there was elegantly carved furniture atop the largest rug Belford had ever seen, woven into an intricate design which included both the Mark of Kings and the royal fox crest. A tall pitcher of a rosy wine and several ornate glasses stood on a counter against the near wall. Tapestries lined the chamber, just like in the palace above, and there was a large dark mirror built into the far wall. As usual, the room was lit by electric light bulbs.

"Wait here," said the steward. "Lord Ethan will be with you shortly."

The steward exited the room, leaving Belford to himself. Belford immediately walked over to the mirror on the opposite side of the chamber. Something was odd about it. His reflection was too dark. Not all of the light was bouncing back. When he got his eyes close and held his hands up around his face to block out the rest of the light from the room, he thought he could make out distant shapes behind the glass.

"Very perceptive," said a voice from behind him.

Belford turned quickly, dropping his hands from his eyes. A man, barely older than himself, dressed in a fancy, white button-up shirt stood at the entrance to the chamber. He was poised nonchalantly against the frame of the door. There was a smirk on his face. Something about the high, angular architecture of his cheek bones combined with his bright-blue eyes seemed familiar to Belford, though he couldn't quite place him in his memory. Belford had met with so many people since arriving in Erotos that he could hardly be expected to remember them all.

"Hit that switch, just to the left there," said the man, pointing beside the mirror on the wall.

Belford hadn't noticed the switch; it was partially obscured by one of the tapestries. He reached out and flipped it. Immediately the mirror became translucent: A glass window overlooking a huge cavern, larger than anything Belford expected to find this deep underground. A roaring river flowed across the cavern floor and through the turbines of a massive power plant, built right in the center of the hollow. His assumptions had been correct, but it was even more spectacular than he imagined.

"I hope I haven't kept you waiting long," said the familiar man.

Belford turned and stared blankly at him. "Will Lord Ethan be joining us any time soon?" he asked.

The man's smirk grew larger as he walked over to the counter and poured himself a glass of the rosy wine. He clearly didn't care about Belford's status. Over the past month, Belford had gotten used to people bending over backwards to please him. He was starting to feel almost entitled to the treatment.

"You should be more cheerful," said the man. He took a long sip from his glass. "We are going to rule this whole world one day, you know."

Belford narrowed his eyes.

The man laughed. "Oh, forgive me," he said, "I know this must be confusing. I just wanted to see if you'd be able to figure it out. I don't blame you, though—it must be so odd. It seems every time we meet I look completely different." The man put his glass back down on the counter with a hard clink.

Belford continued to stare at him, confused.

"You never knew me when I was this young, so I didn't really expect you to recognize me." He pulled the sleeve of his white shirt up, exposing a Mark of Kings on his bicep.

Belford could hardly believe it. "Lord Ethan…?" he asked. He knew the answer before he even opened his mouth. He really needed to stop letting things surprise him.

"In the flesh. Though please, just call me Ethan, no more of this 'Lord' nonsense—we are equals." Ethan walked over and placed a hand on Belford's shoulder. "Thanks to your medical knowledge, Doctor Crane and I were finally able to figure out how Garrett has been rejuvenating himself all these years. Not a simple process, I assure you."

So this is where all of Crane's inquiries were leading….

Ethan's blue eyes were more than familiar, Belford realized—in fact, he knew the face well; an old friend's. His curly, brown hair was cut short like Belford's—generally a sign of nobility in Aragwey, though Belford kept his short more out of habit than anything else. Most people couldn't afford the regular haircuts that were required to keep shorter styles from looking shaggy, though that wasn't as much of a problem here in Erotos. The city was full of prosperity. When Ethan was an old man he looked so different—his white hair straight and thin—Belford would have never guessed it to be so curly in his youth.

Belford couldn't stop grinning at the sight of him. He wasn't sure why Ethan's return to vitality made him so happy. Yes, Ethan had defeated old age, which was exciting in itself, but that was not what made Belford so cheerful. Perhaps it was the realization that no one would be expecting him to lead the Ver'konus anymore. That was a huge weight off his shoulders. Deep down, though, he thought it might just be the fact that he finally had somebody he could really talk to, someone who would truly understand what it was he'd gone through.

"I hate to cut the pleasantries short," said Ethan, the smirk instantly fading from his face, "but there is business to attend to...." Ethan's eyes became blue flames. "I've called you here to ask for your assistance on a very important mission."

Belford dared not move under Ethan's intense stare.

"Together, we are finally going to kill Garrett Rames."

CHAPTER

4

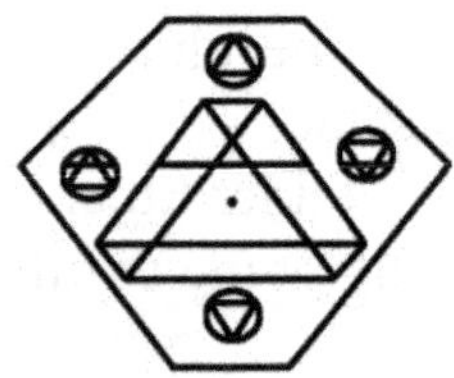

A Moment of Clarity

The lights seemed to flicker, everything going dark for brief lapses of time as Belford's eyes stopped interpreting information correctly. His brain was reeling from Ethan's words.

A mission to assassinate King Garrett? It's reckless— beyond reckless, it's insane!

Ethan was staring at him now, not even a hint of amusement on his face. "If you fully remembered Garrett—knew what he'd done—you wouldn't be so hesitant," he said, his brow lowering into a frown. "So many lives destroyed because of him…. It was his actions that led to the war that ended our world."

Belford had no memory of exactly how their world was destroyed, but he didn't doubt Ethan's story. He felt he could trust Ethan. He knew firsthand the types of atrocities Garrett was capable of committing. Garrett created Wilgoblikan,

42

making the king equally responsible for all of the terrible things Wilgoblikan had done, including the death of Kara.

Ethan had his own reasons for hating Garrett. During their first meeting, Belford learned about Ethan's wife, Michelle. Garrett murdered her shortly after her return to Earth. Belford could faintly remember Michelle's face—an olive complexion with hazel eyes and chestnut-brown hair that ran down in tight curls over her ears. She was definitely one of them—one of the people memorized within the computer. Belford had never heard her listed amongst those with the Mark of Kings, so he could only assume Garrett killed her before she had a chance to reveal her mark to the people of Aragwey.

"I know you must not have much stake in this world," said Ethan. "I for one didn't care for this place when I first arrived, but it will start to feel like home, if it hasn't already." Ethan's tone shifted to one of a more pleading nature. "Garrett has ravaged these lands. He had a head start on me, and carved out his corner of Aragwey with brutality during the Cleansing. We are too evenly matched to go head-to-head, but with your added strength and my returned youth, I just know we can destroy him."

Other than Wilgoblikan, if there was anyone in the world who could find Claire, or at least give Belford some idea of when or if she might return, it was Garrett. Whether he liked it or not, confronting Garrett was Belford's best chance for answers. Perhaps paying him a visit was exactly what needed to be done.

Belford still wanted to question Wilgoblikan, though. The Whune was already in the custody of Doctor Crane, and talking to him would be a much easier and safer option than traveling across Aragwey to try to capture Garrett. Shiara once mentioned that as a Whune, Wilgoblikan was incapable of betraying his master, so whether or not Belford would be able to get anything out of the dark wizard was determinate on whether Wilgoblikan considered the information to be harmful to Garrett. There was no way to know without trying.

If Ethan truly needed Belford's help, that gave him leverage. This was the break he had been waiting for. Ethan would have no choice but to allow him to question Wilgoblikan. "I was wondering," said Belford, "whatever happened to that Goblikan that was captured last month in the Underground?"

Ethan's piercing eyes shifted to Belford's face. "Why do you ask?"

"I was just curious," he said, trying to feel Ethan out. "Aldune thought he might be of some intelligence value."

Ethan grimaced slightly. "That was the hope," he said, "but unfortunately his ties to his master were unbreakable. He was useless to us."

"I know a thing or two about Whune minds," said Belford. "Maybe I could have a run at him? See if I can get him talking?"

"I've heard all about your little experiments on that Whune-girl," said Ethan.

Belford felt a hard knock in his chest as Ethan referenced Kara.

"I might have taken you up on the offer if you'd come to me sooner, but unfortunately the Goblikan was recently put down. It was simply too dangerous to keep a creature like that around once his usefulness expired."

Belford's heart dropped. He tried to not let the disappointment show on his face. Getting information out of Wilgoblikan had been a long shot, but it had been his only goal for the last month. All he had left now was the possibility of questioning Garrett—a daunting task.

Ethan moved on with the conversation: "You may or may not be aware, but King Vouldric of Taris was murdered several months ago, followed shortly by a Kovani and Goblikan invasion force laying siege on their capital, Saldrone. The city has not yet fallen, but their resolve is wearing thin. Soon Taris will be just another part of Kovehn." Ethan took a seat, and gestured for Belford to join him before going on. "I heard you were in North Galdren when King Lodrin was assassinated?"

An image of the Crimson Stalker flashed across Belford's mind. He still had nightmares about those gray eyes. The way he killed, so clinically, so calmly—it wasn't natural. The king of Antara was ripped apart in his study, along with every guard and servant on duty—no witnesses remained—but Belford knew the Crimson Stalker was responsible. He killed everyone in the palace and then vanished without a trace.

"My war room has been in a bit of an uproar as of late," said Ethan. "There's been news from the north: High King Nemos of Graven is dead as well—has been for months actually. They say he died in his sleep, though my sources in the Arcani suspect foul play. We knew about it almost immediately from our spies, but the Arcani are keeping it secret from the rest of the world while they silently jostle over their choices for a successor. Recent events, however, have forced their hand and it will soon be public knowledge.

"A meeting was held in Corton City, one of their northern strongholds, to crown a new high king. The entire Gravish hierarchy was present. It was the only event that could have gotten all of them in one place at the same time. The city was ransacked, and everyone inside murdered, though the details are still unclear at this moment. The Power was used, that much is certain, but the city was heavily guarded by those who should have been able to defend against such an attack. There is no explanation—it should have been secure. No evidence was left by whoever was responsible, but it doesn't take a genius to figure out that Garrett is the one poised to benefit most from the disarray that is already beginning to spread within Graven."

Someone went in, killed everyone in line for the throne, and then disappeared into the night… it sure sounded like the Crimson Stalker to Belford. The mysterious man had been capable of using the Power without the moon—something that defied reason and was simply unheard of within the

Arcanum. Shiara assumed he must have been using Power Artifacts, but Belford had seen him in action—there was nothing in his hands, no intermediary devices to suggest the presence of an Artifact. If he descended upon Corton City while the moon was down, like he did in North Galdren, he would have been unstoppable; tearing through Ver'ati as if they were nothing at all. Ver'ati couldn't defend themselves any better than ordinary men if the signal from the moon was beyond reach. The only explanation that Belford could think of was that Garrett must have found some way of boosting the Crimson Stalker's abilities, and in doing so created a monster even more terrifying than the Whunes.

Ethan stood up and walked over to the door. He motioned for Belford to follow him back out into the hallway. "The Torus Desert is expanding," he said as he led Belford deeper into the labyrinth of tunnels. "It can only be Garrett's doing." Ethan pushed open a heavy door on the right side of the hallway and stepped through into a chamber containing a wide wooden table of dark polished walnut with a giant map of Aragwey stretched out across its surface. Battlements and troops were marked all over by little figurines and flags.

There were four men already in the room, huddled together around the Kovehn corner of the map, running through battle scenarios by arranging and rearranging the various pieces. Belford recognized two of the men instantly. First was Doctor Hilven Crane with his short hair and hooked nose. He reminded Belford a bit of a falcon, the way he looked around with his piercing eyes, and yet he was always so solemn at the same time. The other man Belford recognized was Lieutenant General Cale Fisman. He had been the acting leader of the Ver'konus while General Aldune was away and Ethan indisposed by his old age.

Belford had been required to meet with Cale several times since joining the academy and while he seemed nice enough, Belford got the distinct impression that Cale didn't really know what he was doing when it came to commanding the

Ver'konus. He was in his fifties, with short hair like Doctor Crane—though, unlike the doctor, Cale was balding on top. He was a lanky man; very tall and skinny. He was always rubbing his lower back. The back pain was probably caused by his terrible posture. He was hunched over even now as he studied the map. None of the men looked up as Belford and Ethan approached.

"All we have to go off of are rumors," continued Ethan, "but if what we hear is true, new Whunes are being created within the Torus Desert every day, stockpiled for a war that could make the Cleansing look like a friendly game of chess." Ethan glanced at the four men with mild disinterest. They were pressed together shoulder-to-shoulder as they worked over the map. "Welcome to my war room," he said to Belford, gesturing all around him.

Doctor Crane and Cale Fisman looked up now and nodded to Belford. The other two unfamiliar men glanced up momentarily as well.

"You already know Doctor Crane and the lieutenant general," said Ethan. "The other two are Tannel Cresdale, Head of the Arcanum Council, and his steward Sarbin Raiger." Ethan narrowed his eyes as he said their names. "I've been forced to include them in our invasion planning."

Tannel and Sarbin ignored Ethan's comment, though Ethan purposely spoke loud enough for both of them to hear the distaste in his voice.

"They don't seem to understand that without me, their little *Arcanum* wouldn't even exist," said Ethan. "Garrett would have seen an end to their lot ages ago." Ethan was starting to push it.

"You may look like a child," said Tannel, "but that is no excuse to act like one." He did not look up from the map as he bit back at Ethan. Tannel was a wide man with thick, black eyebrows and a square jaw. He was cleanly shaven, which seemed like a poor choice given that his face was badly pocked with old scaring. A short beard, or even some stubble, would have greatly helped at covering up the ugly marks. He wore vestments that were altogether too ceremonious given the lack of occasion.

Tannel's steward, Sarbin, was a younger man. He had black hair as well, though he kept it long on the sides and short in the back—a strange style even for Erotos. Sarbin said nothing, though it was clear by the frown on his face that his sentiments resided alongside the councilman's.

"Tannel here doesn't have much faith in my abilities," said Ethan. "He doesn't think my strength will be enough to destroy Garrett once and for all, and is refusing to put the support of the Arcanum behind my plan. What he has failed to consider, however, is you." Ethan clasped Belford on the shoulder.

From out of his pants pocket, Ethan drew a white chess piece—the king—and grabbed a white circle figurine off of the map from where it was sitting atop Erotos. It resembled the full moon emblem, Ethan's symbol of choice, and was clearly meant to represent Ethan on the map. He carried both objects over to the other side of the table, to Tavallon, the capital city of Kovehn, where the four men were carefully arranging an army's worth of figurines and battalion flags. Ethan slammed his two pieces down with unnecessary force, sending a black circle, which Belford could only assume was King Garrett's representation on the map, flying off the table, along with a number of other figurines that got in the way of his fist.

"With Aaron joining me in the fight, we can't lose," said Ethan. "Alone, the two of us can accomplish what the entirety of the Phandolian Guard, the Ver'konus and your precious Arcanum has failed to achieve for decades—the end of Garrett Rames. All I need is for your council to prepare the Arcanum to deal with the remaining Kovani forces that refuse surrender."

"To clean up your mess?" Tannel narrowed his eyes. "And if you fail to dispose of Garrett, what then? Every Ver'ati I send will be slaughtered."

"We won't fail," said Ethan, staring unblinkingly into Tannel's eyes.

Tannel matched his intense gaze. "I do agree there is merit to your plan. But if I am to accept the proposal, I have an important stipulation," he said. "Your escort must be comprised of men of my choosing to ensure the success of the mission. I will not see my men killed just because Garrett's strength turns out to be greater than you expect."

It was Ethan's turn to study Tannel's face for a moment now. "This must be a small operation," Ethan argued, shaking his head. "It can only be a few men. We won't make it within a hundred leagues of Garrett if we can't slip by his defenses unnoticed."

"Fine," said Tannel, "but you must bring with you two agents of my choosing, then—competent men."

Ethan considered his options with a clenched jaw before finally agreeing. "Just two," he said.

Tannel nodded. "Then it is decided," he said. "Sarbin, along with the two Ver'ati I select will report back to you before nightfall."

Sarbin appeared just as surprised as Ethan to hear that he was included in the deal.

"You know better than anyone the kinds of decisions I make," Tannel said to his steward. "I trust you to keep the sanctity of the Arcanum intact in my stead."

Though his eyes grew wide, Sarbin bowed submissively.

"Come on," Ethan said to Belford, leading him back over to the entrance of the war room. "Until next time, boys," he said, giving a sarcastic salute as he and Belford stepped through the doorway.

Belford waited until Ethan secured the door shut behind them before speaking. "I'll do it," he said. "I'll go with you to assassinate Garrett."

Ethan breathed a sigh of relief. "You had me worried there for a moment. There wouldn't have been a mission without you," he said in earnest.

Belford knew he would have to be cunning. In order to find Claire he needed to discover how Garrett's man had successfully calculated his return at Darrenfield. He doubted Ethan would be willing to postpone his revenge once he had the opportunity to kill Garrett. Belford was going to need help if he was to pull this one off. He needed to bring people he could trust—people more loyal to him than to the leader of the Ver'konus, or to the Arcanum. "I do have one request though…."

"Anything," said Ethan, the confident smirk already returning to his lips. "Anything you want."

Best Laid Plans

The Whune who was once Salvine stirred at the base of her Calvenite cage, tranquilizers finally wearing off. Mangled nubs resided where her claws once protruded, aching with phantom pain. In her groggy state, she momentarily forgot about the terrible doctor and all he had done to her. She stretched out her hand to run it along the bars, only to have her shortened digits swipe through nothing but air. She reached out a little farther and collided with the cage, sending a spike of discomfort up her arm. The unprotected skin throbbed with a sensation reminiscent of fingernails being pried away from the flesh.

She recoiled as she let loose a deep moan. Pain was a new sensation for her—also courtesy of Doctor Crane. He meddled in her mind incessantly, as he did with all the captured Whunes. She had already watched the life slip from two of her brethren so far. A third was currently locked in a state of complete paralysis, heaped up in a lump of flesh at the bottom of its cage by one of the good doctor's bumbling experiments. Doctor Crane did not speak while he tinkered with their bodies and minds, instead whistling out an eerily cheerful tune between puffs on his smoke stick. At the rate the experiments were progressing, she did not expect to be alive much longer.

Looking around now, she found that her master, cage and all, had been removed from the chamber. New emotions flooded her body. Beyond the worry over her own safety, she also felt a sense of great sorrow at the loss of her master's presence. Those types of negative emotions were as foreign to Whunes as arithmetic to a sheep. Whunes, like sheep, were simple-minded creatures, but unlike sheep, lust for killing was the driving force in a Whune's relatively short life. Sadism and carnage were at their core. Bloodshed was the only thing that freed their shackled minds, albeit momentarily.

Besides herself, there were only five Whunes remaining. Their cages, along with the empty ones of her fallen brethren, stood in a semicircle around Doctor Crane's cold metal examination bench. She and the other Whunes were forced to watch as the doctor worked his torture on each of them in turn. They were transfixed by new emotions of fear and anxiety as they stared out from their indestructible cages. The thick leather straps that kept them in place while on the examination bench were panic inducing in their own capacity. Whunes were only naturally submissive to their master, and to no one else… she feared the worst for Wilgoblikan. She could no longer feel his mental presence. He had always been with her in some capacity since the day he brought her into the world. She hoped the loss of his presence in her mind was due to Crane's meddling rather than the terrible alternative—that Wilgoblikan's life had ended; that her master was no more.

She groggily watched Crane storm around the room in silence, tossing his torturous devices back into their various storage compartments. Crane wasn't whistling today. He was clearly displeased—his plans for Wilgoblikan left unfulfilled, if she was to reckon a guess.

We need to get out of here....

She did not bother resisting the voice in her head any longer. She and the voice had found themselves in almost complete agreement since being brought into this hellish dungeon of a laboratory. The voice was right again this time. She needed to get out of this cage or she would be killed. If by some miracle her master still lived, she was of no use to him dead. But how could she escape? The bars were unbreakable.

We could pick the lock.

She scoffed at the suggestion. The finesse required for such a task was beyond the brutish tendencies of a Whune.

She could feel a prickle of hesitation from the voice, as if it were contemplating its next words carefully.

You could let me... take over our body.

Normally, she would never consider such a drastic course of action. The presence of the odd voice had been a treacherous enemy from within since the moment she first saw the moppy-haired boy and words that were not her own began to echo off the inside of her skull. *Javic! That's Javic! That's my Javic!* It fought her every step of the way and stopped her from completing her master's task.

What other choice do you have? It spoke meekly. *Sit here, all locked up, and wait to die? I can pick the lock—my brothers taught me.*

She had to admit, the presence had a point. They would have to work together if there was any chance of escape. She did not usually address the presence directly, but she did so now out of a sense of comradery. *What will you use? We have nothing.*

The voice lit up at the acknowledgment of its existence. *Just be prepared to slam into the front of the cage with all your might... but only when I tell you to. We are going to need to topple the cage.*

Together, they eyed Doctor Crane with a hateful stare as he finished cleaning up his shiny toys and stomped out of the chamber.

Once the doctor was gone, the presence briefly took control of her body to turn her head and observe a tin case sitting on top of the cabinet directly behind their cage.

Claws, was all the voice said.

She understood immediately. That tin was where Doctor Crane kept all of the Whunes' amputated, razor-sharp claws. If she could get ahold of one, it would be the perfect tool for attempting to pick the lock. The only problem: Both the case and the cabinet it was sitting on were too far away from their cage. Even tipping it over wouldn't get them within arm's reach of the cabinet base, let alone the case on top.

Be patient. I have a plan.

She waited for some elaboration, but the voice remained silent. She could sense a bubbling of optimism rising up from the portion of her mind where the presence resided. Foolish optimism, perhaps, but it was contagious none-the-less. She would go along with whatever the voice had planned—give it control if it so wished. At this point, she had nothing to lose. As foreign as giving up control would feel, it was nice to be in agreement—to not be at odds with herself any longer. Right now, fighting the enemies on the outside was more important than fighting herself from within.

All we have to do is watch and wait, the voice said. *Have faith. A moment will present itself. With my intellect and your strength, I just know we can get out of here.*

CHAPTER

6

The Road to War

"The term *Ver'ati* is derived from the ancient Aragwian dialect—loosely translated 'hand of God.' Its usage has become relatively synonymous with *wizard*, though only wizards who have completed training with the Arcanum can claim the title rightfully." Professor Arius Vanton glanced around the auditorium in an accusatory manner, as if all his students were guilty of making such false claims.

Javic had never heard of anyone daring to call themselves Ver'ati until after completing the Dance of the Elements—the ancient rite of passage that every Ver'ati undertook at the culmination of their training. It was not until after they passed that final test that a member of the academy finally earned their title and was accepted into the Arcanum.

"The Arcanum is the oldest order of Power users, dating back to the first cycle of the Gravish Standard calendar, all the way to John Graven himself," continued Professor Vanton.

"The ancient city of the Arcanum was called Sultrim, the Sun City, now lost within the Arid Hills to the west; initiates of the Arcanum at one time would make pilgrimage to Sultrim to train in the ways of Mast."

The slight shake of a distant Echo rattled the windows at the sides of the auditorium. Professor Vanton didn't seem to notice the apprehension in his students' faces. Thoughts of Laudry Hall were surely running through all of their minds. Javic, for one, couldn't get the image out of his head—the entire structure rearing up and twisting over.

How quickly it vanished into the earth....

It was the reason Javic was here now, back in Conset Hall with Professor Vanton, instead of listening to the history lecture Professor Lian had been preparing last night in his office, regrettably located within the basement of Laudry Hall. Lian was the only casualty Javic knew personally. Rather than canceling the class, the Ver'konus opted to instate Arius Vanton as guest lecturer until a more suitable replacement could be found.

"In the first years of the second Cycle of the Mark, the time of Emily Fox," Professor Vanton went on, "loyalties within the Arcanum splintered. Some were bound to the kings of Graven while others believed in the authority of the Mark of Kings, which Emily Fox possessed. The two factions warred for several decades over their differences. The Gravish Arcanum, calling themselves the Arcani, or Children of the Arcanum, moved their home city to Dreythor, while the Phandolian Arcanum named their faction the Vestori, meaning The Shield, and moved here to Erotos nearly seven-hundred years ago—forever sworn to protect the bearers of the Mark of Kings."

Rylin was seated next to Javic in the large auditorium. He tapped Javic on the arm and then gestured towards Baxton Crigs, seated down one row and to their right. Bax was the third member of Javic and Rylin's trio. They lived in the dormitories together—Bax's room was located straight across the hall from Javic and Rylin's. Javic wasn't as close with Bax as he was with Rylin, but this was mostly due to Bax not having the time to spend every waking moment with Javic the way Rylin did. A year older than Javic, Baxton had already graduated out of initiate status and was now a cadet within the Ver'konus. This carried with it a heavier class load, as well as a greater emphasis on military training which kept him on a strict schedule.

Bax's girlfriend, Sima Pahel, took up much of his time as well, though no one could blame him for wanting to spend time with her. Sima was gorgeous—long dark hair, dark skin, dark eyes, with a bit of an exotic quality about her which Javic found subtly alluring. Although she'd been born and raised within the city, Javic was sure she had at least a little bit of outlander blood in her. She was a very quiet girl and a hard worker—the complete opposite of Baxton Crigs, who was boisterous and always joking around with his peers. Sima was a cadet as well, sharing many classes with Baxton, including this one. She was sitting to Bax's right, taking ample notes on Professor Vanton's lecture.

Bax held up his notepad for Javic and Rylin to see. He'd sketched a picture of the professor, wrinkled face drooping halfway to the floor, standing atop his podium to show off a pair of woman's undergarments. Javic smiled to himself. Bax had done a fine job at capturing Professor Vanton's likeness. A pair of young women seated directly behind Javic started giggling at the sight of the artwork.

"Pay attention," Professor Vanton warned sternly, swinging his head around to focus on the girls. "You *will* be tested."

The girls stopped their snickering at once and sank back into their seats with reddened faces.

The professor continued on as if no disruption had occurred. "After the split in the Arcanum, initiates stayed in their homelands to train rather than seek out the knowledge that resided within Sultrim. Years passed, but after the death of Emily Fox in the year forty-eight of the second cycle, the feud fizzled out, only a stalemate remaining. Emily Fox was credited with the peace that followed her death, though in reality it was her presence in the first place that split the Arcanum."

Many of the students frowned at Vanton's words. One typically did not speak ill of Emily Fox within the capital, as she was universally considered to be the most beloved figure in all of Phandolian history. The professor did not seem to care one way or another that his lecture was causing discord.

"As the heat of battle became merely a memory, initiates on both sides of the Arcanum attempted to rediscover the path to Sultrim. Many who went searching for it, however, never returned. Those who did come back often brought home tales of wandering the wilderness for a fortnight, stalked by wolves and other creatures, all the while beaten down by the biting winds of the deadly mountain passes, only to scale a final ridge and find themselves back in the foothills overlooking Barhele, the city they set out from.

"A few came back raving mad, spouting nonsense, while others returned altogether mute, unable to speak of what, if anything, they had found within the Arid Hills. Some purported that the Paerto'sul—Guardians of the Sun—may have been responsible for the missing pilgrims, though most believed the guardians were already extinct by that time. The guardians were hybrid creatures, created with the Power during John Graven's era. Genetically similar to bears, they had massive bodies and walked on four legs, but they also had wide wings that made them capable of short flight. Highly intelligent and always loyal, it is said that the Paerto'sul could understand and partially mimic human speech, though few records remain as to the extent of their language abilities. They were tasked in protecting Sultrim, and each would have done so until their dying breath. Being an artificial species, research suggests the guardians would not have been able to survive more than a single generation after human abandonment, as successful procreation under such circumstances is highly unlikely.

"Regardless as to whether or not the Paerto'sul could possibly have been the cause of the missing pilgrims, it did not take long for both the Arcani and the Vestori to ban the pilgrimages outright, which was in year sixty-five of the second cycle. The city of Sultrim was deemed altogether lost in the decades that followed."

Everyone scribbled down dates and events in their notepads, unsure of what, if anything, they would be expected to remember from this lecture when it came time to take their exams.

"Hannah Davis rose to the Phandolian throne in the three-hundredth year of the second cycle, closing out the Cycle of the Mark and initiating the transition of the calendar into the third cycle. Sultrim already resided solely in the arena of myth and legend by that time, and with no more notable references to the ancient city in the Archives, we will skip ahead another three-hundred years to the beginning of the fourth cycle, with Garrett Rames as he began to vie for the Kovani throne one century ago. This was also the start of the Cleansing, commonly known as the Fall, or the Goblikan Wars depending on the source. The Cleansing is notable to our discussion of Sultrim because artifacts believed to have been lost within the city began to resurface all across Aragwey at that time."

Talk of King Garrett always drew Javic in. As Javic understood it, Garrett was directly responsible for ordering the executions of his parents, Bartan and Kali, and his grandmother, Teresa. Because of Garrett, Javic and Elric were the only ones left with the Elensol name. Strangely, hearing mention of him now did not evoke an emotional response within Javic the way it once had. Garrett was like a disease on Aragwey—a black taint that spread across the land with poisonous tendrils. Javic would have loved to see Garrett eradicated, but it was his minions that Javic hated most—people like Wilgoblikan. They were the ones who carried out, firsthand, the vast majority of evils contributed to Garrett.

"When Garrett took power, initially the Phandolian Vestori flocked to his side, rallied by the Mark of Kings, but it was not long before Garrett began to break the most sacred laws of the Arcanum. Garrett secretly Compelled many of the Vestori council, creating the first Goblikans, and killed all who opposed him. He created the Whunes to wage his war. The Vestori was all but destroyed from the inside out by its own leadership, twisted to do Garrett's bidding. The remaining Vestori in Phandrol and the Arcani in Graven allied together to fight Garrett's expansion until Ver'ati of all sects, Goblikans included, had dwindled from numbers in the thousands down to only a few hundred. The Whunes killed nearly a third of the non-wizard population of Aragwey by the end of the conflict as well.

"The final battle of the Cleansing took place on July fifth of year nine, fourth Cycle of the Mark, when one of the long lost artifacts of Sultrim—the fabled Orb of Parphim, now commonly referred to as the Orb of Saldrone—was used to eradicate the Goblikan army in the Battle of Eversted. The city of Eversted was also obliterated by the Orb of Parphim at that time, forming the Torus Desert wastelands. It was considered to be an acceptable price to pay for ending the war, though the scar it left behind is a substantial one. It was said that anybody who looked upon the orb's light was destroyed instantly.

"After that day, the Power could no longer be reached at the origin of the blast site. Surrounding areas soon followed until the whole desert became a dead-zone for the Power. Although the orb resides within Saldrone now as a reminder of that brutal past, its power was all but drained during the Battle of Eversted. Today, it sits atop an obelisk overlooking Saldrone's harbor, waiting for enemy ships to pass. It is still capable of sinking vessels with a narrow beam of energy, though its days of mass devastation are long over.

"The properties of the Orb of Parphim have been of renewed interest in recent years because of reports that the Torus Desert is expanding. Ver'konus agents in surrounding towns and villages have reported that the dead-zone for the Power is expanding into their areas as well, even faster than the rolling sand dunes. It is unclear whether residual energy from the artifact is responsible for the continued degradation of the environment after all these years, or if something more insidious is at work. Rumors of new Goblikans breeding within the Torus Desert have spread fear throughout the Gestrcho region, though the accuracy of such claims is unknown.

"After the Cleansing, Garrett Rames was not entirely defeated, of course, but without his army of Goblikan soldiers he was forced to cease his war march. He still managed to expand Kovehn to over twice its original size when all was said and done, though. So I ask you all to ponder this," said Professor Vanton, looking across the entire class, meeting the eyes of many of his students. "If the rumors are true, and the Goblikans really are returning, what will the price of freedom be now that we no longer have the Orb of Parphim to aid us? You are all training to become Ver'ati—to become soldiers. When the time comes, you must be willing to lay down your lives to protect your countrymen, your brothers and sisters in arms. The Gift of the Arcanum is not the Power bestowed upon you; rather, you are the gift, given by the Arcanum to the people of Aragwey. If you cannot make the sacrifices necessary of you, I suggest you find some way of leaving now; slip away into the night and never return, because when the time comes and people really are relying on you, it will be too late to run."

Everyone stared at Professor Vanton. He seemed to have forgotten that he was talking to a room full of initiates and cadets, most still children, tested by the state and put into this classroom because their blood indicated they could touch the Power.   They were not battle-hardened Ver'ati, or even volunteers for that matter. Vanton somehow managed to turn a history lecture into a most depressing look into the soul. As the class let out, Javic thought he saw Professor Vanton give him a small wink as he walked past.

"Is it just me, or is Professor Vanton starting to go a bit batty?" asked Rylin as they exited the lecture hall.

"Starting? I'm pretty sure he's already lost it," said Baxton as he attempted to slide his arm around Sima's back. She skirted away from his touch and doubled her stride to stay ahead of him. She was clearly not as amused with his antics as the other girls in class had been. Baxton bounced forward trying to catch up with her as they descended the marble steps of Conset Hall to Garson Square below.

Javic caught a glimpse of the hollowed-out ground around the ruins of Laudry Hall through the skeletal trees. The sinkhole was no longer expanding, but still no one risked going within two-hundred paces of the upturned building. The spires of the hall's roof dug into the side of the pit like pointy fingers, bent back as far as they would flex under the massive weight of the rest of the hall pulling down on them. They were all that was stopping the building from plummeting even farther into the hole. King Garrett wouldn't need to start a new war to destroy Erotos at this rate. The Power was pulling the city apart all by itself.

With sundown quickly approaching, the temperature was beginning to drop. Javic decided to head back to his dorm room to put on some warmer clothes before his next class. Professor Herin had warned everyone to bundle up because the lesson would be held outside tonight. Javic was actually somewhat excited to see what sort of activity was planned. Professor Herin was a Builder—a Ver'ati engineer—and that meant most of his classes were indoor lectures about architectural structure and design. Javic hoped that having class outdoors was a sign that things would become a little more hands on with the Power. Javic got to try his hand at creating Calvenite during an in-class activity last week and it was quite an enjoyable experience. The creativity that design work required came from a place within Javic that he'd never tapped into before. Professor Herin, impressed with Javic's natural ability to work the stone, used Javic's completed model as an example during the following lecture.

Ver'ati architecture fascinated Javic. To form Calvenite, ordinary slate needed to be created in the desired formations and shapes first before being converted into the unbreakable substance. Sometimes a design called for a structure that would be perfectly sound for hardened Calvenite, but which in its slate form would not be able to hold up its own weight. Slate was brittle, making it a challenge to work with.

The Etwel and Etwon Bridges were good examples of this—they lacked any conventional support structure that would allow natural materials to span such a large distance. During their construction, massive support pillars needed to be driven deep into the channels below to stop the slate from sheering off and crumbling into the Rivers Etto. After the slate was positioned correctly, it was converted into Calvenite and the support pillars were removed, once again allowing ships to pass freely up and down the channels.

Javic left Rylin and Baxton behind at the south edge of Garson Square. The whole class was to meet there at the entrance to Anshaw Hall, the architecture building. All the Builder apprenticeship students called the building The Fortress, and for good reason. The cathedral-style structure looked like a miniature version of the Arcanum headquarters in the Old City. Elongated stain glass windows stretched from the ground nearly to its eaves, at which point breathtaking spires took over, piercing into the sky almost as high as the towers of the Queen's Palace. They could have gone higher still, but city ordinance forbade any structure from surpassing the height of the palace.

Javic still had a little time before Professor Herin's class started. The moon would be down for another twenty minutes or so, and the class always began a few minutes after First Sense—the period of time just after moonrise when one first felt the presence of the Power. He hurried back to his dormitory, down one block from Anshaw Hall and to the east. It was a large, unimaginatively square building where all of the initiates were required to take up residence. Most of the cadets resided there as well as it was difficult to find accommodations elsewhere in the city. The dorms were cramped, two students to a room, sometimes three.

There wasn't much space for personal affects—after the two cots, dressers and a pair of writing desks, the space was nearly filled up—but this suited Javic just fine. What few belongings he still had from Darrenfield filled only a single pack, though he had accumulated some additional clothing since arriving in Erotos. Some of the other initiates—mostly the ones from more affluent backgrounds—complained about the limited size of their rooms, but here at the academy, everyone was treated equally, at least until they started gaining rank.

Rylin, coming all the way from Shian City, had brought more toys than anything else. His belongings spilled over onto Javic's side of the room. Javic didn't mind the clutter— it was better than a bare desk to look at when his mind needed a distraction from his homesickness. Their chamber was on the first floor, which was fortunate. It saved Javic considerable stair-walking time which many of the other students had to calculate into their schedules.

The building was already mostly empty when Javic entered. Everyone had class immediately following First Sense during this time of the moon cycle. The city's schedule may have been built around the moon, but people still preferred to sleep when the sun was down. Classes were always planned to be over as early into the night as possible when the moonrise came as close to sundown as it would tonight. A few stragglers were headed out as Javic traversed the hallways towards his room at the end of C-block.

He rounded the last corner and found that his door stood ajar. He slowed his stride. He was positive he closed and locked the door before leaving with Rylin earlier. After a brief thought of Whunes, he shook the idea off—had the creatures really been present, he would have been able to smell their stink from far down the hallway.

All worries of thieves and monsters quickly subsided as Javic pushed the door open and found Belford sitting on the edge of his bed. He was dressed in a slick leather jacket, fancy trousers, and the same bizarre shoes he'd been wearing when he first appeared in the quarry outside of Darrenfield. On the tip of his index finger he had a beautiful curved blade balanced at its mid-point. *Still safely in its scabbard, thank Mast.* The blade toppled over as Belford caught sight of Javic.

"About time," said Belford, hopping up from the bed. "I was starting to think I wouldn't find you before it was too late."

"Too late for what?" asked Javic, unable to hold back a grin any longer. It seemed like forever since he'd seen a familiar face.

Belford was smiling as well. He clasped Javic on the shoulder before answering. "How would you feel about coming along on a secret mission?"

CHAPTER

7

A Debt Repaid

Revenge, justice—it didn't matter what anyone called it—King Garrett was finally going to pay for his crimes, and Javic was going to get to participate in bringing him down. It was a very satisfying thought! Belford hadn't been able to say much regarding the details of the plan, only that Javic should pack his bags and head to the harbor as soon as possible. There, he was to board the Rosa Marsa. That meant more familiar faces in Javic's future.

He'd gotten to know Captain Bundles and his crew quite well during their journey along the Crimson Waters. The steamer was scheduled to depart within the hour. Belford assured Javic that word had been sent to his grandfather as well. Elric would be meeting them at the docks. Javic couldn't wait to see his grandfather most of all. Before the academy, Elric was present for every part of Javic's life. Even though he knew his grandfather was just across the city from him, the distance might as well have been a thousand leagues.

Belford apologized for not being able to stay longer—he still had some arrangements to finalize before setting off. He departed, leaving Javic to figure out exactly what he wanted to bring with him.

Javic tore his dresser apart, grabbing mostly at his cold weather clothing. While rushing around the room he tripped over a stuffed animal that belonged to Rylin. It was the only toy of its kind that Rylin brought with him to the dormitories. Rylin never spoke of the stuffed animal, clearly embarrassed to own something so childish. He even attempted to hide it from Javic during their first week in the dorms, but Javic spotted it on their very first night together and merely pretended not to notice.

Rylin held it close every night while he slept. Its body was made from real fur. Javic wasn't sure what kind of animal the toy was supposed to resemble. It had four legs and a head with a snout. There were no other clues. Every other feature—ears, eyes, nose, tail—had long since fallen off or worn out. Javic didn't think less of Rylin for keeping the stuffed animal. It was sentimental to him, and Javic understood the importance of such things.

In his rush to leave the farm in Darrenfield, Javic accidentally forgot to pack a very precious photograph of his father, grandfather, and himself, taken when he was an infant. He had looked at it so many times growing up that the image was still burned into his mind. Leaving it behind was one of his biggest regrets—it had been the last tangible piece of his father. Now, nothing remained.

If Rylin's stuffed animal meant anywhere near as much to him as that photograph had to Javic, he knew Rylin would be devastated if anything ever happened to it. He placed the critter back down gently on Rylin's pillow and let out a short sigh. He really was going to miss the kid.

Despite his excitement for the impending mission, he knew he couldn't just leave his new friends behind like this—at least not without saying a proper goodbye. He owed them that much. The journey would take several months, if everything went to plan, and that was a long time to be absent with no explanation.

As soon as he finished packing, Javic hurried over to Garson Square where he hoped to find Rylin, Bax, and Sima still waiting for class to start. As he approached Anshaw Hall, he felt the moon crest the horizon, bringing with it the increased sense of awareness that had become so familiar over the last month. The ground beneath his feet felt like an extension of his legs. His consciousness drifted out to consume all that was around him. He was tempted to reach out for the Power now—to let it fill him with its churning energies... so many countless possibilities—but he let the feeling subside.

It was always like that during First Sense: An old lover calling to him—one night apart already far too long. It wasn't until after he started using the Power regularly that the longings settled within him. He was told it was always like that for initiates—a thirst, growing stronger with each subsequent sip. Professor Vanton said the Power was like a drug. In time he would learn to master its allure, but the yearnings would never entirely go away.

As he rounded Anshaw Hall, Javic found that his classmates had already departed without him. At first, he wasn't sure how he was going to find where Professor Herin had taken everybody, but then he spotted a group of students gathered near the sinkhole on the other side of the square. It only took him a moment to spot Baxton amongst the crowd—he was at least a head taller than most of the other students, making him easy to locate. Javic ambled over in his direction, stopping only momentarily to readjust the strap of one of his bags as it dug painfully into his shoulder.

Professor Herin was poised precariously at the edge of the sinkhole along with two other Arcanum Builders. Their robes gave away their occupation—the hem of each of their wide sleeves was dyed brown to represent the earth from which their grand structures were carved. Every sect within the Arcanum had its own markings or colorations which altered the stock appearance of its members' official Ver'ati robes. Not every group was mutuality exclusive, however; Javic realized that much after seeing an Ameliorator displaying the usual blood-red hem of that sect, also adorned with the serpentine hood clasp of the Archive Historians. Although wearing the official garments was not at all a requirement for members of the Arcanum, most Ver'ati chose to proudly display their affiliations.

As Javic joined the throng of students, he found no lecture or lesson in progress. Professor Herin's back was to the class, as were those of the other Builders. All three men were focused intently on the upturned building in front of them. The class was only there for observational purposes—to see the Builders in action. Rylin and Sima were alongside Bax. Javic joined them just in time to watch the Builders erode the final spires of Laudry Hall, already bent far beyond the breaking point for any normal material. The spires snapped quickly, sending out deafening cracks as the Ver'ati transmuted the material back into slate. With its claws snipped, Laudry Hall began to groan and shift position, grinding along the wall of the chasm. It turned farther onto its side, banging against the stone precipice before falling straight down and vanishing entirely beneath the surface. A brief moment of silence passed before it reached the bottom of the pit. A violent impact shook the square with a crash that echoed out of the hole as Laudry Hall found its final resting place.

Javic realized Rylin was looking at him funny. Baxton and Sima glanced over at him as well as he placed his bags on the ground.

"Going somewhere?" Baxton asked, cocking his head to the side.

Javic nodded. "For a while, yes," he said, pausing awkwardly. He knew he wasn't allowed to give any details, but it was difficult not to say anything.

Baxton seemed to understand. "Something to do with your friend? The one with the Mark?" he asked knowingly.

Javic didn't need to answer; it was obvious.

Rylin was looking at him pensively, clearly concerned.

"Just be careful, won't ya?" Baxton said.

Javic nodded again. He didn't know what else to say. There was nothing he could say.

Rylin continued to stare at him searchingly.

"I'll be fine," said Javic. His voice faltered slightly. He tried to change the subject. "I suppose you'll already be a cadet by the time I get back," he said to Rylin.

Rylin clasped him around the waist in a tight hug.

"Mast, watch over you," said Sima, placing a hand on Javic's shoulder.

"Thank you," said Javic. Rylin still hadn't released him from the hug. Javic let him take all the time he needed. He suspected Rylin would have a rough time with his absence. He hoped Bax and Sima would look after the boy while he was gone.

With Javic still engrossed in his final goodbyes, the Builders tore through the side of the sinkhole, sending chunks of rock and sediment cascading down into the pit. Water was already seeping slowly into the hole, but as the Power ate away at the wall, the flow turned into a geyser. The force of the Etwel River was momentarily redirected to fill the dark depths of the chasm below. One of the Builders began igniting bits of rock into white-hot spheres of molten stone and dropping the pieces into the pit at even intervals. Professor Herin and the other Builder conducted their work under the light of the stones. They transmuted the water collecting at the base of the chasm into solid rock, filling the hallways of the dilapidated Laudry Hall and raising the floor of the pit closer to ground level. They did this in stages, waiting for the sinkhole to fill a bit between transmutations. They were forming a dense foundation. Eventually, a new building would be erected in Laudry Hall's footprint. Javic couldn't get the thought out of his head that the new structure would be like a grave marker to the old hall buried beneath.

He didn't stay long enough to see it formed. Rylin was unable to speak as Javic whispered a more personal farewell in his ear. "Stay strong," he said. "You'll do brilliantly. Make everyone proud."

Rylin stared back at him with sorrowful eyes, too choked up to utter even a single word. In that moment, Rylin reminded Javic of Kara, the way she had been both absent and present at the same time, almost as if lost to the throes of imagination. Unlike Kara, though, Javic could tell exactly what was running through Rylin's mind. He'd already had his family taken away from him—his whole life replaced with the academy—and now Javic was leaving him as well. It made him feel cruel; callous. Even so, Javic felt a greater pull inside of him. It forced his arms to pick up his bags and made his legs start walking, drawing him towards the Rosa Marsa.

It felt like destiny to Javic—this mission would change the face of Aragwey. Belford mentioned briefly to Javic that Lord Ethan would be leading their journey—in fact, this was Ethan's personal mission upon which they'd both been invited. Javic knew Lord Ethan hated Garrett. The fact that Ethan would put himself in harm's way to see the mission through could only mean one of two things: Either their success was all but ensured, or Lord Ethan had grown increasingly reckless in his old age. By the end of this, one of them—Garrett or Ethan—would be dead. A final duel.

Sima, Bax, and Rylin all looked genuinely sorry to see Javic leave as he made his way south across Garson Square. He caught a ride from a peddle-taxi as soon as he reached the main street. The driver took him along the river's edge and then over the South Bridge. It was wide enough for two royal parades to march side by side. A steady stream of carriages and taxis crossed back and forth over the slow flowing water. Javic glanced past the railing as they wheeled along. Behind him and down the river he could clearly make out the pit, still filling with water. Pulses of green light flashed from out of the hole, illuminating the murky dusk with bursts of unnatural lightning as his teacher and the other Builders transmuted the river water into the next layer of foundation.

The taxi passed through splotches of light cast from Lord Ethan's orbs high above in the Calvenite lampposts. The lights were placed every thirty paces or so along the road, leaving more light than dark on the Queen's Boulevard. The ropes of shadow between the luminance fell across Javic's face as mere flickers compared to the pools of light. As he approached the harbor, the lights grew even closer together until the splotches converged and no darkness remained at all. The taxi took a right and then a left onto the boardwalk promenade, bringing the sprawling docks into view.

Javic paid his driver with the few coins that remained from his life before the academy and set out on foot down the long stretch of dock.

The marina was full for the night, all the fishing vessels and cargo ships having already returned from their daily travels before dusk. Most ships sat silent, their crews asleep or departed to land, waiting for the first light of morning to draw them from their slumbers and back into the fray. The docks themselves had knee-high lampposts, pumping out more of Lord Ethan's light all along both edges of the walkway. Javic could hear unintelligible singing coming from within one of the broad vessels to his right. The drunken, cheerful voices were muffled by the boards of its curved hull.

Ropes creaked as the wind put strain on the many lines holding the ships in place all across the harbor. The weather was picking up and it was starting to rain. Each gust of wind carried with it a spray of tiny water droplets which lashed against Javic's face like stinging ice. He hadn't yet learned the Ver'ati trick for repelling moisture and cold, but even the chill couldn't dampen Javic's spirits now. He kept his face turned down as he stepped gingerly towards the Rosa Marsa.

He rounded the bend in the dock, and the seemingly too-large silhouette of Thorin McGowlin came into view. Half an arm taller than an average man and twice as wide, Thorin had a most menacing stature. Next to him, dwarfed by Thorin's tree trunk legs, was Shiara Nighfield. She was scowling. Her black hair, braided tight, ran down her back like a coiled viper, tensed and ready to strike. Oh how he'd missed them both!

The slickness of the damp dock was all that stopped Javic from running to greet them. The Rosa Marsa floated at their side, its port waterwheel looking just as rusty as Javic remembered. The whole side of the ship was streaked with a crimson stain just above the waterline. No official vessel, especially one with Ver'ati amongst its crew, would ever have rust on its hull. It hardly even looked seaworthy, which made it the perfect camouflage for their mission—such an unassuming vessel to carry the founder of the Ver'konus into King Garrett's realm.

Crates sat all along the dock. They were being slowly loaded onto the Rosa Marsa by a team of Ver'ati. The wizards worked in silence, their black robes and cloaks giving them the appearance of specters, barely visible in the darkness as the raindrops bent around them. One of the crates was too large to be lifted by hand and so a small crane had been erected on the dockside. Part of the Rosa Marsa's roof was removed in order for the large container to be lowered into place within the cargo hold. A dockworker operated the crane, closely watched by one of the Ver'ati. The dangling crate shifted about in the wind, but the crane operator lowered it with precision.

Javic could just make out Captain Artimus Gupree with his salt-colored hair pacing back and forth along the Rosa Marsa's bridge area, clearly distraught. Captain Bundles—as his friends called him—loved his ship dearly. It must have been difficult for him to see the roof peeled back like a used up tin can. Thinking about it now, Javic doubted the captain would have ever agreed to take his ship and crew on such a dangerous mission by choice, no matter how great the compensation. He wondered if Bundles knew the objective of their mission. It wasn't fair to drag someone into something like this without at least giving them a choice in the matter. The captain had his son Eben and his crew to look out for after all.

Just as Javic reached Shiara and Thorin, he was grabbed playfully around his middle from behind. The subtle scent of country lilac enveloped him, sparking off memories of spring and all the freshness that follows a good rain during that time of year. Mallory's jovial giggling hummed in his ears as she clutched onto him tightly. He felt her breasts push up against his back and instantly felt heat rising in his face. By the time she let go, he feared his blush must have resembled sun stroke.

"How have you been?!" asked Mallory, her smile dimpling her cheeks as it went all the way up to her large, round eyes.

Arlin, behind her, was watching Mallory closely. He was being more attentive towards her than Javic had ever seen him before. Usually Arlin remained aloof when it came to matters beyond the sword, but he eyed Mallory now with a wary regard, as if she were a dangerous predator capable of tearing him apart. Javic felt a nervous flutter in his stomach, but he wasn't sure whether it was Arlin's odd disposition that was causing it, or if his entrenched feelings towards Mallory were finally catching up with him.

"I've been good," said Javic, scratching at an imaginary itch on the back of his left arm. He forced his hand to stop moving as soon as he realized he was doing it. "What about you and Arlin?" he asked.

"We've been great," said Mallory. "We really missed you a lot though…."

Arlin didn't even glance up at the mention of his name. He was entirely absorbed with staring into Mallory's back.

Is he angry with her or something?

Whatever was going on with Arlin, at least it didn't seem to have anything to do with Javic. Arlin had never viewed Javic as competition for Mallory's affections, which was insulting in a way, but greatly preferred over hostility.

Mallory must have sensed the eyes on her back. She turned around with a sudden twist and returned Arlin's stare. Her expression saddened as she read the look on his face. She turned back towards Javic.

"Come back safe, alright?" she said, her eyes cast slightly downward.

"Wait," said Javic. "You're not coming with us?"

"No…" she said, "I can't.…"

"It's too dangerous," said Arlin. "Mallory must remain in Erotos."

Javic couldn't help but feel disappointed. It was true that Mallory would be safer here than if she joined them, and Javic certainly was not enchanted into thinking that there could ever be anything romantic between them, but he had still been looking forward to spending time with her while on the mission.

Shiara had a curious look on her face as she watched the exchange. Surprisingly, the two women hadn't spent much one-on-one time together during their journey south, but even so, they had formed a special understanding which connected them at times on a level beyond words. Javic couldn't quite understand it, but he made no attempt to sort it out; he knew women's matters were beyond his comprehension, and so he just let them be.

"Look after yourself," Shiara said to Mallory.

Mallory gave a curt nod.

Everyone waited on the dock while the Ver'ati finished loading the supply crates. As the last box was carried onboard, a procession came around the bend in the dock,

Belford bouncing enthusiastically at its lead. He was still wearing the leather jacket he had on at the dormitory, as well as the shiny, curved blade, latched awkwardly against his hip. Another dark-haired man, about Belford's age, walked at his side, dressed in a simple white button-up shirt which was far too thin for the foul weather. The rain curved around the entire group, though, not a drop landing on them.

Behind Belford, a young woman no older than Mallory was dressed in a pale-green, fur-lined bonnet and a cloak which she held wrapped tightly around her shoulders. She kept close pace with Belford, followed immediately by an escort of black-robed Ver'ati which included Captain Grine and Lieutenant Canbel whom Javic remembered from his jaunt in the Underground. Javic did not recognize any of the other Ver'ati. The young woman looked around with wide eyes, the sense of adventure clearly not lost on her. Captain Grine gazed at her with a misty-eyed expression as they progressed—only interrupted by their sudden halt upon reaching the Rosa Marsa.

"Has Sarbin Raiger arrived yet?" the young man in the white shirt next to Belford asked one of the Ver'ati who had been loading crates.

"Yes, Lord Ethan," said the Ver'ati. "He's already onboard with his entourage."

Javic took a closer look at the man in white. He had heard stories of King Garrett making himself younger every few decades with the Power, but it was still a shock to see the Lord Ethan of his grandfather's stories appearing so youthful. It made sense in a way—his piercing blue eyes were calculating and determined, as if he were two moves ahead and already contemplating a third in a high-stakes game of Crowns. He didn't have any of the mannerisms of a typical inexperienced youth—the sort of person Javic happened across frequently at the academy. He was relaxed in his position of command, though there was a touch of tiredness to his limbs.

A pattering of feet brought Javic's attention back to the end of the dock. His spirits rose as he saw his grandfather, coat held over his head, bounding recklessly down the wet walkway towards him. All of the Ver'ati became uneasy with his urgency, several even freeing up their hands in their wide sleeves as if expecting an ambush. Elric slowed to an uneasy trot as he saw Javic and the others staring at him. He was breathing heavily by the time he reached the Rosa Marsa.

"Elric Elensol!" Lord Ethan cried out, a boyish grin appearing on his lips. The other Ver'ati relaxed slightly with Ethan's joyous greeting. Ethan clapped his hand down on Elric's shoulder. "It's been too long! I didn't think I'd ever see you again!"

Elric looked exhausted, as if he'd gone the entire distance between the Hotel Willows and the docks in one long sprint. The confusion on his face was only momentary as he took in Lord Ethan's younger form. "I can hardly believe my eyes," he said. "For a second there I thought you must have been your own son!"

Lord Ethan shook his head. "I never did find time to have any children, though I suppose that possibility is open again for me now."

"I suppose so," said Elric. "You always did claim you'd find a way to defeat mortality, but I'll be damned if I ever thought it would really come to pass...." A twinkle of wonder flashed in Elric's eyes but then faded away just as quickly when he glanced over at Javic. His face drooped into a concerned grimace at the sight of his grandson. Elric's graying wrinkles—eerily accentuated by the flat light of the knee-high orbs—seemed to have multiplied several times over since the last time Javic saw his grandfather. Elric turned back towards Ethan, keeping the grave expression on his face. "I need to speak with you privately," he said, already leading Ethan away from the rest of the group.

Ethan gestured for his escort to stay behind as he and Elric walked down the dock together. Elric's jaw was set, which meant whatever he planned to say, it would not be up for discussion. Elric could be stubborn when he wanted to be, and he always got his way on such occasions, but this time he was talking to Lord Ethan. Once they reached a significant distance away from the Rosa Marsa, he began speaking quickly in a hoarse whisper which Javic couldn't quite make out over the wind, even with his senses heightened by the Power dancing across the fringes of his consciousness.

From their body language it appeared Elric was chastising Lord Ethan, as unbelievable as that was. Elric stood in the same forward-leaning, intimidating stance that he used to use when scolding Javic for shirking his daily duties around the farm when he was a child. Lord Ethan never once opened his mouth—he just listened intently to what Elric had to say. He continued to stand in silence even after Elric finished.

Javic couldn't help but be impressed by the amount of pull his grandfather had over Ethan. Elric, a commoner, was ordering around the leader of the Ver'konus! Javic knew Lord Ethan and his grandfather had a bit of a history together, but Elric never went into much detail about their relationship. Javic certainly didn't expect his grandfather to be able to get away with telling Ethan what to do.

From down the dock, Lord Ethan scanned his sapphire eyes across the crowd of people standing in wait beside the Rosa Marsa.   Everyone else was watching the odd one-sided conversation closely as well. Lord Ethan's eyes stopped when they locked with Javic's. His gaze caused Javic's breath to catch in his throat.

"You," said Lord Ethan, "Javic Elensol, son of Bartan, son of Elric, may not depart on this journey."

Javic felt as if he'd been punched in the chest.

What did Grandfather say to bring down such a decree? I'm being punished for his insubordination!

A quick glance at his grandfather showed a look of relief on his face.

He's happy about all of this....

Everything suddenly came together like a thousand needles stabbing him in the heart. This was Elric's resolve; the stubborn order he'd forced upon Lord Ethan.

My own grandfather has betrayed me… deprived me of my destiny.

Two of the Ver'ati from Ethan's entourage grabbed hold of Javic's arms roughly. He hardly felt their touch at first, though it jarred him substantially. After a moment he was pretty sure their hands were all that was holding him up.

"Gently, please," Lord Ethan said to his men.

Javic slumped slightly as they loosened their grips.

Lord Ethan made his way back over to the group. "If I'd realized you were part of the friends Aaron wished to include on this mission, I would never have allowed it. Phandrol is indebted to your family for its past sacrifices," he said to Javic. "Your parents gave their lives in service to the Ver'konus. You, personally, have done quite enough already for our cause simply by bringing Aaron to me unscathed—"

"—but that was nothing at all!" Javic tried to interject.

"Silence!" ordered Ethan. "There will be no argument. Your path does not lie on the road we take. You will remain here, at the academy, until you've finished your initiate training and are no longer a danger to yourself and those around you, after which you will be released into Elric's custody until such time as you become of age and are granted the right to choose your own path by the laws of this land."

Javic looked around at the faces that surrounded him. Few met his eyes, but those that did were filled with pity. "But I want to go! I'm nearly seventeen," said Javic. "My birthday is in less than two months…."

"And until then, Elric is your guardian," said Ethan. He dismissed Javic with a gesture. "Return him to the dormitories, and keep watch to be sure he doesn't attempt to follow us. I know all too well the determination that resides within the Elensol blood."

CHAPTER

8

Ek'radam

The Rosa Marsa's engines started up with a deep rumble, the smokestack already frothing at its tip with dense exhaust fumes that billowed over the sides. They drifted downward to float across the water like a supernatural mist. All Belford could do was watch as Javic was escorted away through the fumes by the guards.

There was barely time to say a disheartened goodbye before Javic disappeared around the bend in the dock. It was a disappointing turn of events, to say the least. Out of all of his friends, Belford had been most looking forward to reuniting with Javic. There were very few people with whom Belford could share his secret intentions of interrogating King Garrett. Javic was the first person he had intended to tell—the only one Belford was absolutely certain would have his back no matter what.

Despite Shiara's promise that she would do whatever she could to help him find Claire, he knew there were limits to how far she would go. Her allegiance was split. When it came down to choosing between listening to Ethan or himself, there was no telling whose orders she would follow. Belford had no idea how he was going to go about questioning King Garrett when Ethan only wanted him dead.

He had considered going directly to Ethan with his plight, but if he asked permission and Ethan refused, Belford suspected he would be kept far away from Garrett during the final takedown. He doubted he would get a chance to go against Ethan's decision at that point. Belford knew Ethan was incapable of being unbiased about this. After the death of his wife and a feud that already spanned at least one lifetime, Ethan was not about to let Garrett live a moment longer than he had to.

Just before boarding the Rosa Marsa, Belford approached Elric. He felt like he needed to say something to him. He had not considered that Elric might be so against Javic's involvement in the mission. It was clear from his lack of baggage that Elric did not intend to join them on the trip either.

"I'm sorry," said Belford, "I never meant to put you in such an awkward position."

Elric narrowed his eyes slightly at Belford's words. "You're just as reckless as *him*," he said, shooting an annoyed glance over in Ethan's direction. "Always assuming things are going to turn out for the best. He's certainly lived long enough to know things rarely go exactly as planned." Elric lowered his eyes and let out a long exhale. "No, I must apologize," he said shaking his head. "This isn't your fault. I shouldn't put this on you. It is only natural for you boys to seek out adventure—to want to make a difference… it's just *this* mission.…" Elric tugged at the chain around his neck.

Belford realized a while back that Elric's deceased son's wedding band rested at the bottom of that chain. Elric often fiddled with it when he was reminded of Javic's parents. The butterfly pendant under Belford's own shirt suddenly felt very heavy. Elric's ring and Belford's pendant were both reminders of those they lost. Belford kept his so that he would never forget his failures. He didn't want to make the same mistakes again. He couldn't let anyone else die because of him. He wondered if Elric kept his token for a similar reason. Sometimes it was easy to forget that he was not the only one who had lost people.

"This is the same mission," said Elric, continuing softly, "the same exact one." He let out a short sigh. "I couldn't bear to see him go—not the way my son Bartan did…. This isn't the first attempt Ethan has made on King Garrett's life, you know. Kali, Javic's mother, and her sister, Meldreth— they were sent on a very similar mission a couple of years after Javic was born. Ethan believed Garrett would be more vulnerable while traveling out on one of his rare inspections to his eastern territories. He gave the order and the sisters journeyed out, all alone, to slip by Garrett's defenses. Kali would have done anything for Ethan. She trusted him like a father." Elric clenched the dangling ring tight in his fist until his knuckles whitened. "As soon as my son discovered the truth about her mission, he couldn't stand the thought of Kali being out there facing such danger without him. He believed the girls had been sent on a suicide mission, but there was nothing he could do but wait and hope for the best."

Elric had to collect himself with a deep breath before continuing. This was clearly an uncomfortable subject for him.

"After learning that Kali and Meldreth's mission had failed and they were captured by Wilgoblikan, Bartan set out with a few men. Together, they attempted to free the girls, but only Damian Sarvo, one of Bartan's friends, returned. No one else survived. Bartan was an excellent swordsman, but he stood no chance against Wilgoblikan's dark powers. Damian barely escaped with his life. He brought back some of Bartan's personal affects and told me what he could of the location of his burial."

A glossy sheen passed over Elric's eyes. He grabbed hold of Belford's shoulders tightly.

"You need to promise me something right now," he said. "If things go wrong and the mission is compromised, you must promise that you will get out of there! Just save yourself and get out. This is Ethan's war, no one else's. You could become the king of all of Aragwey one day, as long as you don't let Ethan's obsessions drag you down before your time. Sacrificing yourself, even to save Ethan, won't be doing anybody any favors. He may be an old friend, but Aragwey needs somebody like *you* to lead her into a new era— somebody compassionate and caring. I used to think Ethan could be that man, but for many years all he has truly cared about is destroying King Garrett. It has festered inside of him—consumed him. Aragwey cannot be united by hatred— that can only corrupt the lands further."

Belford stared back at the frantic expression on Elric's face. He truly felt for him. Elric had lost everyone he cared about apart from Javic, leaving him understandably wary.

"Promise me!" Elric insisted.

Belford couldn't help but feel awful for inviting Javic along in the first place now that he knew the truth about Elric's past. "I promise," Belford said. Although he had no desire to be king of Aragwey, he didn't have any intention of sacrificing himself either, so the promise was easy enough to make.

Behind him, Captain Grine and Lieutenant Canbel boarded the Rosa Marsa, followed by Ethan and his personal maid, Vera. Belford met Vera once before, albeit briefly, during his visit to Ethan's chambers when he was still an old man. Although Ethan no longer needed the medical assistance that Vera was capable of providing, he apparently found her useful enough in other aspects of his life to keep her around now that he was young again. She did not look very pleased to be going on the mission, however, and had adopted a sort of permanent grimace. Her pale-green cloak whipped at her ankles as she stepped aboard, ignoring the outstretched hand of Captain Grine, offered out to her to assist her across the gap.

That was it for Ethan's entourage—very limited, just as he promised in his war room. Elric bid Belford and the rest of the passengers farewell as they filed onto the steamer one by one. Arlin was the last to board. He stood with Mallory, locked together in a desperate embrace that continued on until Captain Bundles' son, Eben, with his curly mop of a hairdo peeking out from under his cap, and Garcenus, the always glowering deckhand, released the final ropes holding the Rosa Marsa in place. Arlin hopped on just as they pushed off.

"He's a good man," said a woman lurking to the right of Belford in the shadows of the rear-compartment's seating area. She was in her late twenties, dressed in a white cotton shirt with a dark-brown bodice overtop. Her long legs appeared to have been poured into her formfitting, black breeches. They rode low on her waist, shamelessly showing off the deep curves of her hips.

She had a dark-olive complexion which reminded Belford a bit of the gypsy women whose caravan he briefly traveled with on the journey south last month. Her ash-brown hair was woven into a tight braid like Shiara's, but instead of running down the middle of her back, hers draped over her left shoulder and sat atop a shelf of pushed up cleavage. The lady watched Arlin as he turned away from both Mallory and the docks. Mallory lingered reluctantly by the now empty slip with a forlorn expression as the steamer putted farther away from her, towards the harbor's entrance.

The only people onboard the Rosa Marsa that Belford had yet to meet were the two Ver'ati that the head of the Arcanum Council, Tannel Cresdale, promised to send along with Sarbin Raiger, his steward. That meant that despite her disarming appearance, the woman must have been a decorated Ver'ati within the Arcanum. Tannel had vowed to send only his best, after all.

"Do you know Arlin?" Belford asked.

"No, not personally," said the woman "but judging from that Talus Shard blade at his side, he must be a Guardian of Truth, *Paerto'radam* they are called, and already a master swordsman at that. I must say, he is very young to have earned such a weapon. Both of my brothers attempted to join the Order of the Blade when they first became of age, but they had neither the swordsmanship nor the determination required to earn a novice blade, let alone a Talus Shard."

"The Order of the Blade?" asked Belford.

The woman continued watching Arlin curiously as she answered Belford's question. "The Order is to normal men what the Arcanum is to Ver'ati—a top place of tutelage where those with the talent and spirit can refine their skill with the sword. Young men and women from all over Aragwey are drawn to the Elswani Monastery at the edge of the Scar of Phandrol to train, though only the best of the best are initiated."

The woman began playing with the end of her braid, brushing it back and forth across the center of her cleavage in a teasing fashion.

"It's a very prestigious title to hold—Guardian of Truth," she continued. "When a guardian completes his training, he is bound to the Order, swearing fealty to the Ek'radam monks— to protect them if they are ever in danger. A very fascinating bunch.... The guardians take an oath to never strike down another blade-brother or sister—that's their only written law, as far as I know. They are an honor-bound society... I have never heard of anyone ever breaking that cardinal rule."

"Why would they need a rule stating not to kill each other?" asked Belford. "Isn't murder already illegal everywhere?"

The woman laughed. "The guardians are from all over," she said. "After they complete their training they are allowed to return to their homelands and use their talents however they see fit—militaries, swords for hire—whatever they want. Sometimes two blade-brothers will meet as enemies on the battlefield, but they must not kill one another. Otherwise, the offender is cast out from the Order and marked for death."

"Oh," said Belford. They stood in silence for a moment. Belford had learned many unexpected things since his awakening in Aragwey, but for some reason, a loner like Arlin Calary being a sworn protector of monks still surprised him. "Arlin… a guardian for monks…."

"Well, the Ek'radam monks don't actually have much need for warrior defenders these days, but a thousand years ago during the Founding, when John Graven and the monks were first spreading the word of Mast—*ek'radam'ati*… the truth of God," she added upon noticing Belford's blank expression, "they needed competent swordsmen to defend them against the savages and cannibals that plagued these lands all the way from the Scar to the Northern Sea…. I can't wait to talk with him. I'm sure he has quite an interesting tale!" The lady eyed Arlin with a lustful look that could only mean trouble.

"I'm Belford, by the way," he said. "I have the Mark of Kings on my arm, and I'm very interesting as well…."

The woman laughed. "I know exactly who you are, Aaron Levy. There is very little of which the Arcanum is not aware," she said. "You better go pick a cabin before all the good ones are taken." And with that, she tossed her braid over her shoulder and walked away from Belford with an overly exaggerated wiggle in her hips. She flashed a flirtatious smile in Arlin's direction before stepping below deck through the hatchway.

"Who was that?" Belford found himself asking aloud.

Captain Sharith Grine, seated nearby, grunted with annoyance. "Livian Niern," he said, "an Illusionist of the Arcanum. I'd watch out for that one…. They call her the Black Mist because of what she did during her Dance of the Elements, back when she was first raised to Ver'ati status."

Belford cocked his head towards Captain Grine, waiting for him to continue, but he merely shrugged.

"You should ask Lieutenant Canbel—he was raised that same year and actually got to see it firsthand…. Livian modified the council's perception of her test by producing a dark cloud of mind altering spores." Captain Grine's lip curled up slightly, as if he caught a whiff of something rancid. "Tampering with a person's mind against their will is Compulsion, and normally would have earned her an execution, but at that time there were no rules against the creation of spores that did any such altering for you. It was just different enough to slip between the laws. It sure got her a lot of notoriety at the time, though, and even coined a new discipline, Microfloration—the study and creation of biological spores—which was immediately banned all across the board for being too dangerous and too easy to abuse. It's now restricted to research-status only, locked away in the basement of the Arcanum. She blurred the lines between Illusion and Compulsion, and opened the door for many truly scary possibilities… just think of it, spores that can kill, or Compel more maliciously than the black mist that Livian invented, capable of destroying whole populations in a single conjuration."

It was biological warfare combined with the Power. Belford realized the implications immediately. He could remember some of the news stories from his old life—stories of subway attacks and airport threats; hundreds dead, their lungs burned out by invisible clouds of gas; men, women, and children, it made no difference, death did not discriminate. Even so, Belford could think of several poignant uses for brain spores that might effectively solve his current dilemmas.

What better way to convince Ethan to let me question King Garrett than to change his mind for him.

It would also make getting the truth out of Garrett once they captured him much easier.

Of course, getting Livian on his side was easier said than done. Convincing her to break Arcanum law for him was probably impossible. Still, he felt it might be worth a shot. He would have to keep a keen eye on Livian regardless, for Arlin and Mallory's sake. Livian definitely had her sights set on Arlin. Even with Arlin's one-track mind focused on the mission, Livian would be impossible to resist if a dose of specialized brain spores ever happened to find their way into his system....

Would the Arcanum's laws really stop Livian from using her ingenious creations?

She could just as easily make any witnesses forget anything even occurred. One thought that struck Belford as particularly troubling was that, for all he knew, Tannel Cresdale may have sent Livian along on this mission specifically to use her spores against Ethan and his team. There would be no better way to ensure the Arcanum's control over the mission. After meeting the sly man, Belford wouldn't put anything past him.

Belford tried to let his paranoia settle. He remained up top, staying out of the way of the crew as they performed their final preparations for travel. Garcenus latched down fenders and stowed moorings in a compartment by Belford's feet. He nearly took Belford's sneakers off with the ropes as he threw them into the storage space. He still blamed Belford's group for forcing Captain Bundles to leave Weni behind, the Rosa Marsa's old first mate, in North Galdren before their harbor escape. Garcenus and Weni had been romantically involved. Belford could hardly blame him for holding a grudge, but if they had delayed their departure from North Galdren long enough for Weni to return, the royal guards would have surely captured them all and tried them for the Crimson Stalker's crimes—namely, the assassination of King Lodrin.

They hadn't been left with many options. No news had reached them yet as to what had become of Weni. Belford knew exactly how Garcenus felt—the not knowing was the worst part. Garcenus let his anger simmer, ignoring the passengers in their entirety for the most part.

Although Captain Bundles usually tried to avoid cruising after dark, he was equipped to do so when necessary. A guide torch fueled by an oil canister was lit, its flame projected out in front of the Rosa Marsa by a large curved mirror that amplified the light. Garcenus used it like a spotlight, turning the mirror back and forth to illuminate their path. To keep a low profile, no one was allowed to use the Power during the duration of their voyage, especially not to light the way. Even here within Phandrol, there was no telling how many of Garrett's eyes and ears were integrated amongst the country-folk.

Eben Gupree sat by his father as he piloted the vessel. The boy kept vigilant eyes on their course, watching the river for any sign of obstacles such as floating logs or turbulent riffles of fast moving water which indicated a shallow lay below. Periodically, the boy or his father would check on the spread out charts that sat beside the helm. The pages were old and tattered, but the river did not seem to have changed much since its mapping. Detailed notes warned of rocks and sandbars periodically along the Etto's sides. Captain Bundles kept the ship at the center of the channel at all times. For the most part, he just used the charts to spot landmarks that would indicate their progress downriver.

After a while Belford grew bored and decided to head below deck. He quickly realized he should have heeded Livian's advice and selected a cabin earlier in the night. The only room still available was located within the crew quarters area, right between the kitchen and cargo hold. Every time somebody climbed the grated steps to go between decks or walked down the hallway to visit the mess he could hear their boots clanging on the metal.

As Belford double checked the passenger cabins up front to make sure he hadn't skipped over any empty rooms on his first pass, Ethan, who was already set up with Vera in the cabin Belford had shared with Javic the last time he was onboard the Rosa Marsa, beckoned Belford over to join him for a cup of tea. At a glance from Ethan, Vera poured Belford a cup before he even had a chance to accept the offer, and then left the room to give them some privacy. The silent disapproval coming off of Vera as she passed by Belford was palpable.

"Tumultuous, little firecracker, that one," said Ethan once Vera was out of earshot. "Don't take her attitude personally. She's like that with everyone. I just keep her around for that gorgeous ass of hers!" Ethan chuckled to himself, sloshing tea out of his cup and into his saucer.

Belford forced a grin.

"Now that we finally have some downtime, I've been meaning to talk with you about a few things," said Ethan. "I assume there are still quite a lot of gaps in your memory, and I know how frustrating that is. I can imagine you probably have many questions about what happened to our world… how we ended up in Aragwey…. Well, I could spend the next couple weeks telling you everything I remember, though it all happened so very long ago for me that I've probably forgotten half of the details myself, or I can show you how to unlock your original memories in their entirety."

There was no question which route Belford preferred. Just the thought of getting his memories back was enough to cause him to nearly dump his own cup of tea into his lap. He placed it down on the table before his excitedly shaking hands caused him to accidentally burn himself. With his memories back, he would finally be able to remember how he first met Claire, along with all the other little details of their time together that still eluded him no matter how hard he tried to bring them back. It was the most precious gift anyone could give him. The only thing better would be if Claire was back in his life in earnest.

"It's a meditative technique," said Ethan. "The Ek'radam monks taught it to me when I first appeared in Phandrol. It facilitated the return of my memories in days rather than months. Without them, Garrett's initial plots to murder me may very well have succeeded. Do you know much about the monks?"

Belford shook his head. "Only that John Graven used them to spread the teachings of Mast across Aragwey."

Ethan smiled harshly. "Crafty bastard, that John Graven. He appeared a thousand years ago, the first of us to return, and found himself in a land full of superstitious, head-shrinking, barbarian fools—literally hundreds of tiny tribes, all warring over women, livestock, what-have-you; a quarter of the population dying every winter from lack of food. He gave them a unifying religion and they treated him like a god, allowing him to carve out a civilized kingdom for himself. If only we had it so easy."

Ethan pulled a metal flask out of a case beside one of the beds and added a splash of hard liquor to his tea.

"Anyway, that's beside the point. People were frightened by the Mark of Kings on my arm when I first appeared, which isn't surprising after what Garrett put the nation through with his Cleansing. I was lucky that the monks found me first before any of Garrett's assassins. They helped me remember who I was—opened up my mind—which in turn allowed me to take full control over my abilities. I destroyed those sent to harm me, and continue to do so year after year as Garrett repeatedly tries to end my life. And now it's your turn to unlock your true potential… and Garrett's turn to die." He said it simply, with no emotion in his voice. "Lie down on that bed and try to relax. I will walk you through the process." Ethan finished his tea with a large gulp and then turned his seat to face the bunk.

Belford took off his shoes before lying out on his back, his hands overlapping on top of his stomach.

"Close your eyes and breathe deep, like you are trying to fall asleep," said Ethan. "Let your mind wander wherever it wants—to the places it needs to go most."

The steady pattering of the Rosa Marsa's waterwheels helped Belford relax. The first image to appear in Belford's mind was Claire—no surprise there.

"Your mind knows where it needs healing—which pathways have become shut off or are missing between your memories and your consciousness. You must feel out these missing strands so that the connections can be revived. Let your mind wander. Do not force it."

Belford allowed his thoughts to drift. Claire's face faded away, slipping through the blackness of the underside of his eyelids. He let her go, his mind turning itself back towards the empty recesses of his past... but they weren't really empty, he realized, they were just cut off. A dark chasm stretched out before him, just like the one he had seen before in his dreams. When he first came across the chasm, he was afraid to jump in, but after doing so, fragmented memories resurfaced with jarring images of destruction juxtaposed with the faces of his friends and intense feelings of fear and love.

"Do not let your emotions overwhelm you," Ethan said. "Once you find a path to your missing memories, it will collapse again if you do not control the flow. Like water in a canal made of sand, if you let too much through your gate, it will wash through faster than you can comprehend it and destroy the gate in the process. You must focus on one memory at a time—your earliest thoughts that pertain to the subject that initially drew you in. Your mind has sought out this missing chunk of memory, which makes it the most important. The best way to retrieve it is to follow the thoughts through in an order that makes sense to you now."

It was Claire that drew him in. She was hidden somewhere in the void. Unfortunately, Belford did not know his first memory of Claire. He didn't remember how they met, so he wasn't sure where to begin.

"You have probably noticed that when your memories have returned to you thus far, they have been most complete and allowed you to recover the longest stretches of time when followed through chronologically. Your thoughts are not actually stored in this manner—they are more like data on a computer hard drive, grouped together around subjects and feelings that branch out into hundreds of thousands of unique pathways. It is easy to let whole chunks of memory slip by unrecovered if you focus on feelings rather than reconnecting with each memory in the order it was created. Unless you revisit the memories in sequence you will never revitalize more than a handful of pathways at a time. Otherwise, you will just be shooting in the dark, frivolously grabbing at disjointed thoughts as they float by like leaves in the stream until you finally collapse your gate with the overload. Always start with what you know, and then be mindful to only allow the rest to come in at one logical step at a time, not all haphazardly as it is stored within you."

Belford focused on the last thing he could recall in its entirety—his last full memory before the fragmented thoughts of Claire overwhelmed his mind: It was when he took the test at the Gothenburg Convention Center; Wes Flairity, the strange Swede with a knack for technology, altering their scores; the certainty that he would be picked for a job that he knew absolutely nothing about, except that it would be both dangerous and somehow important; fearing that somebody would discover the truth about Wes's cheating; getting the call, congratulating him for being selected... *that part was new*... the Crimson Stalker had interrupted his dream with the brass spyglass Artifact before he had a chance to get that far into his memories... *Ethan's method is working!* Belford redoubled his concentration, delving deeper and deeper into his forgotten past—closer to Claire....

CHAPTER

9

Strangers

Despite the early morning hour, the airport was a bustle of arrivals and departures as Aaron made his way over to the ticket counter. He had a nervous tickle in his stomach all week ever since Wes altered their test scores at the convention center. When he was officially chosen for the project, he was completely beside himself—a bundle of useless nerves. On top of his fear of getting caught for cheating, news of another plane being shot down just three days ago, this time over Warsaw, put him on edge even further. When it came to flying, safety was merely a relative term these days. Statistics said you were more likely to die on the drive to the airport than on the plane itself, but no one was shooting missiles at cars, at least not in Sweden. Aaron had never enjoyed flying, even before rising tensions brought televised executions and suicide attacks to his living room on an almost daily basis.

The woman behind the ticket counter took his passport and typed his name into her workstation. "You'll be departing from gate C12," she said as her printer sprang to life. It spit out his ticket, provided to him free of charge by his new employers. She passed it over and returned his credentials before turning to the next person in line. The ticket had the gate and departure time on it, but strangely no destination was listed. "It's been privately chartered…" was the best explanation the attendant could give him.

Aaron was early, so he bought a snack from the bagel stand in the terminal before making his way to the holding area. When he arrived, the only other person waiting for the flight was Wes. Sitting in a window alcove with his hood drawn up over his blond hair, Wes was staring downward, completely immersed in his tablet computer. He didn't even notice Aaron as he walked over and stood right beside him.

"Breaking into airport security?" Aaron asked jokingly.

Wes jerked up, pulling his touchscreen to his chest. "Of course not," he said as he recognized Aaron, "I was just reading some news."

Aaron took a seat beside Wes in the chair nearest the window ledge. "Have they told you anything?" Aaron asked. "I'm still completely in the dark."

Wes frowned slightly. "No," he said, "but I did some digging of my own."

Aaron raised an eyebrow.

"CIOX Laboratories hired us," he said, keeping his voice low. "They're a subsidiary of Reblan Industries, an Israeli company which does a lot of research and development for Allied military applications. But because it's a public corporation they have to keep public records of their earnings and any grants they receive. So I looked into them."

Aaron leaned forward in his seat. "What did you find?" he asked.

Wes laughed. "Nothing at all. All of their records were perfect, every cent accounted for… but that was exactly what made me suspicious."

Aaron cocked his head to the side. "I don't get it."

"Corporations like these have literally thousands of transactions to account for every day, and with all the bureaucratic red tape that they have to deal with under international law, they should have had at least some minor discrepancies in their books. Everyone else does. But their records were perfect." Wes shrugged. "The books are cooked," he said, "I don't know why yet, but I assume it's because they have money coming in from somewhere they don't want to report. CIOX is just a shell company."

Aaron narrowed his eyes. He had never been one for conspiracy theories.

"Don't believe me?" Wes asked with a laugh. "I know I'm right. They made a rookie mistake really. If you don't want to get caught cheating, don't give yourself a perfect score," he said. "Only give yourself the highest *believable* score. There's a reason we're both sitting here today—I let a couple of people score above us on our test."

Aaron still wasn't entirely convinced, but the conversation ended prematurely as a couple in their early thirties stepped into the holding area. They sat down on the opposite side of the terminal, farthest from the gate, and began chatting between themselves. Even so, Wes did not pick the conversation back up.

After a little while, a small jet, unmarked by corporate logos, taxied up to the gate. The whirr of the engines died down and a hatch folded out from the bulkhead, forming stairs. An attendant signaled Aaron, Wes, and the couple over to the gate. "Small crowd today," he said. "Watch your step as we go out onto the tarmac." The attendant opened the door to the gate and checked their tickets one at a time before leading the group down a flight of stairs and out into the open air.

The tarmac was extremely windy and noisy with all the other aircraft coming-and-goings making a constant clamor. A maintenance vehicle and several long baggage-cart trains sped by, going back and forth between the terminals. Wes and Aaron followed closely behind the attendant, staying within the green painted walk lanes.

"Have a good flight," he said to them as they stepped up into the jet.

Onboard there were only six rows of seats, four seats to a row, broken up into groups of two by the central aisle. Apart from the pilots, sealed off in their own compartment, there was only one other person already onboard the plane: A short, middle-aged man with glasses and a tidy beard, poised in front of the backwards-facing seat typically reserved for a flight attendant.

"Aaron, Wes, good to finally meet you," he said, extending a handshake to each of them as they entered. He was an Irishman, judging from his accent—clearly not there to serve them inflight beverages. "Mr. and Mrs. Miller, it's an honor, truly," he said to the couple from the holding area as they stepped on behind Wes. "Please, take a seat anywhere you'd like." The Irishman was dressed as if he were about to go out on a safari—a beige, short-sleeve, button-up shirt and khaki cargo pants with matching work boots. "My name's Dana Farris," he said, "and I'm going to be your Project Manager for the next seven or eight months. We have one last quick stop to make at Copenhagen International to gather several more of our team members and then we're off to our final destination!"

"And where exactly might that be?" asked Wes as he and Aaron sat down across the aisle from one another in the second row.

"I'm not at liberty to say," said Dana. "I'll tell you when we get there."

"You can never be too cautious," Wes said sarcastically.

"I'll also need to take any wireless devices you have on you now as well," said Dana, "for security purposes."

Four phones were passed up to the project leader, one from each of the passengers, without any argument, but Wes pushed the bag containing his tablet computer farther under his seat with his foot. Wes really wasn't very good at following rules.

The married couple sat down in a pair of seats in the third row behind Wes. "Aaron and Wes, is it?" the man asked, his accent somewhere between British and American English.

Aaron and Wes nodded after turning around in their seats to face the couple. Aaron knew the man's accent all too well—he employed it himself from time to time. The British half of the man's accent, like Aaron's, was a farce, put on simply to deflect the animosity that most European people held towards Americans. Ever since the United States' economic collapse brought down the rest of the world's markets there hadn't been much love for Americans within the Union. Rather than bear the brunt of the prejudice, Aaron found it easier to pretend to be someone else. His mother actually had been British, so it wasn't too much of a stretch for him to take on the vocal mannerisms.

"I'm Ethan, and this is my wife Michelle," the man said, his strikingly blue eyes glistening with moisture. He didn't seem to blink them quite often enough.

"Hello," said Michelle, giving Wes and Aaron both a warm, motherly smile. Ethan's wife appeared to be of Greek descent—hazel eyes, dark skin, and short brown hair that was styled into wide curls that bounced around on either side of her face—though her accent was distinctly posh British.

Dana Farris strapped himself into his backwards seat as the pilots started up the jet's engines.

"So, that was quite a test they had us take, wasn't it?" Ethan asked loudly, above the drone of the turbines.

"A real doozy…" responded Wes.

Aaron shot him a cautionary frown from across the aisle.

"We must all be geniuses," Wes added, laughing. Wes truly was impossible.

"I believe Michelle and I were chosen because of our previous defense work," said Ethan. "You two must really be something special, though, if you don't have any ties to the company…."

Aaron sensed suspicion in the unasked question: *Why were you selected?* "Prior defense work?" Aaron asked, doing his best to drive the conversation away from himself.

"Oh, yes," said Ethan. "We worked on the HAMMER Project last year… missile defense."

"It stands for High Altitude Multiple Missile Eradication Ray," added Michelle. "I came up with the name."

"You guys developed HAMMER?" asked Wes, the excitement bubbling up in his voice. "Which parts were you responsible for?"

Michelle lit up as well as she began talking about her work. "I programmed the targeting system with a team of engineers. Ethan was the project leader, though—he spent most of his time on the power system and laser amplification matrix."

"The technical feat alone…" said Wes, clearly awed.

Aaron had heard of the HAMMER Project as well. The news called it a safety net, catching any tactical ballistics that happened to find their way into European airspace via the Middle-Eastern corridor.

"Two more platforms are already being deployed this month alone, so we should have total blanket protection by the end of the quarter," said Michelle.

The safety net couldn't come soon enough. The cold war between the European Union and the East Asian Coalition was simmering hotter than ever. It was taking a harsh toll on the morale of the Europeans. For years there had been an atmosphere of wartime—no one ever knowing when or where the next bomb would go off, only that there would be a next bomb, and another one after that. Paris, Barcelona, London… nowhere was entirely safe, even with all their surveillance. The terrorists had become more sophisticated to match the Union's countermeasures, and while some cells were uncovered, many plots were not found out until after sifting through the rubble.

The power gap that the United States left in its downfall needed to be filled. The EU and EAC differed on their opinions of who should take over. Once again, the Middle-East was being used as a pawn between two superpowers.

Look how well that turned out for the United States last time, thought Aaron.

Even with the old regimes toppled, daily pop-shots from hand-held rockets still landed along the border countries of the Union from Syria and Jordan. Turkey and Greece had taken the brunt of the bombardment—Israel too, though that was hardly news—but since the first HAMMER station was developed, more than ninety percent of the missiles were successfully destroyed before impact. It was true that a plane over Warsaw had just been shot down, but that missile was launched by terrorists who were already on the ground in Poland.

Aaron glanced back at Ethan. Based on his knowing expression, Ethan must have noticed Aaron's American heritage slipping through in his accent as well. A silent understanding formed between them. They had both sought out a better life after what should have been the end. America was practically a third-world country now, bankrupt and broken. Their homeland couldn't provide for them anymore, and so it had been time to leave. It was adapt or die, and Aaron felt no shame in choosing life. In actuality, he had already been overseas with his father when the collapse happened, but they didn't make any effort to return home after the dust settled—there was nothing left for them in America.

The flight only lasted twenty minutes or so before they found themselves on the ground again, pulling up to the gates of Copenhagen International. Aaron peered out his window as the jet taxied in—hangers and pavement—just like every airport he had ever been to; impossible to distinguish. Wes, staring out the opposite side of the plane, suddenly unbuckled his seatbelt and jumped up into the aisle, nearly hitting his head on the overhead compartment in the process. "Scoot over," he said, hastily grabbing his bag out from under his seat and shoving it under Aaron's.

"What's going on?" Aaron asked.

Wes had a huge grin on his face. "A couple of girls are about to get on, and I want them to sit here so I can talk to them," he said, gesturing towards his old seat.

All Aaron could do was shake his head as he undid his own seatbelt and shifted over to the window seat.

"Dibs on the brunette," Wes said as the hatch opened, letting in a brisk breeze that relieved the stuffy cabin air.

Dana Farris greeted the girls as they stepped aboard the aircraft. "Isabelle, Claire, come right on in."

The first girl to enter was the brunette that Wes apparently fancied. Her mousy-brown hair hung to her shoulders in a straight cut with side-swept bangs. Her skin had a natural tan hue that was far too dark for her to be native to northern Europe. She had a cute smile on her face as she shook Dana's hand.

"Oh, Ms. Reblan, I have a message here for you from Yosef," said Dana. He handed her a physical piece of paper—an unusual sight with most things being digital these days. Her smile instantly faded as she read the printout.

Wes, who had been poised to offer her his old seat, had a sheepish look on his face. "Reblan?" he whispered. "As in *Reblan Industries*, the people that hired us?"

The girl overheard the remark and turned on him with a fiery look in her eyes. "Yes," she snapped, crumpling up the printout, "my bastard uncle is Yosef Reblan, Founder and CEO." She had a heavy Israeli accent.

Dana shifted back and forth on his feet uncomfortably.

"Do you have a problem with that?" she asked, staring Wes straight in the eyes. Despite her youthful, skinny-girl appearance, she had quite a bite to her. Aaron wasn't sure if it stemmed from pride, anger, or both.

Wes, growing increasingly wide-eyed, shook his head like a chastised child.

"Oh, Isabelle, I'm also going to need any wireless devices—" Dana began.

The girl handed her phone over her shoulder without looking at Dana. She walked past Wes to the last row of the plane and took a seat by the window, as far away from everyone else as possible.

The look of shock faded from Wes's face, quickly replaced by a smitten, puppy-dog expression. Strangely determined, Wes jumped up from his chair yet again, this time nearly plowing over the second girl as she started down the aisle. Wes shuffled to the back of the plane and swung into the seat beside Isabelle, effectively trapping the Israeli girl.

"Sorry about Wes," said Aaron, glancing over at the other newcomer for the first time, "he can be a bit careless…." Aaron's breath caught in his chest, his stomach fluttering nervously as he took in the beauty of the girl that stood before him. He had never been very good at talking to women… especially not pretty ones… and this girl wasn't just pretty, she was absolutely, stunningly gorgeous!

"Is this seat taken?" she asked, running her hand through her slightly disheveled auburn hair. The color reminded Aaron of the bark of the giant redwood trees he had seen once before in his youth, their cherry hue taken straight from the setting sun. He had been in awe of their grand scale—you could drive a car right through a tunnel carved in their massive trunks—it made him feel so tiny; insignificant.

He barely managed a squeak of consent as he moved the metal clasp of the seatbelt out of her way.

"My name's Claire," she said as she settled down beside him. She was Irish, like Dana, although her accent was nowhere near as thick as the project leader's. She had the most beautiful green eyes Aaron had ever seen in his life. It took all his effort not to shy away from their gaze.

"I'm Aaron," he said, trying to sound confident as he shook her hand. Her fingers sent off sparks throughout his whole body with their delicate caress. It was like stepping into a hot bath, the condensing beads of steam tickling him as they dripped down his spine. "So… you're Irish?" he asked. *What kind of stupid question was that? Of course she's Irish!* He was too tense; acting like an idiot….

Claire nodded. "I lived in Dublin until I was ten," she said. "That's when the riots started, so my ma took me and Aiden out of the country—Aiden's my little brother."

Aaron found himself distracted by the cute freckles on her nose. They weren't overly dark, just a perfect sun-kissed spattering. She smelled like springtime; sprigs of fresh flowers—lilac—with a hint of honey and crisp lime in the after note…. She was still talking…. *Pay attention! She will never like you if you can't even listen to her!*

"We moved to London for a time," Claire continued, "then had to come here to Copenhagen to find work—I'm a biologist. What about you?" she asked.

Aaron could feel Ethan's eyes on him without even looking. "Oh, I'm from all over," he said, putting a little extra British emphasis into his vowels. "I was an army brat, so I never stayed in one place very long growing up…." It wasn't a lie, really. He had been an army brat, it just happened to have been the US army that his dad was in. "My father died in combat when I was twelve," he said, "so I went to stay with my mum after that, she lived in London too, so it's possible we were there at the same time."

"Small world," Claire said with a smile. "She must be worried sick about you now—your mother I mean—mine's been beside herself all week since I was chosen!"

Aaron merely nodded. His mother wouldn't be worrying about him, or anything else for that matter. She was long dead, having passed away from cancer the same year his father was struck by the IED. He didn't think about it much anymore—how he had moved from the army base where his father was stationed, to a hospital to watch his mother's final deteriorating weeks, to a foster home, to another foster home, to another, back and forth for three long years until he finally turned sixteen and was allowed to live on his own. It was a dark time in his life and he preferred to pretend it hadn't happened. He tried not to feel sorry for himself—there were plenty of other orphans from the war; not having parents did not make him special.

Claire's soulful eyes peered straight into his, making him second-guess himself. For some reason, leaving out even a single part of the truth made him feel like he was lying to her. It made him uncomfortable.

"I moved to Sweden for school, to become a doctor," he said, trying to mask the shadow that had briefly fallen over his face. As much as he was impelled to tell her everything, there was no point weighing her down with such troubles.

Claire seemed intrigued, but then a long breathy yawn, escaped her lips. She covered her open mouth with the back of her arm. "Apologies," she said, "you're not boring me or anything, I just haven't had much sleep." She smiled, causing tiny dimples to appear in her cheeks. "Can you wake me when we get to… wherever we're going?" she asked.

"Sure thing," said Aaron.

Claire's arm brushed against his as she reclined her seat the few inches it would go back. She leaned against the chair sideways, her head facing Aaron, and fluttered her eyelashes for a moment before settling down for a nap. Aaron continued to watch her for a while until her breathing deepened and she slumped lower in her seat. Her face was the perfect picture of innocence.

Giggling coming from the back of the plane brought Aaron's attention to Wes and Isabelle. The girl was laughing, so whatever Wes was doing, it must have been working. Aaron wished he knew how Wes managed to turn that situation around so quickly. Wes's unabashed determination was truly an asset.

With nothing to do, time passed slowly. The flight continued on for what felt like hours. Aaron wasn't sure exactly how long it lasted; his only clock was on his phone, currently at the bottom of Dana's handbag. Wes and Isabelle talked throughout the entire flight while Ethan and Michelle busied themselves with magazines. Aaron read for a bit as well, but soon grew bored. He began trying to figure out roughly where they were headed based on the landmarks that passed below. He knew they were flying south—the sun was on the left side of the plane all morning long. He began to grow hungry for lunch at the same time the land beneath them was replaced by seemingly endless water. After heading south over Europe for so long, Aaron figured it could only be the Mediterranean Sea.

The jet began its descent even before land was visible. Claire managed to sleep the whole time until a bout of minor turbulence shook her from her nap. She woke yawning and stretching as the plane made a hard left turn, filling the windows with blue sky.

"Hi, there," Aaron said as Claire looked over with sleepy eyes.

She squinted from the bright sky. The plane leveled out, then turned back to the right a little ways. "Oh, look!" she said, pointing out the window.

A sprawling metropolis of gray and white buildings stretched out below them all along the coast as far as the eye could see. Farther inland a bleak landscape of dirt and sand carried on into rocky, low-lying hills. The city was the divide between the churning sea and this desolate landscape. Skyscrapers seemed to rise right up out of the harbor, grouped together in a dense cluster that overlooked the water. The buildings tapered off as the dusty lowlands enveloped them, the structures becoming smaller and smaller and increasingly widespread. Green palm trees were speckled amongst the architecture, as well as several larger parks whose lush vegetation was at odds with the desert beyond.

The city was thick with minarets—tall, narrow towers from which Arab prayer services were projected over loudspeakers for all to hear. Aaron had seen minarets before while traveling with his father through Turkey when he was young, but even then he did not remember there ever being so many all in one place. Halfway between the high-rises of the main city and the distant hills of jagged rock, a sand-blown airstrip waited for their arrival. The jet descended, its landing gear thumping as it skidded across the pavement. Everything shook in the cabin. The windows rattled heavily as the roaring wind beat against the wing-flaps, slowing their forward motion with air resistance.

"We are now in Tripoli, Libya," announced Dana Farris after the jet slowed to a controlled crawl and began taxiing towards a large hanger.

All of the passengers looked at each other in confusion. Other than Libya's recent induction as the newest member of the European Union, there was nothing of specific significance going on here—at least nothing that had been reported in the news. It was just another economically shattered region, incorporated in the hopes of spreading stability.

Only Isabelle and Dana showed no wonder over their odd destination.

CHAPTER

10

The City by the Park

The plane stopped moving as it reached the hanger's entrance. Dana stood up and opened the hatch, letting the smoldering air from outside seep into the cabin. The heavy scent of jet fuel floated in with the heat. It was even stronger outside on the tarmac as they disembarked; Aaron wrinkled his nose while stepping through the hatch. The humidity was harsh under the midday sun. Aaron's skin immediately became sticky as his non-acclimatized body furiously sweated.

Just beyond the tip of the wing, an unmarked white van pulled up to relieve everyone from the blistering sun with its air-conditioned interior. Dana sat in the front passenger seat while everyone else piled into the back. Aaron followed Claire inside, sitting next to her in the middle row. Michelle and Ethan got into the back. There were three seats to a row, so Wes sat on the opposite side of Aaron, and Isabelle filled out the back row. In the tight quarters, Claire's leg and side were pushed up against Aaron. Again, he felt an intoxicating electric sensation coarse through his veins at her mere touch. He couldn't take his mind off of her smooth legs rubbing up against him as the van bumped along the derelict road that connected the airport to the highway. He could feel her chest expanding with every breath. Aaron made no attempt to brace himself as the bumps forced their bodies together.

The van traveled north and then east for a few miles where it approached one of the overly green parks Aaron had noticed from the air. The area housed a new development, only partially completed. A strip of muddy buildings surrounded the north side of the park—the outskirts of Tripoli proper— while the south side was mostly bare dirt from the edge of the road continuing out as far as Aaron could see into the rolling hills in the distance. Within the barren expanse on the south side of the park, a complex of three modern buildings sat clustered together. Based on the orange cranes still attached to their rooftops, they were either at the tail end of construction or just preparing to start an expansion.

Their driver stopped at a red light while attempting to turn onto the park road. All the street signs were in Arabic. Most had been spray painted with graffiti; some were even riddled with bullet holes. A lot of the newer signs even had damage from small-arms fire. Aaron sank lower in his seat as a local man dressed in a high-necked robe, all white from head to toe, glowered at them as he crossed the street.

"Oh, don't mind him," said Dana. "The locals are still rather conservative here—they don't like the ladies wearing short-sleeved shirts."

"What are we supposed to do?" asked Michelle. "It's so hot here…."

"Don't worry," said Dana, "you won't be spending much time in the city. We will be keeping you all quite busy throughout the duration of the project."

The light turned green and the van sped on down the nearly abandoned stretch of road that curved around the south side of the park. When the complex of new buildings was right in front of them the van slowed. They approached the middle building.

"Research Headquarters," said Dana as the van came to a final stop. "The Libyan government has been kind enough to grant us this land for use during the extent of our study. Sorry again for all the secrecy, but everything will become much clearer after the orientation briefing."

A man waiting at the building's entrance approached the van and slid the door open. Two other men poised purposefully at the doors to the building were dressed in black blazers and ties. Their jackets bulged out slightly on their left sides. Each man's left arm was held rigid above what Aaron could only assume was a concealed weapon. For some reason the armed security did nothing to make Aaron feel any safer. Stepping out of the climate-controlled van, Aaron had almost forgotten how dense the air outside could really be. It fell on him like a physical weight, making his every motion labored.

Dana hurried everyone through the heavy entrance doors— two sets to keep in the building's cool air—and into a tile-floored lounge and reception area. Dana waved at a woman behind the front desk. She hit a button that buzzed open a security door to the left of the group. After a long hallway they took a right turn and found themselves in a cafeteria.

"Go ahead and grab a bite to eat while you can. I don't want you starving during orientation," said Dana. "The other candidates should be arriving any minute. They've already settled in—been waiting around now for two days for our arrival—but they haven't had orientation yet either, so they will probably be a bit antsy to get started."

Even before Dana finished speaking, a man and woman in their early thirties, dressed in glossy-black uniforms reminiscent of track outfits, walked into the cafeteria.

"About time you all showed up," the man said with an Australian accent. His light-brown hair was styled up into a faux-hawk that made him look like a bird in the middle of mating season. Although he had a youthful grin, his tanned skin was creased with wrinkles around his soft-blue eyes, giving away his true age. His teeth were bleached-white shards of perfection, flawlessly aligned and shaped—no one's teeth were that straight naturally.

The woman at his side looked the group over, a pleased expression on her round face. She wore dark-rimmed prescription eyeglasses that gave her a nerdy appearance. This was only further stressed by the lack of attention given to her black, shoulder-length hair, which hung straight down in wiry strands on either side of her head.

"The name's Travis Garrison," said the man, "and this lovely lady is Brooke." He lightly placed his hand along the woman's lower back as he said her name.

She let out a nervous chuckle and pulled away from his touch. "Brooke Thomas," she said, keeping the introduction formal.

"Oh, come on darling," said Travis, "don't let my intensity frighten you!"

"Now, now, Travis, leave Brooke alone," said Dana, forcing an apprehensive laugh himself. "You know fraternization amongst the team isn't allowed." He hesitated for a moment, turning towards Ethan and Michelle. "Except for you two of course, since you're already married."

"There's no harm with a little fun between friends," said Travis with a wink. "It wouldn't be a distraction," he added, a sly smirk appearing on his face. "You can't keep us apart forever!"

Brooke blushed deeply. She pointedly refusing to make eye contact with anybody—especially Travis.

Dana's face grew stern. "Although it is true that any relationships formed here could significantly disrupt and distract from our project, that is not the reason you must stay apart," he said. "The real danger we aim to avoid is the unexpected alteration of your brain chemistry. Over the next few months while you are undergoing our trials, any unaccounted changes could cause any number of side effects within you. Something as mundane as falling in love actually has a profound impact on the human brain—the first symptom of which is the release of dopamine at levels comparable to cocaine usage. The risk of harm when combined with our trials would be extreme, and that is to say nothing of the erroneous results that it would provide for the study."

A slightly overweight man in his early forty's, short hair receding over his temples, approached Travis from behind and placed a hand on his shoulder. "You heard the boss," he said, his gray eyes flashing. "Don't get too happy or it might just kill you." The man made no attempt to disguise his American accent. It was standard Midwestern, just like all the newscasters back in the states. That made three American's so far on the team—a surprisingly high number considering the search for subjects took place in the EU.

Travis scowled at the sound of the man's voice. He did nothing to mask his distaste as he turned around. "And what brings the magnificent Garrett Rames to the dining hall?" he asked sarcastically. "I thought you weren't taking meals with us riffraff any longer."

Garrett stared blankly at Travis for a moment before turning towards Dana in disinterest. "John and the women wished me to inform you that they've received word of your arrival and are currently waiting in the conference room for orientation to begin." He shot a quick glare over in Ethan's direction, a look of fiery recognition in his eyes. "Don't keep us waiting," he added, glancing back at Dana. He ignored the rest of the new arrivals entirely as he spun on his heel and exited the cafeteria.

Aaron looked over at Ethan questioningly. Ethan was frowning and slowly shaking his head back and forth.

"Garrett worked on the HAMMER Project with us," said Michelle once Garrett was out of earshot, "that is, until Ethan fired him. He was brilliant, but just too difficult to work with."

"Narcissistic jackass," said Ethan.

"All piss and wind," said Travis, "the lousy bastard's two shakes away from a beating 'less he gets his roos in check."

Everyone stared at Travis momentarily, trying to decipher what exactly he just said.

"You know, his roos…" Travis reiterated, "as in kanga… big ol' poofs floppin' around…." He gave up as the stares continued. "Never you all mind," he sighed.

Dana stepped out in front of the group. "Everyone please *do* try to get along with each other now, no matter what histories you may have. We need all of you to be able to work together efficiently. Garrett knows this as well. I expect everyone to maintain a high level of professionalism throughout the project." Dana picked up a banana from out of a fruit arrangement. "Quickly grab what you want, then I'll lead everyone to the conference room…. Oh, and welcome to the Arcadian Project!" he said with a smile that didn't quite extend to the tired look in his eyes.

As the group dispersed to gather their lunches, Aaron doubled back to peruse the fruit arrangement. Dana, unaware of Aaron's close proximity, began speaking quietly with somebody over his ear-com. The tiny flesh-toned speaker was tucked deep in Dana's ear canal, making it nearly impossible to see even when looking straight at it. If it wasn't for his muttering, Aaron wouldn't have even realized Dana had the unit in place.

"…a bunch of children," Dana said, speaking softly, almost under his breath, "I swear, you really know how to pick them." He paused for a moment as whoever was on the other side responded. "You don't have to lecture me about it," Dana continued, "I know their DNA is more important than their personalities, I wouldn't be putting up with any of this nonsense otherwise… you know, things could very well get messy again. Of all people you can appreciate the delays another termination would cause—finding a new set of candidates has already set us back several months…."

Aaron pretended to be engrossed in deciding between a slice of pineapple and an array of cantaloupe as Dana turned around and saw how close he really was. Dana jerked in place, stopping his conversation abruptly. Aaron felt Dana's nervous, calculating eyes piercing through the back of his head. He quickly selected a random piece of fruit from the tray and nonchalantly walked back over to join the rest of the group on the other side of the cafeteria.

Welcome to the Arcadian Project, indeed.

CHAPTER

11

Arcadians

After finishing up a quick lunch in the cafeteria, Aaron and the rest of the candidates rode a lift up to the building's fifth floor. They followed Dana Farris down a long linoleum-tiled hallway to the conference center. Dana was becoming increasingly exasperated as he made calls on his ear-com to the various department heads of the facility. The head lab technician, a man named George Cartwright, was apparently supposed to be meeting the team at the conference room to aid Dana with the orientation briefing, but he wasn't picking up any of his calls. Dana left several biting voicemails for him before attempting to contact anyone else.

Next on his list was Miriam Gerard, the French doctor who conducted Aaron's interview at the Gothenburg Convention Center. She was the lead psychiatric doctor for the project. Miriam answered, but she, along with several other department heads that were supposed to be present for the orientation, were all off-site having lunch and wouldn't be able to join them on such short notice. With the time table for the briefing moved up at Garrett's behest, everything was falling apart. Dana's level of irritation reached a critical point by the time they reached the conference room.

Inside, a long rectangular table lined with low-backed chairs took up the majority of the floor space. Garrett—face twisted with scorn—was seated on the far side of the table with his arms crossed over his chest. Beside him sat an equally impatient man with a strong Russian nose and two eager-eyed women, all in their early forties. The women quickly ended a hushed conversation and looked up at Dana as he walked in. Aaron sat down beside Claire, followed by Wes and Isabelle. The rest of the candidates filed in, filling out the remaining seats around the table. Dana placed himself at the head of the room in the only chair that had armrests. Aaron felt like a CEO at a board meeting.

In total, there were twelve candidates for the mysterious project—a diverse group. They looked like a true cross-section of society. The only thing each candidate seemed to have in common was their superior intellects. Aaron couldn't shake the feeling that he didn't really belong here. He was only chosen because Wes changed his test score for him; he didn't measure up to the rest of the candidates.

Dana went through a quick list of introductions, reading off the names of each person around the table in turn. "Let's start with our young ones," he said, naming Isabelle Reblan first, the Israeli born girl; niece of the CEO. Dana smartly avoided mentioning her uncle again after the defensive outburst it caused on the plane.

Next was Wes Flairity. The Swedish boy still had his tablet computer hidden away in his bag, clutched tight to his side. Aaron was next. He realized Claire was already watching him with an unabashed gaze even before his name was called. Her stare made him so self-conscious that he momentarily stopped paying attention to anything else and nearly missed Dana's introduction for him entirely. Aaron waved awkwardly after catching an expectant scowl from Dana from across the table. Claire's amused grin made his cheeks go flush.

"Claire Birch," called Dana. "A fellow Dubliner and distinguished biologist." He cracked the first real smile Aaron had seen him make.

Claire nodded gracefully, though it was already quite obvious to everyone that she was the Irish girl to which Dana was referring. Her auburn hair and fair skin were enough to give her away. Aaron couldn't get the thought of her soft cherry lips out of his head—how they would feel pressed up against his own. Without even trying, she had him flustered in every way imaginable.

As Ethan's name was called, Garrett gave an exaggerated yawn. Although Ethan tried to maintain an outward calm, the turmoil within him was palpable. It seemed to be taking every ounce of self-control he had not to lunge across the table at Garrett. Despite the open animosity, Ethan really was an amiable person with everyone else other than Garrett. The fellow secret-American had kept a respectable distance after recognizing Aaron's own fake British accent, and for that Aaron was grateful.

Dana called Michelle Miller next. "Ethan and Michelle are the brains and brawn behind the HAMMER Project," he said. A slight turn of Garrett's head pointed his right ear towards Dana, making it obvious that he was actually paying keen attention to the project leader's words despite his feigned disinterest. A tightening of his jawline gained a meaningful glance from Dana, intended to quell Garrett's anger. The bad blood remained just beneath the surface.

Dana continued on, introducing Brooke Thomas, the nerdy woman from the cafeteria. She was a Spaniard, although Aaron would never have guessed it from her pasty skin and the lack of any Spanish accent when she spoke English. Dana said she was a linguist, fluent in nine languages. *A walking brain with a pair of glasses on it.* Her massive intellect did nothing to alleviate Aaron's concern over his own lack of qualifications.

Travis Garrison was next. The Aussie grinned, showing off his perfect pearly whites. A hand-to-hand combat expert and martial arts weapons master, Travis was a former jiu-jitsu world champion—purely an athlete, and surprisingly not a brainiac like the others, at least as far as Aaron could tell. Aaron didn't possess anywhere near the physical prowess of Travis though, so even the Aussie's apparent lack of intellect did not make Aaron feel any better. Aaron had no extraordinary talent, no shining résumé; he had earned his doctorate, which would have been impressive around some crowds, but the other candidates weren't just ordinary people. Aaron wasn't stupid, but he wasn't the type of person that liked to solve calculus equations in his head while sitting on the toilet either.

Dana called Garrett Rames after Travis. Garrett looked up at a large analog clock on the far wall of the room—a silent protest which clearly indicated that he thought the introductions were a complete waste of time. Dana quickly listed off several projects that Garrett had taken part in before moving on to the next candidate. Of the list of accomplishments, Aaron was only familiar with the HAMMER project.

"John Graven," Dana called. The Russian man sitting beside Garrett looked up. He had a powerful, chiseled face; a slight ridge at the base of his nose formed the most prominent of his hardened features. Now that the orientation was underway he no longer shared Garrett's impatient expression, rather, he held a look of deep concentration, studying each of his fellow candidates as if they were to be his competition. He was clearly a no-nonsense type of person. Dana did not delve into any of John's qualifications, rushing through the list faster now that he was almost through.

Dana introduced Hannah Davis next. Seated beside John, the small woman's raven-black hair hung loose, reaching down to the middle of her back. Her chair was pumped up as far as it would go so that she could sit at the table at a reasonable height, but she still looked as if she needed a booster seat. Somehow she managed to match John's commanding attitude pint for pint with her own serious demeanor. She did not smile as Dana said her name, merely nodded and folded her hands in front of her on the table, spurring him to continue.

The last candidate was Emily Fox. With an angular face to do her name justice, her slightly upturned nose and wavy blonde hair gave her an interesting mixture of soft, feminine features and harsher, more accented ones. "It's been a long week. Can we just get started already?" she asked.

Dana put away his roster with a sigh. Going off script was clearly not his strong suit. "The Arcadian Project," Dana began, looking around at each of the candidates. "You've all been chosen to participate in a series of trials for a newly developing technology that will revolutionize *everything*." He paused for emphasis but was only met by blank stares. "When I say that what we are doing is groundbreaking, I'm not talking about creating a larger screen dimension on some new tech toy or coming up with a smarter algorithm for sorting packages in a warehouse. I mean that what we do here over the next few months will literally change the way the world works."

Although Wes was already hanging off of Dana's every word, the rest of the candidates were much more reserved.

"Over the last decade, we here at CIOX Laboratories have been developing a method for remotely manipulating matter. I'm talking about controlling the movement of molecules with a signal from our supercomputer—the ability to alter the physical structure of the atom with a simple wireless command."

Dana's description seemed to have gone right over Travis's head. The rest of the candidates, however, were now beginning to look a little more enticed. Wes literally scooted up to the edge of his seat, looking about ready to burst with excitement. Aaron glanced over at Claire and their eyes met briefly. Aaron turned away with a blush. Realizing that Claire just saw him blush made him redden even further. He found a spot on the wall towards which to concentrate his gaze, hoping to limit any additional embarrassment.

"We pretreat the matter with special markers that allow the computer to dynamically read the makeup of atoms and molecules within a vicinity. We then send signals to the markers to tell them how we would like to re-sequence the matter—using the atom's own innate powers of repulsion and attraction to move whole clusters around. We can force state changes, making the atoms drop or seek out electrons, alchemically transforming the material into any element on the periodic table, stable or otherwise."

With a startling bang, the conference room door swung open, revealing a heavyset scientist, winded from a run. His round head seemed too small atop the sea of white that was his lab coat, draped across his body. Dana's eyes darted towards the man in annoyance of the interruption, but instantly the project leader's face lit up and began to fill with relief.

"Let me introduce to you George Cartwright, our lead lab tech," said Dana. "Nice of you to finally join us," he added, speaking through gritted teeth. "George is here to tell you all exactly how you will be fitting into the project." Dana shifted his chair over to the side of the table.

With no more seats left, George was forced to address the room from a standing position. He took a small clicker device out of the right front pocket of his lab coat and pushed its chrome covered button. A square portion of the center of the table rose up to expose a projector. Its lens flashed on, blinding George with a shower of white light until he moved to the side of the table to escape its beam. "As Dana mentioned, I am the head lab technician here at Echo Facility.

I also oversee the labs in the Atrium and Battle-Cove Test Range from time to time—"

"—those are the buildings to the east and west of here," said Dana, clarifying for Aaron and the rest of the new arrivals who hadn't had a chance to explore the complex yet.

"Yes," said George, still breathing a little hard from his run to the conference room. "Have you already covered the CMM or the VRP?" he asked.

Dana shook his head. "I told them a bit about the markers, but haven't gotten into any technical details yet."

"Alright," said George, "I'll start with the VRP then." He cleared his throat and pushed on his clicker several times, skipping past the introductory slides of his prepared presentation. The words *The Arcadian Project* flashed across the wall briefly as well as a map of the three-building facility. He stopped skipping ahead when he reached a slide titled *Virus Replication Protocol*. A diagram of a tiny molecular structure filled the wall. "This is Marker model V7, the current model," said George. "It's a self-replicating iron-carbon nanotube device used to scan nearby particles and receive instructions on what to do with them from our computer. Each marker houses a gathering of millions of special neutrino particles which have been attracted to it via a high-frequency current."

Several eyebrows went up at the mention of neutrino particles.

"Yes, yes, I know what you're all thinking," said George. "While it's true that normally the tiny neutrinos would pass right through matter without interacting, we discovered a few years ago that we could tune an electro-magnetic current so that it would attract a swarm of the curious particles. Once the neutrinos are amassed, further application of electric currents at specific frequencies was found to have predictable and reproducible effects on all particles in the vicinity of the mass. In short, we can alter a nearby atom's nucleus, combining it with others or even ripping its quarks apart to produce different molecular weights. The electron count, and therefore the atom's properties of attraction and repulsion, is also altered."

This caused a rush of murmurs to break out amongst the candidates, the responses ranging from disbelief to excited laughter. Emily Fox and Hannah Davis on the other side of the table put their heads together, speaking quickly in a high-pitched chatter that sounded like two chipmunks fighting.

Dana put his hand up to silence everyone, but it still took several moments for the room to settle down. "Go on," he said to George.

"It's truly a miraculous discovery," said George. "The markers themselves are not typically affected by the neutrino mass because of the properties of iron within the iron-carbon nanotubes that make up the markers' structure. Each iron atom acts like a tiny lightning rod, absorbing the energies directed towards it, protecting our device from alteration. Iron can be affected as well when higher frequency currents are passed through the neutrino mass, but doing so will destroy the marker, ultimately scattering the neutrinos, though not before altering other iron particles in the environment. The self-replicating nature of the markers allows them to regenerate quickly to fill in any gaps in the network's coverage should one or more become damaged or destroyed at any time."

Most of the candidates were following along with George Cartwright's complicated presentation. Aaron had heard of things like quarks and neutrinos before from science shows and classes, but hearing the names in passing and actually understanding the science behind what Mr. Cartwright was talking about were far removed from one another.

"The markers work somewhat like a virus, although they're not biological in nature," George continued. "The VRP, or Virus Replication Protocol, is the programming that we have passed to the markers to tell them how far they are allowed to replicate. The density of markers required within an environment to detect every atom present is about five hundred units per square centimeter. Whenever a marker detects a gap within the network's coverage it autonomously creates a new marker from material within the environment, which then self-generates a current of electrons to gather a new neutrino mass, and positions itself in the environment to fill the gap. Right now, the markers exist only within the Test Range and several of my labs across the complex, but when testing is complete, we will alter the VRP to increase the radius of their expansion, allowing them to reach out as far as required."

"Umm…" Travis interrupted, looking quite confused, "how about an explanation in English for us non-scientists…."

It was Cartwright's turn to look flustered.

Dana stepped in to help. "The computer tells the markers what to do, then the markers use the neutrinos to manipulate the matter around them," he said.

Travis nodded slowly, but the blank expression on his face wasn't encouraging.

George pressed his clicker and a new projection appeared. "CMM," said George, "Cognitive Matter Manipulation. This is where all of you come into play. You see, the problem with the markers is that they can only scan particles within their range, which is quite small. Although there are many markers, which overall cover every particle in a given area, it takes a lot of computational power to determine which markers need to be accessed in order to affect a large-scale area. To solve this problem we have developed the CMM serum—a huge advancement in cognitive communications technology. Once injected into a subject, they… or rather, you, I should say… will develop a mental link with our supercomputer, and your spatial input will be used to figure out which markers are closest to the material that you wish to alter."

Travis started to open his mouth again, but Dana jumped in before he could ask George for clarification. "We inject you with a substance that allows you to telepathically connect to our computer," said Dana. "You can then send it instructions about how you would like it to manipulate the matter around you, and the computer uses a combination of the visual data coming from your eyes and your spatial awareness to determine which markers it needs to relay commands to in order to fulfill your objective."

Travis narrowed his eyes. "So, it's like we're playing cricket, and I'm the coach deciding which players to put on the field?" he asked.

"Not really," said Dana, "more like you are the coaches ability to see the field, and the part of him that has the drive to play the game, but the computer is the rest of the coach, and only he can see the players and decide which ones to use, which are the markers, and the bat is the neutrino mass, affecting the ball, which is each of the particles you want to manipulate to get to your desired outcome...."

"That's a terrible analogy," said George, provoking a glare from Dana.

"Basically, you will become a biological interface for our computer," Dana reiterated. "You will mentally pass it instructions on how you would like to manipulate the environment, and the world will change around you. You lucky ones are about to be given the powers of creation and telepathy rolled into one... godly powers... just think of it, the full potential of the atom unlocked; boundless, safe, clean energy at your fingertips. You will be able to produce any material known to the universe in any shape, form, or size at zero physical cost apart from the stock matter that the transformations require. And trust me when I say that there is plenty of stock matter to go around—enough to transform the entire world."

The passion behind Dana's voice was moving. He stood up from his seat and pressed a switch on the far wall of the room. The panels retracted, revealing a window that looked out over the endless waves of sand dunes south of the city—unused matter that could be turned into anything their hearts desired.

The whole world was their stock material.

"In mythology, Arcadia was an unspoiled paradise, a utopia where man lived in harmony amongst nature. That is exactly what our project will create out of the world," said Dana. "There will be no more starvation, no more debt, no more needs or wants left unfulfilled. Infrastructure for an entire city can be built up over night. We will have the power to create anything the world needs, free of cost. The modern day capital of Arcadia is right here in Tripoli, so it really is a most poetic backdrop for what we will accomplish over the coming months. Together, we will usher in a new golden age for mankind!"

CHAPTER

12

Needles

The orientation concluded with a buzz of high energy—no one quite sure if they should truly believe what they just heard. Dana left the candidates with George Cartwright as he went off to meet with the other department heads that missed the orientation. George led everyone back to the elevators and down to the main lab in the basement of the building to receive their CMM serum injections.

"We piggy-backed our serum into empty flu-virus shells," said George as he retrieved a black plastic case full of syringes from a locked cabinet. "That way it disseminates throughout your whole body in about seven to nine days, creating the link by altering your genes in every cell with which it comes in contact." George pulled out one of the syringes from the case and inspected the clear liquid under the florescent lights. "Of course, the important thing is that it propagates within your brain, but since it spreads around each person's body differently, we will have to wait the full

incubation period before beginning any of our experiments."
He tapped the needle with his fingernail. "I should also
inform you all that you will likely experience flu-like
symptoms as the virus spreads, but with any luck they should
be mild compared to the real flu."   Before pulling the
candidates aside one by one to give them their injections,
George retrieved a second case of syringes with needle tips
easily ten times larger than the first ones.

"Planning on sucking out our bone marrow with those?"
Ethan asked jokingly.

"These shots contain your security chips," said George.
"They will allow you to access some restricted areas around
the complex without an escort. Those of you who have
already been here for a couple of days know I speak the truth
when I say that it's rather inconvenient to need an escort to
move around the facility."

"Can't wipe your ass around here without a security guard
watching you," Travis interjected.

"Yes, well, these chips will eliminate that problem…" said
George, "although they do leave a bit of an ugly scar and a
permanent bump at the injection site."

A concerned look flashed across Isabelle's face. She didn't
seem too keen on marring her flawless skin. Claire, on the
other hand, was already rolling up the sleeve of her blouse,
eager to begin.

"The chip injections are required," said George, speaking
mostly to Isabelle, "but if it's any consolation, rather than
leaving you with a disfiguring scar, I can cover the mark with
a free image graft," said George. "I highly recommend it."

Image grafts were similar to tattoos, but didn't require
piercing the skin to transfer the pigment of the image. The
end result was a high-resolution, flawless, tattoo-like marking
printed directly on your body. They were said to be entirely
painless to receive. It was a new technology, and as such, the
grafts were typically not cheap to come by.

Claire was the first volunteer. George took her behind a dividing curtain to administer the injections. Despite her eagerness, a sharp whimper indicated that the thick needle of the chip injection really was as painful as it looked. Aaron found himself rubbing his bicep in empathy, but it was not long before it was his turn to receive the monstrous needle in earnest.

George led Aaron over to an exam bench and had him remove his shirt. He gave him the small injection of CMM serum first. It pinched as it went in, but was over with little discomfort. The chip injection, however, was excruciating. As the tip went in, Aaron's face immediately began to feel hot. His bicep was on fire, every nerve ending screaming as if his arm were in the process of being hacked off. It was a tearing sensation, as if his muscle had been flayed open and his blood replaced with acid. Only when he thought it couldn't get any worse did Mr. Cartwright finally begin pushing the plunger on the back of the syringe. The pain branched out, molten metal filling his veins. The fingers of his left hand cramped as a spasm ran through his bicep. When George removed the needle, a sickly wet feeling ran down Aaron's arm—a river of blood unleashed. The warm liquid dripped from Aaron's fingertips onto the tiled floor.

"Sorry, that was a bad one," said George. "Let me get some cotton for that." George hurried over to a jar full of swabs.

Aaron was grateful to be seated as he felt himself start to grow lightheaded. On the verge of passing out, he fell back on his unscathed right arm, propping himself up as best as he could. George came back over with the swabs and began mopping up the mess. Bright-red blood was still flowing freely from the open wound in his bicep. Aaron's arm began to feel cold.

George wasn't able to keep up with the flow. "Keep pressure on it," he said, putting Aaron's right hand on the blood soaked ball of wadded cotton. "I must have nicked an artery." George hustled back over to the cabinet of medical supplies.

Aaron felt woozy, but it wasn't long before George returned with an odd device that looked suspiciously like a soldering gun. Aaron diverted his eyes, bracing for more pain as George removed the cotton swabs and placed the tip of the device up against the open wound. Instead of pain, a soothing warmth flowed through his arm. Aaron looked back down just as George finished with the device and pulled it back from his skin. His arm stopped bleeding instantly. All that was left of the wound was a rigid scar.

Miraculous!

Never in all his medical training had Aaron ever seen a device capable of such instantaneous healing.

George, seeing the surprised expression on Aaron's face, answered the unasked question. "Nanobots," he said with a smirk. "CIOX Laboratories is a world leader in nano technology. Mostly medical applications—patents pending."

Aaron should have guessed as much. Nothing else could have patched him up so quickly.

"Would you like an image graft?" asked George, holding up another device that he grabbed off the side table. The end of it looked like a suction cup.

Aaron glanced down at the scar again. It was about an inch and a half wide, dark pink and raw. Not the best look. He nodded to George, who quickly stuck the suction cup end over the scar.

"Don't I get to choose what image to use?" Aaron asked.

"Nope," said George, "only have one queued up. It's cool though."

George pulled the trigger and Aaron noticed a slight tingling in his arm, though it may just have been an aftereffect from the nanobots. It took about twenty seconds, and then the light on top of the device went from red to green. When George pulled it away from Aaron's skin, a branding had been left behind. It was geometric—triangles, circles, lines—Aaron didn't study it for long. The important thing to him was that the ugly scar had been entirely smoothed over. A bump from the security chip remained behind at the center of the marking, but anything was better than how it looked before the graft.

All of the remaining candidates chose to receive the image graft as well. After all the injections were finished, George showed everyone how to access the various terminals around the facility to view their schedules and pull up maps of the complex. Their security chips automatically gave them access to personal schedules and room assignments. All they had to do was move their arms close enough to the terminal for the station to read their chips. The candidates' living quarters were on the eighth and ninth floors of the Atrium—the building to the east of Echo Facility. Many of the other staff lived on the lower floors of that building as well. George released everyone to do as they pleased while they waited for the CMM serum to begin running its course.

It was no surprise when Garrett immediately went off by himself, heading out on the town. Everyone else stayed together, though, walking over to the living quarters as a group.

"You're all going to love the Atrium," said Emily, her lips pouting out as she spoke. "It really is quite marvelous."

Upon arriving, it didn't take long for Aaron to see where the building got its name. The ground floor housed an indoor botanical garden with paved pathways that laced between tall palm trees and exotic plants and flowers, all carefully manicured back from the edge of the walkways. It was like stepping into a climate-controlled park, littered with fountains and man-made streams)and waterfalls. Coy filled the waterways. The lethargic, white and orange shapes shimmered brightly beneath the surface, forming ripples overhead. The ceiling was ten stories high and made of glass, allowing the sun to shine down throughout the entirety of the hollow building. It was stunningly beautiful. Aaron couldn't wait to ride the glass-walled elevator up to the ninth floor where his room was located and see what the Atrium looked like from up above.

Travis addressed the group: "If anyone wants to go out tonight, I scouted out a nice bar the other day. It's over on the other side of the park. We could all grab some brews and get to know one another a little better." The offer seemed to be directed mostly towards Brooke, but the woman skirted Travis's eye contact and disappeared up one of the elevators without a word before any plans were finalized.

"I'm not much of a drinker," said Hannah, giving a prickly expression.

"Nonsense," said Emily, "we'll stop by for a bit." She committed both of them despite Hannah's reservations.

"Great," said Travis, "anyone else who wants to come can meet us down here at six." He gave them all a farewell and went off to have a workout in the gym, located in the basement.

Hanging back from the group, Claire caught Aaron's attention. "Are you going to go?" she asked.

The nervous tingle in Aaron's stomach returned immediately. "I don't know," he said, "I guess it could be fun." Aaron didn't want to admit that the idea of going out into Tripoli without an armed escort frightened him. To him, the bullet holes in the street signs were a clear indication of the quality of the neighborhood surrounding the complex.

Claire took Aaron's hesitant response as affirmation. "I'll see you at six then," she said with a smile that lit up her eyes.

Whatever worry he felt was immediately replaced by giddiness. It shook through his core, sending a wide smile to his own face. He was about to receive godly powers, and yet all he could think about was the girl with the auburn hair.

Dana's words reverberated through his mind, *something as mundane as falling in love actually has a profound impact on the human brain.* Claire's presence in his mind was dangerous.

He tried to get his feelings in check as they rode up the see-through elevator together, but it was no use. He had watched her sleep on the plane for longer than he cared to admit—her chest rising up ever so gently and then sinking back down with soft exhales; her face, a pure portrait of innocence. Aaron lost that enduring child-like quality long ago, starting with his father's death. Though he hadn't been allowed to see the charred body, just the American flag folded across the pristine coffin, the hopelessness that engulfed him was still enough to shatter his sense of childhood.

Moving in with his mother in London was supposed to be his time to pick up the pieces. He locked himself in his room, refusing meals and avoiding all human contact right up until his mother was diagnosed with cancer. The timeline got a bit indistinct for Aaron after that. It seemed like months went by curled up on that cold chair in the chemotherapy center, but he knew it had happened much faster than that. She lost the will to live. Her sunken eyes and pale skin slick with sweat; the pain that grew worse and worse until the drugs kicked in and drained away not only the pain, but everything that made her his mother. She laid there motionless, dull eyes so flushed out with painkiller that she didn't even know who Aaron was by the end.

He didn't try to get his childhood back after that—it was too mangled. Only in the past few years had he managed to push aside that darkness, tucking it away in the less accessed portions of his brain. As long as he always remained focused on the future, his mind stayed clear of the painful memories. It was only during times of weakness that the shadows began to seep back into his conscious mind. Oftentimes it was the moments just before drifting off to sleep when the waves of self-pity and blame would crash down upon him, smothering him, ruthlessly consuming all other thought.

I should have been there for her—not locked away in my room... maybe then she would have fought harder to live.

His interest in medicine wasn't a coincidence. It was the cardinal distraction that finally allowed him to escape from his darkness. Now he could keep going for days, even weeks at a time without wondering how his life could have been different. He wanted to help prevent other people from going through what his mother experienced. Medicine inspired a sense of purpose within him. It was what kept him going.

Claire's innocent expression didn't make him forget about his past, but it did stir something deep inside him that he couldn't quite explain—a sort of nostalgia. He wanted nothing more than to preserve the feeling. Bottle it up and drink it little by little each day for the rest of his life. Just being around her made him feel better; gave him hope for the future. Maybe when all of this was done—when the Arcadian Project was over—he could build up the nerve to ask her out.

As the elevator reached floor eight and Claire stepped off, she turned around and gave a little wave before the doors closed again, blocking her from view. All alone, Aaron looked out behind him through the glass that formed the back of the lift. With the atrium far below, he recognized the shape that the pathways and pools formed. It was the same as his image graft—every line and triangle placed exactly like the etching on his arm. Each of the candidates shared that mark now, setting them apart from the rest of the world. A brighter future really was on the horizon, and they would be right at the center of it.

As the elevator door opened on floor nine, Aaron felt a spike of elation surge through him: Maybe he really could have it all—the girl, the job, a better future—prosperity and happiness unlike anything he ever imagined. He was going to have to buy Wes a drink for making it all possible.

Arcadians, here to usher in a new age.

CHAPTER

13

Quantum Entanglement

Don't Be Cruel, an old Elvis song, rang out from an archaic jukebox sitting near the bar's entrance. Every song on the machine was either a celebration of new found love or a lamentation of love gone wrong. Aaron supposed those were the only two emotions one felt while drinking in a place like this.

The bar was silent when they arrived, which was unacceptable to Travis. After tinkering with the old jukebox for a few minutes it started making noise. Travis wasn't outwardly sulking about Brooke's refusal to join them, but based on the song choice it was clear which of the two emotional categories he was reflecting.

The locals were watching them closely, though they maintained a wide berth from the group. Of the twelve candidates, only Garrett, Brooke, and John hadn't joined the party. That left nine non-Arabs, all dressed in black, formfitting, tracksuit-like uniforms, piling into the small pub.

The white-bearded bartender, done up in embroidered silks and a blue head-wrapping, wasn't pleased by their presence. Aaron half-expected the man to refuse them service from all the dirty looks they were receiving. Travis ordered a round of drinks, and despite the bartenders obvious reservations the beers soon showed up at their tables at the center of the room.

Aaron liked his uniform. It was slimming. The black pants had a thin, white stripe running down the side of each pant leg that elongated him, making him appear taller than he really was. The jacket, although long-sleeved, was made out of a light, breathable material that kept the heat off even as the baked earth sweated out all the solar rays it had accumulated during the day. The women's uniforms were much the same as to the men's, only more fitted. They hugged tight to the curves of the women's bodies, dipping low at the neck to expose more than a hint of cleavage. Aaron ventured to guess that the designer was probably male. A very sexually frustrated male. Considering the conservative nature of the locals, it was also a rather poor choice, culturally.

Isabelle, who didn't have much cleavage to show off, wore the uniform proudly nonetheless. The tight pants did accentuate her butt, though, so she had taken on a bit of a lustful persona to match her outward appearance. Claire, on the other hand, had suddenly become much more reserved, wearing a plain gray sweatshirt over the top of her jacket. There was no way she wasn't getting overheated under the extra layer, but she refused to take it off.

Travis gestured towards the array of beers sitting in front of them. Everybody grabbed one and held them up as Travis made a toast. "Here's to better times, and to new friends," he said.

The words of Elvis played out through the grainy speakers of the jukebox, singing about forgetting the past and of the future looking brighter.

"To a true heart and a brilliant future," Wes said jokingly, nearly repeating the song's lyrics verbatim.

Isabelle cracked up more than Wes deserved for his mediocre attempt at humor. She snorted loudly, making her laugh even harder and slosh some of her beer out on the table as she covered her mouth with her hand.

Everybody else chuckled as Isabelle turned red from embarrassment.

"To us," added Aaron, "Arcadians, now and forever."

With the clinking of glasses, the toast was finished and everybody splintered off into smaller groups. Each table only sat four people at the most, so naturally Aaron found himself alongside Claire and across from Wes and Isabelle.

"Can you believe it?" asked Wes. "We're all going to change the course of history!"

"I just wish I could tell my ma about all this," said Claire with a worried frown. They had all been forced to sign lengthy non-disclosure agreements the moment they were selected for the project. "I've always talked to her about everything in my life, and now to have to keep a secret like this…."

The face of a young boy flashed across Aaron's mind—about twelve years old; auburn hair the same shade as Claire's but more curly; sad green eyes filled with concern. The image was there for a moment, and then gone, settling back into the haze. "What about your brother?" Aaron asked. "You two are close, right?"

Claire's eyes narrowed as she glanced at Aaron cautiously. "Aiden didn't want me to come here," she said. "Eight months is a long time to be away."

A guarded apprehension fell over Aaron. He wasn't sure what had set off the feeling. It was the same tentative storm cloud that descended on him whenever someone asked about his mother—a secretive and overly defensive demeanor that was hard to revert back from.

Claire did not elaborate on her relationship with her brother.

Another image of the same boy jumped through Aaron's mind—this time in a hospital bed with tubes attached to his nose; fresh tears glistening in his eyes; his arms stretched out with great strain, beckoning him closer. Aiden was sick; dying. It was impossible to know, but Aaron felt it to be true.

Proud Mary suddenly erupted from the jukebox. "Oh, I love this one! Dance with me," said Isabelle, grabbing Wes by the hand and dragging him out of his seat before he could respond. There was no dance floor, but she pushed one of the empty tables aside to make room and immediately began bumping hips with Wes in a playful, rhythmic gyration.

Claire's eyes were cast downward. She held her beer between her hands with the sleeves of her gray sweatshirt pulled up over her fingers. Condensation dripped down the bottle, dampening the sleeves. She sighed as she looked up at Aaron. "My brother's not doing well," she said. "I don't usually tell people about this. He has a rare blood disease that we've been treating since he was a little baby. It's gotten worse over the last few years… he has to stay at the hospital now… we don't know how much time he has left, but that's why I had to join the project, to help pay for the medical bills." Tears had formed in her eyes, but it looked as if a weight had been taken off her chest by saying it out loud.

"I'm so sorry," said Aaron with genuine sympathy in his heart. He had no idea how he could have known; it was the strangest sensation—feeling like he had been there at the hospital with Aiden. He knew what he looked like; smelled like; the sound of his voice, beginning to crack now with greater frequency as he entered into the throes of puberty. He couldn't have known any of it, and yet the memory was there, almost as vivid as any other. The only difference was that this *memory* was slightly harder to recall than a normal one, as if it were from many years ago. The details were all there, only they took a second to drum up to the front of his mind.

After another moment, the image of the boy began to fade again, all the intricacies slipping away until the memory felt hollow, like a lingering dream about to be forgotten.

This is crazy... just intuition combined with an overactive imagination, that's all it is. What else could it be?

"I need to use the washroom," he said, excusing himself away from the table. He felt a wave of vertigo rush over his body as he stumbled past Wes and Isabelle and around the corner that led to the toilets. He pushed open the door to the dimly lit men's room. It reeked of stale urine, which didn't aid the uneasiness in his gut.

He looked at himself in the scratched up mirror—a cold sweat dripping down his face.

I'm going insane....

His beer was still in his hand. He chugged it down, emptying the bottle before tossing it into the junk bin by the door. After a few moments his head finally started to settle down, stopping its spinning.

It was just an educated guess—it can't have been a real memory. All the day's excitement just got me worked up.

He grimaced at himself in the mirror when he realized that he was probably messing up his one chance of actually getting Claire to like him. She opened up to him, and he immediately ran off. He didn't want to be remembered as the weird guy who spent the whole evening in the toilet. He rinsed his face in the sink and dried his hands, then took one last deep breath before heading back out into the bar.

Before he rounded the corner to the main room, he heard the yelling. The bartender was out from behind the bar shouting in Arabic. It seemed to be directed at Wes and Isabelle mostly, though his pointer finger swung wildly across all of the other candidates as well. Claire rushed over to Aaron when she saw him lingering by the washroom hallway.

"Come on!" she said, grabbing hold of Aaron's hand and pulling him towards the entrance of the bar.

Her skin felt like lightning bolts across his hand, sparking off in all directions in slow motion. Aaron thought he was growing lightheaded again until he realized it was a rush of endorphins surging through him that was making his mind go fuzzy.   The corners of his mouth were pulled up in a permanent grin.   Aaron would have been content with the moment lasting forever.   Claire let out a playful giggle as she tugged him through the open door and into the night air, followed closely by Wes and Isabelle and more distantly by the rest of the candidates.

Claire changed their grip, intertwining her fingers with Aaron's as everyone ran laughing across the street to the big park that stood between the bar and the complex.   "What happened back there?"   Aaron finally managed to ask.

"They're a bunch of sexist, anti-Semitic pricks!" Isabelle spat.

"I think they just didn't care for her provocative dancing," Claire whispered in Aaron's ear.   They shared a silent smirk.

"I know of another bar down the street," suggested Travis, but no one really felt like venturing out farther into Tripoli.

"I think we're going to call it a night," said Hannah, huddled up closely with Emily.

"Us too," said Ethan, giving Michelle a wink, "anyone want to split a cab?"

Hannah and Emily approved.

"I want to walk back through the park," said Isabelle.

Aaron, Claire and Travis joined Wes and Isabelle while the other four hailed their taxi.   Travis produced several more beers, seemingly from out of nowhere, and gave one to each of the girls as they started off into the park.

"So where did they find you?" Wes asked Travis.   "An Australian jiu-jitsu champion just hanging out in the EU?"

"Pretty much," said Travis.   "I was backpacking across Europe when I ran out of money in Germany—I don't speak a lick of German mind you—so I started doing odd jobs here and there to get by.   Fell in with the day laborers.   Only managed to avoid the refugee camps by pretending to still be a tourist whenever the Jacks were around… that's the Police," he added when it was obvious no one knew what he was talking about.   "Anyway, some of my buddies heard about the cattle call, so I went, and now here I am. I guess they liked my combat and weapons training. It does make me wonder, though, how somebody like me fits into their scheme."

There was no one else in the park as they made their way down the winding paths. It felt odd to Aaron that such a place could exist in a city like Tripoli. The park was well maintained despite the near ruin of the mud buildings and cracked pavement that surrounded it. The skyscrapers of downtown were far enough away that they looked like a separate city off in the distance. Other than the park, this part of Tripoli was a rundown shanty-town.

Someone had invested a lot of money to create this oasis in the desert. But for what? The locals surely weren't using it. In a way, it acted like a buffer between the city and the complex. Perhaps that was the point; they were in the barren landscape of Libya where strife had held the region down for decades. It was a dangerous place—a place nobody would ever expect to house the greatest advancement in technology the world had ever seen. The park separated them from the ailing city. Aaron was probably just being silly; there were other parks in Tripoli as well, he saw them from the plane, though none of the others were quite as large as this. Maybe the Libyan government was just trying to show off in front of the rest of Europe now that they were initiated into the EU.

Claire lingered back from the others as they came across a copse of pine trees. "It's strange, isn't it? These trees aren't native to this area."

It was true. Aaron hadn't realized it until she pointed it out. "All plucked from different regions and replanted here in the middle of the desert, just like us," he said, shaking his head in dismay.

"It's like they're trying to give each of us a sense of home," said Claire.

Aaron's mind immediately jumped to the giant redwood trees he had been so inspired by in his youth. There weren't any trees like those here of course, they would take centuries to grow so thick and tall even if they had been planted alongside the other vegetation, but Aaron recognized various maples, pines and other kinds of firs that were common across America.

Aaron reached for Claire's hand this time. He did it on impulse, and was a little taken aback by his own bravado. A feeling of bravery that was quite foreign to him had somehow taken hold. Claire's soft fingers did not recoil. Instead she aided him in interlocking their grip again.

He raised his eyes from their hands to Claire's face to see what her expression held. A twinkle in her eyes along with her intoxicating smile brought jubilation to Aaron. He didn't want to take his eyes off her as they continued walking, but he made a quick glance up ahead to see where the others had made off to. They weren't far away. Aaron happened to look just in time to see Isabelle turn towards Wes and kiss him on the lips. Without a moment of hesitation the two lovebirds immediately started making out in an over-gratuitous way, leaving Travis to shrug away from the display awkwardly.

"Look at them go!" said Aaron with a laugh, but Claire's eyes weren't focused on Wes and Isabelle; instead she was staring at Aaron's lips.

His heart started racing when he looked back at her, the intention clear on her face. Once again it felt like a static tingle had settled over the park. Aaron wasn't sure what had gotten into him, but he didn't care. He leaned forward, grasping the back of Claire's head gently with his free hand and placed his lips upon hers. His whole body was a torrent of sparks from just the one small kiss, which led to another, and then another. He felt her tongue brush lightly across his lower lip, and then the images began to pour through his mind, enveloping him like waves on a beach, one after another breaking on the sand.

The images were memories, only they weren't his own....

Banana bread baking at Christmas, then spitting out cherry soda all over their board game after Aiden told a joke;

camping by the lake one summer evening, eating snow cones to cool off in the sun; jasmine bushes growing outside her window, filling her room with their heavy fragrance every spring and summer until the white petals blew free, covering the ground in a thin blanket that looked like snow; standing with Aiden outside the old house in Dublin on a particularly bright day while waiting for ma to fill the huge twenty-person above-ground swimming pool—it felt so real, like he had actually been there, just waiting and waiting and waiting until ma told them it was time to go in, then climbing up the ladder and hopping into the chilly hose water. The giant orca whale floaty; Aiden wearing his water-wings, still too young to swim without them; they both had so much fun that they never wanted the day to end, the best most innocent time ever....

But it had never happened, at least not to Aaron.

Aaron pulled back from the kiss, searching Claire's face for answers.

Her green eyes had grown large, eyebrows pressed together now in a worried frown. "Why do I remember driving through giant redwood trees?" she asked. "I've never seen such a place in my life." Her breathing suddenly seemed clunky. "I need to go...." she said as she ran off through the park faster than Aaron knew she could move.

CHAPTER

14

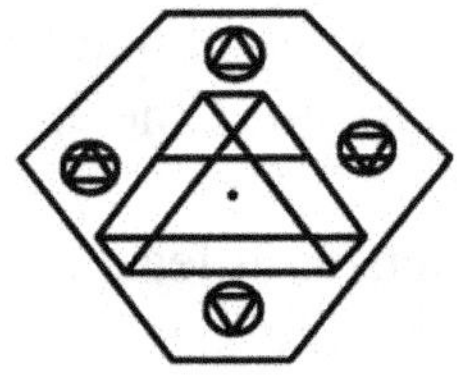

Whispers in the Night

After several days and nights of continuous sailing, the Rosa Marsa was nearing the end of the Etto River. Fort Bastion, the largest of Phandrol's military encampments, stood at the junction where the Bastion River met the Etto and then quickly flowed out into the Great Minthune. The military city, surrounded on three sides by flowing water, formed the forward front of the conflict between Phandrol and Kovehn.

Barracks upon barracks lined the streets—reinforced buildings with sprawling floor plans that covered an acre or more of land each. The bunkers were built out rather than up so that if any portion of their ceilings collapsed during a bombardment multiple floors wouldn't be lost. Countless regiments of ordinary men and Ver'ati alike crowded the docks as the Rosa Marsa sailed into the harbor. Barges were constantly coming and going, ferrying the troops to and from their deployments on the other side of the Crimson Waters.

The uncovered ships—twenty at a time fording the wide river in either direction—were packed shoulder to shoulder with men, some in cream-colored Ver'konus uniforms with a variety of colored sashes—red for lancemen, green for archers, black for cannoneers and artillerymen… the list went on and on—others wearing the blue-fringed tabards of the queen's forces; the Phandolian Guard. The queen's men outnumbered the Ver'konus soldiers five to one. Here and there, a black-uniformed Ver'ati passed by, always in a position of command. A single competent Power user could outweigh an entire regiment of ordinary troops on the battlefield, but, as Arlin pointed out, it only took one well-placed sword or arrow to kill a man—even Ver'ati were susceptible to death.

General Aldune was stationed here at the fort, leading the war march from the relative safety of the main keep. Though the fighting had been on the Kovani side of the Minthune in recent months, many old scorch marks marred the Calvenite walls of Fort Bastion. Whole portions of the battlements were warped well beyond an ordinary material's structural integrity. Attacks of the Power—nothing else could have dented those surfaces.

Ethan planned to use Aldune's campaign as a distraction—an all-out invasion of Kovani territory to keep Garrett busy while the Rosa Marsa sailed right up to his doorstep. With Guther Aldune in charge, the incursion so far had been more successful than anyone dared hope, pushing deep into the Kovani countryside with little resistance. Even so, Ethan had some new orders for his second-in-command.

Captain Bundles piloted the Rosa Marsa down one of the large canals that cut through the fort's many encampments and then tied up against a piling, as close to the main keep as he could get. Ethan stayed below deck lest Garrett had eyes within the city. He sent Captain Grine as his runner to request Aldune's presence aboard the steamer. There was no telling how far Garrett's treacherous network reached, and only a fool would underestimate his enemy with so much at stake.

From what Belford remembered about his past, Garrett didn't seem all that dangerous—more of a jerk than anything else, really—but Ethan insisted that as Belford continued to recover his memories he would understand the true danger that Garrett represented, both to the world they came from and to the whole of Aragwey now. Belford spent every night of their journey, and sometimes large portions of the days as well, meditating with the technique Ethan taught him. He was quite pleased with the increased rate of return of his memories, every session filling in more and more gaps, leading to new discoveries about his past.

The Arcadian Project; his medical training; Garrett and Ethan before they were King and Lord; the Mark of Kings— nothing more than an image graft to cover up the scar of their security chip injections; and most importantly, Claire. He was remembering how they met and fell in love—oh how he cherished those memories most of all! He had developed a strange mental link with her—that much was clear. He was able to see into her mind, experience parts of her past as if they were his own. It was a beautiful thing now that he looked back on it, though he knew they were both quite frightened when they first made the discovery. He couldn't wait to meditate again later that night to see what more he could recover, but for now there was work to be done.

During the day, whenever Belford wasn't meditating in his little room by the stairs, he focused much of his time and energy on trying to find ways to win over the various Ver'ati on board—to get them to trust him more than Ethan. It was a task that was much easier said than done. These were military men and women, and following orders was what they did, by oath and honor. If he was actually able to convince any of them to capture Garrett rather than kill the king when Ethan gave the order, it would be a miracle.

Unfortunately, questioning Garrett was still the best method Belford could think of for predicting Claire's return. It was all he had, really. Rather than simply trying to make friends with the Ver'ati, which was starting to feel like a futile endeavor, he began working on finding ways to manipulate them instead. He kept his eyes and ears open, constantly searching for an opening, and luckily, he managed to find one.

Vera Ekrin, Ethan's young maid, for all the scowling she did, had managed to attract the attention of Captain Grine. He pined over her hopelessly, always casting sidelong looks at her whenever they came across each other in the hallways or ate together in the mess. The captain never stated anything of his feelings out loud, but they were as clear as the sky on a cool winter morning.

What gave Belford leverage was the way Ethan treated the girl—always talking about her as if she were a purely sexual being, despite her conservative attitude and lack of any advances towards Ethan. He made inappropriate comments both behind her back and in front of her face indiscriminately, even going so far as to slap her butt whenever she walked within reach. The lustful look in Ethan's eyes painted it as more than a playful act.

When she wasn't scowling, Vera had adopted a vacant expression, distancing herself from the abuse. Ethan's treatment of the girl bothered Belford greatly, but there wasn't much he could do about it. Ethan was their leader, and now was not the time to publicly undermine him if he ever wanted to see Claire again. What he could do, however, was make sure Captain Grine was aware of Vera's mistreatment at the hands of Ethan, so that when the time came, Grine just might choose to help Belford rather than follow Ethan's kill order.

Belford was pretty sure Thorin and Shiara were already in his pocket, he did have a history with them after all, but he hadn't yet figured out what to do about any of the rest of the Ver'ati aboard the Rosa Marsa. He still thought Livian Niern was the most dangerous of the bunch with her potential ability to generate brain spores, but that was what could also make her the most valuable of them all to have on his side.

The three Arcanum Ver'ati—Sarbin Raiger, Livian Niern, and Deenan Raughel—kept to themselves. They seemed to have their own agenda. Belford just needed to figure out what it was the Arcanum really wanted out of this mission, and then somehow use that to get his way. Convincing any of them to speak was going to be a challenge, however. It was clear that Sarbin didn't trust Belford, probably because he saw him as one in the same with Ethan, whom the Arcanum was constantly running into conflict with. The steward wasn't about to drop any hints as to the Arcanum's true intentions.

Next up was Deenan. He had a long face, and that was pretty much all Belford knew about him. They hadn't spoken a single word to each other, though Deenan did grunt one time when they passed in the stairwell. The dark-eyed man spent nearly all of his time sitting on a stool at the entrance to the cargo area. He and Livian switched off guarding the compartment, and no one besides Ethan, Grine and Sarbin ever entered.

Livian was the only one out of the three that Belford thought he might have a hope of manipulating, but all he had on her so far was her interest in Arlin, and he hadn't yet figured out how to use that to his advantage. For reasons beyond Belford's knowledge, Arlin was too distracted to even recognize the advances Livian made towards him. All Arlin did was practice his swordsmanship. Each day in the afternoon, he and Thorin dueled tirelessly, going through steps on the back deck of the steamer, blocking and striking for hours—a ceaseless clang of lashing steel. Thorin put down his cudgel, donning a thin, long blade that reminded Belford of a katana instead. With Arlin taking all of his meals in private, neither Livian nor Belford had gotten a chance to spend much time with him so far on the journey.

Belford would have to make connecting with Arlin a higher priority if he wanted to use Livian's admiration for the swordsman to his favor.

With the sun setting on Fort Bastion, Captain Grine returned to the Rosa Marsa with General Aldune close on his heels. Sharith Grine, short and scrawny as he was, looked like a child next to Aldune. Guther really was a beast of a man, packed dense with muscle; the same body type as Thorin. Aldune's expression soured when he saw Thorin standing beside Shiara on the back deck. "What are they doing here?" he asked loudly as he boarded the steamer. "They aren't cut out for a mission like this," he spat.

Belford felt a temper rising inside of him. The memory of Aldune's stubborn attitude almost getting everyone killed in the Erotos Underground last month was fresh in his mind. Guther's face was still etched with the scars of Wilgoblikan's searing explosion which had caught them all off-guard. Belford could have healed the remaining marks, but he thought the general deserved the ugly exterior. "They're here with me," Belford said flatly.

Guther looked him over with recognition. "You should be more careful of the friends you keep," he said. "Their inexperience could get you killed." It sounded like a threat.

"Watch your head on the hatch," said Belford as Aldune started down into the belly of the Rosa Marsa. "You wouldn't want to get any more scars."

Aldune was only gone for about ten minutes before he came back up frowning and disembarked from the steamer without another word to anyone. He started towards the keep at a brisk pace and never looked back. Belford made his way below deck as Captain Bundles ordered Garcenus to untie the ship; they were setting out for night travel up the Crimson Waters. Belford stopped at the base of the steps as he heard Ethan and Sarbin exiting the cargo area, just around the corner. "I'll give him that much, he certainly does know how to get a job done," Sarbin said to Ethan. The Arcanum steward may not have had much trust for Ethan, but that surely didn't stop him from being chummy with him now.

"He will do well to relieve the lieutenant general. Cale really is over his head down there anyway," said Ethan. "We need Garrett to think he has a chance at winning against us here so he'll send more troops away from Tavallon. A man is most reckless when he thinks he is nearing victory."

"I'm not sure Garrett could produce a victory at this point even if we left three goats in charge of military operations."

"We just need to make the fool think things are going his way," said Ethan. "Sacrifice a city or two; maybe let him cross back over the Minthune if he gets so bold as to try. We're going for the ultimate victory here, after all."

There was a pause as the men started walking again. "Same time tomorrow?" asked Sarbin. A change in tone suggested a serious nature for the proposed meeting.

"Maybe start an hour earlier," said Ethan. "I like to keep my evenings free."

Belford pressed himself up against the wall as Sarbin and Ethan passed the stairway, headed towards their respective cabins. Neither noticed Belford in the shadows. After they were gone, he peered down the hallway towards the cargo hold. A watchful Deenan Raughel occupied the wooden stool.

Belford was left troubled by the exchange. Aldune was going back to Erotos to replace Cale, and Ethan was letting Garrett take back everything Aldune had worked so hard to achieve.

Sacrificing cities....

Belford didn't think he was capable of making decisions like that; lives lost to give his schemes a better chance at success. It was all just too much. Simply knowing about Ethan's plan made his chest hurt with guilt.

How many people would die simply to throw off Garrett's confidence?

It felt immoral.

But the order was given, and Aldune was gone. They were at the front, almost behind enemy lines now, not to emerge again until they sailed back down the Great Minthune on their way home. There would be no more communication with the Phandolian war machine from this point out.

With nothing left to do but drown himself in his thoughts, Belford stepped past the supply closet and opened the door to his little cabin by the stairs. He intended to meditate—to try to recover more memories of his past—but as he settled down into his cot, he found it difficult to concentrate. He fell asleep before he managed to recover any more of his memories. The metal clang of boots on the stairs outside crashed like distant thunder in his dreams.

As one dream rolled into the next, he found himself surrounded by the people of his past—Claire, Wes, Ethan, Travis, all the Arcadians, drinking and laughing—only, Travis wasn't talking in his usual Australian accent. He was speaking French, or was it Spanish? Italian? It kept changing; all gibberish to Belford. Ethan's face kept shifting—young to old to young again—it was disconcerting to watch.

Garrett was there too, only he wasn't laughing; rather, he sipped from his beer with the forked tongue of a snake. Garrett stared at Belford through the vertical slits that had become his eyes. *Hssssss*, he said, turning fully into a snake now. Glistening, dark scales appeared over his pale skin. His jaw shot open, exposing venomous curved fangs with pointed tips. He sprang at Belford like a steel trap snapping shut. Belford woke with a start just before the fangs could sink into his neck.

He could still hear the hissing; a faint rasp echoing through the ship. He thought it was just his imagination at first, but as it continued on, he realized he was actually hearing the murmur of voices coming through the wall; soft whispers in the night.

He tried to understand what they were saying, but the bulkhead muted the words beyond recognition. It sounded like they were coming from the supply closet adjacent to Belford's room. He tried to go back to sleep, but the whispers proved too distracting. After turning over several times, he was suddenly unable to find a comfortable position. Belford stood up from his cot and opened the door of his cabin. The hum of the engines was louder in the hallway, causing the sound of the whispers to evaporate into the night air. The door to the supply closet was shut.

Belford reached for the handle, ready to tell whoever was inside to find somewhere else to have their late night conversation, but when he opened the tiny closet no one was there—just a slew of extra ropes, lamp oil, repair tools, buckets; all sorts of items that were necessary on a ship like the Rosa Marsa, but only of occasional use. The whispers were louder here, but Belford still couldn't identify where they were coming from. The steamer bumped over a wave, causing the closet door to fly open all the way and knock against the hallway wall. The whispers ceased immediately, though the bang wasn't very loud. Belford continued to listen for a while, but the voices did not return.

He exited the supply closet and walked past the two sets of stairs, one leading up to the back deck, the other down into the bilge, and then glanced down the hallway beyond that led to the cargo area. Deenan was still there, all alone, fast asleep now though he remained upright in a seated position on his stool. He was leaning against the cargo hold hatch which was shut tight behind him. Belford approached the sleeping Ver'ati, but after only three steps the man opened his eyes and pulled himself up straight on his stool. His expression indicated that Belford would be smart to turn around and go back to his cabin, but Belford had had enough of the secrecy. "What's back there?" he asked.

Deenan didn't respond, merely standing up as Belford took another step closer. The Ver'ati tapped the silver stripe that ran through the blue-hemmed sleeve of his robe. It was the same hems that Livian wore—the blue indicated that they were Illusionists, while the silver stripe was reserved for the Arcanum elite. Deenan's gesture towards his stripe was a warning; a gorilla puffing out his chest to ward off rivalry.

Belford didn't heed the warning. When he took another step, a bright light flashed out of nowhere, blinding him. Before he could react, hands grabbed his wrist and spun him around, twisting his arm up and sideways behind his back. The spots began to clear from his vision as Deenan gave him a violent shove down the hall in the direction of the stairs. He tried to turn around to look at Deenan and was met with a heavy handed slap to the side of his head. A second, lighter push brought him stumbling back to the corner that led to the cabins. To avoid receiving another smack, he continued forward on his own without attempting to turn around, but after rounding the corner, he peeked back down the hallway at Deenan. The Ver'ati was already sitting on his stool again, as if nothing had happened. Belford cursed the man under his breath, rubbing the side of his face where the stinging slap struck him, then spun back around to hobble to his cabin.

The supply closet door was ajar. Garcenus stood at the opening holding a dim lamp that cast dancing shadows across the wall behind him. He scowled at Belford—his usual dark grimace—then opened the door more fully and rummaged through the closet before emerging with a case of lamp oil, enough for at least twenty lamps. He latched the door behind him and shuffled down the hallway away from Belford.

When Garcenus was out of sight, Belford opened the door to the supply closet himself, but nothing was out of the ordinary. He returned to his cabin. Only the rumble of the engine and the pattering of the waterwheel broke the silence of the night.

Maybe I can finally get some rest now.

He laid himself back down on his cot and closed his eyes. If he didn't start gaining some respect around here, this was going to be a very long and unsuccessful journey.

Left Behind

Javic absently squeezed the soft lump of clay in his hand, watching the gray putty squish out between each of his knuckles. When he opened his fingers the goop had formed a spiky shape, imprinted with the lines of his palm. He smoothed it over; rolling it back into a sphere before squishing it again for what must have been the thousandth time.

"I think I'm ready to give it another try," said Rylin, seated beside Javic. They were in Professor Vanton's transfiguration class—the first one Javic had been allowed to participate in since being unceremoniously locked in the closet with the task of finding his anchor; a task which he utterly failed. So far he had spent a whole month's worth of classes sitting by himself, fighting boredom while the rest of Vanton's students learned how to become Ver'ati. Professor Vanton still insisted that Javic needed to focus his mind, to clear himself of emotion in order to allow cold, calculated use of the Power—the kind of concentration Javic employed while hunting back in Darrenfield—but there was just too many distractions at the moment for him to have any hope of achieving such a mental state.

Vanton agreed to let Javic spend some time with the rest of the class for the next couple of sessions solely because Rylin had asked that Javic be his study partner. Javic was to act as the boy's assistant while Rylin prepared to take his upcoming proficiency exam. It was only a few days away now—Rylin had been approved to take the test early because of his excellent marks in all of his subjects. Ever since the exam date was set, the boy had become an uncharacteristic bag of nerves, forgetting how to do even simple tasks with the Power. Things he knew forwards and backwards, conversions he had practiced over and over again a hundred times were suddenly tripping him up.

Javic placed the ball of clay down in the groove at the center of the wooden work table next to the three small goblets that were supposed to hold Rylin's final transmutations. He took a step back to give Rylin some room to work. "Alright," said Javic, "now remember, in order to transform it into three different substances, each with different densities but the same volume, you need to use different amounts of clay in each goblet." On his most recent attempt, Rylin split the clay into even thirds, causing the last goblet to overflow all over the table with transmuted water, the least dense of the three materials he was tasked to create.

Rylin looked flustered even before he lifted his hands. The boy took a deep breath and focused his unblinking eyes on the lump of clay, causing it to vibrate slightly in its groove. The ball suddenly split apart like a brittle rock smashed by a blacksmith's hammer, sending shards ricocheting all across the room in an unexpected explosion. Bits of shrapnel landed along the other work stations, splattering on impact and sticking to the clothing of their fellow classmates. Rylin received a few dirty looks, but the clay was too soft to cause any real harm. It wasn't exactly an improvement over his last attempt....

"Rylin, Javic," Professor Vanton called from his desk at the front of the room. He gestured for them to approach.

Rylin gave a sigh and meekly dropped his outstretched arms as he and Javic made their way over to the professor. Before they were halfway there, Vanton waved dismissively. "Never mind, Rylin. Just Javic come here," he said.

Rylin paused, confused by his lack of reprimand. The boy gave Javic a sympathetic expression as he went back to his seat. Javic continued on alone. He was going to be delegated back into the closet, he just knew it. He couldn't help wondering if Vanton simply didn't like him for some reason. He was only brought out to help Rylin pass his exam, but since the boy was doing even worse now with Javic as his partner than he had before on his own, Javic didn't think there was much of a chance he would be allowed to continue working with him.

"Rylin has a bright mind, but he is still very young," said Professor Vanton when Javic reached his desk. "He does not yet have the level of maturity that you possess, a trait he will surely find need for in the days to come if he is to succeed at the tasks set out before him. The proficiency exams this term will be administered by Lieutenant General Cale Fisman while General Aldune is away, but the lieutenant general has no experience working with initiates. There is no telling what sorts of challenges he will present students with during the exam. Everyone will need to be extra prepared for their tests, and so I must ask a favor of you."

Javic narrowed his eyes, wary of exactly where all this was going.

"I can see you have been distracted from your studies, and from the whispers I have heard going around, there certainly are plenty of reasons to be, but if you could try to put whatever troubles are ailing you out of your mind, Rylin could really use your assistance right now." Vanton wrung his hands together. "Ver'ati must be composed internally as well as externally. I believe Rylin just needs a friend right now. Talk to him, figure out what's bothering him, and help him move past it."

It was a strange assignment, to be a friend, but it was what Javic should have already been doing all along. Javic was so focused on his own woes that Rylin's drop from head of the class to the bottom of the pile hadn't really registered with him. Javic had to remind himself that the thought of leaving Rylin behind had been his one regret while preparing to set out on the secret mission. Now that he was staying in Erotos, it was selfish and wrong of him to ignore the boy. Even so, it was very difficult for Javic to get out of his own head. He had been betrayed by his grandfather, the one person he trusted most, and nothing he did now could take his mind off of that. It constantly ate at him.

Being presented with the opportunity to take down King Garrett had felt like destiny, the cosmos finally treating him right for the first time that he could remember. But then Elric took it all away from him. He understood that his grandfather was only looking out for his safety, but going on that mission with Belford and the others had been more important to Javic than anything else in the world—a chance to see wrongs righted, to fulfill what his parents started so many years ago. He wanted to be there when Garrett met his end, to see firsthand that the monster was taken down, and yet Elric had not even bothered to consult him before sealing his fate by talking to Lord Ethan. If Elric really cared about him, he would have seen how much the mission meant to Javic and let him go. He hadn't spoken to Elric since that night and made a point to throw out the daily letters he received from his grandfather unread as well. He was still bristling with anger over the whole situation.

It had been five days now since the Rosa Marsa's departure, but today was the first day Javic was allowed to go out without a Ver'ati escort. The two cloaked men tasked with watching over Javic had made sure to keep their distance during the day, but it was hard to miss two fully trained Ver'ati hanging out inside the initiate dormitories at night. It led to many unanswerable questions from Rylin and Bax, but eventually they stopped asking about the escort when it became clear that Javic was not allowed to explain the presence of the men. The Ver'ati had been there to stop Javic from attempting to run away, as if he were hair-brained enough to try something so dumb after Lord Ethan made it clear that he was not welcome on their journey. The Rosa Marsa was long gone, probably already nearing the end of the Etto River, maybe even heading up the Crimson Waters by now.

When class ended, Javic and Rylin descended the marble steps of Conset Hall into Garson Square and started to head back towards their dorm. Across the way, Professor Herin and the other Builders had made quick work of the new building. It rose out of the earth where Laudry Hall once resided. The new structure had the same floor plan as Laudry Hall, and the plaque at its entrance even held the same name. It was as if nothing happened. Not a single piece of physical evidence remained of the disaster. Professor Lian, Javic's old history teacher who perished in the collapse, was not so easily replaced. After word of Professor Vanton's unorthodox lecture reached the higher administration, the class was canceled rather than have Vanton continue frightening Lian's ex-pupils into fleeing the academy altogether.

It bothered Javic that no memorial was constructed. It was as if the victims didn't matter to the Ver'konus. Their only goal was to gloss over the negative and move on; smooth out the wrinkles and forget the past; it was a dangerous policy. *How many other moments of significance have been swallowed up and forgotten by the Glowing City?*

Javic and Rylin were already halfway back to the dorms before Javic realized the boy hadn't spoken a single word since exiting Conset Hall. "Are you alright?" he asked.

Rylin glanced around to see who Javic was talking to. Upon finding that there was no one else present he blinked several times in confusion.

"You've just been really quiet the last few days, is all," Javic added.

The expression on Rylin's face was still distant. "It's nothing," he said. "It's stupid. Don't worry about it."

Javic stopped walking, forcing Rylin to turn and speak to him face-to-face. "Well, whatever it is, it's obviously affecting you, so it can't possibly be that stupid. Besides, if it causes you to not pass your proficiency exam, how do you expect to help me study for mine?" Javic asked with a grin.

Rylin sighed, clearly hesitant to speak. He diverted his eyes before opening his mouth. "It's Sima," he said, "I just can't stop thinking about her…." Rylin's cheeks went flush as he glanced back up into Javic's face. "She kind of reminds me of my mother…." Rylin's face nearly turned purple as he blushed even harder.

Javic wasn't sure how to take that. Rylin's mother, the loud woman from the boy's stories, didn't seem anything like the slender and exotic Sima, but he didn't argue. Rylin was having his first boyhood crush on an unavailable woman—familiar territory for Javic, though admittedly not a fun position to be in. Javic spent years pining over Salvine before finally making a move—the fateful move that sent her on a course towards her death.

The thought of Mallory obligatorily crossed Javic's mind as well. No amount of feelings would stop her from being Arlin's girl. She had been left behind in Erotos as well, which might have provided solace to his current situation if it wasn't for the fact that initiates were not allowed to have visitors until after passing their proficiency exams. Javic had yet to receive notice of when his exam would take place.

"I mean, I know nothing is going to happen," said Rylin, "Bax is my friend and I would never do that to him anyway, but I still can't get her out of my head...."

Javic put his arm over Rylin's shoulder as they started walking again. "I think I know exactly what you need," said Javic. He was experienced in dealing with heartache, and although it was never easy, he had learned a few tricks to manage the suffering. The best Javic could do for the boy was to help him get his mind off things.

Before Salvine died, when she had been dating one boy after another for years, leaving Javic unable to make a move, the very thought of the girl brought sadness to his heart. The constant longing ate away at his spirit. The only thing that eased his troubles over all those years when she was just barely out of reach was to go hunting. Forcing himself to focus on hitting his targets combined with the physicality of pulling the bowstring was therapeutic for him. There wasn't anywhere to go hunting within the Glowing City of course, but Javic had an idea for the next best thing: Launching rocks into the Etwon River with the Power. So, instead of going back to the dorms, he led Rylin towards the South Bridge, to a spot where he knew they could get down near the water's edge.

"Did I ever tell you about the time my brother Cormick saved me from drowning?" Rylin asked as he tossed a stone into the air and sent it whizzing against the wall on the opposite side of the river. It shattered on the Calvenite fortification, the loud crack echoing between the ramparts.

Javic shook his head. He had heard much about Rylin's family—Rylin had three brothers and one sister, all older than him, and he had told Javic countless stories about each of them—but this one was new.

"Back home in Shian City my brothers used to call me Shrimp," said Rylin, jumping right into it, "not out of meanness—I've just always been little, and also a quick swimmer—anyway, one day when I was nine, I was out with

Cormick in a tiny rowboat he built with my father. He was diving for oysters while I paddled to keep us steady against the currents. Most of the other ships on the coast are fishing boats from the nearby villages—we don't get many large trading vessels south of Shian Point. There isn't much trade to be had between the City and the Scar of Phandrol—the trading companies prefer to ferry their goods up the Minthune.

"There is this one island there, though, where the traders that do make it that far south claim to have seen mermaids playing in the shallows. This was back when I still believed in such things. So I'm rowing, waiting for Cormick to resurface—he can hold his breath for what seems like forever—the wind is picking up and the water is getting a bit rough, when I think I see something bobbing over amongst the rocks of the island. I see long hair, a girl, and there's something shiny. Immediately I'm thinking I just discovered a mermaid, and that I could be rich. Like all the tales say, if you can win over a mermaid she will bestow upon you endless riches that have been lost by man into the depths of the sea. The mermaids have no use for our money I guess— just trade in fish or something—a barter system."

Rylin launched another rock, this one splashing down in the middle of the Etwon. "Well, I knew I couldn't take the boat over to her, because when Cormick comes up he's usually pretty tired and carrying a sack of oysters, but I couldn't just let the mermaid get away without at least trying to talk to her. So I decide to take off my shirt and trousers and just dive in, hoping the boat wouldn't drift too far. I start swimming, but the tide is pushing me back. I just try to keep my eye on the rock where I saw the mermaid splashing, but after a while I can't see it anymore; the waves are blocking my view, hitting me in the face. I look back and the boat has already drifted twice as far from the island as where it started, but I'm a strong swimmer so I keep pushing forward.

"I'm almost there when a big wave comes over the top of me and throws me under, a force so strong I felt like I wouldn't ever be able to pull out of it. You lose your sense of direction in something like that—the sheer weight of it—you don't even know what's up and what's down. I remember being frightened, then finally orienting myself and coming up to the surface gasping for air just in time for another wave to push me back down. I must have hit my head on the bottom or something, because after that I don't remember anything. Cormick must have come up, seen *me* bobbing over by the rocks and rowed the boat over to save me. By the time I came to, we were already halfway back to shore. I was coughing up water, but still managed to ask him if he saw the mermaid, to which he replied, 'I must have, because she already gave me all the riches I could ever wish for—my little brother back.'"

Javic's eyes welled up, touched by the story. Javic wished he had that—a family who cared about him so deeply that they would do anything for him. He didn't feel like he was worth all the riches in the world to anyone. "You must really miss them," said Javic, "your family."

Rylin nodded. "More than anything," he said. "Cormick is going to bring my mother out for a visit sometime after I become a cadet."

"Then we better work on getting you focused and ready for your exam," said Javic, picking up several more rocks from the ground. "See if you can hit the railing on the other side." Javic tossed one of the stones out in front of Rylin.

The boy sent it flying in a straight line. It bounded off the curved railing and shot up into the air, landing somewhere over in the Central District—an impressive shot. It was good to be able to laugh again.

"I bet you can't do that a second time," said Javic.

Rylin smiled. The boy stood up a little straighter and made a face of concentration as he prepared to take on the challenge. Rylin was changing back into his old, confident self. Javic could already tell tonight was going to be a good night after all.

CHAPTER

16

Patience

The door to the laboratory slid open with the grind of ungreased wheels in its track. One of Doctor Crane's assistants stepped into the chamber, clipboard in hand, marking off a list of supplies and noting what needed to be replaced before the doctor's next barrage of experiments. It was like clockwork. The assistant made his way around the lab, as he did after every session, checking each of the cabinets and drawers before approaching the central exam table and verifying the condition of the attached restraints.

The Whune who was once Salvine had been waiting patiently for days, acting meek and docile, leaning against the back of her cage, the way the voice inside her head suggested. When the assistant finished his duties, he walked with an exaggerated arc to avoid her cage as he exited the chamber. Each day she made absolutely sure to show no aggression while in the assistant's presence. She was conditioning him to not fear her—to lure him in closer, so that she could strike. His arc had diminished in response. With any luck, today would be the day.

Get ready.

She silently stood up and moved to the back of her enclosure. It would take as much momentum as she could muster to knock the heavy cage over.

The assistant had no idea what was coming. He turned away from the restraints, satisfied in his observations.

Her pulse quickened. If she did this right, she was about to satiate her much pined after need for blood. The presence in her head knew she would kill the assistant, but for once it remained silent, giving tacit consent over her intended actions.

Now! The voice cried out as the assistant stepped directly in front of the cage. She lunged forward, slamming into the bars with all her force. The assistant, focused down on his clipboard, shot his head up, but didn't comprehend what was happening fast enough to move out of the way. The Calvenite cage tipped forward as the sting of the bars landed across her face and body. Her head spun and the lights appeared to spark and spiral as the heavy cage toppled over entirely, directly onto their unsuspecting victim.

With the young fool pinned beneath her, she wasted no time reaching her nub fingers between the bars and pressing her thumbs into the squishy orbs of his eyes. He screamed, louder than his first cries of shock when the cage initially struck him. The force of her attack against her own amputated digits caused her much pain, but the pleasure she received from pressing her thumbs into the soft tissue of his head and mushing around the bloody pulp at the front of his brain was extraordinary—better than she even thought possible. It had been far too long since her last kill.

She continued to poke into his brain, penetrating deep into the spongy flesh while breathing in the wild ecstasy of the moment. The crushing weight of her and the cage combined would have probably killed him on its own quite soon, but this way was much more fun. Waves of elation flowed through her as the warm blood steamed from his eye sockets. She cried out alongside him, roars of pure ecstasy as she was overcome with the euphoria of the kill. She wished she could have taken her time with it, but knew it would not be long before someone came to the assistant's aid. His cries ceased, life finally rushing out of him. Her heart pounded with delight at the sight of the expanding pool of blood beneath his torn up face.

Rushed footsteps in the hallway culminated in Doctor Crane appearing at the chamber door, smoke stick still in mouth. He took one look at the mangled corpse of his assistant beneath her cage and used the Power to launch her, cage and all, backwards off of him. His anger increased the force of his attack as the cage flipped back upright and slammed into the cabinet against the wall, sending the prized tin of claws tumbling towards the floor. The lid popped open, just as the presence in her head hoped it would, and dozens of claws skittered across the tiled floor in all directions.

The force of Doctor Crane's maneuver sent her into a heap at the base of the cage. Head still spinning, she quickly snatched up the closest claw she could get her hands on and stuffed it beneath the bandage that covered her left index finger nub, hiding it from sight.

Good, said the voice, *now we just have to stay alive long enough for me to pick the lock.*

Once Doctor Crane realized his assistant was beyond resuscitation, he turned towards her.

"Tricky bitch," he spat, fuming beneath his cool exterior. "I'm going to break you—train you to be a good dog." His eyes were steel. "I'm going to make hurting you my personal project."

Her body went stiff as he used the Power to hold her rigid. Every muscle tightened in a deep flex. Soon, the tensed muscles began to ache. After only a few moments they were already at the point of exhaustion, and the pain was excruciating. Doctor Crane did not relent. Her body felt like it was tearing itself apart; lightning bolts through her veins. Every muscle grew white hot.

Neither her, nor the voice in her head had expected such a heated reaction from the doctor. The presence could barely form words through the pain.

Stay strong, it said, *we've got to stay strong.*

The words felt distant as the tearing sensation intensified. She looked up at Doctor Crane's scowling face. Internally, she smiled at the thought of tearing the skin from his flesh. It would be the first thing she did when she got out.

Her head throbbed with heavy pressure, blood pounding behind her eyes and ears. There was nothing she could do as the corners of her vision began to go dark. She closed her eyes. Unconsciousness was welcome—anything to stop the pain.

Suddenly, Crane released her from the lock. She remained crumpled in her cage as the pain slowly began to lift.

"What have you got there?" Doctor Crane asked.

Disappointment coursed through her body.

Oh no! He's discovered the hidden claw… it's all been for naught.

But when she opened her eyes, Crane was not looking her way at all. His eyes were directed back towards the door to the chamber. A young Ver'ati stood wide-eyed at the entrance with a piece of parchment in his hand.

The young man was too distracted by the corpse of Crane's assistant to answer the doctor immediately.

"Well?" Crane didn't hide his irritation.

The young Ver'ati forced his eyes from the dead man. He placed a hand over his queasy stomach. "My apologies," he said. "It's a letter, from General Aldune. He's been ordered back to the city."

"Ah, good," said Crane, his mood switching in an instant. "Then all is going to plan." The doctor extended his hand. "Give it here," he said.

The young Ver'ati stepped forward hesitantly and handed Crane the letter before backing away from the corpse once more.

Crane quickly read through the correspondence before folding it neatly and placing the paper into one of his pants pockets. He looked back up at the young Ver'ati. "Don't just stand there," he said. "Go get a mop and make yourself useful." He gestured towards the puddle of blood pooling beneath his deceased assistant's head.

The young Ver'ati scoffed. "Can't we just use the Power to clean up?"

"We could," said Doctor Crane, "but if you are to be my new assistant, there's no better time than the present to get over a fear of blood."

"But I'm not..." the young Ver'ati gulped as Crane eyed him intently. "Yes, sir," he said.

"Doctor," said Crane.

"Sir?"

"Call me doctor."

"Yes, doctor," the young Ver'ati said begrudgingly as he went off in search of cleaning supplies.

Doctor Crane turned back on her, still crumpled in her cage. "I hope you're happy," he said. "Now I have to train a new assistant."

You know, I think he might be even more callous than you.

Crane gestured sharply, tossing her to her feet by means of the Power. He quickly fashioned a pair of restraints to the side of her cage that hooked her arms in place above her head so that she wouldn't be able to generate the momentum needed to knock the cage over again.

She did not fight against Crane's kinetic impulses. She knew it would be futile, and she didn't want to risk revealing the hidden claw beneath her bandage.

Unfortunately, when Doctor Crane was finished with her, she no longer had free range of her cage. She would need her hands released in order to attempt to pick the lock. From the look on the doctor's face he wouldn't be trusting her with a free hand any time soon.

"You'll learn to be obedient," he said. "Even if it's the last thing you do." He flicked his smoke stick at her before removing himself from the chamber.

Well, at least that halfway worked. The presence was somehow still in good spirits despite Doctor Crane's promised vendetta against her.

She dangled limply beneath her arm restraints, her body aching, too sore from the doctor's muscle-locking attack for her to stand unsupported. Blood was quickly draining from her hands and arms, leaving a pins-and-needles prickling sensation throughout the restricted limbs. The position was certainly a painful one.

Stay strong, the voice said again. *He'll slip up eventually, and we'll get free. Just you wait.*

Condolences

The moon appeared more pale and further away than usual tonight—a trick of the light through the atmosphere. It was another cold, clear night, the sky completely free of clouds apart from a cluster of high, fluffy wisps hanging out just below the hazy orb of the moon, as if forming a safety net for it to land on should it suddenly slip from the sky.

Professor Herin's Builder class had been less entertaining than usual—just another lecture on mineral deposits and pre-foundation prep work for the creation of large structures. With Rylin excused from all of his classes to take his proficiency exam this evening, Javic hoped he would at least have Baxton and Sima to keep him company, but all of the cadets had been pulled aside as well for a military exercise that was to last through the night.

Javic wished he could have gone along to Rylin's exam to cheer him on, but the proficiency exams were private affairs with only the administrators and individually scheduled test takers allowed present, not large-scale spectator events like the annual Dance of the Elements. Each initiate's test date was set some time towards the end of their first quarter of courses. Javic hadn't yet received notice for his exam in the mail, but he was expecting it to arrive any day now. Being raised to cadet status meant the Ver'konus no longer deemed a student to be a high risk threat to himself or those around him.

It also meant that responsibility for the consequences of his Power use would fall wholly on his own shoulders. If a cadet messed up and hurt somebody, it was considered negligence rather than just an accident. Most importantly, for the majority of initiates, becoming a cadet meant being allowed to see family and friends again. Cadets could leave the academy grounds whenever they wanted. It was freedom and responsibility—those always seemed to come as a pair. Javic wasn't quite as excited as he used to be about being allowed visitors. Of course, it would mean he could see Mallory again, but with all of his other friends gone and the anger he felt towards his grandfather still simmering, he no longer expected it to be the homecoming he had been looking forward to since his first days at the academy. Whether or not he would be permitted to even continue at the academy would be up to Elric's discretion at that point.

Despite being less eager, Javic still checked his mail every day for the notice of his exam date. Professor Vanton had been stressing preparedness all week; having Cale Fisman as lead test administrator added a level of unpredictability to the occasion. Javic couldn't stop worrying that his inability to access the Power without using his emotions was going to somehow hinder him on his exam. Professor Vanton hadn't fully given up on having Javic find his anchor, but he had softened his stance on excluding him from class for the time being at least. If he failed his proficiency test, he would be forced to retake his courses, and if it came to that, he had a feeling Vanton wouldn't hesitate to put him right back in the closet. Freedom was on the line, and, almost as important to Javic, his pride was at stake.

Upon arriving back at the dorms after finishing all of his classes for the night, Javic headed straight for the mailroom—down a short tiled hallway that led off to the left after passing through the main entrance doors. Hundreds of numbered drawers lined the walls, each corresponding to a different room within the dormitory. Elric sent Javic a new letter every day, and every night Javic threw it away, unread. He was not even close to being ready to forgive his grandfather for his actions at the harbor. Tonight, Javic was early and the mail clerk had not yet sorted the first floor's mail into the appropriate drawers. The ink smudged man smiled knowingly at Javic as he handed him the small bundle of letters meant for his room.

The top letter was from Elric—Javic tossed it aside as usual—but under that was a message printed on official Ver'konus stock card. Javic's eyes quickly scanned across the document, double checking that it was meant for him and not Rylin and then searched for the all-important date printed at the bottom. One week from tonight. He only had seven days to prepare himself. He suddenly felt nervous. He had known it was coming, but now that the time was set, he felt even less confident than before.

After his exam notice was a letter to Rylin from his brother Cormick. Javic tucked them both under his right arm and half-ran, half-walked back to his room. Nervousness settling deeper within him with every step. A bustle of activity outside in the hallway as he turned the final corner made him take pause. His door stood open, and this time Belford wasn't around to be the culprit.

Three boxes were stacked outside along the hallway wall; it looked like somebody was in the process of moving in to his room. It didn't make any sense—there was hardly enough space for him and Rylin to live in there as it was. Two men in Ver'konus military dress uniforms, deep-blue suits with golden buttons, stepped out of the room as Javic got closer. He did not recognize either man. One had a stubbly beard and was carrying another box which he placed down beside the others in the hallway. The second man had Rylin's prized stuffed animal in his hands. He tossed it into the least filled of the four boxes, on top of what Javic now realized was a whole pile of Rylin's possessions. He ran the last few paces to the dorm room. The men looked up as Javic blocked their way.

"What's going on here?" Javic demanded.

The men glanced at each other, their stiff body language clearly showing their annoyance. It looked as though they had hoped to finish up before Javic got back from class. "We're just following orders," said the man who had been holding Rylin's stuffed animal.

A quick glance into the room showed that they had taken only Rylin's things. All of Javic's belongings were untouched, but on Rylin's side of the room there was nothing left but a bare mattress sitting on its wooden frame. Only the stock furniture remained—the little dresser, writing desk, and chair that had been there when Javic first moved in.

"Whose orders?" asked Javic. "Why are you taking Rylin's things?"

The men shared another quick glance. "A direct order from Lieutenant General Cale Fisman," the first man said impatiently. "Now step aside, we have a job to do."

Javic stood his ground. "You can't just take his stuff," he said. "It doesn't matter who ordered it—that's theft if you don't have Rylin's permission." The Ver'konus took all of its laws very seriously, even for members of the upper-command. When accused of a crime, a military tribunal decided a soldier's fate. If a wrong-doing was clear, the punishment was often severe.

"Not like he's going to need them anymore anyway," said the stubble-faced man who had remained quiet until this point. He purposely bumped Javic hard with his shoulder as he bent down to stack two of the boxes on top of one another. He lifted them up into his arms, readying to leave.

With the shock of being jostled, Javic felt his face growing hot with anger. "What's that supposed to mean?" he asked, snatching Rylin's stuffed animal off the top box, out from under the man's nose.

Eyes flashing with contempt, the man snapped at Javic. "Well, you see, when someone dies they lose all their rights," he said coldly. "So we don't actually need anyone's permission to take them. Now get out of my way."

The first man was less rude, but still spoke without emotion as he gathered up the other two boxes. "The Ver'konus must reclaim space when a resident is deceased. Don't worry, these boxes will be stored and sent back to his family in due time."

Javic felt as if the ground were slipping out from under him. It couldn't be; they had to be lying. It didn't make any sense. In fact, he refused to believe it—it was just too absurd. He had seen Rylin a few hours ago before leaving for class. The boy had been headed out for his exam and everything was just fine. Rylin had regained his composure and confidence and was ready to be tested. No other among the initiates could have been more prepared. There must have been a mistake; Rylin *had* to be fine.

The men left while Javic was still reeling. He stood in the empty hallway, Rylin's stuffed animal dangling from his fingertips. Rylin would be coming back from his exam any moment now, surely advanced to cadet status, and he'd be just as confused as Javic as to why all his possessions were taken from his room. The two letters under Javic's arm fell to the ground in front of the open door.

Can they be telling the truth?

Rylin's exam was the first to take place this term; the first one Cale Fisman had ever administered. Something could have gone wrong. The test could have been too dangerous or maybe Rylin froze up again.

Why did they come in secret and take everything so quickly? They're trying to erase him!

That was the way things worked around here; glossing over mistakes. It made sense that they would handle a student's death the same way they dealt with Laudry Hall. By removing any evidence Rylin ever existed, most of the other students and people who didn't know him well would soon forget the dangers that went along with enrollment at the institution. That's how they operated; just smooth everything over and move on.

It still didn't feel real. Javic sat down on his bed and waited, expecting Rylin to walk in and everything would be alright, but hours came and went, and Rylin never returned. As day turned to night and the room was cast in shadow, Javic realized Rylin's lamp had been taken along with the rest of his possessions. Javic didn't have one of his own, and Lord Ethan's luminescent bulbs did not grace the inside of the dormitory rooms. At some point, while sitting alone in the dark, sadness crept in, overriding the disbelief. It didn't hit him all at once, instead falling over him like grains of sand through an hourglass as the reality of the situation solidified in his mind. Rylin was never coming back—the realization grew stronger and stronger with every passing minute.

A rap at the door pulled Javic to his senses. He wiped the back of his hand across his cheeks in an attempt to disguise the tracks of his tears and then slowly rose to his feet to see who was knocking. A part of him was still holding onto hopes of seeing Rylin on the other side of the door, but the rational part of his mind had already given up on that possibility much earlier in the night. Javic fumbled in the dark for the door handle. As soon as it was open, light filled the air from Professor Vanton's lamp. He stepped in without waiting for an invitation. The sadness on Javic's face must have been apparent, because Vanton's brow drooped lower when he looked upon him.

"So it's true, then?" Javic asked as he sat back down on his bed. He already knew the answer.

Vanton studied Javic's face for a moment. "He's gone," he said simply. There were many emotions below the surface of the professor's face, lost within the endless wrinkles and crevices of his pale skin. "I'm so sorry."

Javic thought he had prepared himself—thought he was resigned in the truth—but hopeless pangs of sorrow threatened to consume him now with those few words from his teacher. He wanted to ask what had happened, but the words caught in his throat; he couldn't make a sound as the lump grew and grew until his whole chest felt like it was cramping up. The dim flame of Vanton's lantern cast flickering shadows across the tiny room, driving the gloom deep into Javic's bones. Although he wanted to cry out, his body wouldn't let him. He couldn't even breathe.

"It happened during his exam," said Vanton. "No one will say exactly how he died, not even to me, but if it were Rylin's fault they would have had no problem telling me." There was bitterness behind Professor Vanton's words. "They messed up, and Rylin paid the price." A silent tear ran down Vanton's cheek before disappearing into the cracks of his skin as if it had never been there. "I'm sorry," the professor said again. "I'm sorry I've been so hard on you as well. It's only because I know you have such great potential."

The words were hollow to Javic. Nothing really matter anymore. Rylin was better than any of them, but in the end it hadn't helped him one bit.

"I knew your mother, Kali, when she was here," continued Vanton. "She was one of my students. The best I ever had, actually. She was so kind, and brilliant—different, like you. You never would have expected so much passion and energy to come out of such a girl."

The talk of his mother somehow unleashed the pit growing inside of him. An uncontrollable sob escaped Javic's lips now, followed by a steady stream of tears running down either side of his face.

"She was taken from us at far too young an age as well, but she left behind something very special. You can be a great wizard one day, Javic. I can feel it within you. I must go now—there are still many questions that need answering—but even though tonight we have had a terrible loss, please don't let it kill your spirit. There is still much to be done." Professor Vanton placed the two letters that Javic dropped outside his room onto the writing desk. "Focus on your studies; it will help. Prepare yourself for whatever Cale might throw at you." With that, Vanton silently slipped through the doorway, blanketing the room in shadow once more as the lamp light faded down the hallway, and Javic was left to mourn for Rylin on his own

Javic clutched Rylin's stuffed animal tight as he lay in bed, letting the soft fur brush up against his damp cheek. It had comforted Rylin, but the stuffed toy was just a ghost now; a hollow gesture. It did nothing to fill the gap that Rylin's absence left inside of him. Several lonely hours passed before Javic finally managed to drift off into a fitful sleep.

CHAPTER

18

Why We Fight

Belford's mind was at peace. The consistent splashing of the waterwheel provided a soothing backdrop of white noise, allowing him to attain the state of relaxation needed to facilitate the return of his memories. He trained his thoughts on the last thing he could remember about his past: The soft kiss in the park, culminating with the discovery of the mental link between Claire and himself.

He was ready to follow it forward, to reignite the synapses that fell dormant somehow during his long slumber within the computer, when suddenly he became aware of quiet footsteps passing outside his cabin door. The slight creak of a turning handle was followed by the click of the supply closet door as it latched shut again. There was a moment of silence, followed by a muffled scrapping sound like a heavy box being dragged across the floor.

When the noises finally ceased, Belford had to fully restart the process of focusing his mind. Meditation did not come easy for him; even little distractions threw him off. Before he was able to make any progress in his renewed efforts, the familiar sound of muted voices carrying through the wall started up again. It was almost every night now that the murmuring conversations were taking place—always late at night, and always when he least wanted to be disturbed.

Try as he might, Belford was unable to pinpoint exactly where the voices were coming from. Since being accosted by Deenan, he stayed clear of the cargo area, but that hadn't stopped him from looking around the rest of the ship for the source of the sounds when they picked back up again the following night. He went up to the top deck, after which he checked down in the bilge to see if the voices might be coming through the floor rather than just through the wall, but nowhere other than his little cabin could he hear the talking quite so distinctly. Last night, the chatter carried on for several hours, just distracting enough to keep him awake and unable to concentrate on his meditations. Tonight, he didn't feel like waiting around for it to finish.

With almost everyone aboard the Rosa Marsa already asleep, there wasn't much to do this time of night, so Belford got out of bed and headed up to the bridge where he was sure to find at least one other sleepless person. As usual, Captain Bundles piloted the vessel during night travel. He was the only member of the Rosa Marsa's crew experienced enough to do so. Beside him sat Sharith Grine, his eyes looking beady and unfocused now that he wasn't allowed to wear his glasses any longer. Ethan had ordered him to take off the lenses for the remainder of their mission because spectacles were not very common in the north and could potentially draw unwanted attention.

With Kovani territory less than a day away, every precaution was being taken to appear ordinary and insignificant—they were to remain unnoticed; just riverboat traders going about their business. Some of the Ver'ati had proven quite capable at fitting in aboard the working vessel, while others still seemed at odds with the situation. Of course, all of the Ver'ati had been instructed to take off their official robes and stow them away in their luggage. Grine was dressed in a fine button-down shirt and black, narrow-legged trousers that didn't quite look like they belonged on a riverboat. It wasn't a working man's attire—such articles of clothing would never be found amongst a crew member's wardrobe, to say the least.

"How's it going?" Belford asked, sitting down beside Grine. Despite finding Grine to be somewhat irritating, Belford had vowed to fully exploit any opportunity that presented itself when it came to winning over the Ver'ati aboard the steamer. It was a rare occasion to find anybody by themselves on such a small ship, and this was as close to alone as Belford had seen Grine so far. Captain Bundles' presence was not a deterrent for what Belford had in mind since the captain had no stake in the mission apart from keeping his ship safe.

Grine turned to look at Belford through squinted eyes. "Is that you, Aaron?" he asked. "Things are only a little blurry in the daytime, but I can't see much of anything in the dark."

"It's me," said Belford. "Are you sure I can't try to fix that for you? It must be quite the headache." Belford had offered several times now to correct Grine's vision. Although Belford had never specifically attempted anything like eye surgery before, he was fairly certain he could perform the procedure— he understood the principles of how the human eye worked well enough anyway. Grine, being an Ameliorator himself, had developed a phobia of the Power being used on him, medically or otherwise. Belford could hardly blame him, given the rudimentary skill level of the healers in Erotos.

This time Grine didn't dignify Belford's offer with a response, merely grimacing in his general direction.

"You might take him up on that, boy," said Captain Bundles. "You ain't much use as a spotter if you can't see!

Nearly ran aground twice now because of this lad," he said, gesturing towards Sharith with mock distaste.

"I told you already," said Grine, "I'm not here to be your spotter. I just can't sleep! Stop relying on me during your piss breaks." He crossed his arms in front of his chest and stared out into the bleakness beyond the bow. Captain Bundles' son Eben was up there somewhere; a dark figure in the shadows, moving the mirrored spotlight device back and forth, guiding the steamer forward with the intensified torch glow.

"If you can't hold your own weight, you ain't much worth on this ship," said Bundles.

Grine sighed. He clearly wasn't going to win this argument.

"Nice that Vera was able to come along, isn't it?" asked Belford, turning the conversation towards the one thing he knew could manipulate Grine.

Sharith's face reddened at the very mention of her name. "Ms. Ekrin?" he asked. "I suppose."

"Ah, don't be like that," said Belford, nudging Grine slightly in the ribs with his elbow. "I've seen you two together—you like each other." In truth, the affection looked to go only one way; Vera had shown no interest towards Grine whatsoever.

"What do you mean?" asked Grine, his face growing redder still.

"Oh, you know," said Belford. "It's in the way she looks at you when you aren't paying attention. If you want to be with her, you just have to ask her, no matter what is going on between her and Ethan."

"Lord Ethan?" asked Grine with a frown. He was feeding right out of Belford's hand now.

Belford nodded, but then decided to vocalize the gesture when he remembered how little Grine could see. "Yeah," he said, "I don't know what's going on between them, but she's clearly not into him like she is with you. I think Ethan might be taking advantage of his position over her…. You can't let

Ethan control every decision in your life, though. Sometimes you just have to go with your gut." The seed was planted. Belford wasn't very good at lying, but he thought he had managed to play a rather convincing role here. Now he just had to get out of the conversation before his kindness and advice started to come across as too forced.

"Careful boys," said Captain Bundles. "Ethan is a dangerous man. I wouldn't want to be the one to try to take away his plaything."

Grine's frown deepened; he seemed lost in thought, though it might just have been his inability to focus that gave him his distant, starry-eyed expression. Belford wished Captain Bundles hadn't said anything. On the one hand, referring to Vera as Ethan's plaything would only grow Grine's distaste for Ethan, but on the other, Ethan's power truly was intimidating. It was a toss-up as to whether fear or love would win out in the fight for Grine's allegiance.

"Have a good night," said Belford, excusing himself away from the helm. He intended to go back down below deck, but when he got to the hatch he noticed Arlin sitting by himself on the long bench seat at the very back of the stern. Belford changed directions and went over to say hello.

His approach didn't register with Arlin. The swordsman's face was vacant, the lack of expression momentarily giving Belford a flashback to Kara's empty eyes. The thought of the girl still made his stomach twist up; the butterfly pendant seemed to burn against his skin. Kara deserved so much better. She could have had such a long happy life if not for him…. It was happening again… the self-blame and sadness bubbling just beneath the surface. He needed to get the thought of Kara out of his head before the emotions started to well up in his eyes.

"Are you alright?" Belford asked, using Arlin as a distraction to push his own feelings back down. The question wasn't completely selfish—he genuinely was concerned for his friend's well-being. Arlin had been acting odd the entire trip.

Arlin only seemed to notice Belford's presence when he sat down beside him on the bench. It took a moment for Belford's words to register with the swordsman before he responded. "I've just got a lot on my mind," he said, "too much."

Belford wasn't sure what to say. Arlin sounded like he was trying to open up, but Belford didn't want to make him uncomfortable by asking any questions that would come across as prying. Arlin was a very private person. If Javic were here he would have known exactly what to say; he was always so much better at navigating social situations than Belford. The funny thing was, Belford learned more about Arlin from his brief conversation with Livian than he had in all his time with the swordsman put together. Speaking his mind was not something Arlin did.

"Kovehn is a very dangerous place for me," Arlin continued after Belford's awkward pause. "It is my homeland, though not a place that would welcome me back any time soon…. May I confide something in you?" he asked.

Belford was more than a little surprised to hear those words coming from Arlin, but he quickly nodded his consent.

"There is much I have not told you about myself," he said. "I believe a man's past is no business but his own, but it is also true that too much piled inside is dangerous if left unattended. I often speak to Mallory on such occasions, it helps me stay focused and battle-ready, but obviously that is not possible right now, nor would her presence be of much comfort to me under these circumstances…."

Arlin was nothing if not cryptic, but he certainly was ready to talk—practically begging Belford to unburden him. "I've been told I am a great listener," said Belford. No one had actually said those words, but he could manage it for a friend in need.

Some of the tension lifted from Arlin's face immediately. "Up until several years ago I was a member of the Kovani military," he began. "I joined to protect my homeland from people like Ethan. Do you know what would happen if Kovehn fell? Its citizens would be treated like dirt. We would be neglected and left unprotected in slums to die from malnutrition, disease and pillaging. Our money would be taken as tax to be spent on the homelands of our invaders, and anyone unwilling or incapable of paying would be imprisoned or killed. The people of Kovehn are not responsible for King Garrett's atrocities, but we would be the ones facing punishment. In reality, the Kovani people have suffered far more than anyone else at the hands of Garrett. That being said, a new king is what Kovehn needs, but *not* a king with foreign allegiance."

Belford was confused. "Wait, so why are you fighting for Phandrol now if that is what you believe will happen?"

"Things do have a curious way of turning out, don't they? As it would happen, there are worse fates than subjugation. But you are incorrect: I do not fight for Phandrol—I fight for you. I believe you could be the leader Kovehn needs in order to heal itself."

That, too, was something Belford hadn't expected to hear. Arlin had been the most resistant of all of Belford's friends to believe in the Mark of Kings on his arm. Elric said something similar to Belford before the Rosa Marsa departed from Erotos—that Belford could unite Aragwey—but it still sounded absurd to him. He knew he wasn't cut out to fix a nation. *What use would I be? I couldn't even save Kara—one helpless, little girl.* He'd failed to turn her back from being a Whune, despite all his medical training. Healing people was the one thing he was supposed to be good at, but when it really mattered, he couldn't even get that right.

Arlin did not give him a chance to show his dissent. "Before we met, I was a wandering fugitive. I left the Kovani military on poor terms. I couldn't follow the unjust, and what

I saw within my commanders was pure evil. They took their queues on how to treat civilians from Garrett. It was institutionalized rape and murder wherever they stopped, all across Kovehn. A military is supposed to protect its people, but under their command the civilians were treated worse than animals, left dying in the streets, abused beyond recovery. It was a terrible thing to see, and I could not stand for it. I didn't remain in the military for long, not when I saw how bad things had gotten. They were the true enemy of Kovehn, so before I left, I went into the command tent and did what had to be done."

None of what Arlin was saying made any sense with what Livian had told him. "Livian said you were a member of the Order of the Blade… a Guardian of Truth?"

"Once," said Arlin, eying Belford suspiciously. That must have been something Arlin hadn't intended to open up about. "Alas, no longer. I trained with the Order before joining the military, but I sealed my fate with both on the same day. One of my commanders was a blade-brother, and killing a Brother is an unforgivable crime within the Order, so unfortunately I was forced to leave both behind that night."

Livian said that to kill another blade-brother was the ultimate sin for a guardian. By oath, any member of the Order would be honor-bound to kill Arlin if they ever got the chance. "You shouldn't carry that sword around anymore," said Belford, worried about the ramifications. "People might recognize it… like Livian did."

Arlin shook his head. "The Talus Shard is a part of me," he said simply, giving a minor shrug. "Throwing it away would be running from my past, which is something I cannot do. If a blade-brother comes across me and recognizes me as a traitor, I will accept their challenge to duel if that is what they believe must be done. It is their right to hold me to my crime. I could not forgive my commanders' transgressions; not even the bond of brotherhood was enough to make me forget what I saw—their injustices were far too great; such actions sully the name of the Guardians. If a Brother comes to kill me, they may have their chance, but I will not go down easy."

A fiery expression burned in Arlin's eyes. Belford had only seen it once before, the day Arlin saved Mallory, Javic and himself from the Whunes in the cave outside Rasile, his blade swinging through the air in a deadly dance. It was the intensity of his soul burning to escape.

"I am not worried about the Order," Arlin continued. "There are few who know my face outside of the Elswani Monastery. I am afraid that is not what troubles me today...." Arlin took a deep breath, reluctant to continue.

After all that, Belford wondered what could possibly be on Arlin's mind that was more worrisome than murder and the retribution of his former company and order.

"It's Mallory," he said. His voice faltered and he had to clear his throat by swallowing. "She is... with child... my child...."

The words fell on Belford with considerable weight. This really was something Javic would have been better at dealing with. "She's... pregnant?" he asked, the idea of it not really sinking in. "What are you doing here? You should be with her right now!"

"We only just found out the day before the mission," said Arlin.

"You didn't have to be here," said Belford. "Family is more important than coming along on some stupid mission."

"But this is for family, don't you see?" Arlin smiled meekly at Belford, looking truly frightened for the first time that Belford could remember. "I believe Garrett intends to start another Cleansing," he said. "How can I bring a child into a world like that? Though the people of Kovehn will suffer under foreign rule, all of Aragwey will be lost if Garrett succeeds in commanding another Goblikan army, and from what I have seen whilst traveling with you over the last few months, I believe the battle may already have begun. If we cannot dethrone him soon, there may not be much of a world left for *any* child to grow up in."

Arlin really had a way of putting the fear in Belford. The weight of their mission never felt so heavy. Although Arlin was truly a man of principle, Belford couldn't help think that perhaps Arlin was simply more comfortable with the idea of risking his life in battle than he was at the prospect of raising a child. There were other capable swordsmen who could have taken Arlin's place on the mission, but he was the only father his child would ever have a chance at knowing. Belford wished he had never gotten Arlin involved in any of this mess. Maybe Elric was right; he really had gotten them all in over their heads with this one. Regardless, there was no going back now.

Although Belford felt more conflicted now after learning the truth behind Arlin's odd behavior, for Arlin, talking to Belford appeared to have eased his mind substantially. Maybe it was just the weight of his secret being lifted off his shoulders, but after he bid Belford a goodnight, Arlin disappeared into the belly of the steamer with a much more present look about him. Belford wasn't sure exactly what Arlin had gotten out of the one-sided conversation, but he hoped that whatever his resolution was, that it would help keep everyone alive. Distractions were never good on the battlefield.

Belford headed back down to his room as well. As he passed the helm, Grine was still staring absently out the front window beside Captain Bundles. Suddenly, his mind games no longer felt all that important. He quietly walked down the metal stairs, taking light, quick steps to avoid making noise because he knew how annoying the clanging could be for anyone trying to sleep in the crew area. He ended up inadvertently startling a pale-skinned, sleepy-eyed Garcenus who was exiting out of the supply closet just as Belford turned the corner. Garcenus cursed at the sight of Belford, and then mumbled something probably just as obscene under his breath. Both of the deckhand's eyes had huge dark circles beneath them as if he hadn't slept in days, but even so, the venom in his glare was just as potent as ever. Although he had appeared to be closing the supply closet door when Belford happened upon him, Garcenus reopened it now and reached inside. He grabbed randomly for the first thing his hands could find, which just so happened to be another case of lamp oil.

Belford mused at the idea of Garcenus's quarters, filled to the brim with a hundred lamps all burning at once—it was the only way Belford could imagine the deckhand going through the amount of oil he had seen him take out of that closet in the last couple days. Although staying up all night in a flaming room would certainly have caused Garcenus's dark shiners, Belford very much doubted that was the actual case. The idea was just silly enough to make Belford smile though, even with Arlin's secret bouncing around in his mind. Garcenus, of course, did not return the smile. After retrieving the lamp oil, he closed the closet door and slunk away into the darkness.

All Belford could do was shake his head. Garcenus might get over his anger of Weni being left behind in North Galdren one day, but for now he wasn't anywhere close to forgiving Belford or the others for taking over the Rosa Marsa on that fateful day. When Belford entered his room, the voices were thankfully absent. He lied down in his bed and let the sound of the waterwheel wash over him. Although he wasn't sure how effective meditation would be with everything else running through his head, there was still some time left to delve into his mind before the temptation of sleep became too strong to resist.

Voices in my Head

The beep of the computer signaled the beginning of the calibrations. The wireless electrode patches attached all over Aaron's skin made him itch. He wanted to scratch himself so bad, but he was not supposed to move during this part of the process. All he could do was try to turn his mind away from the physical discomfort.

"Just a few more seconds..." said George Cartwright, noticing the slight wiggle in the line on the monitor; it danced every time Aaron made even the slightest movement.

Aaron focused on steadying the line. He became a perfect statue and it slowly stopped its wavering.

"Almost there..." said George.

A tickle was building, this time in Aaron's nose, and it was quickly becoming monstrous in size. He flared his nostrils repeatedly and wrinkled his nose in an attempt to ward off the inevitable. With every twitch he could see slight jumps on the monitor. Before George could complain about the motion again, Aaron sneezed, not once, but five times in a row. The line went wild, shooting up into jagged mountain peaks as red error marks flashed all across the screen.

The calibration stopped automatically, the line vanishing as all the readings ceased to record. George was frowning, but there was nothing Aaron could have done—his nose was aggravated well beyond the minor flu symptoms predicted to coincide with the Cognitive Matter Manipulation serum's spread through his body. His muscles ached all over and his head felt like it was going to explode from all of the pressure in his sinuses. Everyone was feeling the effects of the serum more strongly than anticipated, but, thankfully, none of the candidates had gotten to the point of throwing up yet. Aaron hated the sound of vomiting; it could turn his settled stomach queasy in a matter of seconds—even thinking about it now made him slightly uneasy.

The cruelest part of it all was that the project administrators were forcing the candidates to perform physical tasks. They had to get their heartrates up while the patches monitored their brain activity—it was supposed to aid the serum's dispersal throughout their bodies. Moving about was the last thing Aaron felt like doing at the moment, but once his electrodes were calibrated he would have to join the other candidates in tossing a rubber ball around in the court on the other side of the room. Travis made a game of it, setting up garbage cans as makeshift goal posts. As each of the candidates finished their calibrations they joined one of the two teams running around trying to score points on each other.

"Are you finished moving?" Mr. Cartwright asked impatiently.

Aaron wiped his nose with the sleeve of his uniform, leaving a thin streak of snot behind. He then dabbed at the smear with his index finger, curious of its viscosity.

George gave a disgusted look as Aaron rolled his fingers together.

"Oh, shut it," said Aaron. "You're the one who did this to us."

George's demeanor did not improve.

Aaron prodded around the edge of several of the electrodes, easing their itchiness before settling down for a second attempt. Once he became still, George reinitiated the equipment.

It had been three days since the CMM injections. As the serum took hold, Aaron's mental connection to the computer was supposedly growing stronger. Besides feeling sick, however, the only change he noticed so far was the ever increasing presence of Claire's memories and emotions within his mind. He hadn't yet decided whether or not he should mention the mental link to Dana Farris or one of the other administrators. He knew he was contractually obligated to do so in order to maintain the integrity of the project, but he was afraid of what might happen; Aaron was beginning to realize that he was little more than a test rat, and such animals were not always treated kindly when experiments went awry.

Strangely, it wasn't the prospect of being kicked out of the project that worried Aaron—rather, it was the thought of being separated from Claire that made him most anxious to keep the secret. He knew things about her, intimate things she had never told anyone, and his fondness for her was growing greater with every new detail that he learned. She was so kind and caring; a truly selfless person at heart. Her brother's medical condition made Aaron so sad that it might as well have been his own sibling in a hospital bed. The longer he was exposed to her memories, the more difficult it became to distinguish them from his own. He was starting to understand her in a way that people only knew themselves, and as much as it scared him, deep down he didn't want it to stop. Under any other circumstances, or with anyone else, he would have been unable to get over the intrusive nature of their link, but when it came to Claire, his quickly growing feelings for her meant he couldn't get enough.

Love is like a drug....

Aaron looked over at Claire just as the computer beeped again, signaling the restart of its processing. Claire was across the room, sprinting beside Travis as they played against Wes and Isabelle—they were the only four candidates to finish their calibrations so far; the rest were waiting outside the unorthodox lab room for their turn with Mr. Cartwright. Apparently, the younger and healthier the subject, the longer they would need to keep their heart rates up to have the same effect.

The computer made a low tone. "All done," said George, "now go play."

Aaron stood up from his stool. Claire was watching him now as well with a worried expression on her face. Wes scored a point against her during her inattentiveness, but she continued to watch Aaron as if he were a wolf, not concerned at all with the outcome of the game. She had been keeping her distance from Aaron for the last two days, ever since they both realized the spontaneous memory sharing only occurred when they were in close physical proximity to one another. Part of Aaron wanted to get closer to her now—to learn more—but if Claire wanted to minimize the memory leakage, he had to respect her distance.

He had no idea what parts of his mind Claire had seen into so far, but based on the variety of things he learned about her, he had to assume that he was just as exposed in her eyes. He was not at all eager to share some of his experiences but there were no boundaries when it came to their link. From Claire, he'd seen numerous intimate moments, actually feeling her sensations firsthand as if they were his own—it was quite strange, to say the least. Though the connection made him feel like an intruder at times, in a way he and Claire were already beyond such trivial matters as embarrassment. It was as if they were old friends, but more than that, really—as if she was a part of him. He would be lying if he said none of what he gleaned through their link was arousing, but while it would have made him feel like a peeping-tom if the connection had been one way, the knowledge that she was seeing his innermost thoughts and fantasies as well made it more like a sensual mingling of souls.

The ball game stopped as Aaron approached. He was close enough now to feel Claire's presence even without looking at her. It was like an invisible tug, as if he were the needle of a compass drawn by her intense magnetism. Claire retreated as Aaron came nearer, heading for the bench on the opposite side of the court. The nervous tingle in Aaron's stomach felt foreign; Claire's emotion leaking through their bond. She grabbed a towel from a stack and dabbed at some of the sweat on the back of her neck. They both knew they would have to get close together now if they wanted to maintain a normal appearance, but she was feeling resistant to the whole idea.

Wes grabbed a cup of water and made his way over to Aaron. The boy had a grin on his face. "I thought Travis would be better," he said. "We're kicking his butt."

One look at Travis was enough to show that he was as distracted as Claire. He was standing still in the middle of the court, staring off into the distance as if looking through the far wall. His face was drenched in sweat, perhaps from the game, but his skin was sickly pale as well. "It looks like the flu symptoms are hitting him pretty hard," said Aaron.

Wes leaned in towards Aaron and spoke quietly in his ear, "Pretend I'm not saying anything special so we don't draw attention, but I've got to tell you something… something extraordinary has happened."

"If you don't want to look odd, stop leaning in so close," said Aaron in a normal voice. No one was near enough to overhear them.

"You're right, you're right," said Wes, backing off slightly. "This is really exciting, though. I'm not really sure how to describe it, but Isabelle and I can read each other's minds! I know it sounds mad, but it must be a side effect of the CMM serum. Somehow it's connected us to more than just the computer."

Aaron found it somewhat comforting to learn that he and Claire weren't the only ones who formed an extra bond. "Claire and I have the same thing going on, seeing each other's memories and such."

Wes laughed out loud, but then looked around again to make sure no one was watching them. "I guess we figured out the side effect of fraternization. There's no way both of our pairings are coincidental." Dana Farris had warned them about this—of the dangers a change in brain chemistry represented. He had called it unpredictable and potentially life threatening, and yet Wes spoke nonchalantly, no outward worry showing on his face. "Watch this," he said, gesturing over his shoulder with a slight up-nod of his head.

Isabelle was standing over by Claire on the other side of the court. She was carrying the rubber ball from the game in her hands. With a quick glance over at Aaron, Isabelle smiled, and then threw the ball as hard as she could at the back of Wes's head. Aaron flinched in anticipation of the collision, but Wes put his hand up and caught it in a perfect catch without turning around or ever having seen it coming.

"The more you exercise the connection, the stronger it gets," he said. "It's not just random memories and thoughts anymore; we're actually talking to each other right now. I can basically see through her eyes in real time if I try hard enough."

"That's amazing!" Aaron exclaimed. He could sense Claire's questions pouring through the bond already—not the words exactly, but the feelings were clear. After watching the strange interaction between Isabelle and Wes, she must have sensed Aaron's excitement, which only added to her confusion. "Are you going to tell *them* about it?"

Wes shook his head vigorously. "No way! At least not yet."

"Then you should probably stop showing it off," said Aaron. Several of the technicians were looking over at Wes curiously. Aaron flicked his eyes in their direction.

For once, the boy got the hint. He began putting on a show. "You could have knocked my head off with that!" he yelled over to Isabelle.

"Sorry," said Isabelle, already fully aware of the cover-up. "I was trying to throw it to Aaron."

That was enough to satisfy the coordinators' curiosity; they turned back towards their monitors, preparing to receive the next candidate's calibrations.

Wes lowered his voice again. "You can probably do it too. It's incredible—like being a superhero!"

Their conversation was interrupted as Brooke entered the lab through the nearby door. It was her turn to sit still for Mr. Cartwright. George waved her over as he finished placing the temporary adhesive on the undersides of her electrode patches. As she walked beside the sports court, a cry of pain brought Aaron's attention to Travis. The Australian was hunkered over at the center of the court, clutching the side of his head as he grimaced in agony. His hand fell from his temple, a dazed look appearing on his face as he lost consciousness. Aaron saw a trail of blood dripping from the corner of Travis's left eye before he went down, falling face first to the floor. The technicians swarmed over him almost immediately. The first man to reach Travis turned him over onto his back and lifted his eyelids—only the bloodied whites of his eyes were visible, the pupils completely rolled up into his head. Travis's body started to convulse in a violent seizure, his feet kicking out at several of the men who came to his aid.

Aaron's worry for Travis's safety was doubled by Claire's emotions slipping into his mind. The technicians were scientists, not medical doctors, and they were already doing everything wrong. "Turn him on his side," Aaron shouted. "Don't restrict his shaking, that will only hurt him worse!"

Aaron ran over towards Travis as George Cartwright made a page on his ear-com, calling for medical assistance. The other technicians were all looking around in panic as Aaron dropped to his knees beside the convulsing man.

"Don't we have to stop him from swallowing his tongue or something?" one of the lab techs asked, the worried expression on his face doubled in his voice.

"That's a myth," said Aaron. "People can't actually do that. Just keep his jaw tilted back so his airway stays open." A subtle hint of sexual arousal drifted through the bond. He shot a confused glance over at Claire, which caused a storm of embarrassment to radiate out of her. Apparently she liked a man who could take charge. Aaron's own face reddened slightly in empathetic reflection. After another moment he wasn't sure how much of the embarrassment was Claire's and how much was legitimately his own. He wished it was easier to distinguish their emotions.

A medical team burst through the doors pushing a stretcher. As soon as Travis stopped convulsing they hefted him up and wheeled him out of the lab. It didn't take long for George to cancel the rest of the day's tests. When Dana Farris arrived at the lab he wasn't pleased, but he did agree with George's call. It was in everyone's best interest to wait for the doctors in the medical wing to figure out what caused Travis's episode before moving on with the experiments. Understandably, Aaron and the other candidates were worried—not only for Travis, but for their own safety as well. Dana agreed to keep everybody updated on whatever the doctors discovered. He was being surprisingly open about the whole situation. They were even allowed to visit Travis in the medical wing after he regained consciousness. Ultimately, whether they came to support Travis or just out of personal concern, every one of the candidates ended up waiting outside the examination room with Dana Farris while Travis received his brain scan.

Even though Claire was not sitting directly next to Aaron, she was still easily close enough for him to sense. Judging from the jumbled range of emotions coming through the bond, Aaron ascertained that Isabelle was telling Claire about the link between Wes and herself. Intrigue, fear, doubt, excitement; they all flowed together almost indiscernibly as they transferred across the link. When the girls were through chatting, here and there random memories slipped through into Aaron's head as well—an orange tabby cat named Trixie that roamed Claire's neighborhood when she was a young child, always sleeping on the clay shingles of the local abbey's roof during the warm summer evenings; she wondered what had happened to that cat after the riots, if it could possibly still be there to this day, napping and chasing mice. Years later, the smell of lamb stew filled the London flat as it simmered on the stove for hours—amazing how one simple meal could make her mouth water all day long. It wasn't until later, upon seeing an animal activist video, that she fully comprehended where the meat came from. It made her feel guilty for enjoying the tender flavors; the bloody images almost turned her into a vegetarian entirely for a time until cravings for meat finally overpowered her disgust. A third memory came through, this one hazier than the other two: Aiden crying, just an infant, and ma looking so tired and beaten down, trying to remain brave after Aiden's terrible diagnosis; his blood was bad; killing him—that was one of Claire's earliest memories. It was from before her father left. Thoughts of Aiden came regularly from Claire; they were clearly prominent in her mind. She'd spent too much time in hospitals because of her brother's condition. It was no surprise that being in the medical wing now was bringing up such despondent thoughts.

Miriam Gerard stepped out of the examination room; she had been in with Travis and the medical doctors during the scan. "He's regained consciousness," she said in her French accent. "He had an aneurism behind his left eye which caused a misfire of electrical impulses, manifesting the seizures, but he is stable now."

Dana breathed a sigh of relief. "Do we know what caused it yet?" he asked.

Dr. Gerard looked at him for a moment, hesitant to speak in front of the candidates. "We believe it was a side effect from the CMM serum," she said, "something unforeseen. I am going to need to see each of the candidates individually for some psychiatric evaluations to make sure no one else is at risk, starting with Brooke."

A concerned hush fell over the group.

"Why me?" asked Brooke.

Miriam seemed to be searching her mind for the best way to explain. "I believe Travis has developed some sort of... connection to you. Have you experienced anything out of the ordinary in the last few days? Any strange thoughts that might possibly have been... not your own?"

Peculiar vibrations were traveling through the link from Claire. When he glanced over at her, it was as if radio static were playing over the top of his thoughts; there were words there, but he couldn't comprehend them.

Aaron looked back over at Brooke. Her eyes were bugging out of her head with worry. "No, I haven't noticed anything," she said. Her forehead formed deep wrinkles.

"That is good," said Dr. Gerard. "This may be an isolated incident, but I would like to tread lightly here. I will be calling each of you down to my office for more thorough evaluations, and then I would like to start seeing everyone daily to make sure the serum integrations go smoothly. If you would come with me now, Brooke." The two women went off down the hallway in quick succession.

The static was still present in Aaron's mind. He tried to focus it, attempting to decipher the message Claire was sending his way. Instead of understanding the words, images started to spread across the bond. A man stabbed and bleeding in the streets; rocks smashed through storefront windows; fires burning everywhere—the smoke becoming so thick that Claire had to pull her shirt over her nose and mouth.

It did little to filter out the soot. She felt like she was suffocating as the roar of the rioters grew nearer. They were just two streets over when Claire's mother grabbed her and her brother and piled them into the car. They abandoned everything but the clothes on their backs. Anything not taken by looters was burned to the ground that night. The Dublin Riots. Along with the images, muffled words began to feed into Aaron's mind.

Not safe… who's next?

That was all he was able to understand, but the meaning was clear enough. Claire's fears were justified if it really was Travis's connection with Brooke that caused his aneurism.

Dana opened the door to Travis's room. Seeing Travis's timid smile was not nearly as comforting to Aaron as he'd hoped. Travis had a patch over his left eye; his vision completely gone from that side. There was no telling whether or not it would return naturally. One of the doctors, a lanky man with glasses, assured Travis that nanobots could repair any lingering damage, but that it would take time.

A pair of nurses in the middle of an animated conversation in Arabic looked up as everyone piled into the room. They ceased their chatter and quickly cleared out of the way to make room for the visitors.

"How are you feeling?" Dana asked Travis tentatively.

Travis had to turn his head to see Dana with his good eye. "Better now, I guess," he said. "I thought I was going bonkers." He blinked several times as he took in the mass of faces peering down at him. "I could hear voices in my head, a dozen of them, all speaking different languages. They were all talking so fast… I couldn't concentrate one bit… but then I started to understand what they were saying. I don't know how, since I only know English. It makes no sense. But then, after a bit, I realized all the voices were Brooke's; that they were her thoughts, some in French, some Spanish, some German, you name it, all bouncing off the inside of my skull. A minute ago I could even understand those two nurses over there babbling about nearly having to remove my eye, and they were speaking Arabic, which I've never learned a word of. That's how I know this is all real, but it's all gone now. Everything's silent again." Travis massaged his left temple with his thumb and index finger. "I'm not going crazy, am I? I'm going to be alright?" he asked, his voice becoming meek.

Dana ran his fingers through his beard. "I think so," he said. "As long as we keep you far away from Brooke."

It was exactly what Aaron feared most: If he came clean to Dana, he would be separated from Claire, but staying close to her was putting them both in mortal danger. He would have to tell the truth; he didn't have any other choice now.

Not yet. Wait until we know more.

It was Claire's voice in his head. She wasn't ready to give up their link just yet. Aaron wasn't sure inaction was the right move, but he did agree that this wasn't a decision to be made lightly. He tried to send a message back to her:

Let's stay apart for now, to be safe.

He wasn't sure if she received it at first, but she nodded silently and slipped out from the back of the pack, exiting the room. The distance that he could feel her at was already increasing. She was over halfway down the hall to the elevators when the final traces of her presence vanished from his mind. He was all alone now. *Or am I?* There was something else in his mind that hadn't been there before; another external presence. It was small, but it was definitely there. Unlike his connection with Claire, where he could feel her intelligent consciousness prickling against his, this other manifestation was less tangible. It was as if something was watching him, but not in an eerie way—more like it was looking after him. It was a comforting feeling. The new presence didn't have a location in the way that Claire did. Instead it seemed to radiate from all around him.

What are you? He mentally reached out to it, but other than a slight electric tingling in the back of his mind, there was no response.

CHAPTER

20

Solitary Refinement

Miriam went to every extent to make her office a comfortable place for people to share their feelings. Water flowed over rocks in a tiny Zen garden nestled into the middle of the floor, while soothing orchestral music played above the hum of the building's ventilation system. Aaron wasn't sure if he should recline on the rounded couch or not—he had never been to a psychiatrist before. After his mother's death he was supposed to have visited with a child psychiatrist, but his foster family at the time found a way of collecting money from the government for the expense without actually ever taking him in to the shrink. Aaron didn't mind though, he preferred to work through things on his own. Right now, however, he knew if he didn't at least share something credible with Dr. Gerard she would suspect him of holding back. Rather than give her the chance to pry into him with questions that could reveal his link with Claire, Aaron immediately told her about the strange sensations he had been having since his visit with Travis in the medical wing.

"That sounds normal—exactly what you should be experiencing at this point in the serum's dissemination," said Dr. Gerard. "A few of the others are experiencing similar effects—a religious affinity; an overseeing presence. You may also begin to feel a oneness with the world around you as the connection develops."

Just as Aaron suspected, the budding presence in the back of his mind was in fact the computer taking hold. If this new link developed anything like his bond with Claire, he soon would be able to send mental messages to the machine. He wondered if it was already capable of using his eyes to locate the matter markers. It was difficult not to get overexcited at the prospect of having superpowers, but he still had to remember the dangers. The scientists weren't finished working out the kinks with this new technology, as Travis could surely attest.

"Do you think everything is going to be alright with Travis and Brooke?" Aaron asked.

Dr. Gerard bobbed her head back and forth. "Hopefully," she said. "Brooke seems just fine; no symptoms at all. From my talks with both of them it would appear Travis recently developed feelings for her, but that the emotions were unreciprocated. Somehow his mind made a connection with hers using the CMM serum and it was just too much for him to handle. It's an interesting thing actually, his aneurism happened in the Broca's area of his brain. That's one of the brain's main language centers. It just so happens that Brooke's Broca's area is much more developed than Travis's, so it is possible that the extra stress of Brooke's foreign-language-intensive thoughts caused the rupture, although we may never know for certain."

Miriam dismissed Aaron for the day without further questioning. She probably assumed that if he were experiencing life-threatening side effects of the CMM serum, he would have mentioned something by now. Part of Aaron felt like a fool for not telling her the full extent of his mental state, but for some reason his self-preservation instinct had been thrown way off. Keeping himself safe no longer felt like the most important thing he could do. There was no way to accurately assess the dangers of his bond with Claire—it was a guessing game for which no one had an adequate answer— but with the thought of losing her becoming increasingly unbearable, the risk to himself, no matter how high, seemed well worth the reward. He considered for a moment that this change in thinking might be a side effect of the serum as well, but ultimately it didn't matter. He wasn't ready to give up his pursuit of their new relationship, and that was that. The only thing that made him hesitate in his decision was thinking about the possible risk to Claire's safety. He would never forgive himself if something happened to her because of his selfish desire to stay connected. Ultimately, it was the knowledge that Claire wanted to keep their link as much as he did that stopped him from coming forward after such wavering thoughts.

Over the next five days the metamorphosis within Aaron's brain continued its evolution. The "oneness with the world" that Dr. Gerard spoke of settled in, becoming stronger the closer Aaron got to the test range. He assumed it had something to do with his proximity to the matter markers he knew to be housed within. The sensation he felt when he was close to the markers was one of serenity; he became the earth, capable of feeling the environment around him with his mind in a similar manner to how he could sense Claire without actually looking at her.

None of the candidates had been allowed into the test range yet, but that was changing today. Their first trial run at controlling the computer with their minds was scheduled for just after lunch—George Cartwright was to coach them through it. Aaron's connection to Claire had strengthened as well. He could now feel her presence from anywhere within the complex no matter how far away they got from each other. The memory and thought sharing was still only possible when close together, but its range was steadily increasing. With their assigned living quarters being just one floor apart in the Atrium, attempts to avoid each other had proven futile. It didn't take long before they both gave up on that hopeless endeavor all together.

At night, they began to share dreams. When they woke, it was clear that the dreams had been joint manifestations of their minds. Together they roamed the streets of London or toured the Irish countryside; one time they floated high above a bright sunset streaming with every color either of their minds could imagine, the beauty of which was unmatched by anything in the waking world. They did not always realize they were dreaming—it was much like normal dreams in that regard—but whenever one of them became lucid they would always inform the other so that together they could go off on a grand adventure to some far off location within their minds. Aaron was never alone anymore, but for some reason that didn't bother him. Claire was coping almost equally as well with the lack of privacy. Aaron did sense moderate aggravation within her from time to time, especially when he sent her telepathic messages while she was on the toilet. She never told him to stop, though; it was a game they played, sending each other messages at the most awkward or inappropriate times. Aaron was winning by a landslide.

Dr. Gerard didn't suspect a thing, even with Aaron and Claire constantly sending messages back and forth during their daily sessions with the woman. Wes and Isabelle had also decided not to share any information about their link with the project administrators. Apparently, Aaron wasn't the only one willing to risk his life to stay connected. Other than Travis, no other secondary links had been discovered so far.

Travis was cleared from the medical wing, but he still wore the eyepatch over his left eye. It was supposedly only a temporary measure while the nanobots worked on repairing his vision. He needed to get used to the limited range of his peripherals; he kept walking into things. The doctors hadn't been able to figure out how to dissolve his link with Brooke, so instead they were scheduled for evaluations and experiments at opposite times so that they wouldn't cross paths. If his bond was as strong as Aaron and Claire's, Travis must have been able to sense Brooke's whereabouts at all times by now. Fortunately, there hadn't been any further medical concerns for him. Travis was a little depressed about being kept away from Brooke, but he did his best to keep his and everyone else's spirits up by doing pirate impressions. The impressions annoyed Garrett, so Travis made sure to do them constantly whenever he was in the man's presence.

After finishing lunch, Aaron and the rest of the candidates made their way over to the test range. It was located in the building just to the west of Echo Facility. Scanners read each of their security chips before they were allowed through the staunch iron gates at the building's perimeter.

Mr. Cartwright met them at the entrance as they came in. "Welcome to the Battle-Cove Test Range!" he said, excitement gleaming in his eyes. "There's so much in store for you today, I hardly even know where to begin."

He led them down a corridor to a set of double-wide security doors. After another scan, the doors slid open to reveal a massive inner chamber filled with a barren landscape of sand and rocks, the same as what existed throughout the desert on the outside of the building. For some reason Aaron had expected something greater. A team of technicians equipped with hand-held tablets—similar to the one Wes smuggled in—were standing by, eager to get started. To the right, an observation room looked down upon the test range from a bank of windows three stories up along the south side of the range. Nobody appeared to be inside the room at the moment.

"Don't let the appearance of the range fool you," said George. "The important thing is that it contains markers.

With those, you can make this space anything you want." There was more than a hint of jealousy in his voice. "Now, we don't have a lot of time to get you up and running. There's a special guest coming by later this week from the military to see about funding, so we are going to make sure the trip out here is well worth his time. We've cooked up a little something special to get you started: It's a multi-part protocol we've written for the computer, which, with a little practice, you should be able to access with a single command." George looked over at one of the other technicians. "Go ahead, start it," he said.

A youthful looking technician took something out of his pocket and placed it at the center of a red spray-painted cross a few feet away from where the rest of the scientists were waiting. As the man backed away, Aaron could see that it was a small metal figurine shaped like a little horse. The many angles of its polished mane gleamed brilliantly under the array of halogen lights that lit the test range from high above. Everyone moved back a few steps as the technician tapped a button on his tablet. About ten feet away from the little horse, on a second painted mark, an eerie glow of green light started to radiate out of the ground in a circle. Flashes of white shot out from its center as the ground began to vibrate and crack, crumbling apart beneath the area of the glow. The rocky floor was hollowing out, a concave divot manifesting within the stone as the matter streamed upwards into a dense cluster, hanging in the middle of the air. After several popping sounds, an identical horse figurine coalesced from the clump of floating material. It immediately fell into the rounded-out hollow as it solidified. The manifested lights faded away. Aaron glanced over at the original horse. It was only there for a moment longer before crumbling away into dust.

"Teleportation!" exclaimed Isabelle.

Everyone else was in too much awe to speak.

"Not quite," said Mr. Cartwright. "It's actually remote duplication followed by disintegration of the prime object, but effectively it has the same outcome. The original object is analyzed and then a new version, completely identical to the first, is formed. The only difference is that the new object is built from a different set of atoms."

"Why destroy the original?" asked John Graven as he studied the unnaturally smooth curve of the rounded-out area beneath the new figurine.

"We don't have to," said George. "We just do that for the mock-teleportation effect. With a slight tweak in the protocol we could just as easily have kept both. It took days of programming to set up the vectors for this simple demonstration, but by the end of tonight we should have all of you up and running, capable of sending any object to any location within the test range with a single thought."

It was damn impressive. Aaron's bond with Claire already made him feel superhuman, but that sensation was compounded in the test range; here, he was a god. The emotions coming off Claire were equally as enthusiastic.

"That's not all I have for you today," said Mr. Cartwright, as if the power of teleportation wasn't enough to impress the military representative when he arrived. "We've also developed a compound that, once activated, is nearly impenetrable—a force field of sorts."

George broke the candidates up into two groups—the women staying with the young technician to learn about remote duplication first while the men went off with George to learn about the force field compound. The groupings were devised to keep Brooke and Travis apart. Aaron's growing connection with Claire meant that even at opposite ends of the test range, they were still close enough to pass mental messages back and forth.

Mr. Cartwright pulled up a diagram of the force field compound's molecular structure on his tablet after all of the men were huddled around him. "It doesn't matter if you don't fully understand everything you see here," he said. "The system will be able to interpret what's needed as long as you pass the memory of this image to it."

Surprisingly, Aaron was able to understand most of the notation on the diagram—either the chemistry classes he took were paying off, or Claire's smarts leaking through the bond were aiding his comprehension. The compound was a fiber weaving of protein crystals and amino acids built into a tight net—a synthetic spider-web-like material. It would be light and flexible, but that was all Aaron could tell from looking at the structure alone. To activate the compound he would need to feed a stream of electrons into two thin layers on either side of the polymer sheet, and although he had no clue how that could possibly have any effect on the material, George insisted it was somehow essential for its integrity. Unsure of exactly how he was supposed to issue commands, Aaron reached out to the computer in the same way he learned to communicate with Claire. After they were all given the go ahead, Aaron held the image of the compound's structure in his mind and tried to push the thought through the link.

"Make sure you really *feel* it. You have to want it. The connection is driven by your intent and conviction," said Mr. Cartwright.

Each of the candidates chose a patch of earth for their matter conversion to take place and started concentrating. Although the computer only took a moment to determine which markers needed to be manipulated, the candidates needed to get straight in their heads exactly what they wanted to do with the matter before any transformation could begin. The static sensation of the computer link gave Aaron an exhilarating electric tingle down his spine—it was the only indication so far that his mental prompting was having any effect.

Over on the other side of the test range, Claire was making her first attempt at using the teleportation protocol. Isabelle offered up one of her bright-purple hairclips to be the target of the trial. The plastic molding of the clip, shaped like a tied ribbon, reminded Aaron of Christmas morning—when all of the presents were still under the tree, holding such infinite promise; he could never guess what glorious gifts might be hidden away inside the pristine wrapping paper. Although he hadn't celebrated Christmas in nearly a decade, not since the deaths of his parents, Claire had many joyous memories revolving around the occasion. Absorbing Claire's Christmas experiences had, in a sense, reignited Aaron's fondness for the holiday.

With a blur, Aaron suddenly realized he wasn't just receiving Claire's thoughts anymore: He was actually seeing the hairclip through her eyes! The jarring transition made him woozy. It was different from how he had imagined it would be when Wes first told him about the possibility of sight sharing; everything was so extraordinarily vivid. The dark colors were richer than normal, while the lights bled together like an overexposed photograph. Visually, he felt like he was going through all of Claire's motions, but there was no physical sensation to go along with the movement. Instinctively, he felt his body twitch, reacting to the visual stimulation in the same way one dips and bobs their head while watching a video of a roller-coaster. Altogether, the effect was dizzying.

Something slipped into his mind—one of Claire's thoughts—but it wasn't just any thought, it was her directive telling the computer to transport the hairclip. The command went right through Aaron's brain and found the pathway to his own link with the computer.

Aaron pulled away from the visual connection. It was difficult to do, like waking from a deep sleep; he had to blink several times before his eyesight settled back to normal. Aaron knew what was going to happen even before the green glow erupted: The teleportation process was beginning. The patch of earth his eyes had been fixated on—where he had intended to perform his own compound conversion—now became the target location for a duplicate hairclip. Claire's command was doubled by its transmission through Aaron, so as the original clip crumbled into dust, one purple clip appeared beside Claire, and another in front of Aaron. George Cartwright jumped back as white sparks shot up from the middle of Aaron's teleportation site.

"What the hell?!" George exclaimed as the clip popped into existence. "Where'd that come from?" He looked across the way at the girls performing their trials. "There must be something wrong with the duplication protocol. Excuse me for a moment." George ran off, leaving the men to practice forming the compound without supervision.

Wes had a look of consternation on his face. He didn't have to read Aaron's mind to know that this had something to do with the link. Travis was looking at him as well with his one good eye. Aaron just hoped Mr. Cartwright didn't have a way of tracing the teleportation command back to him or Claire. He was going to have to be much more careful with his new abilities if he was to keep his link a secret.

Glancing around, Aaron realized that out of all the men, Garrett's force field attempt was the only one to have succeeded. He must have maintained eye contact with his creation the whole time. It glowed with wispy tendrils of blue light as it solidified into a clear cube. Once complete, the glow faded away, leaving the box nearly invisible. Aaron only knew it was there by the way it slightly warped the light passing through its corners. A lack of concentration by the other men during the teleportation mishap caused each of their structures to melt into piles of clear goo in the sand that looked like a cross between thick drool drops from a giant dog and a family of beached jellyfish. Ignoring the mess around him, Garrett picked up the largest stone he could find amongst the sand and dropped it straight down on top of his cube. The box compressed against the ground like a spring and bounced the rock back up into the air and off to the side. A childlike glee spread across his lips as his cheeks pinched into a smile. "I think I'm going to like it here," said Garrett.

CHAPTER

21

The Rising Storm

The dry air of the test range chapped Aaron's lips. Already cracking, they stung as if split open entirely, though there was no blood present when he lightly dabbed at them with his fingertips. He would have given anything for some lip balm right about now, but unfortunately none of the stores around the complex carried any of the conventional western goods he was used to. The shop owners, for the most part, refused to talk to Aaron, though some shouted at him in Arabic when he tried to ask questions. They acted as if they couldn't speak English, but Aaron was beginning to suspect that it was just a game they played with foreigners. If only he knew the chemical makeup of lip balm, he could have used his new abilities to direct the computer in making a batch from scratch. He was pretty sure that lip balm was petroleum based, but so was crude oil, so that didn't really help. Instead, he moistened his lips with the tip of his tongue, though the relief it garnered was minimal.

It was Capture the Flag Day at the test range. The red triangle flag that Aaron's team was supposed to be protecting hung limp on its post, undisturbed in the stagnant air. The arena was too large for the ventilation system to maintain a breeze, though it did provide a cool temperature along with a painfully drying level of humidity. Tall walls jutted up, forming a barrier around their flag—they called it home base; a simple structure of condensed sand and rock, quickly erected by John Graven at the start of the match. It stopped the other team from being able to simply teleport their flag away from them at first sight for an instant victory.

This wasn't a game, really—it was a training exercise. The candidates were honing their connections with the computer, practicing matter manipulation under every condition the administrators could imagine. Aaron's abilities were quickly becoming second nature to him; an extension of his body, like a soldier and his gun. Ultimately, that's what Reblan Industries was turning them all into: Weapons. The funding for the project came from the Allied war chest, but the creation of super soldiers was very much against treaty stipulations for either side in the cold conflict between the European Union and the East Asian Coalition. Such research was banned and considered unethical, just like human cloning had been for many years. The legality of the Arcadian Project was thus a bit hazy considering the military focus of their training in the "Battle-Cove" arena. Despite the utilitarian talk of rebuilding a better world which Dana touted in the lead up to their CMM injections, it appeared it wasn't peace that motivated the development of the technology.

Far across on the other side of the test range, Aaron watched a competing structure rise out of the earth to swallow up the blue flag. It made him giddy with excitement to watch things like that—matter conversions; huge, shifting structures; walls and doorways quickly growing into existence as if conjured by magic. Two days ago, none of the candidates would have known where to begin at creating something that large, but they had all become quite competent at commanding the computer during the extensive training sessions that took place throughout the week. They underwent grueling trials that lasted long hours, sometimes late into the nights, but it was fortunate they pushed so hard because the special guest from the military, General Rainard, was here today to observe their Capture the Flag session. According to Dana, it was highly important that they put on a good show. The exercise was more than just a personal challenge: They were instructed to show off the technology's capabilities as best as they could in order to help secure the highest possible funding recommendations for the project's upcoming stages of development.

General Rainard was a tall man with wide beefy shoulders, dark skin and stern eyes. Judging from all the pins and ribbons on his uniform, he was highly decorated within the Allied Army. Inside the observation room, Rainard sat alongside Dana, George, and Miriam behind the large panes of shatterproof glass three stories up along the arena's south side. Yosef Reblan, Isabelle's uncle and CEO of the company, was up there as well—he had yet to introduce himself to the candidates, but from what Isabelle told Claire about him, it was unlikely any of them would ever meet him face-to-face. Apparently, he wasn't a very social man. Isabelle had nothing particularly positive to say about her uncle; she openly despised him, if the trail of obscenities following his description was any indication.

Now, with all eyes on the candidates, it was time for them to put on a show. They started the match with a brief strategic meeting, during which John and Garrett bounced ideas off one another while ignoring the presence of the rest of the red team. They soon decided to move in against the blue base with a quick offensive strike. Aaron was left to hang back in a defensive position alongside Claire and Emily while the two older men fanned out from the home base, creating winding trenches behind them as they went. The sixth and final member of their team was Brooke. She was making her way up to the top of the tallest hill in the arena, north-east of the base, to act as a spotter. The whole team was connected via ear-com units. The six remaining candidates—Wes, Isabelle, Ethan, Michelle, Travis and Hannah—were on the blue team.

From the base, the hill Brooke was on looked tediously steep, but despite the difficulty of the climb, she insisted she was up to the task of traversing it. Standing at its peak was the only way to get a full picture of the ever changing arena below. The hill itself was newly formed—created the previous day by Garrett during one of their technical exercises. It was the single largest land shift anyone had performed so far. With the whole complex shaking, the earth had bulged into the air, nearly reaching the ceiling of the test range. It was no surprise when Garrett was called in front of Dana for a stern lecture on safety.

On the other side of the flag room, Claire looked over at Aaron with a longing expression. The constant stream of emotions that used to carry across their link had ceased a few days ago after they stumbled upon a way to more or less control the bond. Since then, they each erected a wall within their minds to stop the leakage of feelings and memories. It was not completely shut down, though—they could still push messages back and forth at will, but apart from the occasional accidental overflow of emotion which happened here and there when they became distracted or tired, all of the sharing was intentional now. The barriers dissolved entirely when they slept, though, so they still walked each other's dreams every night. Aaron was curious about what Claire was thinking right now as she peered silently at him. It would have been simple enough to slip past her mental barrier and read her thoughts, but they both agreed not to venture into each other's minds anymore without an invitation.

Next to Claire, Emily leaned tentatively against the stone wall, her face tense at first but then relaxing after a moment once she was certain the slanted wall wasn't going to collapse on her. "Seems sturdy, I guess," she said.

"I don't like this," said Claire. "We're just fish in a barrel here, waiting to be attacked."

Admittedly, John and Garrett's defensive strategy wasn't very in-depth. They needed to stay close to the flag of course, but perhaps standing in the same room with it wasn't the smartest move. There was only one entrance to the flag room, so if they could find a position that overlooked it, they would be infinitely better off than they were right now.

Emily and Claire were both watching Aaron expectantly. He wasn't usually the leader type, preferring to lay low in the back of a pack, but at least he did know when it was time to stand up. "Alright, let's go," he said reluctantly, making his way out of the flag room and across to the first set of trenches. John and Garrett had done a nice job of carving out the tangled walkways. The blue team would have a tough time working their way through them. The trenches were just deep enough to hide a man if he crouched slightly, but Aaron and his defensive team would be able to see down into them with impunity if they made their way around the north side to the higher ground provided to them by the mountainous hill. With any luck they would be able to spot the blue team before any of them even got close to the flag.

Suddenly, a voice that Aaron did not recognize came over his ear-com. "Isabelle is sneaking along your south flank." It was a message to the entire red team from someone in the observation room. Glancing up through the thick glass, Aaron could see that it was Yosef Reblan who had taken control over Dana's administrative microphone. "Move against her now, and show us what you've got." There was no emotion in his voice. It was odd for him to be interfering with the exercise like this. Isabelle could have very well gotten the jump on them all if not for Yosef giving away her position.

"He's right," said Brooke, still several vertical feet from her intended position at the top of the hill. She paused in her climb and gestured largely with her arm as Aaron looked up at her, pointing out Isabelle's location to the south of the trenches.

"We're close," said John, still on the prowl with Garrett. "Everyone else hold your positions, we've got this."

The channel went silent. Aaron used the down time to form a short barrier out of the stone of the hillside where he, Emily, and Claire could hunker down and wait for an unsuspecting victim to attempt to cross through the trenches. Things looked to be going all too flawlessly when a piercing scream suddenly blasted over the ear-com channel. Everyone grabbed their heads in surprise as the harsh sound pierced down their ear canals. "They got me," Brooke choked out.

Moments ago, she had been safely perched near the top of the hill, mostly hidden within the rock face, so Aaron hadn't expected her to have any trouble. She was nowhere to be seen now as Aaron scanned his eyes back and forth across the hillside. It was as if she simply vanished. Her disappearing act was a bit eerie, to say the least, especially since whoever was up there with her could spot Aaron and his defensive team waiting below. Their little barrier did nothing to stop anybody up above from compromising their position.

"Watch out for—" Brooke's muffled words came over the channel before the communication cut out entirely; someone took her ear-com from her, wherever she was now.

"What happened?" asked Emily.

Aaron and Claire shared a look of apprehension.

The ground rumbled in the distance as Garrett and John engaged Isabelle. The sound of several small explosions echoed off the high walls of the test range. In the closer vicinity, a cloud of sand and dust was beginning to plume up over the trenches. If the rising storm grew much stronger, their visibility of the trench network would be hampered. Having the high ground would be completely worthless at that point once the sand blocked their view.

Aaron glanced back up the hill, unsure which front an attack would be more likely to come from. A flash of light caught his eye from the peak. It was Brooke's glasses, still on her head. She was in a seated position, tied against an outcropping of rocks that Aaron was fairly certain hadn't been there a moment before.

"We could use some help," said John over the ear-com. There wasn't any panic in his voice, but his breath was raspy, as if he'd been kicked in the chest. Isabelle must have been putting up a better fight than they anticipated.

Aaron glanced over at Emily and Claire, hesitant to leave them behind.

"We'll be fine," said Emily.

Go on, Claire thought through their bond. Using mental communication was easier than talking out loud.

Aaron didn't waste any more time. The cloud of sand above the trenches was growing larger, stirred up by some unnatural wind. It was beginning to obscure Aaron's view of the blue base beyond. Aaron made his way across the trenches, jumping from wall to wall above the gaps as he traveled south. His face stung as the sand whipped against him. At one point, on a particularly wide gap, he nearly lost his footing, but managed to regain his balance and throw himself over to the next wall with only a minor delay. There was a slight ridge in the landscape which stopped him from seeing John and Garrett's fight with Isabelle, but as he approached the edge he noticed dark soot pumping into the air. Once over the ridge, Aaron could see the source of the smoke. Several fiery craters were scattered across the arena. The flames were mostly burnt out by now, but the smoke production was still very high.

Down a ways and off to the right, Isabelle was in a defensive position, crouched behind a force field that she managed to construct around herself. John and Garrett were becoming exasperated. They'd already sent everything they could think of at her shield; rocks, explosions, bolts of pure energy—those would only make the force field stronger if Aaron's understanding of the compound was accurate—but at this point they were trying anything they could whip up. No matter what they did, however, nothing was having any effect. All the physical objects bounced right off, and everything else was absorbed. John sent a large stone at it at one point and while it too bounced off, the shield did compress much farther than it had when hit by objects of smaller mass. Garrett took note of this weakness and began gathering a large boulder's worth of material to smash against the force field.

As Aaron got closer, he could see the strain on Isabelle's face. Maintaining the shield against such bombardment apparently was taking its toll on her. For the first time in the test range, Aaron realized how easily things could end in disaster. With Garrett's attack, if Isabelle's shield faltered, she would certainly be crushed to death by the massive stone. Garrett didn't seem to care one way or another about Isabelle's safety, only the outcome of the match. He continued growing the projectile for the final blow.

Off to the left, Aaron noticed movement on the other side of the trenches within the still growing cloud of sand. It must have been Travis based on his muscular frame and the speed at which he was sprinting between the dunes. He was in the best shape of any of the candidates. Though only visible for a moment before disappearing again into the billowing sands, it was clear that Travis was closing on John and Garrett much faster than Aaron was able to hop between the trenches. The thought of warning the two men didn't even cross Aaron's mind—the game didn't matter anymore, he just wanted Travis to get to Garrett and stop him from attacking Isabelle before something terrible happened.

The cloud of sand swooped over John first, and then Garrett, blocking them both from view. Aaron heard a shout in the distance, and then a static buzz began to spill across the ear-com channel. From the sound of it, Aaron guessed that either John or Garrett's unit had become dislodged from his ear and was now being blasted by the sandstorm. The rumbling static became too loud for comfort, so Aaron was forced to take his own unit out of his ear as well.

Travis was like a ninja—a one-man army, seemingly capable of being everywhere at once. It was as if he had intrinsic knowledge of their entire battle plan. The more Aaron thought about it, the more he began to suspect that Travis must be cheating by delving into Brooke's mind. That was the only way anyone could have found her so easily, and with her vantage point at the top of the arena, seeing through her eyes was the easiest way Aaron could think of for Travis to have known exactly how to get to John and Garrett so quickly as well—the arena, littered with pits and blind hills, wasn't exactly a breeze to navigate.

The pillar of sand consumed everything around Aaron. It was focused in front of the observation room windows, making it unlikely that anyone inside could see what was going on down below in the arena. If Travis had been listening to Brooke's thoughts, Yosef Reblan's unfair tip about Isabelle's position must not have gone over very well. Now it looked like the CEO and everyone else up above would be forced to watch sand for the remainder of the exercise as their punishment.

The storm was becoming so thick that Aaron was having trouble breathing. Approaching the end of the trenches, he slowed his movement while he pulled his shirt up over his mouth and nose to protect his lungs.

Emily is down, Claire's thoughts rushed over the bond, *Ethan has the flag.* The message was thick with disappointment.

Aaron spun around; there was still a chance he could head Ethan off if he moved quickly enough. That was the last thought that went through his head before he felt the hands on his ankles. There was nothing he could do by the time he realized someone was hiding within the final trench. With a sharp jerk, his legs were yanked out from under him. The fall knocked the wind out of him as his chest collided with the top corner of the embankment. Luckily, the sand that covered everything in the arena padded his landing enough that he didn't think any of this ribs were broken. Down in the ditch now, Aaron flipped over, coughing as he tried to regain his breath.

Wes was standing over him, the boy's blond hair flush with sand. Wes's body language was tense. "I got you," he said, sounding about as surprised as Aaron felt. Wes's eyes remained locked on Aaron's, searching for any sign of resistance, but Aaron stayed still, already resigned in the loss. It didn't take long for Aaron to notice that the stinging granules of sand that lashed against his skin weren't coming within a foot of Wes's body. In fact, judging from the pattern of the airflow, it appeared that Wes was at the epicenter of the storm; the mastermind behind the swirling winds.

Suddenly Dana's voice boomed over the loud speakers. "Everybody stop," he said. "The demonstration is over—come to the entrance immediately." It took several seconds after the loud speakers cut out for the echo of his words to finally die down within the range.

Wes continued to stare at Aaron as if Dana's message was merely a trap to take him off-guard.

"You just gunna stand there?" Aaron asked.

Wes blinked several times before he extended his hand down to help Aaron to his feet. "Sorry," he said. "It's hard to remember it's just a game sometimes."

Aaron understood the feeling. When the match was underway, the arena became their whole world. It had taken the realization that Isabelle was in mortal danger to fully pry Aaron out of his own competitive mindset.

As they climbed out of the trench, the sandstorm was already settling back to the ground. Strangely, the observation room appeared to be completely empty now. Aaron and Wes met up with Travis, Isabelle, John and Garrett before heading towards the entrance. Garrett's face was swollen; his left eye in the beginning stages of a particularly unattractive shiner—compliments of Travis, Aaron was sure. Everyone was looking worn out, but Isabelle was the worst of them. Despite the cool temperature, Isabelle's face was spattered with beads of sweat. The exertion of maintaining the force field put her in a state of extreme fatigue. Her whole body drooped. She stumbled as she took her first steps away from the goopy remains of her shield, halfway disintegrated and sinking into the sand. Wes shot John and Garrett a rage-filled glare as he ran up to Isabelle. She instantly put her arm across his shoulders without looking up. They were already deep in a mental conversation by the distant expressions on their faces.

When they reached the entrance, Dana was there, waiting for them. He wrung his hands together in a nervous twitch.

"What's wrong with you idiots?!" Wes shouted at him before he could speak. "You nearly let these morons kill Isabelle!" He gestured at John and Garrett.

Dana ignored Wes's complaint. He was looking sheepish as he silently watched Claire, Emily, and the remainder of the blue team approach the double-wide doors. "We've had a security breach," he said once everyone was gathered. "Unfortunately, some of our files have been leaked to the media." Dana spoke slowly, choosing his words carefully.

Along the hallway, Aaron noticed pulsing, white lights all along the ceiling of the corridor—a silent alarm.

"We've gone into lockdown," continued Dana, "no contact in or out of the complex until things have settled down. I'm so sorry this is happening to all of you… we will find whoever did this, rest assured."

"Which files? What does the media know?" asked Hannah.

Dana was clearly hesitant to elaborate. His voice grew higher in pitch as he stumbled over his words. "There are some… allegations… they're saying we've created illegal super soldiers.…"

"Our faces are all over the news!" shouted Wes. He'd managed to pull up a newsfeed on a nearby wall console. It was a local broadcast so the newscasters were speaking in Arabic, but the various driver's license and passport photographs of the candidates appearing on the side of the screen needed little explanation. Everyone turned away from Dana and crowded around the tiny screen.

"What are they saying?" asked Michelle. "Who here knows Arabic? Where's Brooke?"

"Oops," said Travis. "I'll go get her!" The Australian sprinted off into the test range in the direction of the tall hill. Aaron couldn't really tell from this far away, but Brooke must still have been tied to the rock outcropping at its pinnacle.

Dana should have stopped Travis—Travis and Brooke were still supposed to be avoiding each other for the most part—but the project leader was too distracted to enforce the rule.

Multiple sets of running feet caused echoes that carried down the hallway behind Aaron. He turned around to see a group of five men dressed in suits, handguns drawn, hustling towards them. His initial spike of fear subsided when he recognized several of their faces. They were all members of the incognito security force that usually hung around the outside of the complex's three buildings.

"Oh, good," said Dana. "Our escort to the Atrium has arrived."

As soon as Travis returned with a rather disheveled looking Brooke, the security detail led Dana and the twelve candidates through the test range hallways. Once outside, Aaron was surprised to see how quickly news of the project had spread. A small crowd of protestors had already formed in front of Echo Facility, directly between the candidates and their destination. The security guards were forced to find an alternate route to the Atrium. Around the corner of the test range, an outdoor stairwell led down into a utility tunnel that resurfaced on the back side of Echo Facility. Fortunately, the protestors did not take notice as the entourage crossed over to the Atrium from the tunnel's exit. As soon as they were inside, the doors were locked behind them and thick storm shutters rolled down to cover all the windows of the first few floors.

"If they know our names, they could easily get our home addresses," Claire said to Dana. "I need to call my mother and warn her!"

Aaron could feel the worry rising in Claire. Her fears were so great that they were beginning to spill over her mental wall and across their bond.

Dana was already shaking his head. "I'm sorry, that's not possible right now," he said. "No outside contact; it's for your own safety." Dana refused to say any more on the subject. He was already on his ear-com with somebody else as Claire tried to argue. He turned his back on the candidates and went off with several of the security guards into a restricted area.

Claire was fuming now, and she was not the only one. The rest of the candidates looked about ready to take up arms. John swore in Russian, storming after Dana to the edge of the restricted section. The security guards had to physically pull him back as Dana ran off down the hallway. The door latched magnetically shut behind him, leaving the candidates with no one to diffuse their anger on.

From Claire, the torrent of emotions boiling over their link was only a fraction of what she was experiencing. Anger, frustration, sadness—it was enough to start Aaron feeling particularly distraught as well. Their pulses began to rise in tandem. Aaron's mind raced, trying to think up some way to warn Claire's family, but no solution came to him; all of the building's consoles would be completely cut off from outside networks by now while they were in lockdown mode. Claire stomped off towards the elevators, putting as much distance between herself and Aaron as she could. She wanted to be alone with her feelings. Even though the emotional spillover lessened with the increased distance, Aaron could still feel her tension prickling within him as she ascended to the eighth floor and entered her room.

Aaron took a seat on a bench in the lobby. It faced one of the taller waterfalls in the central garden. He watched as it poured over a ledge and splashed down on the rocks below. Its beauty was lost on him right now. All he could think about was Claire—he wished desperately for her family to be safe. As sad as it was, Claire's leaked memories were the closest Aaron had come to feeling like he had a family in nearly a decade. Despite having never met them, not knowing if they were alright made his stomach ache with worry. Anything could be happening to them: Harassment, attacks, kidnappings—his mind went wild. One thing he was certain of was that the EAC, when it came to furthering its agenda, had no problem harming innocent people. The kidnapping and torture of family members of elected officials was already an ongoing issue all across the Union. If the EAC thought they could gain control over the EU super soldiers with the same tactics, Aaron had no doubt they would try.

Wes sat down beside Aaron. "I might be able to help," he said, glancing over with sympathetic eyes. "I think I can get a message to Claire's family. Warn them to relocate, if it's not already too late."

Aaron opened his mouth to ask him how he could possibly send a message during the lockdown, but then he remembered Wes's smuggled-in tablet computer—it would still have a connection to the outside world! He gave Wes a big hug, but released him quickly so as not to cause any delay. "Do it," Aaron said. "Give them a fighting chance."

Wes nodded as he stood up from the bench.

"Oh, and one other thing," said Aaron. "Could you transfer my money to them—the advance from the Project?" He was thinking about Aiden now, stuck in a hospital bed. They would have to change their names and move him to a new hospital. That, or hire a private physician to look after him for the time being. Either option would be costly; much more than Claire's family could afford. "I can give you my account number—"

"No need," said Wes, "I already have it. I collect stuff like that." Wes gave a wink and then began to walk away, but stopped again after only a couple of steps. He turned back towards Aaron. "I should have told you earlier…" he said. "I didn't actually change your score that day at the convention center. You slayed the test. I lie sometimes… I'm not pathological or anything… but I'd hate for you to think you don't belong here because you definitely do." He turned away again and headed towards the elevators with alacrity.

Aaron didn't know what to think. He wasn't sure he believed Wes, but it was a nice sentiment.

Despite Claire's wish to be left alone, Aaron had to tell her what Wes was attempting. She needed to know there was still hope for her family. He reached through their bond and delivered a mental note. Some time went by without any response. Aaron started to doubt if the message even reached her, but then two words fluttered back to him.

Come up.

The words were simple, but there was no hint as to why she wanted to see him. She could have thanked him over the bond if that was all she intended. Perhaps she wanted to say it to him in person. Claire must have been experiencing great relief because the anxiety that had been spilling through the cracks in her mental wall all but evaporated in an instant. Aaron made his way over to the elevators. He still felt moderately worried for Claire's family, but with the news story just starting to break, he had to have faith that Wes's warning would reach them in time. After pressing the elevator button, Aaron waited as the lift that took Wes to his room glided back down the glass tube to the lobby.

A vision flashed into his mind, sent over the bond from Claire. It was only a silhouette at first; too dark to make out any details. The image quickly adjusted and Aaron realized he was looking at Claire's body, reflected in the mirror above her bathroom sink. It only lingered for a moment, and it was still quite dark, but Aaron's heart skipped a beat when it became apparent that she was fully nude. He of course had seen such personal views of her through their shared memories before, but this was different: This was happening right now, and this time she *wanted* him to see.

I'm waiting....

Aaron's heart skipped another beat. The ding of the elevator as it reached the eighth floor briefly shook him back to his senses. He bounced down the hall to Claire's room and found the door already ajar when he went to knock. He could feel his breath quickening; his heart was beating so fast that it was as if he had taken the stairs instead of the elevator.

All the lights were off, but the sun streamed in through a break in the curtains. Streaks of light landed here and there, mostly centered along the foot of the bed. Aaron felt Claire's presence before he saw her, the tingle in the back of his mind directing his gaze over to the chair in the corner of the room. She stood up; a silent greeting. All the modesty she normally possessed ceased to exist, replaced by an animalistic passion. She was fully exposed before him; a hungry look in her eyes just begging for satiation. Aaron closed the door behind him without looking back. He dared not take his eyes off her.

Claire's auburn hair fell across her body. As Aaron approached, she tossed the wavy strands over her shoulders, giving him full view of her breasts. He felt like he was moving through water. It was unreal—a perfect dream. An uncontrollable jitter of excitement shook his body, the anticipation too much to bear. She took a step towards him as well, cutting through the arrows of light that danced between the curtains as they billowed back and forth with the slight breeze coming up from the air conditioning vent. As soon as she was within reach, Aaron placed his hands along her waist and caressed her smooth skin with his fingertips.

I know you've wanted this, Claire thought to him as she stared deep into his wide eyes. *I have as well.*

She lifted her chin, seeking a kiss. Aaron was hesitant to oblige because of how dry and chapped his lips had become during their time in the test range, but he hadn't the power to refuse her now. He brushed his lips gently across hers, so moist and tender in comparison. Pulsating warmth began to rise in his chest, filling him from his core outwards with tingling exhilaration. Claire's shiny, pink lip gloss transferred onto him, flowing across his skin like silk as it filled in all the tiny cracks and crevasses. It smelled of fresh strawberries, so sweet and tempting that he had to taste it, licking the edge of his lips with the tip of his tongue. They kissed again, embracing one another. Aaron could feel her warmth through his clothing as she pressed her firm body up against him. Every inch of his skin cried out in ecstasy at the touch.

Claire's mental wall began to crumble, disintegrating further and further with every caress he landed across her thighs and buttocks. He knew his own wall was breaking down as well. He wanted to be inside of her—mind, body, soul—and she wanted him just as bad. Her sensations flowed across the bond, amplifying his own feelings tenfold. His fingers in the middle of her back sent exotic tingles down his own spine as well as hers. The heightened awareness sent them both into an upward spiral of arousal.

Aaron was still wearing his Arcadian uniform. Claire unzipped his jacket first. He hastily shrugged it off his shoulders and then pulled his undershirt up over his head as well. Claire went for his pants next, sliding them down with slow deliberate intention. Aaron stumbled slightly over his shoes, but in a matter of seconds, he was fully exposed as well. The chill of the air conditioning made the hairs on his arms stand up.

Claire took a step back to observe her handiwork. Her eyes widened and she bit her lower lip, making the cutest face Aaron had ever seen. She blushed slightly as Aaron grinned at her. He could feel her lust clamoring through the link, intertwining with his own. It was beyond intoxicating.

Claire let out a squeak as Aaron brazenly scooped her up off her feet and into his arms. He kissed her once more before placing her back down on the bed's plush, cream-colored comforter. His knuckles trailed across the back side of her inner thigh as he removed his hands out from under her. The touch sent shivers through Claire's body, which were immediately translated over the bond, urging Aaron on.

As Aaron moved over the top of her, Claire sat up, gyrating her hips in small circles against Aaron's pelvis. He locked his body up against hers while she kissed him again and again, stroking the back of his head with her fingertips. He was amazed just how much heat was coming off of her. Her skin radiated against his like warm sand on a beach. Her fingernails were sharp but gentle, massaging his scalp in an effortless tease. Claire gasped in delight as Aaron's own euphoria surged across the bond.

She fell back as Aaron leaned over her and placed his face against her chest. Her breasts were glistening in the dim light—Aaron recognized the body lotion—a sweet concoction of apricot and vanilla extract. There had been a container of it in his own bathroom as well, complements of the Arcadian Project housing staff; they ran the Atrium like a five-star hotel. His hands glided smoothly across her skin, grasping and stroking as he played. Soon, Claire bucked up into him with a soft moan that told him she wanted something more.

They moved as one, Aaron holding his breath as he slowly eased into her. Heat enveloped his whole body, making him flush from head to toe as he breathed a sigh. It was like stepping into a hot bath. Claire's fingers gripped his, her nails digging into his flesh painfully for a moment before quickly releasing. She moved her arms to her sides, bracing herself as she wrapped her legs tightly around his waist. Aaron grabbed hold of her hands, their fingers interlocking. She gripped him back. Her green eyes were glossy with moisture, but she was in no discomfort. Aaron knew her feelings as surely as his own. They were one, both physically and mentally.

Time seemed to stop as they rocked back and forth. He kissed her on the neck, right in the nook where it met with her shoulder. The dots of her freckles there were like stars in the night sky. He traced along them with his tongue, drawing careful constellations that caused her to moan out several more times. Aaron would have been intent with the moment never ending—an eternal bliss—but a storm was rising inside of them both, aching for release, each thrust bringing them closer and closer to that euphoric peak. He could feel Claire's wave slightly outpacing his own, but as her surging sea smashed down on the rocks, a rush of endorphins passed over the bond and pushed Aaron over the edge as well. There was no holding back as Claire spasmed and pulled him against her.

When they were through, Aaron sprawled out on his back beside Claire, thoroughly exhausted. His lungs burned like he'd just finished a race. Claire's thoughts came across to him all jumbled—random snippets of childhood memories, all happy and sentimental, the moments in her life when she felt the most safe and secure. She rolled over onto her side and rested her head on his chest as she attempted to calm herself. She was still breathing furiously hard, twitching with pleasurable aftershocks that shook through her body.

"Will you stay with me?" Claire asked. It was the first clear thought she had been able to form.

Aaron stroked his fingers through her hair, being careful not to snag any strands. "All night?" he asked.

She glanced up at him, her cheeks rosy with blood flow.

Forever, she thought.

The unspoken word washed over him. The gravity of its meaning so vast she dared not utter it out loud. The absolute sincerity behind it brought moisture to Aaron's eyes. He leaned down with the last of his remaining strength and kissed her on the forehead.

Yes, he thought back, *always.*

And she melted into his arms.

CHAPTER

22

Dark Reflections

The stiff air caught in Javic's lungs as the floor rumbled with an innocuous groan. The shaking was not caused by an Echo this time; rather, it was the direct result of the Power being summoned up within the nearby testing chamber. The pointed chandelier that spiraled down from the high ceiling rocked with a gentle motion that reminded Javic of a clock pendulum, though its shape was more like that of a crude torture device.

On the floor, he could see himself reflected in the dark stone that lined the anteroom of the examination hall, its polish so pristine that it looked as if he were standing atop a pool of still water, frozen over into a crystalline glaze. The world at his feet appeared darker than the reality above; his own tormented face staring back up at him fit right in amongst the anguishing shadows. The lofty ceiling formed a pit, while the massive chandelier above became spikes at its base, ready to impale him should he sink too deep into the darkness.

Outside the examination hall, Candeer Fountain spouted wide streams of water high into the morning gloom. The fine mist it produced only made the winter gusts that much chillier. Javic spotted Mallory and his grandfather perched out there along the fountain's edge when he first arrived. He was fairly certain neither of them noticed him as he entered the restricted exam hall. With so many other students passing by at the same time, Javic needed only to keep his head low until he was inside. He hoped to put off the reunions for as long as possible. An official summons was required to go within the exam hall's massive doors, so Mallory and Elric would have to wait outside while Javic completed his proficiency test.

Mallory came to show her support, but Javic didn't really feel up to seeing her right now. Her presence was agonizing, only serving as a reminder of what he could never have— what he so desperately wanted—a connection beyond their current friendship. Elric, on the other hand, came to reclaim his guardianship of Javic from the Ver'konus. Javic was still underage by Phandolian law, so now that his initiate status was about to expire, Elric would soon be back in charge. Seeing his grandfather for the first time since the departure of the Rosa Marsa was even harder than Javic expected it to be.

An idea kept burning in his mind: If he went on that journey with Belford and was absent from Erotos in the week leading up to Rylin's accident, maybe things would have turned out differently. Had he not helped Rylin train, Professor Vanton might have postponed the boy's test, thinking him ill prepared. Countless possibilities jumped through his head. *What if I had delayed Rylin on the way to his exam? Or what if I helped him prepare better? Stayed up later? Pushed him harder? Given him more encouragement?*

Javic still didn't know exactly how Rylin died, so there was no telling what minor detail might have saved his life. It was a futile thought process, he realized, and while he did not blame Elric for what had happened to Rylin, seeing his grandfather brought up a lot of conflicting feelings for Javic at the moment. All the lost chances and possibilities circled mercilessly in the back of his mind, haunting him like restless spirits in the night.

Going into his proficiency exam, concern for his own safety should have been paramount, but instead of a flutter of nervous tingles, Javic simply felt empty. Rylin had been better and trained harder than Javic, but even that wasn't enough to save him. Javic's stomach dropped out from under him every time thoughts of Rylin invaded his mind. His heart beat against his ribcage, clanging like a metal spoon against the inside of a hollow pot. He was emotionally carved out, weakened, with the current washing over him, and there was no one left to pull him out. His self-confidence had reached an all-time low, and yet he didn't even care. If his exam took his life, at least he wouldn't have to try anymore. He would be erased by the academy just like Rylin; just like Professor Lian and all the others who perished in Laudry Hall. Sooner or later everyone died, and when they did, their menial lives didn't really matter at all. None of it made any difference.

The door to the test chamber creaked open a few feet and a boy, another initiate from Javic's class, stepped out. His name was Tyris Orensten, and although Javic hadn't spoken to him much before, he knew him by reputation. A blacksmith's son, Tyris was two years older than Javic, which was odd for a Phandolian initiate since all children in the kingdom were supposed to be tested for the Power when they first turned thirteen years of age.

Most Phandolian initiates were thirteen or fourteen during their first year of training, depending on when their abilities began to manifest. But Tyris's family, living in a small village along the Minthune River, hid him away from the Arcanum recruiters for five years, often leaving him locked up in their cellar for days at a time. They wanted nothing to do with the Power, and even less to do with the Arcanum, so they told the recruiters that Tyris was dead. They even went so far as to dig a fake burial plot for the boy.

Eventually, Tyris's abilities started to mature on their own despite his lack of guidance. Tyris's father locked him up for one final long stint in the cellar before turning him over to the officials. His family feared what they did not understand. Javic could only imagine how terrible the betrayal must have been for Tyris. Both the boy's parents were brought to Erotos to face criminal charges for their deceit of the recruiters, and Tyris was scooped up by the Ver'konus. Needless to say, he did not plan to return home when his training was complete.

"Your turn," said Tyris, smiling at Javic when he saw him waiting in the anteroom. "Don't worry. It was easier than insulting an Antaran during the bloom." Antarans were spiritually sensitive about the annual blossoming of the algae in the Minthune River. Merely talking about fishing the Crimson Waters during such occasions was enough to elicit a good tongue lashing from most Antarans. Tyris walked past Javic with a little extra bounce in his step as he exited the exam hall, clearly excited to have earned his proficiency certification.

Javic started towards the doorway of the test chamber, but before he reached it, Cale Fisman, slightly hunched, appeared at the threshold. Biting at the skin around his left thumbnail, he waved Javic over with his free hand.

"Javic Elensol?" Cale confirmed, glancing at the chart he had been carrying under his arm. There was a slight hesitation in his voice as he read the name. "Are you... Kali's boy?"

Javic nodded as he approached the doorway. His mother seemed to have made quite the lasting impression here; surprising, given the Ver'konus's propensity to forget.

The apprehension in Cale's face drained away, replaced by a wide smile. "How wondrous!" he said, "I knew your mother well!" Cale extended the bit fingers of his left hand out for an awkward handshake. Javic tried not to look at the jagged, stubby nail-beds as their hands interlocked. "Who would have ever thought I'd find you, of all people, standing before me today? You must be very strong, what with Kali's blood flowing through your veins…."

Javic shrugged, unsure of how to respond.

"Where are my manners? Come in, come in," said Cale, stepping aside from the doorway and allowing Javic to enter the test chamber.

A wooden work table, identical to the ones in Professor Vanton's class in Conset hall, sat in the middle of the otherwise empty room. A lump of clay in the groove at the center of the table was joined by three crystal goblets and a weight-scale—the same exercise he helped Rylin practice over and over again in Vanton's class. Tyris did say the test was easy, but this seemed far too simple.

"You know, being Kali's son, I'm sure you already have all of these basics down. Perhaps you wouldn't mind skipping over this child's play and helping me out with a real problem for your certification instead…?"

Javic stared back at Cale in confusion. The nervous look that was Cale's default expression returned with a vengeance as the silence became prolonged. "What kind of problem?" Javic asked, feeling his own apprehension surge as well.

Cale tried to smile, but it showed as more of a grimace. "Well, think of it as a challenge, really. There is something I need, but it happens to be hidden away in a place that I cannot go because of my fully matured age. You, on the other hand, are plenty young enough to cross through the Gateway without developing a schism. Come with me; it will be much easier to show you what I'm talking about."

Cale turned and walked away from Javic, expecting him to follow. Schisms were serious business—localized Echoes that could tear a wizard apart from the inside out. After a moment of hesitation, Javic made a few double strides to catch up with Cale as he led him across the examination chamber and out a doorway on the opposite side. Javic followed tentatively behind the lieutenant general as the hallway snaked and turned several times and then carried down a flight of stairs into the building's basement. Soon they entered a passageway that connected the exam building with the Erotos Underground. A shiver ran down Javic's back as the tight walkways of stone conjured up memories of his previous jaunt through the subterranean system. He had chased after Aldune as the buffoon recklessly led him and Belford right into Wilgoblikan's awaiting hands. The whole experience had become a frightening blur in his mind; a source of many nightmares over the last month and a half since his arrival in Erotos.

"It's just right up through here," said Cale as they rounded a turn and stepped into a rocky chamber filled with dozens of empty crates and shredded packing supplies. At the center of the room, a freestanding stone archway was propped upon a wooden pallet. It didn't look small enough to have fit through any of the passageways that surrounded the underground chamber. At the center of the arch was a strange mirrored surface; it shimmered with a dark reflection similar to the black stone of the exam hall's anteroom floor, but unlike the stone, this surface was far from rigid. "The Gateway," said Cale as he and Javic approached. The odd reflective material flowed like water; the movement of the air forming ripples like a breeze across a shallow pond. Their reflections, already warped, distorted even further. "It's an Artifact," said Cale, answering the unspoken question. "Recently recovered. Quite a fascinating piece."

"What does it do?" asked Javic as he stared in awe at the shimmering curtain.

Cale stood beside him, looking equally enthralled. "It's a portal," he said, "to another place. A lost place that holds many secrets." Cale placed his hand on Javic's shoulder and turned him around so that they faced each other. "You will do it for me?" he asked. "Go to this place and bring me back what I need? There's no reason to be fearful, it will be perfectly safe for someone as young as you; no danger at all. I will tell you exactly what you need to look for."

Cale was quite insistent. His fingers were digging painfully into Javic's shoulder-blade, slowly shifting him towards the portal's entrance.

"It's like a giant, curved tusk," said Cale, "the item you seek—about as long as your arm, but twice as thick. It's the missing core of an Artifact. The core is completely inert on its own, so you need not worry about activating it with your touch. One end comes to a point, while the other should be rounded off. I do not know what color it will be, though it is likely it will be at least partially translucent. It is very important that you bring the core back to me intact. The core cannot be recreated or repaired if it is damaged—Artifacts are finicky like that, so don't break it."

Cale turned Javic back towards the Gateway, but Javic was leaning against the lieutenant general's forceful hands now, hesitant to put himself at the mercy of the Artifact.

"Kali would be so proud of you," said Cale, "helping the Ver'konus like this. I know you won't let us down!"

Javic spun around to face Cale again. "I haven't agreed to go, yet," he said.

The corners of Cale's mouth twitched down into a frown. "What do you want?" he asked, taken aback. "I can promote you to corporal—skip you right over cadet—but I can't do much more than that for a single mission."

Javic hadn't yet decided if a military career with the Ver'konus was something he wanted to pursue—he knew his grandfather would be against the idea—but still, the thought of a free promotion was intriguing. It would move him over a year ahead up the military ladder and allow him a wider selection of classes to choose from. Skipping ranks was practically unheard of within the Ver'konus; such gestures were typically reserved for great acts of valor on the battlefield or post-death honorary rewards. The lieutenant general must have been quite desperate if he was willing to make such an offer.

"I have another condition," said Javic, seizing the opportunity. "I need to be granted all the rights of an adult in the eyes of the law. I want to be able to choose my own path."

Cale's face lit up. "I can do that. Now get in there, Corporal Elensol, and hurry back once you've found the core!"

Javic would finally have control over his own destiny when he was done. Even so, he wasn't really sure he should have accepted the task. The whole situation was altogether strange: *Why did Cale choose an initiate for such an important mission?* He was putting a lot of faith in Javic's abilities, which Javic didn't feel he deserved. Just because his mother was a powerful Ver'ati didn't mean he knew what he was doing all the time. He couldn't shake the feeling that this was all just a game—a part of his exam—devised to see how he would cope under such pressures.

Cale handed Javic a dark-leather glove. Sewn into the palm was a concave metal disk with a pearly surface that flashed a thousand different colors as he turned it back and forth in front of his eyes. It looked like the inside of a freshwater clam shell, except that the disk was perfectly rounded and smooth. "Use this to light your way," Cale instructed.

Javic slipped the glove onto his left hand, his fingertips grazing across the cool metal of the disk as they went in. The proportions of the glove were way too large for Javic's hand, but as he cupped the curved metal within his palm, it began to glow. The brightness soon surpassed Lord Ethan's luminous orbs, the white light flooding away all of the shadows caught within its concentrated beam.

Javic turned towards the gate. Despite Cale's insistence that this was all perfectly safe, the thought of Rylin was weighing heavily on him. There was no way the poor boy died from transmuting a lump of clay into water.

"Good luck!" said Cale. "And don't touch anything but the core…."

Cale's final warning buzzed through Javic's ears as a nudge at his back sent him through the shimmering barrier. He held his breath as the murky sheen poured over him, enveloping him in its dark reflections.

CHAPTER

23

Sancta Sanctorum

Javic awoke with a jolt, encompassed with utter darkness. The emptiness around him was so dense that it felt heavy on his eyeballs. A faint musk drifted in through his flared nostrils. It smelled like an old blanket, left out in the rain, just beginning to rot. The air was motionless, though that didn't stop it from being bitterly chilly; his ears and fingers were already numb before he awoke.

He had no idea how long he'd been unconscious, but it was long enough that his blood was beginning to feel stagnant in the frigid cold. Sitting up, he shook his arms in an attempt to force his heart to pump blood all the way to his extremities. His forearms and wrists tingled as his internal heat revitalized the frozen tissue. The prickling sensation slowly migrated down to the tips of his fingers as the warm blood worked its way through his system.

His shoulder was throbbing as well; a knot was already forming in the spot where he had been resting against the hard ground. He must have fallen on it, though he had no memory of that happening. *Where in Mast's holy sanctum am I!?* The beginnings of an uncontrollable shiver ratcheted through his chest as he shifted his head back and forth, straining to make out anything at all in the impenetrable darkness that surrounded him. The effort was futile.

Deprived of his sight, he forced himself to take steady breaths in order to stop from panicking. The periodic drip of water droplets hitting the ground was all that broke the silence. He racked his mind for any sort of explanation. It felt as if he were trying to recall a half-forgotten dream.

Cale Fisman's pressuring hands….

The stone archway….

The tusk-like relic he had been tasked with retrieving….

It all slowly began to drift back to him.

The ground was slightly damp and unforgivably firm beneath him. Running his hand across the stone, he scooped up a layer of dust and grit between his fingers. He remembered the glowing lens Cale gave him. The ill-fitting leather glove was no longer on his left hand. Javic felt across the ground with both hands, brushing desperately back and forth through the thick layer of filth as he searched for the missing light source.

He wasn't afraid of the dark, but he had never been entirely comfortable with it either. The thought of being trapped forever in the darkness made his heart race with anxiety—he could feel every rapid beat as it pulsated uncomfortably in his stiff fingers. After a few frantic seconds, his hands finally fell across the worn glove.

The leather radiated heat against his icy skin as he snatched it up and shoved his numb fingers into the glove's opening. As soon as the metal disk fell in place against his palm, light surged from the Artifact. Javic's eyes recoiled from the intense blaze as if seeing for the first time. It was like staring into the sun. His head throbbed for a moment as his vision seared with streaks of white, but, quickly, the pain subsided and his eyes began to adjust. Soon he was able to make out the shadowy shapes surrounding him.

At his side, atop a stone dais, stood an archway identical to the one he could faintly remember stepping through in the Erotos Underground. The shimmering curtain fluttered with an infinite depth like the night sky. Thick pillars stood out on either side of the Gateway. More columns in pairs held up the ceiling every dozen paces down the length of the long rectangular room. Javic forced himself to stand up. His legs felt weak at first, nearly giving out twice in the first couple of seconds that he remained upright; his whole body shook as blood surged into his cold muscles. He moved like a pair of rusty wool sheers as he shuffled over to the nearest support pillar, to the left of the dais.

Chunks of black rock crumbled away like rotted plaster as he poked at it with his index finger. It had been Calvenite once, he was certain, but it appeared to have somehow halfway converted back into slate. He had never heard of Calvenite degrading, but there was no other explanation; intentional transmutation by Ver'ati would have turned it gray in color, and, judging by the dips in the ceiling, the violent process would have collapsed the room entirely had the weakening occurred all at once. No, this was the result of many, many years of extremely slow degradation. Precarious didn't even begin to express the structural integrity of the chamber.

Javic shone his light around the base of the pillar. A large pile of eroded Calvenite flakes surrounded it. The dark particles were the source of the dust that covered the room. Javic could see his footprints in the black powder, starting in front of the dais in the stirred-up area where he had groped around in the dark for the glove.

There were other footprints visible in the sandy filth as well. Several tracks led out from the Gateway, cutting various paths across the chamber floor. None led back. Thoughts of Rylin immediately clawed their way into Javic's head.

Could he be here, still alive, somewhere in this darkness?

A surge of urgency rushed over him.

All the prints looked recent, though he couldn't be entirely sure when they were placed. With no wind to move the dust, there was no telling how long the Calvenite particles would take to accumulate in the impressions. Regardless, Javic knew that if there was even the slightest chance of getting Rylin back alive, he needed to investigate or else he would never be able to forgive himself.

One of the more conspicuous tracks was accompanied by a brown smear, as if whoever made it had been dragging their feet through mud. Javic followed the smear with his light beam as it angled off to the side, running adjacent to his own footprints. The trail went around to the opposite side of the pillar he'd just been poking. Stepping around the column, Javic found the smear ended with a dark figure leaning against the dilapidated chamber wall.

Javic's breath caught in his chest.

The frozen corpse of a wizard stared up at him—black robe soaked through with rusted blood.

He stumbled back in horror at the sight, accidentally brushing against the fragile pillar behind him. A large portion of the column sheared off with his light touch and smashed into brittle shards on the ground, sounding like a clay pot knocked from a countertop.

Dust particles showered around him, floating down from cracks in the warped ceiling. Somehow the structure managed to hold. Javic tried to regain his composure as he wiped the sooty powder from his face with his sleeve.

The scent of decay was mild considering how close he was to the body; the decomposition of the corpse slowed by the freezing temperature of the room. The man's face looked like it had been turned inside out. Blood-filled welts covered nearly all of his exposed skin. At this point, the wizard would have been unrecognizable to his own family.

Even the stitching on his robe was tattered, as if it had been disassembled thread by thread and then sewn back together slightly wrong. Some seams ran strangely across the robe's pattern while others were missing altogether, leaving gashes that cut not only through the fabric but down into the Ver'ati's skin as well. Javic could just make out the twisted serpentine hood clasp of the Archive historians attached under the man's chin.

He had never seen a victim of a schism before, but he instantly knew he was looking at one now. The Power had warped the poor man's body, bending him like the reflections in the Gateway's portal. The dark stain beneath him was a puddle of dried blood, deep brown from oxygenation. He had bled out through a thousand misaligned veins and arteries—hundreds of tiny discrepancies each only a hair's width wide, but they added up to terrible effect.

Javic was grateful his stomach was strong. Most people would have puked up their guts at the sight of something so gruesome.

At least it's not Rylin. There's still a chance....

Javic turned away from the mangled body and followed the other footprints down towards the end of the chamber. There were at least three distinct sets of prints leading in that direction—it was hard to tell the exact number since they often ran on top of one another, but they all went down towards the chamber's only exit.

A raised threshold that once held a door now stood empty. Metal hinges were still attached at the wall, but no other scrap of the door remained. Javic stepped over the threshold and out onto a suspended walkway. Although he was more than a little concerned about the severe state of decay that the bridge was in, there was no other path available to him. If there had ever been guardrails, they were long gone now.

Bits of the stone fell away from the sides into the dark abyss beyond as he took his first hesitant step out. He could hear the rock crumbling away, but the pit that surrounded him was so deep that he never heard any impact at its bottom. He didn't dare get close enough to the edges to peer down. Part of him was glad he couldn't see the busted pillars that must have been holding the walkway up from below, as that would have only added to his anxiety. The one thing that kept him from turning back was the possibility of finding Rylin. He forced himself to continue on, one carefully placed step at a time.

The musky scent that lingered in the Gateway chamber filled the air even stronger out here despite the immensity of the cavern. A distant rumble, reminiscent of the earthquakes in Erotos, shook the walkway ever so slightly. Javic froze in place as more fine flakes of Calvenite dust fell from the suspension lines that stretched high into the air above the bridge every couple of paces. For a Calvenite structure to need suspension support, it must have been extremely long— longer than any of the bridges in Erotos. Those lines were probably all that was preventing the weakened material from buckling under its own weight now.

An uncontrollable sneeze racked Javic's body as the falling dust particles invaded his nostrils. The sound carried deep into the emptiness before echoing back. He felt as if he were standing in the middle of a hollowed out mountain. The ceiling vaulted up at such a sharp angle from the Gateway chamber that after only fifteen or so paces out onto the walkway, his light beam was already too widely dispersed to penetrate the darkness when pointed straight up. It was like trying to shine a light on the moon; the ceiling simply slipped away into the shadow.

"You do not belong here," boomed a deep growl of a voice.

Javic spun his beam around wildly through the air. The words seemed to have come from all around him as they echoed off the distant walls.

Sweet merciful Mast! That voice was even lower than Thorin's!

More bits of crumbling Calvenite fell down to the walkway as the steady swoosh of powerful wings enveloped him, whipping up the air. The musk, once light on the air, suddenly became so thick that it nearly made Javic sneeze again.

"Why are you here?" the voice asked. It was closer this time, coming from off to Javic's left.

Following the sound of the wings, Javic shifted his light just in time to catch a glimpse of a huge flying creature before it dived out of sight beneath the walkway. All Javic was able to make out was an enormous mass of brown fur held aloft by a pair of wide, fleshy wings that reminded him of a bat's.

The sound of the flapping circled below. "Are you like the others? Here to steal the treasures?"

Javic turned back towards the Gateway chamber and ran as fast as his shaky legs would carry him. He hadn't made it more than ten strides, however, when the creature swooped past him and landed hard on the walkway, completely blocking his escape. Javic skidded to a halt in the dust as he got his first full look at the terrifying monster. It was like a bear, only with wings. A short, furry snout extended to a black-tipped nose, above which sat a pair of dark, pupil-less eyes which reflected back red when Javic shone his light on them. The creature was easily twice the size of a normal bear. It stood up on its hind legs and flapped its wings several more times before tucking them in against its sides. Javic couldn't help but stare at its mouth full of sharp, gnarled teeth as it spoke.

"Little human should not run," said the monster. It stared at Javic as if expecting a response, though it was impossible to tell what, if anything, the creature was thinking with its enormous face completely devoid of human expression.

A bear with wings... the thought felt oddly familiar. Javic was sure he had heard of such a thing before, but he was having trouble recalling exactly when. His mind, along with the rest of his body, was still feeling groggy since waking up on the floor of the Gateway chamber.

Suddenly, it came to him: Professor Vanton's history lecture—the lost city of Sultrim; pilgrims gone missing; scholars arguing over whether or not the city's ancient guardians could have been responsible for the lost initiates. The winged bear chimeras, spliced together by the Power, were already believed to be long extinct at the time of those debates—and that was more than six centuries ago!

"You're a Guardian of the Sun!" Javic exclaimed, despite still being terrified. The chimera continued to stare back at him. "A Paerto'sul—everyone thinks there are none of you left...." One of the creature's rounded ears twitched as Javic spoke the ancient Aragwian word. Javic decided he better answer the guardian's initial question before the bear became impatient—that is, if the unnatural beast was even capable of impatience. "I'm here looking for my friend," he said. That was half the truth, anyway. Telling the creature that he was sent to pilfer the core of some ancient Artifact somehow didn't seem like the best idea. Javic's voice rang weak in his own ears. "He may be lost... or hurt...."

The guardian glanced off into the darkness to the side of the path, its dark eyes focusing on something unperceivable to Javic. "Little human cannot pass this way any longer. The path ahead is collapsed." The creature turned back to Javic and continued its unrelenting stare. After a moment, though, it knelt down on its front paws and lowered its neck. "Raljaska will carry you to where all the humans go."

The guardian's offer came as a surprise. Javic was hesitant to climb onto the beast, but with the creature blocking the path back to the Gateway, he didn't really have much of a choice in the matter.

"Your name's Raljaska?" Javic asked, stalling for time. He took the bear's silence as affirmation. There had to be some way of declining the guardian's offer without offending it, but every scenario that ran through Javic's head ended with him being eaten.

Even while crouching, Raljaska was taller than a horse. Javic could see no way out of the predicament except to mount the guardian's wide back. He didn't want to make Raljaska angry by pulling its fur, though, so he did his best to be gentle as he hooked his reluctant fingers around the meaty ridge at the base of the guardian's neck. He tried to swing his leg over, but fell short. Raljaska aided him by lifting its head slightly during Javic's second attempt. This time he quickly fell in place, straddled across the bear's shoulder blades. The creature's musk was potent, its fur actually damp in places where glands in its neck pumped glistening oils out onto its surprisingly soft coat.

Without warning, the chimera's long wings sprang out from its sides and began to flap against the stale air. It took two lumbering strides forward, the shifting motion forcing Javic to latch on tight around the bear's neck with both arms. Slipping off became a distinct concern as Raljaska's feet lifted from the ground and they were both tossed wildly into the air. Javic felt as if he were falling in the time between each wing beat, but then the next flap would come along and catch him with its massive vertical thrust just as the weightlessness started to feel permanent.

He strained his fingers as he gripped the bear's fur tighter. The world was once again buried in darkness as Javic's light-glove sank into the creature's dense coat. They went on like this, rising and falling to a steady beat for nearly a minute before a sudden thump signaled that Raljaska's hind legs had planted solidly against the ground. This was followed by the guardian's massive front paws touching down, the force of which nearly launched Javic over the creature's head entirely. Raljaska lowered its neck again and let him down; Javic had never been so glad to be back on solid ground!

He felt as if his heart was pounding a thousand beats a minute. It took several moments for him to catch his breath as he peered around in the darkness. From what he could tell, they had flown in a straight line and landed back down on the opposite end of the suspension bridge where it joined with another Calvenite rock face. A system of tunnels stretched beyond into the distance. "Where are we?" Javic asked.

"Just on the other side of the collapse," said the bear. "We walk from here."

"No, I mean, what is this place?" Javic clarified, gesturing all around him.

An airy noise escaped from the bear's muzzle. It almost sounded like Raljaska was laughing at him. "Guardians of the Sun do not leave the Sun City."

So this is *the fabled Lost City of Sultrim after all....* For some reason Javic had assumed the Sun City would be brighter… and warmer.

Raljaska tucked its fleshy wings in against its side and shifted past Javic to enter the passageway. It barely managed to fit between the narrow walls. As Javic followed behind, he noticed shelf-like alcoves built into the sides of the corridors that splintered off from the main tunnel. Each alcove was filled with dozens of dusty objects, no two exactly alike. Some appeared to be common items—utensils and tools, pots and pieces of armor, fine jewelry and silky garments still in excellent condition despite centuries of abandonment—but most were less familiar in nature—a strange rod with a hook on its end, a twisted hunk of metal, an ornate carving, an odd figurine here, ornament there, baubles and orbs of every shape, color and size. Everything was placed seemingly at random across the shelves. It was an ancient repository of Power Artifacts, Javic was certain. Without activating the objects, there was no physical proof that these were Artifacts, per se, but the lack of any natural rust, rot or decay, even on the delicate clothing items, was evidence enough. A silk scarf couldn't possibly outlast the Calvenite walls that surrounded it without being a very special scarf indeed.

Cale's Artifact core could easily be swallowed up by a place like this—a grain of sand in a vast desert. There must have been literally thousands of unique Artifacts down each of the corridors. Javic had already passed nine or ten passageways on each side of the main tunnel by this point, and there was no telling how far the repository continued on ahead. It would take days, if not weeks, to search through the collection....

"Do not touch the treasures," said Raljaska.

Javic put his non-gloved hand in his pocket; he had no intention of disobeying. Unknown Artifacts were extremely dangerous to experiment with—the dead Archive historian in the Gateway room was just one example of what could happen to a person. The tunnel system continued on, forming a labyrinth of adjoining corridors.

Raljaska led him around several cave-ins that blocked their progression through the main tunnel. The bear knew the way well; always getting them back to the central corridor just on the other side of the collapsed sections. Each time they went down a side tunnels, Javic was able to get a closer look at the relics.

Several of the Artifacts were tuned to activate upon his mere presence. Whether they were responding to his Ver'ati blood or sensed him more generally as a human, Javic did not know. Raljaska paused, ears flattening against the top of its head as one of the "treasures" began to glow. The corridor was illuminated by a soft light, as if from a gas lamp. The shadows of the relics in front of the glowing Artifact were projected against the side of guardian's massive body. Raljaska looked back at Javic, the bear's expression filled with suspicion, but Javic's free hand was still stuffed securely in his pocket. The bear made no comment, but glanced back at Javic with much greater frequency as they continued on.

Down the next side passage, another Artifact spontaneously activated itself. Javic instantly felt as if he had stepped into a bathing chamber where somebody had been running a piping hot bath. The air became heavy with heat and moisture. The chill that had settled inside of him started to seep out of his bones now, relieving his frozen muscles. The hairs on Raljaska's back spiked up slightly. The guardian was clearly more comfortable in the cold. A growl of annoyance escaped from deep in the bear's chest, but soon they moved beyond the range of the Artifact and the air returned to its natural freezing temperature.

They were not far past the warming Artifact when something caught Javic's eye: Within the highest alcove on his right, a relic that appeared to match Cale's description of the core was leaning against the wall. Curved to a point, the mammoth-sized tusk flashed with an orange iridescence that reminded him of Shiara's firestone earrings. Beneath the core's cloudy surface, flecks of red sparkled like rubies as the light from Javic's glove fell upon them. The whole core was shining ever so slightly on its own even without the light-glove. This faint internal glow was what drew Javic's eye to it in the first place.

Amongst all the countless Artifacts in all the endless hallways and recesses that formed the depths of Sultrim, the core was miraculously just an arm's reach away. Had the relic been located just one corridor farther down, it would have been lost within a collapse, never to be seen again—at least not by Javic. He quickly looked away from the Artifact and diverted his light beam as Raljaska's massive head swiveled around to peer back at him.

There was nothing he could do—the core was far too large to conceal on his person, and even if it were no bigger than a thimble, he couldn't do anything without the bear taking notice; not with those wary eyes constantly checking on him. He wasn't about to do anything that might upset Raljaska and he most certainly didn't need any reminder that his main goal was to find Rylin. He had no choice now but to pass up the core.

Back in the main tunnel another ambient glow began to trickle into the corridor. At first, it appeared another Artifact had activated, but as Javic got closer, he realized he was seeing dim light coming in from outside, penetrating down through a collapse in the ceiling. A flurry of snowflakes danced across the tunnel floor as Raljaska brushed through a snow drift that had blown in. Amongst the snow, a cluster of winterbells blossomed up through a crack in the walkway, unperturbed by the icy weather.

The pale-purple bulbs were one of the few types of flowers that could survive in such a cold environment. Javic had seen them before during the winter in Darrenfield, but they were quite rare in the lowlands. Javic was a little surprised to see the night sky above the mountainous terrain when he looked out through the collapse—it had been early morning when he went in to take his proficiency exam. The entire day must have passed since stepping through the Gateway in Erotos for it to have gotten this dark, but his body most certainly did not feel rested, so he doubted he had simply been unconscious at the base of the dais the whole time.

Javic's foot slid as he stepped down on a cylindrical object. Whatever it was shot out from under him and skittered across the floor. He caught himself from falling by placing one hand against the wall, and then looked down to see what tripped him up. A fairly large bone, half the length of his forearm, stained brown and black with bits of flesh and fur still attached to it, sat in the middle of the walkway. It probably belonged to a goat or some other medium-sized animal. Looking around, Javic noticed several other bones, all different sizes, littering the hall. The farther they walked, the more concentrated the bone piles became.

The smell of decay began to permeate the air, growing stronger with every step they advanced. When Raljaska led him into a chamber beyond the final row of relics, Javic already knew what he would find: It was the bear's den. Large mounds of bones and carcasses stood in every corner of the room. The stench was immense; not even the freezing temperature could cull the noxious odors that escaped those rotting piles.

"Mama!" came a screech from above that made Javic jump back with surprise.

A clump of dark fur about twice the size of a sheep dropped from the ceiling and glided down on spread wings. It was followed by two more young chimeras, each detaching from dug out grooves in the crumbling crossbeams overhead where they'd been perched upside-down like bats.

"What did you bring us, Mama?"

"Out of my way, let me see!"

Raljaska was a female…! Javic shuddered at the thought of what the papa bear must look like if Raljaska was this large, but there wasn't time for much conjecture.

As Raljaska nuzzled the first approaching chimera cub, an old memory popped into Javic's mind. Several years ago, after a couple of chickens went missing in the night, Javic found a fox den dug into the tailings at the edge of the old Belford Quarry. The half-eaten chicken carcasses aside, it had been the discovery of a litter of new fox pups that stood out in Javic's memory. With food scarce that season, the mother fox toiled hard to drag both stolen chickens all the way across two leagues of countryside in order to feed her young. It only took a moment for Javic to realize his predicament—this time, he was the meal. The bear had led him unwittingly to his own slaughter!

Raljaska's words fluttered back to him: This was *where all the humans go.* Javic took a closer look at the bones that surrounded him. Top and center on the nearest pile sat the rotted out remains of a human skull. The jaw was missing, and the entire back side of the skull was shattered away, but there was no mistaking that it had once been somebody's head. It was impossible to know if the skull belonged to Rylin or one of the other unfortunate souls who left their prints behind in the Gateway chamber, but tears immediately stung at Javic's eyes as he thought about the horror of such a fate.

Do they plan to eat me alive, or will they shatter my skull first before the feast begins?

Before any of the chimeras could make a move for him, Javic dashed from the chamber like a compressed spring. He didn't really know his plan of action, but he knew the only way he was going to stay alive was if he ran as fast as he possibly could.

CHAPTER

24

Treasures

A chorus of echoing growls pursued Javic as he stumbled down the hall, sliding across the scattered bones of the bears' previous prey. His light beam bounced wildly across the walls in front of him. It was difficult to keep it aimed straight at the speed he was forcing himself to move. His sudden sprint took the chimeras off-guard. That, along with the tight walls of the tunnel system, gave Javic the head start he so desperately needed.

He could hear the claws of Raljaska's cubs scampering across the stone as they began to chase after him. Two unsettling thoughts occurred to Javic simultaneously: Firstly, if he happened to be so lucky as to stay ahead of the bears long enough to reach the open air of the suspension bridge, the chimeras would have a massive speed advantage once they spread their wings and took flight. Secondly—and even more troubling—there was still the collapsed section of bridge

251

to attend with. He had no idea what he was going to do about that.... Raljaska wouldn't exactly be offering to ferry him back across the gap any time soon.

Rather than let his mind race with desperation, Javic used his bubbling fears as an emotional base for accessing the Power. His veins flushed with blood as the invigorating energy consumed him, causing his senses to surge with exaggerated awareness. Some of his heightened senses were helpful—for instance, the path before him, illuminated only by his shaking light beam, became sharper in his eyes—others were not quite so welcome: The foul tang of spoiled meat and bear musk redoubled in his nostrils to noxious effect, turning his stomach over in knots. He could taste the grimy stink on his teeth. It urged him forward as surely as physical nips at his heels, but feeling like he was going to throw up did not help him run any faster. The sound of his feet slapping against the stone walkway rebounded between the narrow walls, nearly blocking out the clomp of the bears' pursuit as they steadily closed in from behind. The thought of joining the rotting carcasses on either side of the path ensured a constant stream of adrenaline pumped through Javic's veins.

Javic realized the only way he was going to escape was by slowing down the chimeras. A plan began to unfold in his mind: Despite being a novice with the Power, Javic still knew a thing or two about manipulating Calvenite. Even in its deteriorated state, it contained the same structural makeup as the material he had been studying in Professor Herin's class. Running full speed down a hallway didn't provide the ideal conditions for performing a transmutation, but if he could turn enough of the Calvenite in the walls and ceiling back into slate he might be able to cause a cave-in that would block off or at least slow down the bears' progression behind him. Building a new wall across the path would have been a safer choice, but putting Calvenite together took twice as long as simply tearing it down.

There wasn't a moment to waste; he could sense the chimeras closing the gap as Raljaska and her cubs became excited by the thrill of the chase. Javic began a frantic version of the transmutation process he had learned in Professor Herin's class, pulling apart as many of the strengthening bonds in the Calvenite molecules as he could while still bounding speedily down the corridor. He focused on a patch of ceiling above him, slowing his stride momentarily as he made the conversion.

Dust sprinkled around him like a fine mist, but it was taking too long. He had to keep moving; with a quick glance behind him, he saw that the guardians had nearly halved his lead in just the one short lull in his pace. There simply wasn't enough time to weaken the target section to its breaking point. The only way he was going to be able to make the stone brittle enough to fully collapse was if he focused his efforts on a spot that was farther out ahead. That would give him more time to erode the structure of the molecules before moving past. It would be very risky, though; if the ceiling collapsed too soon, the stone would come down right on top of his head, trapping him on the same side as the bears… if the falling rocks did not kill him outright. Of course, the only alternative was to give up entirely, which would mean being eaten alive anyway, so, despite the peril, Javic chose an already patchy looking section of ceiling as far out ahead of him as he could shine his light beam and began the transmutation process from afar.

A dust cloud started forming beneath the new target section as small chunks of sandy slate fell to the corridor floor ahead of him. The ground was shaking. Javic thought it was just his nerves at first, but soon he realized it was another tremor, rumbling violently throughout the entire tunnel system.

The walls audibly groaned as the earth shifted around him. Javic lurched sideways as the sheering forces made him stumble, but he quickly regained his footing and continued moving forward. He did not let his concentration falter.

Larger bits of rock tumbled into the walkway from above as he picked apart the Calvenite ceiling strand by strand with his mind.

He was at the target area now. As Javic lunged through the growing dust cloud, he sent a final burst of kinetic energy straight upwards into the center of the weakened section. With a deafening crash the tunnel buckled all around him. Sliding rocks smashed painfully against his back and shoulders, sending him crashing to the floor. He did not land gracefully, his hands taking the brunt of the fall. Though his left hand was protected by the leather glove, the shining lens smashed between his palm and the ground so hard that hairline fissures splintered across its surface. The light immediately began to flicker on and off and became more diffuse, sending out a dimmer, more widespread glow rather than the solid beam it produced before.

During the fall, Javic's right palm slid across the stone as well. Even before the sting settle in, he already knew the damage was serious. Much of the fleshy part of his palm was shredded by the rough, gravelly surface of the tunnel floor. It hadn't yet started to bleed by the time Javic climbed back to his feet, but he knew the flow would start soon—and Mast would it be fierce! The pain hadn't registered with his mind yet; it felt as if he had plunged his whole arm into a bucket of ice water. He wasn't looking forward to his adrenaline wearing off—he would feel everything then.

Javic glanced behind him at the wall of dirt and rock that filled the passageway. The earth had been held back for so many centuries by that Calvenite ceiling.... He couldn't tell how extensive the collapse was or if it would be possible for the bears to get around it, but with the ground still rumbling from the earthquake, Javic didn't wait around for the dust cloud to clear. He needed to follow the path back exactly as he had come if he ever wanted to find the Gateway chamber again, but already things were looking unfamiliar. He was fairly certain he was still on the right track, but every side tunnel looked exactly the same in the wavering light of his damaged lens.

The earthquake was severe enough to knock some of the shelved Artifacts—particularly the round ones—down into the walkway. To avoid inadvertently setting off any of the relics, Javic leapt over everything he came across. Either this was the first major earthquake to wrack the city in the six hundred years since its abandonment, or else the Paerto'sul were keeping the place tidy. A collapse up ahead looked to be the same one Raljaska led him around before their final jaunt up the central corridor. Javic took a right and continued his pained trot down the side tunnel. It wasn't until he hit the wet heat of the warming Artifact that he knew exactly where he was.

He remembered the core Cale was looking for was located nearby. Against his better judgment, Javic turned back around and retraced his steps a little ways until he saw the tusk-like shape, toppled over amongst a clutter of other Artifacts within the highest alcove on his right. It seemed a shame to come all this way and not retrieve what he was sent to get. As he reached for the core, his wrist bumped a pointed relic sitting just in front of it. A burst of energy shot out from its tip and melted a pinprick sized hole straight through his already injured right palm.

Javic cried out—he was surprised more than anything else, really. The bright red beam of light continued out the other side of his hand and pierced through the adjacent wall as well. The device deactivated as soon as his wrist stopped touching it. His nerve endings were already in shock from his fall during the cave-in so the pain wasn't really worsened all that much. Still, watching a hole get burned through his hand was more than a little disconcerting. Thankfully, it was a small hole, and the heat of the beam cauterized his flesh at the same time it pierced through.

Javic's hand was tingling. It felt frozen and on fire at the same time. The pain intensified as he determinedly grabbed the core and pulled it down off the shelf with a sharp motion, sending several other Artifacts flying. He could feel his heartbeat in his fingertips as his whole body shivered in protest of the use of his hand. The core itself remained inert to his touch, just as Cale promised. Javic held the oddly shaped item as securely as he could in his compromised grip. Though the hole in his palm was cauterized, the overlapping wound from his earlier fall was just now starting to flow heavily with blood. As he stepped back from the shelf, the hot, tacky liquid dripped from both sides of his hand and streamed down the length of the core. He tucked the Artifact under his right arm, clutching it tightly to his side as he restarted his desperate shuffle through the long corridor.

Holding onto the connection with the Power caused his physical pain to intensify—yet another drawback of having increased awareness. It was as if he could feel every cell in his body crying out in distress. Releasing his grasp on the Power was his only option. As soon as he let go, the pain blurred back together into one big blob, which made it much easier to suppress than the thousands of individual spikes he felt before. He pushed the sting to the back of his mind and continued to retrace his steps.

It wasn't long before another cave-in blocked Javic's way. He knew he was still on the right path when the side tunnel became illuminated with the soft glow of the lamp-like Artifact he passed earlier. For a moment he considered discarding his damaged light-glove and replacing it with the steady shine of the new Artifact, but the heat radiating off of it was so intense that the hairs on his arm actually began to curl as he reached towards it. He suspected that picking the Artifact up would result in his skin bubbling as surely as touching the inside of a lit oven, so he continued on with only his flickering glove to guide him.

After several more cave-in detours, Javic found himself once again stepping out onto the derelict suspension bridge. He was less concerned about it being able to support his weight this time, since it managed to hold both him and Raljaska at once without collapsing. He started across without any hesitation, but still kept away from the sides; there was no use in tempting fate.

Earlier, the quick flight on Raljaska's back made the walkway seem shorter than it actually was. The guardian's air speed must have been quite great because it took several nerve-racking minutes of stumbling along on foot before Javic finally reached the collapsed segment of bridge.

Suspension lines dangled in the empty air where the platform once resided. He could see the other side, but it was a good twenty paces out, and there was no obvious way across.

A terrifying roar echoed out from the distant tunnels behind him.

Javic's heart dropped: The bears made it past the cave-in much faster than he hoped they would. It didn't appear they had reached the open air above the bridge yet, but they would soon. He swore at himself for wasting precious minutes retrieving the core. Despite having released the Power, he could still feel tiny traces of energy lingering in his veins like a thick sludge. He revitalized the pathways, embracing it again fully as he gripped the connection with every ounce of his being.

As expected, his pain spiked. The edges of his vision grew momentarily fuzzy as the burning sensation erupted from his palm, but he grunted through the discomfort. His body shook uncontrollably as he gritted his teeth. He couldn't stop himself from crying out again, so he just let it happen. There was no ignoring the pain; he just had to work through it. Right now he needed to focus on finding a way across the gap.

He could use the Power to fabricate something, but there wasn't much stock material around for him to work with. Forming a new chunk of bridge was completely out of the question—it would require far too much matter. What precious little material he had access to was already part of the deteriorated walkway, and he dared not weaken that any further for fear that the whole thing would collapse. The only excess matter he could see was in the leftover dangling suspension lines, but they weren't nearly thick enough to provide the substance he would need to build even a narrow Calvenite plank long enough to span the gap. Calvenite was too dense; he would have to build something weaker. He didn't need his patch solution to last for generations, only long enough for him to cross over to the other side.

Without wasting another moment, Javic called on the Power. With a single thought, he snipped as many of the dangling lines as he could and pulled them over into a pile at the center of the walkway. Without really thinking about it, he began to mentally weave the suspension lines into fibrous ropes like the ones Captain Bundles used to moor the Rosa Marsa—they were strong, flexible, and, most importantly, light; exactly the sort of thing Javic needed right now.

He focused his mind and watched as the structure of the detached suspension lines crumbled away and then twisted back together into the new, lighter material. Even though he formed the ropes as thinly as he felt would be safe, he was almost out of stock material by the time he finished making a second line. They would just have to do.

His idea was to attach one rope to the first intact suspension line on his side of the gap, and the second rope to the base of the bridge so that they were aligned vertically at approximately his own height apart. He could then use one rope for his feet and the other for his hands to maintain balance. It would be risky shifting sideways over the nothingness, but it was the best idea he had come up with and there was no more time to think.

Rather than tie the ropes in place, he used a technique Professor Herin taught called *Seaming*, in which one material is literally fused with another on a molecular level. The ropes flowed into the structure of the bridge forming seamless connections more permanent than any adhesive. The Seamed joints would be the strongest parts of the ropes now. Next, he needed to get the other ends of the lines over to the opposite side of the expanse. Javic launched the free ends of the ropes as if they were stones being sent across the Etwon River. Getting them to land in the right spots on the other side of the gap while simultaneously Seaming them in place was even harder than Javic expected it to be—and he had been under no illusion that it would be easy. Between attempts he carefully coiled the ropes so that they wouldn't become tangled during their flights.

With every burst of Power that Javic summoned up, he felt his own energy draining out of him. There wasn't much energy in the form of heat in the environment, so his body was the only source left for the kinetic bursts to cannibalize. The already frigid air dropped well below freezing during the first few attempts. He tried again and again, sometimes his aim was just a little bit off, other times he didn't even come close. He was beginning to feel both hopeless and exhausted when the first of the two ropes finally made contact exactly where he intended, landing across the base of the bridge. He quickly locked it down. There was a little bit of slack left in the line, which he didn't think would be conducive to balancing once he was standing between the two ropes, so he shortened the line with a quick couple of snips to remove a chunk of rope on his end and another Seam of the severed ends.

The second rope needed to hit square on with the closest suspension line across the gap in order for it to be high enough up to be useful as a balance line—a much more difficult shot than the first. With time running out, Javic knew he needed to get a grip on his nerves. He tried to clear his mind of all the clutter by pretending he was back home in Darrenfield skipping rocks across the stream near his farm.

No pressure; just passing the time before supper.

The fantasy half-worked, though the worry didn't entirely subside. It was impossible to forget about the flying bears, closing on him by the minute. Even so, once he locked down his focus, the practice from launching the first rope paid off. After just three more tries, the second line flew across at just the right angle to make contact with the suspension line. Relief dripped from his pores as he fused the rope in place and quickly snipped out the excess so that both lines were taut and ready for his crossing.

With the Artifact core shoved halfway down his pants, Javic stepped out onto the makeshift tightrope. He scooted sideways with his left foot first, sliding his non-injured left hand along the thin upper rope. His right hand was almost entirely useless by now. Blood was freely dripping from his fingertips and he was starting to feel faint.

The higher rope was attached a bit lower on the far side of the gap than on the near side, so with every step he progressed, the vertical distance between the two lines got shorter, reducing the overall effectiveness of the balance line. There was nothing left to do now but pray to Mast and ignore the pain in his right hand as he held on for his life. The top line was at neck level by the time he was halfway across the gap. With his feet wobbling on the lower rope, Javic shakily hooked his right elbow over the top line to stop from falling.

He had only just regained his balance when an ominous rumble began. It came from afar, sounding like a rushing river in the distance. He knew instantly that the earth was shaking again, but since he was in such a large hollow it took a moment before the movement translated through the two halves of the suspension bridge. Without being able to see the sides of the cavern it was difficult to judge the motion, but Javic felt as if the bridge was wobbling in large horizontal circles. Being halfway across, heading back would take just as long as continuing to the other side. He had to keep moving no matter what. With his ropes already stretched tight, if the two sides of the bridge swayed any farther apart... well, at least the fall would kill him instantly.

Ten steps to go....

Something whizzed straight down past the side of the walkway. For a second Javic thought it was one of the chimera cubs flying by, but then a second object fell past him a little farther out in the distance. The sky was literally falling! Boulders the size of wagon wheels streamed past Javic in the darkness, breaking off from the unseen ceiling far above. He could hear the air being pushed aside as the large chunks of Calvenite fell through it. With the flickering of his glove, some stones passed by between pulses of light, masked in shadow, with only the whooshing sound to indicate they were ever there.

Six steps....

Javic could feel the strain in the ropes as the two sides of the bridge began to gyrate at slightly different rates. Both lines creaked and groaned, stretching dangerously close to their limits.

Just four more steps....

"Up there, Mama! The treasures! He's taken one!"

The chimeras were out of the tunnel system—his time was gone! It wouldn't take long at all for the guardians to catch up now that their wings were spread.

"You must not disturb the treasures!" growled Raljaska, already much too close for comfort.

Javic's right hand throbbed in recognition of the guardian's words—Artifacts were far more trouble than they were worth. A pattering of distant crashes reached Javic's ears as the first of the large slabs of Calvenite that fell from the ceiling smashed into the ground far below; he almost thought they would continue to fall forever without finding the bottom. He could only imagine how far down the pit must reach.

Two steps left!

The two sides of the bridge pulled apart as the quake reached a peak in its intensity. There was a snap as the lower of the two ropes gave way under the strain. Javic's legs fell out from under him as the line flopped uselessly against the side of the bridge. If it hadn't been for his right arm being hooked over the top rope, he would have slipped off into the darkness and vanished along with the rest of the debris. He struggled to hold on with his gloved hand as a rush of butterflies surged through his stomach. The quake shook the remaining rope violently, jarring his whole body and making his legs wobble back and forth in a useless sway. The vibration seemed malevolent, as if it were an animal trying to throw him to his death.

All Javic could do was hang on as the two sides of the broken bridge leaned back towards each other, making the line dip with slack. It only lasted a moment before they pulled apart again, stretching the line tight, almost to the point of breaking. Again and again it cycled through—loose, tight, loose, tight—tossing him into the air each time as the fibers strained audibly under the pressure.

He was close enough to the other side that he could reach out and scrape his feet along the edge of the bridge when the rope was in its loose state. Because of the inadvertent slant he had attached the line at, he found that shifting his weight just right when it tossed him into the air made him bounce slightly towards the low end, scooting him a little bit closer to safety each time. Despite being terrified of falling, he forced himself to spring up even harder when the rope went tight in an attempt to hasten the process. He was flying so high that his right arm, still hooked over the line, bounced free of the rope entirely each time.

After several hops he was able to get the toes of his left foot onto the bridge. Rotted bits of Calvenite fell away from the side as he flailed around trying to get a sturdy footing. His body was at an angle now—poised as if repelling down a rock face—his upper half leaning over the abyss while his legs were planted against the bridge. All he needed was a few more good bounces and he might have been far enough along to pull himself up with ease, but the quake had other plans.

With a final snap, the line severed somewhere behind Javic. His body fell back into a steeper angle, but with his feet still braced against the bridge he was able to hold himself from falling. He pulled hard against the rope with his one good hand, grunting as he strained his already aching muscles. His bicep felt like it was tearing and his ligaments were searing, but the pain was hardly noticeable over the fear in his chest. His heart pounded as he pulled with all his might. It would take every bit of strength he had to drag himself onto the walkway with only one arm.

His face became hot; he was holding his breath. He forced himself to breath in and out through his gritted teeth. His arm was starting to give out—he wasn't strong enough. With one last desperate effort, Javic grabbed onto the rope with his bloodied right hand and pulled. It felt like his skin was being ripped off, and in actuality it probably was—what little of his palm was left from his fall stayed behind on the rough rope as he put one hand in front of the other.

The pain was intense, but giving in meant death, so he just kept pulling. Either the light-glove was becoming dimmer or else the sides of Javic's vision were growing dark. If he was going to pass out, he just hoped he wouldn't wake up during the long fall. Before he realized what was happening, he tumbled forward and was sprawled out face first on the bridge. Sweat dripped down his forehead, saturating his densely curled hair. He was exhausted and filthy from all the Calvenite flakes as well as the dirt from the intentional cave-in. His hand was bleeding so profusely that he wasn't sure he could make it to the Gateway without collapsing from the loss of blood.

He knew what needed to be done to stop the bleeding, but he wasn't looking forward to it. As Javic stood up, he drew the Power inside of him and used it to ignite his own blood and flesh all across his wound. The pain took over, gripping his insides. He lost control of his body as the scream poured out of him and he buckled over, back onto the ground.

He had cauterized the wound, but his hand was maimed and useless now. He might as well have been carrying around a block of wood on the end of his arm. His whole body felt hot as his blood pounded in his ears. Again, he forced himself back to his feet; he had to make it to the Gateway before....

One of the chimera cubs swooped past him and landed on the walkway.

Still holding onto the Power, Javic lashed out, attempting to Combust the creature into dust. Disappointingly, the attack had no effect, apart from the bear cub growling in anger. The unnatural chimera must have been immune to the Power, just like a wizard. He needed to try something less direct. He lashed out again, this time with fire. The fluff-ball of a creature shrieked and dove off the side of the platform as the flames licked its hide. Javic's feet floundered along down the bridge, not waiting for the bear to make another pass.

The air was filled with a roar from Raljaska—she was extremely close now; only a few paces back by the sound of her. Javic ignited the Calvenite dust at his feet, bursting its molecules into pure energy as he ran over the top of them. He could feel the heat on the back of his neck as the flames whipped up around him, shooting even higher into the air than he intended. The Artifact core, still down his pants, stabbed him in the leg as he increased his stride. He pulled it out with his left hand and held it in his fist as he ran.

A falling slab of Calvenite smashed into the bridge up ahead on his right, making the walkway wobble even less predictably than it already was. The collision left a hole in the bridge. Javic leapt over it, but he didn't slow down as he sprinted towards the Gateway chamber. He dared not look behind him at the pursuing guardians, instead opting to send more flames into the air every few steps in the hopes that it would ward them off long enough for him to escape. He could see the Gateway chamber; it was only a dozen paces ahead of him now.

Suddenly, Raljaska barreled by on Javic's left, twisting swiftly through the air. The bear swiped at several of the suspension lines, slicing right through them with her massive claws. The bridge started to slant over into an uneven plane, but Javic was already at the raised threshold of the Gateway chamber—Raljaska was too late to stop him as he tumbled through into the pillar-lined room.

The ground was still shaking with the seemingly endless tremor. Several of the shattered columns had crumbled away entirely and sections of the ceiling were collapsed in, forming a gauntlet of obstacles for Javic to climb over and around. The Gateway, shimmering with its dark depths, was still standing atop its stone dais at the far side of the chamber.

Raljaska's massive head poked in through the chamber's opening. Thankfully, the bear was too large to fit any farther into the room, so the chimera just stood there, staring at Javic. The creature didn't say anything, she just watched him as he scooted around the piles of rubble that littered the chamber floor. Eventually, Javic stopped looking back; those emotionless eyes made him too nervous.

As he approached the dais, the pillar to its left that was already halfway disintegrated collapsed the rest of the way, bringing the rest of the chamber down with it. Javic dove for the Gateway as everything crashed around him.

Trail of Crumbs

The entrance to the balcony was chained shut, but with a little effort, Havorie managed to pry open the door with her fingertips just far enough to squeeze out onto the narrow platform that marked the highest accessible point in all of Erotos—the top of the palace's south tower. It had been exactly fourteen years to the day since Havorie's mother, the beloved Queen Nestra Elveres, fell to her death from this very balcony. Havorie was told her mother was alone at the time, and as such the fall was deemed an accident. Although she accepted that explanation when she was a child, recently the story hadn't been sitting well with the young queen.

It just didn't seem reasonable: The railing was too high to fall over, rising all the way to the top of Havorie's chest, and it was impossible to go beneath because of a mesh cross-hatching of Calvenite bars. She couldn't imagine any

scenario where someone could slip off the perch by mistake—
no, not without a helping hand.

Madam Jusair, Havorie's head maid, told her not to worry
over such things—that no good would come from stirring up
the past. *Dead trees cannot bear fruit.* Havorie couldn't help
but hear the woman's voice in her head as she thought those
words; Madam Jusair was always spouting off some such odd
saying like that. Half the time, Havorie wasn't even sure what
the archaic expressions meant.

Looking out over the city, to the south of the palace,
Havorie watched as working men bustled about the docks.
The marina was always a flurry of activity, no matter the
weather. This late in the morning, most of the fishing and
merchant vessels were already set out along the Rivers Etto.
There were more than a few empty slips at the docks, but by
nightfall each one would be filled again as sailors returned
with their daily bounties. People found freedom out there on
those swift moving waters. With the hookjawed trout
spawning upstream this time of year, it was said to be difficult
to cast a net without catching at least a half dozen of the
brawny fish. Nearly every man with the means was out there
today, stockpiling food to last through what was predicted to
be one of the harshest winters in decades by the Arcanum's
Aerologists.

Havorie never questioned the wizards' tellings; the
Aerologists understood the weather better than anyone. They
could conjure and control the flows of air and water with
finesse, turning up the heat to mimic the bake of summer
amidst the throes of a bitter winter, or even bring a chill to the
warmest of days. It had been a regular practice for many
years, always keeping the city pleasantly temperate—that is,
until the Echoes became too extreme to be ignored. For most
of Havorie's life, large-scale weather manipulation had been
banned within the city limits. The seasons immediately
returned to their natural shiftings, but, despite the effort, the
Echoes did not lessen much in frequency. Perhaps the

mandate had come too late to do any real good. *A single bucket cannot stop the in-flowing current*—another morsel of wisdom from Madam Jusair.

Even without Ver'ati meddling, the weather in Erotos was typically mild, at least when compared to the extremes of the southlands. This time of year in the deep country, the snowdrifts from the mountains could gust down a blanket of fine powder thick enough to bury a man all the way up to his elbows in only a matter of hours. Havorie had never been to the southlands—she rarely even ventured outside of the palace—but she had heard stories. In all honesty, the southlands sounded dreadful, but Havorie still would have welcomed an expedition right up to the base of those lofty peaks and beyond, if only for the change of pace. The harsh conditions would probably be less romantic if she ever actually made such a trip, but for now it was a tantalizing dream. The only taste of the wilderness that Erotos still had was the bite of the Rivers Etto. The rivers flowed clean, unlike the algae infested Minthune to the north; the Etwel and Etwon were both born of pure snowpack runoff from the Scar. The waters were always icy, but this far downstream the rivers would never freeze over entirely, not even during the coldest of winters.

Removed from the wilderness, as Erotos was, Mast still held some surprises for the capital this year. Over the course of the last month the water levels of both the Etwel and Etwon dropped to an all-time low. Last summer's drought combined with an early freeze in the mountains meant the snowpack retained what little water it gathered, not to be released again until the spring thaw. Not even the Aerologists predicted the sudden cold snap; it was as if summer had fallen straight into winter, skipping over autumn entirely. The lack of a warning mattered little, though: Had the Aerologists seen the freeze coming they still could not have manipulated a climate change large enough to affect the snowpack—the scale was simply too grand, even for the most skilled of Ver'ati. On a clear day like today, the bleak mountaintops of the Scar of Phandrol were visible in the distance, piercing high into the sky like an arrangement of jagged teeth, impassibly dense and steep—a humbling reminder of Mast's grandeur.

Here in the harbor, with the water level so low, sandbars were exposed in parts of the channel which Havorie had never seen dry before. According to Lord Resoldo Byron, Havorie's steward, a freighter ran aground on one of those patches several days ago. It took until late last night for the work crews to finally finish the repairs on the vessel and tug it back out into the channel. Lord Byron kept Havorie well versed in all the local on-goings and talking points. *A queen must know the plight of her subjects in order to perform her stately duties effectively.* While her daily lessons with old Resoldo often seemed like frivolous exercises in outdated tradition, the lord was actually a much wiser man than she cared to admit. Apart from his grueling emphasis on posture and queenly manners, Havorie was quite fond of her old steward.

A clanking sound from one of the tower's inner doors caught Havorie's attention. A spike of worry traversed up her spine; she wasn't supposed to be out on the balcony. Usually, no one sought to disturb her while she was in repose within the tower—everyone knew her mother died here, so the palace staff kept a respectable distance. Havorie came here to be alone with her thoughts. She cared not if people thought it strange that she liked to secluded herself in the same chambers her mother had chosen. All of Queen Nestra's personal belongings were here—some had been present while her mother was alive, the rest were moved to the tower for storage in the weeks that followed the *accident*. This was the one place Havorie could still feel her mother's presence.

Another nearby door screeched as its un-oiled hinges swung open. Footsteps carried closer to the balcony, meandered past it by a few paces, then looped back around. Havorie stayed quiet, hoping whoever it was would leave without finding her perched out of bounds, but the footsteps came to a final stop on the opposite side of the balcony door. Slender fingers appeared in the gap, pulling the door open as far as the loose steel chain that secured it would allow. The links grated against the door frame with an unpleasant screech.

"There you are, my queen!" exclaimed Ervia Sindel, her face appearing in the opening.

Havorie was relieved at the sight of the little maid.

"I've been looking all over for you," Ervia continued. She wore a hesitant expression on her face as she observed the considerable drop on the far side of the railing. "Won't you come back in?" she added with a squeak.

"Afraid I'll fall?" Havorie asked, glancing over at Ervia incredulously.

Ervia's cheeks flushed with embarrassment. "Of course not, I didn't mean—"

"I supposed it would be problematic for *you* if I were to follow in my mother's footsteps." She was just teasing the girl; it amused her to see how flustered she could make Ervia.

Instead of bumbling over herself with curtsies and begging for forgiveness the way she so often had over the last fortnight, Ervia's brow lowered into a deep frown. "I only meant that you aren't supposed to be out there. There's a reason it's chained shut, you know. It's unstable. Besides, if someone sees you, it will be *I* who receives the lashings for not reporting you to Captain Sarvo."

So the little mouse had grown some spirit. That was good; Havorie could respect that. She thought about arguing further with the girl—the view from up here was exquisite, and the crisp morning air felt exhilarating in her lungs; so rarely did she have a chance to go outside anymore—but Ervia was right: There was always a chance that somebody from the ground would spot her, and Havorie did not wish to bring punishment upon the handmaid.

The young queen pressed her chest up against the door as she squeezed back inside the tower. The sliding motion sullied her dress, but she didn't really care. Madam Jusair would certainly have a few choice words to say when she saw the dark streaks on the fine blue silks, but Havorie doubted the woman would go so far as to chastise her; the palace maids had become experts at stain removal thanks to Havorie's exuberant behavior. She would just have to make certain Lord Byron did not catch sight of her until she had a chance to change. The steward, always proper, became quite distraught the last time Havorie unwittingly paraded past him in a sullied blouse. The current marks on her dress were much worse than the slight stain that had been present on the previous occasion.

Ervia already appeared much relieved as Havorie ducked beneath the chain. The upper chamber of the tower was dimly lit by oil lamps, sparsely scattered across the dark Calvenite stone walls. Ervia held a portable lantern in her right hand. Variations in the flames cast a flat light across the girl's face. There were no florescent bulbs up here, nor any communications panels. Most rooms in the palace were equipped with such modern amenities, but the south tower was skipped over during the palace's renovations two decades ago.

Havorie smiled apologetically. She was indebted to the little maid after all. Several weeks ago when Damian Sarvo nearly caught them spying on Lord Ethan, Havorie fooled the head of security into believing that she had only been out of bounds to see her new friend—just girls being girls. Thankfully, the maid played along with the ruse, even though the two had never crossed paths before that night. The next day, Damian reassigned Ervia to be one of Havorie's personal handmaidens. It was an unusual act of kindness coming from the typically impassive man. A more likely explanation was that Damian just wanted to stop Havorie from straying out of her wing of the palace any longer. At first, she considered Ervia to be just another layer of her imprisonment—a companion meant to keep her complacent within the walls of her chambers. Damian's ploy was laughably naïve—her whole relationship with Ervia was a fabrication; the plan would never work—or so she initially thought. Now, after spending considerable hours with the maid, Havorie had to admit she really was starting to enjoy Ervia's company.

Whenever Havorie thought she had the girl figured out, something new would always arise. If nothing else, Ervia kept things interesting, providing a much needed distraction from the monotony of Havorie's day-to-day duties. A lack of any real power or responsibility made Havorie feel utterly useless the majority of the time. Going to meetings; listening to reports or lectures; giving the occasional speech—none of it really mattered, it was all just a means of keeping her busy while the real decisions were made by others. Havorie's friendship with Ervia made her happy—true friendship was hard to come by for someone in Havorie's position. If feelings of discontent fueled change, then it was no surprise that Havorie was sliding in the opposite direction, becoming increasingly complacent with the direction her life was headed. She could feel the rebellion draining out of her heart on an almost daily basis. Could she really sacrifice her ambition for a mouthful of comfort, sprinkled out to her like crumbs to a starving bird?

No! The throne is my birthright! I will not give it up so easily! I'll show Damian and everyone else my resolve! There was still the question of what that meant for her relationship with Ervia…. Perhaps, if their friendship continued to grow, the handmaiden could become an ally; a supportive cohort in the challenges that lay ahead. Trust was not something that Havorie gave out easily. Residents of the Glowing City often had their loyalties dangerously splintered. She had to be certain of Ervia's intentions before she could even begin trusting the girl. Havorie had no leverage against Ervia. Friendship could be faked.

"Speak, then," said Havorie, turning to Ervia. "Why have you searched me out during my hour of repose?" The question came across harsher and stiffer than she intended, the flames in her heart giving a bite to her words.

With a grimace to show her embarrassment, Ervia did curtsy now, remembering her place in front of the Queen of Phandrol. "Pardon my interruption, my queen," she said, bowing her head low to the floor as she pulled up her turquoise skirt in a deep curtsy.

Havorie nodded for the girl to continue.

"Madam Jusair had me cleaning out one of the old drawing rooms this morning, and I stumbled across something… hidden. It was tucked away beneath the false bottom of a drawer in one of the carved writing desks—the one with the falcon engraved in its cabinetry—I thought it was just an old book at first, but it's a handwritten journal… it's not signed or anything, but I'm fairly certain it belonged to—"

"My mother…" Havorie finished.

Ervia's eyes widened in confirmation. For the first time, Havorie noticed the tattered leather-bound diary held beneath Ervia's right arm.

Havorie knew the desk Ervia described. Half-forgotten memories of her mother clawed their way back into her mind—Nestra sitting in front of that desk for what felt like hours, writing nonstop while Havorie frolicked around the room playing with her toys. It was as if her mother had been born a scribe rather than a queen. The falcon carving, polished to the same dark, glossy sheen as the rest of the mahogany desk, seemed to watch over Havorie as she toddled back and forth. She used to make up rhymes about the strange objects that filled the world around her—the palace was full of all sorts of eclectic ornaments and carvings that made her young imagination bristle with creativity.

Nestra would pause in her writing and listen to Havorie as she recited her poems in song. When she was finished, Nestra would continue the tune, picking up where Havorie left off. Such a lovely voice her mother had, like no other she could recall hearing before or since. The melodies that drifted back to her now were haunting, but perhaps that was just an effect of the distortion of memory through time. The tunes used to rock her to sleep at night. Snippets of song still popped into Havorie's mind from time to time, though she rarely stopped to reflect on where they had come from.

Falcon stirring in the deep,

Lift me up from whence I sleep.

Soaring high to distant lands,

Within the clasp of talloned hands.

It matters not what's left behind,

Nor where I go, nor what I find.

Through love and strife I dance and weep,

And live the life I wish to keep.

She could no longer remember which words she made up and which ones her mother filled in for her.

For some reason she could not explain, Havorie hesitated when Ervia offered the journal out to her. Its cover was cracked and worn from heavy use, the natural oils of the leather long ago having dried up. The spine was creased and flimsy from being opened too far, far too many times, but it still held tight to the pages. Havorie had to force her hands to reach out to it. This was a tangible piece of her mother…. As soon as her fingers grasped the edges of the journal she could already feel its warmth, as if it were alive—a breathing, thinking organism. Havorie's breath caught in her lungs. She mused at her nervousness as she let the air escape, almost in a sigh. Before she could open the diary, Ervia spoke again.

"There's one more thing," she said, reaching into her skirt pocket and retrieving an envelope. "A love letter, written to your mother. It was inside the journal—it isn't signed either…." From the look on Ervia's face, there was something very troubling about the letter. She passed the envelope to Havorie. "This is why I sought you out with such haste."

An odd feeling began to rise in Havorie's chest as she opened the envelope and unfolded the fragile note. As she began to read, her immediate observation was that the handwriting did not belong to her father, King Amador Lewis. From what she remembered of her father's writing, it had been much stiffer than this; he had always scrawled with the sharp movements of a hurried hand. The lines in this letter were curvy in comparison, each word formed with a steady deliberateness that would have been as foreign to Amador as playing the lute.

Havorie had never been close with her father. Throughout most of her childhood he was away from the capital soldering in the Kovehn conflict. He returned briefly to the palace after her mother's passing, but kings did not rule Phandrol; his place had always been on the battlefield. He was a skilled swordsman, taught by members of the Paerto'radam, though he hadn't joined their ranks. His training with the Guardians of Truth led to many victories on the battlefield. He was a proud warrior, but when it came to fathering, he had always been a stranger to Havorie. Two years after her mother's death, Amador was slain while leading a raiding party across the Crimson Waters. Havorie took the news without emotion. It was as if a distant uncle had died.

Regardless of her lack of attachment to her father, news of a secret suitor was still a scandalous surprise. As Havorie furiously scanned her eyes across the letter, her curiosity was soon replaced by dread: It started out as a typical love letter might, doting on her mother, drawing metaphors between the shine of her eyes and the light of the moon reflecting off the clear waters of the Etwel on a warm summer's eve. After several more flowery sentences, including one which nearly made her blush from its frank sexual innuendo, the mysterious suitor asked her mother to a rendezvous.

What was certainly the cause of Ervia's alarm also jumped out at Havorie: The suitor asked Nestra to come to the top of the south tower—specifically to the room where Havorie and Ervia now stood—and the meeting was set to take place on none other than the day her mother fell from the highest point in all of Erotos. There was no mistaking it; the date marked upon the page had been engrained in Havorie's memory for fourteen years now.

Queen Nestra's death was no accident... *my mother was murdered!*

Carnivorous Thoughts

A sharp tug by Madam Jusair on one of Havorie's stubborn locks of curly, blonde hair brought a beaded tear to the young queen's eye. The droplet clung to her lashes, forcing her to blink several times before her vision became clear again. She vocalized no complaint over the head maid's roughness in un-knotting the tangled mess—Havorie was too absorbed in thoughts of treachery and assassination to as much as wince at the pain in her roots. Her hair be damned—someone had seduced her mother, and then lured her to the top of the south tower to end her life! The thought was enough to fill Havorie's chest with an icy pain that was a thousand times worse than any physical affliction she had ever experienced. Her heart welled with the sting of the un-graspable emotion. She didn't know where to direct her fear or anger, so the feelings permeated all around her indiscriminately.

Trying to deduce the likely suspects made her head spin. The killer would have needed access to the palace, but with guest housing located adjacent to the south tower in the east wing, the assassin could have been anyone—Arcanum, military, diplomat, palace staff—the list was extensive. Contemplating possible motives for the assassination didn't make the pool of suspects any less diluted. There were simply too many reasons someone might want to dispose of a queen. Amongst the deluge of emotion that was pulling Havorie in every direction simultaneously, it was overwhelming sadness that ultimately took hold of her. She found it difficult to consider such dark possibilities without a pain twisting in her gut that made her abdomen feel like a stretched hide atop a ceremonial drum, her heartbeat churning out empty thuds against her ribcage.

Madam Jusair grunted as she ripped through another hopeless knot on the top of Havorie's head. The queen's chin jerked up like a marionette as the brush bristles intertwined with the clump. Madam Jusair froze in place, anticipating a backlash. After a moment, when it didn't come, the woman hesitantly repositioned the brush and then began a slow massage with her fingertips to loosen the tangle. "What's the matter, dear?" she asked as she separated the offending strand from the rest of Havorie's curls. "Clearly, there is something on your mind."

Havorie shifted her eyes across the mirror to Madam Jusair's reflection. The head maid's attention was still focused downward on her work. The woman's newly graying hair, tied up in a loose bun on top of her head, wobbled back and forth as she leaned in to find a better view of the knot. Valyne Jusair had been head maid since before Havorie was born, so it was very possible that she might have some insight into whom her mother was seeing around the time of her death. The woman was one of the few people Havorie felt truly had her best interests at heart—she had been Havorie's wet nurse after Nestra found she was unable to breastfeed, for

Mast's sake! Madam Jusair was the closest thing to a mother figure that Havorie had these days.

Still, Havorie was hesitant to tell anyone else about Ervia's discovery—at least not until she had a chance to read through the leather-bound diary more carefully for clues. After making Ervia swear a vow of secrecy, she hid the documents away in one of the south tower's many storage chests. It would be much safer if no one knew she was searching for the identity of the secret suitor within those pages—best if no one knew any pages existed at all, really. If the wrong person learned of her hunt, she could very well end up the victim of her own tragic *accident*.

Unfortunately, there was no guarantee the answers she sought would be found within the diary at all. Her mother wrote many of her references in code, and it was proving to be quite difficult to decipher. Every name within the journal was replaced by an animal, and every location or object was switched out in accordance with some metaphor that Havorie had not yet begun to understand. Havorie knew she was in for a struggle from the very first page:

"The baboon's chest must be sore after the brazen display at the hunting grounds. No amount of chest pounding will change my mind on this matter. The red dove stays, and that is final. I've no doubt the phoenix will rein in his monkeys once I remind him that he is here on my volition, and that invitations can be withdrawn. It's always a struggle with that one, but I know he will fall in line in due time. In this case, he truly is a hen in the Fox house and not the other way around."

In the pages that followed, Nestra started referring to the secret suitor as her "nightingale," always calling upon her late in the night like a chattering bird in search of its lover. Her mother was clearly smitten—a fact which made the subsequent betrayal only that much more heartbreaking to Havorie. Between the monkeys, birds, and mythical creatures, all the masked references in the diary piled on top of one another, making the young queen's head hurt.

After a few moments, when it became obvious to Madam Jusair that Havorie intended to remain silent to her inquiry, the woman ceased her efforts in untangling the knot and turned her piercing eyes on Havorie through the mirror. "A carnivorous thought can damage the soul. It's best to let such things out."

Havorie sighed. She knew the idea of discovering her mother's assassin was consuming her; it had been two days now since Ervia brought the little leather-bound book and fateful letter to her attention, but already it felt like an eternity had passed. This was not the type of thing she could simply liberate from her mind by speaking out loud. Knowing the killer walked free was enough to keep Havorie awake at night. Whenever she was alone in the darkness, she felt as if an evil presence was looming over her, watching her from out of the shadows. Havorie wouldn't feel safe again until she found justice for her mother, and for that to happen, she needed to get some answers.

She wasn't sure if she was making the right decision, but if she couldn't trust Valyne, there really wasn't any hope left for her anyway. She decided to just come out with it. "Did my mother have any… *men* in her life, other than my father? Romantically, I mean."

Madam Jusair seemed to stare through Havorie.

Perhaps carnivorous thoughts are contagious….

She only caught a brief glimpse of the glossed over expression that lingered on Valyne's face before the woman snapped back to her senses. Madam Jusair's eyes darted away from the mirror and back down to Havorie's scalp, her fingers springing to work, once again picking at the massive knot. "Of course not," she said. "Why do you ask?"

The lapse was subtle—Havorie might not have noticed anything odd had she not been staring into Valyne's eyes when she asked the question. The words stirred something deep inside Madam Jusair—Havorie could not be sure whether it was an old memory resurfacing or perhaps just some long forgotten inkling of suspicion that found its way back into the woman's conscious mind, but one thing was clear: Valyne Jusair knew something. The false calm expressed on the woman's face was belied by a slight tremble in her usually steady hands. Havorie hadn't the time to play such games. "Tell me the truth!" she pressed on. "What do you know of the affair? Who was—?"

"These are dangerous questions," Valyne interrupted. Her grip on Havorie's golden locks grew uncomfortably tight as her fist clenched. "Why tarnish your mother's reputation with such inquiries? A royal *affair…*" she whispered the offending word, "such an accusation can only bring shame upon house Elveres… upon the whole royal office."

"I know of the secret suitor," Havorie continued. "I must learn this man's identity."

Madam Jusair released Havorie's hair and spun her around in her seat so fast it made her head spin. "These questions are inappropriate," she said. "I will not be a part of dredging up the past. You know nothing of what you speak. How can you? You were just a babe! Your mother was a good woman and does not deserve to have her name sullied like this—not now, not ever."

Havorie was surprised by the ferocity in Valyne's voice. The head maid did not appear to comprehend the true stakes of Havorie's line of questioning. This was not simply about scandal or reputation—she aimed to catch a murderer.

"The consequences…" the woman continued, almost pleading now. "Just stop. Dead trees cannot bear fruit—you must not speak of this again, not to anyone!"

A flicker of movement in the shadows behind Madam Jusair caught Havorie's eye. She would have gasped at the revelation of an eavesdropper had she not immediately known the man's identity. The lack of surprise did not make the circumstance any less dreadful, though. No one but Captain Damian Sarvo could move with such stealth through the chambers of the palace. The bulky man shouldn't have been so adept at hiding—nor so light on his feet—but it was he who stepped from the shadows. His usual scowl was eerily replaced by a faint smile that looked all too foreign on the captain's gnarled face. Havorie's heart dropped. Damian was the last person Havorie wanted to see right now. There was no telling how much he overheard.

"Always finding new ways of antagonizing the staff, I see," Damian said jovially.

Madam Jusair nearly leapt out of her stockings as he spoke. She hadn't noticed his approach at all.

"What did she do this time," Damian asked, "tear her dress climbing about the south tower?"

Both women remained awkwardly silent, unsure of how to respond. Havorie got the impression she was spotted during her brief stint on the balcony the other day. Things always had a way of getting back to Captain Sarvo, but it was best not to openly admit to such things unless she was directly accused. Havorie just prayed he truly missed the subject of their current discussion.

"I hope all is well today, Valyne." Damian's eyes remained locked on the queen as he addressed the head maid. "I don't mean to interrupt, but I need to steal Havorie away. The Ver'konus briefing has been moved up an hour."

Madam Jusair's breathing hadn't quite returned to normal since her scare, but she did her best to mask the anxiety. "We're all finished here," she said, putting on a fake smile.

Valyne quickly shifted Havorie's hair around to hide the knot—there was still quite a bit of work to be done in untangling that mess.

The young queen felt the head maid's eyes linger across her back as she stood up from her seat and followed Damian out of the chamber. *How long was he standing in the shadows?* The hard heels of the captain's boots made echoing clomps against the dense tiles of the sitting room's floor. He must have taken great care to enter her study without producing so much as a tap. Havorie made no attempt to converse with Damian as they stepped gingerly out into the marble-lined corridor; when it came to Captain Sarvo, she preferred to walk in silence.

They proceeded down the wide hallway towards the reception room where Havorie received her audiences. Her feet, held by slippers, made no noise as she quickened her pace to keep up with the captain's long strides. Damian glanced back several times to make sure she was still following, but of course she was always right on his heels. Havorie learned long ago to always keep up with the captain if she wanted to avoid his scorn. His speedy pace had become so engrained in her over the years that she lingered behind only briefly as a soft vibration of unnatural energy tickled against the underside of her left wrist.

The tingling indicated that one of the three working dials on her Detector was making a sweeping change. She dared not consult the Artifact now—if Damian recognized it as a Power Artifact, he would surely confiscate the device without discussion.

The Detector had been behaving queerly over the past few weeks, ever since the night Lord Ethan and Aaron Levy, the strange boy with the Mark of Kings, departed from the harbor. The two most powerful Ver'ati in the city traveled rapidly, due north, under the guise of darkness. Despite the lord's otherwise successful attempt to keep the expedition a secret, the Detector tracked their movements along every bend in the

Etto River until they traveled far enough downstream for the dial to be swayed towards the next most powerful Ver'ati still within the Detector's vicinity. Not surprisingly, the needle meandered east, in the direction of the Ver'ati training academy where most of the magic users in the city resided. A week after that, though, things started to make less sense.

One morning the dial went from pointing steadily at some Ver'ati who was as of yet unknown to Havorie—the strongest wizard remaining in Erotos—to jumping around sporadically from one target to another, as if the powerful Ver'ati it was watching suddenly ceased to exist. Havorie expected to hear news of some great wizard's death when Lieutenant General Cale Fisman came to visit her several days later for the Ver'konus briefing—that was last week's meeting—but the acting-leader did not volunteer any such information. Death was the only way Havorie could think of for a wizard to so abruptly vanish from the Detector's all-seeing vision. It may have been her imagination, but Cale seemed more agitated than usual during his last visit to the palace. He was a nervous man by nature, but whether he was simply feeling flustered from the stress of leading the Ver'konus in the absence of Lord Ethan and General Aldune, or whether it was a sign of something more sinister, Havorie had no way of knowing.

After only a few more steps towards the reception room, Havorie's curiosity proved too great for her reservations to suppress. She convinced herself that it was unlikely Damian would recognize the golden band clasped around her wrist as a Power Artifact even if he did happen to glance back in the quick second it would take her to consult the dials of the Detector. She still felt a flutter of nervousness in her abdomen as she flipped back the sleeve of her frilly dress and peeked down at the faintly glowing contraption sitting loosely against her forearm.

It took only a moment for Havorie to recognize what had changed: The Ver'ati detecting dial no longer danced randomly—it once again was fixated due north, focused on a single powerful entity. Havorie's first thought was that Lord Ethan was returning to the city, but upon closer inspection, the needle was already locked steady on its target and giving off a faint glow—a direct indicator of proximity. By her best judgment the target was almost certainly already within the city limits. The dial did not make a gradual shift, the way it would have had Lord Ethan's ship been navigating back up stream.

Her moment of contemplation was cut short as a familiar voice up ahead brought her attention to the open door of the reception chamber. It was the gruff, throaty heckling of General Guther Aldune.

"Bring me another one!" he snapped at some unseen server. "A real bottle this time, mind you. Piss water may pass for wine in the gutter you call a home, but I'd have to be gone from civilization for a lot more than two cycles to find this slosh even remotely drinkable."

The voice grated at the young queen's ears. Havorie quickly hid the Detector back under her sleeve—Damian hadn't glanced back at least, but that one morsel of good fortune hardly outweighed having to spend a single moment with the abominable Guther Aldune.

To Havorie's dismay, the foolish young server that Aldune was conversing with attempted to offer an explanation to the general rather than simply bowing from the room the way a more experienced staff member would have done. "But, sir," he said, "Lieutenant General Fisman specifically requested this bottle be put on layaway for the occasion." A moment of silence followed, in which the young server probably realized how grievous a mistake opening his mouth had been.

"Do I look like a twat?" Aldune spat, sounding already on the verge of irate. "Do you see a lanky, balding, fish-eating twat standing in front of you!? Cale can request all the piss water he wants, but that doesn't mean I have to be offended by its presence!"

Havorie's wrist tingled with another warning from her Detector—Aldune was conjuring the Power. Channeling was forbidden within the palace, but clearly Aldune had no qualms about breaking the rules. Havorie cringed; nothing good would come next. The sound of shattering glass was followed by a desperate cry of pain as the server scampered backwards through the opening into the hallway. Havorie recognized the young man that stumbled out in front of Damian. It was Caspin Byron, one of Old Resoldo's grandsons. Blood streamed from his right cheek and temple where shards of Aldune's goblet lacerated his skin. He was a simple boy, which only made Havorie feel worse for him as he dashed down the hallway clutching his cut-up face.

Damian shifted his hand towards the hilt of his sword, but then let it fall back to his side, no doubt realizing the defensive posturing would only anger the general further. When Damian and Havorie entered the reception room, however, Aldune was surprisingly at ease.

Guther shifted slightly in his seat upon hearing their approach but kept his back towards the entrance of the room. He was reclined comfortably in a chair on the near side of the long, narrow table that served as a barrier between negotiating parties when the reception chamber was used for such purposes. A second server, standing perfectly still in the southwest corner of the room, maintained a wide-eyed stare in Aldune's direction, watching as if the general was a ravenous beast. No indication of the outburst remained in Guther's demeanor, but the puddle of red wine and broken glass was evidence enough of his simmering anger.

"Bring me your best Antaran brandy," Aldune grumbled, dismissing the second server without looking up. The frightened man fled from the room with no need for further prompting.

Damian stepped back out into the hallway, taking up his position beside the open doorway. Havorie guardedly scooted around the slowly expanding puddle of red. Bits of glass crunched beneath her slippers as she made her way to the far side of the table and took her appointed seat across from Aldune.

"Havorie," said the general with a blank expression on his face. It was an unceremonious greeting, but the best she could expect from the man. Aldune seemed haggard. His eyes were bloodshot and his skin drooped as if he hadn't slept in quite some time.

"How goes the fight at Fort Bastion?" she asked, feigning interest. "I had not heard of your return to the city."

Aldune turned his head slightly, pointing his ear towards the open doorway, as if listening to some distant conversation that Havorie could not perceive. Ver'ati had heightened senses when consorting with the Power, so there was no telling where the general's attention had wandered.

Havorie often likened Ver'ati with cats: Both tended to stare off creepily into the distance, as if listening to the wind. Some Aragwians, especially the Kovani, believed that cats could see spirits—that when the wise creatures stared intently at nothing, they were actually seeing through an invisible veil into the world of the dead. Some said Ver'ati had the power to see ghosts as well, but Havorie had been around wizards enough to know the true limits of their abilities. Havorie believed cats and Ver'ati stared off for the same reason—an overall disinterest in ordinary human matters. While cats might be contemplating how best to catch a mouse or watching a refraction of light dance across the ceiling, the ruminations of Ver'ati were a much greater mystery to those looking in from the outside. Certainly, the only type of spirits Aldune communed with were the kind he could pour into his glass.

General Aldune abruptly turned back towards Havorie as if there hadn't been a lull in their conversation. "The Minthune will be lost to us by month's end," he said. His tone was casual, but there was more than a hint of pain behind his bloodshot eyes.

"I had heard the fight was going well," said Havorie.

"It was," said Aldune. He volunteered nothing more.

Havorie was truly surprised. Every report she received so far about the northern campaign promised great success. Aldune was withholding something—that much was clear from his conflicted gaze. When it came to information, Aldune demanded much, and provided very little. Havorie wondered how her mother had dealt with the astringent general. He had been Lord Ethan's second-in-command for decades, so surely Nestra must have sat through many similar meetings. She would have demanded to know everything, and settled for nothing less than every miniscule detail.

A quick rap by Damian against the door's frame indicated that somebody was approaching the chamber. Havorie and Aldune both turned their attention towards the portal as none other than Lord Resoldo Byron himself stepped through the doorway carrying a bottle of fine Antaran brandy wine. Aldune certainly did not miss the deadly glare in the old man's eyes as the master steward uncapped the rosy spirit and splashed three fingers worth of drink into a tall glass. From the confused look on the general's face, he must not have been aware that the young server he accosted was Resoldo's grandson.

"Raging baboon," Lord Byron said under his breath.

"Excuse me," said Aldune, rising to his feet, his temper immediately starting to flare again.

Resoldo didn't back down. "You're nothing more than a savage beast!" he shouted. "Always picking on the weak."

Havorie had never seen Old Resoldo act like this before. He was generally such a proper and polite man, but Aldune's attack on his kin pushed him too far. The general's eyes bulged out of his head in response, a vein visibly pulsing in his right temple. Havorie jumped to her feet as another tingle against her wrist warned of imminent doom. The Power was beginning to course through Aldune, flowing in to fill his every capillary—an invisible process to all but the Detector.

"General!" Havorie cried out in as stern a voice as she could muster.

Aldune spun around, caught off-guard by her authoritative tone. Havorie flinched away from his gaze half-expecting to be struck by whatever devious attack he was planning against Resoldo, but nothing happened. Instead, Aldune's new glass innocuously fogged up with condensation as he exploited the Power to chill his beverage.

Havorie quickly regained her composure. "Do sit down, general," she said. "I believe we still have some matters to discuss. And as for you, Lord Byron," she directed a meaningful look towards the master steward, "go see to Caspin's wounds. And take that bottle with you. The good general has already consumed more spirits than I daresay he deserves."

Resoldo was still enraged, but he made a curt bow towards Havorie and departed the room without another word. Lord Byron's choice of insult—calling Aldune a raging *baboon*—had not gone unnoticed. Her mother wrote of a brazen baboon in her diary pages. The animal fit well with the general's brutish demeanor. If Aldune was indeed the baboon from her mother's diary, perhaps the pages weren't so indecipherable after all.

Aldune retook his seat. This time, his demeanor remained hostile. He glared at Havorie across the table as he threw back the entire glass of brandy, downing it in one swallow. It was a wonder the cup did not break as he slammed it against the table. Havorie maintained a calm gaze, but under the surface she was more than a little anxious to be dealing with the beast of a man while he was in such a state—half-drunk and with his hackles already raised. She needed to appear unaffected by his antics—it was her only defense against his bullying.

"What do you mean we are going to lose the Minthune?" Havorie let irritation sound in her voice to mask any weakness she might otherwise exhibit. Aldune stubbornly maintained a blank stare. "If we lose the Minthune, we will have lost our primary shipping lane," said Havorie. She knew she was stating the obvious, but she continued anyway. "Without the shipping lane, we will have to rely on Antara and their limited hospitality to transport all foreign goods across land. With so much at stake, why would you, our most decorated battle strategist, relinquish your command at the forefront of the conflict?" Aldune's glower deepened with every word. Havorie saw an opportunity for leverage and pressed on. "Was it fear that led you to abandon your station—leaving Phandolian soldiers to die at the hands of a ruthless enemy?" It was a dangerous gamble, implying that Aldune's actions were both cowardly and treasonous. Such accusations demanded explanation, which is what Havorie was counting on. It felt like the type of thing her mother would have done to pry information from a difficult adversary.

At first, Aldune's lips tightened, but soon he realized he could not remain silent under such scrutiny. He shook his head in disbelief; Havorie had backed him into quite the corner. "It wasn't my choice," he said, picking his words carefully. "I was commanded to return...." He didn't say where his orders originated, but Havorie knew Aldune only answered to one man. The timing of Aldune's return was right in line with what Havorie would expect if Lord Ethan delivered the command in person during his journey north, so she continued on with that assumption.

"Why would Lord Ethan want our armies to falter?" she asked.

Aldune slumped low in his seat, realizing he already gave away more than he intended. Havorie hoped he would divulge more information, but Aldune was not a stupid man. He knew that by admitting to receiving orders, he at the very least managed to deflect her accusation of treason. He was intent on staying silent now, not wanting to accidentally reveal anything else.

Havorie wasn't so easily deterred. She decided to fish for more information by watching Aldune's expression carefully as she spoke what she already knew to be the truth: "Lord Ethan is heading north, and he has taken that young man with the Mark of Kings with him."

For the first time that Havorie could recall, Aldune appeared genuinely fearful of what Havorie might say next. Perhaps he thought she had deduced the entire meaning of Lord Ethan's secret expedition. Havorie let him sit in that moment a while longer as she contemplated what to say next.

If she appeared to already know everything, perhaps Aldune might let a few more details slip. She needed to be careful though—if she guessed incorrectly at Lord Ethan's intentions, the general would surely lock up again, realizing Havorie's knowledge exhausted. She could think of several reasons for the lord's departure—meeting with the Arcani; plotting against Kovehn with Gravish officials; maybe something to do with the Antarans and the recent death of King Lodrin— though she couldn't think of any reason for taking the man with the new mark along for the ride. Aldune's dismissal from his post at such a crucial time in his campaign didn't make any sense to the young queen either. Phandrol would lose ground—surely Lord Ethan realized that. The Kovani would only be emboldened by the shift in momentum and fight all the fiercer for it. There were too many unanswerable questions, and none of her possible explanations satisfied them all.

Havorie had no choice but to go with a vague reference and hope Aldune would bite. "If Lord Ethan just wanted to stretch out his new body, I dare say a simple jaunt around the palace would have sufficed."

Aldune seemed to become dead sober at the mention of Lord Ethan's new body. He leaned over while rising in his seat, puffing out his chest to loom over Havorie. The baboon really was quite intimidating. "I don't know where you got your information," he snapped, spittle flying from his mouth, "but know this: Lord Ethan is on his deathbed, withering away in the east wing right now."

Havorie matched his posturing, attempting not to show any fear. "We both know very well that that is not true," she said.

Aldune leaned in even closer across the narrow table and continued in a rushed whisper. "It would behoove you not to make up stories. You never know who may be listening." He gestured over his shoulder with a tilt of his head towards where Damian was keeping watch on the other side of the wall. "Even queens can fall."

Havorie lashed out with an open hand and slapped Aldune across the face with a crack that silenced the room like a strike of lightning.

The threat was not subtle, nor was the stink of brandy on the general's breath. Aldune maintained his deathly stare as he rose to his feet. Without another word he turned away and exited the chamber.

The queen remained seated for a long moment after Aldune's departure, surprised by her own bravado. Whatever Lord Ethan and Aldune were up to, it was definitely serious. Havorie had never been so openly threatened—not by anyone! But if Aldune thought he could frighten her into submission, there was a nasty surprise coming his way.

The general hadn't divulged much. She still couldn't grasp why Lord Ethan would willingly lose the Minthune River— perhaps it was he who she should be levying treason charges against. It just didn't make any sense—Lord Ethan practically ran Phandrol—his life was at stake right beside hers if the kingdom were to fall. He had a good thing going here, so why would he want to let King Garrett encroach on that? It was like setting fire to his own house and then stepping back to watch it burn. People were going to die! All of Garrett's soldiers would bear down on Phandrol to exploit their weakness—locusts devouring a crop. The Kovani might even take Fort Bastion if they pushed hard enough, and that would be a huge tactical loss in the region.

All of Garrett's soldiers... the thought stirred something within Havorie. It would take much fighting for the Kovani to take the Minthune. Garrett would have to mobilize every available troop at his command to ensure his success. *That was it! Of course!* Havorie was surprised she didn't seen it sooner. Garrett would not be able to resist swarming the Minthune with everything he had—lowering his defenses as he made the offensive strike. He would be so distracted, his mind so swamped with battle plans, that he would not see what Lord Ethan had cooked up for him. The two strongest Ver'ati in all of Phandrol could very well be deep into Kovani territory by now. Havorie couldn't help but smile to herself at her keen deductions. It was the only plan that made sense— and a quite clever one at that, playing to Garrett's ego.

Havorie shuddered to think what would happen if Lord Ethan failed. This was an all-or-nothing ploy. At this point, Phandrol was already set to lose many soldiers—there was nothing she could do about that—but if Ethan failed, retaking the Minthune would be even more costly, and maybe even impossible. If all went well, though, King Garrett would be paying for the Crimson Waters with his own blood.

Lord Ethan was gambling with the future of Aragwey. Everyone would be affected by whatever happened next, and ultimately, there was nothing Havorie could do to change the outcome—not with her rule minimized as it was. Either Ethan would gain a great victory for Phandrol, or Garrett would expand his domain. The best she could do now was reclaim her rights as queen and get herself into a position to either prosper from Ethan's success, or, if it came to it, aid in the clean up after his devastating defeat.

Eventually, Damian poked his head around the corner into the reception chamber to see what was keeping Havorie so long. She gathered her wits and made her way back around the puddle of red wine. As Havorie departed the reception chamber, an oil painting against the wall caught her eye for the first time in years. It depicted a royal boar hunt—men on horseback following a pack of dogs through a clearing; long pikes holding a massive pig at bay amongst the brambles and hollowed out logs of the forest floor. The colors were drab, and the violent struggle of the boar had always been off-putting to Havorie. She must have passed it by at least a thousand times without ever really looking at it. What transfixed her now was not the painting itself, but the title etched into the tiny bronze plaque at the bottom of its frame. "The Hunting Grounds," it read. The same words her mother used for the location of the *baboon's* chest pounding.

The clues to deciphering Nestra's diary were all around her, hidden in the walls of her home and on the tongues of her subjects. Havorie just needed to start seeing things from her mother's perspective. If she looked hard enough, she knew she could identify the secret suitor—this *nightingale*—and bring him and anyone else who aided him to justice. She could not remain in the shadows, fearful of oppressors, if she was to truly be queen of these lands. Her first act after reclaiming her command would be to rout out the perpetrators of her mother's murder and rip the poison from these walls. Under the light of truth, and with the steel of justice, the *nightingale* would sing no more.

CHAPTER

27

The Key to Destruction

Javic wanted to give up. Severe fatigue and numbness flooded his muscles as the unbearable sting in his right palm brought a cold sweat to his brow. The twitching pain in his hand was the only sensation he was aware of over the icy grip that filled the rest of his body. The cold pressed in, biting down on him from the tips of his toes to the backs of his closed eyelids. He felt as if he had been fitted with frozen coins, placed over the eyes of the dead as payment to the gatekeepers of the afterlife.

Javic already passed through a gateway, but he was in far too much agony to be dead. Spirits didn't lie on their stomachs on the hard ground, matted in sticky blood, gasping for air whilst praying to Mast that somebody would happen by and save them from their despair. Every time Javic regained his breath, he began to cry out again for help, but after an hour or so of throat-tearing shouts, still nobody answered.

He wasn't in Sultrim any longer—thank Mast—but he wasn't where Cale sent him through the Gateway in the Underground either.   He was in a narrow alcove-like chamber—it appeared to be a storage area. Luminescent orbs in the dark stone hallway beyond spoke to the likelihood that he had returned somewhere in Erotos, and that the Gateway had simply been moved to wherever this place was. Like before, the portal rested atop a wooden pallet, but the black, shimmering sheet at the center of the Gateway that once rippled with an invisible breeze and infinite depth was no more—its magic extinguished by the destruction of its twin on the Sultrim side. It was just an ornately carved stone arch now.

Javic tried to stand up, but his body was completely wrecked; he couldn't even climb to his hands and knees, let alone his feet. He was beginning to think this narrow room would become his tomb when the murmur of distant voices brought him out of his stupor.

He cried out as loudly as he could until the fire in his hoarse throat became too intense and he was forced to cease. Listening intently, he found that the voices had stopped, but then a quick pattering of feet sounded from outside in the hallway. Javic cried out once more despite how it grated against his vocal cords. The footsteps—two pairs—sped up, his saviors converging towards his desperate call. The relief that poured over Javic, even before anyone appeared in the opening, was like warm water, seeping deep into his muscles to soothe his aches. It was as if he were finally awakening from a feverish nightmare, and only now could he begin to relax.

From around the corner of the hallway, Tannel Cresdale, head of the Arcanum Council, appeared with General Guther Aldune right on his heels. Both men wore confused expressions on their faces as they took in Javic's pitiful figure, sprawled out as he was across the floor.

"What the hell happened...?" Aldune began, but then froze as he eyed the faintly glowing Artifact core lying beside Javic.

Tannel moved past the core without taking notice and knelt his wide frame beside Javic. The councilman cupped Javic's head in his hands, and immediately the feebleness faded from his limbs. An energetic strength surged into Javic's body from out of Tannel's fingertips. It trickled through his veins, giving him a pins-and-needles sensation everywhere it wandered. The Power revitalized his worn out muscles, making him feel as if he could jump up and run circles around the room, but then his energy reverted back to a more normal level as the council leader retracted his touch. "People usually use that technique on horses, but that should help," said Tannel. "You should still see an Ameliorator about that hand."

Javic was able to sit up on his own, though every motion still sent twinges of pain from out of the cauterized hole in his right palm. By the time he got to his feet, Aldune had already scooped up the Artifact core and was gazing through its transparent, orange surface at the flakes of red suspended beneath. Javic had the sudden urge to reach out and snatch the core from the general's grasp, but he suppressed the inclination. Distrust for Aldune aside, an odd protective instinct had come over Javic—he nearly died retrieving the core. Seeing it in the hands of such an oaf brought a pinch of irritation to his already tight jaw. Aldune casually slipped the core beneath his jacket.

"What happened to you, boy?" asked Tannel, pulling Javic's attention away from Aldune.

Javic took a breath to settle his temperament. He knew the council leader by reputation only, but it was said that the well-established rivalry between the Arcanum and the Ver'konus was the result of Lord Ethan's distaste for Councilman Cresdale. Tannel was a former member of the Vestori, the sect of Ver'ati that initially bolstered their support behind Garrett Rames before his evil nature became apparent.

Garrett betrayed them all of course—corrupting most of the Vestori leadership into his first Goblikan Whunes during the Cleansing. Few Vestori survived that bloody war. Tannel was much too young to have lived through the Cleansing, but he did join the Vestori and learn from those battle-hardened old wizards before the reformation of the Arcanum in Erotos during Ethan's rise to power.

From what Javic gathered from Professor Lian's history lectures before his life was cut short by Laudry Hall sinking into the earth, the reformation of the Arcanum was fundamentally just a rebranding of the Vestori name, meant to strike out any negative connotations that may have lingered from their association with King Garrett.

Tannel had the highest seat of power within the Arcanum now, and as such, he was the only Ver'ati that could challenge Lord Ethan's claim over militaristic command in Phandrol. It made sense that Ethan would dislike such a rival, but Tannel didn't seem like such a bad guy to Javic. Of the two men standing before him, Tannel was the only one who bothered to help him just now—Aldune's attention had been locked up in examining the mysterious core.

"Lieutenant General Fisman sent me through the Gateway," said Javic, answering Tannel's question. He gestured at the stone arch. "It transported me to Sultrim."

Tannel quickly eyed the broken Gateway, mentally putting the pieces together. "Are you Rylin Gansly?"

Javic narrowed his eyes. Perhaps his optimistic judgment of Tannel's nature was a bit premature. If the councilman thought he was Rylin, the boy must have been sent through the portal after all. He had to wonder how aware the Arcanum was of Cale's *perfectly safe* mission.

"No," Aldune answered for Javic. "This is Javic Elensol, son of Kali Genavil. According to the records that were turned over to me when I returned this morning, he was reported dead nearly two weeks ago."

It took a second for Javic to comprehend his words. *Two weeks? That's impossible!* He rounded on Aldune. "But I was in Sultrim for less than an hour!"

"Curious," said Aldune, "a delayed transfer time." He glanced over at Tannel, but the councilman merely shrugged.

An image of the poor bled-out Archive Historian in Sultrim's Gateway chamber flashed across Javic's mind. He thought about telling Tannel what he'd seen, but his instincts told him the Arcanum was already well aware of the loss to the historians. Javic hoped the Gateway truly was broken for good—no one else deserved to die from a terrible schism, let alone the vicious claws and teeth of the Paerto'sul.

"Perhaps you can tell me a little more about your experience," said Tannel. "Did you see any Artifacts?"

Before he could answer, General Aldune grabbed hold of Javic's left sleeve and yanked him towards the alcove entrance. "It'll have to wait," he said. "The kid needs to see a doctor. I'll take him to Crane."

"Just a minute, now," said Tannel, grabbing Javic's other sleeve. "I already Invigorized him—he won't be expiring on the spot. There's no harm in answering a few questions first."

Javic was caught between the two men as they stared one another down.

"The boy is not Ver'ati yet," said Aldune. "The Arcanum has no claim over him." He pulled Javic a little closer.

Javic could clearly smell alcohol on the general's breath. For a moment, he was honestly torn between which of the overbearing men he wanted to win this little tug-of-war. His prior experience with Aldune was not pleasant, but Tannel was an unknown variable. It was obvious to Javic that Aldune didn't want him being questioned by Tannel—and if *questioning* was just another word for *interrogating,* Javic was glad to have Aldune on his side.

The Arcanum had a reputation of always getting the answers it sought, no matter how unsavory the means of procurement. While Javic didn't care to hide anything about his mission to

Sultrim on Cale's behalf, Tannel's awareness of Rylin's fate was enough to unnerve him. If the Arcanum sanctioned Cale's use of initiates, in Javic's mind that made them equally culpable for Rylin's demise. It might be in the Arcanum's best interest to cover up such an obvious disregard for the well-being of students. All it would take to close the matter permanently would be the fulfillment of Javic's already filed death report. He wanted to make like a gravel-hopper and get the hell out of there, but all he could do was wait for Tannel and Aldune to come to a decision.

"He is only an initiate," said Tannel. "The Ver'konus has no claim on him either until he is given a real rank. Now since we happen to be standing in a restricted section of the Archives, the boy falls under my jurisdiction."

Aldune appeared to be at a loss. The irritation was clear in his eyes, but after a moment of hesitation he released his grip on Javic's sleeve. The sly smirk that found its way onto Tannel's face made Javic shudder, sending another spike of pain up his right arm. Fortunately, Tannel had unwittingly provided him with a way out.

"Actually," said Javic, "Lieutenant General Fisman promoted me to corporal before I went through the Gateway."

Tannel's smirk faded instantly.

Aldune gave a chuckle. "A *real* rank. Looks like the boy's coming with me after all," he said, the smugness clear in his voice. "Good evening, Councilman Cresdale."

There was nothing Tannel could do as Aldune turned and departed from the alcove, dragging Javic along behind him. They had already taken half a dozen quick paces down the long corridor before Javic was able to pull his arm free of Aldune's grasp. The general let him go, allowing Javic to walk more dignified beside him as they navigated through the twisting connections of the Arcanum Archives.

Although Javic didn't look back, he could sense Tannel's angry glare piercing into him right up until the first turn in the hallway finally relieved him from the councilman's line of sight. Javic wondered what Aldune and Tannel were doing down here together, just the two of them, so deep in this maze of catacomb-like corridors. There was certainly no friendship motivating their meeting. Given the apparent vastness of the storage facility, it was a miracle that anyone happened by in time to stop Javic from succumbing to his wounds.

Every wall was lined with alcoves identical to the one Javic arrived in. Exposed wires connected a string of luminescent bulbs that ran the length of the corridor, shining out every ten to twelve paces. Some compartments were bare, but many contained Artifacts—never more than one relic per alcove, though. The Archives were well organized, unlike the cluttered mess of shelves that filled the halls of Sultrim. Every compartment was marked with a sequence of numbers and letters—a serial code for record keeping. The end of every corridor was labeled as well. The tunnel system containing the Gateway was marked *R39*. Restricted section number thirty-nine, Javic realized. Many more restricted tunnels lined the central walkway in both directions.

"Promoted to corporal?" Aldune asked once he was sure Tannel wouldn't be able to overhear them even if he had tuned his heightened Ver'ati senses in their direction. "Did you make that up?"

Javic shook his head. "A small reward for my troubles."

Aldune clasped him on the shoulder. "Well, good thinking bringing it up," he said, "it just saved your hide."

It was odd how kind the general was acting towards him, but it did not curb the anxiety tugging at Javic's thoughts. "What will happen with the core?" Javic asked, eying its outline beneath Aldune's jacket. "Why did you hide it?"

Aldune frowned. "I'll handle it," he said. "It'd be best if you forget all about that."

"I was nearly killed..." said Javic, "and Rylin... why did Cale—"

"Lieutenant General," Aldune growled, always one to harp on the etiquette of subordinates despite his personal lack of manners.

"Why did the lieutenant general send us—?"

"I'll handle Cale," Aldune interrupted again, waving his hand dismissively through the air. "The man's an idiot. It was a terrible judgment call sending you kids—albeit surprisingly effective... but that's over now. I'm running things around here again, so you don't have to worry about any of that. You report directly to me now."

Javic didn't think he liked the idea of reporting to Aldune very much, but knowing Cale was no longer in charge was definitely a relief. Javic opened his mouth to stubbornly ask what disciplinary actions would be taken against the lieutenant general, but another growl sounded in Aldune's throat.

"Have I not been clear? You are not to speak of any of this. Not ever. Not to anyone—I don't even want to hear it," he said. "Whatever happened in Sultrim stays there. Tannel will try to question you eventually. As far as he is concerned, you stepped through the Gateway, then came back immediately. There was no core; you've never even heard anything about any core; you saw nothing while you were there. Cale did not order you through—that was a lie—he showed you the Gateway for your studies and you became so overwhelmed with curiosity that you had to venture in. That's the whole story, and not a detail more."

It was an order, not a suggestion. Aldune did not wait for agreement from Javic before continuing on down the corridor. As far as the general was concerned, the conversation was over. Javic hustled along behind him, but already he found himself struggling to keep up. His legs were starting to feel heavy again, as if he were wading through a shallow pond with a muddy bottom. He could almost feel the imaginary silt sticking to his feet and ankles as sluggishness crept back into his muscles.

His stride faltered and he stumbled across the flat walkway, taking several staggering steps forward before he finally managed to recover. The boost of energy delivered to him by Tannel's touch was fading fast. Javic's pulse pounded in his head simply from the effort of walking—he knew it wouldn't be long before the strain grew too great and he would be forced to stop entirely. Aldune was pulling farther and farther ahead, forcing Javic to push his deteriorating body to its limit. After only a few more pained strides, Javic realized he wasn't going to make it.

"Wait," Javic cried out through panting breaths, but it was already too late. Javic watched helplessly as the edges of his vision began to grow dark. Everything seemed to slow down around him as a rush of warm blood flowed to his head. He tried to reach out and brace his arm against the wall to steady himself, but the signal from his brain never reached his limb. He felt his body tumbling forward as gravity took over, and was already unconscious before he hit the ground.

As his mind swam aimlessly across the void, he was not aware of General Aldune lifting him up, nor the remainder of their trek through the vast Archives. The waking world only peeked in on him twice: Once as Javic caught a glimpse of the masterfully painted, high-arched ceilings of the Arcanum Cathedral's entrance hall, and then again as he was placed down into the back of a rickshaw taxi and sent bumping along the Queen's Boulevard. His world was a confusing dome of spinning colors and sounds. He felt as if he were being pulled apart in all directions. The next thing Javic knew, he was resting on a padded table with a terribly bright light shining into his eyes and Doctor Hilven Crane's hooked nose staring down at him in a solemn frown.

Javic felt the room spin again as a burning sensation enveloped his right hand. It felt like poison creeping through his veins as the fire spread to his wrist and slowly slid up the length of his forearm to his elbow. From there, tiny bolts of lightning seemed to spark out in all directions. His muscles tensed painfully in a rapid twitch. Sweet relief finally came as a cooling sensation filled his right palm and the electric charges faded. Javic didn't need to look to know that his palm had been mended and all of his nerve endings reattached in their proper positions.

The inescapable pull of sleep lowered Javic's eyelids. His wounds may have been healed, but his body still needed to recuperate all of its lost energy. He felt like he could sleep for a year and still not be satisfied. Whispering voices caught his attention, but they mingled indistinguishably with the internal dialogue that was starting to flow through his mind. He could hear the laughter of his friends, telling animated stories that sounded like they were coming from somewhere off in the distance, another room, just beyond reach of his comprehension. Rylin's adolescent squeak, Thorin's low hum, his grandfather's raspy chuckle—it was all comforting, like returning home after a long day of chores to find a warm fire blazing and a hearty meal heating on the stove. The waking world once again faded away as a fog settled over his mind.

In his dream, he was home in Darrenfield. It was late autumn, in the evening, and a healthy breeze was flowing through the tall grass. Sounds of laughter came from a long table, set up outside in the field between the farmhouse and the pastures. A massive feast was laid out and all of Javic's friends were gathered around to enjoy the celebration.

The autumn harvest festival was underway, and the Elensol farm was somehow at its epicenter. The autumn-pole, usually placed outside the inn at the center of town, stood high at the other end of the field, its many-colored streamers dangling down into the hands of every boy and girl of the village as they danced in a clockwise circle, weaving their lines together. It was a tradition for the boys to attempt to entangle the streamers of their crushes while the girls giggled and avoided every one of the boys' best laid plans. Salvine was among the girls. Javic felt a deep twinge of sadness as he looked upon her. She smiled and twirled effortlessly, pulling her streamer high to slide free of a knot several of the younger boys inadvertently made with each other by running in the wrong direction.

At the beckoning of his friends, Javic turned back towards the long table. His eyes drifted across a glistening roasted pork dish and a large assortment of jellied garnishes. When he looked up again he found that all of the chairs were suddenly empty. All except for one. Mallory sat by herself at the end of the table with a welcoming smile on her face. Javic walked towards her, past the holiday spread, barely noticing the transition. Without a word, Mallory grabbed hold of his hand and ran with him over to the autumn-pole where they each took up a ribbon and joined the juvenile dance.

For once, his attention was not on Salvine as Mallory playfully looped her green streamer directly around Javic's body several times, wrapping him tightly with the soft silk. He let his own ribbon fall as his hands became tied to his sides. After a few more circles, Mallory stopped in front of him, her grin replaced with a misty-eyed expression that made Javic's stomach flutter with anticipation. He would have reached out to her if his arms weren't restricted, but he could only watch lustfully as her chest swelled, rising and falling with her quickening breath. He knew what she wanted—the thought alone made Javic shudder excitedly. She wrapped her arms around his neck, leaning in to kiss him. Oh how he longed for her embrace! She was so soft, so delectably sweet; he could hardly contain himself as her lips brushed ever so gently across his own.

Someone cleared their throat behind Javic, causing Mallory to pull away with a wide-eyed expression. Javic's heart dropped; they'd been caught! Surely it was Arlin, ready to fight him for Mallory's favor. The ribbon holding Javic in place vanished, along with Salvine and all of the village children, though he did not notice the disappearances.

He spun around, expecting to see the blond swordsman, clad in full armor with his steel drawn, but instead, he found Cale Fisman standing behind him. The middle-aged man looked haggard beyond his years. He had dark bags under his eyes as if he hadn't slept in weeks. His skin had turned pale and gray since the last time Javic saw him, and his forehead shined with a thick layer of grease which he dabbed at now with the sleeve of his wrinkled uniform.

"Sorry to interrupt," said the lieutenant general. "You looked like you were having a pretty good time there, but this can't wait until you wake. I must know, did you find the core?"

Javic was confused at first, his mind still wrapped up in the idea of Arlin catching him with Mallory. His nerves soon began to settle though, and as they did, Cale's words sparked memories within him. The world spun around the two of them, the air becoming cool as the autumn evening evaporated, turning into the perpetual darkness of the pathways of Sultrim. They stood now on the derelict suspension bridge, Calvenite flakes speckling the air in front of the light beam that was once again shining out from a glove on Javic's left hand. The tusk-shaped core was tucked down the front of his pants.

"Good! You did find it!" said Cale, the majority of the anxiety draining out of his face in an instant. The nearby roars of Raljaska and her cubs echoed across the wide cavern. Cale glanced around, apprehension already beginning to filter back into his expression, but he soon refocused on Javic. "What has become of the core?" he asked.

Another roar sounded. Javic knew they must run. "They're going to eat us!" he cried out the warning to Cale as he tried to make a dash for the Gateway chamber.

"Stop," Cale commanded, grabbing Javic's shoulder with a grip that he could not pull free from. "Tell me what has become of the core!"

"There's no time," said Javic, "Raljaska is nearly upon us!"

With a flash of fur, Cale was knocked to the ground by one of the bat-winged cubs flying straight into him from behind. He grunted in exacerbation. "Fine, take us from here," he said. "Think of when you came back." He had to shout now as a rumbling earthquake violently shook the bridge from side to side, nearly drowning out his words. "Did you still have the core with you?"

The rumbling faded away and the chimera cub vanished as the bridge wrapped around itself to form the tiny alcove in the Archives where Javic's rescue occurred. The events shifted naturally in Javic's mind as the memory began to replay.

Aldune and Tannel came running around the corner to find Javic in his desperate state of exhaustion. Cale's face drooped again as he watched the general pick up the core and slide it beneath his jacket. "This is quite unfortunate," said Cale. "General Aldune cannot be trusted. It is vital that we retrieve the core from him, or else everything will have been for naught." His voice became pleading. "You must go to him—earn his trust—it is the only chance we have! He will never let me close enough to find it."

As Javic stared back at Cale, a wave of alertness flowed through him—his conscious mind beginning to stir. Immediately, he became aware that he was dreaming. One realization led to the next as he took in Cale's amused expression—he couldn't say exactly why, but he was certain the lieutenant general was more than just a figment of his imagination.

"That's right," said Cale, catching the glimmer of understanding in Javic's eyes. "A physical meeting would have been too risky—both the Arcanum and Ver'konus are keeping a very close watch on you."

Cale must have been using the Crimson Stalker's brass spyglass—it was the only logical explanation. The Ver'konus confiscated the dream-walking Artifact from Belford when they first arrived in Erotos. It was supposed to have been delivered to the Archives for the Historians to study—the

Arcanum claimed ownership over all Artifacts—but clearly it had found its way into Cale's hands instead. The intellectual understanding of how Cale was in Javic's mind did not make him feel any less violated. If he couldn't count on his dreams for privacy, there was truly nowhere else he could retreat.

"Do you understand me, boy?" asked Cale. "You must find out where Aldune is keeping the core!"

Javic could have almost laughed. Trusting Cale over Aldune was like relying on a hungry wolf to lead him around a serpent's den—even if the wolf saved him from the snakes, the beast would still sink its own fangs into him in the end. Even so, Javic thought it best not to let Cale know just how uninterested he was in helping him—it would only make the situation that much more dangerous. "I understand," said Javic, trying to mask his true feelings, "but I doubt Aldune will ever trust me."

"Ah, but that is where you are wrong," said Cale. "He and your mother were close—closer than he lets on. You can use that to get him talking. Once you establish a rapport, tell him that Tannel told you the secret of the core, and then hint that he may intend to steal it for the Arcanum. After that, I am certain Aldune will check that it is still secure, either in the waking world or subconsciously in his sleep—either way, I will be waiting and watching. We can do this yet! I have faith in you, boy—you're very resourceful, just like your mother!"

The plan was as clever as it was devious—Javic could respect that, though every mention of his mother made him squirm a little inside. Normally, he loved hearing about Kali, but when Cale talked about her, it made him feel uneasy. Cale must have thought him naïve; it was obvious that he was trying to manipulate him. He decided to turn it back around and use Cale's desperation against him to finally get some answers. "There's just one problem," said Javic. "I don't actually know what the core does."

Cale studied Javic's face for a long moment before beginning a slow nod. "You're right," he said. "I must trust you with the truth if we are to be successful." His gaze wandered off as he contemplated his next words. "The core is a power supply. You've heard of the Orb of Parphim—the Artifact that ended the Cleansing with the formation of the Torus Desert? The orb was depleted during the event, but combining it with the core will make it whole again. I needn't explain to you how dangerous it would be for such a device to fall into the wrong hands. The Torus Desert was the result of just one burst of the orb's energy, but with the core, the orb can be recharged repeatedly. A warmonger like Aldune wouldn't be able to resist using it. He has admitted as much to me himself—!" Suddenly, Cale ratcheted his neck back to peer straight up into the air as if something troubling had caught his attention.

Javic glanced up as well, but could see nothing to warrant such scrutiny.

Cale continued scanning his nervous eyes all across the ceiling, only giving Javic half of his attention as he spoke again, this time with a more tentative tone. "Even directed at our enemies, the energy of a single blast from the reconstructed orb would still cause irreparable harm to Aragwey—it burns at Mast, ripping her soul out of the very stone we walk on, leaving behind wounds that fester and will never heal. How long can Mast bleed before she dies? When her essence is gone, the planet dies with her." Cale stopped watching the ceiling and focused back on Javic. He let out an audible sigh as he observed the incredulous expression on Javic's face. "I know it must look bad, the things I have done, sending you through the portal into such danger, but I really had no other choice, you must see that! The core was fabled to be in Sultrim, and with the Gateway recently recovered, I knew it was just a matter of time before somebody went looking for it. I needed to make sure that whoever found the core would be somebody like me—someone who would keep it safe, otherwise we are all damned."

As Cale finished, again his attention began to wander. He craned his head back once more, but this time, the distant sound of a door creaking open caught Javic's ear.

"I must go now," said Cale with haste. "Someone is coming…. Good luck, corporal. The free world is counting on you." And with that, Cale blinked out of existence, leaving Javic in a sea of emotional contortions. Cale placed the key to destruction in his lap, and now Javic needed to decide who could possibly be entrusted with such responsibility.

As his mind reeled, the dream-scape shifted with every new troubling thought that occurred to him. Everyone knew war was looming, though no one but Professor Vanton dared speak openly about such things. A visible tension had been steadily growing within the expressions of every military man and woman on campus since Javic first arrived in the Glowing City.

If the rumors of a Goblikan army amassing in the Torus Desert were true, that could only mean King Garrett planned to invade shortly. It was common knowledge amongst Ver'ati that Whunes did not have long lives—the bodies of the twisted could not hold out for much more than a year or two under such strain. Garrett would certainly make whatever move he was planning before they expired.

Javic thought about Lord Ethan and Belford. Even if their mission succeeded, the fate of the Goblikans was still uncertain. *Will the dark wizards be freed from Garrett's enslavement once the king is dead? Can they become human again, or are their minds twisted beyond concern for their master's mortality?* Javic's dream came crashing down around him. The walls of the little alcove became unstable, melting away and rushing back, leaving him in a void of emptiness. His consciousness was grappling for complete control over his body now, and the process was quickly rousing him awake.

Cale was right about Aldune; the general would surely use the Orb of Parphim against the Goblikans without hesitation. The orb might be their only chance at defeating the nightmarish horde if Garrett's demise didn't free them from their mental bonds. If the only other options were death or slavery at the hands of the Goblikans, the impact of the orb's energy on the environment didn't really seem like all that high a cost... as long as Cale was incorrect about the world actually dying as a consequence.

With a subtle shift, the void of nothingness that surrounded Javic turned into the backs of his eyelids. He could feel his body again. In his groggy state, he began moving his legs about, testing the snugness of the padded sheets that held him to the unfamiliar bed. The vividness of the dream remained in his waking mind as his heart thumped an uneasy beat. He immediately noticed an uncomfortable weight on his chest from some object sitting on top of him. It was difficult to open his eyes, but he forced them wide when he realized the object on his chest was moving.

A pair of yellow eyes flashed at him out of the darkness, only a hands-width away from his nose. Javic jumped nearly halfway out of the sheets before the tightly tucked blankets pulled him back down against the mattress with a bounce. The creature flew up into the air as well, screeching like some sort of demon before landing back down hard on Javic's chest with four pointy paws. It scampered off the bed, across the room and out the door before Javic could even comprehend what was going on. If his heart hadn't been beating fast before, it certainly was now.

A series of quick footsteps sounded from the hallway beyond the half-opened door. Javic couldn't see much—it was night—but a little bit of light did filter in through the window from the streetlamps outside. He was just barely able to make out the silhouette of a person as they moved into the doorway, forming a slightly denser void of darkness than the empty air around them. A hand began to fumble along the inside of the wall for the small switch that Javic knew would fill the room with intense light. He was already used to the idea of the luminescent bulbs and their ability to cast such brilliance in an instant, but the shine was still disorienting to Javic's eyes as the room became flooded by the concentrated glow.

"You're awake!" exclaimed the melodic voice of Mallory Worvon. "You scared poor Buttercup nearly half to death—he came running out like the room was on fire."

Javic's heart swelled at the sound of her words. Never before had he heard such welcoming tones. A long absent feeling of being home filled his lungs, stinging like cold air in his chest as he breathed in. The rising emotion brought moisture to his eyes, but for once, he was unabashed by his tears—they were tears of relief. He had to blink several times to clear the sleep from his eyes before he could see straight, but finally he was able to take in the welcome sight that stood before him. Mallory was dressed in a loose fitting, slightly sheer, red and black nightgown that cut off midway up her exposed thigh. Javic's heart thumped a few extra beats as his eyes slid across her body. He was so enthralled that he almost didn't notice the extremely agitated tan and white cat in her arms until it made an angry howl-like meow.

Buttercup was far too cheerful a name for the disgruntled little fellow. He had a notch missing from his left ear, knots in the fur around his face, and a kink two-thirds of the way down his bushy tail.

"I adopted him," said Mallory, "or more accurately, he adopted me."

Buttercup glared across the room at Javic with unblinking eyes—the cat knew exactly who was to blame for his unpleasant flight. The long-haired feline wriggled around in Mallory's arms until she gave up trying to hold onto him and placed him back down on the floor. He shot Javic one last look of disgust before trotting out of the room.

"How's your fever?" Mallory asked.

Now that she mentioned it, Javic's head was feeling a bit hot. His whole body was covered in a thin layer of sweat, though, which meant he was starting to regulate his heat properly again. "Not too bad," he said as he scooted the rest of the way out of the blankets to cool off.

To his chagrin, he found that he had been stripped down to his underwear, and that the underwear he was currently wearing was a different pair from the one he had on before. His face reddened at the thought of Mallory seeing him naked. He hoped the flush of his fever covered up the embarrassment forming in his cheeks, but the small smile that appeared on Mallory's lips indicated that it had not. Javic wanted to bury his head back under the blankets and never come out.

Mallory had a way of making him felt like a novice bumbling around with his master's tools. The last time Javic saw Mallory, her fine brown hair had been shaggy and grown out from the months of travel she spent on the road with Arlin. It felt like just that morning she and Elric were waiting beside Candeer Fountain to celebrate the completion of his proficiency test. He regretted avoiding them that day. Mallory's hair was cut short now—it would have fallen just shy of her shoulders had it not been tied up into a high ponytail on the back of her head. New side-swept bangs flowed across her forehead as well, separated out from the rest of her hair by a band of dark-blue cloth.

"You changed your hair," said Javic in an attempt at small talk—anything to avoid thinking about her seeing him naked.

Mallory's large chocolate eyes instantly became puffy as tears started to stream down her cheeks.

Javic's mind raced frantically, trying to determine what he could have possibly said wrong. "No, I like your new hair, it's very pretty!"

Mallory rushed across the room and wrapped her arms around Javic's shoulders, holding onto him just like she had in his dream, but instead of kissing him, she sobbed into the nook of his neck. "They told me you were dead…" she said, squeezing onto him even tighter.

Javic held her, caressing the back of her head and neck with his fully healed right hand—only a slight scar remained to mark the spot where the energy beam tore through his flesh in Sultrim. His whole body tingled with heightened awareness under Mallory's embrace. This was where he belonged—he felt at peace with her in his arms. The subtle aroma of lilac filled her hair, flirting with his nostrils as he pressed his face against the side of her head. Javic continued to hold onto Mallory until she pulled away on her own and brushed the tears from her eyes with the backs of her hands.

"I'm sorry," she said. "I should have told you immediately." The look of sadness on Mallory's face deepened. "It's Elric… he's gone…." Again, her eyes began to well with moisture.

Javic froze in place, his whole body filling with dread. *Gone? As in dead?* He didn't want to jump to any conclusions, but his mind immediately wandered to every dark place imaginable. *Was there an accident? An Echo? Grandfather wasn't so old as to be taken by old age yet, was he?* When Javic was little, he always assumed Elric would be with him forever. He was no longer under such illusions, but the thought of never seeing his grandfather again still tied his stomach up in knots. He had been so callous, throwing out every letter he received from Elric while he was in the dormitories. He was just so damn furious about not getting to go along with Belford and the others on the Rosa Marsa. As unwelcome as his grandfather's meddling was, he knew Elric was only trying to keep him safe. If Javic's childish temper was the last memory his grandfather ever had of him, he didn't think he would be able to forgive himself.

"Oh, no!" said Mallory, reading Javic's expression. "Not like that! I mean he left the city!" Mallory cringed at the cruelty of her misleading words.

"What happened?" Javic asked, still on edge.

"I'm so sorry. I didn't mean to scare you like that," she said. "It was after they told us you were dead. Elric became very distraught. I knew he was taking it hard, but there was nothing I could do. The day after your exam, I went to see him, and he was already gone—left the city on horseback. Didn't even check out of the Hotel Willows or take half of his belongings with him—just up and left."

Javic swung his legs over the side of the bed. He needed to find his grandfather right away—to let Elric know he was alright—but Mallory stood in front of him and stopped him from getting to his feet. Javic tried to move her aside, but her eyebrows lowered into a stern frown and she reached out and pushed Javic back down into the blankets with unexpected ferocity.

"Where do you think you're going?" she demanded. All signs of her tears were completely gone. "It's the middle of the night and you need your rest!"

"I need to find him!" said Javic, starting to rise again.

Mallory pushed him back down to the bed a second time, this time climbing on top of him and straddling him between her thighs so that he couldn't make a third attempt. She was considerably stronger than she appeared. "Running out of here right now in your underwear isn't going to help anything," she said. "Elric left two full weeks ago. He could be over a hundred leagues from here by now. You don't even know which direction he was headed."

Javic felt foolish. Mallory was right of course; it had been a purely emotional impulse. Figuring out where Elric went was going to take time. Javic would need to recruit help, and he wasn't going to find anyone in the middle of the night. He let out a sigh of defeat. Despite it all, he still felt like he should be doing something.

"Will you rest?" Mallory asked, hesitant to release Javic.

Perhaps that was all he could do—bide his time and regain his energy while he concocted a real plan. Lying beneath Mallory, he couldn't help but notice how warm her caramel skin felt against his own. As much as he actually enjoyed having her so close, he nodded quickly, agreeing to cease his struggle so that she would get off. He was ashamed to admit it, even to himself, but worry for his grandfather was quickly being replaced within his mind by a growing arousal. With how little they both were wearing, he knew that in just a few more seconds things would become extremely awkward if Mallory didn't remove her bare thighs from his waist and let him shimmy back under the blankets. The physical manifestation of his arousal would soon be pressing up against Mallory's inner-thigh in an entirely inglorious and unsubtle way.

When it came to Javic's feelings for Mallory, it was as if there was a magnetic pull over him that he could not turn away from. She was a real woman, radiant and strong, but still ever so soft to the touch. Now more than ever she had a certain glow about her that made her tantalizingly attractive.

As Mallory slid off of Javic, he was pretty sure she recognized the excitement budding inside him. He wanted to withdraw into a cocoon until his embarrassment faded, but he knew if Mallory was ever to start seeing him as a man, he needed to stop acting like a little boy. He wondered what Arlin would do in a situation like this.

"I really missed you," he said to her. He wasn't sure what he was going to say next until the unfiltered words poured out of him. "Will you stay with me tonight?" He instantly regretted opening his mouth. It was as if someone braver than he had taken over his body for a moment. Javic had never been so forward before; it gave him a sick feeling in his stomach. Now that the words were out, he couldn't take them back, so he just held his breath as he waited for her response.

Mallory stood silently, rubbing her lower back as her eyes wandered across the empty wall behind Javic. "I set up a spot for myself out on the sofa," she said, still avoiding his eyes.

Javic hadn't realized she gave up her own bed for his recovery. It only made his feelings for her that much stronger. He slid beneath the covers and scooted over far enough for her to climb into the bed beside him if she wanted. Mallory remained hesitant for a moment longer, but then she walked away from Javic without another word and turned out the bedroom light. Javic was disappointed, but not the least bit surprised.

I really messed things up this time.... Of course Mallory doesn't want to stay in the bed with me—she's still Arlin's, even if he is half a kingdom away.

What hurt most was the knowledge that if his and Arlin's roles were reversed, Javic would never have left Mallory behind to go on some king's errand. Javic would have stayed with Mallory, and no prospect of revenge or personal glory could have ever pulled him away. Arlin didn't appreciate what he had. Javic couldn't think of anything that would make leaving Mallory's side worthwhile, even for a moment.

He had to mask his intense shock as the bed springs compressed beside him and he felt Mallory's warm body snuggle up against him, her back touching his side. Javic turned to face her, placing his right hand against the curve of her hip. He moved without thinking, before fear of rejection could undermine his impulses. He still couldn't believe his own boldness as he dragged his fingers across her thigh and didn't stop even as he reached the edge of her nightgown. His heart was pounding with a mixture of absolute terror and optimistic exhilaration. Moving slowly, one finger at a time, he slid farther and farther into uncharted territory.

He didn't know what had come over him, but the fact that Mallory still hadn't pushed his hand away made his heart flutter even more wildly. Eventually, his fingertips brushed up against the short hairs of her pubic region. His heart was pounding. She breathed in sharply and her legs tightened together into an impenetrable gate. Javic's hand froze in place, all of his fears and doubts crashed down upon him.

What was I thinking? I'm such an idiot... Mallory doesn't want me. I've gone too far.

Javic quickly retracted his hand as Mallory rolled over to face him. He was half-expecting her to slap him, but instead, she leaned in and gave him a slow, tender kiss right on his lips. Javic could have floated away. He wanted nothing more than to continue kissing her, but she pulled back and laid her head down on her pillow.

At the same time, Buttercup, with a loud meow, jumped onto the foot of the bed and walked between them. The strange cat locked its yellow eyes onto Javic as it curled up against them both. Javic hadn't expected the kiss; he could still feel the lingering sensation of those angelic lips against his…. It was his first real kiss…! *It really happened!* It was wetter than he imagined… *but still good! But what does it mean?* The question snuck in like weeds in a barley field. *Is she inviting me for something more?*

He knew he was overthinking things. He just needed to let everything happen as it would. With a final sense of abandon, he began to lean over the top of Buttercup, intent on stealing a second kiss, but the cat made a low growl and Mallory scooted slightly farther away to give the tan feline more space. Mallory remained facing Javic, but her eyes were closed now as her head sunk deeper into the pillow. Javic was still trying to calculate his next move when it became clear that she had already drifted off to sleep.

Her steady breaths taunted him; she was so close, and yet so far away. For well over an hour, Javic watched Mallory and the bothersome cat sleep. Javic's mind was far too full of unanswered questions to allow him to retreat into his dreams. Eventually, though, the exhaustion of the day's ordeal caught up with him, and not even the uncertainty of his future with Mallory or the unknown whereabouts of his grandfather could stop his body from settling down for some much needed rest.

CHAPTER

28

Necrotic

Doctor Crane's revenge for the death of his assistant was both brutal and merciless. If it hadn't been directed at her, she would have admired the sadistic pleasure he took in inflicting his torment.

The Whune's bones were painfully broken and reshaped; her mind prodded and tweaked. Since the doctor's last meddling, she was now constantly tired and actually needed to sleep.

Whunes weren't supposed to sleep!

He was making her weak, like a human.

There was little rest to be found while hanging from her restraints, however. The pain in her arms consumed her. Her hands felt like lead-filled sacks, her appendages useless slabs of meat wrenched above her head; dead weight. The only thing worse than the pain of her bloodless limbs was the sensation when the doctor released the restraints in order to conduct his experiments. That was when all the blood rushed back in with a swift torrent—ice shattering in her veins.

Despite her exhaustion, she had never actually experienced sleep before, but she knew the vulnerable state would eventually overtake her. Her eyes were sluggish and her head gave a woozy throb every time she shifted her neck too quickly. Every minute was a struggle between the pain and fatigue.

"This one's not looking too good," said Doctor Crane's new assistant. The young Ver'ati that cleaned up the previous assistant's remains was gesturing in her direction

Her head spun as she shifted her gaze upon him.

"I don't pay you to make observations, only to clean up and help me restock," said Doctor Crane.

"You don't pay me at all," said the assistant, frowning, "the Ver'konus does."

Doctor Crane rolled his eyes.

"No really, look here," said the assistant. "The flesh on its hands and wrists is starting to look necrotic—lack of blood flow."

The presence in the back of her mind perked up at the assistant's words. It had been lying dormant for quite some time now. It couldn't stand the pain either, and so retreated away from the conscious portion of her mind.

"If you keep it strapped up like this, you'll have to amputate soon."

Doctor Crane approached her cage, his hooked nose seeming to deepen the lines of his scowl as he observed her dying flesh. "Amputations can be fun," said the doctor. His face showed no hint of emotion.

"You should really take better care of them," said the assistant. "You only have three left, and there's still so much we can learn. Who knows when, if ever, we will get a chance to study Whunes up close like this again?"

Doctor Crane merely shrugged. "I don't tell you how to do your job, so how about you don't tell me how to do mine."

The assistant gave a slow blink. "But you always tell me how to do my—"

"—I know," the doctor interrupted, "because I'm your superior in every way." He dismissed his assistant with a wave of his hand. The young Ver'ati left the chamber with his face held in a tight pinch.

As soon as his assistant was gone, Doctor Crane turned towards her. "I didn't want to give the little bastard the satisfaction, but he's right," he said. "Your hands are already halfway rotted off." He chuckled slightly and shook his head. "Honestly, I was curious to see how long it would take."

He wants *us to lose our arms...!* The presence in her mind was on the verge of hysterics.

Several drops of moisture coalesced in the corners of her puffy eyes. The realization hit her in a strange wave of emotion at the center of her chest. She knew cruelty—inflicted it upon others as often as possible—but never had it been directed towards her in such an extraordinary manner. She was fond of her arms. They helped her kill things. They made her useful.

The doctor was staring into her face. He made a curious click with his tongue before turning away and walking over to one of the cabinets. He continued to speak to her. "I have been attempting to increase your higher brain function recently, though I doubt your brutish mind will have noticed the difference yet. Even so, perhaps you can understand this: I've been hurting you as punishment for knocking your cage over onto that boy. He was a good assistant. Didn't talk back. I am punishing you because you defy me. You need to learn who gives the orders around here. Perhaps you have already learned."

The doctor turned back towards her, the hook implement that could undo her restraints now in the palm of his hand. He approached her cage once more.

"I could let your arms die, rot off, and kill you, or cut them off before they take your life. Without your arms you would certainly understand who owns you." His eyes held no remorse. "But you are more useful to me whole. At least for the time being." He slipped the metal hook between the bars and poked the pointed end through the ring at the end of the first strap. He tugged it towards him, releasing her right hand.

Her arm flopped to her side like a sack of rocks. She howled as the pain brought more moisture to her eyes. The blood flowed back into her stiff limb with the sting of a thousand needles. It burned like fire, aching as if the doctor severed it.

Doctor Crane made his way around to the other side of her cage. "You are going to be an obedient little dog, aren't you?" He used the hook to release her other arm.

The claw hidden beneath the bandages on her left index finger stayed in place as her arm fell against her body.

She wanted to slam into the side of her cage and crush Doctor Crane the same way she killed his assistant, but she knew she must remain composed. She didn't need the voice inside her head to tell her that this was the moment they were waiting for. With her arms released, her freedom was imminent.

"Remember what a nice thing I've done for you today," said the doctor, "letting you keep your arms."

Oh, you have no idea. There was fire in the silent voice.

She couldn't lift her arms yet, but the blood would revitalize her limbs with little time. Whunes healed fast. Doctor Crane hadn't taken that gift from her yet. As soon as she was alone, she would allow the presence to take control. Together, they would pick the lock and finally escape.

But then what? She hadn't really reasoned out what to do after breaking free of the cage. Maybe it was Doctor Crane's alterations to her higher brain function that got her thinking, but she was starting to realize that escaping the cage was very different from actually being free.

After we get out, we'll go find Javic. The voice chimed in. *He'll know what to do—keep us safe.* The presence was more enthusiastic than ever.

She wasn't so sure about that part of the plan. She had no interest in seeking out Javic. *Why would he help a Whune? We are just another monster to him.*

The presence did not share any of her skepticism. *You do know I was a girl before all of this, don't you? My name was Salvine, and Javic and I....* Emotion was welling up within the presence.

In truth, she didn't know much of anything about Salvine or who she was before her master changed her. She never really thought about it or cared. She was as aware of her life before becoming a Whune as much as a butterfly remembered being a caterpillar. They were the same entity, but somewhere along the line they'd been turned into soup and reformulated into something new.

He'll recognize the dove charm and know it's me. The silver chain was still clasped tight around her wrist. *He'll know it's me. He has to. We... we love each other.*

Love...? Even with the influx of new emotions floating around inside her head, love was still too foreign of a concept for her to comprehend.

Salvine pondered the inquiry for a moment before responding. *It's kind of like the way you felt for Wilgoblikan. You would do anything for him. Love doesn't just go away. Javic will figure out how to save us. He'll make everything better.*

It made a little more sense now, but she would still have to take Salvine's word for it. Regardless of Javic's feelings, there was one problem with the plan as far as she was concerned. It was a thought that she needed to keep locked away from Salvine: Even if Javic did help her, he would want to turn her into a human. If he had his way, he would kill her, and leave Salvine in control. That was something she simply could not allow to happen. She was a Whune, and she intended to stay that way.

She would let Salvine think she was going along with the plan, but when she got the chance, she would take back control permanently. She would be the Whune she was always meant to be, killing everything that stood in her way. Salvine was right about one thing—she would do anything for her master, alive or dead. She knew what he would want from her: Find the boy with the Mark of Kings, and kill him, once and for all. Complete Wilgoblikan's mission, with or without him.

Cloudburst

Javic raised the hood of his tattered cloak and pulled the fringes in tight around him like a blanket to insulate his body from the rain. In all his years, he had never seen a downpour quite like the cloudburst that opened up over the streets of Erotos that morning. The paved roads flowed like rivers, causing the passing carriages to send off sprays of water from their wheels that shot up high into the air. Everyone unfortunate enough to be caught out on foot moved with a brisk pace between the storefront awnings that redirected the rainfall away from their heads. The water ran off the overhangs, splashing down at the edge of the sidewalk, but there were still many gaps in the network of canopies through which sheets of thick runoff descended like waterfalls. The sky was a densely dark shade of gray. The clouds moved in low, nearly obscuring the spire-topped towers of the Queen's Palace on the other side of the Etwel River in the Old City.

The stable boys at the Hotel Willows—where Elric had been staying at the north end of the west city—were very helpful in tracking his grandfather's initial direction of departure. They saw Elric load several hefty bags onto each of the two packhorses that came to Erotos towing Shiara and Thorin's blue wagon, and then saddle up a third horse for himself. Set for a long journey, he rode out due west towards Nesbern instead of taking the road north, which would have been the most direct path for returning to Darrenfield if that was what he intended.

It appeared Elric was not headed home.

Javic couldn't think of any destination that made sense given the reported course. As far as Javic was aware, Elric had no friends in Antara. The thought of his grandfather out there all alone on the road, emotionally lost and broken, redoubled Javic's guilt over avoiding him on the day of his proficiency exam. He had a terrible feeling that his presence in his grandfather's life was the only thing tethering Elric to these lands—his grandfather had already lost so much. The grief and despair Javic experienced after losing Rylin was large, but nothing compared to what Elric must have suffered after receiving news of Javic's death—Javic was the only family Elric had left.

The chimes of a great bell somewhere off in the distance indicated that it was already midday. Apart from now knowing his grandfather's general direction of travel, he was still no closer to actually finding him. Unfortunately, Javic slept most of the morning away. He was already behind in the schedule he made for himself in his head. He hoped to have located and hired a tracker by now so that there would be enough time remaining in the day to gather supplies and head out before nightfall, but that was beginning to look increasingly improbable. With the winds picking up and the rain starting to blow sideways, it was unlikely anyone would be willing to head out until the weather cleared up, but that did not make Javic any less anxious to get going.

The Amelioration he underwent the previous night had taken a lot out of him, but after resting until late into the morning, he now had plenty of energy to devote towards worrying again—not that he ever really stopped. This city had a way of keeping him on edge. He never managed to bury the uneasy feelings entirely; it was becoming an incessant habit for Javic to chew on his fingernails whenever the anxiety started to build.

He remained in a deep sleep throughout the night and morning until the sounds of the rainstorm pelting hard against the country-style tin roof of Mallory's apartment roused him from bed. The Blue Fox Inn, where Mallory had taken up residence, was a fairly upscale establishment, situated just across the Etwel River from the palace.

Mallory was already gone when he awoke, her pillow commandeered by Buttercup, curled up in the indentation left behind by her head. The cat was glaring at Javic even before he looked over at the feline; such judgmental yellow eyes, mocking his romantic failures. Buttercup gave one slow, dismissive blink and then began to lick himself.

The new found confidence he inexplicably came by the night before had abandoned him to the pit of worry he was becoming so accustom to. It slowly deepened in his abdomen as the morning progressed. His nails tasted bitter from the cake of Calvenite dust still encrusted beneath the jagged ends. He found himself biting at his cuticles instead in an attempt to avoid the acerbic flavor. Javic could only attribute last night's uncharacteristic boldness to his exhaustion. The part of his mind that held concern for the consequences of his actions must have shut down first as his body surrendered to fatigue. At this point, he had no idea whether he utterly destroyed his friendship with Mallory, or if he miraculously transformed it into something greater.

It was difficult to think through the events of the previous night. Ever since stepping through the Gateway the first time in the Erotos Underground, many of Javic's memories felt unsolid—separated from time and space as if he were recounting a dream.

Mallory kissed me! That much he remembered clearly.

Just the thought of her soft lips brought an excited tingle to his stomach. Her smooth hips—rolling his hand slowly up her thigh—he reveled in the memory, though at the same time fretfully wished he could take his actions back. *What does she think of me now?* If his touch was unwelcome, he had vastly overstepped his bounds in a severely irrevocable way. But then again, she did kiss him.... He was eager to see Mallory, but also glad to have some time to formulate his thoughts first.

The state of physical weakness he was in last night, drifting in an out of sleep, made him question the authenticity of some of his other memories. It was difficult to sort out the real from the imagined; even defining what *real* meant was proving to be difficult when he considered Cale and the brass spyglass.

He was so sure in his dream that Cale was actually there, but even that was an uncertainty now. Perhaps the whole meeting was just a figment of his overactive imagination—recovery after Amelioration was known to occasionally have strange effects on the mind. He had undergone so much emotional and physical trauma in the past few days that if somebody told him that everything he experienced was just some elaborate fever dream, he would gladly accept the explanation. Only the scar at the center of his right palm proved irrefutably that at least his memories of Sultrim actually occurred.

Assuming his dream-conversation with Cale was real as well, there was still the problem of deciding who could be entrusted with the Orb of Parphim—and ultimately the future of Aragwey.... As small as his personal troubles should have been in comparison to something like that, Javic's utmost concern right now was locating his grandfather. Worry over what would become of his relationship with Mallory was a not-too-distant second in his thoughts. Everything else from

Aldune and Councilman Cresdale to Cale and the Orb of Parphim was peripheral. Each added to the pressure he was facing, but he could only focus on one thing at a time. Until he knew everything was alright with his grandfather, he had no hope of concentrating adequately on anything else—that was the excuse he told himself, anyway, to stop the guilt of ignoring the greater good of the nation from creeping in too heavily.

A streak of lightning flashed across the sky directly overhead, its crackling roar sounding concurrently with its display. A second flash, just as close, soon followed. Within a matter of seconds, everyone still braving the elements hastily cleared the street. A shift of the wind brought the subtle scent of ozone to Javic's nostrils.

Determined to reach the western gate, he ignored the obvious signs of danger. If the stable boys from the Hotel Willows were accurate, Javic could be confident Elric passed through the west gate. The guards stationed there might be able to give him a better idea of Elric's whereabouts—they routinely queried travelers as to their intended destinations. It was altogether odd that Elric would go west; it was possible that the stable boys just made up the story to coax a few extra marks out of Javic's pocket, but their descriptions of the horses Elric took with him were accurate enough.

With the street suddenly clear of all its usual traffic, Javic soon realized he was being followed by two separate tails. First, a pair of black-robed Ver'konus soldiers bumbled along behind him about half a block back, matching his every move. Javic recognized the men as the same duo that followed him around campus for several days after the Rosa Marsa first departed without him. Another half a block behind them was a less conspicuous second tail. A solitary man dressed in civilian garb progressed down the opposite side of the street, undeterred by the weather—an agent of the Arcanum if Javic had to reckon a guess. He looked to be keeping an eye on the Ver'konus pair as much as he was watching Javic. Both tails maintained their distance, content with merely hanging back and observing for the time being.

Javic quickened his pace as another lightning bolt crackled across the sky—he could see no reason for making their jobs any easier. He turned a corner and was stepping briskly past a tavern when a pair of calloused hands reached out and pulled him in through the open doorway. He was so focused on the men behind him that he completely forgot to pay equal care to the rest of his surroundings.

"Are you mad?!" asked the slender, wild-haired man to whom the hands belonged. He was in his late thirties to early forties by the looks of him. His scruffy beard was overgrown even for an adventurer, which, from his tattered, windblown cloak and dirt stained trousers, he appeared to be. Wearing a suit of dark-ringed chainmail beneath a soiled, cotton over-shirt, he smelled in great need of a bath. His skin was darkened by a combination of sun and a thick layer of grime, accumulated over a long period of travel; he looked to have spent more days on the road than off. "Get in here," he said. "One bolt could strike you dead!"

Javic let his fears of being attacked subside as he glanced around the bar and saw a multitude of other displaced city folk, all hunkered down at the various tables to wait out the storm. "I have urgent business to attend to," said Javic, turning to leave again.

"That's no ordinary storm out there, boy. It didn't just blow in overnight—it formed right on top of us!"

An Echo… of course… yet another delay….

"Best to remain indoors until it passes," he said, moving his left hand to the hilt of the sword strapped across his chest.

At first, Javic perceived the gesture as a show of force, but the scabbard was angled for the blade to be drawn with the right hand, not the left. The man rested his left palm on the nub end of the grip in a habitual fashion. With Javic's eye drawn to the hilt, he noticed an opal peeking out from between the blood-red wrappings. It glinted ever so faintly in the dull glow of the tavern's solitary light bulb, shining down from above the bar.

Javic had seen a sword just like this before—curiously, it appeared to be a twin to Arlin's blade, though Arlin's wrappings were black, not red. There were deeper wear marks across the stranger's wrappings as well, etched into the cloth by a consistent finger placement over the years.

"You're being followed," the man said in a low voice, shifting his weight to his toes so that he was ready to spring out in any direction if the moment called for it. His subtle change in stance probably would have gone unnoticed by Javic if it hadn't been for the small amount of weapons training Thorin, Arlin, and his grandfather put him through on the road south to Phandrol.

Javic rotated around just far enough to use his peripheral vision to confirm that the two Ver'konus soldiers from outside had entered the tavern behind him. They were both dripping wet and had frowns etched into their faces. "Don't worry about them," said Javic, "they won't do anything."

Despite Javic's dismissal of the situation, the stranger's tension did not diminish.

"Your blade," said Javic, "the gem in the hilt, I've seen a sword like that before."

The man cocked his head, a skeptical look appearing in his narrowed eyes. "Another Talus Shard? Doubtful. There are only thirty-seven living blade-brothers and sisters who have earned the right to carry such an armament, and out of those, only a dozen or so have stepped foot outside of the Elswani Monastery in the better part of the last decade."

Blade-brothers... the Elswani Monastery.... "You're a Guardian of Truth!" Javic exclaimed. He had read about such warriors in his books—bound by honor to protect the Ek'radam monks with their lives. He heard several stories about them from his grandfather as well, but it had been years since the last time Elric recounted any of those tales. The Guardians played a pivotal role in many of the early battles that shaped Aragwey into the nation it was today. The Order of the Blade gradually diminished over the years, though; it was no longer the vast army of peacekeepers it had once been.

Javic never thought he would actually meet a blade-brother—they had always just been the subject of stories to him, like Ver'ati and Whunes up until about two months ago. *Did the opal mean Arlin was a blade-brother as well? He certainly was a worthy talent with the sword.*

"Paerto'radam," said the man, nodding in affirmation. "The name's Orris Fen, at your service."

"Javic Elensol," said Javic, in awe as he shook Orris's hand.

Orris's grip tightened as Javic said his name, a bemused expression appearing on his lips. "Elensol…? I know that name…. Any relation to a… Bartimus? Bartly?"

"Bartan," said Javic. "My father."

"That's the one!" Orris gave a wide grin. "I knew him, long ago—trained with him." He clasped his palm down on Javic's shoulder. "I don't think Bartan was much older than you are today, but I must say he was devilishly skilled. A pity he dropped out; would have made a fine brother. Is he here with you in the city?"

"No," said Javic, "he died when I was two years old." Elric never mentioned his father training with the Guardians of Truth.

The grin left Orris's face in an instant. "I'm so sorry," he said. "Forgive me for bringing up such things." His tone was so sympathetic that it almost made Javic feel as if the wound of never knowing his father was still fresh.

The sadness that bubbled up to the surface was not for Bartan though, he realized, but for his grandfather—everyone Elric ever loved had been ripped violently from him. "Did you know my grandfather, Elric Elensol, as well?" Javic asked.

"Your father's father? Yes, I recall the man," said Orris. "He and Bartan came to the monastery together, but your grandfather trained under a different master than Bartan and

I." Orris must have recognized the gloom spreading across Javic's face. "Has something happened? I can see a weight behind your eyes."

Javic looked away. He didn't like people seeing into him like that, he was just so emotionally vulnerable right now. Elric had kept much from him.

Across the room, the Ver'konus soldiers were watching Orris just as intently as Javic. Given the sensitivity of the situation with the Orb of Parphim, General Aldune probably hadn't even told the two men why Javic needed watching. They maintained a healthy level of suspicion and alertness as they looked upon him. From the expressions on their faces, Javic knew, without a doubt, that neither the Ver'konus nor the Arcanum would be allowing him to leave the city to track down his grandfather any time soon. He knew far too much, and they wanted to keep him close. Javic supposed he should be grateful Aldune opted to have him watched rather than coming up with a more *permanent* solution to keeping him quiet.

As if on cue, the low rumble of a distant explosion sounded from somewhere out in the city. The crash echoed back and forth off the buildings outside, masking its true direction. Half a second later, the glowing bulb that lit the bar flickered one last time and then flashed bright white with a shower of sparks inside its glass casing before going dark.

The whole tavern was plunged into shadow. The patrons all gasped at once as the light abandoned them. At first, everything remained still, but then a scuffle broke out near the tavern's door. A gurgling sound was followed by a series of pained grunts and a thump as someone collapsed to the floor. Javic could just barely distinguish the outline of Orris Fen as he unsheathed his sword and moved quickly in the direction of the disturbance. Confusion from the light going out was combined with cries of fear from the patrons as metal rang against metal. Javic fell back against the bar and ducked low, keeping himself as small a target as possible in case a wild swing should bring a blade in his direction.

Javic didn't believe in coincidences anymore: He assumed this attack was aimed at him. To remain elusive, he dropped to the floor and crawled across the sticky ground, through spilled drink and food, bumping into bar stools and people's legs alike.

Another flash of lightning outside briefly lit the scene as Orris side-stepped a long dagger and dug his own sword into the flesh of the aggressor at the same moment. The man quickly tumbled to the floor beside Javic and did not try to rise. Soon, a sulfur-tipped match was struck up and a dusty oil lamp ignited, filling the room with a hollow, trembling light. Javic was grateful to be able to see again, though as he took in the carnage before him, he wasn't so sure it was a blessing.

Both black-robed Ver'ati lay dead by the tavern's entrance, each stabbed multiple times in the neck. Their eyes were already glossed over, though terror still lingered in their expressions. Orris was splattered with blood, but not a drop of it appeared to be his own. He held his sword high as he shifted his eyes back and forth across the bar, searching for more threats. At his feet was Javic's second tail—the man dressed in civilian garb that was trailing behind the Ver'konus soldiers. A dagger was still clutched in his hand. He was as good as dead; disemboweled by Orris's blade, he sputtered blood from his mouth as the life seeped out of him. Earlier, outside, Javic assumed the man was an Arcanum agent, but the murder of two members of the Ver'konus in the middle of the city was a bit brazen, even for the Arcanum.

"We should go…" said Orris.

Javic had no argument.

The barroom maintained a stunned silence as he climbed to his feet and stepped around the fallen bodies to follow Orris out into the street. The electrical storm still churned away overhead. The shock of seeing the dead bodies faded quicker than Javic cared to admit—he was starting to become desensitized to such things. Nothing could be worse than the half-mummified, bled-out Archive Historian, or the de-fleshed human skull he saw in Sultrim.

Outside, Javic realized it wasn't just the tavern that had gone dark. All across the city, every one of Lord Ethan's luminescent bulbs was out.

"Mind telling me who I just killed?" asked Orris.

"I wish I knew…" said Javic.

Orris smartly sheathed his sword after watching a bolt of lightning strike a nearby tin roof. He was already enough of a target for the electricity because of his chainmail without holding the equivalent of a metal rod above his head. The streets were still devoid of life.

"Come," said Orris as he began a sprint down a side street. "I know a place where we will be safe to talk."

Javic chased behind Orris, just barely able to keep up with his gait. They turned several times, running down the length of a long alley and then out onto a street within view of the western gate. Orris led Javic up to the stoop of one of the houses there. He knocked on the door, and then they waited. The blood that was splattered across Orris's clothing mixed with rainwater, turning pink where it soaked deep into the fibers of his shirt and cloak. He dragged the less sullied of his two sleeves across his forehead, wiping most of the diluted blood from his brow. There was no hiding it—he obviously just killed a man.

Slow footsteps approached from the inside of the house. Someone fumbled with several locks, and then the door creaked part way open to reveal an old woman with stark-white hair and a gray shawl standing in the entrance. She stood feebly, hunched over, but she did not shy away from the bloodied Guardian. The hallway behind her was lit by a dozen burning candles, all lined up along shelving in the walkway. Without a word, Orris turned the hilt of his blade so that the woman could clearly see the opal—*Talus*

Shard?—displayed between the wrappings. She immediately opened the door the rest of the way and stepped aside.

"You may take the sitting room," she said as Orris and Javic rushed in. "Just down the hall and to the left." She made no inquiry over the blood stains as she closed the door behind them and began to re-latch all the locks.

"Thank you, ma'am," said Orris as he headed off into the dwelling. "A friend of the Order," he explained briefly to Javic.

Upon reaching the sitting room, Orris immediately went about taking off his blood soaked cloak and shirt, which Javic now noticed had several dagger holes cut through it that went down into the chainmail beneath. The armor stopped the assassin's blade from stabbing into his gut. Orris winced as he lifted the chainmail, displaying several deep-green and brown bruises that were already forming along his abdomen. As he laid out his stained clothing by the lit fireplace to dry, the expression on his face shifted. His eyes clearly demanded explanation without the need for words.

Javic sat down on a floral patterned sofa on the opposite side of the room from the fireplace and took a deep breath. He had a long story to tell if any of this was going to make sense to an outsider, so he started at the only place he could: Recounting the first time he met Belford.

Javic's tie to the Mark of Kings satisfied most of Orris's questions right up front. He let him believe that the Ver'konus and Arcanum were keeping an eye on him because of his relationship with Belford. The less people that knew about the Orb of Parphim and Javic's involvement with recovering its core, the better. Javic soon realized, though, that explaining why his grandfather thought he was dead was going to be very difficult without first talking about his trip to Sultrim. He settled on a half-truth, weaving a story about secret experiments conducted on initiates by the Ver'konus. He came across as honest when he spoke of losing two weeks of time during his proficiency exam—that part was completely true, after all—though he left out everything to do with Sultrim, the Gateway Artifact, and the Orb of Parphim.

The blade-brother sat through the majority of the story in silence, asking for elaboration here and there, but mostly just taking everything in. His expression was unreadable, but when Javic finished, Orris nodded. "I will aid you," he said, though Javic had not yet dared ask for any assistance. "I am an experienced tracker." It was the best news Javic had heard in months—for once, something was actually going better than he dared hope!

The old woman whose house they invaded brought Orris a set of fresh clothing without being prompted—they were dusty and dated, but much appreciated. Orris changed quickly and then immediately set out by himself to gather supplies for their journey. He thought it best for Javic to remain out of sight.

While Javic was waiting for Orris to return, he realized he hadn't caught their host's name. She appeared to be the only person living in the residence, and though she asked no questions, Javic could see the curiosity budding behind her eyes. To pass the time, she brought him a cup of honey-sweetened tea and took a seat beside him on the sofa.

"Thank you," said Javic. He was glad to be leaving the city; his grandfather was not overstating things when he said that Erotos was a dangerous place. *The currents here could tear a man apart.* The truth of that statement was more literal than Javic cared to admit.

The old woman tried to place the tea kettle down on a stack of books on the side table, but her wrinkled hand shook, struggling to support the kettle's weight once her arm was fully extended.

"Let me help you with that," said Javic, standing up from his seat.

"It's quite alright, dear," said the woman with a chuckle in her throat. "I've had to deal with much harder things than this over the years—I won't let an overfilled kettle get the best of me!" She stubbornly reached out with the kettle again, this time managing to place it securely atop the books before her strength gave out. "There," she said with a beaming smile.

"Do you live here alone?" Javic asked.

"Oh yes," she said, "for nearly twenty-five years."

It was hard for Javic to imagine such a frail old woman being able to get by within a big city like Erotos for so long without any help. This was not a small house, either; it must have required a substantial amount of effort to maintain, not to mention the financial burden of the city taxes each year.

The woman seemed to read Javic's thoughts. "The Guardians put me up here because of my husband's service to the Order. He fought for them all his life. It's been almost a year since the last time a blade-brother stopped by, though— no one ever visits unless there's a problem…" she glanced over at Orris's bloodied shirt with a raised eyebrow, but knew better than to ask.

They continued to sit in silence, facing the warm fire and sipping their pale tea. Javic felt a tug at his heart strings. Elric warned against the competing pulls of the city, but what Javic could not have foreseen was the feelings he would face that had nothing to do with political loyalties. Seeing this old woman, all by herself for so many years simply because her husband chose adventure over staying by her side, made Javic realize the folly of what he was about to do.

It was the thought of leaving Mallory behind as he set off on this journey that felt so wrong. Abandoning her now without even an explanation after everything they had been through was the cruelest thing he could do to her. He couldn't just run off with Orris. His mind was still filled with all the lingering questions from last night's encounter. He knew it would haunt him for the rest of his life if he ran out on Mallory now. For the first time ever, Javic could actually see himself having a future with Mallory.

The realization that Arlin might be a blade-brother didn't make the swordsman any less intimidating in the competition for Mallory's affections, but right now Javic couldn't care less about Arlin's claim over Mallory. Given the choice to stay or go, Arlin chose to leave Mallory behind. Javic wasn't about to make the same mistake.

It wasn't really up to Javic or Arlin to decide which one of them got to spend their future with Mallory, anyway. Javic knew he wanted to be with Mallory, but ultimately only she could choose her suitor.

Will she choose the one who abandoned her, or the one who stays by her side, even in the face of unknowable dangers?

Staying would be emotionally difficult to say the least, but he couldn't think of a gesture more romantic than choosing love when faced with a life changing decision. *Love... nothing else is quite as exhilarating and frightening at the same time.* Javic's gut groaned and twisted into a nervous pretzel as he set his mind to what he must do: Seek out Mallory and profess his feelings to her. If she wanted him, he would stay by her side. If he found himself rejected, he would join Orris on the quest to find Elric. That felt like the best way to decide. His worry for his grandfather was put at ease by knowing Orris would be headed out to retrieve Elric regardless of his own path.

As soon as Orris returned, Javic told him of his plan. The blade-brother was to wait here for two hours—that should give him enough time to locate Mallory and receive her answer—and if Javic did not return, Orris was to go west without him.

"There could be more assassins," Orris warned, the uncertainty of the plan too vast for his comfort. "I hope she is worth the risk."

The nervous tingle in Javic's stomach grew even stronger at those words, but he managed a meek smile. "She's worth it," he said. He wasn't really sure if he was trying to convince Orris or himself. He didn't doubt his feelings for Mallory, but death was an ever looming and permanent possibility, growing stronger every moment he remained in the city.

Perhaps Mallory will be willing to leave with me....

The lights were still dark all across the city as Javic set out by himself for the Blue Fox Inn and Mallory's apartment. The electrical storm had passed and the cloudburst completely evaporated, leaving behind a deceptively blue sky that gave no hint as to the magnitude of the morning storm. The streets were once again filled with traffic as people cautiously returned to their normal routines. The moon started its rise as Javic walked; the urge to grasp the Power filled him with a sense of strength and purpose that only emboldened his willpower to see his decision through.

With all that happened today, it was difficult to resist the draw of the Power, offering to warm his insides and protect him from all the dangers of the world. It always called to him like that; the tantalizing promise of unending power to give him the strength he needed to take what he wanted from life. He did not give in to the call, though—he knew it was a false promise. The elation of the Power could make him feel invincible—capable of anything—but it would not help him express his honest feelings to Mallory. A state of pure emotion, driven by an undercurrent of internal instinct and random whims—the Power had a way of making everything seem clear and focused while simultaneously clouding his thoughts. He hadn't time for such contradictions right now. It was good to be connected to one's feelings, but he could not aptly express himself without retaining at least some semblance of logic.

When he reached Mallory's apartment, all notions of resisting the Power vanished. The door stood ajar. Broken shards of wood from its frame were splintered across the entryway floor. His heart jumped in his chest as he latched on to the Power with everything he had. Professor Vanton would have harped on Javic's continued focus on using an emotional core to draw in the Power, but it was all Javic knew—he still hadn't found his Anchor. The energy filled his veins, pulsing along with his blood in a fiery torrent of rising pressure. He had no concerns for himself as he rushed into the apartment; his only thoughts were of Mallory's safety.

Through his heightened senses he was able to make out a muffled scream that barely managed to escape from the bedroom down the hall—Mallory's melodic voice twisted into a shrill cry—she was being smothered. Energy built around Javic in the air as he dashed down the hallway—it was an instinctual attack. The temperature of the room quickly dropped as he drew heat from his surroundings and converted it into the electric current he required—a trick he picked up watching Belford back in North Galdren.

He was ready to release a deadly bolt at the first intruder he saw, but in his final steps before entering the bedroom he suddenly lost control over his abilities. It was as if the moon had dropped out of the sky; an impenetrable wall fell in place between Javic's mind and the physical world around him. The energy he already gathered dissipated back into the environment in all directions with the release of a thousand static bolts. Unable to stop moving forward in time, the cloud of dispersing energy stung Javic's skin, burning painfully across his flesh as he crashed through the wandering charges on his way to the bedroom. All of his muscles contracted at once, causing him to fall head first into the closed doorway.

The force of the hit dented the wood and broke the top hinge of the door clean off from its frame. The door fell inward, still attached at the bottom so that it hung crooked into the bedroom. Despite the pounding blood in his head, Javic was back on his feet in an instant.

A robed man was crouched over Mallory, holding a pillow to her face. He sneered at Javic, but didn't look the least bit concerned or surprised to see him barreling in through the doorway. The man was holding a glowing talisman in one hand, about half the width of his palm and the length of one of his fingers—clearly a Power Artifact.

Javic knew instantly that the talisman was responsible for cutting off his connection to the Power—its glow intensified as he fought against the mental barrier, scraping along its edges with his thoughts in search for any means of breaking through to the other side. He wished to strike the man dead with his rage, but it was hopeless. He could feel the talisman enveloping his mind, restricting his thoughts so that they merely bounced around against the inside of his skull. Javic could sense the barrier, like the blinding radiance of the sun through closed eyelids. It pressed in around him. The curves of the talisman were projected inversely along the face of his invisible confinement, as if his mind were trapped within a man-sized version of the Artifact.

Mallory's legs twitched as the intruder applied more pressure to the pillow over her nose and mouth, completely ignoring Javic's approach. Javic could see the wild look of fear in Mallory's eyes as she gasped for breath but was met only with a mouth full of cotton. Javic had no weapons at his disposal, physical or mental, except for his own two fists. He lunged at the robed man—he wanted so badly to tear him off of Mallory—but a pair of hands grabbed Javic from behind and a series of blows landed across the back of his head.

The floor crashed against Javic's knees as he went down. The last thing he saw before a dark bag was drawn over his face was Mallory's legs as they twitched one last time and then fell deathly still.

CHAPTER

30

Smoke

Golden evening sunlight streamed across the little London-style tea house. The abandoned restaurant was quickly becoming one of Aaron and Claire's favorite escapes from the monotony of the lockdown. Here, they could pretend things were normal—that they were just two ordinary people out on a coffee date. The tea house was one of several small restaurants housed within the ground floor of the Atrium building—the hotel-like structure that the Arcadians had found themselves confined to since their identities were leaked to the media.

Dozens of saucers and plates of different sizes, colors, and patterns lined the walls, giving the room a very eclectic, cozy atmosphere. The acrylic of the decorative saucers reflected the sunlight across the room, each plate adding its own tint to the color of the light, like the tiles of a mosaic. Claire was silhouetted by the rays as they crisscrossed, making her glow with an aura of angelic beauty.

Although they were seated by the window to watch the sunset, Aaron's gaze kept drifting over to Claire instead. He found himself unable to keep his eyes off of her as she stared out across the horizon sipping her tea. It was miraculous to think that someone so perfect could love him back with such furious passion to match his own. The intoxicating emotion radiated from her like the desert's heat. She knew all of his innermost thoughts and secrets, and yet still accepted him with an open heart.

Making love to Claire was by far the most romantic and intense experience of Aaron's life. Just reminiscing about it made him stir with desire—the way the endorphins sizzled across their joined minds until neither one of them could think straight and there was nothing left to do but wriggle together deep into the throes of ecstasy.

Aaron contemplated running his hand up her thigh beneath the table—the idea of a repeat performance fanning the flames of his fiery passion. The rim of Claire's teacup pulled away from her soft, pink lips as they curled up into a salacious smile. She knew exactly what he was thinking, and she did not disapprove. Aaron needn't any further invitation. He reached for her leg, but stopped as Claire raised a cautionary eyebrow towards the black security camera dome located just outside the tea house's entrance.

Later, she thought to him, *someone could be watching.*

They already risked too much by going out together in the first place. Drawing any extra attention to their fraternization would only be asking for trouble. The tea house's employees were all trapped outside of the facility by the lockdown, but the security cameras were a constant presence, watching their every move from the ceilings above. It was difficult to maintain the illusion of a collegial friendship when Aaron wanted nothing more than to tear Claire's clothes off and take her right here and now on top of the table, spectators be damned! Claire's skin pricked with delighted anticipation as Aaron thought about all the dirty things he wanted to do to her once he got her alone back in his private room, away from the cameras. Outwardly, they both continued to sip their tea in silence, but within they were transmitting the naughtiest of thoughts back and forth across their bond.

Claire teased him with the memory of their first kiss, so soft and tender, out in the night air of the park on the day they discovered the existence of their connection. The memory was so vivid, Aaron could actually feel the heat of her lips pressing up against his own—or was it his lips pressing against hers? The memory was from Claire's perspective, but such distinctions got a bit muddled the more their thoughts combined.

Already, Aaron had forgotten what it was like to be alone inside his head. Claire's presence felt so natural—a part of him that should have been there all along. He never realized how lonely he was before their transformation, but now that he had someone to share everything with, he hoped he would never have to go back to the way things were before—so solitary and empty. Life meant so much more when it could be shared. A sunset was beautiful, but Aaron wouldn't have bothered to watch one before when he was by himself. Now, with Claire by his side, knowing that she was seeing the same pinks and oranges intermingling like rainbow sherbet in the air as the sun dripped beneath the horizon… it just made everything so much more worthwhile.

As much as their ever growing love was a positive influence in their lives, it couldn't entirely distract Claire from worrying over her family. When it came to Claire's mother and brother, Aaron understood that no news was good news—it meant they were still safe. Convincing Claire of this fact was not such an easy task, however. Whenever she thought about her family, Aaron would receive an anxious knot in his gut from all the emotion slipping uncontrollably across their bond. Although there was legitimate reason to worry, Aaron was certain Wes's warning reached them in time. With Claire's face on the news, he knew they would take the message seriously. The money from Aaron's advance for joining the project would be enough to keep them off the grid for at least a month or two, he hoped.

Aaron's main concern was for Aiden—he needed continuous treatment for his blood condition. There was no telling how much of his medication the hospital would allow them to stockpile, and if he needed a private physician to help administer it properly that would complicate things even further. Once the meds ran dry, they would have no choice but to return to society. Even a brief visit to a clinic might be dangerous. Any amount of time back on the grid was risky when it came to the possibility of EAC terrorists finding and kidnapping them in order to gain leverage over Claire. No one saw the Arcadians as people anymore—they were merely assets to be controlled. With any luck, tension between the EU and EAC would die down to its usual simmer before anything bad happened to the Arcadians or their families.

Here in Tripoli, the small protest that instigated the lockdown of the complex had grown into a full scale riot over the course of about twelve hours. Many Libyans feared retaliation from the EAC against their country for allowing Reblan Industries to experiment within their borders. The angry ruckus of the crowd was a constant reminder of the dangers that awaited the Arcadians in the world beyond the facility's gate. Across the EU, political opinions swung wildly from support for Reblan Industries to venomous opposition of their research. Accusations regarding the illegal creation of super soldiers kept rolling in as the news agencies brought in various experts to converse on the subject. It had been the top story playing across every major network since the Arcadians' identities were leaked—*Had it really only been three days?* Time stood still inside the complex now that all the experiments were on hold. For the Arcadians, there was nothing to do but wait.

Dana Farris and the rest of the project management team was still trying to sniff out who was responsible for releasing the classified documents to the media, but so far the mole managed to elude them. All they knew for certain was that the stolen files were accessed from a secure server within Echo Facility sometime within the past week. The versions of the files that were leaked did not exist before then. The server was not connected to any outside networks, so the documents must have been accessed locally by somebody onsite. Apart from the Arcadians and management staff, only a few dozen people had the clearance required to get close enough to the server to compromise its data, making it just a matter of time before the culprit was rooted out.

Over the last few nights, hundreds of small campfires lit up the sea of tents in the park outside the complex's walls. The cover of darkness only emboldened the riotous crowd as stones and glass bottles were used as weapons against the police and private security forces who moved in to protect the buildings. After dozens of injuries, the EU military finally stepped in, launching teargas canisters from helicopters to disperse the crowd. Aaron was able to see all the action clearly from his room on the Atrium's ninth floor—it was unreal, like something straight out of a movie. The air was so full of white smoke from the canisters that it looked like a low fog had descended all across the park. Thankfully, the building's ventilation system stopped the noxious fumes from seeping inside.

Tonight marked the fourth night of the lockdown. As evening approached, the fumes settled, and the park was once again empty, forming a buffer between the city and complex. The rioters were not finished yet, however. After being removed from the park, all across Tripoli, roves of displaced protestors moved in mass, down one street and up the next, smashing storefronts and ransacking businesses as they went.

Aaron watched it all unfold on the news. The roads were littered with more trash and debris than usual—Tripoli hadn't exactly been a clean city to begin with, but things were certainly much worse now. More than a few vehicles were overturned and set ablaze. Just one street away from the complex, a city bus was now a burnt out husk of blackened metal. It smoldered for several hours before extinguishing itself. Aaron could still see the smoke hanging above the horizon to the west, forming a haze across a portion of the sunset.

Claire turned away from the window, clearly distracted. At first, Aaron assumed it was his own negative thoughts about the rioting that disturbed her from the otherwise tranquil view. Losing her childhood home during the Dublin Riots had been on her mind often since the start of the lockdown—the topic always took her to a dark place. It was something else, though, that stole Claire's attention now. She continued to crane her neck around until she was staring directly towards the eastern wall of the tea house. *Something's happening...* she thought to him.

Aaron followed her gaze, but she was not actually looking at the wall. Her eyes remained unfocused as she perceived something beyond her natural senses. Searching his own mind, it took only a moment for Aaron to detect the odd sensation as well. The portion of his brain that could sense the matter markers in the distant test range was starting to tingle. He had only felt something like this once before, back when the CMM serum was first disseminating through his body, creating new connections and mental pathways. Dr. Miriam Gerard told him that the tingling was a physical manifestation of his mind becoming aware of the large mass of matter markers. This time was different, though: New markers were popping into existence and expanding out from the Battle Cove like a giant, rippling wave across the surface of the ocean.

The sensation moved quickly—as fast as the concussive shock of an explosion. His mind suddenly became aware of the contours of the land between the Battle Cove and Echo Facility. In a moment, the wave washed over Echo Facility entirely, consuming the whole structure and internalizing it in

Aaron's thoughts—every laboratory, hallway, desk and chair was swallowed up. The sensation stretched down into the earth and up into the sky simultaneously—a growing sphere of comprehension.

The expanding front reached the Atrium with unbridled ferocity, pulling everything into its domain. It was too much for Aaron's mind to take in all at once. His thoughts spun out of control as the confusing jumble of extra sensory information piled on top of itself like a chorus of dissonant voices speaking out all at once. With every passing moment, the rising clatter made it more difficult to telepathically distinguish the finite details of the marker filled environment. It was as if he had taken several large steps back from a tiny detailed painting to find that the canvas continued on into a giant mural that filled the entire room. Things that were so obvious before faded into obscurity, while the major systems of the geography became even more apparent.

Matter in motion passing through multiple sectors of markers was the easiest to focus on. He could sense the water in the Atrium's central garden; the arc of the man-made waterfalls as the droplets fell through the air and crashed down on the rocks below. It was like feeling his own blood coursing through his veins. The beat of the water on the rocks below was as clear to his senses as his heart pounding in his eardrums. Electrons pulsed through the power cords within the walls—flowing downward to a mess of laboratories hidden beneath the surface. Following the drifting current with his mind led Aaron to the realization that the structure ran much deeper underground than the limited elevator options in the housing area implied. Echo Facility and the Atrium were two trunks attached to the same intricate root system of seemingly endless laboratories and walkways that stretched far beneath the complex.

When the wave of replicating markers passed through the tea house, Aaron didn't need to reach out to the computer to know that he had complete control over the matter around him. While the small details of more distant areas washed together in his thoughts, his immediate surroundings came through clearer than ever. He could sense every miniscule crack and crevice of the floor as his eyes swept across the clusters of matter markers. The markers themselves were invisible, of course, but he knew their presence by the sensations they aroused within his mind.

This is wrong, thought Claire. *Dana would never purposely alter the Virus Replication Protocol without informing us first....*

Claire had a point. The project staff would have wanted to keep a close watch on the Arcadians as the marker pool was slowly expanded. During their first briefing, Dana Farris and George Cartwright left everyone under the impression that the VRP would not be altered until the end of the project when all other testing had been completed.

There was no more time to ponder the situation as a distant explosion rattled through the complex, emanating from deep within the underground hive of laboratories. Aaron and Claire both jumped up from their seats as the fine china lining the walls of the tea house clinked together in a clash of chimes. Claire looked over at Aaron, the concern in her eyes matching the emotion that dripped across their bond. A second explosion hit after the first faded, this one closer than the last. It was near enough that Aaron could sense the motion of the destructive heat as it tore through several more labs. A void formed for a moment in his thoughts as the matter markers within the labs were destroyed by the intense energy and pressure of the blast, but then new markers quickly propagated back in from the surrounding spaces to fill the gap. Several plates fell from the walls of the tea house, shattering against the tile floor. Bits of colored ceramic shot across the room in all directions.

We're under attack! The murmured thought from Claire resonated in Aaron's mind for a moment before he could truly comprehend what was going on.

Let's get out of here, he thought back to her, already moving towards the exit. Broken plate shards crunched beneath their sneakers as they dashed from the tea house. Once they reached the hallway they started for the central gardens. There were several closer exits that they could have taken to get out of the building, but there was no guarantee that outside was any safer than inside right now if they really were under attack. At least in the lobby there would be armed security forces to protect them.

Shouting from up ahead prompted a shared look of concern between Aaron and Claire. Down the hall on their left, behind one of the magnetically sealed security doors that led into the restricted sections, a series of muffled cries rang out, followed by the distinct pops of several handguns being discharged simultaneously. Aaron and Claire stumbled to a stop before reaching the metal door and moved to the side of the corridor, ducking low to take cover in case any of the bullets happened to come out into the hallway.

Two additional gunshots sounded on the other side of the door, followed by more cries of alarm. The shouts were cut short by an explosion that echoed violently like a cannon going off inside an enclosed train car. A puff of smoke forced its way out through the nearly nonexistent gaps between the door and frame and rose up into the air as a wispy cloud. The explosion left Aaron's ears ringing—a high-pitched tone which faded quickly into deathly silence. For a moment, Aaron wasn't sure that his hearing had even returned. The shouts and cries of the security team ceased along with the gunfire. Aaron had no doubt the men were consumed by the blast.

As frightened as he was, Aaron pulled Claire to her feet and dragged her onwards. They managed to put some distance between themselves and the security door, but before they rounded the corner, another blast shook the building behind them. Aaron glanced back to see the security door lying askew against the far side of the corridor, right where he and

Claire had just been standing. He slowed in his stride as he watched the dense, black smoke pouring out into the hallway from within the restricted section. Although most of his vision was obscured by the smoke, Aaron was able to make out the form of a person stepping into the hallway through the hole in the wall. The black pants and coat of an Arcadian uniform was all Aaron was able to distinguish before Claire tugged him around the bend in the hall. She pulled his arm so hard that it nearly came out of its socket.

Claire made no apologies as they both continued on at full speed, careening down the corridor. The fear in her heart and mind, along with the occasional flash of an image across their bond of the fires that followed the Dublin Riots left no question as to the mental state that Claire had fallen into. She was a little girl again, fleeing with her mother and brother from the only home she had ever known while anarchists burned half the city to the ground. There was nothing to go back to as the ashes of her life plumed up into the sky. That night, the fires left an eerie glow across the horizon. The next morning, a wall of smoke hid the true magnitude of the devastation. Her mother told her not to look back, but Claire's eyes couldn't help but wander. The sky was darkened by the smoke, as if the dense shadow of a heavy rain hung in the distance, but where a rainstorm would have cleansed the air, the acrid smoke burned the lungs and eyes without mercy.

Aaron felt Claire's painful memory. A stream of tears ran down her cheek. She squeezed onto his hand so tight that it made his fingers ache, but he was grateful that even with the torrent of emotion twisting through her she did not let go. Aaron didn't slow his stride again until well after they reached the central garden. Security officers were present, as predicted, guarding the main entrance. The stoic men raised their handguns at Aaron and Claire as they came barreling through the lobby, only lowering them again after the lead officer spoke to someone over his ear-com and ordered them to stand down.

Without delay or explanation the security team escorted Aaron and Claire across the lobby to the entrance of another restricted area. A scanner read the lead guard's implanted chip and released the locking mechanism on the door. The officers lead them inside and then down a long white corridor to what Aaron soon realized was a detainment area. Most of the other Arcadians were already present in the windowless cell, each looking more confused than the last. In the corner, Emily and Hannah were whispering together as usual, too deep in their private conversation to even look up as Aaron and Claire were brought in. The others—Wes, Travis, Isabelle, and Brooke—all greeted the new pair with grave expressions. The door to the cell swooshed shut behind them, its final click resonating off the empty walls.

"Do you guys know what's going on?" Brooke asked. "We were all up in our rooms when the explosions went off… they won't tell us anything."

Claire shook her head.

Aaron remained silent for the moment, still mulling over what he saw in the hallway outside the restricted section. He hadn't shared his revelation with Claire—hadn't had a moment to truly wrap his head around it yet. One of the other Arcadians was the traitor! Whoever it was even passed their own personal information to the media along with the rest of the test subjects' names in order to throw off suspicion. Maybe they hadn't expected to be trapped inside by the lockdown—perhaps they thought they could make a clean getaway after releasing the files. If Claire noticed his distracted mind, she wasn't showing any indication.

Wes patted the empty space beside him, gesturing for Aaron to have a seat on the bench. "Funny how when something goes wrong they treat us like inmates," he said. "You'd think they'd want to make nice, considering we have the power to turn their reinforced walls into chocolate pudding."

Over his shoulder, Travis turned away from trying to listen in on Hannah and Emily's conversation and sneered at Wes's comment. "You won't be joking about desserts when they decide we're a threat to national security," he said. The usually jovial man locked his one working eye on the back of Wes's head. The eyepatch over his left eye made him appear sinister. "They know the extent of our abilities better than we do. Do you really think they will stop at rounding us up? They could end us all before we even know what's going on."

Aaron sensed an increase in Claire's respiratory rate, her heart beating faster beside him. Hannah and Emily stopped talking as well and looked over at Travis as if he had threatened them directly. On the other side of Wes, Isabelle's face settled into a sullen expression—a worrisome reaction considering that out of all the Arcadians, Isabelle, being the niece of the Founder and CEO of the company, probably had the best idea of how Reblan Industries might react to the current situation.

"I know why they are gathering us," said Aaron, unable to keep what he saw to himself any longer. Everyone's attention shifted his way; expectant looks that gave him an uneasy feeling in his gut. He continued on despite the discomfort. "Someone wearing an Arcadian uniform was in the restricted area. I couldn't see who it was, but they blasted a hole in the wall to get out—right after the matter markers expanded." He would let them draw their own conclusions.

A hurt look appeared on Claire's face. Aaron immediately realized his mistake. He'd left her in the dark, only filling her in now at the same time as everyone else. Though he hadn't intended it, his actions implied that she was no more important to him than any of the rest of the Arcadians. He felt a twinge of guilt for not having shared his insight with her sooner. How curious it was that Claire felt entitled to his thoughts and experiences... even more curious was the fact that Aaron felt her entitlement to be completely justified. Their connection demanded a level of loyalty between them that went beyond that of normal individuals. She could sense his regret, and although it didn't erase her hurt feelings entirely, it did go a long way towards easing the tension that momentarily arose between them.

"You're saying one of the other candidates is responsible?" asked Emily.

Aaron nodded, his mind pulled back to the larger conundrum at hand. "It sure looks that way."

Only four of the Arcadians were unaccounted for at the moment—Michelle, Ethan, John, and Garrett. Aaron seriously doubted the Millers had anything to do with the sabotage—they both spearheaded the HAMMER project for the Defense Department—they were patriots! That left John and Garrett. A moment later when the door to the cell swung open and John Graven was escorted inside peacefully, looking confused, Aaron was more certain than ever it had been Garrett Rames exiting the restricted section. Aaron shared his thought process with Claire this time in an effort to make amends for his previous withholding. She concurred with his logic.

Garrett betrayed them all. Providing classified documents to the enemy made him a traitor not only to the project but to the entire European Union!

I always had a bad feeling about Garrett, thought Claire, *I just never suspected anything this diabolical.*

"It makes sense in a way," said Travis, ignoring John's entrance. "All the riches in the world couldn't buy a man the power these matter markers give us."

"I don't understand," said Brooke. "What's the point? Won't they just undo the change to the Virus Replication Protocol?"

Hannah was shaking her head. "That wouldn't destroy the markers that have already formed, it would only stop their further expansion," she said. "And if one of those explosions was the marker control center, they won't even be able to do that much."

"What about shutting down the computer entirely?" Emily suggested.

"Impossible," said John, butting into the conversation as if he'd been a part of it from the start. "It is inaccessible. We did not want hackers to be able to take the system offline, so external connections have been given very limited system privileges."

Aaron and Claire shared a fleeting moment of curiosity over how John knew so much about the inner workings of the supercomputer. Despite the deep connection the Arcadians shared with the system, the project officials rarely spoke of the powerful device. They most certainly wouldn't have purposefully divulged intimate details about its security to any of the candidates.

John saw their suspicious looks and offered an explanation. "I was part of the team that helped modify the system's quantum processors with low gravity specifications—specifically for lunar gravity levels. I did not know what it was to be used for at the time, only where it was to be assembled—an unmanned lunar base in the middle of the Sea of Tranquility. No one is turning it off, because if they could they would have done so by now."

Chatter rose up after John's declaration, but everyone fell silent again as the cell door opened and both Michelle and Garrett were led inside by security. If the befuddled expressions on their faces were any indication, they were just as clueless about what was going on as everyone else had been upon first arriving at the cell. Aaron's mind spun as he realized what their arrival signified.

"What's wrong?" asked Wes as he noticed the expression on Aaron's face.

"It must have been Ethan," Aaron whispered. "Everyone else is here."

Before the door sealed shut, Dana Farris and Yosef Reblan filed in behind Michelle and Garrett. This was the closest the CEO had gotten to any of the Arcadians since the beginning of the project. Dana took a seat alongside Garrett and Michelle, allowing Yosef to take the lead. One by one, everyone else began to notice Ethan's absence. By the time Yosef started talking, the Arcadians were all exchanging knowing glances.

"We have uncovered the mole," said Yosef, looking out at each of the Arcadians in turn. His Israeli accent was thick compared to Isabelle's. When Yosef's eyes passed across Aaron, the disdain in his expression did not go unnoticed. Aaron wasn't sure if the CEO had something against him personally or if this was just how he treated everyone. "We knew it was one of you all along," Yosef continued. "Now we know which. Earlier this week, Ethan Miller broke into a secured system and leaked classified files."

Only Michelle looked truly surprised by the announcement—everyone else had come to the conclusion on their own upon noticing Ethan's absence. Michelle stood up from her seat. "That's ridiculous!" she shouted at Yosef.

"Sit down," Yosef snapped back. A slapping sound made everyone jump as a gust of air left a stinging welt across Michelle's cheek. Michelle's knees buckled beneath her body as Yosef gestured violently with his index finger. Michelle's hand went to her face, the surprise of the invisible blow made her cry out just as much as the actual pain.

Aaron looked closer at Yosef Reblan, seeing him fully for the first time. Although it was possible that there was some other trick at play, Aaron knew in his gut where that gust of wind originated. The curly gray-haired man was an Arcadian. He had received a CMM injection and could control the matter markers just as aptly as the rest of the Arcadians.

"Yes," said Yosef, glancing over at Isabelle, who was scowling back at him. "Why else do you think I chose you to be part of this test group? The successful dissemination of the CMM serum in your blood proved its compatibility with our bloodline. So I suppose I must express my gratitude to you for not dying."

Isabelle spat on the floor and swore loudly at Yosef, her speech momentarily slipping into Hebrew. While her tone was the only context Aaron had to go by, he had no doubt she was spouting a string of heartfelt profanities.

Yosef raised his hand to deliver another blast of painful air, this time in Isabelle's direction, but Wes got between them, interrupting their exchange before Yosef could manifest the attack. "Ethan is the traitor?" he asked. "What evidence do you have?"

Isabelle didn't realize how close she had come to being struck. She continued to mutter under her breath.

Yosef shifted his eyes away from his niece and lowered his half-extended arm. "Evidence? Ethan altered the Virus Replication Protocol, which I am sure you are all very well aware of by now, then he blew up the marker control room and the security chip monitoring center. Now he is the only one unaccounted for—the only one with a motive to run."

"Ethan didn't do anything," said Michelle, being cautious not to raise her voice to Yosef again. "I've been with him every moment."

Yosef turned his hateful glare back onto Michelle. She was still rubbing the wicked welt on her cheek. It had risen into a thick red line beneath her left eye. She looked as if she were struck by a cane.

"You are not with him now," Yosef said simply.

"He's not fleeing, he's just…" Michelle hesitated, "he said he was going out on a walk." Michelle lowered her gaze to the floor, realizing the absurdity of her words.

"Out?" questioned Yosef. "During the lockdown?"

Michelle clearly didn't want to continue. Yosef raised his hand again and Michelle flinched in fearful anticipation. She spoke before Yosef could follow through with his threat. "He said he needed some fresh air… that there was an unsecured door on the south side of the complex and a way through the wall… he said it was safe now that the park is clear of protestors."

Michelle's eyes were filled with tears. Aaron wasn't sure if it was fear of Yosef Reblan, the thought of betraying her husband, or the realization that her husband betrayed all of them that shook her the most.

"Likely story," said Yosef. "Obviously, since you are his wife, we can't trust a word you say, but it's good that you have chosen to talk. Take her away," he said towards the wall. "Be sure she continues to speak until you are satisfied she knows nothing more."

Immediately the door slid opened and two security guards came inside. The men grabbed Michelle under her arms and led her from the cell. Michelle didn't struggle at all as she was escorted away. Her gaze remained on the floor until she was out of sight.

"Go with them," Yosef said to Dana.

Dana promptly got up and followed Michelle and the guards out. He hadn't spoken a single word the entire time he was in the cell, but his grim expression was enough of an indicator of how he felt about the situation.

"As for the rest of you," continued Yosef, turning towards the Arcadians again, "Ethan has left quite a mess on our hands. The matter markers are out in the world now, and we may never be able to fully retract them. We have an extremely dangerous criminal on the loose who can control the environment with his mind. Fortunately for us, the only people with a chance at stopping him happen to be sitting in this room right now."

Aaron already didn't like where this was going.

"Take these ear-coms," said Yosef, handing out a fist full of the little flesh-toned bumps. They made squishing noises as they formed a snug fit with each of the Arcadian's ear canals. "There is a lot of ground to cover in the park, but there are only so many places he could be hiding. The military is holding a perimeter at the edge of the city, keeping the rioters out. They have already been informed of the situation, so if Ethan tries to pass them, we will know exactly where he is.

You will split into groups of two and head out with security details to sweep the park. He won't stay hidden for long."

Just as Yosef finished his speech, every florescent light bulb in the room suddenly flashed bright white and then blinked out, casting the room in total darkness. Shouting immediately erupted from out in the hallway beyond the sealed door. Within the cell, one of the Arcadians—it sounded like Emily—screamed as the lights went out. The whole room echoed with the wiry cry. Claire grabbed hold of Aaron's arm as a nervous twitch took control of her fingers. After a moment of silence, a frantic banging on the outside of the door made everyone jump again. Claire's fingernails dug into Aaron's flesh.

"What's going on out there?" came Yosef's disgruntled voice from somewhere in the darkness in front of Aaron.

Everyone grew silent to listen for the reply.

"It's Michelle!" shouted Dana through the closed door, his voice muffled by the metal, "She's escaped! Some sort of electrical explosion. Everything went dark. Can't see a god damned thing out here!"

"Can you open the door?" Yosef asked.

"No, the keypad's fried," said Dana.

A spark of blue light followed by a steady stream of white flashed into existence beside Aaron. It was a ball of glowing energy in the palm of Wes's hand. "Stand back," Wes yelled out to Dana. Immediately, the door began to sizzle and steam, as if it were a molten piece of iron dropped into a bucket of cold water. Garrett and John, the Arcadians closest to the door, moved back as vapors filled the air around the transforming material. The outer layer of the door slopped off onto the ground in a wet heap, followed by the layer under that. In a matter of seconds, a hole the size of a human head formed in the middle of the steel. More and more material fell in globs onto the floor. The hole widened until it was large enough for two Arcadians to fit through abreast. All that was left of the door was a pile of gray mush on the ground.

Yosef was the first to step through, followed by everyone else out into the hallway, hopping over the mound of sludge. By the time Aaron went through, the pile had expanded to the point where he could no longer avoid stepping in the muck. It squished under his shoes like chocolate pudding, though it gave off a distinctively less pleasant smell. After reaching the hallway, several of the Arcadians created orbs of light similar to Wes's until the corridor was lit even brighter than it had been under the florescent lights.

"Are the ear-com's still working?" Yosef asked, pressing his hand to his own ear as he spoke.

Aaron heard the words broadcast into his head by the tiny speaker.

"Good," said Yosef as they all affirmed. "Let's get moving."

Down the hall twenty feet, the security guards sent to escort Michelle were still picking themselves up off the floor—the electrical shock she gave them proving to be nonlethal.

"We now have two fugitives," said Yosef. "Needless to say, they are too dangerous to be taken alive. This is a kill-on-sight operation."

Aaron felt like he'd been transported into an alternate universe where his friends were his enemies and his enemies his friends. Ethan and Michelle had been nothing but kind to him the entire time he'd known them. Everything he knew about those two pointed to them being a loving couple who wanted nothing more than to serve the Union for the good of the free world, and yet here Aaron was, about to work alongside Yosef Reblan and Garret Rames—two of the most despicable individuals he'd ever encountered—to hunt down his friends like stray dogs in the street.

Aaron wasn't sure what to believe anymore. He didn't want to think Ethan and Michelle were capable of betraying the Union, but facts spoke louder than words. *Innocent people don't run.* The words kept repeating in his head like a mantra.

Yosef left the Arcadians in Dana's hands, heading off by himself deeper into the complex. Mr. Farris walked with them down the blacked-out corridor to where several security teams were preparing to break off into smaller search parties. The lights functioned here; they were far enough away from Michelle's electrical disturbance to remain unaffected.

As everyone broke off into pairs, all Aaron could think about was Claire's family. The more he ruminated over Ethan and Michelle's crimes, the angrier he became. The possibility of all-out war between the EU and EAC was closer than ever because of them—or was that Reblan Industries fault? Sending the Arcadians out on a kill-mission was certainly weaponizing the technology—officially turning them into the illegal super soldiers everyone was accusing them of being. The Arcadians were given the power to change the world for the better, but already everything was descending into chaos.

The one thing Aaron could not shake from his mind was the look of genuine shock that appeared on Michelle's face when Yosef named her husband as the traitor. If the accusations were true, Aaron hated the Millers for leaking everyone's names to the media—hated them for what they were putting Claire and her family through—but the more he thought about everything, the less sense any of it made.

Ethan could have done it alone—kept the truth from his wife—but then why would Michelle be running away now as well? If they were both responsible, that meant they were frighteningly skillful liars. A deception this huge would have taken constant acting in order to pull off so seamlessly. If that were the case, why was Ethan's alibi so painfully weak? They should have been able to come up with fifty more convincing excuses for Ethan's absence than simply saying he was "out on a walk" during the lockdown.

The other thing that bothered Aaron was that Yosef hadn't given them any physical evidence against Ethan. Whatever Yosef said, the case against the Millers was purely circumstantial. It was clear that the CEO did not intend to give either of the Millers a chance to tell their side of the story. Yosef was set on destroying Ethan and Michelle; the kill orders were already given. It all added up to make Aaron increasingly dubious.

Across the room, Garrett was being outfitted with a bulletproof vest by the squad of five that would be escorting him and John through the park. The smirk on his lips and the added spring in his step made Aaron wary. He looked like he was having the time of his life. Aaron didn't care how much Garrett hated the Millers, hunting and killing people should never make anyone that gleeful.

Everyone remained silent as the security teams explained the various strategies and hand signals they would be using while moving through the park. A resigned acceptance settled over the room as the Arcadians all prepared to embark on their mission. Two of their own betrayed them, and now they had to die.

In the back of Aaron's mind, Claire's emotions came across their bond as a confused knot. She didn't like the idea of hunting down the Millers any more than Aaron did, but the image of Aiden circling around in her head made her movements sharp as she strapped her bulletproof vest in place. Aaron was certain that she would do whatever was necessary to make her family safe again, no matter the burden it placed on her soul.

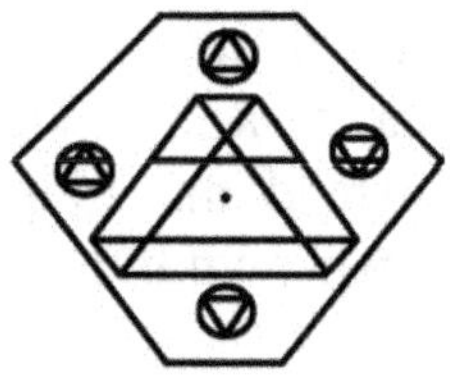

Wildfire

A chilly breeze picked up, blowing in from the east as the sun set along the Altrese River. The Rosa Marsa swayed awkwardly to her starboard side as the wind caught her hull with a powerful gust that roused Belford from his meditation.

His most recent recovered memories buzzed through his head as he sat up in his cot—Ethan and Michelle hiding in the park; the rest of the Arcadians setting out for the hunt. Ethan insisted Belford's memories would show him why Garrett deserved to die. Ethan blamed Garrett for destroying their world, but everything Belford remembered so far pointed towards Ethan being the traitor. Certainly Ethan wouldn't have volunteered to help Belford retrieve his memories if this was where it all led.

Belford shivered as an eerie feeling ran between his shoulder blades. If it actually had been Ethan rather than

Garrett who destroyed their world, and Belford was helping him… he would never be able to forgive himself!

The Rosa Marsa lurched sideways again. The Altrese River was much narrower than the Minthune, making running aground a worrisome possibility if the wind kept up like this. Belford trusted Captain Bundles' piloting skills, but the horizontal shifting back and forth still made his stomach clench up nervously to match every groan of the ship.

The quiet murmurings in the walls had picked up again, though tonight they were less audible than usual because of all the wind whistling through the upper deck. Emotionally shaken by his memories and physically shaken by the storm, there was no chance of Belford finding the inner calm required for meditation again tonight, even with the voices drowned out. The likelihood of him being able to fall asleep any time soon was equally improbable. Though his body was tired, his mind was restless beyond hope. He stood up from his cot and quickly dressed himself as the floor swayed beneath him. He wasn't sure who would still be up at this hour—most of the crew and passengers generally turned in around sunset so they could be awake at first light—but at this point anything would be better than being trapped alone with his thoughts.

If he was lucky, perhaps Ethan would still be awake. He desperately needed the man to tell him his newest recovered memories weren't the end of the story—that Ethan wasn't the traitor; that as more of his memories came back he would see it had all been a vast deception by Garrett to implicate Ethan. Even in his memories he was doubtful of Ethan's guilt, but with how quickly security managed to round up all eleven of the other Arcadians after the explosions, could it really have been anyone else other than Ethan that he saw blasting through the wall of the restricted section? If only he could have seen the culprit's face….

Belford stepped out of his cabin and headed straight for Ethan's room at the bow of the ship. He passed by the galley and mess hall where a clamor of pots and pans striking against one another chimed out with every bump of the vessel. Coriva Lethos, the Rosa Marsa's cook, was still there, cleaning up the remains of dinner before turning in for the night. Never before did Coriva have such a full boat to cook for. Dinner each night came in shifts, starting in the mid-afternoon if she wanted to have any hope of feeding everyone before nightfall. The galley was not large, giving the woman limited space to work with, but the short-haired blonde still managed to satisfy the masses.

With so many mouths to feed, the stock of food from Erotos was quickly dwindling. The Rosa Marsa would have to stop to resupply soon—a dangerous maneuver this deep into Kovehn territory. The city of Melvona had been chosen as their stopping point because of its busy port. The Rosa Marsa would hopefully be able to keep a low profile amongst the other trading vessels that frequented the city. Melvona was still a few days travel, though, and with food already running low, the need for rationing was thrust upon them.

Coriva frowned when she saw Belford step into the mess. Like the rest of the crew of the Rosa Marsa, she was more than a little prickly towards the passengers for dragging them into the middle of this secret mission without consent. "No late night snacks here," she said. "Galley's closed. No nicking things either, else we run out of food before we reach Melvona."

"Just passing through," said Belford, putting his hands up in a gesture of submission.

"You see that you do," said Coriva, narrowing her eyes at Belford. He snatched a bottle of mead off the counter in defiance, taking a few swigs of the amber liquid as he stepped away from the galley. Coriva glared, keeping watch of him until he passed all the way through the mess and out the other side.

He continued to drink as he meandered slowly around the corner, moving into the hallway that contained the first stretch of passenger cabins. Ethan's former caretaker, Vera Ekrin, was sitting there, in the middle of the floor outside of the room she shared with Ethan. Her face was hidden beneath her hands, head lolling between her upward bent knees as the steamer rocked from side to side with the wind. The wavering motion of the Rosa Marsa was even more extreme up here at the bow of the vessel.

Belford drank again deeply before approaching the girl. The sound of his footsteps was masked by the lapping splashes of the river against the hull. At first he assumed she was merely feeling sick from all the motion, but as he got closer he could clearly make out the soft whimpers of her cries. Her head lifted up in surprise as she became aware of Belford's presence. Realizing she was being watched, she immediately began rubbing at her eyes with the backs of her hands, trying feverishly to wipe away the moisture gathered there. Between the puffiness of her face and the short, unsteady breaths that still escaped her lungs, there was no way for her to conceal the fact that she had just been sobbing into her dress.

Belford's face reddened slightly from having walked in on a private moment. He hadn't meant to sneak up on the girl. "Are you alright?" he asked.

Vera shushed him softly, glancing behind her with nervous eyes at the closed door to Ethan's cabin. As she climbed unsteadily to her feet, Belford realized the girl's dress was torn. The fabric was ripped completely clear of her left shoulder. The neckline fell down loose, exposing part of the side of her breast. Vera didn't realize she was hanging out at first, but upon seeing the concern in Belford's face as his focus shifted abruptly downward, she snatched the cloth back up to cover herself and turned away in embarrassment.

Belford opened his mouth to ask her what happened, but the deathly glare he received from the girl silenced his tongue faster than a slap to the face. He took another swig of mead instead. Vera gestured with her head as she walked off, leading Belford farther down the hallway, away from Ethan's cabin. Once she was satisfied that they would not be overheard, Vera stopped and turned to face him.

"Please don't tell anyone about this," she said in a hushed voice, the tears already starting to build back up in her eyes.

"What happened?" Belford asked, though he had a terrible suspicion he already knew the answer.

Vera's eyes shifted to the floor. She was still holding up her dress with her left hand. Her whole body quivered as she took in a deep breath. "I didn't want him to touch me anymore…."

But he wouldn't take no for an answer. She didn't need to finish for Belford to understand. He knew she could only be referring to Ethan—he'd been treating her like a sex-object for weeks now. Belford felt sick to his stomach. "Did he…?" He couldn't muster the words.

Vera shook her head. "He just pushed me around a little and then kicked me out of the room." The poor girl wiped her arm across her nose as she sniffled. "I'm being stupid. Please don't tell anyone about this," she repeated, still concerned about what everyone else would think.

"He can't treat you like this," said Belford. He couldn't believe Ethan had taken it this far. He could feel anger rising in his chest.

"Please…" Vera begged. "He is the most powerful man in the world. It's not a big deal, I was just being dumb. I should have let him do what he wanted and it would have all been over by now."

Belford shook his head in disbelief. She was actually blaming herself! Ethan had her so brainwashed and frightened that she was willing to let him take her body if that meant staying in his good graces. *It was sick! Deplorable! Inexcusable!* "Has he forced himself on you before?" he asked, his eyes set in steel.

Vera must have recognized the look that appeared across Belford's face because she grabbed hold of his arm as if to stop him from turning around and marching right into Ethan's cabin. "Without him I would be homeless, living on the streets of Erotos," she pleaded. "He's the only hope we have of ridding the world of Garrett." She squeezed her fingers tight around his wrist.

Belford sneered. "Ethan isn't the only one with the Mark of Kings on his arm," he retorted. "And just because he's given you a job doesn't excuse this…."

"Don't," said Vera, locking eyes with Belford. "You will only make things worse. He's had a lifetime to refine his abilities; he could easily kill you if he wanted. And don't fool yourself: He doesn't need your help for this mission—he only used you to get the Arcanum Council's approval. Now that we are away from Phandrol, you are just as disposable as the rest of us."

Belford didn't know what to say. He wondered how accurate Vera's insight was.

"Besides, it's not your place. I'm an adult. I can take care of myself." Vera's tears had stopped and she was staring Belford down with her jaw held tight.

Belford sighed. Vera didn't want his help, but allowing Ethan to continue abusing her like this didn't sit right with him. If Ethan was as dangerous as Vera believed, Belford didn't know if he was even capable of helping her, though. It wasn't fear for his own safety that held him back, nor Vera's warning—the only thing that stopped him from confronting Ethan was knowing that doing so would hurt his chances of finding Claire. The moral conundrum bit at Belford's insides like fire ants beneath his flesh. He knew he was being selfish, even though he was following Vera's wishes. If the girl hadn't been so adamant about not wanting Belford to interfere, he didn't think he would have been able to hold himself back from confronting Ethan, even if it meant jeopardizing his personal mission. Still, he couldn't just leave her sitting out here in the hallway like this.

"Do you have anywhere to sleep tonight?" he asked. He knew every cabin aboard the Rosa Marsa was occupied—it was the only reason he was staying in such a terrible room himself.

Vera shook her head, a little bit of her fortitude draining from her face.

"Let's go," said Belford, leading her back down the hallway. "You can sleep in my room."

Vera hesitated for a moment, but then matched his stride. They hadn't gone far when Belford realized Vera was having trouble holding up her torn dress while walking. He stopped briefly to use the Power to mend the fabric. He was familiar with using his abilities to do intricate work such as this— compared to the full flowing gown he formed for Kara after transforming her body back from being a Whune, this was exceedingly simple. Vera flinched slightly as Belford reached towards her, but relaxed again as he slid his fingers gently across the surface of the damaged area, flattening the fabric out and shifting it into proper alignment over her shoulder. The strap reformed, cinching together one thread at a time until it looked as if it were never damaged.

Belford pulled back when he was done, but Vera reached out and clutched onto his left arm with both hands as they continued down the hallway. Coriva was hidden away in the galley when they passed through the mess. Belford was grateful not to have the woman staring down his neck this time around. He went to take another swig of mead and realized he'd already finished off the whole bottle. He placed it down on a table as he passed. Once he reached his cabin door, he immediately bid Vera goodnight. Besides the fact that it wouldn't have felt appropriate for him to stay, there was only space enough for one to fit comfortably on the narrow cot in the tiny closet of a room. Vera needed her rest right now more than he did. Thankfully, the voices that typically kept Belford up at night had receded.

Before he could close the door, Vera leaned over to Belford and gave him a soft kiss on the corner of his mouth. He thought she was aiming for his cheek, but their lips met together with the silent peck.

She felt so warm….

Vera scrunched up her face momentarily as she retracted. It was the first non-glaring expression Belford had seen her make. She lingered in the doorway. Belford stared into her dark-green eyes, still glistening with moisture. They grew wide with anticipation.

Belford couldn't deny that he found Vera to be attractive. The twinge of excitement he felt as her lips brushed gently against his was immediately followed by an intense wave of guilt in his stomach. He shouldn't have enjoyed her touch so much! His breath caught in his chest as she leaned in again. Despite his reservations, his lips parted ever so slightly, accepting her kiss as she placed her mouth upon him.

His heart was pounding; his head swimming with arousal. Without even thinking, he put his hands on her body, holding her hips atop the newly mended dress. They shifted backwards together into the cabin. The passion that came over him was sudden and unexpected. He didn't even bother to latch the door behind him as he guided her to the cot. He followed her down onto the bed, their lips not separating for even a moment as he positioned himself over her.

Desire gripped him as he slid her dress free of her shoulders. It had been too long since he'd experienced any intimacy. Vera moaned softly as he shifted his mouth down her body, kissing her neck. His wandering hands found their way to her breasts. Excitement was rising like wildfire in his belly. He moved his mouth lower, kissing her exposed chest, flicking her hardened nipples back and forth with his tongue and fingers. She moaned again as his hands danced effortlessly across her skin. Her breath was becoming faster.

Unexpectedly, Vera took hold of his right hand and pulled it against her, placing his fingers beneath her dress, between her legs. He could feel the wet heat through her panties. Her eyes shined in the lamp light streaming in through the cabin's open door from down the hall in the well-lit mess. Belford stared into her dark, oval eyes, begging him to continue. His motions felt foreign to him, as if someone else had taken over his body. His urges were animalistic; in the moment; without worry or care. Vera reached out again, helping Belford tug his shirt off over his head.

She gasped as Belford pulled her panties to the side with a sudden tug. He placed his fingers against her bare skin, shaved and soft, so tender beneath his fingertips. She immediately bucked against his hand, enveloping him in her wetness as the tips of his fingers sank inside of her.

He wanted more.

He wanted to feel close to someone again.

Needed to.

He couldn't resist. He pushed in deeper, feeling the rise and fall of her chest beneath him; their bodies pressed together, grinding against one another, skin on skin. He kissed her again and again, stifling her moans with his mouth as he slid his fingers faster.

Vera grabbed hold of his head with both hands, intertwining her fingers in his hair. She gripped hard against his scalp as he forced another moan to escape her mouth. She gyrated against his hand.

He could tell from the look in her eyes that she wanted something more.

She pushed his head down, inching his tongue closer towards her glistening lips. She pulled her dress up to expose her stomach. Belford felt goosebumps arise on her legs as he kissed across her fair skin, sliding ever lower. Vera bucked up into the air as Belford gripped onto her panties with both hands, aiding him in sliding them free.

As he leaned back down he ran his tongue up the inner side of her left leg starting from her knee. Vera shivered with anticipation as he reached her thigh. When he finally got to the top she grabbed his hair once more and pulled him against her, burying his nose in her wetness. Belford felt his own body tingle now as she grinded against his face. He lapped out with his tongue, tasting her. His mouth watered as his head spun with intense euphoria. He dove in fully, licking her again and again, drawing small circles as he went, each one making her twitch. The Rosa Marsa swayed. Belford braced himself against the wall of the cabin as he teased her with his tongue.

"Take me," Vera gasped out between moans. "Take me now!" All of her little twitches and shivers were driving Belford wild with lust. He hadn't the willpower to resist.

Footsteps in the hallway approached quickly from the mess. His excitement was interrupted as he took notice of the sound. Thoughts of Ethan catching him with "his plaything" sent ice through Belford's veins.

He shot up in an instant, jumping out of the cot just as Shiara pushed open the unlatched door. She glanced into the room, her eyes falling across Vera, fully exposed with her legs spread eagle. Shiara's eyebrows lowered into a saddened frown. She turned on the spot and headed back towards the mess without a word.

Belford shared a quick, wide-eyed look with Vera. "Shit," he said, under his breath.

Vera was blushing, but she bit her lip at Belford, playfully urging him to continue despite the interruption.

He didn't feel right just letting Shiara walk away after seeing that, though. "Stay here," he said.

Vera cocked her head to the side with a raised eyebrow.

"I'll be right back," said Belford. He rushed out of the tiny cabin. "Wait up," he yelled out to Shiara as he shut the door behind him and pulled his shirt back on over his head.

Shiara quickened her pace. She was already through the mess and out the other side by the time Belford caught up with her.

"Shiara, wait!" he said, but she continued to walk away. He moved out in front of her and placed his hand against the wall, trying to stop her with his arm. The dark expression on her face soured further as she shoved his hand aside and continued on towards her cabin. Belford ran in front of her again, this time placing his whole body in the doorway to her cabin to stop her from running away. She couldn't push past him this time.

"What the hell do you want from me?" Shiara snapped.

Belford didn't know how to respond. He stood frozen in place in front of her.

"You can't be with me because you're in love with Claire, but you can be with *that* hussy?" Moisture was gathering in Shiara's eyes.

Belford's chest throbbed at the mention of Claire. A sick feeling lingered in his gut as Shiara physically shoved him aside and entered her cabin. "It's not like that," he said. "It wasn't planned!"

Shiara spun around on him. "You can tell yourself whatever you want: Claire's probably dead; you just wanted some quick, easy piece of ass; one last romp before we risk our lives. I don't care anymore! It's none of my business who you fuck. Just leave me out of it. Goodnight."

Shiara slammed the door in his face.

He was left feeling confused. It made sense that seeing him with Vera would hurt Shiara, but he never would have expected such a strong reaction from her. He must have underestimated her feelings for him.

He began a stumbling walk back towards his cabin. The mead was starting to take control of his legs.

It had been too long since he felt another person's warmth against his skin. As sick as it was, it was his longing for Claire's touch that made him so ravenous under Vera's kiss. Despite the high probability that Claire really was gone from him forever, the experience made him feel like a cheater. Belford sighed.

When he reached his cabin, he peeked inside to find Vera fast asleep. In all honesty, it was a relief. He didn't want to let her down, but didn't feel up for sex at all anymore. The guilt was too heavy in his stomach.

What would Claire think if she could see me now?

Belford sighed again.

He turned away from the door and began to wander aimlessly.

CHAPTER

32

The Stowaway

Having already given up his chance at sleeping for the night, Belford wasn't sure what to do with himself. He no longer wanted to speak with Ethan. He couldn't trust himself to talk to *that* man right now—there was a good chance he would end up punching him square in the face for the way he'd treated Vera. He thought about going up to the helm to hang out with Captain Bundles, but he wasn't much fun to talk to when he was focused on piloting. When Belford reached the stairway, instead of climbing up, he stepped down into the bilge. The familiar orange glow of the furnace room bled out into the narrow pathway in front of him, shining across the pipes that ran along the walls. Already he could feel the heat of the inferno radiating out from the heart of the Rosa Marsa.

Beyond the bulkhead was the engine room. The sounds of a shovel scraping through a barrel of coals made a rhythmic beat which was joined by a pair of voices belonging to the fraternal twins who worked the furnace. Ader and Mikel Naffeim were just the sort of company Belford needed right now. The cheery outlanders were singing in their own language, and though Belford had no idea what they were saying, the emphasized rhythm of their tune made for some contagious head-bobbing as Belford neared.

"Hello, Belford!" yelled Ader over the sizzle of the furnace as Belford stepped through the bulkhead. Mikel, the shorter of the brothers, turned around as well, putting his shovel down and greeting Belford with an arm clasping handshake. Ader flipped an empty stool upright and moved it over so that Belford had a place to sit down.

Belford had truly missed the Naffeim brothers. They worked the furnace at night, constantly shoveling coal, and slept through most of the day. With Belford spending his evenings attempting to meditate, this was the first time since departing Erotos that he'd seen the brothers for more than a moment in passing.

"Not sleeping?" Mikel asked as he picked up a charred rake and began adjusting the last shovel-full of coal that was thrown into the blazing furnace.

Belford shrugged. He didn't want to get into everything that had just happened with Vera and Shiara. "I have the little room by the stairs," he said. "Voices have been keeping me up at night."

"Voices?" asked Ader, looking bemused.

"Yeah," said Belford. "I can't figure out where they're coming from. They only talk at night and I can only hear them from inside my cabin. I thought it might have been you guys down here at first, but now I suspect Garcenus has something to do with it—I keep seeing him skulking around the supply closet."

Ader and Mikel looked at each other, a serious expression suddenly falling over both of their faces. "Closet by main stairs, up there?" Ader asked, pointing back behind Belford to the staircase.

"Yeah…" said Belford. "Why?"

The brothers shared another look, having a silent discussion with just their eyes. They were hesitant to share whatever they were thinking. Finally, Ader turned back towards Belford. "There is passageway there… secret compartment," he said, "for hiding things… like smuggle?"

Mikel was nodding. "Smuggler's area," he said, "for cargo that is not allowed. Helps get through inspections, you know?"

"A smuggler's hold?" Belford asked. "In the supply closet?"

"Yes, yes," said Ader and Mikel together. "Is secret," Mikel added, "only crew supposed to know, so don't tell."

"So you think Garcenus is talking to somebody back there?" Belford asked. His first thought immediately went to Weni, the old first mate that Garcenus was having a relationship with before she was supposedly left behind in North Galdren—but that was several months ago! It made no sense for someone to be hiding back there—*what could be the purpose?* Belford couldn't think of anyone else Garcenus would be sneaking off to see.

"Maybe he talk to himself!" said Ader. The brothers laughed hysterically at their joke.

It *was* a possibility, Belford had to admit. Garcenus was a bit *off*. Every passing week since leaving Erotos, his odd behavior only grew more apparent. Belford stayed with the Naffeim brothers for another hour or so, but the whole time he was in front of the furnace, he couldn't get the thought of the smuggler's compartment out of his head. If Garcenus wasn't going mad, that meant he was talking to somebody in there, long conversations that lasted all hours of the night. The more he thought about it, the more he wondered if there might be a stowaway hidden aboard the Rosa Marsa.

A friend of Garcenus's from Erotos? Weni?

Belford had no idea, but his curiosity was palpable.

After saying goodnight to the brothers, Belford exited the bilge with the intention of discovering once and for all who had been keeping him up all these nights. As he ascended the stairs to the main level he heard a strange thumping noise coming from the short hallway that led to the cargo area. Belford peeked around the corner to see Livian Niern on guard duty for the night. From her seat on the stool by the cargo area, she was throwing a small black rubber ball against the floor and bouncing it off the wall. It returned perfectly to her outstretched hand every time.

Belford still hadn't made any headway towards gaining Livian's trust. After Arlin's bombshell about Mallory being pregnant, Belford hadn't the heart to ask him to pretend to be interested in Livian. The Illusionist still sent flirtatious vibes out at Arlin, but the swordsman never wavered in his devotion to Mallory.

Ever since being accosted by Deenan Raughel, Belford had learned not to bother anyone who was guarding the cargo hold door. Whatever the Ver'ati were keeping back there, only Ethan and Sarbin were allowed access beyond the hallway. The two men met back there for hours every day.

Livian noticed Belford peeking at her and sent him a fluttering wink as she continued to throw her ball—a steady *thunk, thunk, slap* as it hit the two surfaces and then returned to the palm of her hand.

Belford let her be, turning the opposite way to place himself in front of the supply closet. He opened the door and stepped inside, latching it behind him. As soon as the door was shut, Belford was lost in darkness. He could sense the walls tight around him, though he couldn't see anything through the pitch black. He lifted his hands and quickly formed a light orb. As soon as the milky glow filled the closet, Belford began looking around to see if he could figure out how to access the secret compartment. Through the thin wall to his right was his cabin where Vera lay fast asleep, and to his left was the stairwell, so he focused his attention on the back wall of the closet.

Lamp oil, ropes, a box of drying rags, a metal wedge on a stick that appeared to be a rust scraper, a thick-bristled brush—shelves full of all sorts of random clutter. Belford searched back and forth shifting things around to see if there was some sort of hidden lever or clasp behind any of the objects that could be manipulated to form an opening to the hidden chamber.

After several minutes without making any progress, the room cooled to near freezing levels from Belford's light orb sapping all of the energy out of the air. He was about to give up his search and let the orb falter when one of the items suddenly struck a chord of curiosity within him. The rust scraper, never before used based on its brand-new sheen, stared up at him from the right side of the middle shelf. Judging from the amount of rust that was plastered all over the belly of the Rosa Marsa, no one had ever attempted to use any such device in the life of the vessel.

Belford picked up the scraper by its thin wooden handle and inspected it in the light of his orb. There didn't appear to be anything odd about it other than the fact that it had never been used. Looking closer at where the scraper had been sitting, though, he noticed a slight gap between the wooden board of the shelf and the side wall that adjoined with his cabin. On a whim he wedged the thin blade of the scraper between the two boards and used the handle like a lever to pry to the side. The whole back wall of the closet shifted sideways with a scraping sound, leaving a gap large enough for Belford to squeeze through behind the false wall.

He hesitated. It would be a tight fit to say the least, and he had no idea who or what might be back there waiting for him. At least if someone was hiding they would probably think he was just Garcenus coming back to talk some more. There hadn't been any sound so far to indicate that anyone was there, but Belford still got butterflies in his stomach as he stuck his head through the hole to inspect the hollow.

It was a narrow walkway, leading aft along the side of the Rosa Marsa towards the main cargo hold. The corridor curved with the hull of the ship, leaving him unable to see beyond the first few feet of the walkway. A large part of him wanted to turn back now, but he knew he wasn't going to find any answers by standing still.

Belford pushed through his jitters and climbed full on into the secret passage. With the wall against his back, he shifted sideways down the narrow corridor past the stairwell that resided on the other side of the wall. He could hear the *thunk, thunk, slap* of Livian's ball on repeat as he moved closer to the cargo area. After the stairwell, he found the main chamber of the hold. It opened up a bit wider; just enough room for two people to stand side by side if they pressed their shoulders together. It was a long rectangular room that looked to run the entire length of the cargo hold. The chamber was empty apart from a small wooden chair and several half-drank bottles of booze. That was it for the secret cargo hold; there was nowhere else to go from here.

Apparently Garcenus had been talking to himself after all, coming back here every night to drink himself into a stupor. Belford felt genuinely sorry for him—Garcenus lost the person he cared about most. Belford was a little disappointed that he hadn't found Weni stowed away. With the mystery solved, Belford turned around to squeeze his way back down the pathway, but just as he was about to leave, something glinted, catching his eye. He froze in place, shifting back and forth on the balls of his feet, trying to see exactly where the flash came from.

After a moment he saw the glint again—a yellow reflection, shining between two of the slats that formed the wall between the secret room and the regular cargo area. Looking more closely now, he realized that some of the boards that made up the dividing wall were loose, as if they had been removed and replaced numerous times.

He stepped up close to the wall and peered between the boards. It was too dark to make out much, but he could see a pair of small, identical spheres lined up horizontally on the other side of the divide. When Belford lifted his glowing orb up to the gap to shine some light through to the other side, the spheres suddenly blinked and retracted out of sight.

Belford jumped back in fright, the light orb bursting apart in a blinding flash as he lost his concentration. *Eyeballs! I was staring directly into something's eyes from less than an inch away!* He shivered at the creepiness of the whole situation. *What kind of eyes reflect yellow?*

"Who's back there?" Belford asked, his voice cracking slightly as he scrambled to create another light orb.

A chuckling laugh sounded from beyond the wall, sending another shiver down Belford's spine.

"Who's hiding back there?" Belford asked again. He didn't wait for an answer. Once his orb was reformed in his palm, he reached up with his free hand and pried one of the loose boards free of the wall. Light immediately filled the second chamber, illuminating the stowaway.

Belford hadn't known what he was going to find on the other side of the wall, but he certainly wasn't expecting this. He immediately recognized the pale, wrinkled face that stared back at him. Even with his gnarled, gray beard and overgrown hair making him look like a savage, wild animal, Belford could never mistake those dark, soulless eyes, reflecting yellow in the orb light. Wilgoblikan's jaw curled up into a wide grin; a face straight out of his nightmares.

CHAPTER

33

Persuasion

Wood splintered in all directions as an explosion of debris ripped through the Rosa Marsa's cargo hold. It was as if a cannon had gone off. Belford hardly even realized what he was doing as he gestured again, sending another shockwave of energy straight through the dividing wall, aimed at the dark wizard who was crouched somewhere out of sight on the other side. Shards of wood soared like arrows through the air, embedding themselves into the far wall of the chamber. Belford plowed his whole body through what remained of the wall's feeble structure, crashing into Wilgoblikan's hiding place.

The Goblikan Whune was sprawled out on the floor, half-covered by fallen boards. The dark wizard hadn't yet made an attempt at channeling the Power, but Belford wasn't about to give him the chance. Belford knew he could not kill another wizard with the Power directly. A safety measure built into the system prevented him from being able to pull apart the molecules of anyone who shared a mental connection with the supercomputer, but he was still able to use more conventional methods of attack. He straddled Wilgoblikan and immediately began to rain down blow after blow with his clenched fists. Belford felt the sting growing in his knuckles as he pounded away. The dark wizard didn't even attempt to defend himself.

The door to the cargo hold burst open, filling the air with lantern light as Livian Niern sprang into the room. Wilgoblikan stood no chance now! Belford continued to pummel the dark wizard as Livian took in the destruction and then sprinted across the broken boards to Belford's side.

As he raised his fist again, about to smash it back down into Wilgoblikan's battered face, Livian slammed straight into his side with all her weight. Belford was thrown off of Wilgoblikan as Livian tumbled over on top of him, knocking Belford onto his back against the side of the cargo hold.

Livian hadn't tripped. *She smashed into me on purpose!* The Illusionist's ash-brown ponytail dangled over her shoulder and into Belford's face as she pinned him against the floor. Fortunately, Wilgoblikan was already beaten into a daze and did not rise now that Belford was no longer on top of him.

Out in the hallway through the open door, Vera popped her head around the corner, awoken by all the commotion. She disappeared just as quickly. Belford could hear her footsteps running up the metal staircase as she went for help.

"What are you doing?" Belford shouted at Livian. "Get off me!" Belford continued to struggle against her until she kneed him in the groin. The shock of the blow made Belford's whole body clinch up. The impact wasn't hard enough to make him throw up, but the pain left his head swimming as his innards rumbled terribly. *Livian is working with Wilgoblikan! She is going to kill me—or worse, infect me with her brain spores!* She could turn him into a soulless

Goblikan; just another one of Garrett's lackeys, willing to murder indiscriminately for the joy of it. *I would rather die!*

The clang of footsteps, coming back down the metal staircase this time, gave Belford a sliver of hope. Around the corner came Captain Bundles and Sarbin Raiger, led by Vera.

"Get Ethan," Sarbin immediately said to Vera upon seeing the destruction in the cargo hold. The girl disappeared again, running back down the hallway.

"What in the Light of the Starcaller is goin' on down here?" cried Captain Bundles. "What've ya done to my ship!?"

"Stand back," said Sarbin, placing his arm out in front of Captain Bundles to stop him from getting any closer to Wilgoblikan.

The captain's eyebrows lowered into an outraged frown at the steward giving him an order. He pushed past Sarbin's arm in disgust. "Who's that conch-blower, and what's he doin' on my ship?" he asked, pointing his finger down into Wilgoblikan's bloodied face.

Sarbin ignored Captain Bundles as Ethan came sprinting down the hallway. No expression appeared on Ethan's face as he glanced over the scene—not until he saw Belford straddled beneath Livian, anyway. "How hard is it to keep watch over a god damn door?" he asked, a blue spark of fire appearing behind his eyes.

Livian was fuming now as well. "It's not my fault!" she cried out. "He didn't come through the door—came smashing through the wall over there like a madman!"

Ethan's head shifted towards the secret compartment, now gaped wide open by Belford's blasts. With Livian distracted by Ethan's presence, Belford used the opportunity to squirm out from under the buxom Ver'ati.

"Are you idiots not seeing Wilgoblikan lying right there?" Belford asked, fending off Livian while making another grab at the dark wizard.

"Calm down," said Ethan. "He's been de-clawed—injected with inhibitor. You don't have to worry about him using the Power anymore."

"Yer transporting a prisoner on my ship without my permission?" Captain Bundles was irate. His face turned red as his blood pressure skyrocketed.

Ethan stepped up to the captain and shoved him hard against the wall. He held Bundles there with his forearm as he stared him down. "You may be the captain of this rusted-out hunk of metal you call a steamer, but this is my mission," he said in a low voice. "You should have told me there was a smuggler's compartment." He pulled the captain away from the wall and shoved him back towards the cargo hold's entrance.

The captain stumbled as he practically fell through the doorway.

"Go back to piloting," Ethan said. "Who's steering this damned thing right now anyway?"

Captain Bundles looked like he wanted to kill Ethan, but he held his tongue. He knew Ethan could destroy him with a single thought.

"I'll have more words for you when I'm finished in here," said Ethan. He turned his focus away from Captain Bundles, ignoring the captain's lingering glare. The captain eventually slinked away, back up the stairs to the bridge, his pride vastly deflated. Ethan turned towards Belford now, the anger draining from his expression, replaced with disappointment. "What are you doing in here?" he asked Belford as he gestured for Livian to step aside. The woman went over and began to inspect Wilgoblikan's injuries.

Belford was still trying to wrap his mind around everyone's nonchalant behavior towards Wilgoblikan. "You said he was dead!" he said, glaring at Ethan.

Ethan sighed. "He's a state secret. All information on him was on a need-to-know basis."

How easily Ethan lied to me....

"*I* needed to know," Belford said. "What if he can tell me how to find Claire?"

"Quite frankly, you didn't need to know. There are much more important things at play here than trying to find your girlfriend."

Belford's jaw tightened as anger began to rise in his chest.

"Now tell me what you were doing back here," Ethan ordered.

Belford barely managed to restrain himself from lunging at Ethan. He vary badly wanted to punch him in the face. He answered begrudgingly: "I kept hearing Garcenus sneak into the smuggler's hold. He was talking to someone, so I came back to check it out."

Ethan narrowed his eyes. "Garcenus? Is that the scowly one? With the dark hair?"

Belford nodded. He still wasn't sure how much he could trust Ethan after the doubt cast by his recovered memories. Belford glanced over at Vera, still standing outside of the cargo hold entrance. Just seeing the girl lit a fire inside Belford's heart as he thought about the horrible things Ethan did to her. It was Ethan that should be doing the explaining. "Now tell me, what is *he* doing here?" Belford wasn't so much as asking for an explanation as he was demanding one.

Ethan considered his words carefully. "Wilgoblikan is how we are going to kill Garrett," he said. "We are using him to gain first-hand knowledge of Garrett's security measures."

"He can't be trusted," said Belford. "He's too dangerous!"

"He's nothing more than an old man now that his connection to the Power has been severed," said Ethan. "Though, you are correct that honesty would be too much for us to hope for from a Whune. The Compulsion that Garrett put him under prevents him from saying anything that would betray his master."

"What's the point, then?" asked Belford. "Why bring him along if everything he tells you is useless?"

"It is precisely his inability to betray his master that inevitably leads to the truth coming out."

Belford stared at Ethan in confusion; he was talking in circles.

"I'll show you what I mean," said Ethan. He turned towards Livian and the battered Whune. "Could you go get Captain Grine again?" he asked the Illusionist.

Livian was frowning over the mess that Belford made of Wilgoblikan's face, but she got up without question and departed the cargo hold. Sarbin closed the door behind her, blocking out Vera from sight, and then removed a small, cloudy crystal from his pocket. It looked like something a spiritual healer might use to cleanse a person's chakras. Sarbin placed the crystal in the middle of the floor and then tapped it gently with a small metal rod, producing a high-pitched tone.

Immediately, it was as if Belford's ears stopped working. All of the usual sounds of the Rosa Marsa—the hum of the engines, the pattering of the waterwheels, the splashes of the river lapping against the side of the hull—all fell away, going silent as if time were frozen. Belford could still feel the steamer's motion as it was tossed about by the storm, but even the sound of the howling winds was now absent from the cargo hold.

"A sound dampening Artifact," Ethan explained. His voice sounded odd. It was as if he were speaking from within the dead vacuum of space. "As useless as the Arcanum usually is, they certainly have some valuable resources to offer."

Sarbin ignored the half-insult as he stood back up from placing the crystal.

"Why do we need that?" Belford asked, his words sounding as hollow as Ethan's.

The door to the cargo hold opened. With its sound absent, Belford wouldn't have noticed the change if he hadn't been looking in the general direction already. Captain Grine stood in the doorway, his eyes wide with concern behind his spectacles. He wasn't supposed to be wearing his glasses anymore now that they were in Kovehn, but no one mentioned the infraction. Sarbin gestured for Grine to approach. He closed the door behind him; there was no click as it shut—Belford felt like he was underwater, looking up through the surface at a silent world beyond. He could hear Grine's footsteps only after he took several silent steps forward first. As he crossed the invisible barrier made by the Artifact, his sounds returned, though they remained dampened like their voices.

"Fix him," Ethan ordered Grine, gesturing towards Wilgoblikan. The Whune had regained consciousness and was starting to shift around slightly upon the pile of broken boards.

"You said we weren't going to do this anymore for a few days," Grine complained.

"Plans change," said Ethan.

Grine sighed as he approached Wilgoblikan and laid his hands on the dark wizard's face. Wilgoblikan flinched, pulling away from the pain caused by Captain Grine's pressure. Grine's hands began to glow as he used Amelioration to heal the Whune's injuries. Wilgoblikan shook from the intense stinging sensation of Grine's heavy-handed method. As soon as the Ver'ati finished, though, Wilgoblikan's whole body relaxed and he was able to sit up under his own strength.

"Let me show you what I was talking about, now," said Ethan, stepping over to the disgruntled looking Whune. Wilgoblikan had a defeated look in his eyes even before Ethan retrieved a pair of clipping sheers, handed to him by Sarbin. "Hello, Wilgoblikan," Ethan said, shifting the sheers back and forth between his hands. They looked like something someone would use in a garden to prune bushes or thin branches. "I'm going to ask you a simple question, and I want you to answer with a *yes*. If you remain silent, or respond in any other way, I will cut something off."

As much as Belford hated Wilgoblikan for everything he did to Kara and the people of Bronam, he felt sick to his stomach watching the polished sheers dancing between Ethan's hands.

"Does Garrett usually take his supper in his personal chambers?" Ethan asked.

Wilgoblikan glared at Ethan through eyes that were still puffy despite Grine's healing.

Ethan raised the sheers to Wilgoblikan's left ear, placing his pale, dangling lobe between the pristine blades.

"Yes," said Wilgoblikan through gritted teeth.

"What was that," said Ethan, continuing to hold the sheers steady.

"Yes," repeated Wilgoblikan more clearly.

"And in a full sentence now so I know you aren't pulling any tricks."

"Yes, King Garrett usually takes his supper in his personal chambers." Wilgoblikan cast his eyes towards the floor.

Ethan lowered the sheers and turned back to Belford. "Because Garrett has Compelled Wilgoblikan's loyalty, the Whune is physically incapable of providing any information that could affect his master negatively. Since Wilgoblikan knows we intend to kill Garrett, he cannot tell us anything that will aid us even marginally, like where he takes his meals, for instance. From his answer, though, we now know that Garrett usually does not take his dinner in his personal chambers. If Garrett did, Wilgoblikan would have been unable to tell us about it." He turned back towards Wilgoblikan. "Does Garrett usually take his dinner in the palace's main dining hall?"

Wilgoblikan remained silent, shifting uncomfortably in his ragged clothes.

Ethan raised the sheers to his ear once more. "Answer now or I'll cut it off," he said simply.

A bead of sweat formed on Wilgoblikan's brow, but he did not verbalize a response.

With a quick clench of Ethan's fist, Wilgoblikan's shriveled, white earlobe fell to the deck as the Whune let out a bloodcurdling scream. The sound dampening Artifact captured the cries, making them only slightly more bearable to Belford's ears. Blood drizzled from the cut line at the new bottom of Wilgoblikan's lobe. His eyes rolled into his head as the pain seared through his body. Ethan snapped his fingers at Grine, and the Ver'ati quickly sealed the wound with a flash of white light.

"I'll ask you again: Does Garrett usually take his dinner in the palace's main dining hall?"

Again, Wilgoblikan did not speak. He was shuddering uncontrollably from the pain.

"Say *yes* or I'll take the right one too," he said.

"Yes," said Wilgoblikan after only a moment more of hesitation.

"Yes, what?" asked Ethan.

"Yes, I am going to rip your heart out of your chest and EAT IT WHILE IT'S STILL BEATING," screamed Wilgoblikan.

Another snip, another terrible cry of pain, and another chunk of Wilgoblikan's body hit the floor beside the withering old man. Ethan let it bleed for a little while before letting Grine seal the wound this time.

"Hurt a normal man enough and you can get him to say anything," said Ethan, "but no matter how much pain you inflict on a Goblikan, he will be unable to give up a piece of information if it is damaging to his master. The tough part is being sure you have pushed him past his breaking point. You must get him to where he will say anything to make it stop— anything but the truth that is. Then you know to believe the opposite. After enough cuts, we will learn the truth."

Belford felt like he was going to be sick. He hadn't felt this disgusted since the day he learned that Whunes were innocent people transformed by the Power. He felt the bile building at the base of this throat and could do nothing to hold it back as he retched onto the floor.

Ethan looked over with sympathetic eyes. "It does take a strong stomach. Distasteful, I know, but there is no other way to find out what we need to know to ensure this mission is a success." Ethan gestured to Grine again and the Ameliorator immediately went about re-growing Wilgoblikan's earlobes. The Whune hissed as the white light enveloped the sides of his head. "Come on," said Ethan, putting his arm over Belford's shoulder, "let's get you something to settle your stomach."

Belford wanted to push Ethan away from him, but there was nowhere to run. Ethan handed Sarbin the blood spattered sheers as he led Belford out of the sound catching bubble. As they exited the cargo hold, Belford noticed a metal bucket propped up against the wall. Inside were hundreds of pale, bloodless fingertips and toes, earlobes and noses, and only god knew what else. Belford felt his face grow hot as another round of vomiting clenched his gut.

CHAPTER

34

Sabotage

The Whune gave Salvine control over her body. She watched in awe as Salvine used her hands to wriggle the claw back and forth in the lock with finesse. With a click, the last pin fell in place and the cage door creaked open with a gentle push. It took far less time than she'd anticipated; Doctor Crane wouldn't be back to check on them again for at least another hour, assuming his schedule stayed consistent. With so much time to spare, the only logical thing to do was recruit some help for their escape.

The other two remaining Whunes watched with intrigue in their eyes as Salvine moved across the laboratory and jimmied the claw into the next lock. As soon as the cage clicked open, the Whune slammed into the front, making quite a racket as the door swung all the way open and banged against its hinges. Running from the laboratory, it let loose a throaty roar before bounding out of sight down the hallway.

Maybe letting them out wasn't such a good idea....

She concurred with Salvine. There was no time to release the second Whune now with the first one being so stupid. They would have to use the lumbering fool as a distraction rather than an ally. *Was I ever that idiotic?*

That much and more, Salvine mused.

Doctor Crane's alterations to her higher brain function were definitely having a positive effect on her intellect. It was hard to imagine being the thoughtless beast she once was. The other two remaining Whunes combined were dumber than a box of rocks compared to her now.

Her feelings of superiority were short lived as a wiry cry rang out from down the hallway—her mindless counterpart already stumbling across some hapless human. Salvine, still in control, moved her legs quickly to the entrance of the laboratory, but just as she reached the sliding door, Crane's assistant came rushing in through the opening and crashed headlong into her meaty chest. He bounced off like a barrelhen thwacking into the side of a barn. He rebounded with a pained cry and landed in a heap on the ground. He certainly hadn't expected to find her loose. Though she wished to tear into him immediately—to sink her jagged teeth into the tender flesh of his neck and relieve him of his throat—she saw the wisdom of Salvine as she moved her arms to capture him instead.

We will make him lead us out of here.

The moon was down, judging from the Ver'ati's lack of an attack with the Power, but she had no way of knowing when it would make its rise again. The risk was worthwhile, though, for without a guide, they would be fumbling around blindly until they were recaptured or killed.

Salvine picked the young man up by the front of his black robe and propped him roughly onto his feet again. The terror and confusion in his eyes was palpable as she spun him around and pointed a gnarled finger towards the door, motioning for him to lead the way. Salvine gripped the back of his neck, holding onto him tight in case he should attempt to make an escape. With a light shove, he began to walk forward.

Realizing how odd it was that he was still alive, the young Ver'ati began to beg for his life. "Please, let me go," he said. "I didn't want Doctor Crane to hurt you! I helped you! Convinced him to untie your rotting arms!"

Both she and Salvine ignored his plea, squeezing his neck slightly harder to shut him up. Out in the hallway, however, they already needed his help. Holding their hostage steady, Salvine gestured one way and then the other down the corridor. "Muuuarp!" she vocalized, trying—and failing—to communicate her question.

The Ver'ati looked at her with a raised eyebrow, fascinated by her un-Whune-like behavior.

Salvine lifted the man up and shook him towards the left and then towards the right in turn, trying to emphasize their need for directions.

"You want to know… the way out?" he asked as he was placed back down on the floor. Perhaps the young Ver'ati wasn't so clueless after all.

"Muuarp."

The man nodded in vague understanding. "Okay," he said. "Just, please, don't hurt me."

Salvine continued to hold the back of his neck as he led them to the right—the same direction the other released Whune had taken. Fifty paces down the hallway, a disemboweled Ver'ati lay dead in a pile of his own organs. Crane's assistant eyed the corpse wildly, though he did not slow his stride.

Another scream from up ahead told of the other Whune's rampage continuing on in the distance. The young Ver'ati led her through its wake of destruction, only slowing when it became clear that they were nearing the ruthless creature. A fight ensued around the corner ahead of them. It sounded like the Whune was winning. Salvine stopped and waited, not wanting to engage in the battle.

"You're smarter than the other ones, aren't you?" Crane's assistant asked.

She gave a grunt of affirmation, bringing a twitch of a smile to the young Ver'ati's lips.

Don't encourage him, Salvine thought to her, *the less noise the better.*

"I knew there was something different about you. You planned all of this, didn't you?"

Salvine growled threateningly.

With a final gurgling scream, the other Whune finished off the last of its foes. The young Ver'ati shut up immediately as the fight ceased. The menacing clomp of the other Whune's feet was all that remained. Crane's assistant stood stiff as the footsteps drew nearer.

Uh-oh.

Wandering aimlessly, the lost Whune rounded the corner, snarling as it recognized the presence of the young Ver'ati. She knew what was going to happen next—the predictable creature did not have the restraint to leave the human alive, despite his death meaning a likely end to their escape.

It lunged at him, still held tight in her grip. Salvine was in primary control of her body. She threw the assistant to the side of the hallway as the other Whune swiped at him with its declawed fingers. Even without its claws, the Whune's attack could easily have been deadly.

Don't let it get him!

She snatched back control from Salvine—as astute as Salvine had been at picking the locks, when it came to a fight, they both knew who should be in control. She grabbed the other Whune's arm and pulled with a swift maneuver that brought the beast to the ground.

The other Whune, dazed by the attack, roared in pain as she twisted its right arm behind its back and wrenched up with all her might. A snap sounded as its elbow blew out. She continued to pull on its arm as she placed her foot down on the back of its neck, grinding its face roughly against the tiled floor.

With a flourish of black cloth, the young Ver'ati brought a hidden dagger out from beneath his robe. She had no time to react as he brought the knife down into the base of the other Whune's skull. Its death was instantaneous. She dropped its arm, preparing to strike back at Crane's assistant before he could stab her as well. Suddenly, he withdrew his hands, placing them into the air while leaving the dagger buried deep in the dead Whune's brain.

"Easy there," he said. "I'm not going to try anything. You saved my life."

She stared the Ver'ati down, daring him to make a move.

"I promise I won't hurt you. My name's Theilo, by the way," he said, hands still raised in the air. "If I put my hands down, you aren't going to kill me are you?"

She grunted again. Despite his cooperation, Theilo made her nervous.

He lowered his hands to his sides as he rose back to his feet. "I never wanted to hurt you, you know. I don't like the way Doctor Crane is running things down here. I'm training to be an Ameliorator. We are supposed to help people, not maim them worse."

Theilo, smartly, did not attempt to retrieve his dagger as they continued on around the corner. He walked without prompting this time. They approached a door on their left. Within were two sets of stairs—one going down and the other up.

"The surface is one level up," said Theilo, "but if you go out into the streets in the middle of the day you'll be killed before you even step off the sidewalk."

Salvine didn't want to hear any of it. She snatched back control of their body and grabbed at Theilo again.

"Whoa, now," said Theilo, dodging her swinging arm. "There's another option. A better one."

Salvine stayed her hand.

"Instead of going up, you could go down, deeper into the Underground. It's a labyrinth down there. You bide your time and then come up later, somewhere unexpected. It won't be easy, but the way I see it, it's the best chance you have."

It made sense, she had to admit. The dark, twisting tunnels of the Underground were where Wilgoblikan got her into the city in the first place. From the hidden Goblikan railway, a set of conjoining passageways formed a breach into the Erotos Underground. She doubted she could find her way back to the railway, but the vast tunnel system would be the perfect place to hide, at the very least.

She allowed Theilo to lead her downward, out of the tiled hallways and into a narrow, rocky tunnel. Almost immediately, her acute senses picked up an odd rumble. It was distinct from the natural churn of the nearby river that flowed overhead. Faint, though it was, she could hear an oscillating hum, mechanical in nature. Her mind immediately went to the train that brought her and her brethren south, but that was unlikely. Still, the sound piqued her curiosity.

They delved deeper into the catacomb-like tunnels, lit sporadically by glowing orbs. Theilo slowed his pace. He paused entirely at a split in the passageway. "I must admit, I do not know my way around down here all that well," he said.

The oscillating hum was still faint, but directional. Her curiosity drew her towards the sound. She prodded Theilo to the right. The young Ver'ati noticed her intentional choice. A look of understanding fell across his face.

"You're going towards the power plant..." he marveled, "you really are a smart one, aren't you? You could take out the lights to the whole city!" He appeared more excited than concerned.

The revelation of a power plant was news to her. She didn't know what a power plant was, really, but the context was obvious. If all the lights went out, her ability to see clearly in the dark would be a great advantage over anyone else she might encounter during her escape.

A slight smirk danced across Theilo's lips as the pathway descended deeper into the earth to dip beneath the river above. Water dripped into the passage at regular intervals, forming puddles that slowly seeped through tiny cracks in the stone. She rushed ahead, following the sounds of the distant machinery. Theilo stayed close, running by her side when the corridors were wide enough, and just behind her when they were not. He kept up with her stride by moving at the upper limits of his feeble human body. The young Ver'ati was panting heavily by the time they stopped at a tunnel that slanted downward at a steep angle. He placed his hands on his knees, his chest heaving from exertion.

The power plant was close. With her sensitive hearing, she could hear footsteps, several pairs, sounding from down the tunnel. Theilo heard them as well. "Let me go ahead and scout the place out," he said once he managed to catch his breath.

The Ver'ati had proved useful so far, but neither she nor Salvine trusted him enough to allow him to go ahead on his own. It was far too likely he would use the opportunity to escape and raise an alarm against her. She gripped him hard on the back of the neck as he attempted to move ahead of her.

"Fine," said Theilo in frustration. "I just wanted to avoid unnecessary bloodshed."

As much fun as bloodshed would have been, she knew such actions taken without necessity could only serve to hinder her escape. She held back with Theilo until the footsteps began to recede into the distance, and only then did they proceed down the ramp.

The deeper they went, the more dense the air became. Thick cables lined the walls on either side of the corridor, filling the limited ventilation shafts with their girth. The machinery was loud here, possibly drowning out the sounds of guardsmen up ahead. She could tell Salvine was nervous, her stride slowing to a more cautious pace. With every split of the passageway the roaring rumble settled deeper into the stone.

Without warning, the shaft suddenly opened up into a vast cavern with smooth Calvenite walls. Down a steep embankment a dark river flowed quickly towards a mechanical structure. Wide blades spun with a furious whir as the water jetted through shafts and out of sight beyond the cavern.

"Magnificent!" shouted Theilo. He had to yell to be heard over the crashing waters. "This is my first time seeing it myself! It turns the kinetic force of the river into the energy that fills all the glowing bulbs across the entire city."

She did not really understand it, but it truly was magnificent. Now she just had to figure out how to break it.

Those blades look strong, thought Salvine. *I doubt throwing anything against them would do any good.*

Scanning her eyes across the cavern, she could see several glass windows looking out over the river. The glass was opaque, hiding what lie behind, but she got the distinct impression that more than one set of eyes was following her every movement. Theilo had a curious expression on his face.

She felt boxed in, even with such a wide space surrounding her. With an aggressive grunt, she dashed forwards, running along the slanted ledge of the chamber. Theilo trotted along behind her, unable to keep up with her all-out sprint. She chose the nearest window and jumped, kicking out with both feet as she collided with the clouded glass. It shattered easily under her weight. She crashed to the ground as several cries of terror rang out. There were three men in the room, all wearing long jackets. They fled the small chamber at once, scrambling to distance themselves from her.

Theilo reached the window behind her, climbing gingerly over the ledge littered with broken glass, and into the carpeted room.

Salvine, still in control, got to her feet and scampered out of the chamber. It would only be a matter of time before an alarm was raised. She took a left, darting down a narrow corridor—the opposite direction of the fleeing men—back towards the spinning blades, but this time from the inside of the strange facility. Theilo had every opportunity to escape, but he stayed at her back for whatever reason.

She reached the end of the tunnel. A closed door stood between her and the machinery she needed to destroy. She kicked at it and beat on it with her fists, denting the thick metal. It did not take long before the hinges bent beyond their integrity and the door fell inwards.

Before her was a confusing nest of levers, gears and panels. She had no idea how any of it worked, and so wasn't sure where to start with her sabotage. She grabbed a random lever, pried it all the way in one direction, and then kept pulling until the bar ripped free of the wall entirely. Nothing of consequence seemed to happen. She tossed the lever to the ground and then moved over to a crank that was attached to a series of pipes.

Before she had a chance to mess with it, Theilo spoke up: "I wouldn't touch that one," he said. "It appears to control the outflow tunnels. If you close them, the water could back up and flood the Underground…."

She glanced over at Theilo, weighing her options. Salvine was deep in thought as well. *That would certainly break things,* Salvine mused, *but if the Underground floods we won't have anywhere to hide.*

A flood would be a great distraction, she retorted. *We only need to remain hidden until nightfall, then head to the surface under the protection of the dark. Besides, how fast could the river possibly flood all the passageways?*

Salvine didn't have an answer. *I guess that's as good of a plan as any.* She grabbed onto the crank. It looked dainty in her massive hands. According to the diagram above, a clockwise rotation would close the outflow tunnels.

"No!" Theilo cried. "I told you, that's too dangerous!"

Salvine, still in control, ignored his complaint, continuing to turn the crank as warning lights began to flash across several of the control panels. With a sudden thud to the back of her head, her vision blurred. A second blow quickly followed, knocking her against the wall as she stumbled forward. Salvine mustered up a growl from her throat as she blocked a third strike with her wrist. She turned on Theilo in an instant, knocking him to the ground with a head-butt. The broken lever Crane's assistant was using as a weapon fell from his hands, clanging as it bounced wildly across the control room floor.

Theilo scooted backwards, trying to rise to his feet, but Salvine reached out and gripped ahold of his ankle before he could get away. She yanked him back towards her, dragging him across the smooth stone floor. She placed her forearm on his throat, pinning him in place.

"Stop," commanded Doctor Crane's voice.

Salvine looked around in confusion. No one else was present.

"Release Theilo, please." The words were coming from a tiny metal box high in the corner of the room. She glanced around again to be sure she wasn't mistaken. "No, I am not actually in the room with you. I am just transmitting my voice from a distance, but I can see you. I know what you are trying to do, and let me assure you, it will not work."

A subtle smirk appeared on Theilo's lips.

"I only let you think you were escaping to test your intelligence," said Crane. "Do you really think I left those extracted claws in reach by mistake?"

Theilo shook his head at her mockingly. The smugness in his expression was infuriating. They'd both been toying with her all along.

"You've done well, but I'm afraid it's time for your little excursion to end. You may be smarter now, but you're still not smart enough."

"Get off me," ordered Theilo, shoving her arm away from him.

Salvine allowed Theilo to rise to his feet. She was too shocked by the deception to resist. Theilo immediately turned the crank back to its original position.

They tricked us…. Salvine's thoughts were lost in a jumble of rage.

She was a passenger in her own body as Salvine slowly shifted closer to Theilo.

I won't let them hurt us anymore. I won't let them win….

Something was wrong—not with Salvine's actions—she wholeheartedly approved of what Salvine had in mind—rather, something was wrong with the machinery. Theilo's attention was locked on the flashing warning lights. Reopening the outflow tunnels only made them blink faster.

Theilo sidestepped over to where the lever was snapped free from the wall. His entire demeanor changed as he inspected the damage. "What did you do…?" A siren began to sound, blaring as lights flashed.

Salvine gripped Theilo by the back of the head and smashed his face into the panel with all her might. She held onto his hair, pulling him back and then slamming him forward again and again. Eventually, all his teeth were dislodged and his features turned to mush, but she kept hammering his face against the metal panel until his skull caved in entirely and her hand became too slick with blood to hold onto his matted hair any longer.

Salvine's fury rolled out of her with a bloodcurdling scream—pure emotion with no clear thoughts running through her mind. When she was finished, she retreated from her position of control, delving back into the deep recesses of her mind.

With Salvine gone, she retook command of her bloodied limbs. Normally, she might have attempted to take more pleasure by further mutilating Salvine's kill, but her increased intelligence warned her that time was of the essence.

Somewhere, pressure was building. She could hear the pitch change in the nearby machinery. She gave the outflow crank a hard twist, closing the tunnels once again for good measure before bounding back through the broken doorway and into the passageway beyond.

"You'll regret this… there's nowhere you can run that I won't find you!" came the final words from Doctor Crane through the metal box before she was out of earshot.

She retraced her steps, jumping back through the shattered window of the observation room and running along the embankment of the underground river. With the outflow tunnels sealed off, the water was no longer flowing past the spinning blades. The chamber steadily filled with the incoming current. The water level was rising faster than she imagined possible. She lost herself within the seemingly endless tunnels.

A deafening roar sounded as an explosion ripped through the earth. Every glowing bulb suddenly flashed bright white and then blinking out entirely.

We've done it, she thought to Salvine. *We stopped the Glowing City from glowing!*

The girl stirred from her safe place deep in her winding thoughts but made no response.

She wanted to revel in the minor victory with Salvine. She reached out to her again: *You know, you aren't as bad as I thought.*

Salvine was rippling with hostility. *This is your fault! You're the one with homicidal tendencies.*

I do what feels good, she retorted. *But you ended Theilo all on your own.*

There was a twinge of guilt—an unfamiliar feeling to her. It escaped the area of her mind where Salvine resided.

I did what I had to do. For survival. You kill for fun.

Killing gives me purpose. It's what I was created to do. You killed Theilo in anger, for revenge. Don't tell me you didn't enjoy it, at least a little bit.

The twinge grew.

Of course not.

She knew Salvine was lying, or at least not entirely telling the truth. She sensed the spike of adrenaline, recognized the hint of elation coming from Salvine while she was in control of her body. Salvine did not savor in the carnage the way she would have, but she didn't regret her actions either. Salvine hated her foe, and destroyed him viciously.

You satisfied your hatred, I satisfy my desire, she thought to Salvine. *Are we not the same?*

She sensed Salvine's annoyance.

We are not. Salvine was stern.

We are the same, she repeated, *deep down.*

We share the same body, but we are not the same. The words came across weaker this time.

We share a mind. Separate, but together. You may as well embrace it.

There was a grumble of resentment from Salvine, but she gave in to the prodding; a semblance of understanding forming between them.

Perhaps you're not so bad either. Salvine admitted begrudgingly. *Perhaps.*

The Terrible Truth

The bag wrapped around Javic's head made breathing difficult. His abductors had drawn a string at its opening, pulling it tight across his throat. The wet heat of his panting breaths built up quickly inside the hood until he couldn't stop himself from panicking. He thrashed about in the chair he was tied to, but his bindings held secure. His wrists were strung together behind his back. The glowing talisman Artifact was still close by, preventing him from reaching the Power. He could feel its cold edges boxing his mind in place within his skull. The more he struggled against it, the harder it squeeze against his temples. It felt like his whole head was stuck in a vice grip.

Javic lost track of time as the minutes dragged into hours. Inside the bag, the only moment was the present. He battled to suck in air through the damp cloth. No one around him spoke, but even through the bag Javic could sense his abductors were close by. After what felt like forever, the bag was finally lifted. Cool air rushed over his face and hair. He had almost forgotten what it was like to be able to breathe normally. His whole face dripped with the built up condensation of his breath. The first thing he noticed was that the city's lights were still out. A flickering lantern lit the windowless room while a lone luminescent bulb dangling from a cord in the middle of the ceiling remained dark. Behind and to the side of him, three men stood in stoic silence, waiting as a pair of footsteps approached the solitary entry point of the otherwise empty cell.

Fiery hatred rose inside Javic's chest as he recognized one of the sneering goons at his side as the man who used his entire body weight to press the pillow down over Mallory's face. He lashed against the glowing talisman's mental barrier once more, wishing he could melt the wicked sneer right off his face, but the attempt only tightened the talisman's grip, leaving him with a splitting headache.

The footsteps reached the metal door and it swung open, revealing the wide frame of Guther Aldune. Javic wasn't surprised to see the general. He had assumed either Aldune or Tannel Cresdale was behind his imprisonment—other than Cale, they were the only ones who knew anything about his trip to Sultrim. Javic wasted no time with pleasantries. "Where's Mallory? What have you done with her?"

The general ignored the question as he walked over and took a seat across from Javic in the only other chair in the cell. "Two of my men are dead," he said. "Good men—loyal men. Tell me what happened to them."

Javic didn't care about Aldune's cronies. His nostrils flared as he pictured Mallory squirming under the sneering man's weight. He'd been suffocating her simply because she was friends with Javic—torturing her to find out his whereabouts. Javic owed Aldune and the Ver'konus no answers.

"I have several reports of a swordsman cutting people down…?"

Javic's focus remained on Mallory's well-being. "If anything happens to her, you won't have to worry about the Orb of Parphim anymore—I will destroy you."

Although Javic wasn't in a position to be dealing out threats, the crazed look in his eyes must have been disturbing to the general. Aldune turned frantically towards his men and gestured towards the door. The other captors immediately departed the cell without a word, though they did share a look of curiosity amongst themselves at the mention of the Orb of Parphim. As soon as the door shut them out, Aldune grabbed Javic by the front of his shirt. "What do you know of the Orb? Who told you about it—was it Cale?" He spoke in an angry whisper, just quiet enough to remain unheard by his men on the other side of the door.

Rather than answer, Javic worked up a ball of phlegm from deep down in his throat and spit it straight into Aldune's already fuming face. The general responded with a powerful backhand that made Javic's teeth rattle. The blow whipped Javic's head to the side and sparked flashes of color across his vision. It probably would have knocked Javic's chair clear over if the legs weren't permanently attached to the floor.

Wiping the mucus from his face with his left hand, the general retook his seat. Surprisingly, he regained his composure quickly—quite unusual for the tumultuous man. When Aldune spoke again, he did so calmly, with no sign of the rage that had just escaped him. "Your little girlfriend is just fine," he said.

"Then let me see her," Javic said through the creak in his stinging jaw.

"Not until you tell me what I need to know," said Aldune. "Now, who told you about the Orb?"

Javic spat again, this time on the floor, a combination of thick saliva and blood. "Tannel Cresdale," he said. "The councilman intends to take the core from you." Javic found himself spouting Cale's lie, though he hadn't previously planned to aid that weasel. Despite his misgivings for Cale, his anger for Aldune outweighed all other considerations.

"And what about my men?" Aldune asked.

"Arcanum assassin, I suppose," said Javic. "The killer was the third body at the tavern—the one with the dagger."

Aldune nodded slowly, as if trying to put the pieces together in his head. "And who killed the assassin?"

Javic was already fed up by the questioning. "Untie my wrists and I'll let you find out first hand." He wasn't about to bring Orris into all of this. The blade-brother needed to make it clear of the city so that he could begin tracking down Elric.

Aldune grunted with annoyance. "You've put me in a tough position," he said. "You weren't supposed to find out about the Orb. I already told you not to speak about any of this, and yet here you go blabbing your mouth off in front of everyone without a care…. I think maybe I will have to teach you a lesson—keep you locked up in here until Lord Ethan returns. Maybe then you will think twice about disobeying orders."

As furious as Javic was, he held his tongue. He knew Aldune was very capable of following through on that threat. Lord Ethan wouldn't be back for at least another month, assuming all went well, and Javic had no wish to remain imprisoned for a moment longer than necessary.

A knock at the door pulled Aldune's attention away. A soldier peeked in and whispered something into the general's ear. After the soldier left, Aldune turned back towards Javic. "It seems you are a popular boy today," he said with only a hint of contempt in his voice. "The Arcanum is desperate. Councilman Cresdale has forced one of your professors to nominate you to this year's Dance of the Elements. It would appear Tannel wishes to raise you to Ver'ati, or at least see you die trying."

Javic was flabbergasted. He was barely out of initiate status… *die trying is right…*. The Dance was a dangerous trial of practical knowledge that required mastery of many aspects of the Power in order to complete successfully. Javic may have been strong with the Power, but he wasn't anywhere close to ready for something like the Dance. He hadn't even been in the top tier of his initiate class after the whole fiasco with not being able to find his anchor in Professor Vanton's course. "Can I turn down the nomination?" It was just wishful thinking at this point.

"No," said Aldune, "once nominated, you have no choice but to attempt the Dance."

"When…?" Javic asked. Everyone had been talking about the upcoming Dance before he lost track of time with his trip to Sultrim. He hadn't really paid it much attention since only Ver'ati and various state officials were allowed to watch the trials in the Arcanum Cathedral anyway, but by the excitement that had been building amongst the more advanced students who had already reached Ver'ati status, Javic was pretty sure the event must be coming up within the month.

"You have five days," said Aldune.

Alright, maybe a little bit less than a month….

"I think we can use this predicament to our advantage, though," said Aldune.

Javic perked up, hoping for some good news.

"It doesn't take a genius to see what Tannel is planning. If you do manage to pass the trials, he will surely lock your placement offerings down so that you only receive one from him personally. In the case of a solitary placement offering, you have no choice but to accept. He wishes to keep a close watch on you, but if you survive I trust that the Ver'konus will be able to count on *you* to keep a close watch on *him* instead." The threatening look in the general's eyes indicated that he did not actually trust Javic, but that Javic's life would be made exceedingly difficult by the Ver'konus if he did not comply. Placing Javic as a spy within the Arcanum may have been a silver lining for Aldune, but it would not help Javic make it through the Dance alive.

"I guess I better release you to start your training—I dare say your life depends on it." Aldune untied Javic's bindings.

His hands felt cold and tingled as the blood began to flow back into his fingers past the line where the rope had cut off his circulation. It took all of Javic's willpower not to reach out and strangle Aldune right there on the spot—he knew it wouldn't end well; Aldune was three times his size, after all, but it sure would have felt good for a brief moment as he choked the air out of him—that was how Mallory had been treated. He managed a calm glare of hatred as the general led him over to the door and held it open for him.

"Your girl is three rooms down on the left," said Aldune, unprompted. As Javic stepped out of the cell, Aldune leaned in and whispered in his ear once more: "Speak openly of the Orb again, and you won't live through the day."

Javic didn't look back as he hurried down the dark hallway to where Mallory was being held. He had no doubt in his mind that Aldune would keep his word. The Orb of Parphim had the power to change nations.

With a sudden release of pressure, the glowing talisman's hold over his mind blinked out of existence. He immediately grabbed at the Power on impulse and felt its sweet currents wash over him like a rumbling river. It was as if the world had been masked in gray, but now every brilliant color of the cosmic spectrum returned to his vision all at once—so vivid and solid; everything within his grasp.

An eerie howl rang out from off in the distance, its exact direction masked by the twists and turns of the hallway. Javic could hear the shrieks well with the Power coursing through him. Whunes—he would never forget their bloodcurdling cries—one was somewhere within the complex. Down the hallway, a pair of soldiers stood by nonchalantly, guarding a doorway to a stairwell. The lack of panic indicated that the presence of the Whune was not an attack, rather, the Ver'konus was holding the beast captive. While that was an interesting development, there were more pressing matters at hand.

It only took him a moment to reach the third door. He swung it open without delay and stormed inside. As the door banged against the wall, Mallory sat up with a start from the examination bench where she was lying. She was the only person in the room. Dressed in a thin medical gown that wrapped across her like a sheet, she was left vulnerable and exposed. Her eyes were red and puffy from crying. The wavering lantern light cast her in a dim orange hue, but Javic could still tell that her makeup was smeared down the lengths of her cheeks. Her face lit up when she saw Javic, though. Javic didn't stop moving until he was across the room and she was held tight in his arms.

"Are you alright?" Mallory asked, new tears already starting to flow.

"Am I alright?" asked Javic. "What about you? I thought they might have killed you!" He clutched the back of her head with his hand, tangling his fingers in her soft hair.

Mallory was tense at first, but then relaxed into his arms. She rested her cheek on his chest and latched her hands around his waist as if he were the only thing stopping her from floating away. Perhaps, in a way, they were grounding each other. In Javic's stomach, butterflies jumped and fluttered about, making him feel as if he were drifting slightly above the floor tiles. Throughout everything, the thought of Mallory had been his one constant source of hope. Finally being together and knowing she was safe filled Javic with a relief that was beyond words.

A man cleared his throat behind Javic, making him jump slightly. He pulled free from Mallory's grasp and turned around to see Doctor Hilven Crane glowering at him from the open doorway. The hook-nosed man was carrying a clipboard which he briefly glanced at before tucking it under his right arm. "I've got good news," he said, "the spotting you experienced was minor and nothing to worry about. I believe it was likely the result of stress. The baby should be fine, as long as you take it easier from now on."

Mallory remained frozen in place, staring at Doctor Crane with wide eyes. Javic looked back and forth between them, not immediately comprehending what Crane was talking about. "Baby?" he asked. "What baby…?" When he looked at Mallory she shied away from his gaze. It didn't make any sense. *Crane can't possibly be saying that Mallory is pregnant—that's just absurd!* Javic may have been a bit behind some of his peers when it came to sexual knowledge and experience, but he knew what it took to make a baby. *I only touched Mallory down there with my hand—there is absolutely no way I could have gotten her pregnant!* The obvious answer came crashing down on him like an overfilled sack of potatoes. *It's Arlin's… Mallory's been carrying Arlin's child this whole time….*

Javic's mind froze. The thought was too horrible to face. If she was having Arlin's baby that meant Mallory had been leading Javic on. She knew they couldn't be together, and yet she let him think he had a chance. Javic felt like an idiot—a complete fool. He had actually tricked himself into believing that he and Mallory could be together, but it was clear now that she already chose Arlin long before Javic came into her life. Everything he thought he knew was unraveling in front of him. *Why did she let me go so far with her?* It was cruel—ruining their friendship and toying with his emotions when she knew all along they could never be anything more.

"I'm so sorry," said Mallory. "I meant to tell you…."

Javic had heard enough. He should never have ignored his instincts—Mallory was always Arlin's girl. No amount of wishful thinking could change that fact. He supposed this was what he deserved for trying to swoop in while Arlin was away.

Now what am I supposed to do, just forget everything?

The playful vibrato of her laughter.

The sweet scent of lilac on her hair.

The tender touch of her lips as her warm body slid so gently against his.

The way she could steal a moment with those soul-catching eyes—never-ending pools of dark chocolate—or flash him one of her mischievous, little smiles that spoke of a thousand untold secrets, any one of which could make him blush for hours on end....

No, those memories would linger within him forever. He was beyond saving. What a torturous trick to play on his heart!

In an instant, his vision of a future with Mallory was dashed to pieces, never to be recovered. All of his intentions of telling Mallory his true feelings—of spending the rest of his days by her side, caring for her, loving her—it was all nothing more than a silly fairytale, never to come true. His stomach became tight as it twisted on itself. It was not like the anxious knot he experienced earlier during his tragically hopeful trek across the city to Mallory's apartment—rather, his insides seemed to have collapsed on themselves, forming a dreadful husk around the empty core that was his center. It was as if his heart were the pit of a plum, left out to rot after all of its meat was picked clean by hungry crows.

He couldn't stand to look at Mallory anymore, her sympathetic expression mocking his very existence. Doctor Crane smartly made an exit while Javic was still reeling. Javic followed the doctor's lead, despite the pleading cries from Mallory for him to stay. He backed out of the room and then fled down the hallway. Mallory chased after him at first, her medical gown flapping loose behind her, but eventually she stopped when Javic refused to look back. He couldn't look back—he didn't want to lose his resolve.

She is having Arlin's child....

No matter what she said, there was no place for Javic in her life. He couldn't go back to being just friends—a line was crossed and romantic inclinations would always arise again within him.

The hallways were like a maze. The distant howls of the captured Whune faded into obscurity long before Javic emerged from the Ver'konus building and stepped out into the streets of Erotos. He was somewhere on campus. It looked unfamiliar without the glowing bulbs. Much time had passed since his abduction—night had descended upon the city. Javic didn't bother trying to regain his bearings, he just kept running. He felt like he should be crying, but the emotion dripped off of him, unwilling or unable to take hold within his body. Slowly everything drained away, until he felt entirely hollowed out.

People passed by in the dark, looking on curiously as he ran at a full sprint, but Javic did not slow. He didn't care where his feet were taking him—he just needed to keep moving, as if he could outrun the truth of his existence. Everyone he loved was gone; his whole life had abandoned him. His parents; his innocence; Salvine and his home in Darrenfield; Belford and his other friends on the Rosa Marsa, along with his chance at glory—his chance for revenge. And then there was Rylin, the little brother he never had, and his grandfather... the same cruel fate stripped them both from his life. Orris was long gone by now as well, out in search of Elric. Javic wished he could be out there on the road alongside the swordsman, but he was stuck here waiting for the Dance of the Elements and possibly his own death. *What's the loss of some girl on top of all that?* And yet, the thought of Mallory brought him the worst pain of all.

He didn't realize where his feet had led him until he looked up and found himself staring at the eves of Conset Hall. Across the way on the other side of Garson square, students were filing into the newly formed Laudry Hall, classes about to begin for the night. How odd that life just continued on for everyone else. Javic stood still for several minutes, his feet rooted to the ground. He had nowhere to go; nowhere to call home any longer. His dorm room surely belonged to someone else by now—it had been weeks since he was reported dead— plenty of time for the academy to assign somebody else in his stead. There was no way he was going to head back to

Mallory's apartment. He didn't know if he would ever be able to face her again—every thought of her pricked his heart like a needle. He was emotionally lost, completely directionless, and beginning to shiver. The sweat from his time with the bag over his head made the gusts of wind that blustered through the square sting all the worse. As his fingers became numb he knew he couldn't stay outside any longer. His sense of self-preservation hadn't completely abandoned him, but he did find it difficult to get his feet moving again.

He climbed the marble steps of Conset Hall and pulled open the heavy door just far enough to scrape inside. It wasn't much warmer within the building, but at least there was no wind. He created an orb of light to help him navigate the blacked-out hallway, using the technique he learned from Belford. Soon, he found himself in front of a familiar room. Not so long ago it housed his least favorite class— transfiguration with Professor Vanton. Despite having disliked the class, Javic couldn't help but long for the simpler times when his biggest worry was studying to pass his tests. He peeked inside through the narrow window in the door and found that the room was vacant. It was as good of a place as any to wait out the night. He turned the knob with a click, but before he could step inside, a familiar voice called out to him from down the hallway.

"I thought you might come," said Arius Vanton. "This way, now. We best talk in my office."

Javic turned to see the professor leaning out of a doorway halfway down the corridor. The lack of surprise on Vanton's face at seeing Javic alive might have seemed odd if he hadn't already been told one of his teachers was forced by Tannel Cresdale to nominate him to the Dance of the Elements.

Vanton didn't retract back into his office until Javic started walking towards him. He peeked out once more when Javic was almost upon him; a grave frown visible on his lips. "Inside, quickly," he said.

Despite being a poor student in Vanton's class, Javic had never visited the professor's office before. It would have been a fairly spacious room if it wasn't for all of the clutter that lined every wall. Cabinets stuffed full of books and journals stood with teaching apparatuses stacked in front of them, forming a narrow walkway to Professor Vanton's desk. A dusty lantern sat upon his desk casting long shadows across the room. Not surprisingly, the desk was piled high with even more books and loose papers.

Vanton shut the door behind them and moved a cold, half-eaten bowl of noodles from a chair onto the floor so that Javic could take a seat. He then made his way around to the other side of his desk to his own chair, stepping nimbly around the teetering towers of hazards that threatened to collapse at even the slightest bump.

Javic released his light orb with a brilliant flash before tossing the gooey casing into a trash bin. As he leaned down, an herbal scent escaped from the old bowl of noodles on the floor. Javic couldn't remember the last time he'd eaten anything. His appetite had been virtually nonexistent since returning from Sultrim. Mentally, food was still the furthest thing from his thoughts—physically, though, his body craved the pressed flour and egg yolk, boiled to perfection in a broth of beef and vegetables. Although the bowl had been sitting for quite some time, the aroma of the meal was still intoxicating. The scent of garlic and basil mixed with fresh lime, making his stomach growl in protest of its neglect.

Mallory set out some food for him that morning in her apartment, but Javic hadn't partaken before heading out to visit the Hotel Willows. The thought of Mallory sent another twinge of pain through his heart. She'd always been so kind to him... so *motherly*.... The word burned at him with its new context. Perhaps Mallory never had romantic feelings for him at all. He could have just mistaken her growing motherly instincts for a deepening personal connection. *But she kissed me!* He wasn't sure which explanation he preferred: That their love was mutual and real but impossible, or that he had been a delusional fool this whole time. Either way, Mallory was having Arlin's child, and there was no place for Javic in that equation. He would *not* be the one to tear a family apart.

While Javic was lost in reflection, Professor Vanton rummaged through one of his desk drawers. He came up with a thin crystal that appeared to be some sort of cloudy quartz, and a small metal rod about the length of his little finger. Javic began to open his mouth to speak, but Vanton shushed him even before he uttered a single word.

The professor cleared some of the papers from his desk and then balanced one point of the crystal on the dark-stained wood so that it was standing up between them like a miniature obelisk. He used the tip of his index finger to hold the crystal in place while he tapped its center with the tiny metal rod in his other hand. A high tone rang out as it vibrated. When the sound faded, the cloudy surface began to glow internally with a faint white light. Vanton removed his finger from the top of the crystal, letting it stand on its own in defiance of gravity. "It is safe to talk now," he said. "No sound will leave the room while this glows." His voice sounded odd—instead of a normal reverberation, the words disappeared as soon as they reached the walls of the office, deadened completely as if absorbed into a thick blanket.

An anti-eavesdropping Artifact—Javic marveled at the ingenuity of the Archive Historians who figured out how to activate the crystal's property by tapping it with a metal rod. He definitely did not envy the Ver'ati who went into that dangerous profession. Artifact research could turn deadly far too easily for Javic's taste.

"I must apologize," said Vanton, a frown appearing on his wrinkled face. "I've done something I wish I could undo."

Javic was pretty sure he already knew what the professor was going to say. Vanton must have felt guilty about caving in to Tannel Cresdale's demands. Putting Javic in the Dance of the Elements was practically a death sentence, given his youth and inexperience, but he could not blame the professor. The Arcanum was far too powerful for a lone teacher to resist. Tannel would have found another way of getting Javic into the Dance even if Vanton refused. "It's alright," said Javic. "I already know about my Dance of the Elements nomination. I forgive you; I know you had no choice."

Professor Vanton's frown deepened. "It is true that I am responsible for your nomination, but that was a calculated decision, and not where I have erred. I have full confidence that you will do just fine during the Dance if you follow my guidance over the next few days. No, the mistake I made was with your grandfather. He is attempting to rediscover the path to Sultrim, and I am afraid I am to blame for his vain quest."

Javic immediately focused on the professor's words, forgetting all about the hunger pangs that still gnawed at his insides. There was no way Elric could have known to go searching for him in Sultrim, especially not two weeks ago when only Cale knew the truth about his fate.

"I have a former student among the Archive Historians who passes me information from time to time," Vanton explained. "The week before Rylin's proficiency exam, several Artifacts went missing from the Archives. The Gateway was the first to vanish—stolen without a trace. Historical records indicated that the Gateway was likely a portal to the lost city of Sultrim, but, as far as my source knows, none who ventured through ever returned to confirm the theory. It was labeled as a high schism risk and placed under restricted access after several historians went missing. Since schisms are more common in adults than adolescents, I began to put the pieces together after Cale reported your death. One student might have been an accident, but two deceased children with no remains to bury, so shortly after a high risk Artifact was stolen… it was far too great a coincidence—especially since you and Rylin were two of my most promising students!"

Javic's mind didn't register the compliment. He was too preoccupied trying to follow Vanton's logic—from stolen

Artifacts to fishy death reports, Professor Vanton had somehow correctly deduced that Javic was sent to Sultrim!

The professor continued: "Your grandfather came to visit me the day after your exam. Rylin's brother, Cormick, arrived in Erotos that same day, hoping to retrieve Rylin's body. Of course, there was no body to relinquish, and they were both about to leave emptyhanded when I received word that the missing Gateway had suddenly been recovered. A worker happened across it during maintenance in the Underground. Its proximity to the exam hall reaffirmed my suspicions, so when I met with Cormick and your grandfather I could not look them in the eyes and tell them their loved ones were dead, not when I did not believe the reports."

"You told them we were trapped in Sultrim?" Javic could hardly believe what he was hearing.

Vanton nodded. "I knew if you boys had survived the transfer, you wouldn't give up without a fight, so I gave them all the resources I had on the general location of Sultrim— lifetimes of research done by far greater scholars than myself—and they departed that very day. As slim as the chances were, I believed sending them was the best hope you boys had for survival… but I know now that I have made a grievous error. I've sent them out on a fool's errand!" Professor Vanton's eyes shined with moisture.

Javic was completely speechless. His grandfather had set out on a mission to rescue him from the thousand-year-old lost city despite the immense odds stacked against him. Javic could only hope that Orris would find Elric and Rylin's brother before the Arid Hills swallowed them up for good.

"I have to ask," Professor Vanton said, "when Councilman Cresdale had me nominate you to the Dance earlier today, I knew you had returned, but I've heard no word about Rylin. Was he…? Did he make it?"

Javic wasn't sure what to say. He too had hoped beyond reason that Rylin might still be alive, but with the winged bears wandering the lost city, and the cave-in destroying the

Gateway, he doubted Rylin's chances. "I saw no sign of him," said Javic. "But the Paerto'sul… there were piles of remains… some definitely human." Javic needn't say more.

Vanton lowered his head in lamentation. "I see," he said.

The anti-eavesdropping Artifact stopped glowing and fell over, no longer able to balance on its point without the Power coursing through it. Vanton stood it up again, tapping it several more times with the metal rod until it reactivated.

"I sent out a tracker this morning to find my grandfather," Javic said, once he was sure it was safe to talk again. "He's a member of the Order of the Blade, a man named Orris Fen. I pointed him west—that was all I knew of my grandfather's departure at the time."

"I'm glad to hear it," said Vanton. "I'm not familiar with this *Orris Fen* specifically, but the Paerto'radam are a competent lot." Vanton's demeanor was already lightening up significantly. "It is fortunate that the historical texts I provided Cormick and your grandfather will take some time to decipher—perhaps even long enough for your man to catch up." Vanton suddenly clapped his hands together with a loud slap. It sounded sharp and quick with the crystal dampening its echo. "Well, you're here, and you're alive, so we best prepare you for the Dance of the Elements!"

Professor Vanton's excitement felt callous in the wake of Rylin's demise. Javic had to remind himself that nearly a month had passed for Vanton since Rylin's death was reported, giving him several more weeks than Javic to come to terms with the situation. Vanton was right, though—Javic had a lot of work to do if he was to have any hope of coming out of the Dance alive. Still, flashbacks of sitting in the tiny closet while the rest of the class participated in activities made Javic question if spending his limited prep time with Professor Vanton was really such a wise idea.

Vanton looked to him expectantly. "So," he said, "have you managed to find your anchor yet?"

Javic sighed. This was going to be a long five days.

CHAPTER

36

The Hunt

Dusk settled over the park, the light quickly fading, making the shadows play tricks on Aaron's eyes. He kept seeing motion in his peripheral vision. At first he thought he was imagining things—every time he turned to look, there was nothing there—but then he finally caught a glimpse of a creature as it flew by. He assumed it was a bird, but then it made another pass and he realized a bat was darting around silently overhead, snatching at the slew of insects that came out to play in the dimming sky.

All five of the men that made up the security team accompanying Aaron and Claire moved just as stealthily as the bat, stepping light on their feet to avoid making any clomp or crunch that could potentially give away their position. Aaron, on the other hand, couldn't figure out how to stop his Arcadian uniform's pant-legs from swishing together as his legs slid past one another. Claire's leggings, being much tighter to her body, were not giving her the same trouble. She glanced over at Aaron with annoyance—a feeling surely shared by the rest of the squad, though all five men remained stoic in demeanor. Aaron shrugged. Short of stripping down to his underwear, there was nothing he could do to avoid making noise while they were moving at such a quick pace.

It was unlike Claire to be so irritable, especially since she knew Aaron wasn't making noise on purpose. She was on edge—the gravity of their mission weighing on her demeanor. She did her best to compartmentalize her nerves, packing them away to the back of her mind, but some of the negative emotions inadvertently slipped across the bond to Aaron. She didn't even notice she was doing it. The search for the fugitives was all that mattered to her as she scanned her eyes back and forth across the spattering of vegetation that stretched out in every direction before them. Aaron's own jitters were multiplied by Claire's unintentional contribution.

The other four squads, made up of two Arcadians and five heavy-assault-rifle-toting security members each, were all out searching through different sectors of the park. Aaron and Claire's team headed out northwest, but Aaron quickly lost track of their progress as the sky dimmed, hiding distant landmarks. Fortunately, their squad leader appeared to know exactly where they were meant to be. The farther they walked, the more heavily wooded the park became. The transplanted pine and oak trees that once reminded Aaron of being back in America had taken on a sinister vibe. In the breeze that blew in with the darkness, the branches creaked and shifted, possibly giving cover to Ethan and Michelle. They could literally be anywhere, just waiting to strike. Each of the Arcadians was a predator in their own right—the hunters could easily become the hunted.

As they reached a large thicket of overgrown shrubbery, the squad leader ordered his men to split into two groups to flank through on opposite sides. Aaron and Claire were separated out as well—Aaron sticking with the squad leader and one other man as they moved in. Their ear-coms were all linked together, so Aaron could still hear the hushed breaths of the other three men plus Claire as they scrapped through the shrubbery on the other side of the thicket. The squad leader set a more cautious pace now; slow enough for Aaron to stop his pants from rubbing together by awkwardly bowing his legs as he took each step. Before long, they reached a clearing in the brush near the center of the thicket. The squad leader silently signaled a full stop and then took a knee as he gestured ahead of them.

They were not alone.

In the clearing, a man was sprawled out across the ground, nearly invisible amongst the shadows. The man—*Ethan?*—wasn't moving. Aaron's breath caught in his chest as the squad leader whispered into everyone's ears through their coms. "Target-One spotted in a clearing, thirty-five meters northeast of my position, lying prone. Confirm area is clear from possible cross-fire."

"All clear," came the quick response from one of the men with Claire.

The muzzle of the squad leader's assault rifle jerked only slightly as the man squeezed his trigger. There was nearly no sound—the weapon was equipped with a hefty suppressor. Aaron's ears only heard the solid thuds of the bullets as they collided with the prone man—three quick bursts, six shots in total, all landing within a tight cluster against the side of his body. Aaron immediately felt sick. Although it was too dark to make out the details, he imagined he could see the life draining from Ethan's eyes as a puddle of red quickly escaped his body. Ethan never moved—not giving so much as a shudder as the bullets tore through his flesh. An uneasy feeling manifested in Aaron's gut.

"Moving in to confirm the kill," whispered the squad leader over the ear-coms as he rose from his knee. He gestured for Aaron and the other squad member to follow him as he carefully stepped out from under the cover of the brush and into the clearing. Aaron trailed a few steps back, again walking with his legs spread wide to avoid making noise, just in case. The squad leader was the first to reach the body. He squatted down beside his kill and pulled back Ethan's head so that he could get a clear look at his face. He squinted at it for only a fraction of a second before dropping it again and jumping back in fright. Aaron didn't want to look, not wishing to see Ethan's lifeless eyes staring up at him, but the squad leader's reaction forced him to move in closer now.

"What the hell is this?" the squad leader said, scrambling even farther away from the body and swinging his rifle around wildly through the air.

Aaron leaned in to see what was wrong. The corpse's head had fallen so that the face was pointed out towards him, but a blank, fleshy surface sat where Ethan's features should have been. No mouth, no nose, no eyes, no eyebrows—just an empty stretch of skin, as if a smooth layer of flesh had been poured over the top of his face. It was truly horrifying to look at. No blood escaped through any of the six bullet holes in the side of the figure either. It wasn't Ethan—it wasn't even human! It was just a creepy, mostly anatomically correct dummy....

Aaron's skin began to prickle as a crackling sound skittered across the air—a trap! The entire clearing distorted in front of his eyes. It was like staring at a mirage in the middle of a desert; the air boiled as an electric charge descended upon them. The shock came from every direction, filling his body with a million pinpricks that sent his muscles into spasm. His limbs went rigid as gravity pulled him headfirst into the earth beside the faceless dummy. His brain felt like an over-flexed muscle, trying to squeeze its way out of his ears. There was nothing he could do to stop the pain. He couldn't even formulate a thought as the current ravished his body. He wanted to cry out to Claire, to warn her through their bond, but the idea was only fleeting and remained unrealized as his vision went dark, his brain shutting off entirely.

* * *

There were no dreams, no wandering thoughts, no fleeting emotions, just a silent emptiness like a dense fog across a still ocean of endless marble. Aaron sat in this impenetrable darkness without concern; no aspirations to escape, to move, to feel. It wasn't that he didn't care, only that the concept of caring did not exist. His consciousness was a near-dormant kernel, like a thick acorn frozen beneath a blanket of winter snow. Slowly, as time passed seemingly without change, the world started to warm—not at any noticeable rate at first, but with a steady shift of incremental progress. A long-stagnant energy began to fill back into the depths of Aaron's body, the ice slowly melting away from his mind as the first cracks appeared in the dense armor of his outer shell. The thaw was revitalizing his mental pathways; his kernel sprouting, growing larger and larger by the moment. The fog was lifting now as well; a stream of awareness bursting at the corners of his consciousness; winter turning to spring.

He became reacquainted with his body—an old friend he hadn't realized he missed until they finally came back together. Time had not treated his old friend well. The cold, hard ground pressed against him. Several pointy rocks were wedged uncomfortably beneath his back, making him ache. He could feel his surroundings, but he could not move, trapped desperately on the edge of sleep. His mind hadn't entirely returned yet, but he knew waking up on the ground wasn't normal. He should be in a bed; somewhere warm and comfortable—somewhere safe—but he knew that was not the case. As his brain scrambled to catch up to his present, the image of the blank mannequin face flashed across his mind. The absence of expression pressed across a human head was terrifying. It filled him with all the revulsion of the uncanny valley—human, but not human; luring him in; a fly to a web.

The image sparked off more memories—the hunt, the wide thicket, the inescapable swarm of electricity. He knew now that he was still in the park. They had walked straight into the dummy's trap.... He regained control over his body as he painstakingly pushed the sleep from his mind. It was still dark when he opened his eyes, the clear night sky speckled with a million white dots. He watched them only briefly before sitting up and turning his attention to his more immediate surroundings. It was clear that some time had passed since his last tangible memory, but he couldn't say how much. The decoy dummy was gone, as were the other men from his squad. Claire was beside him, though, stretched out on the ground with her eyes closed, looking as if she were merely taking a nap. He was relieved to see that she was still breathing.

Around them, the trees were taller and more densely grouped than the brush that surrounded the dummy's clearing. He wondered if they were in the same thicket at all. Aaron put his hand to his ear and found that his ear-com was missing. He leaned over to Claire and shook her lightly, trying to wake her, but she did not respond.

"You shouldn't do that," said Michelle, her voice catching Aaron off-guard as it floated to him from out of the darkness over on his right side. "Let her come about on her own."

Aaron swung his head around, but he could only make out the black form of a thick tree trunk in that direction. Michelle stepped away from the vegetation, the singular shadow splitting in two as she approached.

"She'll be fine," said Michelle, preempting Aaron's concern for Claire. "Might have a bit of a headache, though."

As Michelle got closer, Aaron was able to see her more clearly in the moonlight. Her face was covered in dirt, streaked across her chin and cheeks like camouflage. Her olive skin appeared to be a shade darker than normal. Her hair, usually in tight curls, had fallen flat and was stringing down on either side of her face in a tangled mess. She extended her hand to Aaron. It was stained as well; a dark mixture of dirt and blood across her fingers and under her chipped nails.

"Ethan is dying," she said. "I beg you, please help him...."

Aaron stared back at Michelle, unsure what to do. He had been at her mercy, and she hadn't harmed him—apart from that brutal shock, anyway—but whatever goodwill that garnered did not extend to her husband.

"He didn't do any of the things Yosef was saying," she insisted. "Somebody is setting him up."

The prospect of an unknown perpetrator was even more troubling than the idea of Ethan being the traitor. As unlikely as Ethan's innocence appeared given the timeline of events surrounding the explosions beneath the Atrium, a part of Aaron still wanted to believe what Michelle was saying. Aaron wasn't a doctor yet—he hadn't taken the Hippocratic Oath—but a belief in the sanctity of life was already ingrained in him. Letting somebody die when he could prevent it just didn't feel like the right thing to do. He didn't know if Ethan was guilty or not, but if Ethan never got to tell his side of the story, Aaron would always doubt his decision. Because of that, whether or not to save Ethan no longer felt like a choice in Aaron's mind. Ethan deserved his trial.

"He's over this way," said Michelle, gesturing with her head. "You're the only one who can help him."

Aaron didn't like the idea of leaving Claire behind, unconscious on the cold ground, but he followed after Michelle anyway. He still wasn't entirely convinced he was doing the right thing—the person who blew up the labs was responsible for murdering more than one security guard and put everyone Aaron cared about at risk. If Ethan *was* that person, saving his life could have dire consequences for the future of all the Arcadians and their families, not to mention the rest of the world.

Michelle led Aaron up a hill and down a short decline. In the small clearing that followed, Aaron was surprised to find

Wes and Isabelle sitting alongside Ethan. The injured man was lying on the ground, clutching his side with both hands.

"You're awake!" exclaimed Wes. "Good thing too. I don't think Ethan can last much longer."

"What are you guys doing here?" Aaron asked.

Wes waved his hand through the air dismissively. "Michelle liberated us from our death squad," he said. "Came across her almost immediately after setting out from the complex. We can talk more about that later, but right now Ethan really needs you to get the bullet out of his gut before he bleeds out."

"No one else knows enough about anatomy to patch him up right," added Isabelle.

Wes and Isabelle's endorsement lessened Aaron's concerns about helping Ethan. From the look of things, they had both judged Ethan worthy of life, confirming Aaron's gut instinct to assist the dying man. He knelt down beside Ethan to get a closer look at what he would be working with. There was an entry wound on his left side, upon which Isabelle was keeping pressure. In a search for an exit wound, Wes helped Aaron turn Ethan over onto his right side, provoking a grimace of pain from the barely conscious man. He pulled Ethan's torn shirt up to his shoulder blades but was unable to locate any sign of an exit point. The bullet was still in there somewhere, and would need to come out before Aaron could seal the wound shut. Wes was right—there really wasn't any time to waste if he was to save Ethan's life. The wound appeared to have been bleeding for quite some time now and the skin around it was already becoming necrotic. Ethan was pale and weak, and was taking very quick, shallow breaths. He was somehow still managing to cling to life despite nearly bleeding out.

"What happened?" Aaron asked.

Ethan was too far gone to respond, but Michelle filled him in. "He was returning to the facility from his walk when a security guard approached him and shot him without so much as a word. Ethan didn't even know people were searching for him," she said.

The entry wound was fairly small, probably caused be a nine-millimeter lead bullet. Aaron just hoped it hadn't fragmented inside or it would be much more difficult to extract. Aaron didn't have any experience with bullet wounds, but he knew the longer it took him to get the lead out, the less likely Ethan would live to see the end of the procedure.

Ethan's eyes had grown even more distant in the time since Aaron arrived. There was no doubt Ethan was taking some of his final labored breaths. He reached out to the computer—a process that had become quite natural to him by now—and used his mind to feel his way into Ethan's body. He could sense flesh and bones; blood and muscles. He saw the trail of damage and followed it to a foreign mass, pressing up against one of Ethan's ribs. The bullet was caught on the bone where it was causing a large pool of blood to form around it. He gripped on to the bullet with his mind and shifted it slightly back towards the opening in Ethan's skin. Ethan suddenly became very present, his eyes shooting open wide as he howled in pain. Blood furiously dribbled from the wound.

"Sorry," Aaron said to Ethan, though he doubted the man was in any state to comprehend the apology. "I'm just going to pull it out quick and then see if I can get the computer to patch you up."

He reached back in with his thoughts before Ethan could squirm around too much. He didn't waste any time, mentally grabbing ahold of the bullet again and giving it a quick jerk, pulling the mass out along the path of entry as best as he could. Wes and Isabelle flatten Ethan's arms and legs to the ground as he thrashed about wildly. Blood was gushing from his side in an unyielding flow. The seconds slipped by with Aaron in a tense state of concentration. It felt like an eternity passed by the time the tiny bullet finally slid out of the wound and fell to the ground. So much trouble caused by something so small.

As soon as the lead was clear, Aaron scrambled to seal up the damage. He started by closing the outer skin so that Ethan wouldn't lose any more blood. After that, he corralled the festering pool of blood forming on Ethan's insides back into the damaged blood vessels. He knew how the body was supposed to work, so with his will of intention the supercomputer took over and began to rebuild the rest of the damaged tissue, including the necrosis on the surface.

Small bursts of light, tinted red by Ethan's flesh, flashed under his skin as Aaron directed the computer to use some of the leftover pooled blood as conversion material to strengthen the damaged ribcage and pierced organs. It reminded Aaron of holding a bright flashlight up to his closed palm as a child. The blood inside of him tinted the white light red, and he could see all his veins and blood vessels pulsing. It was as if a flashlight was switching on and off inside of Ethan's abdomen now. By the time Aaron was done, he estimated that Ethan's body was in even better shape than before he was shot.

Although Ethan's wound was entirely fixed, he was still very much weakened from the blood loss as well as the high energy use of the healing process. His eyelids drooped with heavy exhaustion and he immediately drifted off to sleep. Michelle looked worried at first—perhaps thinking he had expired—but Aaron gave her a reassuring smile. "He just needs to rest for a bit," he said.

Relieved, Michelle clasped onto Aaron in a tight hug. "Thank you," she whispered as tears dripped down her dirty cheeks.

Wes was grinning over at Aaron with a smile that ran from ear to ear. "I knew you could do it," he said. "A straight up wizard, this one."

"You know it," said Aaron. "All powerful. Just don't pay any attention to the man behind the curtain." They shared a quick laugh—a motion which felt unnatural given their current predicament.

"I suppose you'd like to know how Isabelle and I ended up here?" asked Wes.

As much as Aaron was curious as to what won his friends' allegiances, he needed to go back over the hill to where Claire was still unconscious. He didn't want to risk her waking up alone and being frightened. "Can we walk and talk?" he asked. "I want to get back to Claire."

Wes nodded, hopping up from where he'd been hovering over Ethan.

"I have more I need to tell you as well," said Michelle.

Isabelle waved them both off. "Go ahead," she said. "I can keep an eye on Ethan."

Michelle leaned down and kissed her husband on the forehead before standing up and following after Wes and Aaron.

"Like I said before," said Wes, "our squad came across Michelle not ten minutes after heading out. She was stumbling over herself—still hadn't found Ethan yet—and our bastard squad leader orders me to kill her. I hesitate—I mean, who wouldn't? She is just running away, terrified, not threatening us at all—and I suggest that we could just capture her instead. The prick puts his gun right in my face and tells me to kill her or he'll blow my head off in three seconds."

Wes paused dramatically for effect until Aaron looked over at him. "What happened next?" he finally asked.

Wes laughed. "He got to two, and then Isabelle telekinetically showed him where he could stick his gun. Right up his own ass—literally."

Aaron cringed at the thought.

"Michelle saw what was going on and zapped the rest of the squad," he said. "You tell him about the chips yet?" Wes asked Michelle.

"Not yet," she responded. "I didn't want to delay getting him to Ethan."

"Good that," said Wes. "You're not going to believe what we found out…. We really can't trust Reblan Industries—I'll let Michelle fill you in. Anyway, after our *discovery* about the chips, we found Ethan lying off on the side of a path with that bullet hole in him. I mentioned that you were good with the medical stuff, so we set out to find you."

"Sorry about zapping you," said Michelle. "Everyone was standing so close together; I couldn't tell who was who in the dark."

They got back to Claire just as Michelle was finishing her apology. Aaron barely heard a word of it, instead focusing all his concentration on Claire's thoughts, freshly stirring within her partially dormant mind. He could feel her brain sparking back to life. Waves of icy slush dripped across her consciousness, shearing off from the frozen layer. He saw his own face reflected back by Claire's mind; felt her concern for his safety; her insides shredded by fear. It was her final memories before her mind had slipped into obscurity: The air was glowing as electrons collided above the clearing during Michelle's attack, a beautiful display of greens, blues, purples, and oranges, shining brilliantly like the aurora borealis during a solar event. She couldn't reach Aaron, though she tried desperately. The electrical storm grew into a swirling mist of flashing colors, biting through her uniform like the sting of a thousand-tentacle jellyfish. Beautiful, but terrible as the poisonous arms wrapped around her neck and forced their way down her throat and into her lungs, choking off her air supply. That was when it all went dark for Claire.

She sat up now, gasping for breath as if coming up from a free dive at the bottom of the ocean. Her chest heaved against her uniform. Aaron immediately reached out to her through their bond, attempting to calm her by telling her that everything was alright, but her thoughts were still in too much of a jumbled panic to comprehend him. She spun around, focusing on Michelle without even noticing Aaron or Wes. She lashed out with a whip of air, just like Yosef Reblan back in the detainment cell, compressed to the width of a razor's edge and projected with precision. Michelle cried out as she recoiled away, covering up her slashed face.

Aaron lunged forward and tackled Claire to the ground before she could strike again. She wheeled on him wildly, her auburn hair twisting about in front of her face. There was no recognition in her eyes as she looked upon Aaron. She continued to flail beneath him until a milky glow filled the air from out of a ball of light in Wes's hand. Claire looked around again in a confused daze as the light filled the landscape. Aaron held her down, pressing his hands against her shoulders. She became still, gazing searchingly into Aaron's eyes as her pulse finally began to slow to a more reasonable level.

Everything's alright, he thought to her, *you're safe now.*

Claire looked over at Michelle, the nervous knot squeezing again in her belly. Michelle was still cowered over, clutching her face. The air lashing left a deep gash across her chin which stretched all the way up to the bottom of her left ear. Today really wasn't her day. Aaron went over to Michelle and stimulated the regrowth of her skin, picturing the layers of dermis rebinding together while he simultaneously relieved the pain impulses coming from her battered nerve endings. He did it so quickly that the cut barely even had a chance to bleed before it sealed back over.

Aaron felt Claire's unasked question in the emotion that came across their bond. *Why are you helping her?* He didn't know how to answer. How could he explain his willingness to aid the people that Claire still believed were responsible for betraying them all and endangered her family? She blamed the Millers for forcing Aiden to run and hide when he should have been resting and recovering from his most recent round of treatments. A gut feeling was responsible for Aaron's change of mind about how to proceed with Michelle and Ethan. Nothing he could say now could translate those feelings into a sensible argument worthy of staying Claire's hand. "You've missed some developments," was all Aaron could come up with.

Claire watched Michelle with a guarded weariness as Aaron went about retelling what Wes and Michelle already told him. Claire's face did not change, but Aaron could sense that she was still dubious about Ethan's alibi of going out for a walk during the explosions. When Aaron caught up to telling about the successful extraction of the bullet from Ethan's abdomen, Claire couldn't suppress her emotions any longer and her expression began to sour.

"There is something else you two need to know," said Michelle, realizing Claire's open-mindedness was quickly waning. "It's your security chips. They aren't exactly what they seem." Wes took a seat on the ground next to Aaron and Claire as Michelle delved into her explanation. "I suspected the chips were something more than just security chips from the very beginning because of their large size and extreme method of implantation." Michelle reached into her pocket and pulled out a cylindrical metal casing about the size of a multivitamin pill, but with several sharp hooks sticking out from its underside. "I duplicated mine outside of my body so that I could take a closer look at it. If all it did was allow us to access restricted sections of the facility while tracking our positions, it wouldn't even have to be a third this size. The rest of the security officers, scientists, and project officials all have normal chips in their forearms that let them into restricted spaces, but you don't see any of them needing image grafts to cover up terrible scars like the ones we received. Our chips are tied to our nervous systems with these hooks so that they can't be removed without causing nerve damage."

"It's an execution device," said Wes, impatient for Michelle to get to the point. "They can remotely kill us whenever they want."

Aaron had been subconsciously scratching at the bump of his implant, but he immediately retracted his hand now.

"All it would take is one quick command from their tracking center and we would all fall to the ground," said Wes. "Permanently."

After meeting Yosef Reblan, Aaron wouldn't put anything past the man. For all he knew, Reblan Industries could have intended to kill all of the Arcadians at the end of the experiment. An unsettling thought occurred to him—if every one of the Arcadians was to suddenly go missing, their employer would merely have to say that they wandered off into Tripoli. No one outside of the company would ever know what became of them.

"Although the tracking center was destroyed, those systems will eventually be brought back online," said Michelle. "The chips can't be removed without causing harm, but I can disable them for you if you let me."

Claire stared into Michelle's face as if she were trying to read the woman's mind. Michelle didn't flinch. "Alright," said Claire after a long pause. "Do your thing."

It didn't take their shared bond for Aaron to know that Claire still did not trust Michelle, but the threat posed by their security chips cast enough uncertainty upon the intentions of Reblan Industries to make her second guess everything else the project officials told her as well. She had taken Yosef Reblan at his word when he said that the traitor could be no one other than Ethan.

"This will hurt," warned Michelle as Claire pulled her shirt down to expose the injection site on her left bicep. "The hooks are wrapped around your nerves, so there is no way to avoid shocking your nervous system at the same time."

"Bite down on this," said Wes, offering Claire a stick wrapped with a bit of cloth torn from his undershirt. "Trust me."

Claire accepted, lying down on her back before clenching her teeth down hard against the cloth.

"Ready?" asked Michelle.

Claire grunted her approval.

Michelle ran her index finger along the bump at the center of Claire's image graft. A gust of unnaturally cold air swept through the underbrush as Michelle cannibalized what little heat energy was in the oxygen and converted it into an electrical current. The tip of Michelle's finger glowed blue like the electrodes of a stun gun, sending an arc of electricity into Claire's exposed arm.

Every muscle in Claire's body tensed at once, the silent strain in her face and neck making it look like she might actually bite all the way through the stick in her mouth. Her back arched up—her body twitching randomly as the electric charge spread throughout her nervous system, firing off random signals to her muscles. Aaron stood clear to avoid getting shocked himself, but it was extremely difficult not to go to Claire's side as she painfully convulsed. He wished he could comfort her through the grueling experience, but there was nothing he could do but watch.

By the time Michelle finally finished, Claire's face was bright red from the increased blood pressure of holding her breath. She was able to relax now and her appearance started to return to normal. The flush faded as she slumped back into the earth with a heavy sigh.

"All done," said Michelle, turning towards Aaron, ready to repeat the process.

Claire passed him the biting stick. There was a sluggishness in her movement as she slapped the spit covered tool down in his hand. *Ouch,* she thought to him. Even the thought felt labored.

Aaron laid himself down beside Claire and placed the stick in his mouth, ignoring the slobber. There was no way to ready himself for something like this, so he just nodded to Michelle and hoped it wouldn't hurt as bad as it looked... but of course, it was worse.

Even the sting of the electrical storm that knocked him unconscious earlier couldn't compare to the biting shock that filled his body now. The *zapping* earlier was devised to shut his brain down quickly, so the pain he experienced was fleeting compared to the incessant stream of electricity currently pumping fire into his veins. It hurt everywhere at once, feeling as if his blood were boiling. His teeth creaked as he bit down hard against the stick—it was the only thing stopping him from biting his tongue as it flexed uncontrollably against the side of his mouth, trying to escape its prison like a worm in a pot of water-saturated soil. His toes curled up in his shoes, every muscle squeezing tight as the shock continued on relentlessly. He began to wonder if it would ever end. The air pushed itself from his lungs in a pressured wheeze, and yet he still felt as if his chest were about to burst open.

One moment he felt like the pain would last forever, and then the next, Michelle took a step back and rubbed her hands together, clearing the sweat from her palms. Aaron's body still ached from flexing muscles he didn't even know he had, but everything was able to relax now. He could feel his face slowly beginning to cool. He was free to move again, but he only had enough energy to spit the stick out of his mouth and flop over on his side to face Claire. His eyelids felt heavy as he looked upon her. She was staring back at him with an equally exhausted expression.

"Can you take first watch?" Michelle asked Wes.

"Sure," said Wes. "You alright, though?"

Aaron glanced up at Michelle. She was bent over, leaning with both arms against her knees.

"Yes," she said. "I just needed to use more energy from our bodies this time—everything is cold and static around here… nothing to grab at. I'll be fine once I sleep it off." Michelle crashed down beside Claire, too worn out to continue standing. She spoke again to Wes without looking in his direction. "You could carry Ethan up here with Isabelle, then start setting up some defenses. I just need a few hours…." Michelle passed out mid-sentence, her head lulling over to the side. She continued to breathe steadily as she settled into a deep sleep.

"Always the last guy awake at the party," said Wes. "You two should get some rest as well, while you can."

Aaron didn't need to be told twice. He used his last remaining strength to reach out and grab Claire's hand. Her fingers felt numb with cold, but she smiled at him. Energy from farther away was starting to seep back into the ground around them, leveling out so that the earth didn't feel quite as cold as it did immediately following Michelle's procedure, but it was still far from warm. Aaron would have done just about anything for a blanket right now, but he didn't have the mental dexterity to reach out to the computer to conjure one. He watched Claire as her blinks became slower and slower—her eyes staying closed more often than they were open.

Several flashes of light nearby stole Aaron's attention for a moment. It was Wes, using the computer to form a large fluffy blanket out of dirt. It still held the appearance of the earth it was woven from, but it clung together in one big sheet. "Camouflage," was all the boy said as he laid it across the three exhausted Arcadians. Wes really was a great guy.

Aaron could already feel the warmth starting to cling to his body as the blanket insulated him from the night air. He might have actually been able to rest easy if Wes hadn't decided to open his mouth one last time.

"The squads think they already cleared this area," he said, "but eventually they will come back around when they realize we slipped in behind them. Be prepared to move quickly if I wake you. We'll need all the bodies we can get when the fighting breaks out. This isn't the Battle Cove anymore."

Nothing could stop Aaron from sleeping at this point, not with how exhausted he was, but his dreams would have been a lot more pleasant without that stark reality check. Arcadians versus Arcadians in the test range was frightening enough—this time they would be fighting for nothing less than their lives.

CHAPTER

37

Scattered

Early morning light shone against the backs of Aaron's eyelids as an eruption of crow caws roused him from his slumber. In the branches of the large dark-wooded maple above his head, every perch was taken over by a dozen or so feathered bodies. The branches shifted as they moved, the whole tree slumping under their combined weight. More of the black birds swarmed in circles in the air above, unable to find open space to land. They didn't seem to care at all that Aaron and the other Arcadians were sleeping directly beneath them, partially obscured by the dirt textured blanket Wes formed during the night.

Despite the ruckus of the crows, Claire was somehow still fast asleep to Aaron's right. On the other side of her, Michelle and Ethan were both sleeping as well. The amount of bodily energy used by the processes of the computer during the night was no joke. Everyone was drained.

A rosy color had mostly returned to Ethan's cheeks—Aaron was proud to see the operation appeared to have been a success. Ethan was well along the path to recovery from what would have otherwise been a fatal gunshot.

Although it was still early in the morning, the dry desert air formed a repressive blanket across the unnaturally lush oasis. Aaron already missed the central air conditioning of the research complex. He climbed to his feet, looking around for Wes and Isabelle as he stretched his tired limbs. He was expecting the pair to wake him up at some point during the night to take over their watch, but for some reason they allowed him and everyone else to sleep well into the morning. Wes and Isabelle were nowhere to be found as Aaron scanned his eyes across the clearing and surrounding thicket.

With a massive flutter of wings, the crows above him took flight all at once, spooked by his motion. They flew off in a swarm, looking like a singular, pulsating organism as they flowed together through the air towards the nearby city. Judging from the dozens of new smoke trails along the horizon, the rioting was still in full force. Maple leaves fell down on Aaron as the crows vacated the tree and the branches sprang back to their normal positions. Curiously, one large black mass remained in the second tier of branches above the ground as the birds departed. It was far too large to be a crow, and too tightly packed to be a group of crows. The branch wiggled as the black form shifted, dropping another slew of leaves on Aaron's head. It moved with purpose—clearly alive.

Aaron barely had time to throw his hands up in a defensive posture as it pounced from the branches and landed directly on top of him. He was slammed to the ground by considerable weight, the concussive shock of the blow sending his head spinning. Prickly, black feathers pressed against his face, stifling his cries for help.

The creature flattened out on top of Aaron, fully restricting his motion. It craned its neck down slightly to peer into

Aaron's terrified face. A nightmarish grin gaped down at him, only about an inch from his nose. "Hello, mate," it said. It was Travis's voice, but the mass on top of him looked more like a giant bird than a man.

Travis's faux-hawk was gone, shaved clean, and black tattooed lines covered his bald head and face in sharp, intricate designs. He looked like a Native American carving—a totem pole man. He was still wearing his black Arcadian uniform, but flaps of cloth now connected his sleeves to his sides like wings and he was covered in crow feathers from head to toe, as if he plucked a dozen or so of the noisy birds clean and meshed the feathers in with his outfit. The odd tattoos didn't stop at his face—they carried on down his neck and went under his shirt, leaving more tattooed skin than open space from what Aaron could see. Travis's eyepatch was gone, but his left eye still wasn't working, it turned lazily out to the side as if he were a chameleon, looking in two directions at once.

"What have you done to yourself?" Aaron asked, unable to hide the tone of repulsion in his voice.

The wild look in Travis's good eye was like a crazed animal. Surprisingly, he sat up and climbed off Aaron, releasing him from the helpless pin. Travis rolled the feathered sleeve of his shirt up off his right arm and drew his finger through an empty patch of exposed forearm. His skin sizzled and blackened beneath his fingernail as it went across. "War paint," he said. "It's a real tattoo, just change a bit of flesh to ink. Easy-peasy, though the conversion burns a tad." He traced back over the same line, drawing the black ink back through his skin to the surface. It seeped from his arm into little droplets which he was able to brush away with his fingertips.

As interesting as it was, the display still didn't explain *why* Travis marked up his body to look like a giant raven. The Aussie grew more and more peculiar with every passing day since forming his one way connection with Brooke. Perhaps he'd finally lost his mind entirely.

"We were starting to think you lot might've been dead," said Travis, glancing across the sleeping Arcadians. "Cartwright got the tracking system back online, but none of your blips are registering."

Aaron watched Travis nervously, unsure of his intentions. The absence of Wes and Isabelle suddenly became much more ominous. "Michelle helped us destroy our security chips," said Aaron. "They're execution devices."

Travis nodded, unsurprised. He stepped past Aaron to where Michelle and Ethan were still cuddled together beneath the blanket. "I'm supposed to kill them if I find them," he said. He glanced back over at Aaron with a blank expression.

Aaron didn't think he could stop Travis if he made a move against the Millers. Travis's connection to the computer protected his molecules from being directly altered against his will, and he was too close to Aaron's sleeping friends to be subdued with an environmental attack without harming everyone else in the vicinity. That left a physical attack as Aaron's only option, but considering Travis's expertise in martial arts, Aaron didn't like his chances. Travis would take him down in a fraction of a second if it came to hand-to-hand combat.

Michelle slowly opened her hazel eyes as Travis's shadow fell across her face. Fear crept into her expression as she took in the feathery form standing above her. Travis was unperturbed by her reaction. He simply reached up to his right ear and removed his ear-com, then placed the flesh-toned bump on the ground and smashed it with the heel of his boot. "I hear you're the lass to go to for disabling killer implants," he said.

It took a moment for Michelle to realize who was talking to her from beneath all the tattoos and feathers. As disconcerting as Travis's appearance was, a smile crept across Michelle's face when she finally gathered that another

Arcadian was joining their cause. Ethan and Claire began to stir at the sound of Travis's voice.

"You're with us?" asked Michelle.

"Of course," said Travis, hurt by the insinuation that he was ever against them. "You think I would trust Reblan Industries with my life after they asked us to kill each other? I'm no wally."

Ethan sat up, struggling to open his eyes in his grogginess.

Travis turned his head sharply so that he could see Ethan with his good eye.

Ethan took one look at Travis and laughed out boisterously. "What's with the feathers?"

Travis briefly moved his neck back and forth like a pecking bird. "The crows respond to magnetism," he said. "Something in their bird brains tells them which way is north I guess. I can call them to me." It wasn't really an explanation. Travis waved his winged arm to stave off further questioning. "Talk of the markers expanding hit newscasts during the night," he said. "The EAC is calling it an act of aggression. It got me thinking, how'd anyone even know to look for the markers so fast? You can't see a difference with the naked eye. Figured someone must've leaked the story, and since you lot have been scuffling around in the park all night...." Travis pulled down his feathery jacket and presented his implanted bicep to Michelle. "Hurry with this, won't you, darling," he said. "If they haven't noticed my ear-com's offline yet, they will soon. Wouldn't want them getting suspicious and making me keel over dead."

Michelle started preparing right away. Her breathing became deeper as she focused on her connection with the computer. This time she was more cautious as she gathered the energy she required from the environment to fry Travis's chip. He wouldn't be drained like Aaron and Claire experienced. Travis took the shock standing up, turning into a rigid statue as the electricity coursed through his veins. Impressively, he managed to maintain his footing throughout the process. He gritted his perfectly white teeth together in a painful clench. When Michelle finished, Travis shook out the muscles in his arms and legs like a swimmer preparing for a meet.

"Woowee!" he yelped. "That got the blood pumping!" Wisps of steam rose up from his bald head, making him look like a burnt out matchstick. It took a moment for Travis to steady his racing heart as he settled against the trunk of the maple. Still breathing hard, he continued speaking casually, as if being electrocuted was an ordinary occurrence for the Aussie. "The way I see it," he panted, "the only chance we have at uncovering the real traitor is to investigate what transmissions went out last night—from within the facility to the outside, you know?"

It was a logical thought, but the logistics of going back to the complex and hacking into the network without getting captured or killed were daunting. Wes might be capable of rooting out the information if he could get his hands on the tablet he smuggled in, but attempting to enter the Atrium while security was on high-alert sounded like a suicide mission to Aaron.

"Where's Isabelle and Wes?" asked Claire, holding Travis with an accusatory stare. After all the commotion of Travis receiving his shock, Aaron would have expected Wes and Isabelle to come investigate if they were anywhere within earshot.

Travis ran his hand across the crown of his smooth head in a nervous twitch. "There wasn't any time to waste," he said. "And it was their idea, not mine…." Everyone was watching Travis with wary expressions. "Wes went back to the facility to hack into the transmission logs," he said. "Thought he'd have a better chance at sneaking in if he went by himself, but Isabelle insisted on going along to back him up."

"That's insane!" said Michelle. "They'll be overpowered by security, not to mention the other candidates! How could you let them make such a reckless decision?"

"Actually…" he said, "they won't have to worry about the other Arcadians at least… I can feel Brooke out to the west, but as soon as Yosef and Dana notice my chip's gone offline they will surely send the squads to my last known coordinates—which is right over there where you shocked the snot out of me. If we can occupy them long enough, Wes and Isabelle will have an open path to the truth. I betcha we've only got a minute or two until they notice my chip isn't broadcasting anymore, and then another twenty before everyone shows up, so we better start preparing now."

Any lingering sluggishness in Ethan's body evaporated at the mention of their position being compromised. "Christ! Are you trying to get us all killed? We need to get out of here while we still can!" he said, grabbing Michelle's left arm at the elbow and tugging sideways, as if to drag her along in his escape.

Michelle laid her right hand on top of Ethan's grip and slipped her arm free from his grasp. "We can't leave," she said. "He's right… it's the only way to clear your name. Wes and Isabelle won't stand a chance at uncovering the real traitor unless we can keep the kill squads distracted." It was a simple truth. Ethan was prepared to argue, but it took only one determined look from his wife for him to realize there wasn't anything he could say that would change her mind. Running away would never prove Ethan's innocence, and Michelle would accept nothing less. Ethan remained silent, letting his hand drop away from Michelle's arm.

Over the next thirty minutes, the time Travis predicted the attack squads to arrive came and went without incident. The anxious Arcadians didn't speak much as they transformed the clearing into a giant open-air fortress. Ethan and Michelle circled the clearing in one direction while Aaron and Claire went the opposite way, forming a wall that was taller than the tallest trees in the surrounding thicket. When they were finished, Aaron couldn't shake the feeling that he was standing in the middle of the Battle Cove again. The makeshift cover wouldn't be of much use against the other Arcadians—it would sustain about as well as a sandcastle to a rising tide—but a structure this large would certainly draw attention, hopefully away from Wes and Isabelle.

While everyone else was building the wall, Travis sat cross-legged beneath the black maple at the center of the clearing. Although it looked like he was deep in meditation, he was actually far outside his own mind, using his connection with Brooke to keep track of the other Arcadians.

"It doesn't make sense," said Travis once the group reconvened at the center of the clearing. "Brooke's squad is still searching out to the west, but they must know where we are by now. It's almost as if—"

With a rattling bang, the first of several fierce explosions erupted against the outside of the fortress wall. In under a second, the whole camp was thrust into chaos. Dirt and chunks of the wall rained throughout the clearing as everyone scattered to find cover. Travis hunkered down beside Aaron and Claire behind the thick maple. Aaron's ears were still ringing from the first blast when the second explosion ripped through the quickly crumbling barrier.

Travis grimaced. "Tricky bastards," he said. "They knew I'd use Brooke to see what they were doing, so they kept her searching in the wrong place!"

Ethan and Michelle rolled into a nearby ditch. Ethan sat up as the last of the debris settled to the ground. He dusted himself off and rose to his feet straight away. "Best not keep our guests waiting!" he said, a fire burning in his piercing, blue eyes as he burst out in a full sprint towards the wall without a moment of hesitation.

Michelle's jaw dropped as she watched Ethan run headlong into the danger without a second thought.

"That bloke's gone bonkers!" said Travis, flapping his feathered arms in admiration. There was a glint of emotion in Travis's good eye as he joined Ethan, abandoning the safety of the tree trunk and charging towards the wall.

Cover was nearly nonexistent within the clearing—while forming defenses, focus was given to building the tall outer wall, with little consideration for what would happen after it was breached. They were only seconds into the fight, and already nothing stood between them and the kill squads. A few smaller trees, Michelle's ditch, and the one large maple were the only prominent features within the encircled clearing.

While running behind Ethan, Travis had only just come out from beneath the branches of the maple when something unexpected happened. Bending his knees as if to leap over an obstacle, Travis was suddenly propelled into the air by a kinetic force of his own devise. It was like his feet were strapped with springs. Travis launched about twenty feet into the air in a straight vertical thrust, then turned his body horizontal to the ground and spread his arms and legs.

Aaron immediately understood the purpose of the extra cloth under Travis's arms—they were functional wings! There was a flap between his knees as well which Aaron hadn't noticed earlier. When stretched tight, the modified squirrel suit allowed Travis to glide at a nearly horizontal angle to the ground. This, coupled with bursts of wind drawn up against his underside, allowed him to remain aloft.

Aaron was fairly certain if he ever tried something that crazy he would instantly crack his head open, but Travis appeared free of worry as he soared just above the treetops. He was able to change direction in midair by aiming the wind bursts against himself at varying angles. His uncanny precision made it look as if he'd been flying his whole life. He zipped back and forth, dipping down and then shooting back up into the air at breakneck speeds, reminiscent of the bat Aaron watched the night before, chasing after insects. This time, however, the other small objects swarming through the air weren't bugs, rather, Travis was dodging bullets as the security teams opened fire from below, straight up into the bright morning sky. Their silenced muzzles gave off dim flickers like Christmas lights in the distance. It might actually have been pretty if Aaron hadn't understood the lethal ramifications of the situation.

The kill squads moved through the breach in the wall, scrambling into the clearing two at a time. The fortress, which seemed like a good idea only moments before, was beginning to feel more like a cage, trapping Aaron and his friends in an open field.

Claire willed an energy shield into existence, but she did not wrap it around them like a dome the way most of the other Arcadians had taken to using the polymer back in the Battle Cove. Instead, she flattened it out into a sheet and stood it up vertically between herself and the gunmen. Michelle and Aaron joined her behind the barrier as several bullets whizzed past the lone maple.

"Get me closer and I'll zap them all to sleep," said Michelle, already focusing her mind so that she could attack at a moment's notice.

"I can't move the shield," said Claire. "The base has to be buried deep in the ground or a hit would knock it over."

Glancing down, Aaron noticed the polymer sheet did indeed slice into the earth with a paper-thin cut. It was like an iceberg, he realized, with more beneath the surface than on top. They were stuck. Several more bullets flew by; one well aimed shot even struck the force field before ricocheting off. The air grew cold, dropping to near freezing temperatures as Claire's shield sapped nearly all the energy out of their surroundings. The leaves on the nearest branches of the maple began to lose their color, turning from a healthy deep green, to a wilted brown, and then finally to black before dislodging from their branches entirely and falling to the dirt. The tree's very life force was being drained away by the hungering shield. It was taking all of Claire's concentration to keep the barrier from faltering as the nearby energy sources depleted.

With time running out, Aaron knew they needed to create a more permanent cover. Thinking fast, he reached out to the computer with a simple request to move earth, forming a trench at his feet. He traced a line with his eyes, blasting soil in all directions as the path carved itself across the clearing. With the dirt so thick in the air, he could only hope the trench would be deep enough to keep them safe.

Beads of sweat dripped down Claire's brow as she labored to hold onto the shield until Aaron was finished digging. Before he could complete his work, however, another bullet impacted with the barrier, and this time, Claire was unable to find enough energy left in the environment to restrengthen the polymer compound. She had no choice but to abandon her efforts as the structural integrity of the shield broke down and it immediately began to melt. The glistening compound oozed sideways like a giant tower of gelatin, collapsing under its own weight.

Aaron, still in the process of blasting dirt out of the trench, had to cease his own transformation prematurely so that he, Claire, and Michelle could all take cover from the steady rain of bullets that were streaking by. Observing his handiwork, the half-finished trench formed a divot just deep enough to protect them from the gunfire as long as they remained prone at its deepest point. Michelle took the lead, crawling on her hands and knees as if she were a commando beneath a sky full of barbed-wire. Claire followed behind her, both women steadily making their way closer to the breach. Aaron flattened himself out in the rear. He was the largest of the three, and so needed to be extra careful not to arch up too high with his back or butt as he scraped along the path.

Overhead, Travis sailed by like a living comic book hero. He procured a fist full of stones and was throwing them one at a time towards the advancing death squads. The Aussie turned on point, soaring back towards the wall again like a possessed boomerang. A moment later, a loud hiss sounded from the vicinity of the breach, followed by screams of agony from the security forces. Against his better judgment, Aaron peeked out of the trench to see what was happening.

Several of the gunmen who had moved through the breach and out into the clearing were dead; their bodies slumped over, making their final twitches on the ground before falling still for good. The remaining squad members were retreating back through the wall at a fast clip. Travis lobbed another one of his stones at the opening, the throwing motion bending his elbow and sending him into a momentary free-fall until he extended his arm back out again. The rock descended towards the trailing forces, but just before impact, it vanished in a puff of white. With another hiss, a quickly expanding cloud of highly pressurized air blasted out from the rock. The dense pocket of pure oxygen shot outwards in a freezing fog. The cloud quickly dissipated, revealing several more soon-to-be-dead gunmen, thrashing on the ground as the membranes of their lungs crystallized in the extreme cold.

Travis turned around to make another pass, but all of the security forces were either dead or already retreated back through the hole at this point. He stayed airborne, patrolling back and forth along the perimeter of the clearing while Ethan maneuvered himself close enough to the breach to begin repairing the rupture. The shattered stone resealed itself. Soon, no sign of the damage remained.

"All clear," Ethan called out. Michelle stood up, a hesitant expression on her face as her eyes darted around, searching for any threats Ethan might have missed. Apart from the dozen or so dead bodies, there was no sign of the security forces within the wall.

Aaron felt the pressure beginning to rise in Claire's chest as she looked upon the corpses. Aaron had the same sick feeling in his stomach—he hated death—but knowing that the men ambushed the clearing with the intention of killing every last one of them certainly took away whatever personal guilt he might have otherwise felt over their passing. He didn't blame the security forces for following orders, but given the choice between Claire's life and theirs, he had no moral qualms about what just happened. He would protect Claire, even if that meant other people had to die. He would do what was necessary. Internally, he put the blame on Reblan Industries for sending the men here in the first place. Yosef and the other higher-ups set all of this in motion.

Travis made an ungraceful landing, tumbling across the ground near Ethan, but was quick to recover to his feet. When Aaron and the women reached him he was still panting for air. Travis made flying look both graceful and easy, but holding his form was clearly strenuous.

"We've got a problem," said Travis between breaths as soon as the other Arcadians gathered around him. "Purple sparks… to the south… emergency signal from Wes."

Aaron searched the horizon all around him, unsure which way south was. He followed Claire's gaze which had settled on a portion of the sky above the wall to the left of their position. Just barely visible above the treetops was a glimmer of violet like a weeping willow firework shimmering against the midmorning sky.

"What's it mean?" asked Ethan.

Travis shook his head. "Nothing good—it would have been yellow if they'd found answers. Wes and Isabelle will be expecting us to—" Travis broke off midsentence and stared blankly through Ethan and the newly mended wall. "Bastards!" he suddenly shouted, a snarl appearing on his lips as he tried desperately to shake off the distant expression. "Dirty snake bastards! They're hurting her!" From the direction of his gaze, Aaron deduced that something must be happening to Brooke. Travis started flailing his arms, grabbing at his own head with both hands, but it didn't stop the tormenting visions from entering his mind.

"Travis! Listen to me," Michelle said sternly, trying to draw him back to his physical senses. "Whatever is happening to Brooke, you need to keep to your own head right now. It won't do any good if you get lost in her fear and pain."

Travis eyed Michelle wildly, still only partially present. Michelle slapped him hard across the face, making his head snap to the side. He inhaled sharply. A red welt was already forming along his left cheek. When Travis turned back towards Michelle his nostrils were flaring with intense rage, but the slap did its job. Travis was back in his own mind. Michelle showed no fear as she met Travis's glare. She knew his anger was not for her.

A voice suddenly boomed to them from over the wall— Garrett Rames, sounding as if he'd gotten his hands on a megaphone, spoke calmly and with an air of authority. "The game is up," he said, his voice echoing throughout the walled-in expanse. "Now kindly turn yourselves in before I'm forced to bring any further harm to Brooke."

From the crazed look on Travis's face, Garrett's proclamation did nothing to drive the fight from the relentless Aussie. "Go to the purple sparks," he said. "Wes and Isabelle need your help."

"What about Brooke?" Michelle asked.

Travis was already bending his knees to once again launch himself high into the brilliant sky. "Leave Garrett to me," he said. He didn't give anyone a chance to argue as he shot himself straight up into the sky and quickly soared out of sight beyond the wall in a furious streak of black feathers.

Aaron and Claire shared a thought of concern. Despite Travis's physical prowess, they both very much doubted they would ever see him again. Outside the wall he would be outnumbered by gunmen and Arcadians alike.

The Millers remained stoically silent, hiding whatever feelings they had over the turn of events. There was nothing they could do for Travis now, so they pragmatically turned their attentions towards Wes and Isabelle's emergency signal.

"How far out does that look?" asked Michelle, gazing towards the slowly fading purple sparks.

Ethan put his hand to his forehead, blocking out some of the glare from the sun. "I'd say it's within the facility." He wiped away several beads of sweat from his brow before withdrawing his hand. The desert heat was getting thicker with every passing moment as the sun climbed higher into the sky. There was no use in further discussion.

They moved as one, making haste towards the south end of the enclosure. There wouldn't be much time before Garrett realized his ultimatum had been entirely ignored. Another assault would be coming soon. Aaron doubted the other Arcadians would hold back from the frontline next time.

Michelle took the lead when they reached the southern-most point of the wall. Ethan stood back, lost in thought as Michelle quickly burrowed a hole through the structure. Once she broke through to the other side, Ethan snapped back to his senses, leading the charge again through the narrow opening.

Aaron half-expected there to be gunmen waiting for them when they emerged from the enclosure, but the park remained quiet as they stepped out from the wall. Other than the slight rustle of branches in the breeze, the park was void of activity—all of the birds in the area must have fled during the explosions of the assault, leaving the park eerily vacant of their usual shrill chirps.

The group soon found a paved path and continued on towards the facility at a brisk pace. Ethan stayed out in lead and never looked back. It wasn't until he'd put some considerable distance between himself and the rest of the pack that Michelle yelled for him to slow down. Ethan reluctantly slowed, though not before shooting a glare of annoyance back towards his wife. "Keep up," he said, "we're almost there."

Sure enough, after cresting the next rise, the trees that surrounded the path opened to reveal the three-building complex on the other side of a large open field of grass. The purple sparks had almost entirely faded, but Aaron could still make out a faint glimmer of the signal—a few curious embers twirled around in the wind above the central Echo Facility.

The field before them was the one used by the protestors as a camp ground for the three days prior to the military chasing them off. Scorch marks and garbage littered the earth, as well as dozens of trampled tents, left behind when the protestors scattered away from the heavy fog of teargas.

Ethan picked his way through the mess, returning to his quick pace. This time Michelle didn't attempt to slow him. As eerie as the park was without its birds, reentering the human world without seeing another living soul was far more disturbing. They were getting close to the facility's gates, and as far as Aaron could tell, no one was guarding the entrance. Aaron had expected someone to try to stop their approach long before now, but only a single metal chain blocked their access to the complex's grounds. They leapt across the last of the ashy pits left behind by the protestors' campfires and crossed the long curving road that ran around the perimeter of the park, connecting it to the rest of the city.

Several rounds of small-arms fire rang out as they reached the chained gate. Everyone jumped, but it was clear the shots were distant and not directed at them.

"The chain's already cut," said Ethan, knocking the loose strand of links to the ground. It made a clang that incited a frown from Michelle.

Wes and Isabelle's entry point, thought Claire.

Aaron nodded. *I hope they're alright,* he thought back.

The gate squealed noisily as Ethan pushed it open. He slipped inside and everyone else followed. The gunshots stayed fresh in Aaron's mind as they moved down the private drive towards the central Echo Facility. A row of palm trees lined the curb. The group moved between them one at a time as if the cover of their trunks was the only thing keeping them alive. They carefully dashed past the entrance of Echo Facility, making their way towards the Atrium where Wes and Isabelle had been headed to retrieve Wes's personal tablet from his room. Up until this point they still hadn't seen any sign of security personnel—but now, as they passed the corner of the building, they came across a group of approximately twenty men, all surrounding a glowing, blue bubble-shield.

Wes was hunkered down inside the dome, which was pressed firmly against the side of Echo Facility. Isabelle was nowhere to be seen. Four of the security guards took turns striking the bubble with long rebar rods, left over from the building's recent vertical expansion. A pile of bullet shells surrounded the men's feet, indicating that the rebar was not their first choice of attack. The guards were exacerbated, clearly fed up with Wes's nearly impenetrable shield. As indestructible as the bubble appeared, Aaron knew Wes couldn't keep it up forever. One of the men who had been standing back until now ordered the rebar wielding guards to move to the side as he drew his sidearm. He recklessly opened fire—the shield sent the hot lead ricocheting wildly around them with every shot. He only stopped when one bullet flew above his own head.

The entire security force was so focused on attacking Wes that no one noticed Aaron's group moving in from behind. Wes, who was facing them, saw what was about to happen. The only warning the men received was the faint smirk on Wes's lips as Michelle sent a crackling cloud of electric energy screaming through their bodies. The men holding the rebar rods received more than their fair share of the shock. Their black blazers smoldered as they fell into heaps of lifeless flesh. The rest might wake again, but if the shock Aaron received the night before was any indicator, they would not be back on their feet for many hours at the very least.

Wes's bubble protected him from the electric storm—its blue glow only intensifying as the energy from the cloud fueled the protective barrier. As the last crackle of electricity faded, Wes stopped feeding energy to his shield and pushed his way through the now useless layer of goop, doing his best to avoid getting the remains in his eyes and hair. He was only moderately successful, still coming out of it looking like he lost a fight with a giant slug.

"Yosef took Isabelle," said Wes, his words rushing together almost unintelligibly. He stepped across the pile of security guards as if they were part of the landscape. "I can still feel her—she's up on the top floor of Echo Facility." He was already moving towards the entrance of the building without waiting to see if the others would follow.

"Wait!" said Michelle. "What about your tablet?"

Wes paused only briefly to gesture towards the bag dangling under his right arm before continuing on. From the look on his face, he was clearly annoyed by Michelle's priorities when it came to Isabelle's safety.

As they started back towards the entrance of Echo Facility, Aaron couldn't help but notice Claire averting her eyes from the still smoldering security guards. The death toll building up around their group was really starting to wear on her. He hadn't meant to pry, but before Aaron knew it, he was slipping past the barrier inside Claire's mind and hearing her desperate thoughts without her permission.

What would you think of me if you ever learn of this? Will you see it in my soul? Will you be ashamed? We have become death, and it will follow us always.

Aaron immediately retreated back beyond the wall. He hoped Claire hadn't noticed the intrusion. He wasn't sure who she was thinking about. Her mother? Her brother? The thought process was disturbing, regardless. The cold surrender behind the words make it all the more unsettling. She felt responsible for the deaths. Even though neither he nor Claire performed the killing actions directly, they were both guilty by association. Aaron felt it too. He wanted to comfort her, but he couldn't say anything without first admitting he violated her privacy. He wasn't sure what comfort he could possibly offer anyway. Her words rang true to him, almost as if spoken in prophecy. They had been transformed into super soldiers, and death *was* a soldier's business after all. It would follow their every move, whether they invited it in or not. They would never be able to forget what had been done on this day.

Claire turned away, running to catch up with Wes and the others. Aaron did his best to push the thoughts from his mind as he followed on her heels. *Can we ever again have a semblance of normalcy in our lives?* Things would never return to the way they were before. They couldn't. There had been both great good and great horror in their new lives since joining the Arcadian Project—it remained to be seen which way the scales would tip by the time all this was through.

Once within Echo Facility, Wes made short work of the security doors that blocked off the entrance lounge from the rest of the building. They hadn't run across any more security personnel so far—it was as if the entire security force had come out to attack Wes around the side of the building like angry bees honing in on an intruder to their hive. Wes paused for a moment at the main elevator bank, contemplating whether or not the speed of the lifts was worth the risk, but as if on cue, the building's power grid suddenly went down, burying the hallway in complete darkness for a moment before the emergency lights flashed on along the edges of the walkway. The lifts did not power back up.

Ethan blasted the stairwell door off its hinges with a fiery force that filled the air in the vicinity with dense, white smoke. With all the doors magnetically sealed and everyone's security chips fried, force was the only option that remained to them. Wes clamored through the doorway right behind Ethan, quickly passing him as he took the stairs two at a time until he was out of sight. Aaron could hear the slap of Wes's feet against the linoleum-tiled steps, already about a floor and a half above them by the time the rest of the group rounded the turn on the second floor.

From what Wes said earlier, Isabelle was on the top floor of Echo Facility, which meant they still had six stories to climb. With how quickly they were falling behind, Aaron was beginning to worry Wes would move on without them when he reached the top. No one else could sense Isabelle's location. When they reached the seventh floor, however, Wes was sitting on the first step of the final flight clenching his right calf muscle.

"Cramp," he moaned, kneaded his leg frantically with his fingertips. Wes was dehydrated—they all were after spending the night out in the park. Aaron was glad Wes's body failed him before he could do something stupid. There was no doubt in Aaron's mind that Wes would have charged forth to rescue Isabelle without even considering the dangers of taking such a bold approach.

Aaron could see the pain in Wes's eyes as the boy cursed his own weakness. "We'll get her back," said Aaron in the most reassuring voice he could muster as he helped Wes to his feet. Ethan and Aaron each took an arm as they half-dragged and half-carried Wes up the final flight of stairs.

When they reached the top, Claire was already cutting through the thick fire-door. It was a quieter approach than Ethan's blast on the ground floor. She aimed her finger like a blowtorch, slicing through the metal as if it were a soft cheese.

Ethan turned towards Wes while they waited for her to finish. "Do you have eyes and ears in there?" he asked— Ethan had put two and two together about Wes's connection with Isabelle and rightly assumed that it must have been similar to what Travis and Brooke had been experiencing.

"No," said Wes. "She's unconscious—only got a location."

"Do you think...?" Michelle proposed the unfinished question to her husband.

"A trap?" Ethan nodded. "It's what I would do. But I doubt he's expecting all five of us." Everyone shared a lingering look of concern. Ethan shrugged. "Lead the way," he said, gesturing for Wes to move into the hallway as the door fell away from its hinges. "What else can we do?"

Aaron helped Claire maneuver the detached door, propping it up against the far wall of the hallway as quietly as possible.

The hum of the ventilation vanished along with the main lights when the power grid went down, leaving the building unnaturally silent.

"That way," whispered Wes, pointing to the left, down the long hallway. Aaron and Ethan took up their positions under each of the boy's arms as they shuffled down towards the door at the end of the hall. Wes's concentration was laser focused, guiding them all the way to a tall wooden door, marked as the office of Yosef Reblan.

Ethan looked into each of their eyes, making sure everyone was ready, and then began a silent countdown with his fingers, preparing for an explosive entrance when he reached zero. *Five... four... three....*

At two, the door to the CEO's office swung open from within. Ethan stumbled back, nearly knocking Aaron over in the process. Wes immediately lunged forward, ignoring the cramp in his leg as he tackled the figure in the doorway. He slammed into Dana Farris, clutching the project leader around the waist in a clean tackle that laid them both out on the floor.

Dana hit the tile hard. In his shock, he did not raise his hands, not to attack, nor to catch his fall. He was as surprised to see the Arcadians as they were to see him, but that did not stop Wes from pummeling him across the face with his fists.

"Easy boy," came the voice of Yosef Reblan from across the room. "There is no use fighting. It doesn't matter anymore."

Wes eased up on Dana, already dazed and battered by the several hard blows Wes landed against his temple. Dana wheezed a pained cough between gasps for air as Wes slid off his chest and turned towards Yosef. Aaron and Ethan moved into the office, spreading out on either side of Wes to support him from the flanks.

Across the wide office, Yosef sat in a tall, dark-leather chair. Behind him, a wall of windows displayed a view of the vast desert landscape that consumed most of the country. The old man seemed relaxed, but a look of sadness in his eyes belied his laidback posture.

"Just take her and leave us be," said Yosef, gesturing towards Isabelle, laid out on a chair in the corner. Everyone was confused by Yosef's lack of fight. They all expected the founder of the Arcadian Project to be a formidable foe.

Claire scooted past Dana, still flat out on his back, and went straight to Isabelle. The girl looked younger than Aaron had ever seen her before, her features softened by the embrace of sleep. Wes followed suit, rushing to Isabelle's side.

"What did you do to her?" he asked as he scooped her up.

"She will wake," said Yosef as he turned away from the Arcadians to face the bank of windows. Outside, the glistening sands shined like water in the sunlight. The wind formed slowly shifting ripples in the frozen sea of dunes. "But it does not matter," he continued in a near whisper, "there will be nowhere for any of us to hide."

Aaron wasn't sure if Yosef meant for anyone to hear the last part. Claire and Wes were preoccupied with carrying Isabelle from the room and clearly hadn't caught a word of it. Michelle, still back out in the hallway, urged them to hurry— if Yosef was willing to let them leave without a fight, no one wanted to stick around long enough for him to change his mind. Only Aaron and Ethan heard Yosef's ominous remark. They shared a quick look before retreating with the others.

Aaron was the last through the doorway. As soon as he passed the threshold, Yosef gestured sharply and the door slammed unceremoniously. The hum of the ventilation system turned back on at the same time—the power returning to the building as the normal lights flickered back on.

Aaron watched relief spread across Wes's face as the boy silently observed Isabelle in his arms. Perhaps he still believed that being with Isabelle was enough—that as long as they were together everything would be alright. Aaron knew better now. They had all been changed, and the world was not about to let them forget it. Death would follow them; there truly was nowhere they could hide.

CHAPTER

38

Friends and Foes

The golden chain of the butterfly pendant necklace dug into Belford's hand, turning the skin beneath it white. He wound it tight around his fist, daring the thin strand of metal to break, but it withstood the pressure. The pinch eventually became too painful, forcing him to ease his grip. The outline of the butterfly remained imprinted on his palm as he let go and allowed the dangling chain to fall into his lap.

Behind him, the door to the cargo hold shifted open with an abrupt scrape—the swollen wood rubbing against its frame. Belford scooped up the necklace and slipped it into his pocket before turning to greet Ethan. As distasteful as the torture sessions were, Ethan's strategy was working. He had formulated an impressive attack plan for Garrett's palace from the information gleaned through Wilgoblikan's lies. That's what Captain Grine said, anyway—the plan was top secret, and Belford was not privy to any of the details.

"It's done," said Ethan, shutting the door behind him.

Before it closed all the way, Belford caught a glimpse of Grine, fast at work re-growing a patch of flayed skin on Wilgoblikan's shoulder blade. Wilgoblikan's head lulled against his chest, his gray hair matted and wet with sweat; defeated and broken. Belford pushed the sight from his mind as soon as the door blocked the Whune from view.

"Did you ask him?" Belford couldn't hide his anticipation. He felt a nervous flutter in his abdomen as he waited for Ethan's response. Ever since realizing Wilgoblikan might be able to deliver him the answers he sought from Garrett, Belford was unable to focus on much else. It was Wilgoblikan who tracked him to Darrenfield almost immediately upon his re-materialization from the depths of the computer, after all. The old Whune had to know something about how Garrett predicted his return so precisely.

"I *asked* him," said Ethan, "but apparently in his mind that piece of information does not harm his master. He was able to answer both yes and no to every question I proposed on the subject, right up until the point where he lost too much blood and stopped answering entirely."

Belford glanced down at the bloodied knife, still held in Ethan's right hand. He had upgraded from the clipping sheers to a dull spreading knife from the galley. Coriva would not be pleased to learn of Ethan's use of her cutlery.

The butterflies in Belford's stomach were once again replaced with the sick feeling of rising bile as the knife dripped several drops of water-thin blood onto Ethan's shoes. He didn't notice the mess as he clasped Belford on the shoulder with his free hand. "Sorry, buddy," he said.

Belford instinctively recoiled from Ethan's touch, as if it were his own skin that had been flayed away. He felt as disgusted with himself for condoning the torture as he was with Ethan for actually carrying it out. Belford dirtied his hands by having Ethan ask his questions, and he hadn't even gotten any answers. Disappointment over the lack of response was the only thing that outweighed the guilt.

Ethan sauntered down the hallway away from Belford, seemingly without a care in the world, twirling the knife in his hands like a toy. In that moment, Belford hated him more than ever. He hated Ethan for what he had done to Vera; hated him for torturing Wilgoblikan; for bringing out his own dark side. The thing he hated most of all, though, was knowing that he was capable of being just like Ethan. Belford breathed deeply through his nose. The anger was self-destructive. The two of them were tied together; brothers in fate.

Vera would not be waiting for Ethan in his cabin, at least. She was still sharing Belford's tiny cot. Belford was grateful for the comfort she brought him at night, despite the close quarters. Their interactions were purely physical. While he wished he was with Claire, it was just nice having someone by his side. He knew the chances of ever seeing Claire again were miniscule, which helped lessen his guilt over obtaining the physical closeness he so desperately needed. If by some miracle he ever did manage to find Claire again, he hoped she would understand.

The door to the cargo hold opened and Grine stepped out. At the same time, Vera descended the metal steps from the upper deck. She locked her sultry eyes on Belford. "Hey, there," she said with a devilish grin. "Do you have time for another fast one before we reach the port?"

Belford's eyes darted to Grine. The young captain's feelings for Vera hadn't been the first thing on his mind when he started sleeping with the girl. Grine brushed past Belford in stoic silence. Whatever headway he'd made towards gaining Grine's allegiance was long gone. Belford let out a sigh.

"I'll take that as a no…" said Vera.

"Sorry," said Belford. "I was about to get some food."

"That's okay, you go. I already ate," said Vera, taking his excuse as an invitation. "Stop by the room when you're done if you have time." She walked past the now boarded-up supply closet and entered their shared cabin. She turned back around, nudging one of the shoulder straps of her dress down her arm. Her dress drooped, exposing a little extra cleavage. She topped the display off with a provocative wink before shutting the door.

Belford watched her go with a slight shake of his head. Her offer was tempting, but he really did have other matters to attend to. He wanted to work on fixing some of the relationships he'd neglected with the other passengers. He made his way towards the mess hall. First lunch was currently being served. Shiara glared up at him from behind her bowl of stew. She and Thorin were eating in silence at their own table in the corner of the room. Grine saw Belford enter and quickly snatched up a bowl and headed for the privacy of his own cabin.

At the larger table, Livian was sitting opposite a man Belford did not recognize. He knew everyone onboard, so the sight of a stranger was perplexing. The Rosa Marsa had been consistently underway since setting out from Fort Bastion. Livian glanced up at Belford, prompting the stranger to turn in his seat.

Belford's mouth fell open. He immediately recognized the face from his past.

Garrett Rames... but how?

There was something off... his skin was loose and droopy, as if he'd gained considerable weight and then lost it again. His features were similar to Garrett's, but not quite how Belford remembered him.

Livian giggled at Belford's expression. "Don't scare him now, Deenan," she said to the Garrett facsimile.

Deenan grunted. The Illusionist had changed his face.

"Creepy," said Belford, turning away and walking over to Shiara and Thorin's table.

Shiara continued to glare as he sat down beside Thorin. "I'm surprised you're joining us," she said. "Figured you'd be deep inside your toy."

"Could you give it a rest?" snapped Belford. "I could really use some support right now."

Shiara narrowed her eyes.

"Hi," said Thorin between bites of stew, ignoring the awkwardness.

"What's with the dynamic duo over there?" asked Belford, more quietly.

Thorin didn't need to look to know Belford was referring to Livian and Deenan. "The Arcanum intends to replace Garrett once he is dead. Take over his rule and establish peace."

It was quite brilliant, Belford had to admit. Livian and her brain spores combined with a fake Garrett would be all the Arcanum needed to take over Kovehn without spilling a single drop of blood—apart from King Garrett's, anyway.

"How are things going with the Goblikan?" asked Thorin.

By now, word of Wilgoblikan's imprisonment within the cargo hold had spread throughout the Rosa Marsa. Belford gave a noncommitting shrug. "Ethan got what he needed from him," he said, "but he wouldn't say how he found me in Darrenfield. The only person left to ask is Garrett himself... if I am to have any hope of finding Claire, I have to speak to Garrett."

Thorin gave him a sympathetic pat on the shoulder.

"If there's an opportunity, will you help me question him?" he asked.

"You aren't stepping one foot off this ship," said Ethan, suddenly behind Belford. "You're too much of a liability, I'm sorry to say."

Belford's eyes went wide. He hadn't heard Ethan's approach.

"I understand your inclination to search for answers, but you would never be able to get the truth from Garrett—not in an hour, not in ten days—and we won't have nearly that much time to take him down."

Belford's face grew hot.

"Your job was done when your presence secured the approval of the Arcanum. You'll be staying behind with Captain Grine, whose job is done now as well. I know you like to meddle where you don't belong, but that's not going to happen this time."

Belford lost his cool. He stood up quickly from his chair, sending it toppling to the floor behind him. Shiara grabbed his wrist as he tried to turn towards Ethan in his rage. She pulled him back around.

"I'm not the bad guy here," said Ethan, his hands pressed squarely to his hips. "I expect more maturity from you."

Belford was fuming.

Ethan eyed him judgingly one last time before departing the mess hall with a bowl of stew. It was only after Ethan was well on his way back to his cabin that Shiara finally allowed Belford to yank his arm free from her grip.

No one spoke. Ethan's words had been final. Shiara and Thorin's expressions remained sympathetic as Belford withdrew from the mess hall in the opposite direction. He wanted to scream in frustration. This was exactly what he hoped to avoid. Rather than win over any of the passengers onboard the Rosa Marsa, he somehow managed to push everyone away, and now he would be nowhere near Garrett when Ethan got his revenge. There would be no answers. Claire was lost. She would stay lost to him. He punched the wall, sending a shockwave through his fist as it struck the hallway's wood paneling with a thud. The harsh sting told him his knuckles would soon be bloody.

Vera poked her head out of their cabin at the sound. Belford quickly shoved his hand into his pockets to hide the injury. Vera cocked her head in confusion. She stepped over to Belford, immediately grabbing his elbow and pulling his hand back out. The butterfly pendant necklace slid halfway out of his pocket as she withdrew his hand.

Vera gasped upon seeing the gold chain. She dropped Belford's arm and quickly swiped the necklace from his pocket before he could stop her. "Is this for me?" she asked in awe, holding the intricate butterfly pendant up to her eyes.

Belford snatched it back, yanking hard when it caught in her slender fingers. The clasp broke, sending the pendant flying to the floor. "Ouch!" Vera yelled, pulling her fingers back in pain. "What the hell?"

Belford dove for the bouncing pendant as it skittered down the hallway. He picked it up and shoved it back in his pocket along with the broken chain. Vera stood before him, scowling with tears already in her eyes.

"Leave me alone," he shouted at her before shoving his way past. He felt like an asshole. He was an asshole. Vera didn't deserve his anger and frustration, but it was too late to take it back now.

Belford kept his eyes down as he took the stairs two at a time, climbing up to the stern. He hated being so hot-headed, but this time he wasn't able to stop himself. He was acting like the old Aaron from his dreams, before the Arcadian Project, before he met Claire and her temperament literally rubbed off on him. Claire had bettered him, but her influence was starting to dissipate. He was becoming someone he didn't like. The pain and darkness twisted in his gut. He wished desperately to be able to go back in time and hold Claire in his arms again.

On the top deck, Lieutenant Sulinton Canbel was beside Eben and Captain Bundles at the helm. The three sat in silence—Bundles had been refusing to talk to any of the passengers since finding out about Wilgoblikan in the cargo hold. He and his son kept their attention on the river. Sulinton smiled politely at Belford as he joined him on the bench seat. Despite Belford's fundamental dislike of Canbel, the inquisitive lieutenant had always been friendly towards him. No one struck up conversation. Belford joined the silent viewing party as Melvona slid into view along the curving river.

The Altrese was wide and slow flowing in this area; a sharp bend in the river eroded a wide swath of land on the bank opposite Melvona. Bundles piloted towards a marina built for trading vessels. Large domed buildings topped with reflective gold towered above the city center. There were eight such structures. They each reminded Belford of the duke's palace back in Bronam—broken now, if Kara's unending nightmare was any indication. Kara never really escaped Bronam. He traced one of the curved wings of the broken butterfly pendant through the fabric of his pants pocket. Part of him had been lost with Kara.

Despite the winter chill that came along with the clear sky, the midday sun gleamed off the crowns of Melvona's domes with a shimmering heat that made the air ripple like water just above the curved surfaces.

The dock was far out from the city center, but the trading port was very much alive. Local fishing vessels dragged wide nets through the murky waters, back and forth, churning up the clay and mud until the water looked like chocolate milk.

Arlin popped his head up from below deck. The swordsman's usual blade was not sheathed at his side. He looked naked without it, his usual calm demeanor replaced with sharp movements.

"Missing your sword?" Belford asked.

"Aye," said Arlin. "There is wisdom in leaving it behind while I help hunt for supplies—it might bring unwanted attention—but it is not easy to part with. The Talas Shard is part of me."

Arlin had said as much before. Belford understood fully. That was how he felt every day when the moon went down and the Power was stripped from him—like losing another part of himself. Arlin's gaze drifted to Belford's bloody knuckles for a moment, but then shifted away. He didn't make any comment. The moon wasn't up yet, and even if it was, Belford wasn't about to risk using the Power to heal himself while in Melvona.

Arlin gestured with his head for Belford to follow him to the back seating area. Belford obliged. Once they were on their own, Arlin pulled a white cloth out from his pocket and began to tie it around Belford's hand.

"Thanks," said Belford. It wasn't the first time Arlin had helped clean up one of his messes. Though the swordsman didn't talk much, he was always there when Belford needed him.

"I've been told I am a great listener," prompted Arlin, saying Belford's words from early on their journey back to him.

It was a kind gesture. Belford exhaled with a sigh. "Ethan isn't going to let me leave the ship," he said. "Questioning Garrett was my last chance at finding Claire, and now it's all gone. That was the only reason I came on this journey to begin with. It's like I've lost her all over again." Belford barely got the words out—they stuck to his throat like flies in honey.

I've lost her….

The corners of his eyes began to sting with tears. Without answers, he had nowhere left to look. No direction. No hope.

"I feared as much would happen," said Arlin, his stoic demeanor returning. "Ethan does not trust you, and you brought me along. If you're being delegated to the ship, it is almost a certainty that I will be as well, but perhaps all is not lost."

Belford cocked his head.

"You may not have noticed, but Livian Niern has taken a fancy to me," he said. "I've been meeting with her in secret for several weeks now, gaining her trust in case we should need her assistance, and it appears that time has come."

Belford actually laughed out loud as he latched on to the shred of hope. It was the plan he hadn't dared ask Arlin to enact. Arlin's apparent obliviousness over Livian's interest in him had been feigned. "You and Livian… did you…?"

Arlin grimaced slightly. "I have done what I must in order to lead her on," he said, "but nothing Mallory would not forgive of me, under the circumstances."

Despite Arlin's reassurance, Belford felt awful for Mallory. Arlin didn't appear too phased by whatever had happened behind closed doors with Livian, though. Ultimately, what was done was done, and Belford was not about to squander the renewed chance that Arlin was giving him.

"I'll speak to her once I return," said Arlin. "I shall see what she is willing to do for our cause."

Once again, Belford was indebted to Arlin. He knew better than to attempt to hug the swordsman, though he was tempted.

"We will be docking soon. You should head below deck to avoid prying eyes."

Belford took the dismissal in stride. He gave a curt nod and left Arlin to prepare for his outing. As Belford headed back down into the belly of the steamer, he wasn't sure where he was going to go. He didn't really want to talk to Vera just yet after making such a jerk of himself. She was probably still in his cabin, waiting to yell at him when he got back. The only people left onboard the Rosa Marsa that Belford wouldn't mind talking to were the Naffeim brothers, down in the engine room. He moved quietly across the metal stairs to avoid drawing Vera out of the cabin.

The heat of the furnace felt even heavier than usual after being out in the chill on the back of the steamer. He stepped through the bulkhead, expecting the jovial welcome of the outlander brothers, but was instead greeted by the ominous glower of Garcenus as he glanced up from working the coal shovel.

"What do you want?" Garcenus asked with a bite in his voice.

"Sorry," said Belford, "I thought the Naffeim brothers would be down here."

Garcenus rolled his eyes as he dumped another shovel full of coal into the red embers of the furnace. "Their shift doesn't start until supper."

Belford realized at that moment that until now he had never actually exchanged any words with the disgruntled deckhand. He turned to go, but stopped as a curiosity fell over him. "What did you and Wilgoblikan talk about?" he asked, leaning against the bulkhead with his left arm.

Garcenus kept his focus down on his work. He didn't answer, though a smirk slid across his lips.

"He's a madman, you know," said Belford. "He'd kill every one of us given half a chance."

Garcenus paused, as if in contemplation. The look of contempt that fell across his face was palpable. "He's the only one on this ship that hates you all as much as I do," he said. His dark eyes reflected the light of the furnace, looking as if flames might actually leap out from them.

Belford frowned. "No one wanted to leave Weni behind, you know," he said. "It was just bad luck."

"Don't you *dare* speak her name!" Garcenus screamed at him. He tossed the shovel to the floor as he stepped up to Belford, puffing out his chest.

Belford stumbled backwards, surprised by the ferocity of Garcenus's advance. "Woah," said Belford, holding up his hands defensively. "I didn't mean anything by it."

Garcenus looked him up and down.

"I know what it's like to lose somebody too," said Belford. "If you'd like, after we're done with all this, we could get a party together to go search for her."

Garcenus's face pinched up in a strange expression. Perhaps the offer surprised him. A smile appeared on the deckhand's lips, though it did not extend to his sharp eyes. With a whip of his neck, Garcenus brought his forehead hard into Belford's nose. The unexpected head-butt brought

Belford to the floor in an instant. Warm blood gushed from his nose. The pain was blinding. Belford cried out in shock. Garcenus merely chuckled. He turned away and picked up his shovel to continue on with his labor.

Belford put his hand to his nose, but the blood was already pouring down onto his shirt. There was no reasoning with a person like this. The hatred in Garcenus's heart ran through and through. Belford picked himself up, keeping his head tilted back as he withdrew from the furnace room. The blood flowed down the back of his throat, thick and warm. When he reached the top of the stairs, Vera was waiting in the hallway, arms crossed, staring at him incredulously.

"I have not had a good day," said Belford, nasally, through the blood in his passageways.

Vera's expression remained unchanged as she gave one slow blink.

"That necklace belonged to someone who's gone now," he said.

Vera pursed her lips to the side. "Come on," she said. "Let's get you cleaned up."

Belford followed her into his cabin. When he was shitty to people, they were nice to him, and when he was nice to people, they broke his nose. He didn't think he should take any sort of lesson from that, but the thought was amusing. Vera had him lay back on the cot and gave him a clean cloth to put over his nose. She helped him carefully pull his bloody shirt off over his head.

"I'm sorry about earlier," he said.

"You don't have to explain," said Vera. "I'm sorry I grabbed the necklace from you. It's just nice to get nice things sometimes."

Belford grunted. He knew she had nothing to apologize for. It just made him feel like a bigger jerk.

"Do you mind...?" Vera asked, crawling up beside him on the cot.

"It's fine," he said, though she hadn't really waited for his response.

She placed her head on his shoulder. Her body was pressed up against him with her arm across his chest. Over time, his nose clotted and the blood stopped flowing out. He eventually fell asleep, napping with Vera in his arms. He had no idea how much time passed before a ruckus of voices arose from out of the mess hall. Vera sat up, yawning widely.

Belford sprang awake as well, rising from the cot. He pulled on a fresh shirt over his head before going out to investigate. The voices in the mess hall sounded excited. Arlin was leading the conversation; already back from his hunt for supplies. When Belford entered, he found the room packed full. Thankfully, Garcenus was absent. Arlin paused only momentarily upon taking in Belford's disheveled appearance—there was a streak of dark, matted blood smeared through the stubble of Belford's unshaved chin.

"Barbarians," continued Arlin. "That's what they are saying, though the sophistication of the strikes implies coordinated leadership unlike what I have heard of them before. All along the Northern Sea—Graven, Taris, Kovehn—all under attack—ships upon ships of invasion forces are unloading and capturing towns. There are wizards among them, and strange beasts which they ride, giant lizards that climb straight up fortification walls. Perhaps some of what is being said is just rumors—I have surely never heard of anything like this in all my days—but one thing that is certain is Kovani forces are being drawn north to the fight— away from the capital. Tavallon will be poorly defended when we arrive, at least until Garrett can call in reinforcements from the fronts in the conflicts to the south and west. He has spread his forces too thin. People are speaking of civil unrest arising all across the kingdom."

"Well that's good news then," said Sarbin Raiger.

"For our assault, perhaps," said Ethan, his eyes sharp with contemplation.

"If Kovehn is unable to turn back the invasion forces, we may very well end up with a new enemy on our doorstep," said Deenan. Belford still wasn't used to Deenan's creepy, droopy Garret-face.

"Exactly," said Arlin. "Killing Garrett may all be for naught if the invasion isn't deflected. The barbarians—if that is truly who is responsible—pose a risk to all of Aragwey."

Murmurs grew from the crowd. Ethan put his hand up to silence the room. "This invasion force is an unknown, but it does not change our mission. Garrett will be disposed, and Kovehn will be taken over by this skin sack." He gestured at Deenan.

"My face will tighten up before we get to Tavallon."

Ethan waved off the interruption. "The rumors are probably blown way out of proportion anyway, but even if they aren't, Deenan will command the entire Kovani military to march north to turn the barbarians away and a peace accord with Phandrol will be formed. What better way to unite two enemy forces than to have a common enemy. We will use it to Phandrol's advantage."

Deenan nodded, sending his drooping jowls wobbling.

"No more talk of this," said Ethan. "We are not in the safest of places for such a discussion. Once the supplies are loaded, someone tell that fat captain to get us back underway."

As the passengers began to disperse, Shiara sent Belford a disapproving frown from the other side of the mess at the sight of Vera clinging to his arm. Belford playfully grabbed Vera's butt while staring back at Shiara. Not one to concede, Shiara approached Belford before he could follow Vera back to the cabin. "Have fun while you can," she said. "If the girl is this clingy now, you might never be able to get rid of her— Mast pray you ever do find your Claire." She walked away, leaving Belford to stew in the thought.

Shiara's just jealous... at least, he hoped.

Ash

The dark water continued to rise. The sloped tunnels ran like rivers of their own, quickly filling the deepest depths of the lightless Underground with the Etto's fury. She was most comfortable in the darkness. It blanketed her; masked her; made her feel safe, despite the rising flood that would soon force her out into the open. Although she was a denizen of the dark, gifted with the ability to see through even the dimmest gloom, there was absolutely no light left within the Underground. Most creatures would have felt helpless in such a place, but she bathed in the shadows, feeling her way along the passageways with budding confidence.

Unfortunately, the chill of the winter water was biting. Doctor Crane's revitalization of her pain receptors made the icy sting nearly unbearable to her rough skin as she submerged herself. Her muscles clenched up like a weak human's, sending her into a frozen shock as she swam down a mostly flooded corridor in search of higher ground.

It was time to make her way to the surface. Based on her best estimates, it should be night up in the blacked-out city. At the start of her escape, Theilo made mention of it being daytime—that was all she had to go off of. She hoped he hadn't thought to obscure the time of day from her. She had to question everything now. Before Salvine killed Theilo, her whole escape had been a ruse, concocted by Doctor Crane to test her intelligence.

Since then, she'd taken over while Salvine retreated into the depths of their shared mind. She moved as far away from the power plant as possible, taking random turns until she had absolutely no idea where she was. She was growing tired. The human restrictions Doctor Crane placed upon her body were a constant nuisance. Fatigue from her escape dragged at her limbs, slowing her stride until she could no longer continue.

She needed to feed. Sadly, the only prey within the Underground were waterlogged rats, swimming blindly to escape the flood. They were an undignified meal. There was no sport in their slaughter. They screeched and swam faster when they smelled her coming, but they could not escape her lumbering strides. Despite her lack of enthusiasm, she used what little energy she had left to snatch up a few of the furry morsels. She consumed them whole, crunching their bones and savoring the warmth of their innards.

Salvine's presence bristled with disgust. *You better not catch us any diseases from that.* Salvine made the emotional equivalent of a sigh. *I really miss cheese….*

You're not the only one who's disappointed. I miss eating human flesh.

Salvine withdrew again, throwing a shade of judgment as she departed. Salvine still thought of herself as human and as such was shackled by the chains of human morality.

When a Whune kills and eats a human, it's no more murder or cannibalism than when a human guts and boils a rabbit.

Salvine ignored her logic, refusing to communicate with her any longer.

After the snack, she continued her ascent. The tunnels became drier as she neared the surface. Although Salvine pretended not to be present, she was watching intently through their eyes.

Ahead, the rungs of a ladder became visible, leading up to a metal hatch. Faint light bled through the cracks around the hatch. Moonlight. Any Ver'ati up above would be able to use the Power. She'd known there was a good chance the moon would be up, but it was still a disappointment. Despite the added danger, the darkness of night provided her only chance of sneaking around the city undetected.

She placed her hands on the rungs and began to climb.

Salvine gave up on her feigned absence. *Javic is up there somewhere. He has to be. We have to find him.* She continued to cling to the thought of that boy.

The last time they'd seen Javic, he was traveling with the bearer of the Mark of Kings. She'd go along with Salvine's plan until she found an opportunity to kill her target. She reveled in her own deviousness. Salvine wouldn't know her true intent until it was too late.

The hatch swung up on creaky hinges. She peeked out of the hole. She was in a square beside a vast fountain basin. No water spouted from its central structure; the pumps had powered down along with the glowing orbs. Moonlight reflected off its lightly rippling surface—a slight breeze gently moving the water. In the distance, several clusters of humans cut paths between buildings carrying oil lanterns to light their ways. No one was close enough to see her as she emerged from the Underground.

One of them might be Javic. We should get closer.

Salvine tried to take control of her legs, but she refused her access.

Wait.

Something wasn't right. Her predator senses knew she was being watched. She inhaled deeply, her mind filtering out her own stink. There was something else here. Something subtle. A sweetness. The anxious sweat of a human, but it was watered down. She spun back around to face the fountain basin, but it was already too late. An ambush was in motion.

No!

Beams of light cut through the cold night air. The sudden onset blinded her momentarily. The splash of several humans leaping up from the fountain basin gave her a direction to attack. Before her eyes adjusted she was already lunging at the source of the beams. A solid thud landed on the back of her head.

"Don't kill it!" cried Doctor Crane's whiny voice.

She could make out blotches now through the light beams. She was surrounded by no less than five Ver'ati.

We can't go back to that lab....

"Did you really think I would let you roam free without putting a tracker on you?" asked Doctor Crane. He was holding a syringe in his right hand and some sort of boxy device in his left. "You continue to disappoint me. Quite a mess you've made."

She let out a monstrous roar—a combination of anger and frustration. In the distance, students traveling between classes fled indoors.

"That's quite enough of that," said Crane. He gestured with a flick of his wrist. The syringe flew from his hand, its long needle stabbing her in the chest and plunging in its liquid before she could yank it out again. "I told you I would find you. You must know, I'm far from through with you. I will make you the perfect specimen yet."

Already, her vision was growing dark, the tranquilizer quickly taking hold.

Must... fight... back.... Salvine grappled for control of her limbs again, but she was already shutting down.

She felt her body toppling over, but she was unconscious before she hit the ground.

Everything grew dark as the world swirled around her. She felt like she was still falling, endlessly downward. There was a heaviness to the air, like she was being dragged through water. Her surroundings slowly changed without her taking notice of the shift. Soon she could hear birds chirping above her. Cool water lapped at her ankles. The glow of a gray dawn lit a featureless sky. She was on a beach, her feet buried in the wet sand as the tide rushed between her legs.

Nearby, a blonde girl in a long white dress sat on the bank, facing the sea. She could feel that it was Salvine, despite having never seen her before. Salvine ignored her appearance, keeping her sad gaze locked upon the water.

She sat down beside her. "Where are we?" she asked, a human voice escaping her lips.

Salvine glanced over, a small frown flashing across her face. "The Gulf of Nerim," she said. "How I imagine it, anyway." Salvine looked her up and down. "I must say, this is *not* how I imagined you, though. Do you even know what you look like in real life?"

She didn't. She'd seen a rippling reflection of her face while drinking from streams numerous times, but she never really paid much attention to her own appearance. "Do I look bad now?" she asked.

Salvine chuckled. "No, not at all. You're much uglier in reality."

She blinked several times, strangely perturbed by the insult. She wasn't sure why Salvine's opinion of her appearance mattered to her.

"Woah, you just grew hair," said Salvine, amused.

She felt the heat of embarrassment rise in her face.

"No, it's nice. Very dark. Feminine. Wouldn't have thought it would suit you so well."

She put a hand to her head and felt the silky locks, perfectly straight. The hair stopped growing as soon as it reached Salvine's hair length.

"That's very human of you," said Salvine.

She silently grabbed a handful of sand and threw it at Salvine.

Salvine shook the sand off her dress. "You know, I never asked before, but what should I call you? Do you have a name?"

She didn't. She'd never thought about such things. She couldn't speak in the waking world. Her master was able to call to her with their mental connection. A name was never necessary. She shook her head.

"Well, what would you like to be called, then?"

A conundrum, to name oneself. She didn't know where to start. Humans tended to be named after other humans. She didn't want something like that.

"Maybe name yourself after something you like?" said Salvine.

She cocked her head, pondering the suggestion. She liked killing things. But she knew Salvine wouldn't approve of anything related to her favorite pastime. She delved deeper, trying to think of an enjoyable experience that didn't involve slaughter. It wasn't easy. She hadn't experience a long life, and many of her early days were already a blur of half-forgotten memories.

One memory did come back to her. It was the first time Salvine appeared in her head: The day her master burned down Javic's farm. After shaking off the odd sensation of Salvine's sudden presence, she had danced around the flames as a plume of smoke and ash rose into the air. It was glorious to see, all the heat and grand destruction. She put out her tongue and caught several flakes of ash as they fell back to the ground to form a gray blanket. She enjoyed the bitter flavor as the flakes dissolved in her mouth.

Salvine wouldn't approve of her enjoying burning down Javic's farm, but she didn't need to know her reasons. "Call me Ash," she said.

Salvine nodded with approval. "Nice to meet you, Ash," she said. "Too bad we'll be dying together soon."

Ash picked up another handful of sand. Using the power of thought she changed the grains into ash flakes and tossed them into the breeze to watch them twirl away.

Field of Stones

A brisk gust of wind jostled Javic's curly hair, sending a fine misting of Calvenite flakes floating away like dandruff. He had yet to shower since his visit to Sultrim—not counting the downpour earlier that morning. He needed a good scrubbing with soap and hot water to have any hope of becoming clean again. His underarms were unforgivably ripe. He kept his arms down for Sima's sake.

Seated beside him with a curious expression on her face, Sima Pahel watched Javic with her dark eyes. He couldn't tell what she was thinking. When Professor Vanton brought Javic out of Erotos through the eastern gates, he had no idea he would be meeting with one of his friends. Vanton pulled Sima out of her Aerology class, taking place just over the distant ridge, and brought them both to a strange valley filled with large, perfectly spherical stones. Javic and Sima took seats upon a pair of stones while Vanton hurried off with his lantern to "gather the rest of the team," leaving them with only the moonlight to see by. There was no telling what Vanton had planned.

Sima's curiosity was biting, but she held the questions from her tongue out of respect. It was clear Javic had been through an ordeal. "I'm glad you're alive," was all she said as she flashed Javic a small smile wrought with concern.

Soon Vanton returned with Baxton at his side. Bax greeted Javic with a one-armed hug and a confused shake of his head. "You're alive!" he mused.

"You can make time for pleasantries later," said Vanton. "We must begin. I sent word to Tyris Orensten to join us as well. His skill with water should round out Javic's training. Let's get started without him, though, so we aren't wasting time."

Bax exchanged a brief smile with Sima as he sat down beside her on one of the stones.

To Javic, it had only been a day since he'd seen Tyris in the Exam Hall before his journey to Sultrim. That was two weeks ago. Javic didn't know Tyris very well, especially compared to Baxton and Sima. What he knew of the boy came from overheard gossip between the other students. The nineteen-year-old was soft spoken and always kept to himself in their shared classes. It was no wonder he was quiet considering the trauma he'd been through—being hidden away from the Ver'konus for years, only to be outright rejected by his family once he developed the Power. He spent most of his teen years locked in his cellar, apparently.

His blacksmith father feared him. During Tyris's final weeks of captivity his father stopped bringing him provision. His parents sat by and waited for him to weaken, expecting him to die of thirst. Miraculously, he persisted. Weeks passed, and eventually his father was forced to contact the Ver'konus to rid himself of his son. The story went that Tyris survived by transmuting some of the stones of the cellar's foundation into pure water.

Javic couldn't help but wonder why Tyris hadn't simply broken free, considering his aptitude with the Power. Tyris had basically allowed himself to be imprisoned and left for dead. Perhaps he'd hoped his parents would change their minds.

"Javic needs training?" asked Baxton.

Professor Vanton nodded slowly. "Our boy here is to participate in the Dance of the Elements next week. I've brought you both here to help him train so that he may be successful."

"And hopefully not die," Javic added dryly.

"Well, it wouldn't be a success if you died, now would it?" Vanton chuckled to himself. Javic grimaced. Vanton's upbeat attitude made Javic uneasy.

Sima and Bax both stared at Vanton, concern heavy on their brows. "That's insane," said Bax, breaking the momentary silence. "Why would an initiate be entered into the Dance?"

Javic didn't wish to discuss the unfortunate series of events leading up to his nomination. "It's a long story," he said, answering so that Vanton wouldn't. "I'm a corporal now, and the head of the Arcanum Council wants me dead because of some things I know…." *Best not to say more.*

Baxton's mouth opened, but he wasn't sure how to respond. His jaw remained hanging slightly askew as Professor Vanton smartly moved the conversation forward.

"I chose the two of you and Tyris because you all studied with Javic and I can trust that you have his best interests at heart. You each also happen to have unique skill sets that will be beneficial for Javic to practice before the Dance."

Javic noticed a dark silhouette moving towards them down the path that led from Erotos into the valley. It was Tyris— his muscular physique apparent even in the darkness. He waved a greeting as he drew near.

"Welcome," said Vanton.

Rather than watch his step, Tyris turned his head up to the dark sky, causing him to narrowly avoid stumbling over several of the spherical stones. "Wow, just look at all the stars!" he exclaimed, a real sense of wonder in his eyes as he gestured broadly to the heavens. "You almost forget how many are up there with the city lights drowning them out." He returned his gaze back to the Earth as he reached Professor Vanton's side. He glanced across the group, his eyes narrowing as they fell upon Javic. "By Mast's light! Javic, back from the dead!" His mouth curled into a friendly grin. "I suppose you have something to do with why I've been asked here?"

Javic nodded. "I'll let the professor explain."

Tyris shook his head in wonder. "Sorry I'm late," he said, looking back over at Vanton. "I guess it's a day for strange occurrences—I was delayed by an escaped Whune scaring everyone over at Candeer Fountain. They recaptured it alive—quite the sight."

Javic frowned. He'd hoped he'd been hallucinating when he heard the roar of a Whune outside Aldune's interrogation chamber. *Terrifying creatures. It would be better if the Ver'konus put them all down and ended their suffering.*

"Strange, indeed," said Professor Vanton. "It's good you have made it. I was just explaining that I chose the three of you to help train Javic for the Dance of the Elements. Sima is a budding Aerologist, Baxton has been training with an artillery unit, and you, Tyris, are a prodigy when it comes to the manipulation of water."

Tyris brushed the complement aside. "How did an initiate wind up in the Dance of the Elements?"

"It's a long story," repeated Javic.

Vanton ignored the interruption. "None of you have ever witnessed the Dance before, obviously—only Ver'ati and state officials are allowed to view the trials, so let me explain what I can of how it works: Every year the tasks are slightly different, but they always follow the same theme. The Arcanum has four Artifacts which it uses to test would-be Ver'ati, one representing each of the four classical elements—

fire, earth, air, and water. Javic will be required to retrieve the four Artifacts within a circular arena where his ability to control his surroundings is limited to only one element type at a time.

"Now, obviously there are many more than just four elements in modern science. The four classical elements actually represent different states of matter. Earth is solids, air is gas, water is liquid, and fire is plasma. Javic will find his ability to manipulate matter only extends to one state for each task.

"Over the next four and a half days, I would like each of you to take turns teaching Javic about the state of matter of which you are most proficient. The flows of air and heat are second nature to an Aerologist. It is a subtle but powerful discipline when mastered."

Sima nodded in agreement.

"I'd like you, Sima, to work with Javic tonight, as I believe this will be the most difficult state for him to grasp, given his predisposition towards its opposite." Vanton glanced at Javic, "You have excellent marks in your architecture class. I could see you becoming a Builder one day. The earth-magic task should not be a hindrance to you."

Vanton turned towards Baxton and placed a hand on his shoulder. "Fire magic is dangerous. Show Javic how to handle such energy without blowing himself up. You'll need to meet out here, as explosions within the city are, I dare say… frowned upon. Don't hold back, though, Javic will have to release his inner fire with great ingenuity to complete his task."

Vanton shifted his gaze towards Tyris. "And you should take him down to the river and show him what can be done when one internalizes a fluid mindset."

Tyris smacked his hands together with enthusiasm. "It would be my pleasure," he said. "I grew up along the Minthune. It's been too long since I've been in the water."

"Excellent," said Professor Vanton. "I foresee this going well." He handed his lantern over to Javic. "I must apologize, I have a class to teach tonight, so I must bid you all farewell for the evening."

Javic wasn't sure what he'd expected from Vanton, but being dumped off to a group of initiates to learn about different states of matter was largely underwhelming. The professor walked off into the night without giving any further instruction. Everyone shared a confused look at his sudden departure.

Baxton waited until Vanton was out of earshot. "A kooky one, isn't he?"

Tyris nodded slowly, staring at Vanton's back until he disappeared entirely into the darkness.

"I guess we should start with the basics..." said Sima, being pragmatic as usual.

"I'm sorry guys," interrupted Javic, standing up from the stone he'd been seated upon. "You don't have to do any of this. There's only a few days before the Dance... there's no way I'm going to absorb enough to pass in such a short amount of time. You all might as well just go back to your classes."

"Nonsense," said Sima. "You're our friend and we're all happy to help." Baxton nodded along.

Tyris stood by awkwardly, scratching his elbow. He was barely an acquaintance to Javic, but he didn't seem keen on taking the invitation to quit either.

Javic sighed. "I barely know a thing about Aerology...."

"Well then it's a good thing I'm here, now isn't it!?" Sima gestured for Javic to sit back down. "You know Aerologists can control the weather. Vanton called it a 'subtle' discipline, but I disagree. I would call it *nuanced*. The best Aerologists can effect a whole region all by themselves, and there's nothing subtle about that. We have to practice outside the walls because years ago the constant weather manipulation inside Erotos was causing too many Echoes and the whole discipline was banned within the city. Out in the countryside, though, the best way to make crops grow is adequate rain, and Phandrol is naturally a rather dry region. Aerologists bring the rain just as John Graven first taught one-thousand years ago." The Rainbringer was one of John Graven's many monikers.

Sima gestured smoothly above their heads, manipulating the air above them. A dark cloud soon formed, blocking out the light from the stars. A tiny misting of rain droplets began to fall from the cloud. Sima suddenly gestured sharply towards a distant stone. A bolt of white lightning flashed out from the cloud, striking the rock.

Javic jumped. The loud crack rattled his teeth. He wiggled a finger in his ear until the ringing faded.

"Clouds form when the air is cooled to the point of condensation for the invisible water molecules that are evaporated within it," Sima explained. "I gathered energy at the center of where that cloud formed and shot it away with that lightning bolt. Basically, less energy in the air makes the air cooler, which forms clouds and makes it rain."

The rain quickly stopped and the cloud dispersed as the cool air spread out to mix with its surroundings.

"Give it a try," said Sima.

Javic took a deep breath to steady himself. He needed to find emotion to draw in the Power. His thoughts began to wander….

In his life, rain always seemed to fall on bad days. It was raining the evening the Rosa Marsa departed without him. It rained the night he met Mallory, too. He almost died that night. Hypothermia settled inside of him before Belford found a cave and started a fire. The flames warmed him just in time to save his life. Mallory laid by his side, unconscious, pale as all hell. He could still remember the way her brow furled into a cute frown as the heat revitalized her body.

It rained today.

Mallory would never be his.

He shook down the emotion before it could make tears appear in his eyes. He grasped onto the core of the feeling, using it to reach out for the Power. He needed to make it rain, and not just on his cheeks.

The Power flowed through him. He reached out to the air above and did as Sima instructed, pulling energy from the oxygen and pressing it tightly together into a tight ball at the center of the newly forming cloud.

"Drag the energy down as the cloud forms around it," said Sima. "If you lose sight of the point where you are collecting the energy you may lose control—"

Javic lost sight of his energy ball just as Sima's warning escaped her lips. A multi-pronged bolt shot towards the group. Bax and Tyris flopped to the ground, covering their heads. Sima had been expecting as much, though, and diverted the energy harmlessly into the distance, an electric snake trailing out and then down into the earth.

"It's ok," said Sima, "keep going. Don't let the cloud dissipate."

Javic was a bit shaken, but he continued, drawing more energy into another invisible ball. This time he kept shifting the ball downward, maintaining the vital eye contact. Finally, the air became cold enough that water droplets began to form. He dissipated the energy with a lightning bolt into a distant stone and marveled at his success as the rain fell upon his head.

"Excellent!" said Sima. "That usually takes people longer to get right their first time."

Javic flashed her a grin, feeling reinvigorated by his success. The rain didn't touch her skin, bending around her the way Javic had seen Belford and other Ver'ati manage. "You'll have to teach me that trick," said Javic.

Sime laughed. "Maybe later," she said, "you could use a bit of a shower first." She wafted her hand in front of her nose.

Javic dropped his arms back to his sides, grumbling to himself.

The rest of the lesson went smoothly. Everyone stayed late into the night as Sima went over more basics of Aerology. Controlling the weather usually meant managing energy to change air temperature. Heat rises. The shifting of air could produce much turbulence, forming huge swirling storms if enough effort and energy were put into them.

Air was all around, of course. It would always move to fill a sudden void with a deafening bang akin to thunder. The atmosphere wasn't very dense, but held a lot of energy. A small stone transmuted into oxygen would expand quickly as the new air molecules spread out. The rock's limited energy was spread thin as well. It could produce a deadly blast of frigid air, flash-freezing its surroundings as the air expanded.

Javic's brain felt overfilled by the time Sima decided to call it a night. The moon was nearly down. Javic was starting to get the hang of air manipulation, but he still preferred working with solids—there were far fewer variables and moving parts to keep track of when all the molecules were tied together.

The four students walked back to the city together.

Baxton laughed to himself. "Wanna know the difference between air magic and fire magic?" he asked. "Artillery strikes can blow off legs, whereas air can only blow up skirts."

Sima frowned at the poor attempt at a joke. She sent a gust of wind that crystalized Bax's hair into a mess of stiff, white tangles. "Don't worry, you won't be blowing up any skirts tonight," she said.

Baxton frowned.

Once they were back through the city gates, Sima invited Javic to stay with her and Baxton at their apartment while he prepared for the Dance. Having nowhere else to go, he gladly accepted. Before his trip to Sultrim, Bax and Sima lived in the dormitories in separate rooms. They'd moved into an apartment together on the north end of campus while he was away.

Sima readied a fresh set of linens for a cot she set up in the common area while Javic saw about cleaning himself off in the small bathing chamber. He spent a good hour scrubbing every speck of Calvenite from his body. Afterwards, he slept like a log. Cale did not bother him again in his dreams like the night before—*Thank Mast.* Javic just needed to focus on making it through the Dance of the Elements. He was glad not to have any added distractions. Everyone slept in late the next day, not rising until it was already nearing First Sense.

Baxton took the lead in training Javic that evening while Sima and Tyris attended their classes. He led Javic back out to the field of stones and went about blasting some of them into gravel. Bax didn't have much to say that Javic hadn't already learned from his time with Shiara and Belford, but he appreciated the refresher. Fire was like a life force—breathing oxygen and hungering for fuel. To manipulate it, one or both of those ingredients needed to be altered. Fire was energy, raw and volatile.

Blowing up rocks was fun. Baxton had him practice directing bursts of explosive energy against the stones in different ways to show him the varying range of effects. If he blasted the very edge of a stone, it shot off like a cannon ball, usually in one piece. When he focused the energy into the center of a stone, the rock would shatter. Bits of shrapnel blew everywhere, showering them with gravel, even at a distance.

If he directed the blast within a stone but towards one side, it tended to fracture, sending the bulk of its mass flying in one direction and smaller chunks in the opposite. He had to be careful about the chunks of shrapnel rocketing straight back towards him with deadly velocity. For safety, he never blew up anything too close. He always had to have enough distance to divert any bits that came his way.

Professor Vanton joined them the second half of the night and gave Javic some pointers. He helped him build up the confidence to generate a massive blast that nearly sent one of the stones out of the valley entirely, leaving behind a crater as deep as Javic was tall.

It was so loud that a pair of Aerologists teaching a class on the other side of the ridge came over to make sure everyone was alright. When they saw it was just Professor Vanton and his pupils blowing stuff up they departed, rolling their eyes. Javic scaled back on the power of his blasts after that and they were not interrupted again.

The following day, Javic met Tyris near the South Bridge, down by the edge of the Etwon where he'd launched rocks with Rylin. Tyris greeted him with a handshake—always so formal.

"So what do you already know about water?" asked Tyris.

Javic squinted his eyes as the low afternoon sunlight gleamed off the channel. "It's wet..." he said.

Tyris nodded. "All the best things are."

Javic raised an eyebrow. "Honestly, I don't know much when it comes to water manipulation. I'm not even sure what the discipline is called."

Tyris laughed. "It depends on how you use it. Water and ice manipulation, when used as an attack, would be considered Destructivism, just like any other elemental attack. General Aldune is a water-focused Destructivist." Javic's face soured at the mention of Aldune. Tyris continued without notice. "When used in weather manipulation it would be considered Aerology, of course. Some Ver'ati sailors use water manipulation to Propel ships. They're called Navigators. Understanding water is a handy skill for any Ver'ati, though, really." Tyris unbuttoned his shirt while he was talking. He shrugged it off his shoulders and laid it neatly on a nearby bench. "You coming?" he asked as he walked over to the railing that separated the pathway from the channel and climbed over onto the steep embankment beyond.

"What are we going to do?" Javic asked, fumbling with the buttons of his own shirt. "Isn't that freezing glacial runoff?"

"Aye," said Tyris, diving in headfirst without a moment of hesitation.

The chill of the winter air was already enough to make Javic shiver as he laid his shirt beside Tyris's. He grumbled to himself as he kicked off his shoes and climbed over the railing.

The water of the Etwon was swift. By the time Tyris reemerged, he was already twenty paces downriver. He turned around to face Javic and shot through the water like a harpoon. He moved with the Power, his arms and legs remaining still at his sides.

"Aren't you cold?" Javic asked from the top of the embankment.

Tyris laughed again. "Not at all," he said. "The water isn't even touching me." His hair was still completely dry, blowing lightly in the breeze despite having just been submerged. "It's pretty much the same trick as keeping the rain off you. The water is bending around me, leaving a small gap of air, and I'm Propelling myself by forcing the water around and behind me."

Javic nodded slowly. "I don't know that trick yet," he said. "I just get rained on."

Tyris rose up from the water. Only his feet remained submerged as the river bubbled beneath him. He stood upon the surface with his arms crossed, effortlessly, as if he were on solid ground. "It's easy, just concentrate on not letting the moisture touch you. Hop on in."

Javic was pensive. "What if I don't figure it out right away?" he asked.

"I reckon you'll learn fast if you want to stay warm."

A small fishing vessel passed by beside Tyris. A young boy on the bow waved. Tyris returned the friendly gesture. He stood on one leg for a second, then dove back into the water. A moment later he came shooting out again, this time flying high into the air. He did a flip before returning to his hovering stance upon a perch of water.

What a show off. Javic had to admit, it did look like fun, though.

The boy beamed back at Tyris, cheering as his troller drifted on down the river.

"Come on," said Tyris, "you've only got a few days left to learn all you can."

Javic grimaced. He already knew this wasn't going to be pleasant if the water touched him for even a second. He took a deep breath, then jumped clear of the embankment. He fell awkwardly, instinctively closing his eyes as the icy water hit him in the face. The water enveloped his whole body. All his muscles locked up as the cold bit into him. After a few moments he finally remembered to kick his feet and he bobbed up to the surface, gasping a shallow breath.

Tyris was standing above him on the water's surface, watching with a slightly amused expression. He stayed by Javic's side, drifting downriver with him. "Show that water what you're capable of," he said. "Repel it from your skin before you freeze."

Javic was already freezing, but he tried to do as Tyris said, holding in his mind the idea of the water flowing around him rather than against him. He immediately felt a difference. The water flowed around his front, but it was still touching his backside. His pants were already soaked and clinging to him as well. "It's too cold-d-d," said Javic, his teeth chattering together as he spoke.

"Hmm," said Tyris. "You'll need to work on that. Here, this should help for now." Tyris gestured ahead of Javic.

The current warmed immediately. A freezing fog formed above the water, the air taking on a bitter chill in exchange for heating the river. The warmth of the water sank into his bones, easing the pain and numbness that had briefly taken over his entire existence.

"Take my hand," said Tyris as he lowered himself back into the water. He dragged Javic to the embankment. "Hurry and climb out," said Tyris. "I don't want to get in trouble for practicing Aerology within the gates."

Javic felt like a drowned rat as he flopped against the stone. The embankment wasn't as steep here. They were parallel to the new Laudry Hall, almost a third of the way through the city from where they started. The Etwon's current was even stronger than Javic realized.

"Try to dry yourself off," said Tyris. "It uses the same principle as not getting wet in the first place."

Javic was able to draw the water from the front of his pants, but just like when he was in the river, his backside stayed wet. "How can I dry my back?" he asked. "I can't see behind myself to use the Power there."

Tyris looked confused by Javic's question. "It's all self-awareness," he said. "You know where your body is, the size and shape… you don't need to see your feet to know they're there, do you?"

"Of course not," said Javic, "but doesn't the Power require physically looking at what you are manipulating?"

"I mean… you do need to know exactly where something is, of course, but you don't *technically* have to be looking at it. I've heard stories of Ver'ati going blind and still being able to manipulate their own bodies. You've created Calvenite before, yes?"

Javic nodded.

"Did you turn only the outer-most particles of the base slate into Calvenite, or did you transmute the whole stone?"

Javic narrowed his eyes. "The whole stone… but—"

"You didn't have to see every molecule in the stone to change its properties because you already knew where they were."

It made sense. Javic just had never thought about it in that way before. He knew where the backside of his pants was, so he internalized that information and focused on pulling the rest of the water out. It instantly streamed away from him, running down the embankment and into the river.

"There you go!" said Tyris. "Ready to take another dip?"

Javic frowned. "Not really," he said. "I think I'll practice in a warm bath first. I doubt the Dance of the Elements is going to require me to stay dry anyway."

"Suit yourself. Let's focus on something else for a bit then," said Tyris. "Before I learned how to keep dry I sometimes used another trick to move along the water. It still uses Propulsion, but you don't have to worry about doing two things at once. I'll show you." Tyris gestured at the surface of the water.

Javic wasn't sure what Tyris was doing—nothing happened instantly—but he continued to watch with interest.

"I don't know what you've heard about me," said Tyris. He kept his eyes on the river as he talked. "Things weren't exactly good for me at home." He waved his hand through the air dismissively. "A few years ago, I briefly ran away. I froze a chunk of the Crimson Waters and floated down river on it. I got halfway to the next town before realizing I didn't know anybody there and didn't have any food or money or anything else with me. I decided to turn back. Using Propulsion I made a portion of the Minthune flow in reverse. It was very confusing for the fish."

In front of Tyris, the Etwon eddied in a circular formation. At the center, a platform of ice began to form. Javic felt a warm breeze blow by as Tyris dissipated the heat from the water into the air.

"Hop on," said Tyris, once his ice raft was large enough for two to ride. Javic stepped down onto the ice gingerly. Tyris followed behind him. They both sat down at the iceberg's center. As soon as they were seated, the eddy dissipated and they began to float farther downriver. "It's your turn," said Tyris. "Make the water push us upstream."

It was much easier for Javic to concentrate now that he wasn't freezing. Propelling the ice forward was a simple task but required constant effort. Unlike launching rocks, where the kinetic force needed only to be placed upon the stone once, the water had to be pushed against the back of the ice raft in a steady stream to avoid causing a jarring motion. The raft lurched forward as Javic began, but he was careful to maintain a steady stream after that. Javic pushed them up to the embankment once they reached the bench where they left their clothing. They both hopped off and let the ice float away.

The city lights were still out, so once it grew dark, it became too dangerous upon the river. Tyris didn't let up, though. He spent the rest of the night showing Javic various tricks with water and ice. Javic practiced moving liquid between buckets and he learned how to create a wall of solid ice like the one he'd seen Aldune make in the Underground on his first day in the city.

By the time Javic was finished for the night, his body was aching for sleep. Three hard nights of training in a row was really taking its toll. Anxiety over what lay ahead still made falling asleep difficult, though. There were only two more days to train before the Dance of the Elements, and although he had learned much, he was still nowhere near ready to take on the challenge.

CHAPTER

41

A Taste of Home

A rap at the apartment door roused Javic from his slumber. Javic rubbed the sleep from his eyes, confused at first by his surroundings as he sat up on the cot Sima had prepared for him. In his dreams he'd been back in Darrenfield. Things had been different, though: There was a wide river out back behind the farmhouse and Rylin and Cormick were out on the water in a rowboat hunting for mermaids. A vail of sadness fell across him as he remembered Rylin's fate. A second rap at the door refocused Javic's attention.

Baxton groaned from the bedroom. It was still early, many hours from First Sense. Everyone had been up late the night before, either staying up for classes, or training in Javic's case, and none of them had planned on being awake before midafternoon.

"I got it," said Javic, just loud enough so that Bax knew he could go back to sleep. He ran his hand through his sleep-matted hair as he approached the door. Unexpected guests made him anxious ever since Mallory's apartment was broken into by Aldune's men. He opened the door a crack and peeked out.

Professor Vanton greeted him with in impatient expression. "Good morning," he said.

"It's early," said Javic, rubbing his eyes some more as he opened the door fully.

"I'm afraid I have some bad news," said Vanton. "Your Dance has been moved up to today, just after First Sense."

Fear instantly gripped Javic's insides. He felt wide awake instantly as his blood began to pump harder. "What? Why? I thought the Dance didn't start for two days!"

Vanton grimaced. "The Dance starts today and runs all week. Your timeslot was originally scheduled for the day after tomorrow, but Counselor Cresdale must have gotten wind of your training, or else maybe this was his intention all along, to further throw you off. I daresay you have made an enemy of that man."

"No kidding…" said Javic. "What do we do now? I'm not ready…."

The professor shrugged unhelpfully. "Two more nights of training would hardly have made much of a difference. Try not to dwell on the lost time and let's just make the best of what's left."

Javic sighed in exacerbation. "If my Dance is just after First Sense, how am I supposed to make anything of my time? I can't reach the Power!"

"It is true that I had intended on using tonight and tomorrow to guide you through some practical trials, but there is still work that can be done. You have not yet developed an anchor. You do not need to actually be able to reach the Power to enter a peaceful state of mind, so that is what we will practice today."

Javic left Professor Vanton outside while he slipped on his shoes and quickly wrote a note for Bax and Sima so they would know what was happening. He joined Vanton, slowly wandering in the direction of the Old City. The Arcanum Cathedral loomed in the distance—it wasn't helping him find peace of mind.

I may very well be marching to my death....

"I'm sorry I haven't been more present the past few days," said Vanton. "My teaching schedule became increasingly full with special guest lecturer *requests* from the Arcanum the last few days. That was no coincidence, of course. And a request from the Arcanum is not really optional, just as your participation in the Dance cannot be avoided. I hope your classmates have been of some help?"

Javic nodded. "I've got a lot of new things in my head. I just wish I had some more time to practice."

"I have faith in your abilities," said Vanton. "Your raw power is vast. You remind me so much of your mother."

Javic stopped walking and turned to look at the professor. "You knew my mother? You never mentioned that before."

Vanton smiled. "She was my best student. I'm sure you've been hearing plenty about her from people around the Academy. You didn't need me piling any more on top. She really did leave her mark around here, though." Vanton was still walking, Javic doubled his pace to catch up. They were already nearing the Etwon Bridge.

"Everybody assumes just because my mother was powerful that I am too," said Javic, "but I don't know what I'm doing half the time."

"I've read your file," said Vanton. "Your blood is very strong. You have Power on both sides of your family. That is very rare these days, ever since the Cleansing. Your mother was of course very strong, and although your father did not have the Gift, he carried it in his blood as well, down from his mother—quite strong as well."

Grandma Teresa. Elric's stories spoke of her power, but Javic never had any reference point to gauge her abilities.

"In actuality, you are stronger than Kali," said Vanton. "Once your powers are refined, you very well may be one of the greatest Ver'ati to come through this city in the last century."

Vanton left Javic to ruminate on that thought as they walked on in silence. After going over the bridge into the Old City, it wasn't until they began to pass the Arcanum Cathedral, rather than going inside, that Javic spoke up. "Where are we going?" he asked.

Vanton chuckled. "It's a surprise," he said. "Suffice to say, we are going somewhere that I hope will aid you in finding your anchor."

Javic was clueless. Soon they crossed the Etwel Bridge. As they passed the road that led to the Blue Fox Inn, Javic felt an extra bundle of nerves pulsing in his abdomen. He hoped he wouldn't run into Mallory. The chances of that happening diminished as they moved farther into the west city.

Javic reached the height of his confusion when they got to the western gate and proceeded out of the Glowing City entirely. It wasn't until he spotted the large fenced in pasture with horses wandering about that Javic realized where they were headed.

Amazingly, Olli spotted Javic even before he saw her. She came prancing up to the fence, whinnying like a wild foal and shoved her soft nose between the fence posts to nuzzle Javic's chest.

"Hey there, girl!" said Javic. "I've missed you so much!" Olli nipped at Javic's shirt. Javic's heart filled as a rush of emotion flooded his body. He hadn't realized how much he truly missed her. She was his most loyal friend and oldest companion.

Olli's sister Amit was by her side, though she was not nearly as excited to see Javic. Her tail flicked back and forth at some flies that were following her.

"I had a feeling you'd enjoy this," said Professor Vanton. "Why don't you go on a ride and clear your head? Meet me at the ranch house when you're done."

Javic didn't even bother getting a saddle for Olli. He hopped over the fence and mounted her bareback. Vanton talked with the ranch manager while Javic took Olli through the gate and out into the countryside. It was unfamiliar terrain, but being back out riding felt like the most natural thing in the world. It had been far too long. He let his mind wander as they explored the rolling hills and valleys together. Nostalgia flowed through him as his body remembered all the countless hours he'd spent with Olli, before his life changed. A large part of him wished he could go back, but he knew it wouldn't be the same anymore—not after everything that happened.

Salvine was gone.

The farm was gone.

Elric was gone.

All his most cherished memories and experiences took place in Darrenfield, but things could never go back to the way they used to be.

Tears welled up in his eyes.

He missed the simple life with his grandfather. Darrenfield may not have been exciting, but it had been home.

For a moment he considered riding off to the west and simply abandoning Erotos and the retched Arcanum. Life would be so much simpler and safer away from the Glowing City. Deserting the Ver'konus was a serious charge, though, and Javic had no doubt the military would hunt him down if he really was as powerful as Professor Vanton believed. He was too valuable of an asset for the Ver'konus to lose, even if Tannel Cresdale and the Arcanum only considered him a liability.

CHAPTER

42

Song of the Nightingale

"Chin up, back straight," said Lord Resoldo Byron. "You mustn't show the curve of your neck. It is a sign of weakness in many Eastern Territory cultures."

Havorie shot Old Resoldo a defiant frown from across the table. She was only leaning forward to take a bite of her poached egg breakfast. "I doubt there is even an outlander within a thousand leagues of here."

Resoldo's forehead wrinkles became exaggerated as he raised an eyebrow. The flat light from the nearby hissing gas lantern deepened the shadows of his creases. "My queen will *not* have bad posture for as long as I am a steward of this house."

Havorie sighed. She knew there was no winning this exchange. She straightened her back and slid forward to the edge of her seat so that she was closer to her food. If she dropped any egg on her blouse, a curved neck would be the least of Old Resoldo's complaints. It was best not to tempt fate. She carefully shoveled in another bite.

"Slow down, my dear," said Resoldo. "Such haste is unbecoming of your position."

Havorie sighed. She was just trying to finish her food so that she could continue her search for her mother's killer. New clues had her antsy to get back on the trail. "Do you really have to sit here and watch me eat my whole breakfast?" Resoldo looked mildly taken aback. Havorie glanced around the dark chamber. Little natural light made it into the dining room. "When are the blasted lights going to be fixed around here?" she asked, quickly changing the subject. "It's already been half a week."

Resoldo frowned at her curse but didn't chastise her this time. "I've been assured the power plant is being worked on, but apparently the damage to the turbines was quite extensive."

Havorie pursed her lips. "What caused the explosion in the first place?"

Resoldo's demeanor darkened. "General Aldune was not forthcoming on that subject."

After Aldune's antics at last week's Ver'konus briefing, the general's already low popularity amongst the palace staff had impressively managed to diminish even further. Poor Caspin Byron's face held several rigid white scars where Aldune's glass lacerated his skin. It was simply unforgivable the way Aldune treated people.

"How is Caspin doing?" Havorie asked.

Resoldo waved his hand through the air. "He keeps telling everyone he was attacked by a bear."

Havorie chuckled slightly. "That's fairly accurate," she said.

Resoldo shrugged. "He's treating the scars like a badge of honor. It's his way of dealing with the shame and fear of the situation. I'll not have him subjected to that wretched drunk ever again. I've reassigned him to the counting house for now."

Havorie frowned. "The counting house?"

"Don't worry, he won't be placing orders or anything, just double checking ledgers," Resoldo reassured her.

Caspin's competence wasn't Havorie's worry. She'd grown up alongside the boy—his biggest fault was with his social skills, particularly his naivety, not his intellect. People tended to underestimate his abilities, but Havorie had always found him to be just as competent as anyone else—more-so, even, depending on the task. "That's about the least social position in the palace," she said. "Are you sure he'd want to be hidden away like that? It sounds rather lonely."

Resoldo caressed his chin in thought. "I don't mean to hide him, I just don't want to see any more harm come to him."

Havorie had an idea. "How about you loan him to me on occasion? I can send him out on little errands. That should help stop him from going batty under all those ledgers." The more Havorie thought about it, the more she was convinced Caspin would be the perfect ally in her search for her mother's killer. No one would suspect the "simple" steward was her spy. An ally in the counting house could also prove beneficial. He would be able to get his hands on any of the palace's records without suspicion. If the books from the year of her mother's death still existed, they would hint at many of the on-goings of the palace. Anything that involved the use of the royal coffers would be recorded. The counting house kept meticulous records.

"I heard from Captain Sarvo that you put Aldune in his place, but still remained stately, after what he did to Caspin. You make an old man proud."

Havorie shied away, blushing at the compliment. "You taught me well," she said.

Resoldo bowed deeply. "If you pardon, I have other duties I must attend to," he said, dismissing himself from the dining room.

Havorie smiled back. "Only if you must."

"Good day, my queen."

As soon as Old Resoldo was gone, Havorie hunched over her plate and shoveled down the rest of her breakfast. She had a fourteen-year-old mystery to solve. Since receiving her mother's diary from Ervia, Havorie had been hard at work deciphering its pages. It was slow going at first, but like any other puzzle, once some of the pieces fell in place, the rest started to become clearer. With a little deduction, Havorie was able to guess that if Aldune was the baboon, then Lord Ethan must be the "leader of the monkeys" her mother wrote of, which also made him the phoenix. It was almost as if Nestra knew Ethan was destined to be reborn from the ashes.

Havorie had taken her own pen to the diary, making notes between the lines whenever she thought she'd figured out another piece of the cyphers. There was a fair amount of uncertainty in her work, but using the hidden references she'd already figured out as a starting point, the day-to-day dealings of Queen Nestra began to reveal themselves throughout the pages. Last night, Havorie took a stab at the diary's final passage, and found she was able to understand the vast majority of it:

The Nightingale sings for me tonight. A rendezvous at dusk upon ~~Mast's crown~~ the South Tower. I've never felt such longings! But what an unsavory scandal we would make.... We were almost caught by the panther last time in the ~~gray mortuary~~ Royal Crypt. How ghastly that would have been, to be caught kissing amongst the dead. They are the only ones without eyes or ears or mouths to scoff at our passion. I fear the panther's friendship with ~~the lion~~ Amador, my father would have spelled the end of our song. I don't want to give it up. Not yet. I'm risking it all, but I've never been so happy, not in my entire life! ~~The magpie~~ Old Resoldo arranged for a photographer to do staff portraits, and now my songbird has gifted me the most wonderful of keepsakes— a photograph tucked into a heart-shaped locket. However, with the panther's increased scrutiny, I've decided to hide my heart in the crown for safekeeping.

She assumed "the crown" was "Mast's crown" from earlier in the entry. That meant the heart-shaped locket was hidden away in the pinnacle of the south tower, the highest point in all of Erotos. If it was still there, Havorie would find it. Inside, the secret suitor would be revealed. From the sound of it, the nightingale was a member of the palace staff, or else the photographer probably wouldn't have taken his photo. If she could recover the locket, she would finally know who had lured her mother to her death.

Havorie's stomach bubbled with anxiety at the thought of uncovering her mother's killer. She was close. She could feel it. She desperately wanted to know the truth, but was also terrified at the prospect. Some of the palace staff had changed since her mother's time, but many of the inhabitants had been around for decades. There was a fair chance she personally knew the secret suitor, this *nightingale*, and regularly interacted with him. It was an uncomfortable thought.

Snatching up the gas lantern, she moved with haste towards the south tower. Out in the main hallway, the lantern wasn't necessary—the sun shone brightly through the garden windows—but the south tower was always dark. Outside, the leaves of all the trees and bushes were frosted over with a pale glazing of ice, the early morning dew not quite thawed. The leaves glistened beautifully in the sun.

She wasn't sure where she was going to start her search for the heart locket once she reached the tower. She'd already been through all her mother's possessions at least a dozen times in her youth. She'd found many hidden treasures, Artifacts included, but she did not recall ever coming across a locket shaped like a heart. Looking through stored possessions was different than searching for secret hiding places, though—maybe with a new mindset she would see something she hadn't noticed before. It was Ervia who found the encoded diary hidden in the false bottom of a drawer in the falcon-engraved writing desk. If today's search was fruitless, perhaps recruiting the young maid to aid in the search would be prudent.

As the hallways curved to reveal the entrance to the south tower, Havorie was disturbed to find a royal guardsman milling about at the door. The guard was one of Damian's younger pupils with whom Havorie had not yet been acquainted. She continued her approach more tentatively. The abandoned south tower had never been a designated spot for a guard posting.

The young guardsman straightened up when he saw Havorie. He stood still as a board, maintaining a serious expression as he saluted sharply. He was positioned perfectly in her way.

"Step aside," commanded Havorie, "I wish to spend some time amongst my mother's possessions." She hoped the pretense made her sound nostalgic rather than quest driven.

"Apologies, my queen, but I cannot allow you to enter the tower," said the guardsman. "The foundation may have been compromised by the subterranean explosion earlier this week. It is not safe."

"Nonsense," said Havorie, "the palace is Calvenite…. Let me through."

"I cannot do that," the guard said again. "My orders come from Captain Sarvo. None are permitted to enter, not even you, my queen. It's for your own safety."

"Mhm. I'm sure," said Havorie.

"You do know, just because the palace is Calvenite, doesn't mean it can't bend or sink. A whole building in the east city—"

"Yes, yes, I heard all about Laudry Hall falling into a hole."

"Then you know if the tower suddenly shifted while you were inside, you could be smashed against the walls or struck by other falling objects and killed in an instant."

Havorie still wasn't buying the excuse. Damian was blocking her search of the south tower, but there was no way he could have known about the heart-shaped locket—at least not from reading the diary. The leather-bound journal had not left her side since Ervia brought it to her attention. Either Damian didn't know what she was searching for but suspected she might find something incriminating in the south tower, or else he already knew about the locket's existence, and upon overhearing her conversation with Madam Jusair, wanted to make sure she wouldn't find out anything more.

Whatever the reason may be, Damian had made a move to stop her from discovering the truth. That did not bode well for his innocence in Queen Nestra's demise. Damian was actively covering up the existence of the secret suitor. The only reasons Havorie could think of for that would be if he was trying to preemptively mitigate the scandal of a royal assassination, or else he was in collusion with the assassin. Worse yet, Damian could be the nightingale himself. Each possibility was more dreadful than the last.

Havorie stared down the young guardsman, trying to think of anything she could possibly say to get past him, but there was nothing. He had his orders. People did not cross Damian Sarvo, especially if they worked for him.

Behind the guardsman, the door to the south tower suddenly lurched open, nearly striking him in the back. The young man jumped forward just in time, the edge of the door barely brushing the back of his uniform.

Damian stepped out into the hallway. If he was surprised to see Havorie standing there, his face did not show it. He ignored her presence entirely for a moment as he fitted a chain through the looping handle and locked the door shut with an iron padlock. He slipped the padlock's key into his pocket before turning back around to address Havorie.

"What are you doing all the way down here?" he asked. "You should be getting ready to attend the Dance of the Elements. Come with me."

There was still several hours before the royal contingence was scheduled to depart for the Arcanum Cathedral, but as usual, there was no arguing with Damian. Havorie shot the young guardsman one last glare before following in Damian's long strides, back towards her chambers.

Havorie was actually looking forward to this year's Dance of the Elements. It was one of the only outings from the palace that she was allowed. Watching all the budding Ver'ati as they tried to impress the audience with their skills was always fun. Havorie loved watching the Power—it made her feel connected to her mother.

Upon reaching her chambers, Havorie was surprised to find Madam Jusair nowhere in sight. Valyne had dressed her every day since she was born. In her place, a new maid, unknown to Havorie, stood by the dressing chair where Valyne always fretted over Havorie's curls. There were far too many new faces around the palace for her liking.

"Where is Madam Jusair?" Havorie inquired.

The new maid shot Damian an unreadable expression. Damian's face remained a mask of stone. She looked back over at Havorie before answering. "Your old maid had a family emergency and needed to take a sudden leave. I'll be filling her position."

Havorie narrowed her eyes. "What sort of family emergency? When will she be returning?"

"I don't have that information," said the maid. "Now, please sit and allow me get to work on that hair."

It didn't make any sense to Havorie. Valyne was a shut-in to the palace as much as Havorie was. She hadn't missed a day of work in her life, and now, suddenly, she had departed for some indefinite amount of time without saying goodbye. Valyne didn't have any children of her own. As far as Havorie knew, Valyne didn't have any family still alive for her to even be visiting!

Havorie had a tingling suspicion that Madam Jusair's absence was a result of Damian overhearing Havorie question her about the secret suitor.

Might he have had her killed?

The possibility was too much to bear. If Damian really was the assassin or covering up for him, Havorie had to come to terms with the possibility that her life may be in imminent danger now that he knew she was investigating. The people meant to protect her were the very ones she needed protection from. Damian had her right where he wanted. There was no way she could continue the investigation on her own, especially when finding answers most likely meant being silenced, permanently.

Damian stood watch from the back corner of the chamber the entire time the new maid worked at re-curling Havorie's golden hair. She felt more trapped than ever.

CHAPTER

43

Day of Reckoning

After riding Olli, Javic had been feeling strangely calm about his upcoming trial—that is, until he heard the roar of the crowd coming from the arena. The windowless waiting room had the most uncomfortable wooden benches lining its walls. With the glowing orbs still dark all across the city, portable oil lamps had been utilized to light the chamber. Javic sat, sequestered with the rest of the Ver'ati-hopefuls that were on the docket for the evening's Dance. He was the youngest nominee by a decade.

No one spoke. The other contenders stared at Javic, some in anger of the mockery they felt his participation in the Dance represented, others in confusion or amusement that someone so young was attempting the same undertaking for which they had spent their entire adult lives preparing. No one seemed to consider that Javic was not here under his own volition.

He did his best to ignore everyone, closing his eyes and running through in his head all the new things he learned over the last few nights. When First Sense arrived, the other nominees began to practice with the Power. Sparks of light and various elemental conjurings put an instant chill throughout the chamber. Javic didn't have a chance to join in on the last minute preparations as an Arcanum official entered the waiting room and gestured for Javic to follow him out.

It wasn't at all surprising that Tannel arranged for Javic to be the first to enter the arena. The councilman's intentions had always been to stack the odds against him. The rumble of the crowd only grew louder as Javic followed the official down a wide corridor to the arena entrance. He was starting to feel like riding away on Olli and deserting the Ver'konus would have been the smarter option.

"Wait here until you hear Councilman Cresdale announce your name," the official said.

A black curtain hung across the doorway in front of them, blocking the view of the arena. Javic's heart was racing. He closed his eyes again and tried to steady his breath.

Tannel's voice suddenly boomed across the arena with unnatural volume. It shook Javic from his concentration. "Ladies and gentlemen of the Arcanum and esteemed guests, welcome to the annual Dance of the Elements! It is my honor to host these trials so that you may all have a chance to witness firsthand the skills of this year's nominees. As usual, after each Dance, those of you with apprenticeship openings may make job offerings to the newly raised Ver'ati."

Javic rolled his eyes. He already knew that if he managed to pass his trial, there would only be one offer coming his way. Ver'ati who received a solitary apprenticeship bid were required to accept. Javic would certainly be placed somewhere Tannel could keep a close watch on him—perhaps somewhere dangerous as well, where an unfortunate accident could befall him without much notice or investigation....

"There is, of note, an exciting alteration to this year's proceedings. Nominees that complete the usual four elemental challenges will now also be required to pass a fifth assessment. I am excited to announce that the fabled Blood Gauntlet of Sultrim lore has been recovered during a dig by our Archive Historians. For those of you who haven't brushed up on your history recently, the Blood Gauntlet is the original Artifact that was used to test initiates before Emily Fox came to power. It was lost for nearly seven-hundred years, but today it will be all of our pleasures to see it in use once more." The crowd cheered, excited for the spectacle to come.

Javic didn't like the sound of a fifth challenge.

Four isn't enough?

"Our first nominee today will be Javic Elensol, son of Kali Genavil. Everyone give him a warm welcome."

The official behind Javic gave him a light shove. "That's you. Get out there."

Javic stumbled forward through the curtain. Despite Tannel's call for a warm welcome, the crowd fell completely silent. A scarred pair of thick Calvenite doors shut autonomously behind him, sealing the pit-like arena. Despite the lack of glowing orbs, the arena was well lit by dozens of torches placed all along the top of a two-story-high barrier that ran the circular perimeter of the arena center. A mirrored ceiling high above reflected the torch light to dazzling effect. Tiered rows of spectator seating continued back some twenty rows beyond the barrier, and while not all the seats were occupied, there were at least a thousand people watching Javic's every move. Javic did his best not to look up at the crowd. He was nervous enough for the task at hand even without an audience.

Tannel stood at a central white stone dais beside a pedestal. Upon the pedestal sat what Javic could only assume was the Blood Gauntlet—a beat up bronze box with a single arm-sized hole in its side. A dark stain streaked down beneath the hole—ancient rusted-out blood. Tannel took a step back from the grisly device. Once he was clear, the base of the pedestal folded up to form a case around the box.

Tannel continued his announcements. "If a nominee retrieves all four elemental Artifacts within thirty minutes and places them into the slots on this pillar, the Blood Gauntlet will be released and the final Dance will commence."

Javic approached Tannel, taking in the setup of the arena as he walked the straight path to the central dais. The circular grounds were divided into four equal quadrants. To his right, a massive column rose nearly to the ceiling. A Calvenite box sat squarely upon its top. The quadrant to his left was flooded with a deep pond of water. Continuing clockwise, the next quadrant mirrored the first with a second column rising just shy of the high ceiling. At the top sat a clear dome casing with a cylindrical stone inside—one of the four Artifacts he was meant to retrieve. In the final quadrant sat a pit. Its placement mirrored the water-filled pond across the way.

As soon as Javic reached the central dais, a flash of fire erupted from the pit. The flames swirled and danced, growing in intensity until they reached the pit's brim, then held steady. Javic had to shield his eyes from the intense light and heat.

Tannel stared at him without expression, the flames at his back. He leaned in close as Javic reached his side. "If you somehow make it to the Blood Gauntlet, make sure to stick your arm in nice and deep."

Javic was given no other instructions as Tannel left him to begin the challenge. The councilman made his way to the double doors. They swung open as he approached and closed again once he was through.

"Begin," boomed Tannel's voice.

The crowd stayed silent. Everyone was waiting to see what Javic would do. Javic looked around again, spinning in a circle as he tried to determine which element each quadrant of the arena represented. Fire was obvious. As was water. That left air and earth for the two with the tall columns. They looked mostly identical, the only difference being one column held a Calvenite box and the other a case that appeared to be glass.

Javic wanted to start with the element with which he felt most comfortable. He approached the column with the Calvenite box, guessing that it was the earth quadrant. The creation and destruction of Calvenite fell squarely within the domain of earth magic. Once beside the column, Javic let his emotions take over, using his fears and frustrations to draw the Power in—*anchor be damned!* To confirm he was in the earth quadrant he attempted to send out a blast of air. Nothing happened, as expected. Javic would only be able to manipulate solids in this part of the arena. He assumed the earth Artifact was sealed in the Calvenite box above.

Fortunately, Javic was well versed in Calvenite manipulation. Most of his classmates could only change Calvenite back into slate if it was directly in front of their eyes, but the process came naturally to Javic. All he had to do was reach out with the Power and envision the layers falling away. Calvenite had a complex structure—infinitely dense compared to natural material. Professor Herin described the process of breaking down Calvenite as being akin to unweaving a tapestry with bare hands, but Javic found it more like washing away a mud castle with a bucket of water.

He worked from the outside in. The box quickly lost its glossy sheen, turning to a powder-gray color as it transformed into slate. Once the box was fully reconfigured, Javic eroded the stone into dust, letting it fall in ashy flakes from the column. The cylindrical Artifact was soon exposed. All that was left was for Javic to get himself to the top of the column to retrieve it.

He considered scooping out chunks of the column to make hand and foot holes as he climbed, but he knew it would be too dangerous, especially on his way back down once his hands were full. Instead, he opted for a safer route. First, he turned the column into Calvenite to ensure its stability, then he formed a spiral walkway around its outside. He had to form the walkway in stages, drawing stone up from the floor of the arena and turning it to slate with a support structure to hold up its weight. There was plenty of material to work with, so it didn't take long before he was ready to convert the walkway into Calvenite and crumble away the support scaffolding. Once he was finished, the walkway spiraled around the column five full rotations before reaching its top.

As Javic ascended the column, he couldn't help but look out upon the spectators. He knew Professor Vanton was somewhere amongst the crowd, but there were far too many faces staring out at him to locate any one in particular. Amongst all the black Arcanum robes a contingent of blue and gold did catch Javic's eye, though. The queen along with several members of her guard were seated in a private box on the side nearest Javic. He looked away as soon as he noticed her, but already his stomach was erupting with a new batch of anxious flutters.

At the top of the column, he quickly brushed away an accumulation of Calvenite flakes and snatched up the earth Artifact. It was smooth to the touch and heavier than he'd expected for its size. He held it against his chest as he carefully walked back down the spiraling ramp to the cheers of the crowd. Soon, the butterflies in his stomach were replaced by a surge of adrenaline. He internalized the excitement of the audience—they wanted him to succeed! It was nice having people on his side. He enjoyed the thought of the look on Tannel's face as he pushed the earth Artifact into the first slot on the central pillar.

He was making good time.

Continuing the trend of starting with the elements with which he felt most comfortable, Javic stepped up to the blazing pit of fire. It was obvious that the Artifact was hidden somewhere amongst the flames. Fire represented the plasma state of matter. Javic would only be able to manipulate energy here. He wracked his mind for a way to keep himself safe from the flames.

Moving the fire aside wouldn't work since the heat could still roast him from a distance. Upon closer inspection, fuel for the flames was being pumped into the pit through a system of grates. On his way south from Darrenfield he'd witnessed Wilgoblikan walk through a forest fire without being remotely bothered by the heat or smoke. If whatever technique the Goblikan was using was taught at the Academy, Javic's classes certainly hadn't touched on it yet. The only way he was getting past the flames was if he could somehow douse them out entirely. His thoughts kept drifting back to the day he met Shiara at the Marrow Tavern.

Fire is like a life force.

The flames had to eat and breathe to continue living. Much like when the Marrow Tavern was burning, he couldn't simply remove the food source. To try to save the tavern, Shiara converted the energy of the fire into smoke to douse the flames. That wouldn't work here either, though, since the fire Artifact would stop him from doing the conversion. Belford's seemingly absurd idea at the time was to use a dome of energy to smother the flames.

Cut off the oxygen supply.

Javic saw Belford create energy fields several times on their journey to Erotos, usually in the form of glowing balls of light. In North Galdren, the dome that protected the Rosa Marsa from the trebuchet turned to goo when Belford stopped feeding it energy. Javic rolled some of the goop around between his fingers that night when he went up on the bow. He had never tried creating such an energy structure before, but it seemed like the best way to deal with the problem at hand.

He took in a breath of hot air as he tried to create a thin layer of the goo on the ground in front of him. At first, the fire Artifact wouldn't allow the creation of the substance, but as soon as Javic thought about drawing in energy from the flames to add to the compound a steady glow of blue light lit the area. Although the goop was some kind of viscous liquid, tying its structure together with energy was enough to allow it to slip past the fire Artifact's limitations.

With gasps from the crowd as his backdrop, Javic used his thoughts to stretch the compound all the way across the opening of the pit like a blanket. He reckoned no one present had ever seen anything like what he was doing. The energy from the fire continued to feed the shield, keeping it rigid without any extra effort. As soon as the fire was fully cut off from the air above, the flames began to wane. In moments, the fire quickly burned up the last remnants of oxygen below the barrier and the flames extinguished.

A ruckus of murmurs arose from the audience, almost covering the hiss of the flammable liquid—no longer ignited—as it was propelled through the floor grates. Whoever had control over the flow of fuel soon turned off the spray.

At the center of the pit sat a solid stone box. Before following a set of steps that led down into the pit, Javic knew he needed to blast it open. He laid on his stomach and peeked over the edge. He wasn't sure how large to make the explosion—he still had a little trouble controlling the intensity of such things. He just went for it, focusing a blast of energy on the side of the container. The top broke free in one large chunk and flew straight up into the air. Screams from the crowd turned to nervous laughter as the stone nearly crested the barrier, but was deflected by an Arcanum official.

Javic grimaced. He hadn't meant to give the blast quite so much power. Regardless, the fire Artifact was exposed. Javic carefully took the steps, slick with oil, down into the pit. He grabbed the Artifact and hurried back out and over to the central pillar.

After placing the second Artifact, he eyed the pond of water, trying to figure out what its puzzle would be. Several wide pipes continuously poured water into the pond while an overflow tube carried the excess away, constantly cycling the water. He walked over to the edge and peered in. He could see the water Artifact below, sitting unobstructed at the bottom of the pond.

There is no way this is as simple as just swimming down there....

Javic removed his jacket and dipped the end of one of his sleeves into the pond. It bubbled and sizzled and eventually disintegrated before his eyes.

This is not *water.*

He was beyond glad he hadn't jumped in without testing the liquid. Getting to the bottom of a pond of acid wasn't going to be simple. He was limited to liquid manipulation, which meant his options weren't plentiful. He couldn't move the acid aside without it flowing back down on him faster than he could push it away. Changing the acid to something inert wouldn't work well either, since the pond was constantly cycling in new liquid. He was going to have to be more creative.

He sat down at the pond's edge for several minutes, trying, and failing, to think of a way to get down to the Artifact. Time was ticking away. Every minute of inaction felt like an eternity, but he couldn't think of any solution that wouldn't end in his skin melting off.

Tannel's voice boomed across the arena. "You do know this is a timed challenge, right?" Chuckles arose from the audience.

Javic did his best to ignore the heckling. After another minute of thought, a realization donned on him: *I don't actually need to go down to the Artifact at all, I just need to bring it up to me!*

Javic stared down at the heavy Artifact and concentrated on drawing energy away from the surrounding acid. A crystalline structure began to form around its outside as the acid froze. He dissipated the heat into the rest of the pool. It would take time for the energy to sink back into the acid-ice, and until it did, the frozen chunk around the Artifact would be less dense than the surrounding liquid.

Once the ice chunk was big enough, it lifted the Artifact to the surface, where it bobbed around in the middle of the pond. With a simple kinetic wave, Javic used Propulsion to nudge the ice block over in his direction. He used his jacket to hook around it and dragged it out of the pond. He was careful to avoid the puddle he created as he warmed the frozen acid. It melted away quickly, until just the Artifact remained, resting on its side. Still damp, he wrapped it up with his jacket and carried it back over to the pillar where he carefully slid it into its slot without touching its acid-covered surface.

Professor Vanton owes me a new coat.

He tossed his ruined jacket into a pile beside the pillar before heading to the final quadrant—air. The clear dome over the Artifact was too aerodynamic for a gust of wind to damage, but if it was glass, it could be broken. He searched the arena floor for bits of stone he could launch, but there was nothing in sight.

Javic backed away from the air Artifact, testing its range. It wasn't until his heels bumped the central stone dais that he was able to manifest a non-gas conjuring. He gripped onto the dais and pulled several fist-sized chunks of the white stone free with the Power. Glancing up at the audience, he realized that if he missed the dome, the people seated behind the column would be directly in the path of the stone. The officials must have read his intentions; a fine-mesh net rose up from the barricade.

Javic lined up his shot, holding the stone out in front of him on his open palm. He couldn't hit the rock with kinetic energy the way he usually did when launching rocks, but he could strike it with a blast of air. His accuracy wasn't as high using an air blast, but it still sent the rock flying hard towards the clear dome.

He nearly missed, but the rock did manage to strike a glancing blow against the top-left portion of the dome, the rock ricocheted harmlessly into the net. A low clang rang out. Glass would have shattered. The dome didn't have so much as a scuff across its immaculate surface. Javic placed the second chunk of stone down—there was no point in launching it—the crystalline dome would hold strong.

His gaze drifted as his mind wandered. He thought about raising the pressure of the air inside the dome until it shattered, but he had no idea how to do that or how much pressure that would take. Javic's knowledge of air magic didn't go much past launching rocks and making it rain. He very much doubted a little bit of rainwater would help him break the dome. His eyes were unfocused, staring in the direction of the acid pond. Suddenly, his eyes refocused sharply, a brilliant idea popping into his mind.

Not water!

He went to work immediately. Although he didn't know the chemical makeup of the acid, using the heat energy from the air he was able to evaporate the liquid molecules into their gas form. The air in the arena grew chilly as he used as much of the heat energy as he could gather for the process. Soon, a low fog formed over the pond. He carefully corralled the acid gas, dragging the whole cloud of floating molecules away from the pond and over to the base of the column. He forced the cloud higher. It creeped up the column until it obscured the clear dome at its top. As soon as it was in place, Javic quickly pulled the heat out of the floating acid molecules, dissipating the energy back into the surrounding air. The acid condensed on the dome, beading against its curved surface. Javic stood back and waited for the acid to do its work. The dome sizzled and smoked as it dissolved. After just a couple of minutes the strong acid ate through all the way and the dome collapsed around the Artifact.

Javic picked up the chunk of white stone he dropped to the arena floor earlier. He took several deep breaths, steadying his heart and mind. With the stone held out on his palm, he blasted it with a stiff gust of air. It wasn't a perfectly accurate shot, but he corrected it with a second blast directed against its left side mid-flight, knocking it back on course.

Thankfully, the Artifact was durable. The rock struck dead center with a solid thwack. The Artifact tumbled off the column, landing with a shallow bounce and a thud as it slammed against the arena floor. None of the condensed acid appeared to have gotten onto the Artifact. Javic picked it up hesitantly, but it did not burn his skin. With the roar of the crowd as his backdrop, he carried the Artifact to the stone dais and shoved it into the final slot in the pedestal.

As soon as it clicked in place, the case housing the Blood Gauntlet cracked open and folded back down into the pedestal's base. Javic nervously eyed the bloodstain beneath the armhole once more. He had no idea what to expect from the final Dance.

Javic pulled the right sleeve of his undershirt up nearly to his shoulder. He peered inside the dark hole, but couldn't see anything. Tentatively, he pushed his hand through the opening.

Nothing happened.

He went deeper, pushing his arm in until his entire forearm disappeared inside the mysterious device.

Still nothing.

He went even deeper. He was halfway up to his shoulder from his elbow when his fingertips brushed up against something rigid at the center of the box. It was warm to the touch. He felt around gently. Whatever he was touching was narrow and latched in place vertically with cool metal brackets. He ran his fingers around its tubular shape, finding it to have many flat edges.

A crystal? He couldn't be sure.

He gripped onto the strange object, making the assumption that that was what he was supposed to do. A mechanical sound clicked within the box. Suddenly the opening of the armhole restricted, grabbing Javic tightly around his bicep. He tried to pull free, but the armhole only held tighter the more he struggled. He couldn't release the central object from his grasp. His palm was smashed up against it uncomfortably. More mechanical ticks sounded from within.

An ominous whirring noise sent a wave of panic through Javic's body. His arm started to burn. Something was pressing into his skin at the forearm, slicing into him. He winced. There was no wiggle room to escape the hidden blade. He felt the heat of his blood as it dribbled down his arm. All he could do was grunt as the blade cut ever deeper. When the blood reached his fingertips, the surface of the object in his grip suddenly grew hot like a stone warmed in a fire.

A rush to his head gave him tunnel vision. He felt like he was falling into a deep hole. The walls were closing in around him. The whole world grew dark as he slipped from consciousness.

CHAPTER

44

The Final Dance

Javic found himself standing in a bright white space—a blank canvas that stretched out forever in every direction. His head swam as he turned from side to side. The sensation of infinity coupled with the absence of any features to mark depth set off a mild wave of vertigo as he gazed out upon the vast emptiness. The uncomfortable spinning grew increasingly intense until he was forced to shut his eyes to stave off the nausea.

"Ahem," said a voice from behind him.

Javic turned around at once. A middle-aged man in a gaudily embroidered tunic fit with a matching cloak was staring down a hooked nose at him. The man had sharp, chiseled facial features and intense eyes that seemed to be focused through Javic rather than on him. A deep scowl was permanently etched across his lips as he spoke.

"Hello, my child," he said. "Yes, it is I, John Graven. I have imprinted this memory crystal with a message for my descendants."

Javic didn't know what a memory crystal was, but he understood immediately that the vision of the founder of Aragwey before him was not an actual person. The crystal must have been what he grabbed inside the bronze box, its powers activated by the touch of his blood. Javic side-stepped to his left and found that John Graven's gaze did not follow his motion. The figure continued speaking towards where Javic first appeared.

"Our bloodline must remain strong. That is the only way to ensure my abilities are effectively propagated to future generations. It is up to you and the rest of our bloodline to maintain order in our glorious kingdom in my absence. I know you have journeyed far, but now it is time for you to be tested to see if you are worthy of carrying on my legacy. Good luck. Only the strong will survive."

The memory of John Graven began to fade away, becoming translucent before disappearing entirely. Interior stone walls appeared from out of the nothingness—a whole world coalescing around him like a beautifully detailed dream. The painter was finally filling his canvas. Javic was drawn into a torch-lit hall—the grand foyer of a palace. Vibrantly colored tapestries were draped across the walls. They swayed slightly as a low rumble shook the ground beneath Javic's feet. He wondered briefly if the rumble was an Echo taking place in Erotos, somehow effecting this dream world, or if it was a recorded memory of a quake from the distant past.

Although it was still daytime in Erotos, high arched windows on either side of the hall showed a dark sky beyond. The walls were lined with decorative columns whose curves matched the architecture of the ones he'd seen in the Gateway room in Sultrim. If this memory crystal housed within the Blood Gauntlet held a vision of Sultrim, there was little doubt in Javic's mind as to where the Artifact had been recovered from. Some Archive Historians must have made it through the Gateway without developing a schism and pilfered from Sultrim's stash of Artifacts before Javic's journey to the lost city destroyed the return portal.

Javic only had a moment to take in the grand foyer in front of him before another voice spoke to him from out of the flickering light. "Hello, human," said a deep growl. The hairs on the back of Javic's neck rose up. The dark outline of a winged bear stepped out from behind one of the columns to Javic's right, filling him with dread. The bear eyed him with an unreadable expression. "You must defeat Ragdon if you wish to survive this day."

Javic, treating the visions before him like a dream, tried to will a sword into existence. Nothing happened. Everything was certainly taking place inside his head, but this was not a dream he could control. The Paerto'sul lumbered towards him, its massive paws pounding heavily against the stone floor with deep thuds. Javic turned to run, but it was already too late. The massive beast thrashed him with its deadly claws across his back.

The sting was immense. Javic felt the claws sink into his flesh as painfully as if the attack had occurred in the real world. His senses were overwhelmed as he laid there flayed open. There was nothing he could do. The bear flipped him over with another swipe of its paw. Javic stared up into its black eyes with horror.

"Ragdon deems you unworthy," it said as it lowered its snout into Javic's neck and bit his throat away.

Javic gasped for air and was grateful to find it. He was back in the real world, on his knees with his arm wrenched up by the Blood Gauntlet. The pain of the bear attack subsided, but a pinch in his arm where the armhole still gripped onto his bicep was intensified by the weight of his body pulling him to the stone dais.

He hadn't time to pull himself back up before a mechanical whir inside the box brought the hidden blade against his forearm once more. He tried to tug himself free, but the box held tight. The fingertips on his trapped hand went cold as more blood was drained from his forearm. He felt the sick wet heat of his escaping blood dribbling down his arm to the memory crystal still clutched in his hand.

Like before, as soon as the blood reached the crystal, he felt himself falling into the dream world.

"Ahem," said a voice from behind him.

Javic turned to find the recorded vision of John Graven repeating his speech. Once he was finished the columned grand foyer appeared once more. Javic knew what was coming this time, but that did not stop fear from making his legs slightly unsteady. He ducked between the columns to his left and dashed away from where the bear would emerge.

"Hello, human. You must defeat Ragdon if you wish to survive this day." The Paerto'sul bounded after him without delay.

Javic reached for the Power. In his panic, it took far too long to enter the state of mind he needed to draw it in. By the time he could muster the thought of an attack, the bear was already nearly upon him. Instinct took over. Javic spun around and tried to Combust the creature. He focused on pulling apart its atoms, trying to turn it to dust, but the attack had no effect.

Ragdon roared angrily. "My Father's blood protects me. Do you know nothing, human?" With one swipe, the bear dislodged Javic's jaw, and he awoke again in the real world.

Javic's cheek was pressed up against the pedestal. His mouth was open and drool was running down his chin.

The Paerto'sul can't be attacked directly with the Power, just like wizards. Javic already knew that from his attempt on Raljaska's cub, but he'd forgotten everything in his panic. He mulled the thought over as the whir started again inside the box. Javic winced as the blade sliced him again, even deeper this time. He was beginning to feel woozy.

If I don't solve this soon, I'm going to bleed to death....

John Graven did his speech, and the grand hall reappeared. Javic ran, just like before, trying to settle his nerves and drum up the emotion he would need to summon the Power at the same time. Being killed hurt. A lot. Avoiding that pain was a great motivator to not die again, but fear of the bear's claws was also a distraction that made reaching the Power more difficult. This time he had a plan, though: He would topple one of the columns right on top of Ragdon's head.

As soon as the Power was within his grasp, Javic turned around and tried to slice a large wedge out of the nearest column. The bear was almost upon him already, but the timing appeared to be sound. Instead of the entire column tumbling over, only an outer layer of plaster crumbled at its base. The tell-tale black sheen of Calvenite appeared beneath the plaster as it fell away. The columns would not be so easy to collapse.

There was no time to do a Calvenite conversion.

Ragdon slammed into Javic with the force of a runaway carriage. The wind was knocked out of him as he fell hard on his back. The bear ripped into him a moment later before he could recover.

Javic's whole body felt cold. He didn't even lean away from the pedestal this time as the Blood Gauntlet ripped into him. His fingers were numb. Soon there wouldn't be much forearm left for the blade to cut into.

Inside the memory crystal the pain and fatigue of his waking body vanished, but the looming threat of the Paerto'sul made the reprieve short-lived.

"Ahem," said a voice from behind him.

As Javic turned around, another figure emerged from out of the whiteness. Javic did a double-take at the unexpected addition. Cale Fisman waved meekly as he approached behind John Graven.

"Hello, my child…" John Graven started.

Javic ignored the recorded message. "What are you doing here?" he asked Cale. "Are you using the spyglass?"

Cale nodded. "It looked like you could use some help. I've been keeping an eye out since we last spoke and Tannel is definitely expecting this Artifact to kill you. An Archive Historian tried it out several days ago and would have died had people on the outside not severed his arm and cauterized the nub before he lost too much blood."

"We haven't much time," said Javic.

"Yes, I know, the winged bear. This Artifact is from a time when people were stronger with the Power—purer blood back then. From peeking in on the Archive Historian's attempts I know you need to access the Power very quickly once the hall appears in order to have any chance. Have you found your anchor yet?"

Javic narrowed his eyes. He wondered how long Cale had been keeping an eye on his dreams.

John Graven faded away and the great hall appeared once more. Cale was still by his side. He slinked off behind one of the columns so that he would be out of sight of the bear when it stepped out.

"What do I do?" Javic asked in a hushed voice. Panic was already settling back over him.

"What makes you feel calm?" Cale whispered back.

Javic didn't want to waste what little blood he had left in his veins trying to find his anchor, but Cale simply stared at him, waiting for an answer.

Javic wracked his mind. Nothing about his current situation was calming, so it was hard to even think about such a state of mind. He thought about Rylin. The boy had used thoughts of his mother as his anchor. She was the most calming presence in his life. Javic didn't have a mother. He couldn't even remember either of his parents. Elric was his only parental figure, but thoughts of his grandfather only ever brought him more worry these days.

There is literally no one in my life that makes me feel purely calm and safe the way Rylin's mother did for him.

It was hopeless.

"Hello, human," said the bear. "You must defeat Ragdon if you wish to survive this day."

Human, thought Javic, *of course. There is no* human *in my life that can be my anchor.* The most relaxed he'd felt in months was that morning when he was riding Olli. No one ever said an anchor had to be a person, but Javic had gotten that notion stuck in his head somehow. The people in Javic's life all caused chaos in his mind, but Olli settled him; grounded him.

Too late....

Ragdon tore him apart.

He kept his eyes closed as the real world returned. He waited for the bite of the blade. The memory crystal was so slick with blood he doubted he would have been able to hold onto it had his palm not been forcibly pressed against it. He was getting very weak. He didn't have many attempts left in him.

Javic wasn't sure why he knew Olli would work as his anchor, but a certainty washed over him at the thought of his oldest friend.

He tried it out, settling his mind with thoughts of a long summer's ride. The Power was instantly within his grasp.

The blade sliced into his forearm and soon he was back inside the crystal's trial.

"Okay, I've got it," he said as Cale appeared by his side. John's speech began as they planned Javic's next attempt. "The columns are Calvenite," he told Cale. "I'm good at manipulating Calvenite, but it will take too long, even with my anchor speeding things along. Does the bear respond to you? Can you distract him?"

Cale glowered at the thought. "I'm not sure, but I've discovered that things that hurt me in dreams hurt me in the waking world as well when I'm using the spyglass… not as severely mind you, but I still don't want to get mauled."

"Man up," said Javic. "You got me into this whole mess to begin with."

Cale sighed as the hall appeared around them.

Javic drew the Power in at once and began transforming the column beside him into slate.

"Hello human," said Ragdon.

Cale stepped towards the Paerto'sul. "Hi, bear," he said.

Ragdon did not continue with the usual speech. The bear cocked its massive head curiously at Cale. "How are there two of you?"

"We are conjoined twins," said Cale, saying anything he could to stall for Javic. "It's a very rare condition. In our dreams we are separate, though, clearly."

"That does not make sense," said Ragdon. "This test was meant for one mind. You are cheating." The bear began its approach, but moved much more cautiously than usual. It was watching both Cale and Javic intently.

Javic wasn't ready yet. He needed more time.

"No, no," said Cale, "there is no cheating going on here." He began backing up slowly towards Javic. The bear continued to approach steadily.

The column was mostly Calvenite still, but Javic had managed to convert a thin swath into slate near its base. He needed to do the same higher up so that he could break the column at those two points and use it as a weapon.

"Could you please explain the test to me?" asked Cale. It was the wrong question to ask.

The bear instantly reset back to its set pattern. "You must defeat Ragdon if you wish to survive this day." It charged towards them.

Cale recoiled away, attempting to run, but Javic still needed a few more uninterrupted seconds before he could break the column free.

"Sorry," said Javic as he shoved Cale back towards the bear.

The lieutenant general screamed as Ragdon slashed into him with razor sharp claws. Cale's entrails spilled out across the floor. Ragdon furiously ripped him to pieces in a rage of bloodlust. Cale and all his severed body parts suddenly vanished as he exited Javic's mind. The bear stood up on its hind legs and spread its wings wide as it roared loudly into the air.

With no time to spare, Javic shattered the bands of slate and used every scrap of determination he had to exude a massive force against the side of the detached column. It rocketed sideways, rotating as it flew through the air like the giant bolt of a ballista. The blunt tip of the column smashed into Ragdon so hard that it speared through the comparatively soft flesh like a pike and left the bear skewered in the center of the hall.

The kill was instantaneous.

The foyer faded away, back to the empty white that the crystal always started with. John Graven was once again by his side.

"You have done well," said John. "Only a true warrior could have defeated one of my guardians. You have earned the right to call yourself Ver'ati. Now go forth, procreate, and watch over these lands so that my legacy may live on."

John and the whiteness faded away as Javic returned once and for all to the waking world.

The Blood Gauntlet released his arm, sending Javic tumbling to the floor. The pressure of the arm-grip had been working as a tourniquet, slowing the flow of blood to the gruesome forearm wound the internal blade had sliced repeatedly into his skin. Now that he was released, the blood sprang forth unabated.

Javic hadn't the energy to rise. He was barely even able to open his eyes. His skin was pale and his whole body was freezing. He began drifting in and out of consciousness. Suddenly General Aldune was by his side. Aldune wasn't the only one. Javic recognized Tannel's gruff voice talking to someone as well, though everything sounded as if it were coming from down a long tunnel. Suddenly, Javic felt a fresh sting in his arm as someone cauterized his wound.

A sudden zap of energy flowed through him next. He recognized the pins-and-needles sensation that spread through his muscles. He gasped air deep into his lungs. He'd been Invigorated. This time, he knew the energized state would only be fleeting.

Doctor Crane was responsible. He was hunched over Javic and helped him climb to his feet. For the moment, Javic felt perfectly fine, but he knew his body was going to need a long sleep and several hearty meals before he could even hope to begin recovering from his ordeal.

"Congratulations," said Tannel, dryly, once again projecting his voice throughout the arena. The audience erupted with cheers. Tannel gestured to silence them before continuing. "Javic Elensol has succeeded at the final Dance and is now Ver'ati and a member of the Arcanum. Unfortunately, something seems to have gone wrong with the Blood Gauntlet, and as such it will be removed as a requirement for the rest of the Dances this season. Let's not let that put a damper on the occasion, though. I would like to take this moment to extend the first offer to Javic on behalf of the Archive Historians." He turned towards Javic. "This is a two-year apprenticeship, during which you will work with the best the historians have to offer to delve into the mysteries of the Artifacts they watch over."

It was basically a death sentence. Everyone knew working with unknown Artifacts was the most dangerous job a Ver'ati could have. The frontlines of war had a better mortality rate.

"Are there any other offers for Javic?" Tannel asked the audience.

As expected, the crowd remained silent. Tannel had locked down the placement offerings. Javic would be forced to accept his offer.

"Well, at least you got one good offer," said Tannel, smiling now. "Alright then, without further ado it is my pleasure to welcome you into the ranks of the Archive—"

"I have an offer to make," shouted a female voice in the crowd. The voice was quiet compared to Tannel's—not magically projected. A surprised clamor arose amongst the spectators.

"I don't think I heard that right," said Tannel, an irritated scowl returning to his lips as he scanned the crowd for the speaker.

"You most certainly did," shouted the voice.

Javic was able to locate the speaker this time. Queen Havorie was standing within her private viewing box. The rest of her entourage looked as surprised as Tannel.

Havorie spoke again. "I would like to extend an offer for the position of Royal Guard to Javic Elensol."

Javic didn't even need to think about it. "I accept the offer!" he yelled back.

Tannel didn't move. He stared up at Havorie with a glare that could kill.

Aldune, standing beside Tannel, began to laugh boisterously, making Tannel's face sour even further. "Well, I guess that does it," said Aldune. "On to the next Dance." He slapped Javic on the back and gestured for him to exit the arena.

Javic still wasn't sure what had just happened, but he wasn't about to start asking questions. He was a member of the Queen's Guard now. Today, he had won, and Tannel lost.

Just before exiting the arena, Javic caught a glimpse of Cale Fisman, standing at one of the spectator entryways.   He looked sickly as he stared back down at Javic. His pale skin made the red welts that covered his face and neck even more obvious. Javic had a feeling the marks continued to the rest of his body as well, where the bear's teeth and claws tore into his flesh.

Javic wasn't sure where he stood with the lieutenant general at this point… he did, after all, just feed him to a bear—but Cale winked at him as Aldune ushered him through the Calvenite doors and out of the arena.

CHAPTER

45

Life and Death

"How much longer will it take?" Michelle asked while pacing back and forth across Echo Facility's entrance lounge.

Wes tapped his index finger against the glossy screen of his tablet several more times before glancing up with a look of annoyance on his face that was not missed by Michelle or any of the other Arcadians. "These are military systems," he said. "This isn't a movie. It's going to take some time."

The abandoned lounge with its cushy armchairs and the gentle breeze of air conditioning provided a false sense of normalcy while everyone waited for Wes to work his technical magic, hacking into the facility's communication logs. He had already been at it for well over an hour without any success. Even if Wes did manage to prove Ethan's innocence with the logs, Aaron wasn't sure it would make any difference. He doubted anyone in the death squads would care about whose identification tags appeared in some system file. People had been killed—frozen, electrocuted,

539

exploded—and that would not be forgiven. No matter who had actually leaked the research files to the media, Aaron and his friends were the ones responsible for the deaths of those men's colleagues. Any evidence Wes managed to dredge up would never see the light of day. Strangely, none of this seemed to matter to Michelle—she was deep on a personal quest to find out the truth no matter how meaningless the answers proved to be.

Aaron knew they probably should have been trying to get as far away from the research complex as they could right now, not sitting in the middle of the entrance lounge waiting for the death squads to track them down again. He considered proposing the idea of fleeing, but ultimately knew they could not outrun what they had become. There was nowhere for them to hide, not with their faces plastered all over the news. Aaron just kept his mouth shut and waited with everyone else for the sake of having nothing better to do.

Claire was seated beside him with her legs crisscrossed atop her seat cushion. She was using her balled up fist as a chin rest; her elbow held in place by her bent knee. She gazed vacantly across the aisle at Isabelle. The girl was laid out on a bench seat, still sleeping off whatever Yosef had done to incapacitate her. Isabelle opened her eyes briefly when they first reached the lounge, managing to make a frown that creased her forehead ever so slightly before slipping back into her unconscious state without a word. Isabelle wasn't the only one who hadn't spoken since leaving Yosef Reblan's office, neither Claire nor Ethan had uttered so much as a syllable in the last hour or so either.

Aaron wasn't sure what had made Ethan so quiet, but he knew Claire's reasoning: She was simply feeling worn down and had retreated into her own thoughts. It was an attempt to distance Aaron from her negative emotions so that he wouldn't have to experience them firsthand. She thought she could spare him entirely if she bundled them up tightly enough inside. Unfortunately, Aaron had already gleaned enough of her mental state from his uninvited visit into her psyche earlier that day and it set off his own downward spiral of sulking pessimism which he'd since been trying to shelter Claire from as well. Being unable to share his feelings with her only made him feel worse, though.

Claire's stomach grumbled with a long, audible gurgle. The uncomfortable twinge drew her back from whatever dark place she was visiting within her mind. She looked down at her own dirt stained Arcadian uniform with a pensive expression as she placed a gentle hand over her abdomen. Aaron knew the feeling well. Neither of them had had a bite to eat since leaving the teahouse the day before. It was already well after lunch time, and their bodies were beginning to file formal protests in the form of whale sounds.

Aaron stood up and offered his hand to Claire. He figured there was no reason for them to starve while there was a perfectly good cafeteria just down the hallway and around the corner. She looked up at him in confusion for a moment, only realizing his intentions when he gestured with his head towards the hallway. Secretly, he was also hoping that being alone with her would encourage her to start talking with him again. The distance that had formed between them felt so unnatural, like half of his brain refusing to talk to the other side.

Claire's palm felt damp as their hands clasped together. The pensive expression faded from her eyes as she looked into his. Overwhelming emotion simultaneously welled up within them both. Aaron wasn't sure if it originated from Claire or from inside himself, but it didn't matter. It permeated their bodies with an undeniable force that drew them together in a much needed embrace. Claire released Aaron's hand, instead clasping him around the middle as she melted into his arms. The emotional energy surged between them, flowing back and forth in a loop that only grew stronger as it continued to feed on itself.

Within the torrent of emotion, Aaron was suddenly hit with an odd sensation as if he were falling into the pit of his own stomach. It only lasted for a heartbeat—a sudden impact that made him feel weightless before quickly retreating to a dull pounding in his ears. Claire pulled away; she had felt it too. Her hands shifted back down to her abdomen as she gave a slight furrow of her brow. When the pounding faded from Aaron's head, he was left emotionally confused—somewhere between a sense of foreboding doom and ecstatic elation. Everything turned on its head in an instant, and though the world had righted itself, Aaron couldn't shake the feeling that something had changed. It was as if somebody moved a piece of furniture in his home, only to return it back to a slightly different position—not far enough away to notice the change at first, but upon sitting down the slight shift in perspective felt unnatural, like you were no longer in your own home— only instead of happening to a room, the shift had occurred over his entire sense of reality.

He looked questioningly at Claire, but she shied away from his eyes, instead staring towards the far wall of the lounge until the immediacy of the experience eased slightly in her mind. "I'm getting some food," she suddenly announced, her tone not suggesting anything odd had just happened at all. She placed her hands deep in her pockets as she started for the cafeteria by herself.

"Could you grab me a bag of chips?" asked Wes without looking up from his tablet.

"And a sandwich," added Ethan. "Ham if you can find it."

Claire nodded. She was going to pretend like nothing had happened, apparently, but Aaron knew she was only putting on a front. Before following after Claire, he glanced over at Michelle, still pacing the room, but she waved her hand dismissively, too distracted to eat. Claire was already moving down the hallway by the time Aaron started after her. She was locking up her feelings again, pushing them deep down inside of her.

"Wait up," he said. He was unsure if speaking directly into her mind would be welcomed at the moment.

Claire didn't stop, but she did slow down slightly in her stride, allowing Aaron to close the distance without running. "What was that?" he asked when he reached her side.

She didn't answer, staring forward with unblinking eyes as they rounded the corner by the elevator banks.

Aaron put his hand on her shoulder, stopping her from moving forward and forcing her to acknowledge him. She spun away from him, pulling her shoulder out from his grasp. She removed her hands from her pockets, crossing them beneath her breasts instead.

"I don't want to talk about it," she said. "And don't you dare try to pull it out of my head!"

Aaron was taken aback—he had no idea where all this animosity and mistrust was coming from. He had only intruded into her mind the one time since they learned to put up the cognitive walls, but it was unlikely she even knew about that.

"I'm sorry," she said upon realizing how harsh she sounded. "I just have some things I need to figure out by myself right now."

She was frightened, Aaron realized. He didn't like that she was pushing him away, but he understood what fear could do to a person. He had lived most of his life in fear—fear that he wasn't good enough; that no one would want him; that the people he loved would leave him or die, just like his parents, or the friends he made and lost while being shipped between foster homes. He learned to retreat inside as well, but now that he'd found Claire he didn't want to let her go—to lose her like all the others. He had to suppress his own bad instinct to cling onto her now as she asked for space. He could offer his support, but he couldn't make her take it. Fear was temporary, like all things, and eventually she would return to him, as long as he didn't make her push him away further with his own actions in the meantime.

They walked the rest of the way to the cafeteria in silence. Aaron couldn't help but feel the pessimistic funk settling back over him. He had no idea how long it would take for Claire to open back up, and every moment he spent on the outside reminded him of just how lonely his life had been before he knew her. The feeling made him anxious.

As they approached the cafeteria, the sound of voices up ahead suddenly grounded Aaron's mind in the current moment. His wariness subsided, though, once he realized it was just a newscast playing on one of the cafeteria's wall consoles that was making the noise. Whoever left the screen on was long gone. The whole ground floor of the building was completely abandoned, apart from the Arcadians.

Aaron and Claire immediately went about collecting food. Aaron found a bag of barbeque flavored chips for Wes and began filling a crate box with bottled water from behind the serving counter while Claire went back into the kitchen to see about gathering up sandwich making materials from the refrigerators that lined the back wall. The newscast droned on in the background. Aaron half-listened in—it was an international broadcast, but they were covering the unrest here in Tripoli. Apparently, the riots sparked protests all across the Union with people gathering outside of Allied military installations with picket signs demanding the end of the Arcadian Project and any other super soldier development programs that might exist. So far, none of the protests had turned violent like the one outside of Echo Facility a few days ago, but the mood amongst the administration was still rightfully tense.

Before Aaron finished packing up the water, the news story suddenly cut off mid-sentence and switched over to an in-studio anchor. Aaron glanced up at the television as a British man in his late forties began to speak in a rushed voice, his eyes scanning quickly across an off-screen teleprompter. "This just in," he read. "There is breaking news out of Cyprus, where just moments ago it was announced that the HAMMER missile defense station has been rendered inoperable by what is being purported as a cyber-terrorist attack." Aaron completely stopped what he was doing now and focused in fully on the newscast. Deep lines were etched into the anchor's face as he continued on with a permanent grimace. "It is believed that East Asian Coalition hackers are responsible for the attack. European Union officials have already issued a state of emergency to all South and Eastern European countries, saying that bombing attacks may be imminent now that the safety net has been disabled. Our coverage will now switch over to the official press conference, currently in progress at the EU Headquarters in Berlin, where German President Lukas Krause is standing beside EU Secretary-General Marcus Ortega to bring us the most up to date information on the situation."

The screen cut to black for a moment before switching to a feed of the secretary-general standing behind a tall podium while fielding questions from the press. "—development of the other HAMMER stations are on hold as well until the vulnerability can be patched," he was saying. An unintelligible clamor of voices rose up from out of the unseen audience.

The secretary-general pointed out beyond the camera and the voices receded to a solitary question: "Is the attack believed to be retaliation for the government's secret development of super soldiers?"

The secretary-general's eyes narrowed into a slight glare. "First off, we are not developing super soldiers," he said. "The Arcadian Project, which you are referring to, received a *technology* grant for research on new methods of infrastructure development, not for creating soldiers—"

"The technology is being used to turn humans into weapons, is it not?" rebutted the unseen press member.

"That is simply not true," said the secretary-general. "Every test subject that was chosen for the project is a civilian.

Saying we are creating super soldiers is like calling a bulldozer a tank, simply because they both run on tracks. Next question."

The clamor started up from the audience again until a single question could be picked out. "Is there any estimate for how long the HAMMER station will be offline?"

"Technicians are currently hard at work patching the affected systems," he began to answer, "but the station will be down for at least—"

The colors on the screen suddenly lit up with a bright light as a low rumble shook the camera. Gasps from the crowd interrupted the secretary-general's answer. Everyone on stage covered their faces with their arms as the light intensified. The feed changed to static, and then everything turned black.

After a long moment of silence, the shot switched back to the in-studio anchor. He was looking away from the camera, unprepared to be taking over again so soon. His face was paler than before as he turned back towards the camera and cleared his throat. "I'm sorry, we seem to be experiencing signal problems at the moment and have lost the feed of the conference."

In the background of the shot, people on the floor of the newsroom scrambled back and forth between desks while every telephone in the studio lit up, ringing off the hook. The anchor paused as he put his left hand to his ear, receiving information through an ear-com.

"I am being told that we have lost all contact with our affiliates in Berlin…" he paused again, staring sheepishly at the camera while the person on the other side of his ear-com fed him more information. "Berlin is gone…?" he said, the shock of the statement almost making it sound like a question. The anchor attempted to pull himself back together. "We are receiving reports of multiple nuclear explosions… huge mushroom clouds have been spotted in the vicinity of Berlin.…"

Aaron's heart pounded in his chest. *The EAC just nuked Berlin,* he thought to Claire. *Come out here quick, it's on the news right now!* He heard Claire scamper across the kitchen to join him in the cafeteria. Aaron felt like he was going to be sick. It couldn't be real! The entire EU government was centralized in Berlin, not to mention the millions of other people that lived there!

Once Claire was beside him, they both glued their eyes to the television set. A map of Europe appeared on the screen and the anchor's voice went up nearly half an octave as he continued. "We are now getting calls from all over the Union reporting more nuclear explosions. We have not confirmed all of these reports, but this map shows which regions are currently believed to have been targeted by nuclear ordinance...." Large red circles covered nearly half the major cities across the EU. "We will continue to update this map as more information becomes available."

Aaron couldn't believe his eyes. The fallout would be immense! The EAC was eradicating the entire continent! He felt lightheaded and had to lean over on the counter as he watched more red dots appear across the map, moving farther west and north in a quickly expanding wave of destruction. He couldn't imagine the dread that washed over him getting any worse, but then a dot appeared over Copenhagen and thoughts of Claire's family pinched at his gut. Claire had shared many memories of her family with him, not to mention the powerful emotions that went along with them. At this point, despite the fact that he had never met them in person, he felt like they were his own family. As pained as he was at the prospect of Claire's mother and brother being dead, he knew Claire was feeling one hundred times worse. She instantly broke down into a blubbering mess on the cafeteria floor, burying her head in her arms.

To Claire, the thought of never again seeing her brother's smile or hearing her mother's voice was just too unbearably cruel. Love for her family was the only thing that brought her here in the first place, and now she was alive, and they were dead.

Aaron wanted to remind her that it was possible that they had traveled outside of the death zone after receiving the warning to flee from Wes, but he couldn't get the thought across as wave after wave of nausea began to flow to him through their bond.

Claire was going through an emotional and physical breakdown, her body working through the motions of vomiting on the floor. Somehow the physical sensation was traveling straight into Aaron as well, making his stomach grumble as it threatened to do the same thing to him. With great effort, Aaron managed to resist the urge. For Claire, even with all her heaving, only a slight amount of bile came up. Her stomach was empty to begin with. Eventually, Claire's body stopped contracting and she rolled over to her side, wiping the corners of her mouth on the sleeve of her uniform as she continued to sob.

It's possible they're still alive—Aaron finally managed to think the words.

"They're dead," said Claire, "or they might as well be. What's left?"

A flash of an image—a memory—slipped into Aaron's mind. It was Aiden, no more than three years old, playing with a toy fire truck. He'd tripped and banged his knee and started to cry. Claire picked him up and kissed him better, stroking a gentle finger across his rosy cheeks to dry his tears. He stopped crying immediately when Claire lifted him into the air—she'd always had that effect on him—*but where am I now? I should be with him, not out here in this godforsaken desert!*

Aaron sat down beside Claire, huddled up in the fetal position against the counter. She placed her head against his leg and he began to stroke her auburn hair with his fingertips. There was nothing to be said; no comfort for what had just happened. Millions were dead. Claire's family was gone—

either dead or lost forever in a world that would never be the same again. The loss was immeasurable. Aaron didn't know what to do with himself—all this death, all this destruction, just because they'd been given the power to change their surroundings with their minds. The EAC wiped out any home they could have possibly returned to; there was nowhere left for them to go.

They stayed on the floor for a long while saying nothing. Claire's memories of her family became a torment, taunting her with what she would never again have. Aaron felt the aching sadness settle into his own soul as well. He wished he could have met them, even just once. It would have been a gift to make memories of his own with them.

At some point the news broadcast cut off and the sound of the anchor's voice changed to continuous static—the station likely gone now as well. Claire looked up at Aaron, their eyes meeting for the first time since the odd sensation that left them dizzy in the entrance lounge. For Aaron, it was like looking into a mirror of despair. The whites of Claire's eyes were bloodshot, the skin around them pink and puffy from crying. Seeing the anguish on her face only compounded his own feelings of hopelessness.

"The thing I didn't tell you before…" she said, still hesitant to open up to Aaron for some reason. She took a deep breath, steadying her nerves as she prepared to speak. Instead, though, she sent the message to him across their bond. *I'm pregnant*… she thought, letting the words linger in his mind. *I can feel her presence growing inside of me.* It was the last thing Aaron expected to hear. Only a few days had passed since they had sex! "I didn't know what it was at first," she said. "I thought maybe it was something different happening with the computer, but I can feel her here now, even though she is only a few cells big." Claire put her hand on her belly, as if caressing the baby through her skin. "I didn't know how I was going to tell you, but I guess it doesn't matter now. There is no future for her… not for any of us."

Aaron's mind was spinning. *We're having a baby... a daughter!* He placed his hand on top of Claire's, searching his mind to see if he could feel the presence Claire described, but she was still too small for him to get a read on her. *Will either of us even be alive in nine months? Will this child ever be born?* He didn't share the thought with Claire—it was too agonizing—though he knew she was already thinking the same thing. Even with everything else, this was the most tragic turn of all—a what-could-have-been, growing larger inside of Claire even now, never to be born. Fate gave him a daughter and shattered the world in the same moment. Tears flowed freely from his eyes as he began to lament, mourning the loss of the future that should have been.

CHAPTER

46

Last Stand

Belford slipped from his meditative trance. He turned away from Vera, fast asleep at his side. Beads of cold sweat appeared at his temples as the memories of his past burned across his mind, their sting as fresh as the day they were first formed. He sat up in the cot and rubbed his face with both hands, trying to pull himself out of the moment that nearly destroyed him. He'd lost more than he ever realized. *A daughter*.... Being uncertain of Claire's fate was bad enough on its own; knowing that she was pregnant only made Belford's mission that much more vital. He had to find her… had to find them both….

After several deep breaths the immediacy of his memories began to fade, as if the past were on the other side of a fogged mirror and no longer right in front of his eyes. The reflection was there, but it was another world, obscured in shadow, just out of reach of his fingertips. As much as he wished to rid himself of the pain of that fateful day, he knew he needed to go back in—to finish out what he started. He witnessed the end of the world; watched as the ash of a civilization rose up to blot out the sky. If he did not remember those people, no one else would.

The blur of his memories began to sharpen into a point—the final forgotten pieces of his puzzle sitting just on the edge of consciousness. If his past contained clues to Claire's whereabouts or any other insight that might help him learn how Garrett predicted his own return back in Belford Quarry, he would not let it go undiscovered. He held his breath as he prepared to go back into his trance, grasping onto the air to remind him of his existence and what had been lost across the pallid surface of his mind.

The sharpening images burned bright like the filament of a light bulb—brighter as he got closer to remembering. He had to squint to see past the glow. The deceased occupied the glass dome fixture of his memories like dead insects—their bodies, black specks that never quite crumbled away, remained encased, as in a tomb, waiting for their moment of deliverance to be upon them, though it had already been many lifetimes since their passing.

As he slipped back through the fogged mirror, a tinge of darkness marred the glow coming from the other side. Steam condensed into beads that ran down; streaks of lines appearing in the cognitive mist. Drawn from tiny imperfections and subtle airflows, they revealed glimpses of clarity, forgotten memories, chasing the tails of the condensed beads.

Mirrors showed the truth—before him a dark figure stirred its outstretched limbs, bending into the foreground as he pivoted his hips to the side with a nervous twist. The shadow mocked him as he sank deeper inside of it, his image of self, warped, skewed, and thrown back, never to be the same again.

* * *

It took all of Aaron and Claire's combined effort to lift their heads up from the cloud of misery that settled over them on the floor of the empty cafeteria. Continuing on felt pointless with everything else gone, but they climbed to their feet and slowly made their way back to the entrance lounge to tell the others what had become of the world. When they emerged from the hallway, not much had changed within the lounge. Wes was still focused downward on his tablet and Isabelle was still unconscious on the bench seat. The only difference was that Michelle had joined her husband in sitting down in the chairs, her feet tired out from all the pacing.

Wes glanced up as they approached. "I got into the system," he said. "Still looking for answers.... Where's the food?"

Aaron and Claire exchanged sullen emotions across their bond. There was no easy way to break the news so they just came out and said it: The world was unhinged; broken at the seams. Aaron explained in detail all he had seen on the news broadcast. There was nowhere to go to escape the nuclear winter that would follow as a continent burned—the radiation was airborne and would traverse the whole globe.

Stillness settled over the lounge as Wes, Michelle, and Ethan all fell under the same spell of aimlessness Aaron and Claire were already experiencing. Nothing they were doing before felt worthy of attention; their lives had been knocked out of orbit and sent careening into the nothingness of the abyss. The leaders of the Arcadian Project aimed to change the world, and they succeeded, just not in the way they hoped.

It would only be a matter of time before this facility met the same fate as the rest of the Union. There was no way the EAC would leave them standing—their abilities made them too much of a threat. Aaron was surprised the complex wasn't among the first targets of the attack. Part of him was starting to wish they had been hit first—at least then the waiting would be over.

Wes put his tablet down and sat silently with Isabelle for several hours until she recovered enough to join the waking world. After she came to, he took her aside to give her the bad news and they didn't return to the lounge until the sun was beginning to set over the park.

Aaron sat with Claire the whole time, their hands clenched tightly together as they looked upon what would undoubtedly be their last sunset. The park lit up with an orange haze as they watched through the tall windows at Echo Facility's entrance. It was just another day from the perspective of the cosmos; an ever changing moment of time, much the same as any one of an infinite others. Distant gasses churned within the star, generating the heat that radiated against their faces as they reflected on the tragically short lives they had lived.

Wes and Isabelle, back from wherever they had been privately grieving, sat down beside them. Aaron was surprised to see Wes once again engrossed in his tablet—perhaps he was just trying to keep busy until the end. Whatever the reason, Aaron didn't bother to ask him what he was up to. Curiosity was among the things Aaron lost in the wake of the world coming to an end. *What does any of it matter?*

As the last golden rays of sunlight dipped behind the distant skyscrapers of downtown Tripoli, a lone silhouette emerged from the tree line on the other side of the grassy field. Claire spotted it first—it was a person… no, two people, side by side with arms interlocked over each other's shoulders. Aaron couldn't tell who they were at first—their meandering approach was quite slow and the low angle of the sun made it difficult to discern much more than their long shadows. Whoever they were, they were limping towards the security gates. Aaron lost sight of the pair as they moved far enough down the sloping field to disappear behind the facility's outer wall.

Everyone saw them, but no one commented out loud. It took several more minutes for the two to close in and slip past the unlocked gate. Once they were inside the compound there was no mistaking the man dressed like a bird or the pasty-skinned Spanish woman at his side. Miraculously, Travis had managed to rescue Brooke from the other Arcadians. The Aussie half-limped and half-hopped as he moved along, using Brooke's shoulders to support his weight. Seeing the grimace of pain etched across his face, Aaron knew the injury must be serious. Travis was tough—if it was anything short of a broken leg, he probably would have been able to shake it off and just walk on.

Even if no one survived the night, relieving Travis's immediate suffering still felt like a worthy cause. Aaron was fairly certain he could fix whatever was wrong with Travis's leg in an instant if only he could get a good look at it. After mending Ethan's gunshot wound the night before, Aaron felt much more confident in his ability to direct the computer in manipulating the delicate structures of the human body. The urge to help his friend was the first motivating force he'd felt since learning of the world's soon-to-be fate.

Aaron rose from his seat, his legs feeling like wooden planks as he moved—stiff and ungainly after the near catatonic state he had fallen into over the last few hours. He was a little surprised to see everyone else stand up alongside him. Even with the world coming to an end, a real kinship had formed within their group. They would go to Travis's aid together. He was one of them, after all; he fought by their side. The six Arcadians ventured out to meet Travis and Brooke along the palm tree shaded drive.

It didn't take long for Aaron to realize something was amiss. He hadn't taken more than five steps from the entrance when the air became noticeably cooler. Even with the sun recently set, the temperature was normally much warmer at this time of evening. A breeze was blowing in from the south over the desert, carrying with it bits of sand that whipped at Aaron's face and neck. He was by no means an expert on the weather patterns of Northern Africa, but an uneasy feeling between his shoulder blades told him that this was no natural storm.

In the time it took Aaron's group to close half the distance to Travis and Brooke, the wind picked up nearly ten-fold in ferocity. The sand stopped hitting them as it plumed upwards into the sky and began circling around like a miniature hurricane—they were right at its epicenter. Realizing the danger, everyone started running, trying to reach Travis and Brooke before it was too late. The swirling sands blackened the already dim sky, casting a dense shadow across the land that made it seem as if it were already the dead of night. The streetlamps, detecting the drop in brightness, flickered on, pouring down pools of glowing, white halogen light that cast across their path like spotlights on a stage.

Isabelle was the fastest. She reached Travis and Brooke first, just as molten droplets of sand began to rain down on their heads. The air cooled further as whoever was controlling the storm transferred the atmospheric energy into the grains and sent them falling back to earth in a hailstorm of fire. Aaron kept his head down as he dashed the last few paces to where Isabelle was starting to erect a force field. The first grains sizzled as they landed against the back of Aaron's neck. They felt like drops of burning oil splashing out of a frying pan. The grains stuck to his clothing, burrowing tiny holes through his uniform.

Initially, Isabelle formed the force field as a wall in front of them until everyone reached her side. She then began to mold it into a dome and lowered it around their heads. As the energy shield settled into the ground, a final burst of air made its escape through the shrinking crack, sending Isabelle's mousy-brown hair blowing wildly around her face.

The dome glowed with a brilliant blue radiance as the molten sand struck its surface. The grains slid off the polymer compound harmlessly, their heat energy absorbed into the hungering shield on contact. The sand's energy strengthened the shield's integrity, but it was not enough to keep the dome powered all by itself. Isabelle's eyes blazed with a fierce intensity as she focused on locating additional energy sources in the surrounding environment.

As the force field aged, its electrons stabilized and its blue glow faded away, casting everyone once again into darkness. Now that the shield was completely transparent, only the slight shimmer of refracted light passing through it marked its position around them. Michelle and Claire, both skilled at energy manipulation, joined Isabelle in finding and extracting fuel from the environment to feed the dome's heavy demands.

Next to Aaron, Brooke lowered Travis to the asphalt and then flopped on the ground herself, exhausted from their trek. The black feathers on Travis's uniform were smoldering where the molten sand had settled upon them, but the pain the sand caused was nothing compared to his other injuries. Aaron immediately crouched down beside him and began to use the computer as a sixth sense to feel his way through Travis's leg. It did not take him long to form a diagnosis: Travis's left ankle was completely shattered, and his fibula had several thin fractures running across it as well! The ankle was the worst break Aaron had ever witnessed. "How were you even upright with this?!" he asked. "What happened to you?"

Travis shrugged. "Bad landing, I guess. Not sure exactly when it happened."

Aaron knew adrenaline was a powerful stimulant, but it had its limits. He was certain Travis was just trying to act tough in front of Brooke. There was no way he could have missed the sickening crunch his ankle must have made when it was turned into the pulverized shards that currently resided there. "This will hurt," Aaron warned as he began the process of liquefying the broken ankle shards. It needed to be done before he could reform them into a solid structure.

Travis may have been acting tough before, but now as his bones turned to mush beneath his skin, he let out a scream that rang back and forth across the inside of the dome. The shield itself wavered slightly as the deafening cry caused Isabelle, Michelle, and Claire to all lose their concentration simultaneously. A moment later, though, Travis quieted down as his bone re-hardened and finished shifting into the correct position amongst his tendons and other sinewy bits. Fortunately, the fibula fractures were much simpler to mend—the bone was already in place and didn't need to be liquefied for Aaron to seal the breaks. Travis probably experienced a burning sensation as the computer filled the gaps, but he showed no outward reaction to the process, putting on a brave face once more.

With Travis mended, Aaron turned his attention towards Brooke. From what Aaron could discern, she had been beaten severely by somebody using their fists or some sort of blunt object. Fortunately, all of her wounds were surface level damage—some small cuts, but mostly deep-red bruising around her face and upper torso. The air glowed blue and purple as Aaron sealed her damaged capillaries to remove the bruising. Brooke looked more radiant than ever when he was finished. In just a few seconds, her skin and outer tissues rejuvenated in elasticity to match that of an infant's.

Just as he finished, a loud popping noise sounded in the distance. Aaron quickly turned his head to search for the cause. From out on the other side of the gate, still in the distance but closing fast, a large mass of flaming material was hurtling towards them. It tore through the gate as if the wrought iron bars were no more than wood and was upon them a moment later. Aaron covered his head with his arms on reflex, but the flaming object impacted the top portion of the dome and ricocheted off at a sideways angle that sent it careening into the side of Echo Facility. The ensuing explosion was so bright that it forced Aaron to close his eyes from the intensity. The shield rippled violently, nearly faltering as the force of the projectile undulated across its surface and left it ringing in a low resonant hum.

Another popping sound reached Aaron's ears as a second fiery object was created within the park and launched towards them. A third and fourth pop followed in quick succession as more projectiles were formed before the second one even reached the shield.

As the first of the three new objects collided with the dome, its impact carried such massive velocity that although it too bounced off, the shield broke down completely, turning to goo that fell around them in a thick, slimy sheet. The molten sand it had been keeping out began to strike Aaron again, singeing his body like crackling embers from a fire.

A drop of the burning sand spattered against Aaron's right ear. It sizzled—a taunting whisper of the searing pain that would soon be his whole existence if they did not manage to reform the shield in time. He knew that there truly wasn't enough time for them to form a new dome before the rest of the barrage found its mark, so, thinking quickly, he willed a thick wall of earth and asphalt straight up into the air in front of the group. The rock wall was immediately impacted by the rest of the volley, the sheer energy of the hit boiling the asphalt back into tar and sending chunks of gravel shooting backwards at them. Fortunately, the girls managed to reform the shield just in time to stop the debris.

During all the commotion, no one—neither attackers nor defenders—noticed the large streaks of light streaming through the dark sky towards them. The first streak descended through the cloud of swirling sand and collided with a skyscraper across the way, instantly vaporizing the building and creating the largest explosion Aaron had ever experienced. He felt like his retinas were going to burn out of his head as the sheer radiance of the blast forced him to cover his face. Another streak impacted before the first flash had time to dissipate. Explosion after explosion wracked the city as the EAC's bombardment of Tripoli commenced in an awe-inspiring display of utter destruction. The ground trembled violently with every impact until there was nothing left of the city on the other side of the park.

The bombardment was over just as quickly as it began. Although the explosions formed huge plumes of dust and ash that joined the sand in the sky, the missiles had not been of the nuclear variety. The Arcadian Complex was spared again. Aaron could only guess at what the EAC had in store for them.

With Tripoli completely destroyed, all that remained of the sprawling city were the debris clouds that hung along the horizon—phantom structures that seemed dense but expanded outward in all directions above the smoldering rubble. Fires burned everywhere, sending off an eerie glow that was reflected back down by the soot filled atmosphere—a fiery hell-scape.

The skirmish between the Arcadians was over. No more projectiles were formed and the molten sand stopped falling from the sky almost at once. Much of the grit still remained airborne, but it ceased its unnatural swirling and began to settle back to the ground at a normal rate and temperature. Like Aaron's group earlier, the other Arcadians were just now realizing the futility of their actions. There was no point in killing each other when the world was on fire.

The girls let the shield deteriorate and everyone stepped out from under the second pile of slime it left behind. They spread out, but no one wandered too far. Standing in a staggered line, they watched with aching hearts as the dust clouds of the collapsing buildings expanded and the distant rumbles crackled like melting glacier ice.

Travis, clearly in shock, pointed towards the burning horizon. "Someone blew up the city," he said, as if they weren't all seeing the same thing. He began to look back and forth across the group when no one responded. "The city's blown up!"

"Not just the city," whispered Aaron. He couldn't bring himself to retell the story of what he saw on the news again, but Michelle quickly filled in Travis and Brooke on the horrid details.

Even though Aaron knew all of Europe was destroyed, it hadn't felt completely real until this moment as Tripoli burned right in front of his eyes. All those people, dead for no reason at all. The Arcadians were supposed to save the world, but there was no stopping *this*. The people of Tripoli expressed their strong opposition to the Arcadian Project, but that hadn't changed their fate. *How little life must mean to the people who launched those missiles.*

He couldn't raise a child in this world, even if they did manage to survive. *What kind of life could she possibly have?* That thought alone was enough to make him want to cry, but he was already so drained he couldn't muster a tear.

He felt the eyes of the dead upon him; empty, black orbs, unblinking. Their silent screams racked the inside of his skull as he replayed their moment of incineration over and over again. All their fear and suffering pooled inside of him, filling his heart until it felt ready to burst with the poisonous tar. He was a frightened child again, alone amongst the sea of screams. Through the cries, one of his earliest memories suddenly came back to him, set off by the orange glow that consumed the horizon.

It was a night in July, before the economic crash that stopped his family from returning to America. He was on his father's shoulders and there were strangers all around him. Fireworks started with a rapid surge, making a brilliant flash that shattered the silence of the lukewarm night. They startled him, sounding louder than anything his small ears had ever experienced. Tears instantly appeared in his eyes and he kicked out his legs in panic, nearly falling from his father's shoulders in the process. He didn't stop kicking until he was placed on the ground, and then he ran, fleeing from the blasts as if his life depended on it.

From around the corner of a building he could still see the flashes reflecting off the windshields of the cars parked nearby. It was only then that he noticed he had lost his father in the crowd. He was all alone, and that realization was more terrifying than a thousand firework bursts. He searched for his father, but everybody looked the same in the dark. They nearly walked over him, all their heads pointed up towards the display. He followed their gaze, staring wide-eyed, never daring to blink as the sky bloomed before him.... The thunderous crashes still made him jump with unexpected intensity, but the golden sparkles calmed his heart once he realized they would not harm him. Before the display finished, his father found him again and scooped him back up into his arms.

There was nothing to calm him now, though, not with the world crumbling before him—no goodness or beauty to chase the fear away; nobody was going to rescue him. There was only fire, ash, and darkness.

"Where are you going?" someone asked from behind him.

Aaron paused. He hadn't even realized he was moving, but he was already halfway to the broken down gate. Although he hadn't thought about it, he knew exactly what he was doing. "I'm going to go sit in the park," he said. It seemed like a more pleasant place to spend the end.

Claire joined him, holding his hand while they walked. Her skin was still as smooth as silk despite the grime of the day. Aaron heard others following behind them as well, but he didn't look back. All he could think about were the eyes of the dead, following him as he crossed the street and walked up the main path that ran through the grassy field.

How old were you? Claire asked in his head.

Aaron jumped slightly. It had been a while now since Claire had last spoken to him inside his mind. He glanced over at her with confusion.

The fireworks, she clarified, *with your father.*

Aaron hadn't realized he'd shared the memory with her, or perhaps he hadn't and she was simply snooping inside his head. The intrusion didn't bother him, though; it was actually nice to feel not alone. *I was probably four or five,* he thought back to her. She didn't respond, merely nodded and squeezed his hand tighter at his side as if to remind him that she was still there. The kind gesture only fueled his heartache, but for the moment the eyes of the dead abated, squirming back into the darker recesses of his mind.

They deviated off to the side of the path where a small hill sat above an empty meadow of wildflowers that overlooked the burning city beyond. It wasn't until Aaron reached the top of the hill that he realized every one of his friends had followed him. He wasn't sure if he appreciated the company or not as he took a seat in the dry grass and dirt. He mostly just wanted to be left alone with Claire and his sorrow. Thankfully, no one disturbed him. They all just stared out beyond the park, still trying to comprehend the unimaginable power of the bombs that ignited the sky.

Aaron removed his jacket and pulled up his shirtsleeve on his right side. He placed the index finger of his left hand on his bicep and drew across his arm. His skin sizzled as he directed the computer to use his own flesh to create the ink of a tattoo, the way Travis showed him earlier that morning—it felt like a lifetime ago. He formed the letter *C*, grimacing slightly from the sting as his skin blackened. The letter burned even after he finished etching it into his flesh, but the pain was a welcome reminder that he was still alive. Claire was the only one he had left in this world, and he would have gladly felt that burn again and again if it meant keeping her by his side. He formed a *B* next, a place holder for their unborn baby—nameless and perhaps destined to remain that way forever.

Lost in his hopelessness, Aaron didn't notice the distant patter at first, but soon all of the other Arcadians were looking towards the east as the noise grew steadily louder. The sound was unmistakable once Aaron was paying attention— helicopters were moving in on them, at least three, though the sky was too dark and too full of soot to make out the exact number. When they got closer, Aaron counted four in total, and it became clear that they were headed towards the research complex. Eventually, one chopper landed on the landing pad on top of Echo Facility while the rest hovered just within the compound, several stories above the ground. Men dressed all in black descended from ropes at the helicopters' sides and disappeared behind the complex's wall.

"What do you think that's about?" asked Travis, rubbing the back of his tattooed head.

"It's the EAC," said Wes. "They're gathering intel."

The certainty in the boy's voice prompted Aaron to glance over at him. Aaron was bemused to find Wes once again engrossed in his tablet computer. Although he hadn't been curious about what Wes was doing before, he couldn't imagine what could possibly make the boy want to spend his precious remaining time with his face buried in a screen. Judging from the expressions of many of the other Arcadians, Aaron was not the only one wondering what Wes was up to.

"I've been digging around in the facility's systems," said Wes, noticing their piqued interest. "At first I was only looking for evidence of someone leaking information to the press about the marker expansion, but when that search turned up empty I started reading further back in the message logs. I got back to the day before the lockdown and stumbled across a curious message with corrupted tags. It was just a string of seemingly random numbers and letters, like a glitched-out piece of mail that had failed to delete properly and was overwritten by erroneous data. I couldn't tell who wrote it, but I ran the content through several decryption algorithms and ended up discovering an encoded message to the EAC."

"Spit it out," said Travis. "Tell us what you found."

Wes was slightly flustered by the interruption but went on anyway. "It has two parts. First is our names and information along with various other sensitive project files, and the second part is the location of a worm," he said, gesturing wildly with his hands, "a backdoor, but not into the Arcadian Project... it's a breach in HAMMER's security."

"I knew it..." said Michelle under her breath. "Garrett... it must have been him.... He was the only one here besides me and Ethan that worked on the HAMMER Project. He's how the EAC was able to take the station offline...." Everyone turned their attention towards Michelle, but she was done talking. The rage in her eyes was only matched by her unrelenting sadness.

There was nothing more to say. They all sat in silence as they watched the helicopters hanging perfectly still in the air. After several minutes, the EAC must have found what they were looking for because the chopper on the roof spun back up and lifted off. The men from the hovering helicopters used mechanized harnesses to propel back up their ropes and into the aircrafts almost as quickly as they came down. All four choppers sped off into the night, their patter quickly fading until every trace of the raid was consumed by the darkness.

"It doesn't matter anymore," said Ethan, echoing the words they overheard Yosef Reblan mumble as he shut them out of his office earlier. Aaron wondered if Yosef had already known what was coming. "We did this. Don't you see," Ethan whispered, "this is our fault."

Aaron felt a hollow thud in his heart as Claire began to softly weep, burying her face in Aaron's shirt to hide her tears. Aaron stroked the back of her head as he glared up at Ethan. "What do you expect us to do?" he asked venomously.

Ethan sighed, glancing back over at the burning city. "For them...? Nothing." He looked down at his feet. "It's too late to fix this."

Aaron looked away. He knew how Ethan felt; every one of the Arcadians was filled with some sense of guilt. The world was destroyed because of what they had become. It was not their intention, of course, and others would have replaced them had they chosen not to join the project, but that did not change the fact that their presence here was the primary motivation for the EAC's attacks. It was impossible not to feel at least partially responsible. The eyes of the dead weighed heavily upon Aaron, judging him, blaming him for sending their souls down into the dark depths.

Ethan sat in the grass with his back to the city. "But it's not too late for us," he said.

Aaron froze in place, hearing Ethan's words but not fully comprehending them for a moment. "What are you talking about?" he managed to ask. "How can we survive?" His heart latched on to the hope with fluttering anticipation.

Ethan stood up again with sudden haste, his back and neck going rigid as he stared back down towards the research facility. "We'll need his help," Ethan said, pointing behind Aaron, across the open field.

Everyone's heads spun around so fast they must have looked like a herd of nervous gazelle on the prairie. Their predator was more dangerous than a lion—one of the other Arcadians was walking towards them from across the grassy field. Travis swore under his breath. Even in the darkness, Aaron was able to recognize John Graven's formidable outline. The tall Russian was walking straight towards them at a steady pace, keenly aware of their presence.

Without warning, the air between John and the group began to shimmer as energy built up in the atmosphere. Aaron felt the tingle of a static charge dance across his skin and tensed up, expecting an attack.

John stopped walking and raised his hands above his head in a gesture of surrender.

"No, wait," said Ethan, placing his hand on Michelle's shoulder.

The air continued to shimmer for a few moments longer, but then Michelle dropped her gaze and the energy quickly dissipated back into the earth. With his hands still above his head, John took one hesitant step forward, and then another into the formerly shimmering space, his pace returning to normal once he was certain there were no lingering atmospheric effects that might harm him. As soon as he reached about twenty yards away from the group, Ethan yelled out to him. "That's close enough, John."

The Russian stopped immediately, eying the group with a rock solid expression that gave away nothing of his intentions or emotions.

"What do you want?" Michelle yelled out to him.

John locked his eyes on hers. "A truce," he said as he began to slowly lower his arms back to his sides. "Our disagreement hardly seems important anymore, now that…" he trailed off and gestured towards the city where the plumes of soot and ash made the ground indistinguishable from the sky.

"What about Garrett?" Michelle asked.

John nodded. "I speak for him, and Emily and Hannah as well. None of us want to fight anymore."

Michelle looked unconvinced.

"Listen up, John," said Ethan, "I have an idea that might just save all our lives, but we will need to help each other out."

John raised an eyebrow. "I'm listening."

Aaron watched Ethan now as well, hanging off his every word and hoping beyond hope that he had a way out of this.

"The teleportation protocol," said Ethan, as if the answer was obvious. "We have a tablet, and access to the facility's server."

Wes hugged the tablet computer closer to his chest as he watched Ethan with frightened curiosity.

"You know the inner workings of the supercomputer better than any of us," Ethan said to John, "seeing as how you helped build the thing. With a little luck we should be able to download the protocol and alter it to work on living tissue."

John scoffed at the idea. "Even if we could get it working, where could we possibly go that the radiation will not touch?"

Ethan smiled, his piercing blue eyes flickering with the light from the distant fires. "The future, of course."

CHAPTER

47

The Black Mist

Belford paced the corridor nervously outside the forward cabins. Arlin was in with Livian Niern, making one more attempt to gain her assistance. Their destination, the great city of Tavallon, was close at hand. Most of Ethan's raiding party was enjoying one last meal in the mess hall before the Rosa Marsa was scheduled to dock. Livian's door opened with a creak. It was Arlin, beckoning him to enter. Belford hustled through, and Arlin shut the door behind him.

Livian's back was to Belford. She was standing behind a neck-high paper screen. The outline of her curvy body was silhouetted across the white paper with lamplight. She finished tying the belt of a pink robe around her middle and stepped out to greet him. Her ashen hair was messy, her cheeks flush with blood and she was still breathing heavily from her activities with Arlin. She smiled at Belford. Arlin sat down in a chair in the corner of the room without a word.

"Did you already make the *spores*?" Belford asked, finishing in a whisper.

Livian walked over to her dresser and pulled a tiny glass vial out of the top drawer. She removed its cork stopper and sat down on the edge of her unmade bed. Her eyes focused intently at the air above the open vial. A vaporous mist began to form—it floated down into the vial in a dark swirling cloud.

"There you go," said Livian, recapping the vial and tossing it through the air at Belford.

He fumbled with the tube for a second before securing it in his palm. He held it up to his eye and marveled at the tiny particles. "The Black Mist...."

"This one is more of a gray mist," said Livian. "It's tailored specifically for the Whune—I would be careful not to breathe any of that in, by the way. No telling what it would do to you. For Wilgoblikan, it will make him much more amiable under your questioning."

"Thank you," said Belford.

Livian nodded. "Wait until we've set off, though," she said. "I'd rather no one finds out I broke Arcanum Law for you."

"Isn't using your spores what you were sent here by the Arcanum to do in the first place?"

"Of course," said Livian, "but yours is a personal matter. My involvement would be frowned upon. I shouldn't have helped at all, but your friend was very persuasive." She glanced over at Arlin and shot him a quick wink. "Now get out of here, I need to change."

Belford and Arlin left together. "You okay?" Belford asked once they were sufficiently far from Livian's room.

Arlin nodded, though he stayed silent.

Belford was worried about Arlin. He hadn't expected Livian's thirst to be so great. Even though it was Arlin's choice to trade sexual favors for the spores, using the swordsman like a prostitute was extremely uncomfortable for Belford. The cost of the mist was no less than Arlin's honor.

Livian could not be swayed to question Garrett, but these brain spores would at least give Belford a chance to get the answers he needed from Wilgoblikan. At Ethan's order, Belford was to stay aboard the Rosa Marsa. Arlin was not to disembark either, as predicted, while Ethan led his attack force straight to Garrett's throne room.

Sarbin Raiger and Sharith Grine were the only other Ver'ati not accompanying Ethan on the assault. Belford needed to find a way to question Wilgoblikan without either of the men interfering. Unfortunately, Belford was fairly certain Captain Grine hated him. Grine had been avoiding Belford ever since the whole Vera thing. Sleeping with the woman a man liked was not the best way to make friends.

Shiara exited her cabin as Belford was walking by. Arlin went on ahead as Belford lingered behind to speak with her. Shiara was aware of his plan—Arlin told Thorin, who in turn informed Shiara—and he hoped she might have some advice for him regarding Captain Grine.

"I know I've made a mess of things," said Belford, "but I wasn't trying to hurt you. If you can forgive me, I could really use your help right now."

Shiara sighed. "You're a real bonehead, you know that?"

Belford's mouth tightened into a frown.

"Did she give them to you?" she asked, her voice hushed.

Belford nodded. He put his hand in his pocket to retrieve the tiny vial but Shiara grabbed his wrist.

"Not here," she said. Shiara looked back and forth down the hallway before stepping back into her cabin. She pulled Belford along behind her. Once inside, she allowed Belford to show her the swirling particles. "Fascinating…" she said, tilting the vial back and forth. "If you have this, what's the problem?"

"Getting to him," said Belford. "Captain Grine is going to be guarding the cargo hold during the raid and we aren't exactly on good terms."

Shiara's eyes never left the vial. "Pity we can't just make some more of this to convince him. The particles are too small for me to see how they're made."

"Livian said it's tailored specifically for Wilgoblikan anyway."

Shiara handed the vial back. "I'm glad she's on our side…."

"So what should I do about Captain Grine?" Belford asked.

"Apologizing to him for being such a dick would be a good start," Shiara said flatly.

Belford wasn't sure what else he had been expecting Shiara to say. He grumbled in protest.

"Well don't look at me," said Shiara. "I'm not going to sleep with him to get you what you want."

The words stung like a slap to the face.

"You know what you have to do," said Shiara. "Go be a man. You've been a jerk, but it's not unfixable. You're a good guy deep down, even if you haven't been showing it." Shiara blushed slightly and diverted her eyes. "I don't know why I always let you get me so flustered." She glanced back up at him again. "Stop looking at me like that!"

Belford reached out and grabbed her shoulders. He leaned in and kissed her on the forehead. She seemed to shrink several inches. "You're right," said Belford. "You're always right."

Over the next hour, the Rosa Marsa docked in Tavallon's sprawling port and Livian used some of her brain spores to turn away a pair of guardsmen who were sent to inspect the vessel. The men sat on the floor by the helm for about twenty minutes with dazed expressions on their faces before standing up, deciding everything was in order, and disembarking to continue their duties elsewhere.

Belford waited until Ethan's raiding party set out and then went to speak with Captain Grine at the entrance to the cargo hold. The young Ver'ati glanced up at Belford as he came around the corner and started down the hallway towards him. A slight pinch in his face showed his discomfort.

"Hi, Sharith," said Belford. Grine continued to stare at him. This was already awkward. "I just wanted to say that I'm really sorry about how things went. I didn't plan anything with Vera, it just sort of happened."

Grine's face tightened further.

This wasn't going to work if he held back. He took a deep breath and dove in head first. "Ethan was abusing her. I found her crying outside his cabin, her dress torn halfway off. I took her back to my room so she could get some rest. I really do care about her, but she and I aren't meant to be together.

Grine's face went from hatred to disgust to confusion in a matter of seconds.

"There's a girl from my past. Her name's Claire—"

"—I know who she is. Ethan briefed me on your history," Grine interjected.

"Ethan doesn't know the half of it." Belford kept his voice level, though he was immediately irritated by Grine's comment. "I didn't even know the whole truth of it until recently. Claire's my soulmate… she's carrying my unborn child…." Belford had never said those words out loud before. He was hit by a wave of emotion that seized his throat for a moment. "I need your help. Wilgoblikan is the only one who might know how to find Claire."

Grine shook his head, though his expression was sympathetic at least. "We already tried to get him to talk. He wouldn't say anything, despite what Lord Ethan did to him." Grine grimaced.

"Ethan didn't have this," said Belford, taking the vial of spores out of his pocket. "Courtesy of Livian Niern. Wilgoblikan will tell us everything we want to know once he breathes this in."

Grine looked genuinely angry. "You mean to tell me that Livian could have made questioning Wilgoblikan easier this whole time, and she just didn't bother to mention it?"

"Seems that way," said Belford.

"I've been healing his wounds for weeks, had to watch him be tortured, skinned, maimed… for weeks! And it all could have been avoided with a tiny, illegal vial of that shit!?"

"Yup."

"The things I've seen are going to live with me for fucking ever. Fuck Livian Niern!"

"Ethan must know what Livian is capable of too—she was brought along on this mission to use her spores."

"Fuck Ethan too, the abusive prick!"

Arlin poked his head around the corner as Grine finished shouting. "Pray tell, are we ready to start now?" he asked.

Grine's eyes shifted back and forth between Arlin and Belford. "Fine," he said, after only a moment of hesitation. "Let's see what the poor bastard has to say."

Once within the cargo hold, Belford went straight for Wilgoblikan. The Whune was tied to a chair with a bag over his head. Ethan hadn't taken any chances with Wilgoblikan after the fiasco with the smuggler's hold. Belford removed the bag and was met by an expressionless stare. Wilgoblikan looked more bored than anything else. Belford held the vial up to Wilgoblikan's nose and removed the cork stopper. "Breathe this in," he said.

Wilgoblikan took a slow whiff while gazing into Belford's eyes—the same uncaring expression held throughout. He sucked about three quarters of the spores up his nose.

Belford recorked the vial and placed it back in his pocket.

"How long do we have to wait?" asked Grine.

Belford shook his head. "No idea."

"It was instantaneous for the guardsmen upstairs," said Arlin.

"Okay then," said Belford. He put his hands on his knees, bending over to stare into Wilgoblikan's face. "How did you know I would appear near Darrenfield?"

Wilgoblikan did a slow blink. His distant expression suddenly focused in on Belford. "I didn't know it was going to be you," he said.

"What do you mean?"

Wilgoblikan exhaled in annoyance, clearly not wanting to elaborate, but Livian's spores didn't give him a choice. "I didn't know which of you would appear. It all depended on the order in which you were originally memorized by the great device. My master didn't know who was next."

"How did you know where to look?"

Wilgoblikan laughed. "The moon, you simple boy," he said. "Darrenfield was approximately the closest point on Earth to the moon at the exact moment of your return."

"How could you possibly know that?"

"Math," he said simply.

"Okay, but how did you know when?"

"It was scheduled. That was the day and time my master chose for his rejuvenation. We learned from previous experience that each time he makes himself younger, someone new returns. The procedure taxes the great device so much that it must push someone out in order to compensate."

Belford glanced over at Arlin and Captain Grine. "Ethan made himself younger too…."

"Then someone else has already returned," said Wilgoblikan.

Belford's heart jumped at the thought that Claire might already be back. There was no way of knowing which one of his friends had returned, but somebody from his past was back. With their memory washed away, they were trying to navigate this unfamiliar world all alone. With all the possible dangers of appearing at random, part of Belford hoped that it wasn't Claire. If he could repeat Garrett's process, he could pull everyone else out safely one at a time in a predictable location.

An odd sensation came over Belford. He realized, for the first time in forever, all of his lingering questions were answered. Now he just needed to think everything through and generate a new plan for retrieving Claire. He began to retreat from the cargo hold when the dark wizard's words caught him off-guard. "It doesn't matter what you know," he said. "My master knows you are here, and every last one of you is going to die."

Grine let out a gasp. Belford stopped in his tracks, turning back around on the spot. "What are you talking about?" Belford asked.

"We have agents in Erotos, and he can sense my proximity. He knows the ship is in the port. Ethan's attack is going to fail. My master has an Artifact that stops everyone but the holder from reaching the Power. He is waiting for Ethan to make his move, and then he will destroy all of you."

"What do we do?" Belford asked Grine and Arlin.

"There is nothing you can do," said Wilgoblikan.

"Shut up, I wasn't asking you." Belford put the bag back over Wilgoblikan's head.

"I know Ethan's plan," said Grine. "We might be able to catch up and warn them if we leave now."

Belford's heart was racing. "Wait," he said as Grine turned to run out the door. "You're too conspicuous with your glasses. Let me fix your vision."

If Grine hadn't looked worried before, he certainly did now. His perfectly rational fear of developing a schism made his hands shake as he begrudgingly removed his glasses and opened his eyes wide for Belford to operate on.

"Tell me when things get clear, I'm going to slowly warp your lenses." Belford filled himself with all the possibilities of the Power. He reached out to the computer and tried to bend Grine's eyeballs. There was resistance; Grine was stopping him. The Ver'ati grunted. "Come on, just let it happen," said Belford.

"Okay, okay," said Grine. He took a deep breath. Belford tried again. Grine contorted his face. "This feels so weird… bad pressure… wait, I think it's working! Keep going."

Belford reformed the correct curve for Grine's eyeballs, bulging his flattened inner lenses out slightly.

"Stop!" said Grine.

Belford thought he hurt him at first, but Grine's eyes shifted across the cargo hold as if seeing it for the first time. "All good?"

"Yes, let's go."

Before they could leave the cargo hold, though, Sarbin Raiger was standing before them, looking furious. "What do you think you are doing back here?" He wheeled on Grine. "Why did you let them in?"

"Lord Ethan and the raiding party are in grave danger," said Grine. "We used Livian's spores on the Whune and he told us that Garrett knows we are here. It's a trap!"

"What are you talking about?" Sarbin scoffed.

"It's true," said Wilgoblikan, muffled by the bag. "You're all already dead. You just don't know it yet."

"You don't actually believe a thing that snake-tongued monster told you, do you?" asked Sarbin.

"Garrett has a Power Artifact that stops anyone but him from reaching the Power. We need to go now if we are to have any hope of warning our people!" said Belford.

"No one's going anywhere," said Sarbin. "And you've been ordered to stay on the ship!"

Arlin struck Sarbin in the back of the head with the hilt of his blade. The irritating man crumpled to the deck with an unceremonious thud, unconscious before he hit the floor.

"We should stop wasting time," said Arlin.

Belford and Grine were right on Arlin's heels as they all sprang from the cargo hold, leaving Sarbin drooling where he landed.

CHAPTER

48

The Farmer and the Viper

Wilgoblikan smiled as the hood was drawn away from his face once more. Garcenus stood over him with a nervous glower. What a fortunate surprise it had been when the foolish deckhand happened upon him through the wall of the smuggler's hold early in the journey. A few late night conversations and one big false promise was all it took to convince the stupid boy to help him.

With Wilgoblikan's Power suppressed with inhibitor he needed to dispose of the unconscious Arcanum lackey before he awoke. Garcenus was wasting time, staring at him, hesitating to do what they agreed upon.

"When I let you go, you won't back out of our deal, will you?" Garcenus asked.

Wilgoblikan gave him the most innocent expression he could muster. "Of course not," he said. "You will have your revenge on the Ver'ati, and I will personally see that your Weni ends up safe in your arms. The Goblikans have agents everywhere. They will know how to find her."

Garcenus nodded slowly. "They wronged us both."

"Exactly. We must work together." Wilgoblikan held in his excitement as Garcenus got down on one knee and began untying his restraints. The sting in his wrists from the tight ropes grew as the blood rushed back into his hands. His fingers tingled and throbbed from the sudden increase in circulation. He stood up, flexing his legs and cracking his neck before turning his attention towards the last threat that remained to him. Sarbin Raiger twitched on the floor. "Help me with him," he ordered the deckhand.

Garcenus obliged, using the rope that had been Wilgoblikan's restraint to quickly lash down Sarbin's arms and legs. His knot tying skills were quite strong. "The moon is up," said Garcenus. "Won't he just be able to escape using the Power when he wakes?"

Wilgoblikan picked up the spreading knife his captors used to flay his skin. "A funny thing about the Power," he said. "You need your eyes to focus the energies."

Garcenus quickly slipped the hood over Sarbin's face, not realizing that Wilgoblikan had intended to put his eyes out entirely.

"Hmm," he said, slipping the knife into his pocket. "I suppose that will work."

Garcenus looked up from his handiwork, pleased.

"Did you bring the lamp oil as I requested?" Wilgoblikan asked.

Garcenus stood up from where he was crouched over Sarbin and retrieved a jug of oil from against the wall. "Here," he said, handing it over. "What are you going to do with it?"

Wilgoblikan uncapped the jug and immediately began pouring it all over Sarbin. The Ver'ati sputtered awake as the fuel soaked his hood. He began to struggle helplessly against his bindings.

"You shouldn't do that!" cried Garcenus. "You'll burn the whole ship down if it ignites!"

Wilgoblikan dropped the jug at Sarbin's feet and then spun quickly, retrieving the knife from his pocket and plunging it deep into Garcenus's neck all in one motion. His jugular was severed. The fool's hands went straight to his throat and pulled the knife out. Now, nothing would stop him from bleeding out. Garcenus collapsed to the deck. His frantically beating heart pumped a thick pool of blood from his veins.

Wilgoblikan stepped back from the arterial spray, avoiding most of the spatter. "Thank you," he said. He picked up the lantern Garcenus brought in with him and smashed it on Sarbin. The Ver'ati flailed violently against his bindings as the flames leapt across his body. Within moments he was entirely consumed and the fire began to spread to the rest of the cargo hold.

Garcenus's hands fell away from his pale face as the blood flow slowed to a drizzle. He looked up at Wilgoblikan with his dark eyes frozen in horror. Sarbin eventually stopped struggling as well as he succumbed to the flames, but by then, Wilgoblikan was already gone.

CHAPTER

49

The Lion's Den

The first thing anyone noticed when looking upon the great city of Tavallon was the mega-pyramid structure Garrett erected as his grand cathedral. It did not surprise Belford that Garrett would fancy himself to be like the pharaohs of old, especially with how close the city resided to ancient Cairo. The massive, gilded structure was several times larger than the pyramids of history ever stood. The Power allowed for such extravagant constructions where conventional building techniques would have faltered. To the people of Aragwey, the concept of the pyramid was new; the rich history of Egypt was long forgotten to the ages. The irony that Garrett lived in a tomb was not lost on Belford. At this point, it was merely a question of whose tomb it would become.

Belford, Grine, and Arlin disembarked from the Rosa Marsa and ran up the dock towards the towering structure. Arlin was moving light on his feet despite the heavy chainmail he wore layered beneath his tunic—it was still lighter than his regular suit of armor, and also less conspicuous for moving around the city.

Grine took the lead. He was the only one privy to Ethan's attack plan. Following Ethan's trail was not difficult. Livian's brain spores were hard at work on the people of Tavallon. Every resident present when Ethan's party passed through was sitting on the ground staring vacantly into the distance just like the guardsmen tasked with inspecting the Rosa Marsa. Everyone else who happened by since the mist cleared was running around frantically trying to figure out why an entire street full of people had suddenly become unresponsive. Belford's group used the discord to their advantage—sprinting through the chaos didn't garner them any extra attention.

"How will we find them once we reach the pyramid?" Belford huffed, holding the curved ceremonial blade sheathed at his side steady with one hand as he pushed his body to keep up with Grine. The scrawny Ver'ati was surprisingly agile.

"The what?" Grine asked, slowing his stride as he looked back at Belford. "You mean the cathedral?"

"Yes," said Belford. "They were called pyramids where I'm from."

"We follow the catatonic bodies, I suppose," said Grine. "It's said to be a labyrinth in there…."

Their lack of a plan made Belford nervous. Although mostly absorbed in his worry, while sprinting through the streets of Tavallon he couldn't help but notice that the capital gave off an affluent vibe of prosperity and cleanliness despite Garrett's ruthless regime. The people were all well dressed, many in long colorful robes whose hems brushed against the smooth stone streets as they glided about with exaggerated posture. Men and women alike wore gemmed, golden jewelry, dangling from their necks, wrists, ears, and various facial piercings. There were no homeless or poor masses like he had been greeted with in North Galdren. Belford doubted this was because Garrett took care of his people. It was more likely the lower classes had simply been killed, forced out, or turned into Whunes.

The port was not far from the entrance of the pyramid. Getting there was simple—but getting inside would not be so easy. Just like in the streets, some guards at the pyramid entrance were dazed by Livian's mist, while others had already arrived to aid the fallen. Though no alarm sounded, all of the guardsmen Belford could see from across the promenade were fully aware they were under attack.

A bald, pasty man dressed in dark robes appeared at the wide entrance to the pyramid. He reminded Belford of Wilgoblikan, the way he glared about menacingly with subtle disinterest at the guardsmen around him. The man approached an incapacitated guardsman and grabbed him by the jaw with his bone-white fingers, shifting the guard's head back and forth, testing the extent of the man's unresponsiveness. Belford would have bet his skin the pasty man was a Goblikan.

Captain Grine saw him as well and stopped his approach suddenly. "Sweet Mast," said Grine. "He's a member of the Special Guard—a highly trained Goblikan contingent. I'm just an Ameliorator, I've never even been in close combat!"

Belford, still breathing hard, shrugged off his jacket and handed it to Grine. "Stay behind me. Handle the guardsmen."

Belford had been around death more than he cared to recall, but he had never actually ended a life—at least, not to his knowledge. Destroying the trebuchet tower in North Galdren may have killed some people, but that destruction had been dealt out on instinct, and whether or not anyone actually died was unknown to Belford. To kill was against everything he stood for as a doctor, but Shiara and Thorin's lives depended on him reaching Ethan's party before it was too late. His friends were only here because of him. He wasn't about to let this Goblikan stand in his way.

He did his best to channel the pure strength and concentration John Graven and the other Arcadians displayed in his memories, compartmentalizing his feelings as he grabbed a boulder-sized chunk of the street with his mind. He ripped the molecules apart, creating a jagged seam that glowed red-hot as he cut the stone from the walkway. He wrenched it upwards and then hurled it like a bowling ball at the single pin that was the pasty Goblikan wizard in the distance.

A guardsman cried out and the wizard lunged to the side just in time. The boulder crumbled into a mass of rubble as it struck the shiny, jet-black Calvenite wall at the back of the pyramid's entrance room.

Belford began his charge anyway. Grine and Arlin joined at his flanks. They dashed across the open promenade. The Goblikan stood his ground. He was wide-eyed, but less perturbed than Belford would have expected from someone who just had a boulder thrown his way. Behind the Goblikan, from either side, two more figures emerged from deeper in the passageway. They were wearing the telltale black robes of the Goblikans as well. A yellow-haired woman and a young man—they hadn't the skeletal appearance of the first man, but the wide-sleeved robes and the fiery malice in their eyes told Belford all he needed to know.

As they got closer, the young Goblikan unlashed two circular blades from his hip and held them up conspicuously in the palms of his gloved hands. They looked like toothless table-saw blades. The dark metal of their construction was reminiscent of the axe's Wilgoblikan's Whunes used— tempered with the Power; with enough force they could shatter ordinary steel.

The blades flew from the Goblikan's palms like drones with intelligent control, soaring in opposite curving trajectories out to either side of the promenade before cutting back in. The deadly disks sliced through the air with a whirr. Belford held up his right arm—he had just enough time to form a personal-sized energy shield. He took molecules and energy from the air around him—there was no time to be choosy—and braced the curved shield against his forearm. A loud pop sounded simultaneously in Belford's ear as air rushed to fill the void left behind by the shield's creation. The environment cooled, leaving him feelings as if he'd stepped into a blast chiller.

The disk to his right struck the shield. The force of the impact shook his bones, but the blade glanced off with a hollow thud. On the left, the second disk drove home. Arlin swung his Talas Shard blade up at it, striking the bottom of the disk and redirecting its trajectory above their heads with a shower of white sparks. Belford reckoned the Talus Shard was *not* ordinary steel!

The young Goblikan raised his hands into the air and the disks sailed straight back to him, landing gently in his open palms. At the same time, the yellow-haired Goblikan slid an amulet out from under her robe and held it up in front of her with both hands. A stone at its center was already glowing. It looked like a massive diamond, about the size of a small chicken egg. Belford knew enough about Power Artifacts to know that anything glowing meant danger. She aimed the central stone directly at him as she stepped out from the shadow of the pyramid. The glow intensified as sunlight struck the stone's surface.

"What do you think that amulet—?" Belford's query was interrupted by a blinding beam of white energy. It erupted from the gem in a brilliant torrent of concentrated fire.

The beam was continuous. It blasted into the promenade, instantly forming a molten streak through the stone as the woman adjusted its trajectory. Belford held his shield up as the beam shifted towards him. He knew the polymer compound could absorbed energy, but the extent of that property was untested.

The young Goblikan's disks were airborne again.

The beam of light struck Belford's shield. He was blinded by the glow as the transparent barrier lit up with the blast.

The over-charged ions radiated with a white glare that felt like looking into the sun. The temperature of the air spiked—waves of heat flowing around the shield. The dry heat licked Belford's skin. It was hotter than the inside of an oven. The glare beat against his face, forcing him to squeeze his eyes shut tight.

"It's reflecting the beam!" Arlin cried. "Quick, rotate a hair to your right!"

Belford couldn't open his eyes, but he did as Arlin instructed, adjusting his forearm to shift the shield ever so slightly.

"A hair more!"

As soon as he moved, there was a clang—the sound of metal hitting the stone of the promenade. The beam ceased abruptly, allowing Belford to see once more.

"Look out!"

Belford spun to his left as one of the young Goblikan's disk-blades closed in. He blocked it with the shield, sending it bouncing off down the street. The disk on the right was already grounded—a hole burned straight through its middle by the reflected energy beam.

The broken disk did not return to the Goblikan when he called for it. He threw one of his gloves on the ground in irritation as the remaining disk sailed back to him alone.

The yellow-haired Goblikan hadn't learned her lesson yet. She lifted her amulet back into the sunlight. Arlin and Grine got behind Belford. Before the stone finished gathering sunlight for another blast, Belford got an idea. He reversed the shape of his shield, bending it from a convex shell over his arm to a concave lens. He placed a layer of material behind the back layer of electrons—a dark cloth. There was another pop as he used more air molecules to form the fabric. He hoped it would block some of the glare from the beam.

The white light found its way to Belford more quickly this time, but he was ready, aiming the shield right back at the three Goblikans. As soon as the beam struck the shield, the young Goblikan cried out, but it was already too late. He was roasted by the reflection, his robes igniting into flames as the beam sliced through him. A surprisingly clean cut. His body fell lifeless to the promenade.

Belford shifted the beam back towards the yellow-haired Goblikan. It swept across in front of her feet, missing her by the smallest margin. She stumbled backwards in surprise. Even though Belford missed, the woman accidentally turned the amulet around on herself as she fell. The fire continued as her screams ceased. The beam burrowed through her chest, the walkway, and down into the earth. The blaze didn't stop until the amulet slid into the hole, blocking it from the sunlight. The woman's corpse smoldered.

Belford immediately felt nauseous, but he didn't have time to dwell on the sight. The pasty Goblikan—the last present threat—had been busy while the others were fighting. Hanging back in the shadows, he transformed three guardsmen into his version of Whunes. The monsters were on their feet, and even more hulking than Wilgoblikan's variety. The pasty Goblikan shoved something into each of the Whune's mouths. Belford was too far away to see exactly what he was doing, but one by one, each of the creatures rushed out into the promenade after receiving their master's offering.

Belford released the shield. He needed to refocus his concentration. He shifted his intentions, imagining picking apart the closest Whune. He called upon the computer, asking it to pry flesh and muscle from bone. He pictured its skin melting away; using the poor creature's internal energies against it; forcing fire to erupt from its very pores—but nothing happened. It was as if it were a wizard—the computer unable to touch it. Belford couldn't affect it directly with the Power. He tried to attack the next Whune back, but the effort was futile. The creatures were extremely fast, bounding over a pair of planters that stood in their way like track stars leaping hurdles.

Belford glanced at Arlin, there was no time to talk, but the swordsman thankfully understood the distress in his expression. Arlin burst forward just in time, his Talas Shard blade still pristine as he directed its point at the first Whune.

The speed of the monster carried it through the blade until the Talas Shard was buried to the hilt in the creature's abdomen. Arlin lost his grip as the Whune's blood covered his hands. The monster thrashed to the side as Arlin attempted to retake the blade, unperturbed by the sword lodged in its middle.

Belford drew the curved ceremonial blade lashed to his hip and tossed it to Arlin with a shout. The swordsman snatched it from the air and swung for the Whune's thick neck. The strike should have severed its head, but to Arlin's chagrin, the blade glanced off, striking some dense, unseen bone placed there by the pale Goblikan to ward off such an attack.

The Whune roared at Arlin, saliva spraying from its mouth. It swiped back at him with its jagged claws. Whatever its master placed in its mouth must have been swallowed.

"It's stomach!" Belford cried out. His instincts told him the small, mysterious object was responsible for preventing him from dismembering the Whune with the Power.

The second of the three creatures was nearly upon them.

Arlin dodged the first Whune's swipe and brought Belford's blade across the creature's abdomen. The weapon tangled with his own sword, still lodged in the monster, but several of its organs splashed out of the gaping wound regardless. The Whune roared again, amazingly still putting up a fight despite the blood and organ loss.

Belford glanced over at Grine. The captain was crouched low to the ground. He was using the Power to slice a stone the size of his head out of the walkway. The second Whune was upon them, joining the first in striking at Arlin. The swordsman scrambled back, nearly tripping over Grine as the Ameliorator hefted the dislodged stone above his head.

Everything seemed to slow down in Belford's eyes. He called upon the computer, directing energy at Grine's stone. Arlin was too close to the first two Whunes to risk aiming at them, so Belford sent the stone lurching sideways with uncanny accuracy towards the third creature, still several paces off. The rock collided with its head, removing it entirely from its shoulders.

He turned back towards the first Whune, trying again to destroy it with the Power. Whatever was stopping him before must have been within the pile of organs at the Whune's feet, because this time the creature's blood boiled. It collapsed into a steaming pile of flesh.

Arlin retrieved his blade, wielding both swords at once as he expertly picked the last remaining Whune apart. It was still alive, but incapacitated with many of its tendons severed. It gurgled on the bloodied promenade.

The pasty Goblikan fled out of sight, back into the pyramid.

The Whune's extra-thick skull prevented Arlin from ending its life. He handed Belford back his blade before crouching down beside the still writhing creature and sliced its stomach out, lifting the organ up in his hands. Belford quickly finished it off with the Power. Globs of black blood poured down Arlin's arms as he squeezed the contents of the stomach back through the severed esophageal tube. The guard's mostly digested breakfast was joined by a small metallic orb that looked like a silver marble. Arlin quickly wiped the device on his tunic, removing as much stomach goop and blood as he could before tossing it in his mouth. He shifted it to the back of his throat, making a pained expression as he swallowed it down.

Belford grimaced.

Arlin caught the look of repulsion but said nothing.

"That's an Artifact! You've no idea what it might do!" warned Grine.

Arlin spit several times to clear some of the tainted saliva from his mouth. "If it stops the Goblikans from using the

Power against me, I'll take the risk," he said once he was finished.

Grine and Belford shared a look of concern as Grine handed Belford back his jacket. They didn't waste any more time. With the pasty Goblikan somewhere ahead of them, they raced into the heart of the pyramid like foolish prey into a lion's den.

CHAPTER

50

Abomination

"Didn't we already try this passageway?" asked Lieutenant Canbel. "I swear we passed this painting already." He pointed at a fresco of a giant winged grizzly bear eating a barbarian. The barbarian was still alive, trying to crawl away from the mythical creature, though half his body was already consumed. The artist had spent considerable time etching the veil of death falling over the barbarian's expression—horror, shock, regret.

Imaginative, thought Shiara. She couldn't help but roll her eyes. Garrett's palace had a brutal aesthetic. Always with the death and dismemberment. *We get it, you're a scary overlord who kills everyone who stands in your way.*

"No. It just looks similar," said Thorin. "The walls are getting slightly closer together the deeper we move."

"But the painting…."

"Keep moving," said Livian. "The whole palace is built like a maze—we did pass an identical painting, no doubt intended to confuse invaders such as ourselves. We are on the right path."

"Hmm," said Deenan, frowning. "I'm not so sure we are. That one was supposed to depict a coiled snake under a log, if Wilgoblikan's words were true." Deenan's transformation into looking like King Garrett was complete. His skin was tighter now, but he was still offputtingly ugly. He glanced over at Shiara, his frown deepening as he caught the disgusted expression on her face.

Shiara broke the eye contact first. She let out a sigh as the group continued walking through the endless corridors.

"How certain are we in our directions?" Canbel asked Ethan.

Ethan didn't respond, focusing only on the path ahead. Shiara could read uncertainty behind his deep blue eyes. Ethan slowed at the next intersection, studying the unmarked walls for any indication of the correct path. He started down the right branch—a random choice.

It had been some time now since they'd happened upon anyone in the hallways. This close to their target, the lack of guards was disturbing. Gas torches lit the path, stretching shadows across the smooth plastered walls. Their footsteps echoed down the corridors, paved with sandstone blocks.

Ahead, a high-ceilinged, tiled chamber promised a possible end to the maze of passageways. Ethan entered slowly at the front of the pack. A strange feeling coalesced in Shiara's gut—something wasn't right. At the center of the wide room stood a hulking statue of a monster quite foul. With a massive lizard tail to balance its weight, it stood upright on its thick back legs, its head nearly scraping the ceiling of the two-story high chamber. Its front arms were short to the point of uselessness, but its massive head housed a set of jaws big enough to swallow a horse whole with teeth sharp enough to chomp one in half. Its snout would have looked right at home on a giant crocodile. Shiara had never seen anything like it before, and hoped she never would, especially if the statue was to scale.

Ethan stood in stunned silence as the rest of the raiding party filed in behind him. "He better not have any god damned dinosaurs," Ethan said under his breath.

Everyone spread out to get a better view of the unnerving statue. Lieutenant Canbel stepped up beside Shiara. "The Goblikan didn't say anything about this," he said, shaking his head.

Shiara stared up at the mouth of jagged teeth. The fine detail on the statue made it feel almost alive.

Beside her, Canbel shifted forward on his feet. In a stroke of fatefully bad luck, the Lieutenant's boots compressed a hidden trigger in one of the floor tiles.

With a scrape, a huge block of sandstone dropped from the ceiling. Thorin's hand shot out and grabbed Shiara by the wrist. He yanked her sideways, jarringly. Shiara clung to his massive bicep as she slammed into his chest. The falling block missed her by a hair. Canbel was on the floor beside them, having barely managed to dive out of the way in time. Bits of tile shot across the chamber as the multi-ton block pulverized a wide swath of flooring around its point of impact.

Shiara looked up at Thorin. She didn't need to tell him how grateful she was. He patted her on the head as he set her down squarely on her feet.

"Way to go," Livian said dryly. "You've barricaded us in."

Canbel's limbs twitched as adrenaline coursed through his veins. The expression on his face indicated a change of pants might be in order. He climbed slowly to his feet, red with embarrassment.

Shiara was shaken as well. The nervous pinch in her gut intensified.

"Move the block," ordered Ethan. "We may have to come back this way."

Deenan approached the fallen block as everyone else cleared out of the way. The powerful Illusionist took a deep breath. The heavy stone would take more concentration and energy to move than Shiara was capable of conjuring.

Suddenly, Deenan cried out. He cradled his head in his hands, agony etched across his twisted face.

"What's wrong?!" asked Livian.

Deenan shook his head violently from side to side. "It's the Power… something's stopping me from reaching it!"

The statement caused a sudden panic. Across the room, everyone attempted to conjure the Power simultaneously. Everything felt normal to Shiara as she filled her body with energy, but as soon as she attempted to channel it outwards, a burning sensation flashed like fire behind her eyes. The pain nearly dropped her to the floor. The searing heat continued like a sharp migraine even as she released her hold on the energy. She, too, found herself shaking her head as if she could pour the fire from her ears. No one else was any more successful.

"It must be some sort of Artifact…" said Ethan. Worry was clear in his voice. In all their planning, a possibility such as this had never even been considered.

The floor and walls of the chamber began to rumble again. Everyone's eyes shot to the ceiling, watching anxiously for more falling blocks.

"The statue!" cried Canbel, bringing Shiara's gaze back down. Chunks of stone fell like melting plaster from the statue's scaly underbelly. An outer shell was falling away, exposing a rippling hide of real nightmarish flesh beneath.

"Run!" boomed Thorin's deep voice.

Shiara looked back. Ethan was already halfway across the chamber, sprinting towards the only unblocked passageway on the far side of the room. Shiara joined the rest of the raiding party fleeing towards the exit. A mighty roar from the awakened beast nearly shook her heart out of her chest.

Before she reached the exit, the tile-shattering bang of the monster's steps sounded behind her.

Clomp. Clomp. Clomp.

In the hallway ahead, the ceiling remained high, and the walls wide enough for the giant beast at their backs to pursue them—and it did. The rumbling footsteps picked up pace.

Clomp, clomp, clomp, clomp, clomp.

Just in front of her, Lieutenant Canbel glanced back at the gaining monster. The look of sheer terror on his face was enough to motivate Shiara's legs into the fastest sprint she'd ever attempted. She overtook Canbel and was right on Thorin's heels.

A moment later, Canbel's scream pierced the corridor.

Crunch.

His cry was silenced. The monster stopped only briefly to swallow its snack. Canbel was devoured completely.

Clomp. Clomp.

It was moving again.

Clomp, clomp, CLOMP, CLOMP.

In a flood of panic, Shiara reached for the Power once more, filling it into every fiber of her being.

Please, Great Goddess, let it flow through me!

Still running, Shiara tested her connection, attempting to conjure a small burst of air, but whatever was blocking her connection remained strong. Fire stung at her brain and clouded over her eyes with its soot. She stumbled forward, losing all control of her sprint.

Thorin slowed his stride. He took Shiara's hand and helped steady her failing legs, keeping her moving.

"Stop saving me!" Shiara puffed. "You're going to get yourself eaten too!"

Thorin gripped tighter onto Shiara's hand in response.

"We can't outrun it!" Livian shouted up to Ethan.

Everyone was straining to keep up their pace.

"What else can we do?" Ethan wheezed.

Livian stopped suddenly, reaching into one of the pockets of her petticoat as she turned towards the demon-spawn behind them. She withdrew a vial from her pocket. Whatever her plan, Livian's bravery was inspirational—Deenan and Ethan slowed and looked back, though perhaps they were simply too winded to continue. Shiara shook free of Thorin's grasp and went to Livian's side. Thorin, not one to shy away from danger, stopped as well. It was time to make a stand.

Livian held up the tiny glass vial. It was marked only with a black inked *X*—some premade batch of spores. While only Livian knew what the spores might do, the ingenuity of her plan got Shiara thinking as well.

Shiara knew she could not channel the Power, but perhaps her firestone earring was immune. Artifacts channeled differently than wizards—she could even use the firestone when the moon was down. It was worth a shot, and there was no time for hesitation. Shiara focused her thoughts on the jewel dangling from her right ear. It was the same concentration she used to reach the Power, but instead of reaching inward on her own ability, she put her mind into the core of the Artifact. The gem could draw energy from the environment, more than should have been able to fit into such a tiny space. She urged the gem to absorb energy in front of her now—it took a gentle hand, rather than a commanding will as most people who knew of the Artifact's abilities assumed.

Unleash your mighty touch, my friend, she thought to it, treating it with the respect it deserved. The air rippled in front of the monster as it barreled down upon them. She could already feel the stone radiating with captured energy. She hoped it could hold enough to stop the massive beast.

The monster crashed into the cloud of distorted air without hesitation. A static shock burst from its chest, singeing Shiara's earlobe as the gem sucked up every electron it could find.

The creature was not subdued the way a smaller animal or human would have been, but it did stumble from the shock. Livian used the opportunity to strike. She threw her vial of spores at the monster's face. The glass shattered against its jagged teeth

The beast roared, sending a shudder of horror down Shiara's spine as she thought about poor Lieutenant Canbel.

"Don't breathe any of that in!" Livian warned as she turned to run.

Shiara followed suit. She spun around, cringing slightly as the now scalding-hot gemstone bumped against the side of her head.

Thorin did not join them. He readied his cudgel defiantly.

The combination of the spores and Shiara's Artifact was already taking its toll on the monster. It snapped at Thorin, but he dodged sideways, simultaneously clocking it upside its snout. Several teeth broke loose, falling to the floor like raining stalactites.

Thorin dueled with the creature. Its attack slowed with every missed snap of its jaws. Thorin's cudgel was unforgiving. Every dodged attack was another strike of the mighty hammer against the beast's face.

The monster's demeanor suddenly changed. It hunched its head forward and opened its jaws wide as if to roar, but instead of a mighty growl, a geyser of dark blood erupted from its gaping maw. Thorin barely dodged the stream of bloody vomit. The creature collapsed onto its side, rattling the whole hallway. It continued to spew blood until the puddle was twice the size of its massive body.

"The spores have done their job," said Livian.

Deenan and Ethan rejoined them, watching the beast's final moments as it writhed around on the floor, its stubby arms twitching all the while.

"You truly are a scary wench," said Deenan.

"Thank you," said Livian.

Shiara clasped onto Thorin's arm, hugging him tightly. His muscles eased beneath her grip.

"What on Earth was that abomination?" asked Deenan.

Livian threw her braid back over her shoulder. "Whatever it was, there's no turning back now," she said. "Let's find Garrett and end this madness once and for all."

They all turned away from the deceased beast and moved deeper into the palace. The winding corridors continued until a static tingle in the air signaled yet another deadly threat. Unstoppable glowing tendrils flowed through the hallway; ghostly arms that slid through stone and flesh alike. There was nowhere to run and nothing to fight as the streams of energy entered their bodies and gripped onto their minds. Thorin tried to shield Shiara from the attack, spinning her around and embracing her in a tight hug. Shiara's last thoughts were for Thorin—her noble companion. He had always been there for her, through all of their many struggles; numerous near disasters, barely averted. Perhaps they'd tried their luck one too many times.

His arms squeezed unbearably tight as the electric shock took hold of his muscles. There was no defense against the stinging energies. It filled their surroundings. Darkness came in an instant, leaving a nothingness that was all encompassing.

CHAPTER

51

Shadow

"Where the hell did he go?" asked Belford. The pasty Goblikan hadn't had much of a head start, but somehow he'd evaporated into the sprawling complex of tunnels without a trace.

"I'm not sure, but I think we're lost…" said Grine.

Belford glanced around helplessly. "Isn't that the same painting as before?"

Grine and Arlin stopped beside Belford. All three studied the painting for a moment. "It does look the same…" said Grine, "could we have looped back around?"

"I haven't a clue," said Arlin with a shrug. "I've just been following you."

Down the hall, the path split in two directions. "Which way did we go the last time we were here?" asked Belford.

Arlin narrowed his eyes in thought as he gazed down the corridor. "I do believe we took the left branch."

Belford set off down the right branch this time, taking the lead from Grine. He picked up the pace when a nearby crash shook the stone beneath their feet. As they neared the source of the clatter, a bend in the passageway prompted renewed caution. They slowed and crept up to the blind corner. Suddenly, Belford's own shadow caught his eye, giving him a start. A change in the lighting sent it stretching long against the wall. It loomed above him like a dark cloud. He tried to shake off some of his nerves before peering anxiously around the corner.

There was movement ahead. He withdrew his face before being seen and threw a gesture towards Grine and Arlin.

He drew a deep breath and went to peek out again, but Arlin tapped him on the shoulder. Belford turned around. Arlin pointed to the curved blade sheathed at Belford's side and mouthed the word "reflection." Belford nodded in understanding. He silently unsheathed his shiny blade and held the tip out just far enough around the corner to use it like a mirror to spy upon the passage without being noticed.

Just ahead, the pasty Goblikan stood at the end of a sealed passage. A massive block of stone filled the doorway there. The Goblikan's attention was engrossed in studying the rock wall to the left of the barricade. His boney fingers slid along the cracks between the rocks. He pressed in once he found what he was looking for and a narrow passageway opened in the previously solid wall.

From within a panel just inside the secret passage, the Goblikan pried a cylindrical tube free from some wiring and discarded it on the floor. He disappeared into the tunnel and did not reemerge.

Belford's group cautiously approached the secret passageway. It was dark inside, but clearly ran deep, snaking between the walls of the main passageways. Belford picked up the tube the Goblikan had discarded. It was made of metal, but was warm to the touch. Looking inside the panel it was removed from, it was clear to Belford that it was some sort of massive battery. There was no indication as to what it had been powering.

Before Belford could give it any more thought, a soul-rending roar echoed from beyond the blocked passage. The screams that followed could belong to no other than Ethan's party.

My friends are in trouble!

Throwing caution to the wind, Belford immediately filled his body with energy and took aim at the barricade. He directed a massive burst of force at the block. It should have been sufficient to throw the mass of an elephant or two across the room, but his gathered energy had other plans. Instead of flowing outward, the energy stagnated inside of him. A static field escaped his fingertips—a million tiny lightning bolts bursting from his flesh. The pain of the energy leaving his body was nothing compared to the feeling in his brain. The veins in his temples constrict, spiking his blood pressure and making him feel as if he'd been kicked in the head.

He fell to his knees, landing hard as he cried out. Arlin and Grine glanced about the hallway for external enemies to explain Belford's behavior, but found none. Once the pain began to subside, Belford climbed unsteadily to his feet.

"I can't use the Power," he explained. "Garrett's Artifact must be restricting my control already."

Grine yelped as he made his own lesser attempt.

The ramifications of not being able to use the Power were more than just worrisome. Belford kept his curved blade unsheathed, though his skill in using it was non-existent. He looked to Arlin, the only capable fighter amongst them. Panic clutched his insides. "What do we do?!"

Arlin put his palm to the barricade, feeling its unmoving mass. Another roar from the chamber beyond was followed by pounding footsteps moving into the distance. "I do not believe going back is an option at this point." Arlin turned away from the blocked passage and strode into the secret tunnel. "Follow me," he said. The Talus Shard blade gleamed in his hands. "I will keep you safe."

The passage was dark and at times barely shoulder's width wide, but Arlin lead them forward with reckless abandon. Belford's thoughts were calmed by the realization that if Garrett's Artifact was responsible for stopping them from reaching the Power, that meant only Garrett would be able to channel within its vicinity. The pasty Goblikan and anyone else would be left at the mercy of Arlin's sword.

After a few twists and turns left the passageway in total darkness, Arlin slowed his pace. Belford's anxiety spiked. He never used to have a fear of the dark, but feeling along with his fingertips against the wall suddenly stirred up the memory of the dark cave in which he and Arlin first became acquainted. The claws and teeth of a Whune could be around any corner. Belford wished he could create some sort of light source, but Garrett's Artifact rendered him completely useless. The moon might as well have been down.

Belford gave a sigh of relief as the hidden passage came to an end, opening back into another oil-lamp lit corridor. His relief was short lived as footsteps became audible ahead. Arlin paused, still in the lead. The tension in his back was like a compressed spring—a jungle cat ready to pounce.

The pasty Goblikan ambled by the opening, breathing hard. He was looking back as if being followed. Arlin held his position within the secret passage, though he had been ready to strike. Another set of footsteps approached from the distance. Arlin waited.

The adrenaline pumping through Belford's veins made the seconds pass by at a crawl.

"We'll take the next one first, then go after the Goblikan," whispered Arlin.

Finally, a guardsman's uniform flashed across the opening of the passage. Arlin lunged. The attack caught the guard by surprise, but the man deftly avoided Arlin's blade as the two tumbled to the floor. An instant later, a ring on one of the guardsman's fingers flashed blue and Arlin was propelled into the air with uncanny force. He smashed against the ceiling and landed hard on the floor with a thud. He did not rise immediately.

The guardsman turned towards Belford and Captain Grine, still standing within the narrow hidden passage. The man was no guard… Belford recognized him immediately.

The Crimson Stalker!

The last time he saw those malicious gray eyes, the monstrous man was slitting the throat of a young street urchin in North Galdren.

Belford tried to strike out with the Power, forgetting for an unfortunate moment that he was still under the influence of Garrett's Artifact. The fear in his heart held the pain that followed at bay. Once again, Belford was face-to-face with evil, and once again, he was powerless to stop it.

The Crimson Stalker pointed at Belford and immediately his lungs compressed with pressure as if a rock were weighing on his chest. The terrifying man was using the Power even though Garrett's Artifact should have stopped him.

Always doing the impossible.

Belford wanted to run—or attack—or do anything—but he was frozen stiff. He was paralyzed just as the poor street urchin had been, right before his slaughter.

Belford tried to turn to locate Captain Grine, praying for some sort of help, but even his head was frozen in place. Every muscle within him constricted at once. His whole body felt like it was cramping. The pain blinded him—his range of vision literally going dark around the edges. It was a wonder he even remained on his feet.

With his ability to move gone, Belford's mind searched desperately for a solution to his precarious predicament. His connection to the computer would normally have prevented him from being attacked directly with the Power, and yet here he was, frozen. His head felt like it might explode from the pressure. Garrett's Artifact must have completely blocked the computer from recognizing him as a protected user. His ability to even comprehend what was going on was fading quickly.

The Crimson Stalker walked up to him with recognition clear in his gray eyes. Although he hadn't seen Belford in North Galdren, the man appeared once in his dreams using the brass spyglass Artifact. There was absolutely nothing Belford could do to defend himself. The Crimson Stalker just stood there, looking at him with silent contempt in his stare. His eyes shifted behind Belford as a thud sounded several paces back.

Belford guessed Captain Grine was held stiff as well, but had been less secure on his footing and toppled over onto the floor. He would be of no help. The Crimson Stalkers eyes returned to Belford without worry.

Arlin, just within Belford's line of sight in the hallway, rose to his feet and used the minor distraction of Grine falling over to leap onto the Crimson Stalker's back.

The Crimson Stalker grunted as he tried to throw Arlin from him, but Arlin was already locked in around the man's throat with his forearm. The Crimson Stalker gestured several times at Arlin's legs as they flailed from side to side, but his attacks had no effect on the swordsman.

So he can attack me, *a Ver'ati, with the Power, but he can't use it on Arlin, an ordinary swordsman.... None of this makes any damn sense!*

Belford's only guess was that the Artifact Arlin swallowed was preventing the Crimson Stalker's attack. At least there was some limit to the man's abilities.

Before Arlin could subdue him, the Crimson Stalker's ring flashed blue again, this time aimed at the floor. Both men flew violently into the air. Arlin took the brunt of the hit against the ceiling, falling from the man's back as they landed again hard.

Arlin rose to his feet quickly, this time scrambling for his sword. It was lying against the side of the hallway. The

Crimson Stalker gestured at the blade just as Arlin reached for it. Belford felt a magnetic tug on his own blade, still sheathed at his side. The pull nearly yanked him onto his face, but his feet were planted squarely. The magnetic tug pulled Arlin's weapon out of reach, towards the Crimson Stalker.

Although the Crimson Stalker couldn't affect Arlin with the Power directly, the armor he was wearing was apparently not protected by the Artifact in his stomach. The Crimson Stalker used his magnetism control to repel Arlin's armor now, effectively pinning him against the wall. Arlin struggled against the hold of his chainmail, but could do little more than wiggle under the pressure of the linked metal.

The Crimson Stalker drew the straight razor he had used on the little boy in North Galdren from his pocket and slowly unfolded the blade as he approached Arlin.

Helpless.

Arlin continued to thrash about for a moment, but ceased his struggles when he realized the futility.

The men looked each other over one last time.

The Crimson Stalker raised the razor to Arlin's throat.

Arlin accepted his fate. He lifted his chin, fully exposing his jugular vein, and gave the Crimson Stalker the most steely-eyed stare Belford had ever seen.

Nooo!

Belford wanted to cry out, but his vocal cords were frozen along with the rest of his body.

The blade ran deep.

Neither Arlin nor the Crimson Stalker flinched.

Blood poured endlessly down Arlin's front.

The Crimson Stalker wiped the blade clean on Arlin's sleeve before letting go of his magnetic hold over the chainmail.

Arlin crumpled to the floor.

The Crimson Stalker gave Belford one last irritated glance before continuing down the hallway in the same direction as the pasty Goblikan.

CHAPTER

52

The Smell of Blood

A twinkle appeared in the darkness, like starlight from a solitary sun glimmering in the distance. Just a pinprick at first, but it drew her forward, calling to her from out of the vast nothingness. Her existence was bleak; so cold; frozen in a world of permafrost. The light flashed and spun and sent tiny sparks drifting to her subdued consciousness. Little promises—gifts of heat and sensation. She reached for the light, but it was too far away. The shadows danced around the glow in a mesmerizing spectacle.

She'd been content in the void—no feelings, no pain, just emptiness—but now she couldn't imagine her world returning to darkness. She stretched out as far as she could, determined to touch just one spark as it drifted by. An ember took pity on her, drifting toward her outstretched limb. She snatched it up as soon as it came within reach.

It sunk inside of her.

Changes began immediately.

The star pulsed and grew, heat filling back into the world. She knew the sensation was familiar. It brought memory with it. The softness of her mother's touch; the curious intrigue of childhood; her first brush with the Power—it stung like a static shock across her nerve endings, but became pleasurable as she went on, almost addictive as she sipped in the energy again and again. The world bowed to her.

Shiara breathed it in.

The memories multiplied, one leading to the next in a surge of conscious energy. A more immediate memory came to her: A terrible jolt—the one that locked her in this nothingness in the first place. She'd been filled with a biting pain that froze her stiff and pinched at her mind unforgivingly.

She had no idea how long she'd been trapped—there was no sense of time in the void.

Her mission came back to her—Tavallon, King Garrett, Ethan's plan, the horrifying monster that devoured Lieutenant Sulinton.... She remembered being blocked from the Power by some Artifact—something no one anticipated. Livian and Ethan led the way deeper into the twisting maze of a palace with Deenan at their heels. Thorin stayed by her side— always the protector. There was a concentrated intensity in his movements. Even without the Power, he would smash the skull of any fiend who dared oppose him.

As consciousness slowly returned to Shiara, pain became the primary sensation in her mind. There was the general ache of her exhausted muscles—tired from being strained during the electric shock that put her under—and the bite of the hard floor beneath her spine, but there was also a burning sensation like a hot poker pressing against the side of her neck. The searing pain quickly out-weighed everything else. It screamed at her to wake up—to do something—anything— to stop the burning.

She was pulled from her haze in a jarring instant.

Before she even opened her eyes, she knew the cause of her torment: Her firestone earring Artifact had yet to cool down after draining the life force from the giant monster. The gem was against her skin. She immediately turned her head to the right so the dangling Artifact would fall away from her frying flesh. The pain, of course, continued, even after the earring shifted into an air-gapped position.

Shiara sat up, panting as she opened her eyes.

Up a short set of steps, a young man sat upon an overly ornate throne. He had a bored expression on his face as he tapped his fingers across a scepter in his right hand. It took Shiara a second to realize who she was looking at: Garrett Rames—chubbier and considerably more youthful than Deenan's version. He locked his eyes on Shiara. Interpreting her pained expression as fear, he smiled menacingly.

Shiara tried to rise but found a metal collar fitted around her neck, chaining her to the throne room floor. It yanked her back down to her knees. Her eyes scanned her surroundings.

Garrett's throne room was vast. Tall tapestries lined the walls on either side of the throne. A second-story balcony ran along the sides and back of the chamber, overlooking the court from beyond a banister fit with arches. The balcony was supported by dozens of narrow pillars that joined the arches above.

The rest of the raiding party was lined up on either side of her, chained down as well. To her right, Deenan was on the end, followed by Ethan, and then Livian. Livian sat cross-legged with her arms across her breasts. Her blouse was torn, only held up by her hands. She scowled at several guardsmen standing to the right of Garrett and his throne.

To her left, Thorin was chained in a kneeling position. He glanced over at her. His eyes blazed with fury, but softened ever so slightly when he took in her concerned expression. Shiara had been the last to wake. Apparently, her return to consciousness was what Garrett had been waiting on.

The King rose, using his long scepter like a cane on the shiny marble flooring. A clear gem at the scepter's top glowed white with a faint shine.

Garrett opened his mouth, but before he could speak, a bald Goblikan in a dark robe hurried into the chamber from an entrance to the left of the throne. Garrett shot him a dirty look, but waited as he approached. He ran up the steps of the throne platform and whispered something into Garrett's ear. A fleck of concern crossed Garrett's face.

"Secure the hall while I speak with our guests," Garrett commanded.

The guards to his side hustled to join several others at the side of the chamber, disappearing through the doorway from which the Goblikan entered.

"Excuse my rudeness," said Garrett. "This here is my Monster Master, Dhron Cain. I believe you've already met some of his handiwork."

Dhron's lack of any hair, including eyebrows, made him look like a naked mole rat as his beady eyes panned emotionlessly across the Ver'ati chained at his feet. His bald head shined with reflected light from the flames of the many oil lamps that lit the chamber.

"I'm sure you have noticed by now that you cannot reach the Power," Garrett continued. "You are entirely cutoff, but I am not." He tapped his glowing scepter idly with his fingertips. "This is how I create my Goblikans," he said. "You cannot resist me." He left Dhron beside the throne as he stepped down the stairs towards Ethan.

His nonchalant attitude was terrifying to Shiara. He knew he'd won. They were entirely at his mercy.

"You're looking youthful as well, I see," Garrett said in a cheerful tone once he was face-to-face with Ethan. "Did you enjoy that shock I gave you?" He leaned in close, just out of Ethan's reach. "I learned that trick from Michelle. Zapping, she called it. It was a pity I had to waste such talent. She cried out for you in the end."

Ethan screamed and flailed uselessly at Garrett. His face turned beet red. Garrett stared at Ethan, unflinching. He waited until Ethan subsided and sat back on his legs.

"All of you will serve me," said Garrett, glancing up and down the line. "Well… almost all of you. I can't let this little attempt on my life go entirely unpunished, now can I?" He began to pace in front of his captives. "You see, one of you has to die." He stopped in front of Shiara, looking her up and down with a smirk. He glanced back over at Ethan. "Don't worry, my old friend," he said, "I'm not going to choose you. You're too powerful to waste."

Shiara held her breath as Garrett's eyes returned to her. She felt filthy under his gaze.

He studied her for a moment longer before starting to pace again. When he reached Deenan he laughed openly. "And this one!" he shook his head, grinning. "How'd you get him to look exactly like the *old* me? Hmm. This nose isn't quite correct, but I still wouldn't feel right killing myself." Garrett cocked his head. "I think I might have some use for you after a few alterations. Having a body double around could come in handy." He turned away from Deenan. "That just leaves the oaf and these two fine ladies. So which one of you will it be?"

The clink of Thorin's chains stole Shiara's attention. She took her eyes off Garrett for the first time since his approach. Thorin grabbed his chain with both hands and pulled with all his might. Garrett watched, unconcerned, while Thorin tried to break free. The metal creaked and groaned but the chains held strong. After nearly a minute, Garrett grew tired of Thorin's thrashing. With the tinniest of gestures, a flash of blue energy shot out from Garrett's fingertips and into Thorin's body. He collapsed, convulsing for a moment while steam drifted up from his head.

"Don't make me do that again," said Garrett.

Thorin gave up. He struggled to sit back up on his legs, exhausted. He was breathing hard. "Choose me," he said.

Shiara's heart dropped. There was nothing she could do. She reached for the Power despite knowing it was useless. The pain of being blocked by Garrett's Artifact pounded behind her eyes. The gem in Garrett's scepter glowed brighter as she made her attempt.

Garrett laughed again. "Did you really think I was going to let you decide? You are powerless. The death is mine to choose." He walked up to Livian and extended a finger to caress the side of her face. "And I think I've made my choice."

Livian's expression was far less concerned than it should have been. Shiara couldn't figure out why the Illusionist didn't look terrified. In an unexpected move, Livian dropped her hands to her sides. Her blouse fell, exposing her left breast. She shimmied her chest slightly, shaking the right one free as well. Shiara spied Livian's hand disappearing into her pocket while Garrett was distracted.

"You don't get a free pass just because you have nice tits," said Garrett.

"But I'll be a good girl for you," said Livian, giving them another shake. "Don't you want a touch? I won't bite."

Shiara imagined she could see the animalistic urges pulsing through Garrett's veins. *Might he really be so stupid?*

Garrett sneered. "What makes you think I didn't already get a feel while you were unconscious?" He chuckled to himself. "Besides, if I were to lean forward, I have a feeling you might try to do something with whatever that is you have gripped in your fist."

Livian withdrew her hand from her pocket like a scorpion's tail and threw a glass vial with deadly precision at Garrett's face. It smashed against his temple as he tried to dodge. The vial shattered, releasing a concentrated dose of spores right to Garrett's nostrils.

"I didn't actually need you to come closer," said Livian.

Garrett jumped back, his temple bleeding where the glass shards sliced into him. "What did you do, you bitch?!"

Dhron, the Monster Master, rushed to Garrett's aid, but Garrett put his hand up to stop him. Shiara couldn't help but smile. It was Garrett's turn to start spewing blood, just like the giant monster!

Livian looked over at Shiara and Thorin. "I'm sorry," she said, with a small frown.

Shiara didn't understand. Garrett sat on the bottom step of his throne platform, staring at Livian.

"What...?" Garrett started, a confused expression on his face. "Such perfection..." he said. "This woman! This woman...! You shall be my queen!" Garrett exclaimed.

Shiara finally understood. The spores Livian used were not the same as the ones that killed the monster.

"May my friends be pardoned?" Livian asked.

Dhron gasped. "No, my king!"

"Silence!" shouted Garrett, rising from the step. "You shall be my queen, but you have no say in such matters. These people tried to kill me, and they must be punished. Now, where was I?" Garrett honed back in on Shiara and Thorin.

"I'm so sorry," Livian whispered.

Garrett walked up to Thorin and put his finger in his face. "This one," he said. "Dhron, take the brute's head."

"But, Master, the Ver'ati witch has manipulated you..." said Dhron.

"You dare question me?!" Garret screamed.

Dhron drew a long dagger from his belt and approached Thorin hesitantly.

Shiara's heart was racing. She wanted to scream, if only it would do any good. Thorin was her closest friend; her confidant; *my protector*.... There were tears in her eyes as she looked upon him. Each teardrop stung as it came out. "Please, no..." she begged.

But Dhron did not listen. He put his blade to Thorin's throat.

"It's okay," said Thorin, still stoic. "I'll see you in another life."

Shiara could hardly see through her tears. "But you don't believe in such things...."

Thorin shrugged.

Dhron watched the exchange with mild interest.

"You'll be okay," said Thorin. "Tell my story one day."

Shiara sobbed.

"My king?" asked Dhron.

Garrett sneered. "I said do it, already."

The first slice was all Shiara saw. She buried her head in her arms. As Dhron went to work, Shiara lowered her face to the floor and rocked back and forth. The sound of the sawing was sickening. The metallic scent of blood permeated the air. A thud sounded as Thorin's body fell to the floor. Dhron did not stop until the job was done.

"Here you are, my king," he said, presenting Garrett with Thorin's severed head.

"Gross, I don't want that," said Garrett. "Throw it away, and have someone clean up your mess."

Shiara felt wetness touch her arm as the pool of blood quickly expanded. It was still warm. She had nowhere to go as it washed over her. She dared not open her eyes. The oblivion of the void would have been a dream come true. She wished to turn her mind off again.

No pain, no emotions, no memories....

Soon she would be twisted into one of Garrett's minions. Perhaps it would come as a reprieve. At least then she would not have to feel like herself anymore.

Triage

Arlin's severed jugular was gushing blood at an alarming rate. His tunic, saturated, turned almost black in the low-light of the corridor. A puddle formed beneath him, and his head lulled forward, tucking the gaping wound between his chin and chest. He had little time left, but there was nothing Belford could do without a connection to the Power. Frozen in place by the Crimson Stalker's unbridled abilities, Belford could only watch as the life drained from his friend's eyes.

With a head rush akin to vertigo, the Crimson Stalker's hold over Belford's body suddenly dissipated. The haunting man vanished out of sight down the long hallway. Belford's muscles loosened and his blood pressure diminished to a more natural level. On wobbly legs, he stumbled to Arlin's side.

Behind him, Captain Grine climbed to his feet—freed from the Crimson Stalker's grasp as well. Grine sighed. "Two experienced Ameliorators, an easily sealable wound, and yet there's nothing we can do…" Grine lamented.

Arlin, somehow still conscious, fluttered his eyelashes.

Belford couldn't stand by and do nothing. "Give me your shirt," he ordered Grine. A tourniquet wouldn't save Arlin's life, but with luck it might slow his bleeding enough to move him out of the Power-blocking Artifact's range.

Grine stared at Belford, confused. He was so used to using only the Power to heal that he lacked basic medical skills.

With no time to waste, Belford grabbed Grine's arm. "Don't move," he said. Wide-eyed, Grine did as he was told. Belford awkwardly unsheathed his curved sword and placed the tip of the blade against Grine's sleeve at his shoulder. He sliced at the fabric with one hand, tugging hard on the sleeve with the other. Grine winced as Belford's blade dug too deep and grazed his flesh. Finally, Belford was able to rip the cloth free.

Kneeling down, Belford tipped Arlin's head back to expose the wound. The flesh was cut smoothly. A gush of blood pulsed out. Air bubbles wheezed through the slit as well—Arlin's esophagus was punctured. Belford wrapped Grine's sleeve around Arlin's throat, swiftly tying it into a knot. He tugged the sleeve snug, making it as tight as he dared.

As soon as Belford finished, Arlin coughed, rocketing a throat-full of blood onto Belford's shirt. More blood dribbled down Arlin's chin, adding to the goopy mess below.

Belford grabbed Arlin's right arm while Grine, finally understanding Belford's intentions, got under Arlin's left arm.

They moved together, Arlin's dangling feet dragging between them. The hidden passage they emerged from was too narrow for the three to walk abreast, so they shuffled down the hallway in the opposite direction as the Crimson Stalker instead. Belford just hoped they would be able to get away from the Power-blocking Artifact in time.

The area of the pyramid they first entered while in pursuit of the pasty Goblikan was a maze, built to stop or delay intruders, but here, beyond the secret passage, they found themselves in the portion actually used by Garrett and his staff. They passed servant sleeping quarters and dining halls, closets and drawing rooms—all empty. Garrett must have removed his staff from the premises in preparation for Ethan's assault. Belford was grateful to avoid everyone. Any delay would spell a swift end to Arlin's chances of survival.

Farther ahead, a guardsmen's barracks held a startlingly grizzly sight. All of the guards were dead. Body parts were strewn about. It was impossible to say how many had been present for the massacre. The blood bath coated the ceiling and walls. An arm was literally dangling from one of the chandeliers! It looked as if every one of the men spontaneously split into fifty pieces and splattered all over the chamber.

Belford's stomach turned.

Could our raiding party have done this?

Belford reached for the Power and attempted a tiny kinetic burst against the air to test his connection. He felt the pinch in his head that told him he was still under the Power-blocking Artifact's influence. There was nothing natural about the scene in front of him. With no bloody footprints leaving the chamber to suggest a physical attack, Belford knew this was done with the Power.

The Crimson Stalker? Or some horrible Artifact?

He had always assumed the Crimson Stalker was one of Garrett's agents. Perhaps his assumptions were wrong.... The terrifying man defied all logic.

The worried look on the pasty Goblikan's face earlier when he ran past the hidden passage suddenly made sense. He must have seen what happened here. There wasn't time to ponder the ramifications of the Crimson Stalker being an agent of some unknown third party. He and Grine continued to drag Arlin, now completely limp, down the hallway.

More sliced-up bodies appeared as they retraced the Crimson Stalker's path of destruction.

Why didn't he do that to me? Those chilling gray eyes....

Belford wasn't looking forward to the nightmares he knew he'd have if he managed to survive the day. The Crimson Stalker left him frozen, but alive... it was almost like a dare. Belford was meant to stand there and watch as Arlin bled out—punishment for getting in the way.

Ahead, the corridor ended with a solid wall. Belford's heart sank. They wouldn't be able to move any farther away, and without the Power, Arlin really was dead. Up until now, his periodic attempts at using the Power all failed. With just a few steps to the end of the hallway, he tried again. He could feel the Power inside of him, but still it would not obey. It burned as it slipped from his grasp. With nowhere left to go, he and Grine placed Arlin down at the very end of the hallway.

Arlin slumped onto his back, unconscious and pale as the death that would shortly take him. The makeshift tourniquet was already soaked through. Belford channeled his frustration into one final reach for the Power, though they'd only moved a few short steps since his last attempt. He tried to blow the air in front of him again. Miraculously, Arlin's slightly overgrown blond hairs blew in the artificial breeze. They must have stopped just barely beyond the edge of the Artifact's influence!

With hope renewed, Belford's heart pounded as adrenaline flooded his veins. He quickly removed the tourniquet and drew in the Power fully. Reaching out with his mind, he attempted to seal Arlin's wound.

Something was wrong.

The tell-tale blue and green glow that always accompanied Belford's healing did not occur.

Nothing happened at all.

Grine pushed Belford aside, realizing time was fleeting. He drew his finger across Arlin's neck, using his fast but scarring method of fusing wounds, but still nothing happened. Confused, Grine touched his own shoulder where Belford accidentally cut him. His skin glowed white. He winced as the cut melted closed, leaving a faint scar behind.

"I don't understand," said Grine. "Why won't it work on him?"

Belford was perplexed for a moment, but then had a sudden realization. "He swallowed that orb device that stopped us from using the Power on the Whunes outside!"

Belford immediately tore open Arlin's bloody tunic. All of the buttons ripped off and flew across the corridor. He used the Power to slice through Arlin's chainmail and undershirt, straight down from his chin, so that he could pull them open and have access to his abdomen. He wouldn't be able to cut Arlin open with the Power, but his sword would work. He drew the curved blade once more. There was no time to create a less ungainly instrument. He heated the blade with the Power, hot enough to kill any germs that were present. It steamed as the blood staining the blade boiled away.

"Sorry about this," he said. He used the hot blade like a giant scalpel to cut into Arlin's chest, just below his ribcage.

He sliced deep, applying firm pressure to cut entirely through the outer dermis on his first pass. He cut through Arlin's meager fat layer on the second pass, and then his muscle on the third.

Arlin's eyes opened. The pain must have been excruciating…. He twitched slightly, but there was such little blood left in him that he was barely able to move at all.

"Don't worry, buddy. Just stay with us," said Belford.

He reached into Arlin's chest cavity with both hands and began feeling around for his stomach. Seconds felt like minutes as he groped through the sticky, warm intestines. After several questionable squeezes of what was probably Arlin's liver, he finally found what he was looking for. He moved everything else out of the way and pulled the organ up to the incision. With a visual confirmation, he picked up his sword again and sliced into the exposed stomach. Feeling around with his bare hands, he soon found the hard lump of the metallic orb. He squeezed the stomach, forcing the ball out of the cut. It fell to the floor and rolled away. As soon as it was clear, Belford was able to use the Power to seal the organ back up.

Captain Grine went to work on Arlin's throat while Belford finished the abdominal surgery. He forced the slippery stomach back in place. It proved harder to put back in than it was to pull out. Once situated, he used some of the excess blood pooling in the chest cavity to create new flesh, binding the layers of muscle, fat and skin back together. Before the incision was fully closed, he corralled the rest of the excess blood and forced it back into the exposed capillaries at the incision point. By the time he was done, Grine was finished sealing Arlin's throat.

Arlin was unconscious again, pale as all hell, but still breathing.

"Did you fix his esophagus?" Belford asked.

Grine nodded. "His vocal cords were mangled terribly as well. I may have realigned them a little too tight."

"So he won't be able to talk?"

"Hard to say. We may end up having to go back in later to fix them."

Belford glanced down at his hands, slick with blood. He used the Power to strip the fluid from his skin. It was a simple process—he often repelled water from his body after bathing. This used the same principle. The blood floated off of him in a fine mist and slowly drifted to the floor. Grine backed away to avoid the cloud and accidentally bumped the removed orb device with his foot

Belford snatched it up as it skidded past. The troublesome orb saved Arlin's life from the Crimson Stalker, but also prevented him from being healed. If Belford was to have any chance of saving his friends, he couldn't have the Crimson Stalker freezing him in place again.

He rolled it back and forth in the palm of his hand—dense and unfathomable to his mental probes. It was impervious to the Power. He couldn't even clean the nasty goop off the outside. Instead, he wiped it across a clean spot on his shirt.

Grine knew what he was about to do. The Ver'ati grimaced in advance. Belford took a deep breath, then threw the orb to the back of his throat. It was a little large for swallowing comfortably and hurt on the way down. His stomach turned over in disgust even before the sphere completed its journey down his esophagus. The residue left behind in his mouth had a foul metallic flavor akin to a dirty doorknob. Belford spit a few times to diminish its potency. He turned towards Grine once he was finished. "Stay with Arlin," he said as he wiped spittle from his chin. "I've got to try to save the others."

Grine didn't argue. "Just be careful," he said with a frown.

Belford knew his chances weren't good, but he had to try.

CHAPTER

54

Instrument of Death

Running down the hallway, Belford retraced his steps. The trail of blood left behind by Arlin was easy to follow. Belford paused briefly when he came back across the barracks with the slaughtered guardsmen. A meat grinder would have left less of a mess.

This is what will happen to my friends if I don't hurry.

The Crimson Stalker had a head start.

The bloody trail ended in a puddle where Arlin's throat had been slit. Just beyond the puddle, to the side of the hallway, the Talus Shard blade gleamed in the lamp light. Belford picked up the sword as he paused to catch his breath.

The moment his fingers closed around the black wrappings a strange feeling of ease fell across him. A sense of déjà vu filled his mind, as if he had held the Talus Shard blade before, not once, but thousands of times. The weight of the sword felt natural in his hand. He instinctively knew its balance point. He held the blade steady in front of him. It felt like a scalpel in his trained hands—a perfect instrument of death.

He searched the feeling of familiarity that so strangely settled across his mind. It wasn't natural.

The Talus Shard is a bloody Artifact!

Somehow he could remember holding the blade before—not with his mind, but with his body. The blade was suddenly an extension of himself, similar to how he felt about the Power when he was able to reach it. The mastery ran through him, from his hands, down into his feet. He felt years—*no, decades!*—of training and experience. And not just sparing and practicing stances, but actual battles—life and death scenarios. It was as if every hand that had ever held the blade was his own. He felt their victories, and their bitter losses. With each life taken or spared, the blade learned. It grew stronger, smarter, more fine-tuned.… It was the strangest sensation knowing so much and so little at the same time. If he thought about his knowledge of sword fighting, he knew practically nothing, but when he let his body take the lead, it was all there, literally at his fingertips.

He continued on with a new boost of confidence. He had no idea where he was going, but he continued forward at a sprint with the Talus Shard blade held down to his side in one hand like a ninja in one of the old movies. He ran light on his feet, mostly masking his footsteps. It wasn't until he came across the vivisected bodies of more guardsmen that he knew he was still on the Crimson Stalker's trail.

Whoever the Crimson Stalker was, he clearly wasn't on Garrett's side, but that did not make him an ally.

Ahead, more bodies surrounded a grand staircase that curved down into a wide foyer. Matching ornate doors on both his level and the one below suggested a multi-tiered room beyond—perhaps some sort of forum or court. Belford approached slowly—there was movement below.

The Crimson Stalker, still dressed as a guard, was silently and systematically slaughtering a whole contingent of frozen guardsmen at the bottom of the staircase. Rather than dismantling them entirely in a flurry of blood and guts, the Crimson Stalker was taking a slower and quieter approach— slitting each of their throats in turn with his trusty fold-out shaving razor. It was clear he was making his way towards the ornate doors on the lower level.

Belford bypassed the staircase and went straight for the ornate doors on his floor. He needed to see what laid beyond before deciding his next move. He grabbed one of the door's heavy levers with his left hand, still holding the Talus Share blade at the ready with his right, and pulled firmly, but slowly. He paused in a long moment of dread as the latch clicked free of the strike plate.

No one seemed to have heard.

He took a breath and then opened the door wide enough to peek inside. As he suspected, the door led to a second-story balcony area. The balcony was empty, thankfully, but he was too far from the edge to see down to the lower level. He could hear voices coming from the first floor.

He slipped inside, staying low as he approached the railing. He could hear crying. He'd never heard Shiara cry before, but somehow he knew it was her. He felt a flutter in his heart, but the Talus Shard kept his emotions in check. He suppressed his feelings, remaining fight-ready.

He peered over the railing and took in the throne room below. Not even the Talus Shard could stop his sadness from overwhelming him as he took in the sight of Thorin's headless corpse. Shiara and Livian were chained to the floor to the right of Thorin's body, both women awash with blood. Ethan and Deenan were chained to the floor as well, but far enough away from the puddle to avoid being enveloped by it. Shiara sobbed into the wet stone. Everyone else remained stoic, staring up at Garrett. He was much younger than Belford remembered him, but Belford still recognized him in an instant.

The pale Goblikan was off to the right side of the throne, glancing nervously towards the set of doors through which Belford knew the Crimson Stalker to be finishing up his dirty work. The bastard was holding Thorin's severed head. He held it out awkwardly by the hair as he glanced between Garrett and the doors.

"Why aren't they answering?" Garrett asked. "Dhron, go see what's happening out there."

The pale Goblikan placed Thorin's head on the floor and tentatively wiped his hands across his trousers. He hadn't taken more than three steps when a blast blew the doors right off their hinges. A cry of shock arose, but a moment later everyone was frozen in place.

Belford couldn't see the Crimson Stalker's entrance from his vantage point—Belford was directly above him—but he could hear the solitary footsteps moving slowly across the marble floor.

Belford knew he needed to make his move soon, but there were no stairs within the chamber for him to get down to the lower level. He crept silently along the balcony, in pace with the Crimson Stalker below, until he was parallel with the throne and the large tapestries hanging against the wall beside it.

The Crimson Stalker stopped when he reached Garrett. He glowered at the king, still frozen in place. Garrett's expression was unchanging—the shock of the doors exploding inward was still etched into his skin. With just a subtle flick of the Crimson Stalker's wrist, Garrett's head whipped backwards, folding awkwardly against his shoulder blades. There was no sound apart from a subtle wheeze that escaped his stretched throat.

The Crimson Stalker's invisible force continued to push on Garrett's head until the skin of his neck began to tear. Blood silently poured down the front of his fine garments. His eyes were looking at his own ass by the time his spine finally popped apart entirely. It sounded in a sick crack and his head was sent tumbling free from his body. It rolled across the throne platform, coming to a rest beside Thorin's.

A completely unnecessary second gesture from the Crimson Stalker sliced off all four of Garrett's limbs and sent them flying in four different directions. His bloody stump of a torso fell to the floor while the rest of him was scattered across the throne room as thoroughly as if he'd stepped on a landmine.

The Crimson Stalker was always efficient and surgical with his kills, but the way he took apart Garrett after he was already dead felt oddly personal.

Without a hint of emotion on his face, the Crimson Stalker turned around to look at the prisoners. His dead, gray eyes immediately locked onto Ethan. He began his approach, honing in on his next victim.

Belford couldn't hesitate any longer. He stood up from his hiding place and climbed over the short railing. The top corner of the nearest tapestry was just in reach. He grabbed hold of it and used the Talus Shard blade to start a slice in the cloth part way across. He had to make a leap of faith. The powers of the Talus Shard steadied his nerves as he jumped and let his weight tear the tapestry in half. The thick fabric slowed his decent just enough to avoid injury. His instincts told him to let go towards the end. He did so, and kicked off from the stone wall. For a heart-pounding moment he was laid out in the air like Travis in his squirrel suit, but then he landed with a somersault in front of the throne.

The Crimson Stalker spun around. It was his turn to be surprised. He tried to use his Power on Belford but the swallowed orb rendered the attack inert. Belford sprang back to his feet and bounded down the steps toward his adversary.

The Crimson Stalker was quick for his advanced age. He leapt aside as the Talus Shard bit towards him and managed to scoop Garrett's scepter off the floor in the same movement. Belford was on him in an instant. The Crimson Stalker parried, swinging the scepter like a bow staff. He blocked Belford's next strike as well.

Their feet moved together like a dance. Belford didn't know the names or the particular reasons for his various stances, but he followed his instincts, letting his feet flow from one position to the next. He knew the intent: To edge the Crimson Stalker into a position of disadvantage.

And it was working!

With every parried blow, the Crimson Stalker shifted backwards slightly. He soon neared the corner of the throne room. Belford would make his final blow once the Crimson Stalker ran out of space.

It was taking so much effort to deflect Belford's attacks that the Crimson Stalker was forced to release everyone from the freeze he'd been holding them in. The pale Goblikan shrieked and scampered out of the room as fast as his feet would carry him. Ethan and the other prisoners rattled their chains, turning in place to get a better view of the fight as it unfolded.

With a gesture, the Crimson Stalker sent one of Garrett's severed legs flying at Belford. Belford was forced to divert it with his blade. He lost a step in his progress. The Crimson Stalker struck out with the scepter, landing a solid blow against Belford's left shoulder. Belford winced, but the Talus Shard wouldn't let him be distracted.

"Watch out!" Ethan cried as the entirety of Garrett's heavy throne lifted into the air and flew across the chamber at Belford.

Belford deftly lunged out of the way as it crashed between him and his foe.

"You'll have to do better than that!" Belford exclaimed. He gritted his teeth and released a growl as he spun towards the Crimson Stalker again.

His strike glanced across the glowing gem at the tip of the scepter. The force of the attack fractured the gem. A burst of white light flooded the throne room. Belford was blinded and thrown backwards by an unexpected concussive shockwave.

The Crimson Stalker was thrown back as well, smashing into the wall behind him.

Belford climbed to his feet, rubbing his eyes to try to clear the flash from his vision. Suddenly, the sound of chains falling to the floor sounded from his left. It was Deenan—free from his bonds.

"We can reach the Power again!" he exclaimed, prompting the other Ver'ati to begin breaking the chains that held them to the floor as well.

Belford's vision returned. The Crimson Stalker was back on his feet as well. He threw the broken scepter Artifact to the floor and withdrew what looked like a tuning fork from his pocket. Before Belford could make a move, the Crimson Stalker tapped the metal prong against the stone wall. A high-pitched tone rang out. It resonated throughout the throne room, hanging in the air.

The floor and walls began to rumble as an earthquake similar to the ones back in Erotos erupted. It grew quickly in intensity. Belford barely managed to stay on his feet. The wall the Crimson Stalker tapped with his device was shimmering with an unnatural glow. It became a blur as it rattled more violently than the rest of the throne room.

He'll bring the whole pyramid down on top of our heads!

In an unexpected move, the Crimson Stalker lunged headfirst at the vibrating wall. He moved without a hint of hesitation. Instead of colliding with stone, he passed through with little resistance, as if he'd jumped through the surface of a pond. Not a moment later, the vibrations ceased in their entirety.

Belford ran to the wall and placed a hand against the stone. It was solid once more. Like a ghost, the Crimson Stalker was simply gone.

Across the throne room, Deenan rushed up the steps to the throne platform and picked up Garrett's severed head. Without speaking, he transformed a broken chunk of the dais into a pristine mirror. As soon as the glassy flow solidified and cooled, he picked up the mirror and stared intently at his reflection. Using Garrett's head as a reference, he changed his own appearance to match. The process was painful, judging by the grunts and grimaces he made.

Belford felt cold inside. He wasn't sure if it was the Talus Shard's effect on his mind or simply the events of the day weighing on him.

"Who the hell was that?" asked Ethan, pointing at the wall through which the Crimson Stalker vanished.

Belford's eyes strayed to Thorin's body. He didn't look up as Ethan gestured. "That was the Crimson Stalker," he said, "the man who killed the King of Antara."

Ethan pulled a face. "Probably the kings of Taris and Graven too… he's racking up quite the résumé."

Shiara was still on the floor beside Thorin. She hadn't moved at all. She hadn't removed the metal collar that chained her to the floor either. Her body was going through the motions of sobbing, only without any sound.

"When did you learn to use a sword like that?" Ethan asked.

Belford ignored the inquiry. He stepped quickly to Shiara's side and knelt down in the tacky puddle of Thorin's blood. He set Arlin's sword down just beyond the puddle. Waves of guilt and heartache fell over him like a waterfall as soon as he released the blade and the Talus Shard's influence was severed.

He pulled energy in, feeling the Power course through his veins. It only compounded his sadness. He drew his finger across Shiara's collar, willing the metal to pull itself apart. A hairline fracture formed. He then used the energy he'd gathered to bombard the collar on both sides of the fracture and wrench it apart. The collar clanged as it dropped against the marble floor.

Shiara sat up onto her knees. Her body fell still. She remained deathly silent as she stared back at Belford with her steel-blue eyes shimmering. Her face and clothing were slathered with Thorin's blood. She had put her face to the floor. The blood was even congealing in her eyelashes.

Belford used the Power to strip it all off of her. A pink mist floated away, statically repelled. He held Shiara's face with both hands for a moment, their sorrow combining as they stared into one another's eyes. There were no words.

Thorin came here for Belford, and now he was gone.

Forever.

Shiara collapsed into Belford's arms. Her tears returned as he held her. He felt the warm drops as they slid down his neck. He felt the sting in his own eyes as well. They stayed that way for a long while, pressed together, mourning the loss of their dear friend.

CHAPTER

55

Spring Renewal

The day after the Dance of the Elements, Javic awoke in one of Doctor Crane's examination room cots to a summons from Queen Havorie and a brand-new, freshly hemmed, black Ver'ati robe folded up at the foot of the cot, compliments of the Arcanum. Still fatigued, he dressed in his new robe and made his way to the palace with guarded excitement. He had yet to discover why the queen had extended the lifesaving offer to him.

Just outside the palace's entrance, Javic was surprised to find Lieutenant General Cale Fisman waiting for him to arrive. The red welts where Ragdon ripped him apart were yet to fade.

"How's the…" Javic pointed at one of the welts on Cale's face. No one was near enough to overhear their conversation, but Javic wasn't sure what to call the strange ghostly wounds.

Cale waved his hand dismissively. "They still sting, but I'll live," he said. "I just wanted to warn you about Tannel… he isn't through with you yet. You messed up his plan when you survived the Dance and then again when you accepted Havorie's offer. He doesn't want anyone to know the Gateway ever existed or that the Arcanum was using it to take Artifacts from Sultrim. I'm not sure how he intends to move against you, but from watching his dreams last night I am certain that he will make another attempt on your life soon."

Javic took the news stoically. Tannel wanting him dead wasn't exactly a surprise, but he had hoped the councilman would give up after the Dance. "What about the core?" Javic asked.

A flash of a smile appeared on Cale's lips for a brief moment. "Don't worry about that," he said. "I've discovered where it's hidden."

A young steward with a furrowed brow and several white scars running down his left cheek peeked his head out of the palace entrance. His expression brightened when he spotted Javic. He trotted over, smiling widely. "Would you happen to be Javic Elensol, sir?" the steward asked.

Javic nodded. "That's me," he said.

"Oh good," he said. "My name's Caspin Byron, sir, and I've been tasked by our queen to retrieve you at once." Caspin glanced over at Cale, seemingly noticing him for the first time. He stared fixedly at the lieutenant general's red welts. "What happened to you?"

Cale maintained a blank expression, ignoring the question at first, but Caspin continued to stare. Eventually he caved in. "I got mauled by a bear," Cale said dryly.

"Oh," said Caspin, bobbling his head around. "Yeah, me too." The young steward slowly ran his thumb across the longest of his white scars.

Cale blinked several times, then looked back over at Javic. "Just remember what I said…." He turned to leave, but then spun back around once more. "You know, you might have been better off in the Archives. Knowing you were in the fold, under his watch, may have placated him. For now, just keep an eye out." Cale departed, sauntering aimlessly away from the palace without another word.

Javic pursed his lips as he watched Cale go. He looked back over at Caspin. "Alright then, lead the way," he said.

Caspin smiled again before scurrying back towards the palace entrance. Javic followed on his heels. They ambled across the long anteroom, passing several dozen guardsmen as they made their way down the columned walkway towards the chamber that contained the Charisms. Javic had heard about Belford's experience with the Charisms and was curious to see them in person. Caspin held the door open as Javic entered the small chamber. An altar at the center of the room held a polished-wood box. A soft, yellow light shone from one of the three orbs contained within—a visual representation of his strength with the Power. As Javic got closer, the glowing orb began to hum. A pair of guards had him place his hands on either side of the altar. The vibrations coming from the orb tickled his palms. Once the guards inspected the orbs, Javic was allowed to enter farther into the palace.

"You're quite strong with the Power," said Caspin as they walked along a hallway with a view of the central gardens. "I can see why our queen chose you. Right this way now." Caspin led Javic into an empty stateroom. It was furnished to accommodate small meetings. A wide table held five high-backed chairs on either side. "Queen Havorie will be with you shortly," said Caspin as he departed, leaving Javic by himself.

Javic took a seat on the far side of the table, keeping the door in sight. As he waited quietly for the queen to arrive, a nervous knot began to form in his stomach. *I really get to meet the queen!* The fact that she was even aware of his existence made him giddy. He still saw himself as just a simple farm boy from Darrenfield. *I wonder what she wants with me....*

He didn't have long to contemplate his fate before Queen Havorie appeared in the doorway. She was wearing a powder-blue dress and had her golden hair done up in tight curls. With her chin held high, her eyes shifted up and down Javic, weighting the entirety of his worth in a single glance. Javic let his eyes wander across the queen's body as well. The thin fabric of her dress clung to her modest curves shamelessly.

Havorie cleared her throat.

Heat rose to Javic's face—he had been staring for too long. Not a single word yet spoken, and already he was blushing. "My queen," said Javic, quickly standing up from his seat and bowing deeply. He'd nearly forgotten his manners.

"Hello, Javic, please sit," said Queen Havorie. "Welcome to the Guard."

"Thank you so much," said Javic. "You have no idea how glad I am you made an offer."

"Yes, yes," said Havorie. "I could tell it upset Councilman Cresdale very much." She wasted no time, jumping straightaway into business. "You will technically be working for Captain Damian Sarvo, my head of security—he oversees all of the Guard within the palace—but I have chosen you to be on my personal guard. I expect your full discretion, even from Captain Sarvo... especially from Captain Sarvo."

Javic raised an eyebrow. "Of course," he said. His curiosity was building.

"I will need you by my side at all times when I don't have you out on errands, in case I am in need of protection."

Javic narrowed his eyes. "Are you expecting trouble?"

Havorie placed a hand over her sleeve on her left wrist. "I'm going to be open with you," she said. "Years ago, when my mother died, her death was not an accident. We are going to find out who killed her and bring him to justice."

Javic realized his mouth was hanging open and promptly shut it.

"You are to trust only me. Report only to me. Do not trust Damian Sarvo or anyone else, do you understand?"

"Yes, my queen," said Javic. He tried to hide some of the shock that had fallen across his face.

"Do you know why I chose you to help me?"

Javic shook his head.

Havorie pulled up the left sleeve of her dress, exposing a golden device strapped tightly around her wrist. The face of the wrist-watch-like device held four dials, one of which was pointing directly at Javic.

Javic shifted forward in his seat to get a better look and found the dial followed his motion.

"You must be aware that you are quite powerful. This Artifact tells me that you are in fact the most powerful wizard in all of Erotos at the moment."

Javic didn't know what to say. He knew he had potential, but he'd never suspected his strength was *that* great. He wasn't sure he believed her....

"My life is in grave danger from an unknown killer. I need the best by my side."

Javic gulped audibly.

"Also, you are quite unassuming, which will come in handy," she added. "Caspin? Ervia?" Havorie called out the door. The young steward and a mousy looking maid stepped into the chamber. "The three of you are the only ones who know of my intentions. You may pass messages through one another back to me if you must. It is essential for all of our safety that no one else knows we are searching for the killer."

Javic was starting to think maybe Cale was right—the Archives might have been the safer option after all.

Havorie dismissed Caspin and Ervia before delivering Javic some final words. "Captain Sarvo is aware I've assigned you to my personal guard," she said. "He is not pleased." She wrung her hands together. "I suspect he will not make things easy for you."

"I rarely find things are," said Javic.

Havorie cracked a smile. She gestured for Javic to exit the chamber with her. Javic stood up and quickly made his way around the table. Havorie placed a hand on his shoulder when he reached her side. The subtle scents of rose and honey drifted up Javic's nostrils.

"I'm counting on you," Havorie said softly, lowering her brilliant green eyes as she spoke. The color reminded Javic of the first hints of spring peeking through the soil after a long winter, the promise of new life budding to the surface. She locked her eyes upon his once more.

A fresh blush flowed into Javic's cheeks.

She flashed him another hint of a smile, a wildness appearing in her expression. "I have faith you won't fail me," she said. "Finding this killer is only the first step, you know. My reign is just beginning. We may do many great things together." Havorie led him out of the chamber, her hand shifting to the small of his back as they walked. "Now, go report to Damian Sarvo at once, so that we may begin."

CHAPTER

56

The Illusionists

Once Deenan was finished altering his face to better match the real Garrett's more youthful appearance, he vaporized the dead king's body and severed head into a pile of ash. With that simple—albeit morbid—act, he replaced Garrett in the service of the Arcanum. Of Garrett's men only the pale Goblikan, Dhron, Garrett's monster master, knew the truth. Unfortunately, he was nowhere to be found.

Deenan stayed behind to search for the escaped Goblikan while Belford led the rest of the group back to Arlin and Grine. He walked with Shiara under his arm. She held onto his waist like a life raft.

Belford's emotions were dampened again by Arlin's sword. He handed the Talus Shard blade to Shiara as they walked. She deserved a moment of reprieve more than he did. She wiped the tears from her eyes and gave Belford a curt nod once the Artifact was in her grasp. She pulled away slightly,

635

although she continued to hold onto Belford's arm. He was pretty sure she was doing it for him rather than for her own needs.

Belford realized Lieutenant Canbel was missing from the party. With all the insanity, he almost hadn't noticed. Shiara informed him about Canbel's untimely death, being eaten alive.

"By a god damn T-rex!" Ethan added.

When they passed the slaughterhouse of a guards' barracks everyone grew quiet again for a moment as they observed the carnage.

"Who do you think sent him?" Livian eventually chimed in.

Ethan mulled the question over. "If I had to reckon a guess, I would say the northern invasion coinciding with the deaths of all the monarchs of Aragwey—save Queen Havorie—is too much of a coincidence to ignore. I know Havorie certainly didn't send the assassin. If anything, she's probably his next target…. I should hurry back to Erotos. We've got to be looking at a foreign entity here. Nothing else makes sense."

"You think Queen Havorie's in danger from the Crimson Stalker?" Belford asked. He'd only met Havorie once—the day she announced his Mark of Kings to the people of Erotos. She seemed kind, and from what Belford could tell, despite her youth, she had a good head on her shoulders.

Ethan shrugged. "From what I've seen here, I would say her whole court is in grave danger of being diced into bloody cubes."

Belford grimaced.

"If it wasn't for you, I doubt that Crimson Stalker fellow would have left a soul alive in this whole gaudy pyramid."

That was as close to a "thank you" as Belford was going to get from Ethan.

"It's a good thing we came here," said Livian. "Our plot is the only chance we have at a quick resolution to the Kovehn-Phandrol war. If this invasion force is as organized as they appear, we may need all of Aragwey to put up a united front against them."

"Perhaps," said Ethan. "Once you get your feet under you here, have Deenan announce a peace treaty with Phandrol in order to fight the invaders, then send all the Kovani troops north. That way they can take the brunt of the losses. I'll organize a Phandolian second wave once I get back to Erotos to mop up, if need be."

As usual, Ethan was playing with peoples' lives. It made sense that he would value Phandolian troops over Kovani, but the way he spoke about using them made Belford feel filthy.

When they found Grine, Arlin was sitting up beside him, conscious, and extremely pale. He looked frightened and more than a little anxious. Shiara gave him back his sword and his demeanor immediately returned to its normal stoic state once the wrappings touched his fingertips. Belford wondered if he even knew the real Arlin at all.

How much of his personality is just a reflection of the Talus Shard?

The sword numbed emotion, both good and bad. It watered Arlin down into a pure fighting machine. He always rested his hand on the hilt.

As Grine had predicted, Arlin's vocal cords were stretched too tight during his surgery and he was unable to speak. They would have to go back in later at some point to fix them. Arlin held his hand to his throat, then gestured a show of gratitude towards Belford for saving his life. With a little help, Arlin was able to get up on his feet, and the group made their way to the entrance of the pyramid. Once outside, Livian bid them farewell and went about generating a huge batch of spores that would make anybody who came near the pyramid unconcerned about the events of the day. They would instantly remember her as one of Garrett's top advisers and all of the deaths and damage would be explained away as a failed assassination attempt.

As soon as the group moved out of range, Livian released the spores into the air. They rose up like a dense morning fog, blanketing the promenade in a thick haze.

Everyone paused for a moment at a safe distance to watch. Belford stood between Shiara and Arlin. The great mist crawled across the pathways and into the nearby buildings, making the pyramid look like it was floating on a giant fluffy cloud. "Do you think Livian ever dosed us with anything?" Belford mused.

"Doubtful," said Shiara. "If she had, I probably wouldn't be able to dislike her so much." She glanced over at Belford. "She made Garrett fall in love with her at the end there. It saved her skin." And cost Thorin his. She didn't need to finish the words.

Belford wanted to cry again. The journey had been costly. Shiara put her arm around Belford and rested her head on his shoulder. He exhaled softly.

Arlin tapped him on his other shoulder. He pointed up at the moon and then at Belford's arm where his Mark of Kings resided. Belford understood.

"I got my answers," he said to Shiara, "from Wilgoblikan. The spores Arlin got from Livian actually made the bastard answer me truthfully."

Shiara picked her head up and looked over at Belford.

"Whenever Garrett made himself young, another one of us would appear."

Ethan glanced over now as well, his interest piqued.

Belford hadn't meant for Ethan to overhear him, but he didn't see the harm in everyone knowing the truth. He could see the wheels turning in Ethan's mind. He nodded to Ethan. "Any process that uses enough computational power would cause one of us to be expelled from storage. When you were made younger, someone probably came back too. They would have appeared at the point of shortest distance between the Earth and moon at the time."

"Interesting," said Ethan. "We'll have to be more careful in the future." He glanced up at the sky. "The moon is getting low," he said. "Let's get back to the steamer and get out of here before we become more vulnerable." He started walking towards the docks again.

Arlin gave Belford an unreadable expression before joining Ethan and Grine. Belford hung back with Shiara.

"I'm glad you got your answers," she said. "It means all this wasn't in vain."

Belford felt the tears welling up again in his eyes. He put his arms around Shiara, embracing her in a tight hug. Shiara squeezed him back.

"I'm with you," she whispered into his ear through her own tears. "Let's find Claire. It's what Thorin would have wanted for you. He was always a hopeless romantic, though you wouldn't have known it." Shiara laughed slightly at her own words. She pulled back from the hug, though not before giving Belford a little kiss on his damp cheek.

"I can't ask you to help me anymore," said Belford. "I've dragged you through enough."

"Nonsense," said Shiara. "We all came here because it was the right thing to do. I'll continue helping you if I feel like it."

Belford wiped his eyes with his sleeve. "You really are a better friend than I deserve," he said.

"I know," said Shiara. "Come on, let's go, we're falling behind." Shiara raced to join Ethan and the others.

Belford shot one last glance at the pyramid on the cloud. He came all this way for answers, and although he found them, he'd lost a true friend and ally in the process. No matter what Shiara said, Belford was incapable of not feeling responsible for Thorin's death. Thorin only came on this mission because of him.

It's dangerous to be close to me.

The thought of running away from the group crossed his mind. He could continue his search for Claire on his own, and hopefully not put any more lives in jeopardy, but he knew his chances of success would be diminished if he chose to go it alone. He felt that staying was a selfish choice, but it was also the only choice he could make.

It wasn't just about him anymore.

Claire was pregnant.

She was carrying his unborn daughter when she was memorized by the computer. The simple fact was he would do anything to find her and keep her safe. He would sacrifice a thousand Thorin's if need be, though each one would take another chunk of his soul to the grave. It was a terrible acknowledgement to make, but he knew only he could find that baby and give her a chance to live.

He loved and longed for Claire as deeply as one could for another person, and yet somehow he loved the mere concept of his daughter even more.

I'll find you, no matter how long or how far I have to look. Even if it's the last thing I do.

CHAPTER

57

The End of the World

Each of the Arcadians did their best to stand still as one by one the computer memorized copies of their bodies. Ethan and John sat huddled together next to Wes on his tablet. Between the three of them, they had managed to use Wes's hack to access the facility's network and extract the protocol for teleportation that the scientists had been developing for the defense department. Teleportation was not intended for live subjects. Complicated brain chemistry and constantly changing biological structures meant parts of the base code had to be altered before it could work on living beings. In principle, analyzing and sequencing the matter of a horse figurine or a hairclip was not all that different from scanning a human, but constantly shifting energies within the human brain meant special considerations had to be taken in order to ensure their copies would have brain function when they appeared on the other side. It would have been a difficult endeavor, even under the best of conditions, but now their time was limited to however long it took for the nukes to find the nearby testing facility.

John quickly hashed out the code for a time delay so that their copies would not appear instantly, as the original protocol dictated. Instead, they would materialize sometime in the future—hopefully long enough from now for the world to have recovered from this war to end all wars.

While their copies might one day live, that did not change the fact that they would all die here today on the outskirts of Tripoli as the city sank back into the desert wasteland. Destruction already filled the horizon… it would not be long now. If the newscast had been any indication, whatever was left of the European Union would be gone by morning. Retaliation strikes from the EU and its allies would already be underway by then, all but assuring the end of the EAC as well. There was no telling how far death would spread as clouds of radiation drifted on the winds in all directions across the globe. Whether or not their copies would find a brighter future on the other end of their journey was entirely up to fate.

There was no time to check the calculations, nor any guarantee the process would work at all, but the alternative— doing nothing—didn't really feel like an option.

"It's done," said Ethan as the last Arcadian was scanned. He exited out of the program and let his hands fall to his sides. Michelle reached out and tried to grab hold of his fingers but he dodged her grasp and turned away, hunching his shoulders slightly as if he couldn't bear to look at her.

Aaron didn't understand how Ethan could be so callous towards his wife, especially now as the end grew nearer by the minute. Claire had been squeezing Aaron's hand tight for quite some time now. Her emotions mingled with his own across their bond—fear, sadness, desperation… love. He nearly lost all sensation in his fingertips from her grasp, but he didn't want her to ever let go.

The computer had taken a snapshot of each of them… even Garrett… filling its memory banks with precise schematics of how to recreate them down to their individual atoms, exactly as they existed in the moment they were scanned. It had never been done before—never even attempted. *Will our souls be copied over? Do souls even exist?* It was far too late to worry over such nuances now.

"One day," said Claire, "another version of you and another version of me will get to spend a lifetime together."

She meant to be optimistic, but the words hurt Aaron. As much as he tried, he could not see the second chance they had given their copies as a second chance for themselves. He wanted *this* version of Aaron to get to spend his life with Claire and their unborn daughter.

She felt the emotion drift across their bond and squeezed his hands all the tighter for it. *Every moment that passes from now until the end is ours and ours alone,* she thought to him. It was true; their copies were already stored away, created in the moment of the scan; no new memories would carry over. *There is no redo button, so we will just have to make every second count.*

Aaron leaned in and put his forehead against Claire's. They stayed like that for a long moment without speaking, each trying to find comfort in the other's presence.

"I'm sorry," said Ethan, breaking the thick silence that settled over the group. His words were not directed to his wife as Aaron initially assumed. He addressed the group as a whole. "I guess it doesn't really matter anymore since it's all going to end… Yosef was right about me… I was the leak." It was Michelle's turn to recoil from her husband now, horror etched across her face. "This isn't how things were supposed to happen, of course, but even so, it is my fault. I released our names to the media and altered the Virus Replication Protocol, but only so we wouldn't be limited to the facility. We were supposed to be heroes… change the world… everyone would know we saved them…."

Garrett spit on the ground in disgust.

Isabelle rounded on Ethan. "You've killed us all!" Her hands were clenched into fists, ready to strike.

Wes, John, and even Hannah all started to encroach on Ethan as well from the moment he expressed his guilt. The rest of the Arcadian's were in too much shock to even react. Ethan did not attempt to evade the first blow as Isabelle swung for his face. He fell to his knees as the mob closed around him. Michelle turned away completely, unable to watch.

Aaron didn't want to believe it—he had defended Ethan; put all his faith in his innocence. Ethan took everything from him—everything from everyone—*and for what?* He would die alongside the rest of them. Aaron took a step towards their betrayer, allowing his growing hatred to take control of his movements. He was intent on pounding his face into the dirt, repeatedly. Aaron wanted to tear Ethan to pieces and then stomp on those pieces until there was nothing left.

Claire grabbed onto his wrists and pulled him back around to face her. "Don't let him steal your final moments," she said simply. *Vengeance changes nothing.* Her eyes were sorrowful as she urged him to find restraint. Her body quivered slightly as she held his arms in place.

We will never get to know what we could have become, Aaron thought back at her, *never get to meet our daughter.* Overwhelming sadness slid across his mind, cooling his rage like the ocean lapping against a fresh flow of lava.

Claire frowned. *We have shared more in our short time together than most people do in a lifetime. Can't we be grateful for that?*

While the rest of the Arcadians turned on Ethan with unrelenting anger, Aaron gazed into Claire's eyes. They were brilliant emeralds, shaped to perfection. Tears glistened across their surfaces as she stared back into him, unblinking. Light from the distant fires reflected off the tops of her cheekbones with a soft glow that brought out the warmth of her skin. The moment passed in silence, more meaning crossing between them than any words—spoken or otherwise—could have ever expressed. She gave herself over to him completely, and him to her.

The flash that washed away the facility made Aaron flinch, but he did not turn from Claire. It was blinding, even in his peripherals, radiating outward like an exploding sun as it evaporated the landscape. Aaron couldn't see anymore, it was too bright for his retinas to comprehend, but he knew Claire was still there. He pulled her in close and embraced her with all his strength. The heat of her skin—her body pressing up against his—was all that remained. He felt her shudder within his arms. He was shaking too.

I'm scared, he thought, the rumbling becoming too loud for spoken words to register. The vibrations flowed up through their feet as the earth convulsed, threatening to sweep them both away.

We'll face the end together.

Continue reading for a special preview of:

Howls on the Wind

Book Three of:

The Arcadian Complex

Paul James Keyes

CHAPTER

1

Pillars of Dust

With his whole body pressed firmly to the stone wall, Rylin Gansly listened for any vibration that might indicate the approach of one of the Paerto'sul. The winged bears had formidable senses of smell—if they drew near Rylin they would hone in on him faster than a bloodhound. Guarded by the bears, the ancient city of Sultrim sprawled far and wide in a maze of tunnels and compounds built high in the Arid Hills. Shafts that ran through the interior of the mountain would occasionally open up into breathtaking views—perches and catwalks precariously etched into the exposed cliff sides. The high passes were treacherous at the best of times and, this time of year, were blanketed by heavy snowfall that made them utterly impassable for a human such as Rylin.

With the Gate Artifact that brought him to the Sun City destroyed by a cave-in, there was no way to leave, at least until the spring thaw.

A hollow rumble drew Rylin's attention. It wasn't one of the many quakes that often shook the dilapidated halls. The pattering footsteps of several guardians were drawing steadily nearer to his hiding spot. They'd found him far too quickly.

I shouldn't have stopped moving....

It was too late now. The bears had impeccable hearing as well. If he so much as breathed loudly, they'd be on him in an instant. All he could do was sit tight and hope they would pass him by. The air was stale within the tiny offshoot from the main hallway in which he'd taken up temporary residence. He hoped his scent was contained within the room and did not linger in the hall beyond.

The rumble grew louder. The pattering of the pack moved quickly down the corridor. They were searching for him.

Rylin became absolutely still, focusing on breathing softly despite the surge of adrenaline that was beginning to coarse through his veins. The bears were not easily evaded. Rylin held his breath as they scampered past the opening of the dark chamber. They continued on, maintaining their quick pace. Their motion stirred up the air, wafting the familiar musk of their fur within range of Rylin's nostrils.

If I can smell them, then they can smell me—

The thuds ceased immediately. Several grunts and tongue clicks sounded from down the corridor. The bears could speak Aragwian, but often communicated in more subtle ways when closing in on a hunt.

They turned back around, moving swiftly towards Rylin's hiding spot. The first of the bears burst into the chamber, its claws scraping across the flooring. Rylin slipped his light-glove into place against his palm, sending a piercing beam of light out towards the first approaching bear. It skidded to a halt and reared up on its hind legs. It was just a cub, but still stood as tall as a man.

The bear only paused briefly in the beam before lunging at Rylin. Its huge paws struck him in the chest, taking him to the floor with ease and nearly knocking the wind out of him. It stared down into Rylin's face, taunting him.

"Found you!" Kamila cried out. She licked his forehead before stepping off his chest.

Rylin had trouble distinguishing the bears from one another by sight, but he knew their voices well by now—he'd been living with them for over a month.

Ashran and Besel, Kamila's brothers, were right behind her. Ashran approached Rylin as well and nuzzled his arm. "Rylin found." A pulsing hum, indicating contentment, escaped the young male's throat.

"You guys found me so fast this time!" Rylin laughed, rubbing Ashran's soft nose. "Did you really wait the full five minutes before setting out?" he asked Besel.

Besel flapped his wings, whipping up the layer of Calvenite dust that littered the floor. "We counted to thirty-ten."

Rylin grabbed Besel playfully in a headlock, joke-wrestling the much stronger bear. "I bet you counted too fast!"

"Nah-uh!" said Kamila. "We counted fair. You just didn't hide well!"

Rylin's stomach rumbled with a deep pang of hunger.

Kamila poked Rylin in the belly lightly with her paw. "Mama caught a deer for supper. Wanna go get some?"

"I'm okay," said Rylin. In truth, he was desperately hungry, but he needed to wait for the moon to rise before he could cook the raw meat offerings with the Power. He didn't want to risk falling ill in a place like Sultrim.

The louder thuds of a full-grown guardian sounded from out in the corridor. Rylin and the cubs stepped out of the chamber to see who was coming. Soon, Raljaska, the cubs' mother, stepped around the corner. She focused her black eyes on Rylin as she approached.

"Hi, mama!" all three cubs cried out in unison.

"Hi, babies," said Raljaska. "Hello, Rylin. I need you to come with me. Ma'freit calls upon you."

Ma'freit was the leader of the guardians. A massive bear, wise and ancient, with the strangest ability to see into Rylin's thoughts. When Raljaska first took Rylin in, it had been only upon the judgment of Ma'freit that he was allowed to stay within the Sun City.

"What does she want?" Rylin asked. Ma'freit was an intense presence to be around. Rylin wasn't thrilled to be asked to another meeting.

Raljaska stared at Rylin blankly for a moment. "Ma'freit wants to speak with you." The bears were quite literal and often thought Rylin to be stupid.

"I mean, what does Ma'freit want to talk to me about?"

"You will have to ask Ma'freit," said Raljaska, cryptically. "There is a gathering, and you have been requested."

Rylin gave up trying to get answers out of the bear. He followed behind her lumbering strides as she led him back down the corridor. The cubs trotted along behind Rylin, chattering to themselves about some past hunt, but Rylin wasn't really paying attention. His mind was preoccupied with curiosity over Ma'freit's summons.

Paerto'sul were similar to their natural cousins in many ways. Bears tended to be solitary creatures. Mothers reared their young, but otherwise little time was spent in groups. Gatherings were not common. Whatever sparked the need for a meeting was undoubtedly not good news.

During his first audience with Ma'freit, the old bear gazed into his mind and determined him to be honest and pure of heart. The other bears, other than Raljaska who called the gathering, wanted to kill Rylin for coming to "steal the treasures," as they put it. The guardians were bound to protect the Artifacts housed within the walls of Sultrim.

Rylin was just one of a long line of wizards tasked with pilfering Artifacts through the Gate. The bears were not amused. Fortunately, Ma'freit saw that Rylin had no prior knowledge of the guardians' sacred duty or any intention of continuing to try to steal Artifacts now that he knew of their wishes.

Stealing the mysterious Artifact core was Lieutenant General Cale Fisman's goal—Rylin was just an unwitting pawn, sent on a dangerous task, blissfully unaware.

The corridor became flooded with sunlight as the tunnel opened up to a wide balcony. The crisp mountain air filled Rylin's lungs as he took in the pristine valley far below. Down the range at lower elevations, black spruce and birch trees stretched as far as the eye could see, uninhabited wilderness for countless leagues down into the heart of Antara. Up nearer to Sultrim, the untouched snow blanketed across the many peaks and twisting passes, sparse with vegetation.

Raljaska bowed down. Rylin climbed up onto the back of the giant winged bear without a word. He was used to the procedure by now. Due to the many collapses around the ancient city, the only way to traverse much of Sultrim was by air. Riding the flying bears was terrifying, but exhilarating. Rylin held on tight to Raljaska's fur as the rise and fall of her wing flaps threatened to send him tumbling to his doom. He eased up slightly as he settled in, and began to enjoy the ride. It truly was remarkable getting a bird's eye view of the summit.

What would Cormick think of me now? Seeing things no other living person has ever witnessed!

Before being sent to the Ver'ati training Academy in Erotos, Rylin's eldest brother Cormick had always treated him like the baby of the family. At thirteen years old, Rylin was the youngest of five siblings, so he understood Cormick's view of him, though it was still annoying. He missed his family greatly. Leaving home for Erotos had been difficult—he'd never been away before. Now he was on the complete opposite side of the nation! The Lost City of Sultrim, deep in the Arid Hills, was as far from Rylin's home on Shian Point as one could get while still being in Aragwey. A cloud of sadness fell over him as he thought about his mother. The distance between them weighed heavy upon his heart.

Raljaska glided in for a thumping landing in front of the tall structure the bears used as their meeting hall. Rylin climbed down gingerly and made his way with Raljaska and the cubs to the building's entrance. There were dozens of other guardians already present, standing together in rows. Their emotionless eyes followed Rylin as he stepped inside. Raljaska and her cubs hung back as Rylin made his way alone down the aisle of bears.

The meeting hall looked to have once been some sort of court. Tall pillars held up a patchy ceiling—once upon a time it was all indestructible Calvenite, but the stone had since degraded halfway back into the weaker slate from which the structure was originally created. Holes in the ceiling brought beams of sunlight down into the meeting hall. Fine particles of Calvenite dust blanketed the hall with a misting of gray ash. It was like that all across the Sun City. The more enclosed spaces held piles of dust a hand or so deep in places where the centuries had allowed it to accumulate undisturbed. The bears did not have the opposable thumbs required to handle brooms, Rylin figured.

Corshen, Ma'freit's mate, stood at the front of the bears. Gray skin peaked out where old scars all across his body prevented the guardian's matted fur from regrowing. Only another bear could have caused such damage. He was not slowed down by his age, nor the old injuries. Dense muscles bulged from his shoulders where the scarred guardian's massive wings, currently folded at his sides, attached to his body. He was easily the largest of the bears that stood before him.

Rylin looked around for Ma'freit, but she was nowhere to be seen. He stopped beside Corshen and looked up at the elder bear for guidance. "I have been summoned?" he asked.

A deep rumble escaped Corshen's throat. "There is trouble under the mountain," he said.

All of the other bears watched the exchange fixedly.

"Ma'freit wishes to speak with you, but she is preoccupied. Tell me human, what do you know of the earth shakings?"

Rylin glanced at Raljaska at the rear of the meeting hall for a second and then back at Corshen. "The earthquakes? Not much. In Erotos the ground often shakes with Echoes from the Power being used too frequently in the area."

Corshen exhaled a burst of hot breath through his black nostrils. "It is much the same here. In ancient times, the Sun City shook, but after the human's abandoned the mountain, the earth eventually healed and the ground became steady once more." Corshen eyed Rylin closely. "Over the past season, the shaking has returned. Many new collapses threaten to tear the city down. The walls are not what they once were."

Rylin was confused. "I haven't been channeling the Power except to cook food, just as Ma'freit requested," he said.

"We do not believe you are to blame," said Corshen, "but the Power is being used greatly within the city—or more specifically, under the city."

The bears watched the look of surprise fall across Rylin's face.

"Ma'freit senses humans within the earth. They tunnel beneath our feet. They have not yet found the city, but they are growing closer every day. Do you know of this?"

Rylin shook his head. "No, sir," he said.

"The city must be protected," said Corshen. "The human invasion will be turned away once they breach the walls. To that, what do you say?"

Rylin swallowed nervously. The bears could easily decide to kill him if they deemed him to be a threat to their home. "I don't know anything about an invasion," he said. "My people are from far away. The Gate is destroyed. I don't see how they could be responsible for the tunneling. No one even knows where this city is—"

"Lies!" growled a bear standing in the front row. "He is one of them! He is a spy sent to learn the city's layout and defenses. We should eat him."

"Silence, Tanuk!" roared Corshen. "Ma'freit will judge the human's earnestness." He turned towards Raljaska. "You must not let the boy out of your sight until she does." He looked back over the rest of the bears. "Prepare yourselves for the battle to come. Ma'freit will know more about the invaders numbers when she returns from the depths." Corshen turned and walked away without another word.

Tanuk bared his teeth at Rylin. The gnarled guardian continued to eye him as if he were a snack as most of the other bears began to depart from the meeting hall. Rylin stared back, wide-eyed, at the hulking creature.

Kamila, suddenly by Rylin's side, nuzzled his arm to get his attention. "Mama says to come out fast," she whispered to him. "It is dangerous to linger."

Rylin didn't argue. He followed after Kamila with haste in his steps. He felt Tanuk's eyes on his back as he ran all the way down the aisle and out of the hall.

A Note from the Author:

If you enjoyed my novel, I also have another series which I am very excited to share—Into the Beyond, which I have had bouncing around inside my head for well over a decade. The first three books of the Into the Beyond series are already complete as of this writing, with more to come between Arcadian Complex releases. You can read the synopsis of Part 1 on the next page.

Also, please don't forget to leave a **review** online! That, along with telling your friends and family about my books, is the best thing a fan can do to give back. The more attention my novels get, the lower the financial burden of writing them will become (it takes years). I will continue to share my stories, one way or another, because that is what I love to do!

About the Author:

Paul Keyes was born and raised in Washington State between the beautiful waterways of the Puget Sound and the always majestic Cascade Mountains. Fascinated by the political and social workings of the world, he obtained degrees in both creative writing and economics from the University of Washington. In his spare time, he is an experienced pianist and composer, which has helped him bring a heightened sense of rhythm and emotional resonance to his written passages. Over the years, he has traveled everywhere from China to the Mediterranean, soaking in the many diverse cultures and histories. Throughout it all, there is no place he would rather be than back home, drifting on a boat somewhere between the San Juan Islands and his home port of Edmonds.

You can follow Paul on Twitter **@PaulJKeyes**,
TikTok **@PaulJamesKeyes**,
or visit **ArcadianComplex.com** to become an honorary Arcadian!

Also By Paul Keyes:

Into the Beyond
Series

A tale of *twisted* fate…

High school sophomore Lewis Graham is awakened by a *seemingly all-knowing* creature appearing through a **portal** in his bedroom. The impish fellow tells him he is important later, and that in order to reach his destiny it is imperative he *does exactly as he's told*.

When he follows the creature's instructions, the cheerleader he's been crushing on is suddenly within his grasp—bullies start dropping like flies!

But then a Native American girl sneaks Lewis a note containing three simple words, launching him down a frightening and thought-provoking path:

Don't Trust It.

This time-bending series packs a psychologically spine-chilling punch.

You can find the series on Amazon, or visit the website, **VergePublishing.org**

Thank you for reading!
-Paul